THE LA...

A.N. WILSON

THE LAMPITT PAPERS

INCLINE OUR HEARTS
A BOTTLE IN THE SMOKE
DAUGHTERS OF ALBION

Mandarin

A Mandarin Paperback
THE LAMPITT PAPERS

Incline Our Hearts first published in Great Britain 1988
by Hamish Hamilton Ltd
A Bottle in the Smoke first published in Great Britain 1990
by Sinclair-Stevenson Ltd
Daughters of Albion first published in Great Britain 1991
by Sinclair-Stevenson
This omnibus edition first published 1995
by Mandarin Paperbacks
an imprint of Reed Books Ltd
Michelin House, 81 Fulham Road, London SW3 6RB
and Auckland, Melbourne, Singapore and Toronto

A CIP catalogue record for this title
is available from the British Library
ISBN 0 7493 2116 4

Typeset by Deltatype Ltd, Ellesmere Port, Cheshire
Printed and bound in Great Britain
by Cox & Wyman Ltd, Reading, Berkshire

CONTENTS

INCLINE
OUR HEARTS

FOR
CHRISTOPHER AND DEB

One

'Will you be eating with us?'

Aunt Deirdre, a tin-opener in hand, spoke over her shoulder to her husband without looking round. She let out a little explosion of annoyance at the bluntness of the instrument. It had a large, wooden handle, and a curved blade, much dented from use.

'We really should get a new one,' she said.

I watched my uncle's handsome, pampered, mildly effeminate face. Whether he would be eating his supper with the rest of the household seemed, for that moment, as though it depended upon Aunt Deirdre getting the tin open. At the best of times, she kept us on rather short commons, and my uncle's expression appeared to indicate that if she were prepared to give him some tinned meat, he might spend rather less of his time 'up at the Place'. In those days of austerity, no source of protein was to be sneezed at. The odours given off from the tin, once the opener had punctured it and begun its jagged journey round the top, made my mouth water. But the meat was not for us. She scooped out a couple of spoonsful (in their jelly they made an appetising slurping noise) into an enamel bowl and with sharp, violent gestures she mashed it into the Winalot. Then with the playfully affectionate tone which she more often adopted with animals than with human beings, she called out: 'Tin-ker! Din-dins!'

Still without looking at my uncle (the pair seldom exchanged glances) she held the spoon under the cold tap to rinse off the remaining bits of meat. It was heartbreaking to see good meat go to waste like that. Tinker, a wire-haired dachshund of uncertain temper, devoured his food with greedy gulps and much rattling of the dish on the cold, stone kitchen floor. When she spoke again, my aunt had resumed the slightly cross tone with which she normally spoke. There was usually a vague sense that she

3

was having to argue a case and that her hearers had threatened to turn nasty.

'Only I've made a rice pudding,' she said.

I was not old enough to know whether this was offered as a means of persuading Uncle Roy to dine out or as an inducement to stay.

'I *think* I'd better . . . ' My uncle paused. He ate half his meals at the Place, but there was always this apologetic rigmarole before he set out there. 'Promised Sargie a game of chess.'

'Just so long as I know,' said Aunt Deirdre. I could not tell whether she would have been less cross if he had said he would be eating with us.

'He gets lonely,' my uncle added. Then, with meaning, he said, 'As we *all* do.'

I do not know whether the last bit of that sentence is true. People appear to have different levels of tolerance as far as solitude is concerned. How much Uncle Roy allowed his mind to dwell on his own loneliness, let alone that of his wife, is something I shall never know.

During the period when I was getting on badly with Uncle Roy, I liked to tell myself that ɦ e was a moral coward. It was only much later that I came to reflect that the opposite of moral cowardice is a tremendously rare quality in human beings and, when found, not always particularly attractive. The rice pudding conversation took place, however, before the period of the quarrels. I was still taking my uncle and aunt for granted. However annoying I might find either of them, they were unalterable facts of life, that afternoon in the kitchen as I sat looking first at one, then at the other.

My uncle's crinkly, white hair was his own, but it sat on his head like a wig and somehow gave him the appearance of some Victorian humbug – perhaps one of the cheery old gents in Dickens, or more likely a sybaritic minor canon in Trollope. Probably this was the effect he was aiming for. He had very clear blue eyes which – again, a Victorian touch – were boyishly innocent, childish. His silky, pink cheeks were quite as soft, when you kissed them, as my aunt's; if anything, they were softer; and his lips, too, were prissy and womanish. My aunt, on the other hand, whose Eton crop emphasised a rather stout neck, was much more obviously masculine. She never, to my recollection, wore trousers, but there was always something mannish about her clothes. The tweeds were of a kind dubbed (and perhaps, by some, deemed) 'sensible'. She always dressed in the same style: in summer a skirt and blouse, in winter, a skirt and jumper; little tweed coats almost identical to a man's hacking jacket.

The outfits were very slightly too smart for gardening (which she did all the time) but a bit too countrified for anything else. She never, however, modified what she wore. On the extremely rare occasions when I met my aunt off home territory (at speech-days or, very occasionally, in London) she always seemed less dressed up than any of the other mothers or female relations.

No one, by contrast, could accuse my uncle of being insufficiently dressy. His wardrobe was extensive, idiosyncratic and, in its own way, stylish. Standing there in the kitchen, he wore some beautifully cut, very wide Oxford bags of the palest grey flannel, a tweed coat of brilliant russet with a waistcoat of the same hue. The high collar and the white bow tie must have been old-fashioned when he first affected them in the 1920s.

When my uncle turned to me, I knew that he had abandoned the conversation about supper. It was by now established that he would be eating with Sargie Lampitt. I could see from his expression that he was about to begin one of his disquisitions about the Lampitt family in general. These speeches could burst from my uncle at almost any moment and in any company. When waiting for trains on station platforms, I have seen him accost total strangers – porters, guards, or fellow passengers – and immediately engineer some general observation about the weather or the time of the next train into an account of the family whose history, doings and affairs appeared to dominate nearly all his thoughts.

Usually, if you talk to strangers in England, they resist being drawn. Fear of boredom, quite as much as the possibility that one might be mad or sexually unreliable, explains their reticence. My uncle was impervious to any of the signals which might be given off on such occasions that the stranger would rather be left in peace. So urgent was his need to talk about Lampitts that any excuse must be found.

'Train's late,' he might say. Trains were a good introduction. If

the stranger replied, 'What d'you expect with all this nationalisation?' – a familiar enough response at that date – he could
proudly announce his divided loyalties.

'No one can blame the Honourable Vernon *personally*' – he
laughed aside this unvoiced suggestion, which no one had
made, as an absurdity. 'But then, as all his cousins say, "Vernon,
you are in the Cabinet." Dear Vernon replies, "I suppose I am."
On the other hand, no one should suppose that the Honourable
Vernon has the last word to say about railways.'

My uncle referred to Lord Lampitt's son as the Honourable
Vernon to distinguish him from another Lampitt cousin of the
same first name. By now, his interlocutors would be truly
puzzled, possibly edging away, wondering why this snowy-
haired stranger, an Alice-in-Wonderland figure, sometimes in
tweed knickerbockers, should be addressing them on the
subject of a family of whom they had never before heard.

'I am old enough,' he would continue, 'to remember old Mr
Michael Lampitt, and he was a director of the LNER. Now the
trains really *did* run on time in those days.'

Regardless of whether this assertion met with agreement, he
could then get into his stride. Railways forgotten, he could
concentrate on Lampitts *tout simple*. 'What an extraordinarily
nice man Michael was! Eton and Trinity – I *do* beg your pardon.'

'That's all right, sir,' the porter on Norwich Station might
answer.

'I was momentarily confusing Michael with Hugo. It was *Hugo*
Lampitt who was at Trinity. Michael was up at Clare. Most of the
Lampitts have been Cambridge men, except, as you perhaps
know, Mr Sargent Lampitt, who is the one I know best. His
father Michael was one of the very kindest men I ever knew.'

Such floods of information would have been too much to
absorb, even had his listeners been interested. In spite of a
distinctly rocky friendship with Sargent Lampitt, my uncle was
constant in his devotion to Sargie's family. All Lampitts, great
and small, were the object of fascination for him, and it can
never have occurred to him that other people might not share
his enthusiasm. No moment and no audience ever seemed
inappropriate, as far as he was concerned, for the rehearsal of
some anecdote in which Lampitts figured prominently. And
when the wells of anecdote ran dry, he was quite happy (even

the greatest concert pianists need to practise their scales) to give a simple verbal rundown of their family tree.

It followed, that having lived for over four years under my uncle's roof, I had become, willy-nilly, something of a Lampitt expert myself. Almost my only conversation had been that of my uncle, and that had been primarily devoted to his theme of themes. If required, I could have passed an examination on the Lampitts. Which uncle had the misfortune to develop phlebitis while staying in Mombasa? In what year did Sargie's father join the Labour Party? Which female member of the Lampitt family was deemed by Sargie and others to be a complete doormat? Which member of the Lampitt family was the author of *Lagoon Loungings*, a distinctly sub-Ruskinian work of the Edwardian era, and went on to achieve minor fame as a popular biographer, most notably of the Prince Consort and of Swinburne? Which Lampitt was married to a Strachey?

Even at twelve, I could have answered all these questions with the same alacrity with which other children of my age could have rehearsed the names of cricketers. I actually knew more about the Lampitt family than I did about my own. This was all the more bizarre since I seldom met any of them except 'Uncle Sargie', a reclusive and mysterious figure who was our neighbour up at Timplingham Place.

Sargent Lampitt was no relation. The 'Uncle' – never a formula employed or accepted by my Aunt Deirdre – was a pleasantry devised by Uncle Roy. Kinship with Sargie was something which my real uncle would love to have claimed. As a child, I was dimly aware of this, but unable to explain it. Since, I have had moments of disgruntled anger about the matter. Viewed from a common-sense point of view, it seems outrageous to esteem one group of people more highly merely because they seem to have attracted to themselves money, fame or chic. Furthermore, with an illogical flight into the values which I professed to despise, I might recall that the Lampitts were not, in class terms, anything so very special. True, the Honourable Vernon and his father Lord Lampitt (Sargie's uncle) were in *Debrett* but this was only a Lloyd George peerage. In terms of literary fame, the distinctions were analogously muted. A Lampitt had once edited the *Nation* before it amalgamated with the *New Statesman*; and there was James Petworth Lampitt (Sargie's brother Jimbo), the belle-lettrist. But this was small beer. Why, if he wanted to disown his harmless suburban origins, did my uncle not aspire after something rather more distinguished?

The answer, I suppose, is that snobbery does not really work like that. Like lust, it is seldom omnivorous and nearly always it will look about for particular, attainable objectives. My uncle idolised the Lampitts for the same reason that the man climbed Everest: they were there. Norfolk was sparsely populated. My aunt's taste for society was almost non-existent. Sargie was their nearest neighbour in a village of less than a thousand souls.

Uncle Roy would probably have been horrified to hear anyone accuse him of snobbery: the more so since he had absorbed much of the Lampitt, vaguely leftist, ideology.

If asked to explain his Lampitt preoccupation, he would have said that it had nothing to do with their money (they were a brewing family) or their modicum of good marriages and worldly success. It was hard to avoid the impression, however, that Uncle Roy regarded his own mother as vaguely *infra dig*. The occasions when Granny came face to face with Sargie Lampitt were a torment to Uncle Roy. The reason given was that she spoke her mind – in other words, she saw *through* Sargie. But since she never said anything particularly abrasive, it was hard to see why Uncle Roy hovered so nervously on these occasions, unless it was for fear that she might let slip in her speech signals, unnoticeable to most of the world, but excruciating to her son, of his background and origin in Putney: 'pardon' for 'what', 'settee' for 'sofa'; the usual string of shibboleths by which the socially mobile in the British Isles have chosen to torment one another.

Although in my moments of bitterest hostility to my uncle I have dismissed his fondness for the Lampitts as 'pure snobbery', I have since revised my view. In time, one comes to revise all views, just as one comes to see that very little is 'pure' anything. Snobbery itself, embarrassing as it may be when identified, is not explained simply by being qualified with the epithet 'pure'. In any case, I rather doubt whether my uncle's first call at the Place (years before my own birth) was conducted in a mood of social aspiration. Uncle Roy was enough of a romantic, at that stage before his addiction began, to regret that the Lampitts were not one of the old Norfolk families, like the Whatleys, now extinct, whose tombs and brasses adorned the parish church.

Nor could the religious history of the Lampitts (originally Unitarian, now predominantly left-wing atheist) have made an immediate appeal. To give him his due, Uncle Roy always expressed disapproval in that area. At some stage, he and Sargie had become fast friends. And if I supposed that the terms of the friendship were ignominious (my uncle always having to play Sancho Panza to Sargie's Don Quixote) that was really their business, not mine. What was my business was the fact that when he was at home, Uncle Roy was able to speak for hours on end about the Lampitts, and to expect me to listen.

That afternoon, for instance, as though he had first thought of the fact, he said, 'Your Uncle Sargie is an *extraordinarily* intelligent man, but he can on occasion be exasperating.'

Uncle Roy laughed, a sure sign that one of his anecdotes was to be trotted out. We all knew them by heart. My aunt, who had got the rice pudding from the bottom of the Aga, stirred it with particular vehemence, as if she would really prefer to be stirring Sargie's wonderfully powerful brains.

'Some time ago – it was before the war – when *was* it, Deirdre?'

There was never any 'Stop me if I've told you this before' about Uncle Roy.

'Oh, I don't know,' snapped Aunt Deirdre. 'Nineteen thirty-three.'

'It could have been. Anyway, the telephone rang and it was old Sargie. "Roy! I'm fed up!" ' Already my uncle's voice was trembling and it was uncertain whether he would get through a recitation of this thousand-times-told story without a collapse into laughter. ' "Let's drive to Cromer and spend a couple of nights in that nice hotel there." I said, "Honestly, Sargie, I can't simply drive off to Cromer at a moment's notice." '

Taking a silk handkerchief from his top pocket, my uncle mopped his brow. If he took the story gently he might manage to tell it without the giggles, or actual hysterics, setting in.

My aunt, after her little flare of temper about the date of the historic drive to Cromer, now showed no emotion at all. She knocked the side of the spoon against the edge of the pudding dish and put it back in the oven. A bit of skin clung to the spoon and, rather than waste it, she said brusquely, 'Here!'

I opened my mouth obediently and then protested at the heat of the spoon.

'Get off with your bother,' said Aunt Deirdre.

By now, our gleeman had resumed his tale, and reached the stage of the anecdote where he and Sargie were on the road to Cromer. Uncle Roy was at the wheel of Sargie's nice old Lagonda and Sargie was starting to imagine that the tyres of this noble vehicle had gone flat. They pulled in at the next garage. Sargie leaned over my uncle and tooted the horn to alert the attention of the garage man. Sargie's imperiousness with underlings was a regular feature of the stories. It did not appear to trouble Uncle Roy – if anything, the reverse. On this occasion, when the garage man appeared, Sargie insisted in ill-mannered tones that he blow up the *something* tyres. Swearwords, in my uncle's version of events, were always censored.

'You should have seen the man's face!' said my uncle. 'I really think, for two pins, he'd have struck old Sargie.'

At the next garage, Sargie made my uncle pull up. He railed at the garage man because the tyres were too hard. They had been blown up by a *something* maniac. At the next – somewhere near Fakenham – toot-toot. The tyres were too.soft. And so on, all the way to the coast.

By the time he got to the closing stages of this anecdote, one of his favourites in the repertoire, my uncle was nearly crying with mirth. The fact that it was (as I came to feel) a vaguely ignominious story never came into it. For example, he never suggested that he himself had been wrong, at a moment's notice and purely on Sargie's whim, to abandon his wife and child – and his job – and drive off for a few days by the sea. Nor did he ever suggest any resentment at being treated, when Sargie was in one of his moods, like a dim-witted servant, brought along simply in order to drive Sargie's car and fight his crazed battles for him with petrol-pump attendants, hotel clerks and all the multifarious figures whom Sargie suspected of being out to get him. One of the most mysterious facts of all was why Uncle Roy consented to stop at all those garages, rather than protest that there was nothing wrong with the tyres and that if Sargie wished to be driven to Cromer, he should stop being a prize ass. On the contrary, part of the pleasure they seemed to derive from one another's company was precisely Sargie's exploitation of my uncle's good nature. The Cromer saga in its longer version continued with Uncle Roy having to swap bedrooms with Sargie because his own room had a better view of the sea and because Sargie's bedding was somehow damp or uncomfortable.

'And goodness, it really was uncomfortable!' my uncle would laugh, in a tone which suggested that Sargie's insufferable behaviour was something we would all half admire.

On this occasion, however, my aunt cut him short with, 'We're going to eat at half-past six. Couldn't be easier.'

Those were the actual words, but her tone implied that the whole business of putting a cottage pie and a rice pudding in the oven had in fact been fraught with difficulties which she was too stoical to reveal. 'You'll be at Sargie's.'

With this, she clumped up the back stairs which led directly from the kitchen to one of the landings aloft.

There was over an hour before my uncle was due to set out, but this was her leave-taking, for she said, when out of sight and halfway up the stairs in the mock-jokey tones of reproof which she used for upbraiding Tinker if he chewed a newspaper or shat on the carpet, 'Not too much to drink, mind!'

My uncle, as if man to man, gave me a look suggestive that my aunt's words were somehow preposterous. They seldom complained openly about one another, but their mutual discontent was not a secret. Perhaps they let me know about it because I was not their child. Felicity, their grotesquely misnamed daughter, was not, I guess, treated to any such conspiratorial signals as that glance which my uncle gave me. Nevertheless, the emotional discord of her parents' house was, for Felicity as for me, part of the air we breathed.

Philosophers, such as Felicity was to become, like to remind us that some questions are not worth asking because there is no possibility of verifying the answer. Most of the questions which I have ever found interesting have fallen into this category, not least the question of why my uncle and aunt ever chose to get married. I could never tell – and I don't think they could either – whether they were what is called 'happy together' or whether they hated each other's guts. Perhaps a bit of both. Although both Laodiceans who deprecated displays of emotion, they were both ardently, strongly married. It was a strange thing to grow up with. They weren't capable of leaving the thing be. They were addicted to their marital routines, but somehow aware that whatever was going on between them, it was not for public display. It was as though there was some strangely pungent

11

smell in their house of which they were half ashamed. I went through a phase of believing that my aunt would have seemed less cross all the time if Uncle Roy had taken her out more. But where would they have gone? And if out, would they have wanted to be seen?

The world was kept firmly at arm's length. Sometimes relations or old school friends of Aunt Deirdre's would come to stay. Very occasionally, she would ask a female friend for lunch. But, for most of the time during my school holidays, the four of us were walled up together with Deirdre and Roy's unhappiness, breathing it, avoiding it, allowing it to warp and change us.

An hour or so after my aunt had gone up the back stairs, my uncle sauntered down the front stairs. He had discarded his tweeds and assumed evening clothes which had known better days. The 'black' tie was really a dullish green; so were the lapels on his dinner jacket. In the hall, there was a large hat-stand with a looking-glass set into the middle, encircled with pegs. An array of headgear depended from this hideous object of furniture, all of them in their different ways suggesting versions of Uncle Roy which at one stage or another he had thought of adopting. He paused now, unaware of my lurking presence in the hall, and stared at the glass with undisguised admiration. It was quite surprising to me, what my uncle did next. I have suggested that the variety of hats represented different aspects of Uncle Roy, but it might be equally true to regard these strange objects as items from a child's dressing-up box. If my uncle had ever been able to distinguish between charades and real life he would probably have possessed fewer hats. The deerstalker would have been ideal for playing Sherlock Holmes but looked absurd in the village. The solar topee – Dr Livingstone, I presume. The Mickey Mouse gas mask was in point of fact Felicity's. But what of the *Daily Mail* hat? Uncle Roy must have been the only person in the world to own such an object – apart from Winston Churchill, at that stage out of office thanks to the unpatriotic (in my aunt's terms) activities of the Attlees, Crippses and Lampitts of this world.

My uncle paused before the glass, as though unable to decide between becoming the greatest private detective or the formidable wartime Prime Minister. For the time being, he rejected both possibilities and reached instead for a tall, silk opera hat which, as soon as he had perched it on his head, gave him the look of Burlington Bertie, the decayed toff. The sight of himself thus attired made my uncle smile and then titter. Having had his moment of fun, he put the hat back and reached for his daily wear, a rather battered black trilby.

'Byee!' he called.

The house could have been empty for all the response he got. At that moment a feeling of tenderness for my uncle seized me and I wanted to call out an affectionate good night. I could not do so, however, without revealing my presence in the shadows by the green baize door at the back of the passage, and thus betraying the fact that I had witnessed his innocent charade. So I let him go out comfortless into the night. My aunt never responded to his cries of greeting or valediction as he entered or left the house; and my cousin Felicity, at that date, never used her vocal chords unless positively forced to do so. There was something tremendously sad about my uncle's figure as he sloped out into the spring evening. It was still light and the colours of the garden seemed especially vivid since, after that long winter, there had at last been a thaw.

Within seconds of his departure, my aunt emerged from her bedroom on the first-floor landing and made her brisk descent, this time down the front stairs.

'Nearly time for "The Mulberrys"!' she announced to the world in general.

This wireless programme, to which my aunt was devoted, purported to be a realistic account of life in some fictitious, rural village of England. It had begun, a few years previously, during the war as part of the Government's propaganda, the object in this case being to persuade the populace to dig for victory, eat carrots for their supposed efficacy as optical stimulants and save scraps for pigswill. 'The Mulberrys', however, soon outgrew their origins as a vehicle for government information and took on a narrative life of its own. The family in question were supposed to live in a village called Barleybrook and run a farm of a few hundred acres. Even by the restricted standards of rural life, it was astonishing how, in this particular village, the Mulberrys got everywhere. Dick Mulberry, the paterfamilias, ran Daisy Farm with his wife Elsie and their son Stan. These three all spoke with an invented rustic voice, 'z's for 's's, 'oi' for 'I', loosely based on the dialect poems of William Barnes. Dick's other children were Reg, who spoke with the accent of a completely different region (vaguely North Country with presumably accidental lapses into Irish), and the Cockney Mag who had married rather rakishly and was always getting into scrapes. The supporting cast included farmhands, a doctor, the vicar and a rival farming family, supposed to be less amiable than the Mulberrys, called the Swills.

No village on earth ever bore the remotest resemblance to Barleybrook and no human being ever spoke, thought, or behaved like a member of the Mulberry lineage. How my aunt, a countrywoman all her life and deeply acquainted with villages and their ways, derived pleasure from the programme I don't know. But she did. When my uncle was out, supper could be timed to coincide with the latest drama from Barleybrook. It was an addiction which Aunt Deirdre had passed on to Felicity and, to a lesser degree, myself.

Consulting the little watch which she kept pinned to her bosom, my aunt called again in her jokey voice; it was sort of mock-pompous, as if she were announcing a hymn number in church.

'Nearly Mulberrytime!'

Felicity did not waste breath answering if she were called. She showed that she had heard by opening her bedroom door and galumphing down the back stairs into the kitchen. When it was just the three of us we did not bother to sit in the dining room. It saved the business of the trolley, one of whose casters was loose, and all the palaver of place mats and glasses.

'Kitchen living' is now universal. At this date, I suspect it was slightly unusual, one of the many examples (marrying Uncle Roy had been the most glaring) of my aunt's willingness to behave eccentrically when she chose.

Cottage pie, with some cabbage which had been swimming in boiling water for a good three-quarters of an hour, was dolloped on to our plates and borne to the kitchen table just as the 'Mulberrys' theme tune crackled from the large bakelite speaker on the dresser. I little knew then how ominous that tune was to become in my life.

'Now, old Silas, doan' you stan' there a-leanin' on the gate. You come up to Oak Meadow – there be some ewes a-lambin'.'

'Sorry, Marser Stan.'

The familiar bilgewater of Mulberry dialogue dripped over our heads.

'Wonder if Mag's *really* bought those black-market silk stockings,' whispered Aunt Deirdre; but a glare from Felicity, whose concentration on the programme was total, was enough to silence her.

Of her two parents, Felicity more resembled her mother than her father. She had my aunt's massiveness; I do not mean that either woman was tall, but they were both then – before Felicity lost so much weight – strikingly full-featured. My aunt's large round face never aged much until she got into her sixties. With her short hair and ruddy cheeks, she could have been almost any age from truculent teens to moody menopause. My cousin Felicity had some of her mother's ageless quality in her late teens, only in her face the truculence was much more marked. In some lights, Felicity at eighteen actually looked older than her mother. They did their hair differently. Instead of Aunt Deirdre's short crop (which, like the tweeds, seemed to be announcing itself as sensible), Felicity had a long, thick plait. She seemed, and I think was, permanently cross. Since it was obvious that she did not like me much, it was hard not to take the bates personally.

We ate our cottage pie, which was greyish and devoid of all flavour. The scene of lambing at Daisy Farm changed to the back bar of the King's Head where Reg Mulberry, with his mysterious semi-Lancashire voice, was making up to Flo, the barmaid.

'Lay off, Reg Mulberry.'

'I jus' said how nice you looked in those stockings, love, that's all.'

'You've been drinking, Reg Mulberry.'

'Hic! I 'aven't.'

'I don't know what you're implying, Reg Mulberry, about my stockings, but I'm not the only person who has them. Your sister Mag's got silk stockings, and there are plenty of people who'd like to know where she got them.'

'Oh, they would, would they?' said Reg in his drunken voice. 'Then if you like, I'll tell you, Flo. I'll tell you straight out . . .'

At this exciting point the Mulberry tune interrupted the dialogue, leaving us on tenterhooks for twenty-four hours. I was every bit as gripped by the programme as the women were, an added excitement being the sense that the vaguely sexual overtones of the final scene had disturbed them both. I knew it had been sexual, without knowing how or why, because my aunt, when she switched off the set, said, 'A pity when Reg starts getting silly.'

Aunt Deirdre thought all male lapses from sobriety or chastity were 'silly'. She was probably right. She had even once said that she did not like Sargie making Uncle Roy drink so much because it made him silly, an observation which offered a strange glimpse into the impenetrable world of their private life. By the severest standards it could be said that it did not need drink, or anything else, to *make* Uncle Roy silly; he was, in fact, never anything else. This, however, was not what she had meant by the word.

'Don't let the other boys get silly,' was the only piece of sex education offered to me by my aunt, before returning to school one term.

The small cottage pie which had been dolloped out of its Pyrex dish had been finished at its first serving. There were seldom seconds at my aunt's board. I would have happily eaten another plateful of cottage pie; though dull, it was far from unpalatable and hunger in those days was a perpetual condition.

'All finished?' asked Aunt Deirdre.

'It was very nice,' I said.

Felicity got up and piled our plates.

'The pud's in the bottom of the Aga, darling,' said my aunt, a remark to which Felicity did not reply. Trying to make the silence seem more 'normal', my aunt exclaimed, 'Good old rice pud!' One felt it was the reply which Felicity was *meant* to have given herself.

The pudding dish was brought to the table and its contents were dispersed into three willow-pattern soup plates. Then my aunt spoke again.

'We'll have to start packing your trunk tomorrow, Julian. There's no point in pulling a face, old thing, it's *got* to be done.'

Packing the trunk was always the signal that the school holidays were drawing to a close. About a week before term began, all my uniform, beautifully laundered and with name-tapes sewn into it, was laid out on one of the spare beds – grey shirts, grey socks, games things (cricket flannels this term): prison clobber. Knowing how difficult I found transitions

16

between home and school, Aunt Deirdre always adopted an attitude of breezy jollity about the whole thing.

'I hate packing,' I said.

'Poor old boy! Back to the Dump!' This was a playful allusion to a judgement of my own, sincerely passed on the school after a couple of terms there. 'Still, summer terms aren't so bad, are they?'

Seeing tears start to my eyes, my aunt swiftly turned her attention to Felicity.

'Darling!'

Felicity was 'Darling'; I was 'Julian' or 'old thing'; my uncle was usually nothing at all in my aunt's vocatives.

'Darling, you're all packed up, too, aren't you? Well, you don't need to pack so much because they let you leave quite a lot of your books there, didn't they? Very sensible. Do you have a lot of beastly exams this summer? What are they called? Prelims, isn't it?'

'Part One,' said Felicity with some ruthlessness. The tone implied that any fool, even one who had married an Oxford graduate, could get the names of Cambridge exams right. My uncle, as a tiresome sort of joke, affected not to remember any of the Cambridge slang; my aunt, who had not attended either university, innocently came out with her 'quads' and 'scouts' instead of 'courts' and 'gyps'. Felicity looked furious. She hated talking, but she hated inaccuracy even more; the one had prompted the other.

'Whatever it's called,' said Aunt Deirdre. 'I wonder if you'll go rowing this term – rather fun! Your father said that the girls' colleges do sometimes have a boat. Pity to do nothing except work.'

The idea of Felicity, a poorly co-ordinated girl, being a welcome member of any rowing crew was one which maternal love allowed to take its place in Aunt Deirdre's brain, but it was an incredible one.

The rice pudding was very hot. We all put a spoonful of jam in the middle. My policy was to eat the cooler parts round the edge, working my way gradually into the middle of the bowl. If one gauged it carefully, one's last spoonful could be pure jam. Felicity, by contrast, eighteen years old and an exhibitioner at Girton, stirred up her jam and rice, spattering some of it on the oilcloth. Then she took up great spoonfuls to her lips, blowing at

17

the pudding with noisy smacking of the chops until it was cool enough to eat.

She ate with lightning speed and began to clear the table before my aunt and I had finished eating. Then she started to wash up. Within a quarter of an hour, she was back in her room. Those two syllables – 'Part One' – were the only ones to have been uttered by Felicity in the course of the whole evening.

Trivial as its events were, I shall always remember that evening, and the morning after, as the beginning of the story which follows. For a while, after Felicity had gone upstairs, my aunt and I sat in the freezing drawing room. She turned collars and I turned the pages of my *Boy's Own Paper*. Then we played a couple of rounds of Snakes and Ladders. She won hands down. Then she pecked me on the cheek and said good night.

Later, long after I had switched out my light, I became aware of my uncle and aunt talking animatedly in the hall. I was too full of sleep to make out what they were saying, but it sounded as though something was up. Probably I am reading back into the situation a significance which I only discerned later on, but I *think* I felt excited, the sort of feeling you have when it is your birthday.

The next I knew, it was seven o'clock, which, because it was Thursday, was the time I got up. There was an early celebration on Thursday mornings and during the school holidays I was an altar server. Later on (from about the age of fourteen onwards) I developed very decided views about these matters and felt sure that Christianity was based on various moral and historical falsehoods. At twelve, I just regarded it as something you did, like compulsory games or going to school or wearing a tie. I am not sure that in so many words I believed it, if by 'it' is meant the abstruser formulations of theology. Certainly, I did not associate my uncle, or any of the things he did in church, with what I would have later called 'genuine' religious aspirations of a kind which I had come across in books or wondered if I had not experienced myself. There was certainly no connection between what went on in church and such questions as whether life had a meaning, or whether there was a personal god. As far as I was concerned, it was drill, a matter of certain words, clothes and actions.

The walk from the vicarage to the church in the early morning was never for some reason frightening, even though the same walk in the half-light of evening required a great act of will. Every bush and shadow in the evening felt as if it were inhabited by a hostile stranger, a ghost, a village lout, or perhaps some man (my aunt had given me hints about their existence) wanting to be silly. In the shadows of morning, everything was different. The grey sky was getting brighter each moment. Though it was still cold, there was a feeling of spring in the air. The birds sang overhead in the long avenue of beeches in the vicarage drive, on either side of which, in thick green clumps, the foliage (but not yet the blooms) of bluebells grew in abundance. Once through the gate and out into the lane, the grass verges were thick with primroses, campion and aconites. The walk was a mere quarter of a mile.

We always entered the churchyard not by the wicket gate but through a little gap in the wall on the south side, from whence a path led up to the church, a large, flint, fifteenth-century building with clear glass in its perfectly proportioned Perpendicular windows.

It is for its carvings that most visitors remember Timplingham Parish Church – the rood screen and the misericords which somehow survived the Reformation, and, most distinctive of all, the beam ends in the roof of the nave. Other East Anglian churches are famed for their angel-beams, but Timplingham has a row of choristers in what Uncle Roy certainly regarded as highly 'correct', full-sleeved rochets. The row of plump carved faces and of hands clasped in prayer could not be more demure, or so one thinks until one has made a careful examination of each figure. All down the south aisle, they stare down, these male wooden innocents, with pudding-basin coiffures reminiscent of Laurence Olivier in the film of *Henry V*. Up the north aisle they appear to present a similarly pleasant if dull picture. Carmelites in choir, my uncle always said. (Timplingham had been a friary until the Reformation.) All figures, that is, save one, three from the end, who gazes down just over the pulpit. The face of this figure wears the same placid expression as all the others. But its hands are not clasped in prayer, nor is the linen enfolded at its neck. Rather, the choir garment has been pulled down to reveal not the flat chest of a Carmelite friar but the ample bosom of some fifteenth-century East Anglian girl. My aunt always said that it was a 'pity' that Timplingham should be famed for this *risqué* piece of sculpture, but my uncle enjoyed pointing it out to visitors. Sargie Lampitt, never known to attend divine worship, was also a devotee of what he called the Timplingham Titties.

Uncle Roy always got to church before I did. By the time I arrived, he would be half vested, in amice, alb and girdle, sitting or kneeling at the back of the Lady Chapel. My job was to light the candles on the altar, check that a quantity of bread (my uncle deprecated the use of communion wafers) was on the credence table with the wine and return to the vestry to wait for the service to begin. Sometimes I wore special rig for this, sometimes not. That morning, I seem to remember, I did not dress up.

All the clothes worn in church excited a passionate interest in my uncle. They all meant something. For me, they were just fancy dress. The fact that I knew anything about it, still less that I *wore* it, was a jealously guarded secret which I should hate to have been known by my contemporaries at school. Wearing albs and knowing the word 'alb' was both pansy (almost, in my aunt's sense, silly) and creepy: only a short step away from witches' robes and dabbling with the occult.

Not so for Uncle Roy who was punctilious about the exact shape, colour and function of each liturgical vestment, and who prided himself on being much more 'correct' than other High Church clergymen in the neighbourhood. The idea was that one should be Catholic without imitating Rome. The clothes and rituals with which Uncle Roy cluttered the church services were all in his view authentically English: the full conical chasubles, for instance, were of a kind which you might see in some fifteenth-century English book of hours and were quite unlike the cut-away, fiddle-back chasubles worn at that date by the Roman clergy. Times have changed and Uncle Roy's vestments would nowadays be all the rage in Rome. Not that he was trying to be in the vanguard – quite the reverse. My uncle's outlandish rig in church was all part of his desire to cut a dash and differentiate himself from the rest of the world. As such, it embarrassed me quite a lot and I would have given anything to see him dressed like an 'ordinary vicar' in church, just as I would have preferred him not to attend school speech-days wearing bright green golfing trousers, a matching Norfolk jacket and the inevitable white bow tie.

The claim that, by wearing extraordinary clothes in church,

he was getting back to some more ancient or authentic mode of carrying on later struck me, however, less as a piece of Uncle Roy's tiresomeness than as a symptom of the almost universal human tendency to rewrite and readjust the past. The so-called Sarum Rite, of which my uncle was so enthusiastic an exponent, had really been invented by a Hampstead clergyman in 1899 and probably bore no more relation to anything which had happened in the Middle Ages than did the deliberations of the Honourable Vernon at the Labour Party Conference. No matter. The important thing was that Uncle Roy and a few others had convinced themselves that what he did in church was the real thing. What was the Judaeo-Christian religion itself, except a creative readjustment of history, a ceaseless rehearsal and repetition of past events which, each time they were recited, became further removed from the original events they described and more a part of the mental furniture of the devotees? So that events such as the Jewish Exodus from Egypt or the Exile in Babylon had long ago ceased to be matters of pure history, if there is such a thing, and had become mythological episodes by which the present lives of the faithful were shaped and judged. One could see the same thing happening in national mythology, too – Churchill's period out of office actually helping to make the events of the Second World War, Dunkirk, the Battle of Britain and all that had happened since achieve an Homeric status in the common consciousness, so that each retelling of the stories itself re-forms rather than uncovers the past. Speaking about the past is always, therefore, an example of the truth of a line of Russian poetry quoted to me (ages after the period I am describing) by Felicity – 'A thought expressed is always a lie.'

What is true for nations or communities of the religious faithful is equally true for individuals. Our attempts to recover or uncover the past and what really happened are doomed at the outset to failure because it is we ourselves who are doing the investigation. We move on. We become someone else. The self of ten, twenty, thirty years previous is alien to us. And yet, untrustworthily creative as we know our memories to be, we are prepared to invest them with more credence than those pictures created by the inevitably rougher brushwork of out- siders. Our own lives, that is, as remembered by ourselves, are probably fictions, but they are more reliable fictions than other

21

people's reconstructions of our own lives. Of all liars the most arrogant are biographers: those who would have us believe, having surveyed a few boxes full of letters, diaries, bank statements and photographs, that they can play at the recording angel and tell the whole truth about another human life.

Strange to say, it was on that April morning in Timplingham Church that the story began which, more than anything else which has happened in my life, has sharpened this truth and put it into focus: the story of Hunter and the Lampitts.

I have mentioned that the colours worn in church were of particular significance to my uncle. Unbleached linen for Lent (it was considered very *infra dig* to wear purple during this season). Scarlet for Passiontide. Green for those long, lazy Sundays after Trinity. Since it was shortly after Easter, I should have expected my uncle to be wearing vestments of white damask. It was something of a shock to see black vestments spread out on the chest in the sacristy. There was no talking before Mass – not so much as 'Good morning' – so the gossipy question of who had kicked the bucket would have to wait. My first horrified instinct was to believe that it was Granny – but then I realised that my aunt would surely have told me and not allowed me to learn so horrible a piece of news in so roundabout a way. On the other hand, since my aunt was the Mercury of the household, why had she not told us the previous evening at supper of the passing which these black vestments commemorated? Her stream of commentary about Timplingham and its affairs provided us with an episodic village drama every bit as interesting as anything dreamed up by the scriptwriters of 'The Mulberrys'. If someone in the village had died, Aunt Deirdre would certainly have told us over the cottage pie.

And besides, if some village person *had* died, it would not have been usual for my uncle to say a requiem mass for their souls. He wore his black vestments on Remembrance Sunday, or for the funerals of those who occupied some special place in his pantheon. I am not quite sure whether 'village people', Uncle Roy's phrase for his parishioners, actually possessed souls. If not, it would clearly have been superfluous to pray for them. Certainly, when soul and body were both in one piece, few enough of the good Timplinghamites ever came to watch my uncle in action. Even by the minimal standards of the day, Uncle Roy's flock was almost scandalously small.

The identity of the deceased would, however, soon be revealed. My uncle had come into the vestry and was putting on the last of what Sargie once disrespectfully called his 'glad rags'. First the black stole, which he always kissed before placing it around his neck; then the huge black chasuble over the head; finally the maniple over the left wrist. Then he picked up the chalice and paten, loosely covered with a cloth (he considered the burse and the chalice-veil Roman and therefore common) and he nodded to me that he was ready for the off. I rang a small handbell and we made our way to the Lady Altar.

The congregation that morning could not be said to be overwhelmingly large. Felicity no longer attended, which eliminated a high percentage of the worshippers. (It was never talked about, but generally assumed that she had lost her faith.) Mrs Batterbee, who helped my aunt in the house, sometimes obliged my uncle by making up the regulation two or three without whom the Prayer Book decreed that it was improper to celebrate the Sacrament. On this occasion, she was away, perhaps with her sister in King's Lynn. Eirene, who did the rough, had the excuse of being chapel, so was not expected to come to the services. So, that morning, only my aunt was in church.

My uncle reached the altar, bowed and kissed it. Then he turned round and spoke in his rather beautiful liturgical tones:

'Of your charity, pray for the repose of the soul of James Petworth Lampitt, who died yesterday . . . '

So! I might have guessed that this liturgical extravagance heralded the passing of no ordinary mortal. Sargie's brother Jimbo had gone to meet his Maker. One could only hope (I suppose that was the point of the requiem) that the Lampitts were as highly regarded in the Kingdom of Heaven as they were in Timplingham Rectory.

All my uncle's judgements of the Lampitts are fixed involuntarily and indelibly in my mind. I sometimes think what a well-stocked brain I would have if, instead of grinding on about the Lampitts, he had read aloud to me from Homer and Plato.

'Old Jimbo is in many ways like Sargie – both very highly strung and *highly* intelligent. What a man Jimbo is! A true belle-lettrist!' My uncle was innocent of the idea that 'belle-lettrist', in modern literary circles, is a term of opprobrium. 'I dare say that there will be fuller lives of Prince Albert, but none more elegant, none more concise, none more *delicious.'*

I had never set eyes on Jimbo, who wrote under the name of James Petworth Lampitt and whose flow of mannered prose had dried up a goodish while before the war. His visits to Timplingham were rare after their mother died, but he and Sargie were said to keep in touch, to write letters and to meet in London. Unless one counted the transitory glory of sitting in the Cabinet (as the Honourable Vernon now did), then Jimbo was probably at that stage (even before he was immortalised by Hunter) the most famous of the Lampitts. The idea of a requiem, I believe, is that the sins of the dead person are in some way cancelled out by the power of Christ's sacrificial offering. None of the three present in church that morning had the smallest inkling what those sins might be. It was Hunter's task to unravel those for us. Had my aunt been aware of *quite* how silly Jimbo had allegedly been, she might very well have gone home to prepare the breakfast, rather than waste time praying for him.

My uncle was a stickler for the 1662 Prayer Book, so that at each celebration there was a complete recitation of the Ten Commandments.

He stood on the altar steps and peered down into the shadowy aisles and the rows of empty pews.

'Thou shalt not commit adultery,' said Uncle Roy.

Alone in the body of the church, my aunt's Angela Brazil tones responded, 'Lord have mercy upon us and incline our hearts to keep this law . . .'

Over breakfast, Uncle Roy told us that Jimbo Lampitt had died the previous day at about half-past five in the afternoon. With my passion for times of death, derived from reading detective stories, I made a mental note that 'the deceased' had died at the very moment that Aunt Deirdre had been putting the rice pudding in the oven.

It was an upsetting death, which was at present unexplained. Jimbo (as my uncle referred to him throughout this narrative) had fallen into the area of his London house from a top-floor fire escape: a distance of some sixty feet. He was not quite seventy years of age. Apparently, he was in the habit towards the end of day of strolling out on to the fire escape on the top floor of his house to admire the roofscapes and treetops, the views and the

24

skies. Sargie said this reminded Jimbo of Italy, though why such reminiscences should be afforded by the sight of Manchester Square in the rush hour was never made altogether clear.

'Sargie was very fond of Jimbo,' said Uncle Roy – 'I think we shouldn't say too much about the *way* he died. It really is too upsetting – the worst death really' – he meant the worst Lampitt death – 'since Gerald died of that tumour thing in . . . '

'Mombasa,' said my aunt.

'No,' I said. 'It was Vivian who had phlebitis in Mombasa. Gerald had a tumour in Johannesburg.'

'He's a clever boy, this,' said my uncle, delighted that I should be so well versed in my Lampitt catechism.

'Of course,' conceded my aunt.

'I suppose that there'll be a family funeral and then a memorial service afterwards for the *literary* world. And we all know what a hotbed of gossip and misinformation *that* is.'

'Quite,' said my aunt.

As it happens, this was a perfectly reasonable exchange, though I don't know what it was based on; my uncle and aunt were as ignorant of the 'literary world' as I was.

'Sargie's very anxious that people won't start saying it's a repetition of history. Angelica all over again.'

'Angelica?' My aunt really did not *concentrate* enough on her Lampitt lore. One even got the impression that she was sometimes frivolous enough to think about other things.

Angelica Lampitt, an unmarried aunt of Jimbo and Sargie's, and a keen supporter of Women's Suffrage, had taken her own life – cut her wrists in the bath – upon the marriage of her close friend Miss Bean. The emotional undercurrents of this tragedy were lost on me then – indeed, I am not sure that I understand them now – but the facts were clear enough. Angelica's death was so dramatic that it seemed to me nothing short of fantastic that anyone could have forgotten about them. 'Angelica' was now synonymous with suicide. My aunt couldn't have forgotten this. Perhaps she considered that that sort of thing, the emotional life of the unmarried, was an unsuitable topic to discuss in front of a child.

'You *know*.' My uncle spoke irritably.

Coming quickly to heel and evidently remembering the Angelica incident, my aunt said, 'They surely don't think it's *that*?'

25

'There's going to be an inquest,' said Uncle Roy.

Again, echoes of Agatha Christie and Dorothy L. Sayers! It was often at the inquest that Poirot or Lord Peter would first see the suspects. I felt thoroughly excited. The violent and unexplained death of a minor literary celebrity whom we hardly knew could not but be the cause of excitement, even pleasure. But death makes hypocrites of grown-up persons. My uncle's line, as a professional, was the reverse of sentimental when it came to the deaths of village people.

Not long before, in Holy Week, my aunt announced the death of a bedridden old woman whom she had been visiting almost every day for the previous year.

'Evie Tarrant's dead,' she had said.

'At last!' was my uncle's only response. Then, about an hour later, he had put his head around the kitchen door and said, 'Does that mean that I have to take the funeral?'

Lampitt deaths were different. They required a sort of possessive solemnity. We had to pull especially long faces to show how 'in' we were with the family. Equally, it behoved us to be cagey about the whole thing with strangers, implying that we who were more or less family knew a thing or two which it would be unsafe to divulge to the hoi polloi.

'I think we shan't talk about Jimbo's death in the village,' said my uncle.

'Of course not,' snapped my aunt. 'You always speak as if I were the one who went round Timplingham gossiping.'

My uncle winced as though she were hitting him with a rolling pin. At the same time there was a look of pleasure in his eyes: he liked getting a rise out of her.

'Anyway,' said my aunt, 'I can't imagine the subject coming up. It's fifty years or more since Jimbo *lived* in the Place and Sargie has retreated so much into himself that people hardly *know* about the Lampitts any more.'

Clearly, the idea that people did not know, care or think about Lampitts was too outlandish to be worth answering. My uncle sighed.

'Dear old Jimbo,' he said. 'Do you remember his dropping in here once when he was staying with Sargie?'

'He was rather rude,' said my aunt.

Obviously, this couldn't quite be gainsaid, because my uncle merely replied: 'It was when he was writing that short book on

26

Archbishop Benson. He wanted some advice about the ecclesiastical background. People like that know *nothing*.'

'I didn't like him saying – "Oh, you're Sargie's tame parson." ' My aunt adopted the all-purpose mincing tones which in her speech signified 'someone else speaking whom I don't happen to like'. As a matter of fact, I believe Petworth Lampitt *did* have rather a squeaky, mincing voice but, had my aunt taken a dislike to Paul Robeson, her 'imitation' of his voice would have been no different.

'He shouldn't have spoken like that,' she said firmly.

'Oh, it was all right,' said Uncle Roy.

'You didn't like it at the time. You didn't go up to the Place for about three weeks. "I thought Sargie was a friend," you kept saying. "How could he call me his *tame parson*?" '

'It wasn't the only time I met Jimbo,' said my uncle. 'He came to Hilda's eightieth birthday party in Ashley Gardens.'

This was a Lampitt family dinner to which my aunt had not been invited. The memory of it rankled as much as Jimbo's visit to the Rectory.

'It was extremely kind of them to ask me,' said Uncle Roy. 'Jimbo was certainly in cracking form that night, cracking form: memories of Rupert Brooke, Baron Corvo, he even went to see Oscar Wilde in Paris, you know.'

At this my aunt glared. When she was in the mood, my aunt glared easily. I had no idea who Oscar Wilde was, nor what he might have been doing in Paris, but my uncle had clearly sailed too near the wind. He began to generalise.

'Good style and beauty of language are undervalued today, but my guess is that old Jimbo will last. The Prince Consort biography is a classic – and some of the essays. That lovely thing about the death of Tennyson – do you remember it? Him clutching *Cymbeline* and the evening light falling on his beard. "No sound from those lips, no breath" ' – my uncle had quite a lot of Jimbo's purple prose by heart – ' "He slept, as Arthur slept in Avalon; and, as another Arthur, who lay in the chu. chyard at Cleveland. The widowed race was run." '

'I expect he'll cut up pretty nicely,' chipped in my aunt brusquely. 'Will Sargie inherit the lot or will they divide it between the remaining siblings?'

'I haven't asked. He seemed much more worried last night about the possibility of an inquest and all the publicity.'

'Oh, *Lord*!' said Aunt Deirdre.

Then with a silent shrug my uncle went to sit in his study to do whatever it was he did there, and my aunt announced that she would be going to the village and would I come with her?

Before we left, we packed the trunk and carried it to the front porch, ready for collection by the railway van.

'One more label perhaps,' said Aunt Deirdre, who was a dab hand at all activities such as packing, tying parcels, or tidying cupboards. 'Will you stick it on, or will I?'

I let her do so, and stared at its newness, wishing that the name on the label had no connection with the address, but realising with misery that the trunk and the label represented an inevitability.

MASTER JULIAN RAMSAY
SEAFORTH GRANGE SCHOOL
GREAT MALVERN
WORCS

I was always embarrassed by my aunt's continuation of the already obsolete custom of calling me Master Julian Ramsay. It conjured up a picture of Little Lord Fauntleroys, Eton collars and the sort of school stories which my uncle probably read in his own boyhood.

'That's done,' said my aunt. 'Now we can go down to the village.'

'You couldn't get me some stamps if you go into the post office?' asked my uncle, coming out of his study.

'Let's hope we don't meet that wretched woman again!' said my aunt. 'She's *everywhere*. Yesterday, she was in the post office and said' – once more my aunt put on her mincing voice – ' "You call me Debbie and I'll call you Jill." Well, I mean, she's only been in the village five minutes!'

'I expect Jill could cope,' said my uncle, lighting his pipe.

'Oh, she ignored it. She gave the woman quite a nice smile, but there was no question of Christian names. It's just so *silly*, trying that sort of thing on.'

I had witnessed the Wretched Woman's blunder. It would be pointless to have told my aunt that Mrs Maddock was only trying to be friendly. That was just the trouble. When my aunt disliked people (she called it 'taking a scunner against them')

28

she could not be reasoned with. It was never explained why she had such a scunner against Mrs Maddock who had moved to the village with her husband not two months before. They still had not learnt that you pronounced it 'Timming 'em', rather than the way it is spelt. Mr Maddock, a weedy little man with glasses, taught in a school in Norwich. She – the Wretched Woman, that is – did not do anything, but she was a Cambridge graduate. 'And don't we know it!' my aunt would always add when recounting this piece of information. 'I could have told her about Felicity being up at Cambridge. That might have shown her that she wasn't the only person to have been there.'

There was no evidence that the Wretched Woman did subscribe to any such extraordinary belief. Just what beliefs she did *not* subscribe to were made all too clear one day in the greengrocer's when she had called out to my aunt, 'You must tell your husband that we'd love to come to support the church, but we just can't believe there's such a thing as a personal creator.'

My uncle seemed most annoyed that the Maddocks had made a joint decision in the matter. It was the 'we' that annoyed him. My aunt averred that the least she could do, the wretched woman, was to keep such ideas to herself and not to go shouting about them in village shops.

The control of information in Timplingham was something in which my uncle and aunt took a strong interest. They did not themselves take a daily paper – Sargie's copy of *The Times* was sent over from the Place several afternoons a week, when he remembered. Otherwise, there was the wireless set. Neither my uncle nor my aunt actually said that they believed that these were the only means by which information from the outside world could legitimately reach the village, but they behaved as though this was what they thought. For instance, in the matter of Jimbo's death, they both spoke as if only those within the charmed circle of the Lampitts themselves might be privileged to know of it. Since Sargie was so seldom out and about, the burden fell on the Rectory to decide what the outside world should or should not know about the Lampitts. The previous year, Sargie's Aunt Hilda had died in a nursing home aged eighty-six. There were no suspicious circumstances. Nevertheless, Uncle Roy treated this story as classified information. He decided that it would be a bad thing if the village 'got talking about it' and we were all sworn to secrecy about Hilda's death. No one in Timplingham had ever heard of Hilda, so it was hardly surprising that bootfaced yokels did not stop my aunt as she walked down the village street in order to quiz her about this most unremarkable passing. Both Uncle Roy and Aunt Deirdre, however, attributed the village people's silence purely to the efficiency of the Rectory's censorship.

A similar line was to be pursued in relation to Jimbo's demise.

While I put on my blue school gaberdine, Aunt Deirdre adjusted her felt hat in the hall glass. It was her only hat, at least thirty years out of date, vaguely cloche. She checked that she had her purse and her shopping list in the bottom of the basket. With her passion for planning everything down to the last detail, she never went out without a list, even if she was only going to post a letter and buy some tobacco for Uncle Roy. She could easily have done the bulk of the shopping on one day each week, but she preferred to do the rounds of the shops every day, disseminating and suppressing news. Like any good agent in the field, my aunt believed in collecting as much information as possible while giving almost nothing away in return.

'Now, we shan't say anything about Jimbo dying,' she repeated to me in the drive.

'Is Uncle Sargie very sad that his brother is dead?' I asked.

'Of course it's a shock – the *way* Jimbo died. But people don't go on for ever.'

It occurred to me – one of the thousand totally false impressions which I harboured as a child – that grown-ups might conceivably not feel things at all. They got into bates; but, by feelings, I meant needing to blub. Grown-ups hardly ever blubbed. I therefore thought it conceivable that feeling was something which you might outgrow, like short trousers.

There had been no mention of Sargie blubbing, even though he *was* one of the grown-ups who sometimes did lose control. Once, when down in the dumps, he had allowed my uncle to buy him lunch in some hotel in Norwich; the salmon was past its best and Sargie had burst into tears. Salmon was worth Sargie's tears, but not the death of a brother. This seemed queer to me.

I agreed with my aunt that nothing should be said of all this in the village; and I believed completely in her power to prevent anyone in Timplingham hearing anything about Jimbo. If Uncle Roy and Aunt Deirdre felt that the village was vaguely hostile or alien, their feelings can have been as nothing to my own. I dreaded the place, hated the idea of having to talk to anyone encountered there, and believed, when I did show my face in the village street, that they were all talking about me. Just going into the shops could be embarrassing; I always had to screw up my courage to do so.

The first port of call was the butcher's. My aunt had the words 'Scrag end' written neatly at the head of her list, words which heralded one of her Irish stews in the near future. As soon as we stepped into the shop my aunt allowed herself an angry 'Tut!' – which was easily explained by the sight of the Wretched Woman standing at the counter.

'You don't have a chicken, Les, I don't suppose?'

'Sold my last, m'dear.'

Mr Harris, the crimson-faced and game-legged butcher, called all his customers, male or female, 'm'dear'. His glistening, lecherous features possibly suggested pleasure at being called Les by this young lady. One suspected that no one, except his darts cronies – and possibly his wife – had ever called him Les since he was a child.

'It's Derek's birthday on Saturday and I wanted to cook something a bit special, you know, perhaps *coq au vin*.'

Mr Harris leered, entering into the spirit of what he took to be some bawdy joke, while the two women behind Mrs Maddock in the queue turned to my aunt. Everyone exchanged glances of horror. Rationing was still in force and the idea of foreign food in Timplingham was somehow not quite nice.

'What about lamb then? Some chops?'

'Right out of chops, m'dear, but I'll tell you what I could do you. A nice bit of scrag end.'

He wiped the cleaver on his old apron, which had once been white and which was now brown with stale blood. Then he clonked a few bits of red and white bone on to the wooden counter.

'I suppose it'll have to do. I can make him a *navarin*.'

Deborah Maddock was tall, blonde, slim and twenty-five years old. If it weren't for the teeth, she would really have been quite pretty. There was a stylishness about her which I admired. I was also fascinated by her voice. Having just about emerged, by the skin of his teeth, from the lower middle classes, my uncle set enormous store by 'good speech', his own voice being in the

31

highest degree mannered and posh. My aunt, who was anyway of a slightly higher social class than her husband, shared Uncle Roy's feeling that educated people should speak what they called 'BBC'. Those who had the misfortune or challenge to grow up speaking 'ee bah gum', as my aunt called any regional variations of speech (northern or southern), jolly well took elocution lessons.

That was Aunt Deirdre's view. Mrs Maddock, evidently, was brazen enough to think otherwise. Although, by today's standards, her voice was barely 'accented' at all, she was thought at the Rectory to 'make rather a thing of being ee bah gum; I should just ignore it if you come across her'. This meant that Mrs Maddock had short North Country 'a's and a few other hardly discernible local variations of speech. I thought she had a nice voice.

While Mr Harris was wrapping the last of the scrag end in newspaper and rolling it into a small haggis-shaped parcel, Mrs Maddock turned round and caught sight of my aunt in the queue behind her.

'Deirdre!' she called. 'Have you seen the news about naughty old Petworth?'

Readers will simply have to take on trust that this is what Debbie Maddock said. At the time, I admit, it seemed incredible. First, one could not believe that she was calling my aunt by her Christian name. One had felt, until that moment, that all my aunt's signals had been so clear that she was somehow keeping Mrs Maddock under control. Evidently not. Secondly, one was astonished that she should have got hold of this top-secret information about the death of James Petworth Lampitt. Thirdly, she was yelling it over the tops of village people's heads as though the Lampitts were just anyone, and even a bit of a joke.

'Ah,' said my aunt, 'good morning, Mrs Maddock.'

'Debbie – *please*. Dr Leavis used to say that Petworth Lampitt was the worst writer of this century with the possible exception of Humbert Wolfe,' pursued the Wretched Woman. The extraordinary thing was that she did not seem to notice my aunt's face as she was saying it. Not only was she prepared to insult the Lampitts, she was also prepared to admit that she had been discussing them with her doctor. This was surely not something you shouted about in shops.

'Still,' she said, impervious to my aunt's icy demeanour, 'you feel sad when they go, don't you, these old literary landmarks. They actually called him the Albert Memorial, you know.'

My aunt was icily silent while Mrs Maddock blurted out these phrases, derived, as she freely confessed, from that morning's *Manchester Guardian*. It was my first glimpse into the rather horrifying fact that certain people – authors evidently among them – have private lives which are considered to be public property. Had Petworth Lampitt been a local grocer or solicitor it is questionable whether even someone so avant-garde as Mrs Maddock would have yelled about his death in quite such tones.

'You do know who I mean, don't you?' she tried, when she saw that she was getting nowhere with Aunt Deirdre. The people behind Mrs Maddock in the queue were becoming restive. 'Petworth Lampitt. He was an author. His brother lives up at Timplingham Place. They say he's a tremendous recluse and a bit of a boozer, but that's probably just village gossip. Anyway, Petworth – that's the author – fell out of a window or something, or he might have jumped off a roof. It was in the paper. They do quite often commit suicide, of course.'

'I don't know what you are talking about, but whatever you mean, it is a very dangerous line of talk,' said my aunt, who had blushed tremendously.

'Poor old things. A blackmailer gets hold of them and that's it – or they just get overtaken by the sadness of life passing by. They think of the days of their golden youth. It's sadder for them.'

The mention of suicide made everyone in the queue stare even harder. Mrs Maddock got out of the way, allowing the other women to approach the counter to buy what little Mr Harris had left.

None of us at this date had any idea that Debbie Maddock, with her teeth and her twins in a pram, regarded herself as an author. There must already have been a novel in the pipeline, though it was several years before she got it published. In other words, with the death of Petworth Lampitt she felt it necessary, as a fellow scribbler, to note his passing and salute it as best she could.

Quite unconscious that she had said anything in the least offensive, she pushed back her floppy, blonde hair from her forehead and turned to me. She said the one thing which I was trying not to think about.

'Well, young man, you'll be going back to school soon.'

I was really just as shy as Felicity. Even had I wanted to answer this tactless quip, I would have been unable to do so. I just felt myself going red and left Aunt Deirdre to do the talking.

'Next week.'

'Is it awful?' pursued Mrs Maddock. Seeing that I went even redder, she adopted those 'concerned' tones with which I later became so familiar. 'No, I mean it. If it's awful, you should say so. Some of these private schools are positively medieval, Dickensian. I don't know why you don't go to a day school.'

She spoke as though I had some choice in the matter. She couldn't, if she had tried, have trodden on stickier ground. The school, however inadequate, had been chosen by my parents. No doubt it suited my uncle and aunt to have me off their hands for rather more than half the year, but my suspicion is that they might have considered taking me away from Seaforth Grange had it not been Daddy's choice. There was an element of piety to his memory in leaving me at quite such an expensive place and at such an inconvenient distance away.

'The wonder is they don't do away with private education altogether,' said Mrs Maddock. She got absolutely no response from Aunt Deirdre to this little morsel, but she battled on with a self-confident laugh: 'It'll come, it'll come!'

By the time our turn came to stand by Mr Harris's filthy wooden counter, there wasn't much meat left. He tried to sell Aunt Deirdre a bluish joint of pork which he said he had been keeping specially.

'And keeping for some time by the look of it, Mr Harris,' said Aunt Deirdre. In the end, she bought half a pound of mince.

'If in doubt, give them mince,' she announced, as though it were a useful general principle to carry through life.

Once outside the butcher's, she stood on the pavement to consider our next move. She was badly shaken by her encounter with Mrs Maddock and it was obvious that we must avoid bumping into her again that morning.

'We'll hang back.' My aunt spoke with the quiet seriousness of a platoon commander who knew that enemy snipers were lurking in every tree and rooftop.

One of the most difficult things about constructing a truthful review of the past is knowing how to chronicle feelings: to say just when I felt this, and when I began to feel the opposite.

Everything gets coloured by one's most recent feelings; about Debbie Maddock, my feelings have been so different that it is hard to get any of them into focus. I can't actually remember what I felt about her before she began her career as a novelist, but I *think* that even then, on the morning we met her in the butcher's, she represented rather a romantic world to me, one of which I did not yet dare to think I would be a part, but a universe which represented the most exciting contrasts with that of the Rectory.

Even while I relished my aunt's extreme dislike for Mrs Maddock (just as a spectacle, in the way that some cruel people enjoy bullfights) I was aware that Mrs Maddock awoke in me the dream of other worlds. Was this what Uncle Roy had felt when he first developed Lampitt mania? For him, the excitement was something which I have cruelly dismissed as snobbish, but he was not in the mean sense a worldly man. He did not love the Lampitts because he hoped to get on. Rather, he loved them at first for what they represented and later, quite simply, as people. After he met Sargie, the world was a bigger place for Uncle Roy, it contained larger imaginative possibilities. Rank, status and fame were only part of the picture, not the whole of it. Money, except in so far as it allowed Sargie to do nothing, and therefore to be endlessly available to waste my uncle's time, played very little part in the picture. None of these things would have meant anything to me aged twelve. But Debbie Maddock, from a very early stage, suggested worlds of which one might dream: a bohemian atmosphere in which people spoke their mind, unfettered by the habits of politeness and concealment with which my uncle and aunt chose to imprison themselves, a world of meals served any old time, of foreign recipes and literary talk . . . I don't know, it was all too nebulous to define. But her presence, just her existence, excited me rather. If Sargie had opened a doorway for my uncle into an enchanted garden, perhaps Mrs Maddock, precisely because my aunt disapproved of her so forcefully, would open a gate for me into another.

Perhaps a large part of the charm derived simply from the fact that she was still a young, personable woman, only about a dozen years older than myself. This too was a new area of things of which I had only the smallest intimations. School, appropriately, was where I was learning. At Seaforth Grange, we had an undermatron scarcely out of her teens called Vanessa Faraday.

Her (for those days) short skirts and unmistakably ample figure beneath woollen jumpers made a vivid impression when she supervised bath nights and dormitory drill. In our dorm, she permitted us all a good-night kiss, allowing us for some moments to hold her against our flat pyjamaed chests and to press our lips against her own. In that austere environment, these kisses were deeply consoling.

Among all her admirers there was active speculation about Vanessa's real boyfriend, who was said to live in her home town of Bromsgrove, Worcs. Was he handsome and what was the extent of the favours extended to him? Although we all prided ourselves on our acquaintance with 'the facts of life', our ideas were almost inconceivably mechanical and crude. In point of fact, there was very little imaginative connection in my mind between the wonderful sensation of kissing Vanessa's full, moist lips, while her breast was clasped to mine, and the cruder levels of dormitory talk after she had switched out the light and left us alone. Although it was a full year or eighteen months since Darnley had informed me how our parents had begotten us, the information had not properly sunk in. A good deal of scepticism remained. If, as seemed to be the case, our mothers had truly allowed this extraordinary invasion of themselves to occur, one could be fairly sure that they did not make a habit of it. Since I was an only child, the evidence suggested that my parents had only had to do it once. Poor Darnley's mother had wanted a large family and had had to do it four times. I now understood, and shared, my aunt's disapproval of Roman Catholics who had been known to do it anything up to eight or ten times.

This being the level of my knowledge and sophistication, it is unnecessary to explain that most of Debbie Maddock's talk about naughty old Petworth, blackmailers and golden youth sailed over my head, and meant absolutely nothing to me. Imaginatively speaking, they still mean very little. The difference between my perceptions now and my twelve-year-old vision of things lies largely in my greater capacity to make connections. Just as I would never have connected good-night kisses from Vanessa with Darnley's anatomical jokes and chit-chat, nor would I have associated Petworth Lampitt (after all, he was a *Lampitt*) with the manifestations of inversion which had so far come my way. These fell into the two general categories of things which had happened to Darnley on scout camp (regaled to the rest of us amid fits of giggles after lights-out) and those more melancholy episodes back at school when the Binker (our word for the Headmaster) was being a Dirty Old Man.

The fact that the Binker was a DOM awakened in us all at various times a mixture of fear, amusement and distress. But, like his cruelty and his verbal mannerisms, it was something peculiar to the Binker, something of which, on his behalf, we felt ashamed and which I would not have found words to describe to any grown-up. I hated the Binker and I should love to have disgraced him; but it was impossible to speak of such things to anyone, least of all to Aunt Deirdre and Uncle Roy. I had never been his victim, but Darnley had been made to go into the Binker's study and take off all his clothes, while many others had suffered one of the Binker's little talks on the sofa, hands straying, or been visited at bathtime – 'Is that water warm enough? Don't move! Nothing to be afraid of!'

The victims imitated the Binker saying this, telling the rest of us in those terrible whispers after lights-out. Sometimes we listened in complete silence and sometimes we let out chilly laughter. No, it never crossed my mind that Mrs Maddock was shouting about *this* sort of thing on that morning in the butcher's shop in Timplingham. I could not imagine why she thought Petworth Lampitt was naughty. Had I realised, I should probably have understood and shared my aunt's rigid horror, as she hovered in the street, determined, at least during that morning's shopping expedition, not to bump into that Wretched Woman again.

'Felicity!'

Silence.

I was standing outside her bedroom door. I knew she was in there because I could hear her turning the pages of her book. Also, from time to time, I heard her crunching a raw carrot which she had found from somewhere. It is unlikely that my aunt's larder afforded such riches. I suspected Felicity of raiding a neighbour's rabbit hutches.

'Felicity, it's me.'

'Cleo – nmph.' That squelching, chewing sound. Perhaps it wasn't a carrot. Perhaps she was just sinking ravenous teeth into a raw potato.

'Felicity, I really have got an aquarium now. Like to come and look?'

Silence.

It was incomprehensible that anyone could be informed of the existence of a new aquarium in the house without wishing to view it. A mixture of hurt and fury welled through my body to think of Felicity sitting there, with her solid, red face, not answering.

'Oh, come *on*, Felicity.'

Her bedroom door opened. She stood there holding a copy of Camus's *L'Etranger*.

'There's an aquarium in my room now.'

'So you said.'

Triumph! I had actually got Felicity to mouth some syllables. She scowled, knowing that I had scored a point here, and shook back her thick, reddish hair from her freckled brow.

'I was just helping Aunt Deirdre with the garden and it was lying there. You're a lazy pig anyway, not helping – we've laid out the spinach and all the lettuce: we've sown radish seeds and stock. Anyway, I thought it was dead at first and I picked it up to stop Tinker eating it.'

'Eating what?'

On the rare occasions when she addressed me, she had a ponderous way of speaking; I was prisoner in the dock and she was the presiding magistrate, aged a hundred and eighteen rather than eighteen.

'Then it jumped. It's lovely, Felicity, come and look.'

'Is this a joke?'

'Aunt Deirdre says I'll have to release him, poor little chap. I'd hoped I might breed them.'

'If it's a frog . . .'

Felicity obviously did not know what she would do if it was a frog. It was a foolish sentence to have started. She ought to have known that, even with her powers of cleverness, she could not change frogs into other things – handsome princes or anything else. With extreme reluctance, my cousin followed me into my bedroom. On the surface which served as dressing table, desk, storage space and laboratory bench, I had placed a large mixing bowl full of water in which a toad was swimming, a beautiful little creature with black and gold markings and glossy black eyes.

'I knew it would be a frog. Put it back in the garden at *once*, Julian.'

She was trying to act nonchalant, but she was scared as hell. I had not brought the toad indoors with the purpose of tormenting her. I was enraptured by its beauty and genuinely wanted to share my joy. Seeing how rattled she was, however, it was tempting to make her suffer, just a little.

'But it's a toad.'

'I can see that.'

'Why say it's a frog then? Would you like to hold it?'

She wasn't staying for this. She turned and walked back to her own room.

'Look at its lovely eyes,' I said.

'I am aware that toads have eyes,' said Felicity, before she slammed her bedroom door.

Darnley would have understood. He had sisters who were even more putrid than my cousin. He also had an extensive knowledge of natural history. I would have asked him to stay with me during the holidays. Aunt Deirdre often urged me to ask a friend and said that she wished I mixed more with boys of my own age. I think Darnley would have enjoyed it. I couldn't bring myself to ask him, though. I was lonely during the holidays and would have valued a crony, but I was too ashamed of the oddness of my family, of the whole Rectory set-up, to risk a friend coming to stay. Darnley would find out that I helped at church and then next term it would be all round the school. Or my uncle would have waylaid him and talked endlessly about the Lampitts. No, having someone to stay in the hols wasn't on. Besides, little as I enjoyed either, I wanted school and home to be quite distinct. The idea was that the holidays were tremendously enjoyable. I think if I had seen the Rectory through the eyes of a friend, I should have realised that this was not quite true. Instinct made me shield myself from the knowledge.

Whatever the reason, the transition between the two worlds was something which I was unable to manage. There was a half-truth in my aunt's brisk 'He'll be all right once he's *back*,' and 'He's much better off without a lot of fuss.'

When I came downstairs with the toad still cupped in my hand, my uncle and aunt were having one of their conferences. These discussions about arrangements were often unpremeditated; they took place suddenly, often in unlikely places, with one person standing halfway up the stairs while another peered down from a landing, or both sitting on the substantial marble-topped table in the hall. On this occasion, my aunt was hovering by the green baize door, with her apron and her air of crossness a parody of the stage domestic. My uncle (the mad employer? the tyrannical butler?) was standing on one leg in the further recesses of the corridor, a coal hod in hand. He was in the middle of stoking the Aga.

'That may be better in any case,' said Aunt Deirdre.

'I don't think Sargie could object.'

'I mean, it might avert, you know . . .'

I instantly grasped that they were discussing the travel arrangements for my return to school. These always threw them into an unreasonable panic because I was unable to take my leave of them without violent displays of emotion. They were lucky if they got away with tears on the station platform. More than once there had been actual hysterics at Paddington and I had had to be forcibly carried on to the Malvern train. They were always devising new means of conveying me back to school without such an outburst. I was as anxious as they to avoid the embarrassment of such involuntary displays. (I had long ago abandoned any hope that they would take me away from the school and I had only a couple more terms there to run.) They had tried both accompanying me. I had clung to them and screamed. Singly, and the same thing had happened. They had sent me by car with Mr Padley the gardener. That was the time I had to be carried on to the train by a porter, and Mr Padley had subsequently handed in his notice. Now, it seemed, they had hit on a new method.

'Felicity thought it was a frog!' I said. 'I'm going to start an aquarium.'

I opened my hands and showed the quivering little toad to my uncle.

'Wouldn't he be happier in the garden?'

'Please, Uncle Roy.'

'I'll have to have that mixing bowl back in any case' – it was always an ominous sign when my aunt sided with my uncle in a conversation. 'Mrs Batterbee will be wanting it.'

I could see the wisdom of all this. We were pretending to have a conversation about the toad. Actually, we were talking about the fact that, in three days' time, I would not be there. It was an example of that touching human propensity to behave as though there were a future even when reason declares that there isn't. The man on his way to the gallows asks permission to stoop down and tie his shoelace. The Jewish woman brushes mud off her husband's shoulder in the queue for the gas ovens, though clothes (muddy or otherwise) and life itself are soon to be surrendered. These are not the actions of foolish optimists. Rather, instinct keeps them straining towards the sun, even when they no longer believe in the future.

Comparisons as strong as this will strike home to readers who reacted as I did to the English Gulag, and will be dismissed by others as tasteless and trivial. English frivolity, the inability to take serious things seriously, the tendency to treat unserious things – dogs or school – as other races might treat war and death – these are difficult waters to chart. As any navigator knows, it is the shallows where vessels come unstuck. Much of the difficulty derives from the fact that emotions cannot be faked up. It may be that we *should* mind about some things, rather than others, but 'sensation is sensation'. I am sure that I am not the only English reader of the Russian prison novels of the Stalinist period, Grossman or Solzhenitsyn, who feels, from the moment of the protagonist's arrest, a complete familiarity with all the emotions through which he passes. The actual deprivations and hardships of an English school may be worse than a Soviet labour camp, and the food about on a level. What counts is that the inner torment is identical – the sharing of insanitary conditions with too many uncongenial people, the strange friendships and distrusts which grow up among fellow prisoners, the same fear of the system which never quite leaves you. The only major difference is that *their* Gulag was something of which the Soviet Government was ashamed, denying its very existence, whereas the English system of private schools is openly boasted about, one of the glories of the world. So powerful is the effect of propaganda that even those who have been through the system and know what it is like are prepared to whitewash their memories and pretend that the dear old place was not so bad as weeds and sneaks such as myself might claim. The other day I had an invitation to the centenary of the foundation of Seaforth Grange. It is a bizarre fact that people will have attended this function and even paid £5 for a buffet lunch. It is rather as if former inmates of the Bastille or the Lubyanka

41

were eagerly to revisit their place of torment, attending a service of thanksgiving in the chapel for all the benefits which such institutions have showered upon humanity; hear a sermon by some former inmate, now a bishop, extolling the virtue of warders whom he knew at the time to be cruel or insane; and even contemplate putting down the names of their own children for a spell in clink.

All this is as much as to say that I could see that there was no future in my aquarium. My aunt told me to give her back the bowl and to dispose of the toad, which I did. I suppose it was cruel, because I might have guessed the ultimate fate of that beautiful creature.

That afternoon, standard Lubyanka procedure, I was taken to the village barber to have my hair cropped. It might be thought strange that there was a barber in such a small place. Haircutting was only by appointment with Mr Sykes, a retired man who operated from his front room in a small house near the Methodist chapel. 'He cut hair in Kingsway,' was always the boast, though I have never heard since that this London thoroughfare was particularly famous for its high-quality barbers.

Uncle Roy, who always accompanied me to the barber, used to say it every time we approached Mr Sykes's door.

'It's a jolly good bob's worth – and don't forget, he used to cut hair in Kingsway.' Evidently, in my uncle's belief, it was like saying a doctor had once had a Harley Street practice or that a tailor, though now operating from a front room in Timplingham, had once cut clothes in Savile Row. Sometimes, when recording in Bush House, I have walked up Kingsway and tried to identify the barber's shop where Mr Sykes was once employed. At some periods, unless I am mistaken, there have been no hairdressing establishments there at all. More recently, the kind of unisex salons which have sprung up all over London have seemed a world away from the smelly little parlour where this alleged expert in the coiffeur's art spluttered over his combs and razors, and hovered, with blunt scissors and quivering hand, so perilously close to one's ears.

'I hear there's been a sad bereavement up at the Place,' said Mr Sykes, solemnly blowing some of the scurf from his comb before applying it to my scalp.

'It is very sad, a great loss,' said my uncle's voice behind me. I could see his face in Mr Sykes's looking-glass. For the quarter of an hour or so which it took Mr Sykes to give me the shorn appearance of a Soviet army private, my uncle lectured him on Lampitt lore. Mr Sykes, before his illustrious career in Kingsway (I often wondered whether sweeping the floor rather than cutting the hair had not been his vocation, wherever the barber's shop in question), had been born in Timplingham and lived there for much of his life. He probably knew as well as I did who all the Lampitts were and could remember the days of their youth. On one occasion, he had even told me how Sargie had run away from Winchester. But he was patient, while my uncle recited his credo.

'The eldest brother you may remember – Sir Michael Lampitt.'

'He who was a director of the railway, sir? Yes, yes. I remember Master Michael, though him we always thought of as the second son, sir, there having been young Master Martin who died when he was a lad.'

'I meant the eldest survivor,' said my uncle shortly.

'And then there was Mr James.'

My uncle smiled tolerantly. This was the mistake people often made, to forget about Vivian Lampitt. Mr Sykes fully conceded defeat here.

'Went to live in Africa, did he, sir?'

'Mombasa,' I chipped in.

'And *then* it was Mr James,' said Mr Sykes.

'Martin; Michael, who was killed at Mons; Vivian, James Petworth, Sargent, Sybil,' said my uncle, just to make sure that there would be no mistakes in future.

'And Miss Sybil, she's now Lady – what *is* her name?'

'Lady Starling.'

'And still going strong, sir – her ladyship, I mean?'

'Oh, rather!' said my uncle. 'What a *charming* person she is. Gentle to a fault and of course a very great beauty. In her youth, as you will know, she really moved in very high society indeed.'

'Well, is that *so*, sir?'

'Oh,' said Uncle Roy airily, 'presented at court. The lot. But completely modest with it. Too kind, some would say. Mr Sargent always says that his sister is a complete doormat, lets people walk all over her.'

'Is that so, sir?'

'Yes,' said Uncle Roy, and they paused for a moment's respectful silence as they contemplated the beauty of Lady Starling's character.

'And then there's Mr Lampitt who's in the Cabinet, isn't there, sir?'

'Ah, that's the Honourable Vernon – he's the son of *Lord* Lampitt, who is Mr Sargent's uncle. They live at Mallington Hall.'

'Out beyond Downham Market, that would be, sir?'

'That general direction. It's one of the most splendid houses in the county,' said Uncle Roy.

'And to think they just started off no better than you and me, brewing beer in King's Lynn,' said Mr Sykes with a sigh.

This egalitarian line of talk would not do. My uncle leaned forward to survey the few hairs left on my head and said, 'Just a little more off the back, if you please, Mr Sykes.'

'More off the back, sir? Right you are.'

I was never consulted about the length of my own hair.

'We'll have you all nice and smart for the summer, won't we, young sir? Be playing a lot of cricket, I expect.'

'Not if I can help it,' I said sourly.

I was fed up with Lampitt talk. I loathed having my hair cut. I rather hated Mr Sykes and I hated all forms of organised sport. Mr Sykes attempted a weak laugh which evolved into a lung-wringing torrent of coughing, only relieved by taking a some-what crinkly cigarette from behind his left ear, applying it to his lips and lighting up. The rest of the work with clippers and scissors took place in billows of Woodbine smoke, so that in this incense cloud I was more than ever like some shorn, sacrificial victim.

My uncle went on reciting the names of Lampitts all day. Evidently, he was going through in his mind all the members of the family who could be expected to put in an appearance at Jimbo's funeral. Rather as at certain times of year the rabbis recite those enormous genealogies from the Book of Numbers, rehearsing the names of the Hebrews who crossed the Jordan with Joshua into the Land of Promise, so the Rector of Timplingham spoke of Lampitts throughout the morning and the afternoon. Technically, he had an audience: at lunch, my aunt, myself and Felicity; during the afternoon, a mixture of myself and Mr Gillard who did rough work in the garden; and during the evening, the family once more.

I am fairly sure that the recitation would have continued even if he had spent the day alone, interrupted only for the quarter of an hour when, clad in Canterbury cap and MA gown, he went over to church at four p.m. to read evensong. And perhaps, even then, there was no controlling a man's thoughts. It is hard to imagine a recitation of the Magnificat, with its mention of the mighty in their seats, without the mind involuntarily straying to the Honourable Vernon in the Cabinet, or to Dame Ursula Lampitt, the principal of an Oxford college. Similarly, the exaltation of the humble and meek, promised in the same canticle, could not be read without some thought of Lady Starling.

I cried a bit during that evening's episode of 'The Mulberrys', hoping that nobody could see. Supper, which, my uncle being present, was at seven, after 'The Mulberrys', was sausages with mash, followed by Eve's pudding with custard. These were my favourite dishes. On any other day of the holiday, I would have wolfed them down. The eve of departure, however, was always enough to bring a sick dread into my stomach. I pecked at custard which on other days would have not had time to cool on my plate.

When the meal was over, we all played cards. When the silently erubescent Felicity had twice, by the luck of the draw, been declared an Old Maid (a verdict which Fate, in real life, looked all too likely to endorse) her parents hastily switched to gin-rummy. Then bed – and a good-night kiss from my uncle and one from my aunt. Even Felicity grunted before slamming her bedroom door, an action which was normally accomplished without utterance. She treated me like a brother, that girl.

I went to my own room and listened. Felicity was a long while getting undressed. I began to fear that I might fall asleep before I heard her. Probably, it was not much more than half an hour, but it seemed like an eternity. Then, more satisfyingly loud than I could possibly have hoped, her under-worked vocal chords were given more exercise than they had had for years. Her screams could have been heard in the village.

'Oh – the *pig*!'

Doors were flung open.

My aunt, who was still downstairs, called up to ask what was the matter.

'The frog –' gasped Felicity. 'Julian put the frog in my bed. I felt it on my toes.'

'Put your cap on, I should,' said Uncle Roy.

'I should' was his strongest imperative. In this case, was his sentence, taken literally, believable? Would he, in any circumstances, be prepared to walk through the village wearing an electric-blue school cap, with the initials 'S.G.' (for Seaforth Grange) emblazoned above the peak? Perhaps he would. I was made of feebler stuff.

I had eaten my breakfast. My bag was packed and in my hand. My mac was on.

'Goodbye, old thing.' My aunt pecked my cheek. 'I'll write. And Granny will come down to see you in a few weeks. We'll get down when we can – anyway for the sports.'

I was being phenomenally good. There was not so much as a crack in my voice as I bade farewell to Aunt Deirdre.

Felicity, who was also standing there in the hall, smiled with unconcealed relief at my imminent departure. The toad incident had not been mentioned. I heard my aunt, while I was dressing, telling Felicity not to start getting me upset; to which Felicity had replied, not unreasonably, what about her?

'You have *got* your cap, haven't you?' asked my uncle when we were in the drive.

'The thing is, I packed it in my bag,' I improvised. Actually, it was in my mackintosh pocket.

I could see that Uncle Roy would not force a showdown about the cap. Already his mind was full of the day which lay ahead. Within a matter of hours, he would be feasting his gaze on a crematorium chapel packed with Lampitts. He wore a white shirt and a black tie to mark the occasion. Aunt Deirdre had talked him out of wearing the opera hat.

'They'll think you're one of the undertakers, especially since you're driving.'

In the event, he wore the *Daily Mail* one and a black suit which was unseasonably thick.

'Your Uncle Sargie will be very upset,' said my real uncle as we walked along. 'He hates funerals. He always expects me to . . .' Here he began to laugh. ' "Save me from my relations,

Roy!" ' he said in his Sargie voice. 'The last family gathering of any size to which I accompanied him was Gloria's funeral. He somehow managed to quarrel with his sister Sybil. It was about the transfer of some shares, I seem to remember. Good old Sargie.' More chuckling. 'He said, "My sister drives a *very* hard bargain." And this of Sibs, who's the most charming girl and submissive to a fault, as Sargie, in more enlightened mood, is the first to admit.'

'Does Uncle Sargie not really like his family?'

'Sh, sh, sh. You mustn't say things like that! The Lampitts are all very highly strung. They are apt to fly at one another's throats somewhat,' he said admiringly.

By now we had crossed the road, passed the lodge cottage, where Sargie's housekeeper lived with her husband, and followed the drive up towards Timplingham Place, a rather handsome, red-brick affair, 1750s, with two wings and a graceful flight of steps leading up to the grand, central front door. This was the entrance we used. My uncle invariably walked in without knocking.

'Coo-ee!' he called as we entered the large hall. 'We're here! Oh, good morning, Mrs Marsh.'

'He's not up yet,' said this long-suffering domestic. She savoured the shock produced by this remark and then, out of pity, she began to mollify it.

'Well, he's *up*, but not dressed.'

She cast her eyes upwards.

('This time, Mr Sargent, you've gone too far,' Sargie liked to imitate her saying. Unlike my uncle and aunt, he was a good mimic and captured Mrs Marsh's Norfolk lilt to perfection.)

'Is he in the bedroom?' asked Uncle Roy, putting the *Daily Mail* hat on the huge refectory table which stood in the hall.

'Oh, no. He's in the library.'

Another raising of the eyes aloft.

Completely ignoring me, my uncle strode through the passage and the drawing room which led to the library. As Uncle Roy opened the door, I could hear Sargie's anguished voice call out, 'Mind! Don't let Joynson-Hicks out!'

There was a rush to the door and my uncle just managed to prevent the exit of Joynson-Hicks, a rather flatulent marmalade tom who, though all of fourteen, was still quick on his pins.

'All ready to go?' asked Uncle Roy hopefully.

'Roy, you'll have to go,without me,' said Sargie in pathetic tones. 'I find that, after all, I can't face it.'

'Say hallo to Uncle Sargie,' said my real uncle. He was flummoxed by Sargie's announcement and played for time by turning attention to myself.

'Hallo,' I said, going round to shake Sargie's hand. Although the days had passed when my uncle made me kiss Sargie, I could still smell the distinctive, spirituous flavour (almost neat gin with a dash of dry vermouth) of Sargie's breath.

'Poor old man,' he said to me, with a gesture to my uniform which made clear what he meant. For some reason Sargie's allusion to my imminent departure to concentration camp did not upset me. It was genuine boy-to-boy stuff. There was nothing of adult condescension in it. 'Let's both do a bunk, eh? I don't want to go to this bloody funeral and you don't want to go to your bloody school.'

I would have welcomed the scheme, even in Sargie's company.

'If we don't set out soon, Sargie, there won't be any time for lunch and Julian will miss his train.' My uncle could plainly see the whole day going wrong. There was panic in his voice and face.

'Joynson-Hicks says I don't have to go,' said Sargie, slowly, seeming to savour the effects of the gin on his sibilants. 'And he says that Julie doesn't have to go back to school either.'

I was close enough for Sargie to ruffle my hair. Then he picked up Joynson-Hicks and stroked him instead.

'You're a wise old campaigner, aren't you, Joynson-Hicks?'

Sargie had all the Lampitt features too strongly to be in any sense handsome: a long, bony face with a pronounced Roman nose, beneath which was cultivated a moustache, at that date a brindled grey though the hair on his head, sleekly combed back and perhaps even brilliantined, was mysteriously dark. He wore horn-rimmed spectacles and the smouldering cigarette in its bone holder was so often between his lips that one thought of it as a permanent extension of his physical features, like a tusk or a unicorn's horn.

'Come *on*, Sargie,' said Uncle Roy, nearly stamping his foot.

'You see, I think Cecily will be there. She's always at these things.'

'She won't necessarily be.'

'Yes she will. She and Jimbo were as thick as thieves. You know how she poisoned his mind against me.'

'I'm sure that's not true.'

'Well, we were reconciled a year or so ago, in spite of her. Otherwise, I shouldn't be able to stay on here. I really need Jimbo's money. Well, it's not all his money, it's Mama's. Did I tell you I was the sole heir?'

'No.'

'Well, the idea was that the others were more or less set up. Now it's just me and Sibs anyway, and she's rich as Croesus. And I have this place to keep up. I've been thinking of some of the improvements I shall make here now I have a bit of cash.'

'Does the Place need improving?' I asked.

'Lord, yes.'

He stood up, holder still between his lips, dropping ash down the front of his dressing gown.

'You don't mean that I have to come to this bloody thing of Jimbo's?' he asked.

'I should if I were you,' said Uncle Roy.

'Oh, Julie! He's a hard taskmaster, your uncle!' And then the next sentence Sargie intoned. It was hard to see its relevance, but perhaps it just signified that he was getting in the mood for a funeral service. The voice was not mock-parsonical; on the contrary, it was sonorous, almost moving. 'Now we see through a glass darkly, but then face to face. Well, I'm half done as you can see, my dears.'

He flung open his plaid dressing gown to reveal a long shirt, whose tails stretched to his knees; a stiff collar, black silk tie, black socks, suspenders tied from the knee, highly polished black shoes.

'I got disheartened before I put on my trousers. What are we meant to be wearing anyway? I can't tell from your rig-out, Roy. It won't be morning coat will it? Surely they won't have all that bloody nonsense just for Jimbo. A black coat and striped trousers, I thought.'

'I'm sure that will be all right.'

'What are you wearing?' – he turned to me – 'Oh, you're not coming.'

He left us for a remarkably short space of time, coming downstairs as smart as paint and carrying a well-brushed bowler.

'Michael's old hat. Used to wear it to meetings. Look here, Roy, you're going to have to drive, is that all right?'

'Perfectly.'

'Will you be safe on the back seat, Julie?'

'Oh yes,' I said. And soon, with my little case, I had sidled on to the large soft back seat of the Daimler.

Sargie's life had been sadder than most, the turnings falser, the ends deader. Uncle Roy could not avoid hyperbole when talking about that family, but I have heard others say that Sargie had been brilliant. He was a scholar of Winchester, a Fellow of New College and then had come the rather surprising marriage to Cecily. No one in childhood told me exactly what had gone wrong here, but his dread of his wife was something about which he was always vocal. It was some time during the First World War that they had got married.

By the end of the First World War, Sargie must have been about thirty. The distinguished monograph on the House of Lords (written from an abolitionist point of view when he was only twenty-one) had never been followed up by the large work of grand political analysis of which everyone had believed him to be capable. Felicity, after she became a don, heard someone say that Sargent Lampitt was the only Englishman since Hobbes who had it in him to be a great political philosopher and thinker. Something happened, though. By the time the Great War had ended, so had his marriage. There was, I believe, a spell in an asylum. The attempt to resume an academic life had not been wise. Not long after my uncle, very young, had been appointed to the living of Timplingham, Sargie had come home to live with his mother at the Place. When old Mrs Lampitt died (not long after the outbreak of the Second World War) the rest of the family were all settled elsewhere. They had no wish to come back and run what Sargie, with a mixture of irony and true snobbery, used to apologise was 'only a bought house'. So he stayed there and ran the place as best he could, with the help of Mr and Mrs Marsh, and one or two other makeshift domestics and amateur gardeners. His only companions were my Uncle Roy and the gin bottle.

The desire to chicken out of that morning's melancholy expedition was typical of Sargie's neurotic behaviour. In later years, I need hardly say, the whole day had become one of my uncle's anecdotes.

'We've got plenty of time,' said Sargie.

'Oh, plenty,' said Uncle Roy.

'That doesn't mean that you have to drive at a snail's pace.'

Although in a nannyish way my uncle bullied and cajoled Sargie, he seemed fully to accept his role as a sort of glorified servant. Rather than question Sargie's right to nag about the driving, he put his foot on the accelerator and the car sped out on the road towards Newmarket. It was a reasonably straight bit of road and the scene was one of haunting beauty. The vast sky dominated. The picture was seven-eighths sky; the rest, elms and horse-chestnuts coming into leaf, fields and hedges tinged with the first green of the year, thorn and may already in blossom. After a very few minutes of swirling through this canvas by Hobbema, Sargie let out a deep moan.

'Do slow down, silly. Are you trying to kill us?'

This fast-slow nonsense punctuated the whole drive, a very merciful accident, because although I felt slightly sick in the back of the car and I was dreading my handover to the prison guards at Paddington station, I found the bickering of the two men wonderfully amusing.

Uncle Roy obviously thought that I was crying when I tried to disguise my giggles by stuffing a handkerchief into my mouth. I could see him in the driving-mirror, avoiding my gaze. Sargie was far too absorbed in his own thoughts to be thinking about me. Occasionally he resorted to a small hip flask and that pleasantly spirituous exhalation which I had discerned in the library at Timplingham filled the limousine. The more he imbibed, the more the death and the approaching funeral of his brother appeared to impinge on his consciousness; the higher, too, grew his estimation of Petworth Lampitt as a prose-writer.

'He wrote some books, didn't he, old Jimbo?'

'He certainly did,' said Uncle Roy. 'Particularly the Prince Albert.'

'It's a little masterpiece, isn't it? Bloody little masterpiece. And the one about Swinburne. And you don't need to go to Venice if you've read his Venetian thing, you know, whatever it's called.'

'*Lagoon Loungings.*'

'That's the fella. Another bloody classic.'

'It is excellent.'

'And yet – I say, Roy, slow down on the bends, can't you?'

'Sorry, Sargie.'

'They had it in for him, those buggers, didn't they?'

'I'm afraid they probably did.'

'Any excuse to denigrate quality, to run down good writing, genius.'

One of the views which appeared to unite Sargie and my Uncle Roy was the idea that there was a gang of people – their precise identity remaining something of a mystery – who were committed to bring to pass all the things of which they themselves disapproved. It sounded as though the motive of these people, the buggers, was pure spite. No erotic preference was indicated by the term. Debbie Maddock was in this sense a bugger, who had learnt from Dr Leavis (a bugger if ever there was one) to denigrate Petworth Lampitt's work, when in fact all Jimbo's books were masterpieces.

'Bloody masterpieces,' concluded Sargie. 'So were the articles he wrote in the Sunday papers. I know it's a sad thing when people descend to writing for the papers, but Jimbo made an art of it. Gems, they were. Did you read the thing he wrote only last week about the French merchant?'

'I hadn't heard of him before,' said Uncle Roy. 'Jewish, I think. Jimbo made quite a lot of that.'

The Lampitts were famous pro-Semites. There is even a Lampitt Street in Tel Aviv, in consideration of the numbers of refugees from Hitler rescued by Sargie's uncle, Lord Lampitt. But everyone in that circle still spoke about the Jews in terms which would nowadays sound offensive.

'Proust,' said Sargie. 'He wrote this bloody great novel all about his own childhood and then a whole lot of characters all linking up with the big house where he used to spend his summer holidays. They all turn out to be pansies.'

'As you know, I don't really read novels, except for 'tecs,' said my uncle.

'We all read them when they started to trickle over here. Haven't looked at them since. Jimbo had. He read everything. I thought his thing on Proust was bloody brilliant.'

The vehemence with which this was spoken was really addressed to all those who had asserted otherwise, the philistines, the buggers, Mrs Maddock, Dr Leavis and all.

'You're right,' added Sargie. 'He was a Jewboy, now you

mention it. All happened at the time of Dreyfus. The French have different ideas about all that sort of thing – I say, for Christ's sake, Roy, we may be going to a funeral, but do you *have* to drive so slowly?'

Although unused to the Daimler, Uncle Roy got us to London remarkably smoothly and, considering all the fuss Sargie was making, in a remarkably good temper. There was the occasional expostulation ('Sargie – honest*lee!*') but no sharp retorts.

Seeing London always thrilled me as a child. It thrills me still. The passing seasons are no less marked there than in the country. As we drove westward, we passed bombsites vivid with green; daffodils in window boxes; beneath trees, grass was purple and gold with crocuses. We purred along to Sargie's club in Mayfair.

'Like to come in for a snifter?'

Sargie was quite without side. If I had said that I would like a glass of brandy and soda, he would have had no hesitation about taking me into his club, clad in blazer and shorts.

'I think . . .' Uncle Roy consulted his fob and had no need to finish his sentence. My train left Paddington in not much over half an hour.

We had parked by the kerb and were standing on the pavement in Brook Street, awkwardly sniffing the air before we took our farewells. Suddenly departure was chillingly imminent.

'I'll come back to lunch with you,' said my uncle to Sargie.

'We can either eat at the club or go to Claridge's. There'd be time.'

'Plenty. The funeral's not till three.'

Their ability to talk about these events, which were to take place after my own departure, was intolerable to me. A figure lying close to death would have felt the same if watchers round the bed began to discuss their plans for what to do after his demise. Sargie became aware of their insensitivity. He had been far from a model schoolboy himself and I always knew, without his having to explain anything, that he *understood*. He turned on me a look of genuine, unmistakable sympathy, the one thing at that moment which could have been calculated to topple my equilibrium.

'Well, my dear, chin chin,' he said.

Even as he pressed a large, white, crinkly five-pound note into my hand, I burst into tears.

Two

My earliest memories are of screaming and crying. In my dread of being separated from my mother, there must have been some element of premonition. As a young child, I always screamed myself to sleep unless one of my parents, nearly always my mother, consented to sit by my bed, stroking my brow with her hand. If she were to leave me a moment before I actually fell asleep, I woke up completely and started to cry with panic. Telling Felicity about this phenomenon, years later, I discovered that my good-night screams were already a part of family legend.

'You were a spoilt little tick,' was her probably quite legitimate judgement.

If spoiling was the reason I screamed, my parents must have rued their mistaken softness towards me. My involuntary demand for companionship last thing at night was so powerful that I was incapable of releasing them from it, even when I was old enough to reason with myself and to long *not* to be a nuisance. If they were at home, one of them had to sit with me. On those occasions (and, poor things, I suspect they were pretty rare) when they allowed themselves to go out for the evening, I screamed and screamed until exhaustion brought its own comfortless, unsatisfying sleep. Quite often, they would return from the film, or the meal out, to find me still wailing at ten or eleven o'clock. I can vividly recollect every stage and element of these paroxysms. First, the eyes watering, tears uncontrollably falling down my cheeks and that unpleasant feeling in the back of the throat which heralded the start of a weeping fit. If my mother was at hand, this first stage could be averted by her smoothing my brow and singing 'Golden Slumbers', sometimes dozens and dozens of times. No other lullaby worked. Mummy must have sung it to me thousands of times, millions. If I hear the tune now, it turns me to gooseflesh.

Granny's anarchic way of getting round the problem, on

those evenings when she was in charge and my parents were enjoying a rare snatch of respite, was simply to get me up. She was far too sensible and too self-protective to put up with two or three hours of someone else's unhappiness, whatever Dr Trubie King may say or write. My parents would therefore get back to the house to find Granny and me building with wooden bricks or, later, for the annoying trick lasted until I was seven years old, playing Beggar My Neighbour.

By then, war had broken out and everything was changed. My father, who in peacetime had been an assistant manager in a shirt factory, joined the RAF. Mummy, whose parents were both dead, moved to a small house in Fulham to be near her mother in-law, who lived in Parson's Green. It was in the garden of that house in Alderville Road that we had the air-raid shelter built and those best of all nights were spent, Mummy and I curled up in the same makeshift bed, clutching one another for fear of the Luftwaffe who never came, for the whole of that autumn.

It was for the first Christmas of the war that we all went to Timplingham – Mummy and Daddy, Granny and I. Apparently, though this was something broken to me at quite a late stage of the holiday, it had always been the plan that Mummy and I should become evacuees and live with Uncle Roy, Aunt Deirdre and Felicity until London was safe again. Before we got to Norfolk, a journey accomplished by train, I can remember my father, in his RAF uniform, imitating the way Uncle Roy said 'invole-ved' rather than 'involved', and 'accomplished' rather than 'accumplished'. There were a whole range of 'aristocratic' pronunciations – 'larndry' for 'laundry', 'blooze' for 'blouse' – which struck Daddy as funny. It made it hard to keep a straight face when we arrived and Uncle Roy's voice was exactly as his brother had rendered it.

Both the brothers had been to one of the 'good London dayschools', as Granny called them. Mummy had been to some awful-sounding boarding school on the south coast. I have no idea what education they would have planned for me in peacetime, but the prep school in Malvern was an idea they had hit upon at the same time as deciding on our evacuation from London. Aunt Deirdre said that it had been recommended to my father by a business colleague; there was no opportunity to inspect it because – that phrase which covered everything – because of the war.

That Christmas was awful. Without the slightest intention of being unkind (never having stayed with us in London, they were entirely unaware of the problem) my uncle and aunt had put me to sleep in a maid's bedroom on the second floor while Mummy and Daddy slept below in a much larger and colder room designated the guest room but hardly ever occupied. The first night that I was left alone, I screamed myself hoarse. I can remember the awful jerks in my voice as I cried out, increasingly incoherently, 'STAY WITH ME, STAY WITH ME!' After ten or twenty minutes of this, the words got lost in mere sound, my cheeks were scorching, my eyes scalding, spittle and snot in great loops like egg-white were festooned across my face and dribbling down the corners of my mouth, and I could not stop.

Not long after the holiday, Daddy went back to his squadron and Granny (wearied, I suppose, by so much talk of the Lampitts and the Sarum Rite) decided to chance what the Luftwaffe could bring. She spent the whole of the war in London, which, as her friend Mrs Webb sometimes said, might have accounted for her nasty heads. Mummy and I were left behind. My nocturnal screamings got no better.

The Rectory policy was that I simply *mustn't* cry and scream. Mummy was forbidden to come to my bedroom after her all-too-brief good-night kiss. After about a week of my regular screams, my uncle was sent up to hit me. If I did not stop crying, he would tell me, he would take me out of bed and give me a jolly good walloping. He was much too nice ever to carry out such a punishment. He had been told to say this by Aunt Deirdre. Felicity, then about thirteen or fourteen, suffered from no such scruples and her bedroom was nearer to the noise centre than Uncle Roy's. More than once, she came in and biffed me. This did nothing to reduce the noise level or to increase the love between the cousins.

The idea of sending me away to school had been planned, I am assured, before my uncle and aunt were aware of the screaming habit. For over two years my nightly shouts made life in the Rectory well-nigh intolerable for everyone else. I have since watched the parents of difficult children and seen how they suffer, both on the child's behalf and from embarrassment. How much anguish I must have caused Mummy! She did not know (nor, I suspect, like) Aunt Deirdre and Uncle Roy very well. She was staying in their house very much on sufferance. Rectory ways were very different from the much more homely atmosphere which surrounded us in London. We did not know anyone who lived in a big house or had relations called the Honourable Vernon. I remember how tense Mummy often looked, frightened, probably, that I was going to scream or, in other moods, worried that I was going to be clumsy. It was hard to imagine that Felicity had ever been a child. Uncle Roy and Aunt Deirdre seemed so very disconcerted by any manifestation of childish behaviour on my behalf. I can remember when Mummy and I were playing French cricket with a tennis racket and an old ball in the garden. Aunt Deirdre came running out of the house.

'Doesn't matter a *bit* if you want to play, so long as you do it well down the lawn, away from the house.' Afraid that she had sounded too severe (and, indeed, her tones would have been rather too panicky if we had been juggling with sticks of dynamite) she added an unconvincingly playful, 'Jolly dee!'

Her fears that I would smash one of the windows with the ball entirely dominated that particular little patch of fine weather. Then, the inevitable happened and, driven indoors by sleet, I had taken to bouncing the ball in the hall. I knew perfectly well that it was a dangerous thing to do and I was not even particularly interested in ball games; simply addicted to bouncing the wretched thing. Mummy's face was so sad on the day I smashed that looking-glass in the hall. The more often Aunt Deirdre said it didn't matter, or that there was no use crying over spilt milk, the nearer Mummy looked to tears.

They had told me that I would eventually be sent to Seaforth Grange, but the reality of it meant nothing to me. Nor did I really imagine that this sending-away would happen for a very long time. There were dozens of warning signals.

'You poor girl, you're simply worn out by that child,' I heard my aunt telling Mummy on one occasion.

And, 'This weepy habit is one he'll jolly well have to break.'

My aunt was quite right; by her lights, she was not being unkind. No one was. I don't blame my family for being unable to understand a phenomenon which, to this day, baffles me. But I do now believe that my mysterious weeping whenever I was separated from my mother was premonitory. My aunt's idea was that, by some accident of upbringing, I had grown too soft. School would toughen me up and stop the caterwauling each evening, since you simply can't shout and wail in a dormitory. If this was the idea, it was a perfectly sound one. I was so shocked by being sent away, shortly before my ninth birthday, that I hardly protested at all. Mummy took me on the crowded train to London and bought me a poached-egg lunch at a Lyons Corner House. Then we had a little stroll in Hyde Park before the unwilling walk to Paddington. I remember how sad she looked.

'It's all for the best, my darling,' she said. And then it was her turn to cry and mine to comfort her. The duty master in charge of escorting the boys back from Paddington was waiting at Platform One. It was September. Almost everyone on that platform was in uniform of one sort or another – school uniform, army or other service uniform, railway uniform. It made those few women who were in civilian clothes look especially nice. Mummy was in a summer frock, a pre-war print thing. That's how I remember her – her thin arms waving, her springy, light brown hair blown by steam and wind; her lovely blue eyes red with crying, her lips very red with lipstick, trembling as she stood there, and we pulled out in our third-class carriage. I didn't weep then.

Five weeks later, she went down to be near my father at Cranwell. They had a few days' leave together and spent it in a nearby hotel. My father had already become a pilot and survived over three years of the war. He had already taken tremendous risks. It seemed as though Providence would spare him for that peaceful little interlude at an out-of-season hotel.

A Heinkel, returning to Germany from an unsuccessful raid, dropped its load of bombs on my parents' hotel, a direct hit. There were only a few guests there that May. It just so happened that Mummy and Daddy were among them.

Thereafter, farewells, partings, transitions from one place or condition to the next have always been difficult for me. From the moment I went away to Seaforth Grange, I was cured of my habit of screaming before bedtime. I did not cry when the Binker's wife told me that Mummy and Daddy were dead. I don't know why that is. But for ever afterwards, when being shoved on to trains by my uncle or aunt, I hollered. On that day of Jimbo Lampitt's funeral, for example, my uncle and the duty master had to lift me on to the train, wriggling and shouting.

'Please! Come on!' my uncle kept saying. 'Think how sad your Uncle Sargie is and he isn't crying.'

I wouldn't have been crying if I had been sitting in the bar of the Savile Club with a large martini and a cigarette, but I was in no condition for repartee.

'Come on! Jimbo's dead. You only have to go back to school, I've got to go to a funeral.'

There is never any point in trying to cure another person's unhappiness by suggesting that someone is worse off than they are. While these reasoned arguments were adduced, I was beside myself, flailing about, kicking and shouting. But when I had been put in the corner of the compartment on the train I did not try to escape. I was so out of control that I was beyond embarrassment. I did not mind that five or six other boys were all staring at me. Though the tears continued to flow, I wasn't making much noise.

'I expect he'll settle down once the train starts up,' said my uncle hopefully. Poor man, I now realise that he must have been in an agony himself, wondering whether he should leave me in the hands of strangers and in such a state of distress. It was rather a spurious character called Mr Rhys who was in charge of the expedition.

'He'll be all right, sir,' said Rhys to Uncle Roy.

'I was just reminding Julian as we carried him in,' said Uncle Roy, 'that we are burying James Petworth Lampitt this afternoon. The author, you know.'

I wonder whether Greasy Rhysy did know about Petworth Lampitt.

'A remarkable loss to literature,' said Uncle Roy. 'Altogether a remarkable family. Jimbo – as they all called Petworth Lampitt – was one of the most succinct and I think I would say *elegant* popular historians in our language. The brother I know much better, of course, is Sargent Lampitt. Again, a man of prodigious accomplishments.'

Greasy Rhysy looked about him anxiously. He had a delicate job to do, herding us all on to the train, counting us, making sure we were all in our seats, attending to other parents and guardians. But, even when he had got off the train and was standing on the platform, my uncle was still talking. He rapped on the window with his fist and made Rhysy stick his head out to listen.

'Mr Asquith himself – Lord Oxford as he became – commended that book on the House of Lords even though, as you probably know, he was far from being an abolitionist.'

'Indeed, sir?'

Snivelling in the corner, I could hear Rhysy's puzzled voice attempting to reply to what had seemed like an urgent summons from my uncle.

'No,' said Uncle Roy, 'old Sargie's a bit of a prodigy. His sister . . .'

He was still talking about the Lampitts as the train pulled out of the station and the summer term had begun.

The prediction that I would be all right, once I had settled back into the routines of Seaforth Grange, was amply confirmed. A fortnight later, if my uncle had been able to witness me talking to Darnley in the queue at break, he would hardly have recognised me as the same being that he had helped to carry on to the Paddington train. The strongest emotions, in my experience, are the most transitory. The despair induced by homesickness or love affairs has always passed away like a squall. Conditions such as my aunt's permanent mild crossness seem unshakeable.

'How many did you get?' I asked Darnley.

'Four.'

'Bloody-oo.'

'He's in a bad mood, I expect.'

'Thanks a lot! We've got him next period. But four, just for talking after lights-out. It's usually three at most. Two, even. If talking's gone up to four, what will we get for serious things, like going in a shop?'

'We shall be *beheaded*!' To pronounce this sentence, Darnley bent double and did a war dance accompanied by extraordinary facial grimaces.

'Be-head-ed! Hung, drawn and quartered! Cas-trat-ed!'

When he had stopped chanting, he stood up straight and said, 'If we went into the bushes, I could show you.'

'No thanks – we'd lose our place in the queue.'

'Garforth-Thoms thinks the Binker's drawn blood this time.'

'What did you show them to Blowforth-Bums for?'

'He showed me his. He got four too – but he handed in prep late.'

61

'Oh, well.' Four for late prep was usual. 'What were his like?' I asked, intending no satire.

'Horrible.'

We both laughed.

This showing of the scars and bruises inflicted by the Binker's instruments of torture (he had a cupboardful in his study) had nothing to do with Eros. We were entirely innocent of the idea that anyone might give canings for fun, and as for the idea that one could enjoy being beaten, I never heard it so much as mentioned in nearly ten years of life in institutions where beatings were a regular occurrence. Nor did I feel the slightest interest, aesthetic or otherwise, in Darnley's bum. The closest parallel which I know to his (purely standard) offer to show me his bruises came in an anecdote told by Uncle Roy in the course of a sermon. After some Council of the Church, Nicaea I think it was, the Emperor Constantine, recently converted to Christianity, entertained the assembled bishops to some kind of knees-up in his palace. It was only lately that these saintly figures had been persecuted for their beliefs. To make the point, they entered the imperial palace proudly displaying the scars of their martyrdom to the guard – pointing here to an eye socket gouged out in gladiatorial combat, here to a stump where some limb had been munched off by a lion. It was very much in this defiant spirit that one might offer, after a thrashing by the Binker, to show the scars to a chum.

Like all the boys in his care – there were about sixty of us – I did everything in my power to keep out of the Binker's way. This was easier said than done. For a start, he prided himself on teaching every child in the school, so one was bound to get him either for Geography or Scripture or (in unlucky terms) for both. When the other teachers weren't teaching, I imagine that they were sitting in the Staff Common Room, sucking at noisome pipes and working their way through piles of exercise books. Not so the Binker, who prowled the school grounds in the fervent hope that he would find a boy infringing one of the innumerable regulations by which our lives were governed: having your hands in your pockets; going out of bounds (this meant not merely stepping outside the school gates, but going anywhere within them except a few paths and a couple of asphalt playgrounds); eating sweets, except on Sundays and Wednesdays; running between lessons; not running on runs –

all these offences were punishable by the cane if the Binker was in that sort of mood. At mealtimes it was the same. He was always there, pacing up and down between the four refectory tables where we ate, looking for breaches of table manners, and insisting that we consume every inedible morsel which was placed before us.

'What's that piece of gristle doing on your plate, Ramsay?'

'Just about to eat it, sir.'

'Good, good. Otherwise Tammie-tawse would have to help you.'

He did not actually use a tawse, but Tam, Tammie, or Tammie the Tawse were among the playful nicknames which he gave to the various rods, garden canes and switches in his collection.

Of an evening, he might turn up at any minute to supervise bathtime and washing. After lights-out, he lurked silently on the landings outside our dormitories in the hope of hearing someone whisper. This had been Darnley's crime on the previous evening. He was a repeated and incurable offender, a compulsive talker quite unable, once a thought occurred to him, to keep it to himself. Punishment may be enjoyable for those who inflict it. One sometimes questions its deterrent effects. In spite of the severest punishments, we went on talking after lights-out. In the eighteenth century, they went on stealing sheep, even though they could be hanged for it and often were.

The queue in which Darnley and I stood edged its way towards the kitchen window where Mrs Binker, a warty lady of uncertain years, dispensed pieces of bread thinly spread with red jam. There was no marg – we only had marg at tea.

When I put out my hand to receive my bread she rapped it sharply with a spoon, taking the skin off my knuckles. One learned not to question such unexplained outbreaks of violence. Then she gave me my bread. As I knew quite well, there was no reason for this assault. She had a very understandable dislike of boys (in general, boys *aren't* nice, and they could be said, in this particular situation, to occupy too much of her husband's attention). Mrs Binker therefore lost no opportunity for tweaking a boy's nose or twisting his ear or thwacking him with an umbrella if she happened to be passing and he happened to be in range. Her acts of violence, unlike those of the Binker, were seldom ritualised, but she did on occasion get the gym master to line us up on the edge of the swimming bath so that she could have the pleasure of pushing us in, one by one. The especially timorous ones she liked to push off the diving board.

Unlike her husband, Mrs Binker (their real name was Larmer; I don't know why we called them the Binkers) was very stout; stout and pale; her warts and moles all sprouted healthy shoots of coarse black hair.

When the boys had collected their bread at the kitchen window, the queue bifurcated to two corners of the playground, where there were milk crates. You helped yourself to a third-pint bottle (courtesy of Messrs Attlee, Bevan and Lampitt). Very welcome it was to swig with that bread which was usually a bit dry. You put the milk-bottle top in the box provided. The tops were collected by Mrs Binker for some charitable purpose (she was well known in the town for her tireless works of charity) and if you failed to do this, you got either a beating or, at least, a week's litter duty.

'Anyway,' said Darnley as we threw our silver tops into the box, 'it's the Binker next. India again.'

'I hate India,' I said.

'I wouldn't mind seeing tigers and elephants. My grandfather was in India. Dad was born there.'

'I don't mean real India. That's great. I mean the Binker's India. Sketch-maps.'

'Then after Joggers, there's *Art*,' said Darnley meaningfully. Somehow, he had discovered my feelings for the new art mistress, Miss Beach, who had arrived that term. He swigged down his milk in a couple of mouthfuls. Darnley had enormous lips which, rather grotesquely, encased the whole of the upper part of his bottle. Thus refreshed, he began to enact the lovesick swain.

'Oh, Miss Beach, I love you. Let me clean your dirty brushes, Miss Beach. Let me kiss you, Miss Beach.'

And with his slobbery lips he kissed the air, sending forth a shower of milky spit.

'Shut up, Darnley.' I felt myself blushing and gave him a rough shove.

'Steady on,' he said. 'Just 'cause you're nuts about Miss Beach isn't my fault.'

'Shut *up*!'

I now got an arm round his neck and prepared to scrag him. Scragging involved getting your opponent's neck in the bend of your elbow and holding it like a vice. He could then choose between standing up and getting his neck broken or being bent in half. Then you could either pull him to the ground (if he was a friend) or (if you didn't like him) you could punch his face with your free hand, kick him in the balls or generally mess him about. It left your options open.

'Hey! Less of that, you two!' The voice was that of Timpson, the head boy. Darnley, in what struck me as a phrase of near genius, had once described Timpson as a 'prize ten-out-of-ten pillock'.

'Any more of that ragging, and you will be sent to the HM,' said Timpson. He was the only boy I ever met who referred to the Binker in this way. 'You two should be setting an example to the younger boys. In less than a year you will have gone on to your public schools.'

'Sorry, Timpson,' I said.

Darnley's specs, permanently bust and held together with bits of Elastoplast, had been dislodged by our horseplay and one of the lenses had somehow got splashed with milk. This clownish appearance did not prevent him following my lead and adopting an attitude of sheepish seriousness.

'So am I, Timpson. Really, really sorry.'

'You were less to blame than Ramsay. He had his arm round your neck, I think.'

'All the same' – Darnley never could resist overdoing things – 'frightfully sorry.'

'I shall overlook it this time,' said Timpson. 'Don't let it happen again.'

He was a cherubic, portly child whose very pursed lips seemed always shocked, forever on the point of giving voice to some well-considered admonition or rebuke.

Carried away by Darnley, I added, 'It was a jolly poor show, Timpson. I should like to put it on record that I am extremely sorry. I should never have scragged Darnley. Not with our both going on to public schools.'

'I am glad that you see it now, Ramsay. As I said, you are both fully old enough to know better.'

'Timpson.'

'What is it, Darnley?'

'I think we've both behaved like nanas – sorry, brutes – and it was frightfully decent, well, sporting . . . '

'The very word,' I said.

'Sporting of you, Timpson, not to send us to the Binker.'

'You mean the Headmaster?' This sage thirteen-year-old had the tone of a High Court judge who had never heard of baked beans.

'Quite, Timpson. HM. Sorry to have called the HM a Binker, Timpson.'

'That's all right, Darnley.'

'Timpson.'

'What, Ramsay?'

'Can I second that apology of Darnley's? I mean, he should never have spoken flippantly like that.'

'Hear, hear,' said Darnley. 'Terrifically, extremely sorry, Timpson.'

Only at a very late stage of all this did Timpson's porcine features register the fact that he was being teased.

'I hope you aren't trying to cheek me,' he said threateningly.

Darnley, a lanky creature already, at twelve years old, at least five foot six or seven, towered over our plump little generalissimo.

'Good Lord, Timpson, no! Wouldn't dream of it.'

It was one of Darnley's particular gifts (being able to fart tunes was another) that he was always able to keep a straight face on these occasions. I couldn't. We both rushed into our classroom as the bell went. In the couple of minutes before the Binker arrived, we put our heads in our desks and howled with merriment.

When the Binker entered the classroom all mirth vanished and we stood in silence. He was a noticeably short man (shorter than Darnley) and his tweedy clothes, slightly too large for him, were suggestive of some Scottish country houseparty. Brindled hair *en brosse;* a slightly florid complexion; glossy brown eyes like a dog's. He spoke in a refined 'Morningside' Edinburgh voice, but would often playfully break into different varieties of Scotchery, as when reading aloud from the novels of Stevenson, Scott, or Buchan, something which he did supremely well. This habit also extended to his reading from the Scriptures. Figures such as prophets or judges were often given special voices by the Binker, so that I always irrationally think of Elijah and Gideon as having spoken with strong Glaswegian accents. Quite often, his heart north of the border, he put on Scotch voices just for the hell of it. This morning, for instance, refreshed by the recent castigation of Darnley and Garforth-Thoms, he had assumed the character of some rustic from the pages of the Ettrick Shepherd.

'And wha's tae distribute yon sketch-mahps?'

This was a rhetorical enquiry. Having pointed them out he then placed the small pile of papers on Craster's desk and this boy (I never kept up with him – I believe he went into the Foreign Office) dutifully dished them out to the rest of us.

Sketch-maps were the Binker's passion – or one of the Binker's passions. Nearly all his Geography lessons began with a distribution of a blank map, drawn by himself (he was a delicate draughtsman) and run off on a stencilling machine. He would then call out the names of places and we had to fill them in on a blank map. Last term, it had been the industrial towns of England. This term, it was India. Since we were only a fortnight into the term, the Binker could be sure that very few of us, except Darnley, would have much grasp of Indian geography. We would not necessarily be thrashed for our ignorance, but there might be the need to be called up to the Binker's desk while, with one hand on the atlas, and the other creeping about our persons, he pointed out the whereabouts of Madras or Hyderabad. ('There's Hyderabad, Craster, and there's no need to flinch – we're all similarly composed'; he was quite open about it.)

Without further announcement, the test began.

'Delhi.'

Phew! He *was* in a good mood. It wasn't going to be a Binker-stinker.

'The Deccan.'

Easy-peasy.

'Karachi.'

Oh, peezeroo.

Like some Homeric deity who sensed hubris in his victims, the Binker smiled.

'Vishakhapatnum.'

After twenty, he had us all on toast. No one got more than about four questions right.

Another boy (Dorset-Lemon, now a publisher) collected up the maps and we then opened a textbook dating from the 1920s. Dorset-Lemon was then required to read out some stuff about tea plantations. Darnley's dad had been a tea-planter, but they had come home before the war. His mum had married someone else quite recently. It was all much more high-powered than anything in my own background.

'Thenk-yor, Dorset-Lemon,' said the Binker.

He laboriously consulted his watch, a thing which he kept on the end of a chain in his waistcoat pocket. Twenty minutes of the lesson had elapsed and there was a quarter of an hour to go. The Binker held forth about India, how it was ours by right since we got it from the French in the eighteenth century, and how Clive of India had showed enterprise and courage ever since he climbed to the top of the church spire at Market Drayton. Another thing was that the King was a King-Emperor who was being betrayed by wicked men who pretended to be his Government but were in fact Communists, determined to hand over the Government of India to another Communist, Mr Gandhi. It amused me to hear the Government spoken of in these terms. It was also baffling. In the Binker's view, Sir Stafford Cripps, the Hon. Vernon Lampitt and others were a gang of ruthless hooligans and pirates, intent on gouging out the finest jewel in His Majesty's Imperial Crown. It was amazing to think of Uncle Roy consorting with such roughnecks. And then I thought of Sargie (who although he wasn't in the Government was the Government's cousin) standing on the pavement in Mayfair and asking me into his club for a snifter.

But it was from the Binker that I heard of the most exciting of all the Government's schemes, something which made me realise that Mr Attlee and his piratical crew were Good Things in spite of so unsportingly beating Mr Churchill in the election.

'There is something worse,' said the Binker, 'worse by far than their desecration of His Majesty's Imperial Crown.'

This was fascinating. I was full of admiration for the Honourable Vernon even before I heard what it was that was *worse* than pulling down everything Clive and his friends had built up and handing over the best-ordered society in the Orient to a lot of ignorant savages (i.e. the people who actually lived there). It was a scheme which would, if once enacted, make all my nightmares vanish away.

'They openly talk,' and in his precise angry tones the last word became 'tok', 'of making private education itself illegal. And we all know what that would mean. Seaforth Grange would be closed down by Mr Attlee's *cheka*. And himself a Haileybury man.'

I had no idea what a 'checker' was, but the thought of it kept me going during the blacker moments of the next couple of terms. I half assumed that it was someone who came and checked up on you. But, by a process of irrational association, the Binker's clipped Scotch manner of saying the word brought into my mind the memory of Robert Donat in the film of *The Thirty-Nine Steps*. At various exciting moments, Donat is chased through the glens and highlands by Scottish policemen, whose peaked caps are encircled with checked bands. O checker! O rend the heavens, come swiftly down!

The Binker's tirade against the Socialists took up the rest of our lesson and then, as Darnley had not needed to remind me, it was Art.

There was a very rapid turnover of art mistresses at Seaforth Grange. Usually, they were young women who could not keep order. They left, usually for mysterious reasons and sometimes in the middle of term. Yet more mysterious than their reason for leaving was their reason for coming in the first place. The money can't have been good. The conditions of work were appalling.

There was a new art mistress, as I have mentioned, and her name was Miss Beach. I had fallen very seriously in love with her. Before it happened, I had never before spoken to anyone about love (I mean the sort you fall into). The subject was aired during Vanessa's dormitory chats, but as something which had happened to her. Clearly, it had happened to Darnley's mother. 'She's still jolly fond of Dad, but you see, she's fallen in love with this other chap,' he had sheepishly confided in me about a year before; it was really the beginning of our friendship. Like all forms of pain, it is totally unimaginable until it happens. I was now in the depths of it.

I took it that Darnley had never been in love himself. In the light of the catastrophe which had befallen his life when the condition afflicted his mother, he could be forgiven for taking a dim view of love in general. This did not make his crude teasing any easier to stomach. Even as we entered the art room, he was moving into his Romeo routine, one hand on his chest and a pink, smooth, knobbly knee looking as if it was about to genuflect.

'I warn you,' I said.

But already my voice was weak, my heart was palpitating, my stomach was churning; for *she* was near and we could hear her surprisingly stentorian tones.

'Come in, no talking – put your smocks on – Garforth-Thoms, where's your smock?'

We all had to wear smocks for Art, even though as it happened we were doing netting, which involved no glue, no paint, nothing with which we might splash our grey prison uniform. Typical, this, of the Binker's unthinking, Stalinist approach to things. Some boy's grey-flannel shirt had probably once been splashed with powder paint. The rest of us, world without end, had to wear smocks.

'There wasn't a smock on the peg, please,' said Blowforth-Bums.

'Nonsense – I can see a whole row of them out there.'

'But they've run out of blue ones, please. The green ones don't match my eyes.'

This playing to the gallery, very annoyingly, worked. The whole class was having the giggles.

'Don't call me "please".'

'Sorry, please.'

The idea was to break the nerve of any new teacher and normally I joined in the ragging with gusto. But, when they ragged Miss Beach, I boiled with indignation. I could easily have killed Garforth-Thoms for his joke about the overalls. I hated it, too, because it established a sort of intimacy between him and Miss Beach. There was something flirtatious about it, to which she responded. When he came back into the room with his smock on, she said, 'Very pretty, Garforth-Thoms.'

This time, the laughs were on her side and Blowforth-Bums was blushing.

She had short, dark brown, bobbed hair and glasses which rather dwarfed her tiny features – a nose so small that it hardly stuck out from her face, miniature ears. She wore a plain green skirt like an Irish kilt; black stockings over wonderful legs; an open-necked man's shirt rolled up to the sleeve to reveal nougat-coloured, freckly arms. The eyes were the liveliest I had ever seen, full of satire and laughter. They seemed to understand everything. She was not in the ordinary sense pretty; certainly she lacked the glamour of Vanessa. She was rather flat-chested. But my adoration for her was not just a spiritual thing. I adored her whole being, I longed for her. Probably at that date she was about twenty-two; no older, because she had only just left art school in London.

Each time I saw her, the being in love got worse. This lesson, for example, when we were meant to be learning the rudiments of how to make nets, everything made me suffer. I was tortured by the fact that I was not able to paint for her, to do something truly artistic. Nets lacked soul. I suppose, to judge from the sketches she did of us while we made our nets, that she thought of us as fisher-boys, like something in the Newlyn School. But I did not see that and it would have given me no pleasure if I had done so. I had loathed being a child ever since I was aware that I was one. Being in love just made it even worse. I did not want her to think of me as a little boy. Then again, I was unhappy because, to her eyes, there was nothing to distinguish me from all the other little boys. I was hatefully conscious of this. Love allowed me no illusion. While Darnley and the rest teased her, I was quite aware that she thought of me as just a silly little boy, misbehaving like the rest. Infuriatingly, she did not seem to *notice* that I was not ragging her. It would have been terrible if she had not been able to control the class. As it happened, she did possess the mysterious gift of making children behave as she wanted them to.

After a while, she put down her sketchbook and wandered among us as we stitched with our string.

'Well done, Tromans, that's coming on very well.'

I hated Tromans for being good at netting. I knew I was not good at it. I kept trying to persuade myself that it was not her idea that we should be doing it, that netting had been forced on her by some higher authority. But there is no reason to suppose that this was true.

'Come on, Ramsay,' she said when she got to me. 'You can't make a net just by sitting looking soulful at it.'

She had a mock-vehement way of speaking which went down well with boys. The tone implied that she was cheering on laggards. Her reference to my 'soulful' expression produced immediate titters all round the art room.

'And Ramsay,' she said, 'your tension is all wrong.'

I could have told her that.

It gave me the chance to be near her, though. Her tiny little white hands took the netting from mine, and for quite ten seconds our fingers were touching.

'Well, let it *go*, Ramsay, or you'll tie us both in knots. Shut up, the rest of you. Get on with making those nets. Sounds like something in the Bible,' she added as a throwaway line. When I got to know her better, I realised that she had a line in very mildly blasphemous jokes. There was nothing offensive in what she said – there was just a tendency for irony about loaves, fishes, walking on water, that sort of stuff.

'Just look at this!' she wriggled my net with more mock anger. 'I know a net is holes tied together with string, but yours is nothing *but* holes. You've dropped about six stitches here.'

I was trying to say sorry, but words would not come. Already, love's terrible tendency to create false hopes was at work in me. Why had she stopped to look at my netting? The rational explanation was that my netting was in a mess. But love did not want this to be the reason. Love wanted me to hope that she was secretly falling in love with *me*. She had stopped just as an excuse, because she wanted our fingers momentarily to touch. She had wanted me to be able to stand with my nose only inches away from her throat, to note the softness of that white, pulsating skin and to smell the wonderful smell of *her* – a particular soap she used, blending with the smell of her hair which was like honey.

In time, she moved on, but I tried to tell myself that whenever she helped another boy with his tangled little bit of netting, it was because his string was really in a mess, whereas she had paused by me because she *knew*.

Some people I have met have told me that they have never been in love. And I have usually replied that they don't know what they are missing. Much the worst thing they are missing is this desire to kid yourself which comes over you whenever you fall in love. You become a kind of lunatic, looking out for telltale signs and secret messages where they do not really exist.

At the end of the lesson, I told myself that she might want me to linger behind. There had been a sign in the half-touching of our fingers as they got entangled in the string together.

'Coming to lunch?' asked Darnley.

There was amusement in his voice, but also the beginning of annoyance that I was making a fool of myself.

'I'll follow you,' I said.

'Aren't you going to lunch, Ramsay?' asked Miss Beach.

'I thought you might need some help tidying up the art room.'

'There's not much to do, is there?'

The way that she peered at me suggested that she thought my staying behind was part of some elaborate tease. There were wary glances at the others, who were drifting out.

'I suppose you could help me put out paper for this afternoon, if you liked,' she said.

I eagerly accepted.

'It's the really little boys this afternoon – Lower III. So that's twenty sheets of paper – distribute them far apart. We don't want them splashing one another with paint.'

'Did you go to an art school or what?' I asked.

'What!' She laughed. 'No, I went to one called the Slade, actually.'

'But I thought the Slade was really good.'

The colossal rudeness of this remark did not occur to me. I took it for granted that everyone knew Seaforth Grange to be a dump, a stinking, hateful pit; the appearance there of anyone intelligent of their own free will demanded some sort of explanation.

'Anyway, how did you come to have heard of the Slade?'

I liked her for not condescending. She did not say, 'Aren't you a bit young to be asking me where I did my training?' She spoke as if we were equals.

With a certain amount of dread, I heard myself having to trot out a line of talk which, if allowed to continue, could have been endless.

'Well, there's this family called the Lampitts. They are terrific friends of my uncle – well, one of them is. Sargie Lampitt. And he's got a cousin who teaches there. Design or something. I've heard my uncle talk about it.'

I thought, when I mentioned the Lampitts, that an expression of faint strain passed over her features.

'There are a lot of teachers and lecturers there,' she said. 'Is your uncle an artist?'

'No,' I said, highly embarrassed. 'No, he isn't.'

She did not ask me what my father did. Had someone already warned her that my parents were dead, or was it just natural tact?

Inescapably, I heard myself being a Lampitt bore.

'They live in the neighbouring large house and they've got hundreds of cousins. One of them is in the Government,' I said.

Miss Beach ignored all this.

'The Slade is *wonderful*,' she said. 'Guess who we had teaching us sculpture last year?'

'I can't.'

'Henry Moore!'

'I've never heard of him, I'm afraid.'

There was a pause.

'I'm really a sculptor more than anything else,' she said. 'Henry Moore is the greatest living sculptor. One of the greatest sculptors in the history of the world. Imagine what it was like to be taught by him. And he is so kind, and so unassuming and modest. And yet he understands so much.'

I wanted to say that I should rather be taught netting by Miss Beach than sculpture by this unheard-of. At the same time, I felt immensely flattered by her treating me to this snatch of grown-up talk. The few sentences about Moore, like Mrs Maddock's Cambridge chat in the butcher's shop in Timplingham, opened up a tiny chink of light: songs from a distant land, promises of future blessedness. I walked on air when I left the art room.

This was the first of many little talks with Miss Beach, talks which began my education. They were always snatched at odd moments – the ten minutes before lunch, the five minutes before the end of break when she was getting the art room ready for a lesson. Sometimes, in a rare moment of free time (and there were precious few of those in an average Seaforth Grange day) we might have as much as half an hour together: for example, if she were on duty on Sunday afternoons. She was always attentive, she never treated me like a child. For instance, on the first occasion when we met after our Henry Moore conversation, she produced some photographs of his work to show me. I was bitterly disappointed to discover that it was 'modern art', something which Aunt Deirdre (I had assumed, rightly) regarded as preposterous. Not so Miss Beach, who explained to me that the distinction between ancient and modern in these areas was largely artificial, a division made by people incapable of making the much more useful one between good and bad art. Moore's fascination with plasticity and form, and the problems which he so successfully tackled, would have been familiar, she said, to Rodin, to Michelangelo, to the sculptors of ancient Athens. Next time we met, she had illustrated books ready, to explain what she meant. I did not need convincing. I believed everything she said and became instantly a convinced Modernist. I don't think she was in fact partisan. Like all true artists, she was interested in *all* aspects of her subject and anxious to find merit in undiscovered areas. Picasso, for example, was a passion with her, which she passed on to me. She even showed me some of her own paintings, angular, two-faced heads in asymmetrical designs which soon seemed very beautiful to me, once I got my eye in. She explained about the growth of abstract painting and showed me reproductions of some of the great early twentieth-century English abstract painters; in particular, we both came to share a great fondness for Ben Nicholson's white paintings, pictures which seemed to combine the purity of mathematics with the romance of snow.

If she had not enjoyed our talks, it is inconceivable that she would have allowed them to continue. She must have early on guessed that I was crazy about her and no doubt she considered that this was an acceptable way of dealing with the situation. How much is it ever someone else's responsibility if you offer them the (usually unwelcome) burden of total devotion?

There were hundreds of other reasons why she might have enjoyed these talks. She was homesick for the arty world she had left behind in London. There were few enough people on the staff of Seaforth Grange who had even heard of Picasso and it was a safe bet that those who had would detest him. To have found an audience was, in a way, a stroke of luck for her; and there were many reasons why she might have thought it unlikely that our friendship could go any further: I was twelve years old, I only came up to her shoulder, I wore ridiculous baggy shorts which flapped about my bare, hairless, pink knees, my voice had not broken, I called her Miss Beach and she called me Ramsay. The embarrassing disparity between our ages was something which, little by little, I came to disregard, though she must have been aware of it all the time. I was deeply, seriously, passionately in love. The pains of it were so terrible that I believed that they must end with my getting what I so earnestly desired: to be with her for ever. I had not worked out the details, but somehow Miss Beach and I would win through. We would be together. I have no idea whether she guessed how very deep the wound was going. Obviously, she was aware of something. Perhaps she called it a 'crush' to make it seem less serious. Perhaps, to her, it was not serious. I was deep in the classic mistake, repeated so often in my life, of thinking that because I cared so passionately, I had somehow bought her, that because I had suffered for her, there was something which she owed me.

Sexual feelings unquestionably contributed to these disturbing sensations but they were very far indeed from being the whole of them. The humiliating activity in which my poor parents had had to indulge in order to generate my entrance into the world was not something which I ever intended to do with Miss Beach. It did not cross my mind, I don't think. I wanted to go for long walks with her on the Malvern Hills. I wanted to stroke her pale, freckled arms. I wanted to kiss her and to be hugged by her. But nothing filthy. Indeed, as the association deepened, and Miss Beach became more and more important to me, I instinctively found that smut had vanished from my mind, so that a lot of Darnley's more hair-raising conversations, and many of the things said or done in my dormitory after lights-out, struck me as repulsively alien.

Even the good-night embraces of Vanessa were now to be loyally eschewed. If I could not kiss Miss Beach, I didn't want to kiss anyone. I expect that this was odiously priggish, but if so, the priggery was instinctive and not willed. I did not have to struggle. I no longer wanted anything in my life except Miss Beach.

That did not stop me from being wholly fascinated, as before, by Vanessa's flow of gossip about herself, the school, the world in general, when it was her turn to come round the dorms in our house last thing at night. When it was the turn of the art mistress to come in for Vanessa's searching analysis, her words were torture to me and yet I wanted to know everything. And it was in this way, from Vanessa, and not from my beloved herself, that I began to discover why Miss Beach was in Malvern.

We had all washed and brushed our teeth and got into bed one evening when Vanessa came into the dormitory. As already indicated, she was a Teutonic-looking girl, tall, with a full figure shown to advantage by tight woollen jumpers, pleated skirts, black stockings. Shoulder-length blonde hair was held back from an innocent, oval face by an Alice band. Sometimes the hair was in a ponytail. With her large, blue eyes, her full lips, her little waist and her large hips, Vanessa was what we artlessly called 'a pin-up'. (We did not in fact possess any photographs of beautiful girls and it would have been out of the question to display them if we had, drawing pins being among the thousand items forbidden by the Binker.) Vanessa having entered, the rituals were then gone through. We all knelt in silence by our iron bedsteads for two minutes, hands clasped, eyes shut, little Christopher Robins lost in prayer. My thoughts invariably remained below on such occasions, I think because I then imagined that there was something distasteful, not to say blasphemous, about talking to God at times designated by the Binker.

When we were all in bed, Vanessa came round and said good night to us. There were about ten in a dormitory. For the younger boys, Vanessa's good night was little more than a peck on the cheek, but for the older boys, myself included, they were full-blown embraces, modelled closely on what Cary Grant or Humphrey Bogart appeared to do when pressing their lips against those of a starlet. ('French kissing', appropriately enough, I only discovered when I went to France.) But now, after Miss Beach, things were different. When it came to my turn to be kissed I no longer pressed my lips against Vanessa's, but merely rubbed my cheek against hers, as, once in a blue moon, Aunt Deirdre might do to Uncle Roy – if, say, he were going away for a few days with Sargie by the seaside.

When we had all been kissed and Vanessa was seated at the end of the dormitory captain's bed, the gossip could begin. Like all good gossips, Vanessa was omnivorous, wide-ranging and quite unafraid to swoop from generalities to the particular. Who was the most handsome man in the world (she thought, on the whole, Prince Philip of Greece, who was going to marry Princess Elizabeth) alternated with the really much more interesting question of what was the Maths master's middle name.

We all knew that he was A. J. Rhys and some weeks before Vanessa had let slip that the 'A' was for Alan. When written down, this information looks commonplace, but any information is interesting if it starts life as a closely guarded secret.

'What's the "J" for, Vanessa?'
'Dunno.'
'You do! You must!'

'I don't!' Girlish shriek. (Vanessa was exactly six years older than I was.)

'You're in love with Mr Rhys, Vanessa,' pronounced Bowen, the dorm captain. 'Vanessa's in love with Greasy Rhysy.'

This suggestion had us all in fits, including Vanessa. We all knew it wasn't true, because she had told us that she had a really wonderful boyfriend back home in Bromsgrove, who drove over to see her twice a week during term. Also we were all, Vanessa included, young enough and therefore cruel enough to suppose that no one *could* be in love with Greasy Rhysy. We all still believed that love affects only the young and the beautiful and that no heart beats inside such lank-haired, collapsed-looking individuals as A. J. Rhys.

'He's married, anyway!' protested Vanessa. She knew as well as we did that this made the Greasy Rhysy joke all the funnier.

Then someone blurted out, 'What's Miss Beach's Christian name?'

There was a bit of silence; then someone else said, 'Ask Ramsay.' More splutters of mirth. Other people being in love always has joke potential: Greasy Rhysy, me, what difference did it make to them? Anything is good for a laugh.

'That's enough,' said Vanessa. I think she genuinely wanted to spare my feelings. 'Why should I tell *you* things all the time? You tell me what's going on. Are you going to win the matches on Saturday against the Downs?'

'Come *on*, Vanessa, tell us!' some young voice protested. 'What's Miss Beach called? It's B.R.B. Is it Barbara Beach, Betty Beach?'

I could not bear the *tone* in which these questions were being fired off, just as though Miss Beach were some kind of joke in the same league as Greasy Rhysy. At the same time, I was more anxious than anyone to know the answer.

'Beatrice Beach!'

'Bertha Beach!'

'Bottom Beach!'

'Shut *up*, Torrance.'

'Just 'cause you're spoony, Ramsay!'

Perhaps to allay any further unpleasantness, Vanessa just came out with it.

'It's Beryl,' she said.

An extraordinary wave of sadness came over me. The others were jabbering, repeating the name, laughing about it.

'How common,' said Bowen: exactly the words my aunt would have used had she heard of someone called Beryl.

I loved her no less. If anything, were such a thing possible, I loved her more, being in possession of that hitherto secret talisman, her name. But I was in love with someone called Beryl. I must confess that I would have been happier with a Beate, a Bathsheba, a Brünnhilde. Beryl lacked poetry.

'Has Miss Beach – has Beryl – got a boyfriend?' asked some cheeky little voice.

'Ramsay!'

More laughter. I got out of bed and prepared to sock Torrance, but Vanessa suddenly turned all schooly and told me to get back or she would send me to the Headmaster.

'That's quite enough,' she said.

By then it was time for lights-out and she had another dormitory to do. But it was too tantalising to leave things in the air like this. When she had switched out the lights in Dorm Five across the landing, Bowen, who, needless to say, was himself crazy about Vanessa, called out to her in a whisper and begged her to come and sit on his bed once more.

'Oh, just five minutes.'

In a remarkably short space of time, Bowen and the others pumped her for information about Beryl Beach. She was, they learned, someone who had done really well at an art college in London, Vanessa forgot the name, and she had already had pictures hung in exhibitions – and statues had been put on show. Everything had been going well, but then she had fallen hopelessly in love with this chap.

(This time, Torrance's repeated interjections of my name struck the others as unfunny and someone, either Pell or Aaronberg, really belted him one.)

Who was this chap?

'He's called Raphael Hunter,' said Vanessa.

'Is he handsome?'

'Very.'

'Vanessa's in love with him, too!'

'Shut your mouth, Torrance, or we'll do it for you.'

'Sorry, Bowen.'

'Does he live in London, this bloke? Who is he? Is he an artist too?'

'He lives in Malvern, or his parents do. That's why Beryl took this job, to be near him, you see. He isn't famous yet, but he's going to be a . . .'

We did not, at that point, learn what Hunter was going to be, for at that moment, someone said, 'Sshh!'

There was only one reason for hushing: the stealthy approach of the predator. In the darkness we listened, terrified and silent. To any but the most hardened listener, there would have been nothing in that silence. But instinct told us that the Binker was on the prowl. There was no chance that he could not have heard us all whispering. That could easily mean a beating for the whole dorm, as well as being very awkward for Vanessa. But she was a quick thinker and she was on our side. She went at once to the window, opened and shut it noisily and said, 'There! Off you fly! Settle down now, everyone, it's gone.'

And she briskly left the room. On the landing beneath we heard her voice conversing with the low murmur of the Binker. He was clearly furious that his cover had been blown.

'A bat, you say?'

'It's gone now, sir.'

'Could they not get rid of a bat without tokking?'

Vanessa whispered something inaudible.

Then there was a black silence. None of us knew how long the Binker paced the landings stocking-footed, torch in hand, ear cocked. Better by far, from his point of view, than a mere whisperer after lights-out, would be the detection, by the rustling movement of sheets, of some onanist in the act. But all was still that night.

It was hours before I got to sleep, days before I absorbed all the information imparted that night by Vanessa, weeks before I understood her own silence on the question of whether Mr Hunter was handsome, years before I began to see a connection between this and Miss Beach's own little silence at the name of Lampitt, and decades before the stories which began as gossip about Miss Beach and Hunter took on the distinct shapes and meanings which they possess for me today.

At first, I felt so hurt by what Vanessa had told us that I found it impossible to believe. Miss Beach was in love with a man called

Raphael Hunter. That was her sole reason for having taken a job in Malvern. This information scalded me when I heard it. All the more terrible was that something which affected me so secretly (could *they* know the depths of it?) and so profoundly, should have been the subject of common chat – on the same level of farce as Greasy Rhysy's middle name. This was something on which I felt that not only my happiness, but my actual capacity to survive in this life, depended. The idea that Miss Beach was capable of feeling for a man as I felt for her was something which offered its own cruel sprig of hope. Hitherto I had not so much as considered that she, or anyone else, *could* have feelings which were as strong as those which had taken possession of me. Now that I had learnt that she did feel, that she *was* in love, things were different. If Vanessa had been able to tell us with some infallible and completely reliable authority that Miss Beach was not capable of love, I think I might have felt the beginnings of relief or cure. For the time being, Miss Beach could have remained on her pedestal and I could continue to pour forth to her my secret devotions and oblations. But to learn that she was in the same humiliating and yet glorious condition as myself, but enchanted with Mr Raphael Hunter, this somehow changed everything, made it more highly charged. Since it was knowledge too terrible to be borne, I gradually began to doctor the facts. I forgot Raphael Hunter's name. Then I persuaded myself that Vanessa had invented him in order to spice up her dorm gossip, that he was not real. After a couple more days and another brief encounter with Miss Beach herself, I even managed to persuade myself that Vanessa had been hinting something quite different, namely that Miss Beach was really in love with me. Knowing, as she did, that the other boys teased me about Miss Beach, Vanessa could hardly have been so cruel as to blurt out the true facts of the case to the whole dormitory. I never had any other opportunity to see Vanessa and to talk about things. Supposing Miss Beach had *chosen* Vanessa as her intermediary! Supposing Miss Beach wanted to tell me that she loved me as I loved her, but supposing she didn't dare. She *might* have asked Vanessa to say that she was in love, in the knowledge that I alone would interpret this information correctly, leaving the other boys in the dorm still in the dark.

This theory looks pretty improbable when written down, but I wanted so deeply to believe it that I soon discovered that all the facts of the case fitted. For instance, during our five-minute encounter before lunch two days later, Miss Beach did not call me 'Ramsay', as I was fairly sure she always had done. She did not call me anything at all. And she had found another photograph of Henry Moore's work. It was one of those strange family scenes – a massive mother shape and a tall figure standing behind her, the whole group photographed against some rough bit of country. She explained to me that the sculptor had got his first inspiration as a child when massaging his mother's back; and that while philistines would say that these sculptures were 'unrealistic' I was to admire their qualities of form, plasticity and strength. I did, I do. But, at the time, this talk of an artist rubbing a woman's back (even though it was the innocuous story of a child rubbing its mother) seemed like a code. When, almost casually, she remarked that I could keep the Moore photograph, all my hopes were confirmed. I could not have been surer of her love had the picture been of Rodin's 'The Kiss' and had the back of the picture, instead of being left blank, been covered with declarations of Miss Beach's undying love for me.

During this phase of conceited optimism, I must have been, even more than usually, an embarrassment and a bore to her. Although I did not dare to snatch many little talks with her, I followed her everywhere and was unhappy unless I could be reasonably sure of her whereabouts in the school. There were very few school buildings as such, Seaforth Grange consisting of five neighbouring Victorian houses and their gardens, enclosed by high hedges and purple granite walls. There was a rudimentary gym and a hideous little chapel, put up a few years before the war on the crematorium model. Otherwise there were few new or specially designed buildings, with the exception of the art room, a lean-to arrangement with large windows at the back of House Five, opposite the rabbit hutches. Above these hutches, there was a rockery and, by clambering up it, one commanded a clear view of the art room. Between lessons, or at other odd moments when she might be there, I would stand and look in. Sometimes she acknowledged my presence and waved, but more often she pretended not to see me.

As soon as she left the art room, I would dash round to the front of House Five and wait for her to come out of the front door; occasionally, I would have the courage to offer to carry her books, or to walk along with her. Sometimes, as I now think, to avoid me, she scuttled down the drive, out of the school gate, where I could not follow her, into Albert Road North. (Apart from our walk to the games fields, it was strictly forbidden to set foot outside the prison confines.) Her own room was in House Two. By a brisk walk across the school grounds, I could be waiting at the gate by the time she had walked all the way around Albert Road North and up Como Road. House Two, much the most handsome of the school houses, was Italianate and faced with creamy stucco, unlike the lumpy granite of Houses One and Three, and the brick of Houses Four and Five. House Two contained the school offices, the staff room, the Binker's study, the secretary's office and so on. On the first floor there was a small dormitory for the very youngest boys, who were allowed teddy bears. The other rooms in the house were all inhabited by female members of staff: Miss Duffy, who taught the younger boys and, throughout the school, English verse; Vanessa herself; Miss Beach. Vanessa and Miss Beach were next door to one another on the second floor. The fact doubtless explained Vanessa's familiarity with the art mistress's business.

Miss Beach's window looked eastward into the school; over the roof of the gymnasium she would have been able to see House Three where the dining room was, its lawns and shrubbery leading down past the large Spanish chestnut tree to the gardens of House Four. I spent hours walking about in these regions, with my eyes trained on Miss Beach's window. Sometimes I was rewarded with a glimpse of her. Once, when our eyes met, she had looked troubled, rather cross in fact, and closed her curtains, even though it was only the middle of the day. Sometimes at night, however, she left her curtains open and her lights on; and once or twice I took the supreme risk of pretending I needed a lavatory and sneaked out on to that lawn to gaze up at the lamp-lighted room. It consoled me, though there was no vision of her on such occasions, to think of the presence which the room contained.

The window itself now appears in my memory like a picture framed by the great green mass of the Malverns which undulated immediately above the school and on whose lower slopes we nestled. Seen with the painter's eye (and by then I wanted to be nothing if not an artist) there was an interest in the fact that this large creamy house stood out against a background not of sky but of green, for the hills sloped steeply upward behind the town. Even these huge, solid, geological phenomena which had come into being as a result of volcanic eruptions, aeons before Miss Beach was conceived, appeared to conform obediently to her own taste for abstract mass, tactile shape. Had one of the hills, *à la* Moore, developed a hole in its side, I should hardly have been surprised. As it remains, the icon in my mind is of a window full of light. Whereas the sky, in reality, is the source of light, in my picture of that window, it was Miss Beach who herself radiated and lit up the surrounding forms.

And it was through this window of hers that I first set eyes on Raphael Hunter, knowing with the immediate instinct of the rival in love that it was he, and thereby I discovered, in a horrifyingly short space of time, that everything which Vanessa had told us in the dormitory was true.

It was towards the end of a cricket afternoon. We had come back to the school from the playing fields and there was an hour or so of free time before we had high tea at six. Instead of going directly to change, with the others, I made my way round to the lawn of House Three for a routine glance at Miss Beach's window. I did not expect to see her at that hour, but the sight of the window itself would have been enough to provide comfort of a kind. It was open wide and, as I looked up, I saw at once that the back of her head was framed by the curtains. Her short brown hair fell straight, just covering her pale neck. Her back and shoulders were bare. At first I thought that she was completely naked; then I could see the line of her print frock, low cut, running across her pale, freckled shoulder blades. Holding these shoulders firmly, and then running up and down her back were a pair of hands, evidently not her own. At first I could not understand what the hands were doing there. They seemed like some weird optical trick. Nor, from where I was standing, were they very obviously masculine. They were just hands. They continued to move, stroking her back. One of them even disappeared within the straight, low collar of her frock. And then, like some absurd conjuror's trick, from behind Miss Beach's head there appeared a second head, resting its chin on her shoulders and kissing her bare back. After a moment of this activity, the head looked over Miss Beach's shoulder, out of the window and in the direction of the lawn where I stood. She turned at that point and then they both disappeared from the window. But for an unforgettable few seconds I had seen Raphael Hunter and our eyes had met.

In the first of those seconds, my agony was compounded by thinking that he was another boy at the school. I do not mean that he *resembled* any other boy, but that he was amazingly youthful in appearance, smooth, sexless. His fair hair was rather short in those days, otherwise I might have supposed that Miss Beach was embracing another girl. His skin was very pale and pasty. Even in the short time that I saw him, I believe that from the very first I was touched by something mysterious in Hunter's face, as though he were not at home in his surroundings. In this case, his air of being troubled, embarrassed, was easily explained by the fact that a small boy was watching him kiss a woman. But I was to see that look of sadness on Hunter's face in other circumstances.

All experience, Uncle Roy had once said in a sermon, has a capacity to change us to a certain degree if we let it, or if we want it to. But there are some types of experience called, in religion, 'revelation', after which nothing is ever the same again. Everything which happens before and after is transformed by revelation, the past as well as the future. If this is the case, then my experience on the lawn, staring up at Miss Beach's window, was a revelation and, like the revelations of Scripture, it was not merely all-transforming, but it was also of so shattering a kind that it took me years to put it into any kind of shape, to interpret it. And this was even more the case because the things which happened over the following few weeks were so completely confusing that the original moment of revelation, the two figures clasped together in the window, the white house framing the window, the green hills framing the house, became for a time obscured. I thought at first that it was a revelation purely about Miss Beach; later, as my interest in him grew, I took it much more as a revelation about Hunter. Only lately has it begun to occur to me that it was both these things, but also a revelation about myself, doomed to be as much the tormented spectator as the actor in my own life's drama.

On the instant, though, I was shocked and bitterly hurt. Before changing out of my games clothes, I went to hide my tears in the bogs.

Being in love is hell, it dominates life, it makes life painful, but

85

life goes on doggedly around love and in spite of it. So, school went on being awful and for the first time in nearly five years, its awfulnesses were half consoling, like the good thing about the Blitz being that it kept your mind off the war. The school curriculum continued, undisturbed and unaware, while my heart cracked. The collection of oddballs who constituted the Binker's staff continued to impart to us the curious assortment of misinformation which they had at their command. Very little of what they taught us – perhaps nothing – was of the smallest interest or use to me in later life. The chief interest of their lessons consisted in watching them behave according to type. Each lesson provided us with a new, slightly alarming, performing animal. Mr Finch; had he been a deserter, or was he shell-shocked? Perhaps neither, but we could make him cry simply by calling out, 'What did you do in the war, sir?'

Poor, wispy Miss Duffy was incapable of making us appreciate the gems of English verse in our reader; she was even less efficient at dodging the paper darts with which we regularly bombarded her. Lollipop Lew, the gangling loon who taught French out of a textbook, had apparently never heard the language spoken. He taught us to speak it phonetically –' gee swiss' for *je suis*. Was it all some kind of elaborate joke which he was playing against the rest of the world? One can ask that of any eccentric and the answer is never easy. With Darnley at the next desk, an item of furniture in which he bred slow-worms (once one satisfyingly came slithering out of the hole which should have contained the ink well, just as Miss Duffy was passing – what yelps!), lessons were an hilarious agony of half-suppressed giggles and unremittingly anarchic attempts to undermine the system. The level of wit was excruciatingly low, often non-existent. The laughter was cumulative. Someone started to giggle. Then another person. In such an atmosphere, any sort of interjection, any bit of cheek thrown at the unfortunate buffoon in front of us, was enough to make us writhe with laughter.

'Sir!'

'What is it *now*, Darnley?'

'What's the French for a male hen, sir?'

'Isn't that a contradiction in terms, Darnley?'

'Very droll, sir, very funny.'

To show how funny it was, we all shouted with laughter.

'Shut *up*!'

'But seriously, sir, a male farmyard bird. You know, sir. What's the French for it?'

There were two jokes going on here – one of simple bawdry and the other designed to expose our teacher's total ignorance of French vocabulary. We all pretended not to notice him rummaging through a much-thumbed *Hugo's French in Three Months* which he kept in his desk. So intent was he on convincing us that he knew the language that he completely forgot the way in which boys' minds work.

'What are you looking at under your desk, sir?'

'Shut up, Darnley.'

'But, sir, you *are* looking at something. What is it?'

'I think *coq* is the word you are after, Darnley.'

This produced such a roar of anarchic laughter that Greasy Rhysy had to come in from the classroom next door to quieten us down.

Darnley was in a different dorm from mine. I didn't tell him any of Vanessa's gossip about Miss Beach, but inevitably it leaked back to him. He was merciless enough to refer to her henceforth as Beryl. In grown-up life, you can't really get away with being rude about someone else's lover or partner or wife or husband. You just have to accept the fact that the heart plays strange tricks and that friends in all other respects delightful and intelligent have been stupid enough to fall in love. Politeness to or about the current object of desire is only abandoned at peril to the friendship itself. Darnley and I had not yet reached this level of sophistication. (I am not sure that Darnley ever quite did, but that is another story.) It pained me then that he thought of my devotion to Miss Beach as yet another joke, but I accepted this fact and even though I biffed him whenever he mentioned the matter I could not cease to regard him as a friend. I still assumed, for instance, that he would be coming out for lunch with us when Granny came down for her termly visit.

The visits of my grandmother were always something to be enjoyed, but this one was something to which we looked forward most particularly, because of the fact that I owned five pounds – the five pounds which Sargie Lampitt had pressed into my hand. Not only was it a fantastic sum of money – his lunch that day at Claridge's with Uncle Roy would have cost him only about a pound – but it was illegal to possess it. Sargie's lavish generosity had in fact landed me in an extremely awkward position. Like many other tyrants in history, the Binker was obsessed by currency control. We were forbidden more than a pound per term in pocket money. 'Ten shillings is more than adequate,' his famous 'Notes for Parents' proclaimed. Whatever money we brought back to school had to be handed in at the school office at the beginning of term. Had I handed in Sargie's fiver to the school secretary, it would have been posted straight back to Timplingham with a brisk letter to my uncle, refreshing his memory of the school rules.

It was therefore imperative that we should convert the five pounds into some commodity which could either be kept hidden when we got back to school or could plausibly be described as a present from Granny. This in itself was not easy. Any sort of food 'except' – I quote again from 'Notes for Parents' –'one moderately sized cake given on or near the boy's birthday' was forbidden. No sweets or chocolates – which were in any case rationed – were to be bought. Nor – the Binker's pen here got carried away with itself, for in what circumstances would we ever have been able to break this law? – were 'boys permitted to bring within the school perimeter meats, including sausages, firearms, explosives or any sort of tobacco'. Alcohol, of course, was out of the question. So, too, were the whole range of more obviously wholesome distractions, like books. 'Boys are only permitted to bring one book per term back to Seaforth Grange. This must be submitted to the Headmaster for approval at the beginning of term. There are books available on loan from the school library.' This collection chiefly consisted of heavy masculine stuff with an obsolescent imperialist flavour, not at that time to my taste. There were pseudo-historical romances by G. A. Henty, Stanley Weyman and W. Harrison Ainsworth. There were the memoirs of soldiers and explorers. Then there were the decayed bound volumes of pre-war *Punch*, each joke as fascinatingly unfunny as the last, and a very out-of-date *Chambers's Encyclopaedia*. It was hardly a literary banquet. In consequence I read almost nothing during my time at Seaforth Grange. Even if they had permitted it, though, I would not have dreamed of spending Sargie's five pounds on books. No. This called for the big idea, though nothing much occurred to us as we wandered around together in break or lolled idly on the sun-drenched cricket pitch (there was no rain that term; the weather was an uninterrupted English summer's day) while the others played with bat and ball.

Lollipop Lew, his waist burdened with white jumpers which we had cast off and which he had tied like a cummerbund around himself for safe-keeping, drooped in the slips, tall, red-faced, himself languid.

'Darnley and Ramsay, what the dickens do you think you are doing?'

'Making a daisy chain, sir.'

'Well, get up and go to the boundary. You are meant to be fielding.'

'No, sir, Fielding's batting, sir. Quite a different boy.'

Everything Darnley did or said contrived to be thoroughly puerile and foolish. Yet I have never laughed so much as I did in his company. Instinct must have drawn us together. Ever since, I have been chiefly attracted to those who wanted to make daisy chains while others played the game. Fielding is quite a different boy . . .

My grandmother, I suppose, had reached a rather similar conclusion at an early age, only with her it took the form of being surprised that a game was in progress at all and of needing assistance even with the composition of her daisy chain. Almost everything was either too complicated or too arduous for Granny to do on her own. Certainly, when my parents were killed, it was out of the question that she should have taken any practical part in my own upbringing.

'I brought *two* boys up,' she would sometimes tell me, wide-eyed, as though parents had almost never been so self-sacrific-ing or adventurous. The effort had evidently exhausted her, and would have been completely impossible had it not been for the loyal support and help of her very good friend Mrs Webb. Unlike the saintly Lady Starling (whom I had not at that stage met) Mrs Webb could not have been described by anyone as a doormat. She had a forcefulness of demeanour which left one in no doubt that she could look after herself. Nevertheless, for her own reasons (perhaps simple kindness of heart) she seemed prepared to immolate herself to all my grandmother's whims and needs.

'It's no good asking Thora to *do* things,' Mrs Webb would say with particular vehemence.

Mrs Webb, for instance, did all Granny's shopping. She had done so ever since the war started.

'Thora never could master those ration books' – there was almost triumph in her friend's incapacity – 'and you couldn't see her queuing, not with those feet.'

Granny's feet, even to the biased eye of her own flesh and blood, looked much like anyone else's. Each year at Cromer or (as Mrs Webb much preferred) Westgate-on-Sea, I had seen them: the full complement of toes and the filmy, delicate, white skin of her instep paddling in the waves. But it was apparently an a-priori truth, requiring no demonstration, that hers were not feet which you could expect to stand in a queue. 'Mr Churchill himself would not ask it,' said Mrs Webb, not long before the end of the war, and this was true. He had asked for blood, toil, sweat and tears, but not that. Not from Granny.

'Remember, I can't stand too long,' she would say.

I always did remember it. I remembered it again when I saw the diminutive figure of Mrs Webb waiting at the school gate on the Saturday of our exeat, as the Binker pretentiously called any permitted outing. Mrs Webb's jaunty little feathered hat, new-looking handbag and satin costume suggested, rightly, an air of prosperity not enjoyed by Granny. She had been left, one gathered, 'comfortable' by the demise of Mr Webb, who had owned a number of ironmongers' shops.

She and Darnley had met before. He quite often came out for meals with me when my people were down. Mrs Webb always embarrassed me, but not Darnley himself, by calling him by his Christian name.

'Hallo, Miles.'

'Hallo, Mrs Webb.'

'Hallo, young one,' she said to me. 'Your Granny's in the Riley. We could not keep her standing at the gate, not in this heat.'

It was a perfect sunny day, with a balmy breeze blowing in from the south.

Mrs Webb, who had driven ambulances during the Blitz, was addicted to motor travel and somehow managed to get enough petrol to drive her little Riley. Sometimes with a wink she hinted that she knew the right people. I have no doubt that she did. Her proud conveyance, shiny black with a violently sloping back roof, was parked at an angle on the steep street to prevent it rolling backwards. Granny greeted us as warmly as she could without stirring from her front seat in the little car, and Darnley and I clambered into the back.

'You'll be hungry for your lunches,' she said keenly.

I began to explain about having to spend the five pounds.

'If I was you, I'd save it up,' said Mrs Webb. 'Now, we're going to Bobby's. I always like the drive into Worcester.'

'Good,' said Darnley. And he attempted to explain to Mrs Webb why the five pounds must be spent that afternoon, and why Worcester would be an ideal place to spend it. Not only were there more shops than in Malvern, but there was far less likelihood of being spotted by a member of staff from Seaforth Grange. My grandmother's favourite eating place in the vicinity was the restaurant of a department store in the middle of Worcester, some eight miles away from the school. The service was quick. You could get delicious fish and well-cooked chips for only a few shillings, while a palm court trio, three crones, sawed out Indian love lyrics and numbers from pre-war musicals. When Darnley's mum took us out, it was always to the Foley Arms, the largest hotel in Malvern, where the meals were four times as expensive and took four times as long. How restless we used to become, waiting for those hunks of overcooked meat in their caterer's gravy.

The drive from Malvern to Worcester was soon accomplished – enlivened, after we had turned the steep bend in the road near the lunatic asylum at Powick, by our transformation into loonies, an uncharitable display which made the old ladies laugh and say we were terrible. Actually, on Darnley's part, the loony act was only just beginning to wear off by the time we reached the restaurant. There was a queue, but Mrs Webb walked to the head of it and addressed the manageress directly.

'If we could have a table at once; only on account of my friend's feet.'

This formula was efficacious; we were immediately led through the quite crowded restaurant. Everything at Bobby's was as I remembered it. The waitress, a stubby pencil poised over her greasy pad attached by a piece of string to her waist, was ready to take our order. Against a far wall the three crones shared a tiny platform with a baby grand and a potted aspidistra, and gave forth their melancholy renderings of pre-war songs: 'The Springtime Reminds Me of You', 'The Isle of Capri' and 'Love Is the Sweetest Thing'.

The food came almost instantly; any person anxious about Granny's feet would have been unable to feel equal worries about her appetite. Darnley himself, no mean trencherman, could not compete with her speed when it came to polishing off a pile of chips. The fish was of the freshest, the whole served with thin slices of white bread and butter and a pot of strong tea for four. And it was tea, not hot water poured over a bag.

'Now,' said Mrs Webb, 'I call that a very nice bit of plaice.'

'Enjoy your meal, did you, dear?' The waitress was hovering again.

'Enormously,' said Granny with great emphasis.

'Well, what to follow, what for sweet?'

'Oh, dear,' said Granny.

'Too full?' asked the waitress.

'Certainly not,' snapped Mrs Webb, 'only don't ask my friend to make decisions. She always did find decisions difficult, great or small.'

'There's a lovely bit of Bakewell with custard,' prompted the waitress. 'Or you could have a nice ice . . .'

She had failed to grasp the reality of the situation. Anyone who knew Granny would have recognised that there was something slightly monstrous about expecting her to do a difficult thing like reach a conclusion.

'Oh, *you* decide *for* me!' she said, for a moment vexed.

'What was it, Bakewell tart?' asked Mrs Webb.

'That's right, dear.'

'I think that sounds delicious.'

'I'd rather have the noice oice,' said Darnley.

He was not imitating the waitress's voice. He had an incurable need to embellish, change, or improve the world as he discovered it. Mrs Webb and Granny laughed almost constantly in his presence, and kept exclaiming that he really must go on the stage.

Both old ladies, but Granny in particular, had a highly developed sense of humour. They appeared to be approaching life chiefly on the look-out for diversion, preferably of a kind which would make them laugh. Granny loved all Darnley's jokes, and I admired the delicacy and swift editorial expertise with which he made his repertoire acceptable to an elderly female audience. True, this meant that a whole range of his 'jokes' – and some of the funnier ones – had to be scuppered altogether. But he adapted some of the stories about English-men, Irishmen and Scotsmen, excising the coarser elements, to truly hilarious effect, so that Granny, having made short work of her Bakewell, was driven to exclaim, 'More, Miles, more!'

'Come on,' said Darnley to me, 'you think of some.'

But he had no sooner said this than he had thought of another. Granny found this particular story, the one about two taxis colliding in Aberdeen and fifty-seven people being killed, so funny that I thought she would choke. As they often say of great performers, it was the way he told them. So conscious was Darnley of this, but so fond of the jokes themselves, that he would sometimes ask, rather anxiously, even when the joke had made everyone laugh, 'Do you get?' Sometimes, he would find that though they had laughed fit to burst, his audience had not understood the point of the joke at all and then he would laboriously explain, 'People in Aberdeen are really stingy, you see, so that they'd all piled into just two taxis . . .'

'They used to make jokes like that about the Jews,' said Granny. 'Before the war, of course.'

Anxious to demonstrate that, Hitler notwithstanding, anti-Semitic bad taste could still raise a laugh, Darnley was about to embark on a series of quickfire question-and-answer routines; but something extraordinary happened which interrupted Darnley's flow.

'I don't know,' said Granny, already shaking in anticipation, because she knew that Darnley's answer would make her chuckle. 'Why *are* pound notes green?'

There was such a pause that I filled in with the predictable, 'Because the Jews picked them all before they were ripe.' On my lips it was totally unfunny. Not a flicker of amusement was to be derived from the words. And we all turned, even Granny with her neck, in the direction in which Darnley was staring.

'That's our undermatron, she's called Vanessa, she's terrific,' he explained in a gabble. Gossip was as good as jokes as far as the old ladies were concerned and they were prepared for a change of subject. I desperately hoped that Darnley, with his somehow more sophisticated family background, wouldn't tell Granny that Vanessa kissed us all good night. I felt, without being able to say why, that my pleasure, or former pleasure, in feeling her large woollen chest against my pyjama jacket was not some-thing which I wanted imparted to the family. But I need not have worried. Beneath the larky exterior, Darnley's impeccable tact was unshaken.

'She looks very young,' said Granny.

'She's eighteen,' said Darnley. 'Most of the staff are ancient, but Vanessa is different.'

'You think anyone's ancient,' said Mrs Webb.

'But they're bonkers, as well, aren't they, Ramsay?'

'Yes.'

Darnley then asserted that the thing about Vanessa was that she was a jolly nice person and I agreed. From an aesthetic point of view, she had, perhaps, never looked nicer than on that afternoon. She wore a yellow and white spotted dress with a broad collar cut quite low over the chest. A yellow cardie was draped over her shoulders like a shawl. Her hair was done in a ponytail. She was smoking her Craven A with infinite sensuality.

'I like her young man,' said Mrs Webb.

It was the young man who had arrested my attention. No one else round that table had ever set eyes on him before, but I had. I would have recognised those hands alone, which had reached out to light her Craven A and now were holding her hands across the table. When he turned, it was unmistakable.

' "The oldest, yet the latest thing," ' Granny sang very, very quietly, conducting the music of the trio with her teaspoon. Mrs Webb took up the refrain.

> ' "I only hope that Fate may bring
> Love's glory to you!" '

It was not possible to tell any of them who he was. The terrible pain of seeing Raphael Hunter through Miss Beach's window and holding my beloved in his arms had made any subsequent mention of the matter impossible. Although Vanessa had, only a few weeks before, told all the dorm that Hunter was Miss Beach's boyfriend, only I knew what he looked like; only I had the painful evidence of my own eyes that this man in the restaurant had a claim on Miss Beach.

'I wonder who he is,' said Darnley.

'He's very, *very* handsome,' said Granny, quite spontaneously.

Now that I had the chance to survey him at greater leisure, I did so. My feelings about Hunter, before and since, are far too complicated for me to be able to say whether I shared Granny's opinion. I think, rather, that I was looking at Hunter partly in order to find out what handsomeness was. So *this* was what women found beautiful – a completely smooth face, boyish and on the borders of chubbiness; not much colour, not much vivacity in the eyes, but the features framed into an expression which was obviously meant to be amiable. I think – this really is the *point* of Hunter – I think it *was* amiable. Naturally, I can't really remember what it was like to look at Hunter's face for the very first time, nor for the second time, at leisure in Bobby's. My memory of the whole episode is distorted by all the things which have happened since. But even in these first essays in the difficult business of interpreting Hunter's face I think there was the glimmering of a perception in my mind that he was not so much handsome as inoffensive. I have since come to believe that Hunter's strangely youthful and characterless face is a sort of *tabula rasa* on to which his innumerable devotees have fixed their own criterion of beauty and attractiveness, finding there what they have put there themselves. But perhaps this is what we do with all faces? Anyhow, such perceptions, true or false, lay in the distant future.

My instantaneous reaction, which excited an irrational burst of fury against Vanessa, was that he had asked her out to luncheon in order to discuss Miss Beach. It did not occur to me, even when I saw him holding Vanessa's hand, that one could have the sublime experience of kissing Miss Beach and then so much as look at another woman. Miss Beach was not by conventional standards a beauty. But she was The Woman. It was simply inconceivable that Hunter, who had held her in his arms, did not feel as I did in this matter. Vanessa, known to us boys chiefly as a dormitory confidante, was obviously trying to help Hunter through some emotional crisis with Miss Beach.

'Do you know who he is?' asked Mrs Webb.

'The only thing we know is that he comes from Bromsgrove, don't we, Ramsay?'

'Do we?'

With my literal mind I was on the point of blurting out that Vanessa herself had told us that Hunter's parents lived in Malvern. It was her boyfriend who lived in Bromsgrove, not Hunter.

'Yes, thicko, don't you remember? Vanessa's told us several times she has a boyfriend at home. They see each other twice a week.'

'I think he looks very – well, *distinguished,*' said Mrs Webb. But, at that point, the waitress blocked our view of the pair and gave us our bill.

'You pay over at the desk, dear.' She indicated a glass cage at the entrance to the restaurant. Granny instinctively peered in the opposite direction for the cash till and began to assume a look of vexed helplessness. The impression given was that it was bad enough to have to pay for our food, but to find a cash desk, even when it was pointed out to her, was insupportable.

'It sounds *awfully* complicated,' she said.

'Anything with a queue is going to be difficult for my friend,' glossed Mrs Webb.

As it happened, there was no queue at the cash desk at that moment. Although it obviously was not part of her duty to do so, the waitress decided to take Granny's pound note over to the cash desk for her. She returned with a fistful of change and was ecstatically grateful when Granny tipped her threepence.

The afternoon, between all the jokes at table, had already been mapped out for us by Mrs Webb. A short perambulation of the shops would give us time to secrete as many illegal sweetmeats as could be crammed into a blazer pocket. Mrs Webb thought our idea of spending the five pounds all at once absolutely stupid and said that she would take us all on a nice river steamer. Darnley's mum never arranged outings of this kind. After the drawn-out hotel meals, we would simply loll about with nothing to do in her plush hotel lounge. Uncle Roy and Aunt Deirdre (I never inflicted them on Darnley) had outings planned, when they came down, but they were never of a kind which could give pleasure to a twelve-year-old boy. If they had taken me to Worcester, they would have insisted on spending the whole afternoon in the cathedral and we would not have emerged until we had devoted the closest scrutiny to every bit of coloured glass, every tomb and monument, every carved misericord. As for refreshment, in all weathers my uncle and aunt preferred a picnic to 'some awful café'. We always stayed our appetites in some lay-by sitting beside the car, except on those ecstatically happy expeditions to some little-known relation of Sargie's whom Uncle Roy had promised to look up. A tedious drive to Ledbury for tea with Sargie's cousin Peter stays in my mind. Anyway, with Granny and Mrs Webb, there was none of this. We just had to wait while they had one last cigarette in the restaurant and then the afternoon was ours.

The question on all our minds, when we had explained who Vanessa was, was whether to greet her as we left the restaurant. I deeply did not wish to do so, but Mrs Webb, who thought that they looked an extremely pleasant couple, was of the view that it might seem rude not to. Wiser counsels prevailed and Granny said, 'Perhaps she'd rather be left in peace on her afternoon off. She sees quite enough of you at school!'

So we left Bobby's without alerting Vanessa to our presence there. Granny heaved herself to her feet, announcing to Mrs Webb that it might be an idea, if they were going on the river, to powder their noses, but how on earth she could find anywhere to do this she could not conceive. Mrs Webb (pronounced by Granny a *genius* for the discovery) said that she could see a sign bearing the word 'Ladies'. Darnley and I thought it might be a good moment for a pee and went off to our own place.

When we were standing at the urinals, Darnley said, 'That was a smashing meal – why can't Mummy be like your grandmother?'

'How d'you mean?'

'Mummy never laughs at things.'

'Doesn't she?'

'Do you think Vanessa's let that man stick it up her yet?'

'They don't want a baby, do they?'

I threw out this swaggeringly worldly riposte partly because I thought Darnley was going too far, partly to disguise the fact that I knew that he wasn't Vanessa's boyfriend, but Miss Beach's.

'Did you see them holding hands?' asked Darnley.

Having finished at the urinal and shaken himself dry, he lowered the side of his shorts once more. I did the same. We never bothered with opening and rebuttoning flies.

'No,' I lied.

'They were holding hands. They had that dreamy look like Mummy and David.' He held the door of the Gents for me (there was never any nonsense about washing our hands). As he did so, he said, 'I hate love.'

Since Darnley had no idea who Hunter was, he could not really respond to my idea that we shouldn't mention, when we returned to school, that we had seen Vanessa with a man in a restaurant. I begged him to keep quiet about the matter; I felt that it was an area which could only cause me pain and I was equally sure that Darnley had got it all wrong. But he told his dormitory and by the time Mrs Webb's Riley was speeding back to London, all the school knew that we had spotted Vanessa, being kissed by her boyfriend in a really posh restaurant in Worcester. When it was next her turn to supervise our dormitory, the other boys were merciless in their curiosity. Everyone assumed, on Darnley's authority, that this was the boyfriend from Bromsgrove. She had already told us so much about him – how could she *mind* our having seen him?

Only I knew that this was not quite right; and nobody reckoned on the seriousness of the whole business. Hitherto, Vanessa had been our friend, a figure who was something between an elder sister and a fantasy figure of perfect woman-hood. I always think I understand a little about the conventions of medieval courtly love because of having known Vanessa. How could all the knights of a particular court have loved the same lady? Those who reached out so eagerly for Vanessa's embraces would have known the reason, for there was no rivalry in the love of Vanessa. She distributed her favours equally and this was the convention observed. It was altogether different from the exclusive, secretive passion which I nursed for Miss Beach.

Darnley and I, in bringing back the news of Vanessa in the restaurant, were unwittingly destroying a whole part of our lives: one of the few things which made life at Seaforth Grange bearable. For the Vanessa who was questioned about her lunch on Saturday turned out to be a completely different figure from the dorm pal of yore. It had been perfectly permissible, apparently, to quiz her about the boy from Bromsgrove and to make outrageous suggestions about her chances of seducing other members of the staff. When we had accused her of being in love with Greasy Rhysy, she had laughed as much as the rest of us. But the lunch in Worcester was out of bounds – we were not to question her about it.

Quite a few of the boys in the dorm were slow to pick this up.

Torrance, inevitably, called out, 'They saw you, they saw you!' as soon as Vanessa came into our room.

She took no notice, but the general, high-spirited uproar soon died down when it became obvious that she was in no mood for japes. She was pale and very, very angry. She strode through the dormitory until she came to my bed. For the first time, her bigness, hitherto merely a matter of erotic attraction, seemed positively threatening.

'You *stupid* little boy!' she yelled at me. She got me by the shoulders and shook me. 'Why can't you keep your nose out of other people's business? Oh, yes, it's all just a big joke to you, isn't it?'

'But I didn't . . . '

'Oh, yes you did, you and your little friend Darnley. I saw you in Worcester! Well, let me tell you, little Master Ramsay . . . '

This terrible transmogrification, by which Vanessa had become a grown-up and one of the most obstreperous kind, held the rest of the dormitory enthralled, but not silent. Some stood on their beds, no longer quite able to speak but showing from their gleeful, foolish faces that this was the most amusing episode yet in the real-life drama of Vanessa: miles better than film stars and Bromsgrove.

I was trying very hard not to cry. Other members of the dorm, more sensitive to atmosphere than those who were openly gleeful, sensed that we were about to lose Vanessa for ever, lose her as a friend. They began to support her.

'Honestly, Ramsay!'

'You silly little prat, Ramsay!'

'Ramsay and Darnley do it again.'

There are always people in the world who are prepared to seize on some aspect of one's behaviour which they regard as less than satisfactory and make out that it is a part of a repeated, overall pattern.

Vanessa's little tirade, however, never got finished. Just as she was in mid-sentence, expressing the hope that one day I should find out how much it hurt to have everyone gossiping about me – a more than backhanded curse which could be taken any number of ways – everyone fell silent. Over the shoulder of her blue matron's overall I could see the grey hair, the club tie, the too-large, baggy tweed suit of the Binker.

'Oh hell,' said Bowen.

'Indeed,' said the Binker with grim satisfaction.

The atmosphere was so terrible that one would not have been totally surprised had there been an occurrence like the last scene of *Don Giovanni* in which someone was actually, bodily snatched into the regions of eternal punishment; I took a minute or two to realise that the 'someone' singled out for the role of villain was myself. Foolishly, I had even allowed myself a flash of hope that the Binker's presence would somehow vindicate me, that he would tell Vanessa to stop shouting and allow us all to settle into our beds for the night. This was not the Binker's style and I should have known it.

'Bowen.'

'Yes, sir?'

'Please come to my study tomorrow morning. The offences – using a swearword of the most obnoxious character and being unable to control your dormitory.'

'Yes, sir.'

'Woe betide an army, Bowen, when the troops won't obey the officers.'

'Yes, sir.'

'I shall consider whether or not to allow you to continue as dormie captain.'

'Yes, sir.'

'And wee Tammie-tawse will settle the rest.'

There was silence. Then, like some horrible witness in a Stalinist show-trial, Vanessa rose from my bed to denounce me.

'Ramsay is the one to blame, sir. He was the one who started all this noise and bother.'

'Is this true, Ramsay?'

'No, sir.'

'What! How dare you contradict a member of my staff?'

'Sorry, sir.'

'Well, is it true or isn't it?'

I was silent.

The Binker smiled. He had no idea what was going on, but there could be no doubt that a serious offence had been committed, one which needed the most severe castigation.

'You also, Ramsay, will have the goodness to present yourself at my study tomorrow morning. Now the rest of you are to remain silent and we will have no more of this matter. Miss

Faraday, if you care to come down with me, you can explain what these young hooligans have been up to.'

I felt a touch of sympathy for poor Vanessa as she left that dormitory. She hung her head. She knew that, in the passion of the moment, she had gone too far and that she had just lost herself ten friends. Whatever we did to restore things, there would be 'never glad confident morning again'.

Beatings were so frequent an occurrence at Seaforth Grange that the sensations of anger and dread which dominated the next twelve hours were not new to me. Even when you manage to sleep, in such circumstances, you know in your dreams that a beating is going to happen. You try to tell yourself that you have survived dozens of beatings before; that the pain does not last more than a few days; that, in all the course of the school's history, there have been hundreds, thousands of strokes of the Binker's sticks administered to his pupils and that they have all survived. And yet, for all these attempts to allay fear, it still has its power to torture you. And when you get up you feel sick and the school breakfast seems more than usually nauseating: but the grey, half-cooked pieces of bacon fat must be eaten, partly because it is the school rule and partly as a matter of pride. They all know what you are feeling, the other boys, but you must not show fear in front of them. If one of us had broken down and wept, and implored the Binker publicly for mercy, might not our tears have broken the system? Who can tell? The need to disguise our feelings, to keep a stiff upper lip, was so strong that no one would have contemplated breaking the code. And eventually breakfast ends and everyone stands in silence. Then there is grace, said by Timpson. And then, as if you needed reminding, the Binker says, 'Ramsay and Bowen to see me, please.' And he strolls the leisurely distance from the dining hall in House Three to his study in House Two. The familiarity of the whole routine – it was a daily ritual at Seaforth Grange – did nothing to lessen any part of its horror, and I am only sorry that the Binker is dead and cannot read these words as I write them, nearly fifty years on, as a record of all the needless suffering which he inflicted in the course of his career.

That particular morning, Bowen and I followed him at a discreet distance. He would have looked, to an outside visitor from the town, like a charming old gentleman, pottering through his garden. He paused to have a few words with the gardener, who was already at work, watering some petunias in the cool of the morning. By the time we reached the hall of House Two, it was empty.

It was a large hall. Next to the study was the school secretary's office and, opposite that, the Staff Common Room; above, as I have said, were the little boys in their dormitory and the female members of staff in their various bedrooms. So there was plenty of coming and going; and all those fortunate people who were not going to be punished would look at us and know that we were miscreants.

Strangely, passers-by more often regarded us with scorn than with pity. I sometimes think of my times outside the Binker's study door when I am watching the TV news and some criminal is brought to trial, accused of an offence which at that moment society has decreed to be unpardonable, such as political terrorism or child abuse. The man's head is covered with a blanket, so he is almost invisible. The police hustle him along between the Black Maria and the dock. Yet, the hatred engendered by such figures is so virulent that one sometimes feels it oneself, even while watching them on television. The crowds have hovered to watch, to thump the prison van, to scream abuse at the crumpled, defeated little figure who goes to his punishment.

The Binker's study door opened.

'Ah!' he said genially. 'Bowen, please.'

Bowen was probably in the study for no more than seven minutes, but time is measured by the imagination and not by the clock. My wait seemed interminable. I could hear the Binker's voice meandering on. Occasionally, there was a silence. Probably it was not in fact a silence, but Bowen could hardly find the words to reply. Those about to be thrashed lose their vocal power. What I was anxiously listening for was the actual moment of castigation, for I had told myself that if Bowen got two for his inability to control the dormitory, I might get away with only one. After all, I had done nothing. There was no logic in any of this, but I was convinced of its truth. If he got more than two, I felt that there would be no limit to the Binker's wrath. But, even as I stood there with my ears cocked, Miss Beach came down the stairs.

Because she belonged to the real world and had not yet settled at Seaforth Grange, she did not automatically understand what it signified to be standing outside the Binker's study after breakfast. In fact, she did not even assume that I was waiting for the Binker. Any of the doors in the hall – or none of them – might have been the one I was waiting outside. She probably assumed (what could have been likelier?) that I was hovering about in the hope of glimpsing her. As it happened, I wasn't and the very sight of her on that scene tore me in two excruciating directions. As Miss Beach's aspirant lover, I was ashamed to be doing anything so childish as waiting for a thrashing. I wanted above everything to conceal from her my actual reason for waiting in the hall. On the other hand, still having failed, failed completely, to grasp the significance of my glimpse of Vanessa and Hunter in the restaurant, I believed that Miss Beach was the one person in the world who was capable of saving me from my fate. All she would have to do would be to tell the Binker the truth and I would be let off.

This second view of mine begged so many questions that it is just as well that I never put it to the test. It implied, for one thing, that I was about to be caned purely for spreading false rumours about Vanessa and that the falsehood of the rumour could be established beyond question by Miss Beach. It ignored whatever uncontrollable impulses had actually led Vanessa to lose her temper; still more, it ignored the Binker's need to hit children each morning with sticks. It momentarily ignored the fact that by thus establishing my complete innocence (I had, after all, urged Darnley not to spread the rumour) I would be landing my best friend in the soup. It also implied that Miss Beach would not mind her lover being the centre of this schoolboy drama, in fact the talk of the whole school. More than anything, it implied that she knew all about Vanessa's tryst with Hunter. As I was to realise subsequently, she knew nothing about it at all. This is a mistake which I have often made since: assuming, because the whole world knows that X is having a love affair with Y, that this common knowledge is also in the possession of X's family, or Y's other lovers. On the contrary, those most affected by such events are often the last to hear about them; and if they hear about them at all they are often privy to far fewer 'secrets' than might be the common property of gossips at the very outer periphery of things.

'What are you doing here?' asked Miss Beach. 'Do you want anyone in the staff room?'

She was looking wonderful in an open-necked, white blouse. Her intelligent face was screwed up into its expression of comical curiosity, as though any explanation for my presence there could be expected to make her roar with laughter.

I pointed silently to the Binker's door. Boys seldom entered the study for any purpose other than canings or, still worse, one of his little talks. But Miss Beach did not know this. Looking back on the scene I realised that she did not know *anything*. Even my few shreds of knowledge about Hunter and his whereabouts would have been enough to stop her ironical smile. When I pointed to the study door she just pulled a 'solemn' expression, but only of the cheeky kind that anyone might pull when contemplating the pomps of authority.

'You're coming to me today, yes?'

'Yes.' Art was fourth lesson.

'You don't look very pleased about it.'

From behind the study door the noises had begun. Thwack, thwack.

Perhaps Miss Beach did not hear these sounds. Or, if she did, they were to her ears toneless and without significance, as though the Binker had been knocking together a couple of books, or thumping a cushion to make it more comfortable on his chair.

'See you later then,' she said and she stepped airily into the Common Room. Even though the door opened for no more than a second or two, the smell of tobacco which came from the staff room was almost overwhelming.

Then the study door opened and Bowen came out, rather red, but not actually blubbing. In case I had not heard the last stroke (and I hadn't), he held up three fingers and went his way.

'Ramsay!'

The Binker called my name as casually as if I were a patient awaiting treatment from a doctor's surgery.

'Come in, Ramsay, and close the door.'

He had already selected his weapon. It was lying on the desk, but he was in no hurry and he sat down while I stood before him. He began in his usual humdrum way by saying that he set great store, 'verra great store indid, Ramsa' – his voice always became more Scotch when he got excited – 'by the maintenance of discipline in the dormitory.'

Discipline, it seemed, was the beginning of wisdom. Without it, life itself would apparently fall into chaos. Bla, bla, bla.

'But your offence, Ramsay, is very much worse than that. Very, very much worse than a breach of discipline. There is absolutely nothing which more undermines a community such as our own than common tittle-tattle. Gossip, Ramsay. Do you understand what I am saying, boy?'

'Yes, sir.'

'Of course, you cannot be expected to understand that grownups have feelings and that some things, certain very private things, affect grown-up persons most deeply. These things, Ramsay, these private sacred things, you have held cheap. You have chosen to make them the subject of dormitory ribaldry. Am I right, Ramsay?'

One did not in these circumstances ever contradict the Binker.

'Speak up, boy!'

'Yes, sir.'

'Miss Faraday very delicately did not wish to tell me the nature of last night's ballyhoo. It was very understandable that she should have wanted to keep this thing to herself, but I am glad that it has all come out into the open. Although it has yet to be announced officially, I believe that it is only a matter of time before Mr Hunter – the young man with whom you saw her – and she announce their engagement to be married.'

'No, sir, that's not right.'

'Do not interrupt, Ramsay, or you will make things a deal worse for yourself.'

'But you've got it wrong, sir!'

'Mr Hunter's mother told me about it herself only yesterday – before all this disgraceful matter. As it happens, Miss Faraday is engaged, or about to be engaged, to an old boy of the school, to one of my very favourite pupils. His parents are friends of mine of long standing. They live only down the road.'

'But, sir . . .'

The wrongness of all this, as I still thought it, gave me tongue and courage. I was not going to land anyone else in trouble. I simply found myself unable to let the Binker say things which were palpably false.

'I wish you to make a personal apology to Miss Faraday in

105

writing. You are to show me the letter before you present it to her.'

'But, sir . . .'

'You are a stubborn little man, Ramsay, but you will hear me out and then I think wee Tammie-tawse will teach you a lesson in manners which you will not forget. You will make a written apology to Miss Faraday for the embarrassment which you have caused her. From what she has told me, your conduct last night was filthy and disgusting. I am happy to say that from what she has further told me there will be a happy announcement ere long. The story has a happy ending. It is not often an Old Granger marries a member of my staff. In fact, I think it sets a new Seaforth Grange record.'

He smiled. It was evident that this particular Old Granger was rather special to him.

'Now bend over, Ramsay, and hold the arms of the chair.'

'Even so,' said Darnley, later in the day as we changed for cricket. 'Eight! It makes history.'

'I just thought they were never going to stop.'

'And this Hunter bloke was one of the Binker's favourites – a sort of Timpson-style arse-licker – about a hundred and fifty years ago or something?'

'Looks like it.'

The whole episode was puzzling and painful. When we had got to the art room for our fourth period and found that all Art lessons for the next few days were cancelled, I had told Darnley everything. He promised, this time, not to spread it all round the school, and I now believed and trusted him.

'Crikey,' had been his reaction. 'You should have told me when we first saw this Hunter bloke with Vanessa.'

'I just couldn't. I thought he was still, you know . . .' I couldn't say Miss Beach's name.

'Rather hard cheese on Miss Beach,' said Darnley.

'Very.'

'You see what I mean about hating love.'

For a momentary flicker, as he said these words, I thought that I might release myself, there and then, from the thrall of loving Miss Beach. But then my resolution hardened. I became more in love with her than ever, in love with love itself and, for the first time since I had heard about Hunter, actually hopeful that I might win a place in Miss Beach's affections. After all, if Vanessa could give us kisses, why not Miss Beach? What was to stop Miss Beach kissing me? And then, perhaps, eventually, when I was sixteen, say, we could get married. I was very nearly thirteen. It only meant three years to wait. She could do her sculpture. I could be an artist, too.

'Here, hurry up, or we shall be late for cricket,' said Darnley.

I was still sitting there in the changing room, my studded cricket shoes untied, my white shirt half buttoned.

'There's half an hour,' I said.

'Yes, I know, but we might have business to do on the way.'

'Oh, not more trouble.'

I could see a look of hilarious naughtiness in Darnley's face.

'You know that five pounds you wanted to spend in Worcester?'

'It's always in my pocket.'

'Well, bring it.'

The walk to the games field was the only excursion beyond the prison confines which we were allowed. We were not allowed to deviate to the right hand nor to the left. We had merely to cross Albert Road North, go down a little footpath to the next road, cross that and then follow an unmade-up track to the playing fields. At this point the town touched the countryside. There were open fields. A farm, a smallholding. It was thither that Darnley was bound with my five-pound note. The daring of his scheme was outrageous. I could not believe that anyone would get away with it. He assured me that the smallholder, a Mr Heber, would be only too happy to comply without asking questions, since he had a long-standing row with Seaforth Grange – something to do with the Binker having 'taken' one of his fields before the war to make a football pitch.

'What'll we do if someone asks us why we are setting out so early?' I asked.

'I'll say that Lollipop Lew has sent us on ahead to tidy pads in the pavilion.'

'They'll think we're queering.'

'They won't!'

'Or smoking.'

'Oh, shut up.'

He began to explain more of his scheme. It was impossible, as

107

he outlined its finer points, not to be doubled up with laughter. Our destination was soon reached.

'There we are,' he said. And he pointed to the sign outside Mr Heber's bungalow.

The reality of the situation – that Miss Beach would not come back that term – was slow to sink in. From day to day, I lived in hope that she would come back – her tears dried, her lover dismissed and forgotten – to be mine and mine alone. The practical implications of a return – she would have had to share a bathroom with Vanessa – did not really occur to me.

There had been something between us, though. It was not all fantasy. About a week before the end of term, I got a postcard from Paris – it was a picture by Paul Klee. No allusion was made to the matter of Hunter or Vanessa. But she would not have sent the card had she not wished to absolve me of any guilt in the whole episode. 'It was fun getting to know you! Let's hope our paths cross one day. Paths have that way with them sometimes, like fingers.' Did she know how much I loved her, or how much in the following weeks I grieved for her? At the time, I was so pleased to have been singled out for a postcard that its sad implications took some time to absorb. She did not sign the card with love. Instead, there were the familiar initials – 'B.R.B., or should I say "Please"!!'

I came across the card not long ago in the bottom of a drawer. It was strange to be revisited by this keepsake of a person who was once so painfully dear to me and by her own youthful sense of life being something all in the future, hers and mine. Gradually, perspectives change. One tries to disguise the knowledge of how much of life has gone by with the insistence that the important thing is to live in the present. Either way, one is indulging onself and viewing one's own life as an entity, something with a storied shape which might be of interest to a chronicler. Another sense within us hints that to explain anything so multifarious and self-contradictory as a human life is an exercise in illusion.

Hunter was intelligent enough to know this, which, perhaps, was why his own practice and advocacy of the biographer's art could be conducted with such panache. One accomplishes nothing so stylishly as the thing in which one has no belief: gigolos probably make better lovers than those weak with desire; the best politicians are those who are most like actors; the most influential churchmen are those who seem furthest from the ideals of the Gospel. Hunter wanted to make lives make sense. Perhaps his own painstaking efforts to explain Petworth Lampitt were all part of a need to hide the lack of sense, thread or meaning in his own life. His charming smiles were those of a juggler who knew that one day the reckoning would come, that his concentration would falter and the various balls which he kept floating in the air as if by magic would eventually bounce into chaos at his feet. What I never discerned in Hunter in the early days was the element of tragic heroism, the element which guaranteed that when he fell, it should be with as much sang-froid as he brought to the seduction of girls and the advancement of his own career.

On the simple level of his success with women, many have found it impossible not to be in awe of Hunter. In my own case, there has been an additional factor of coincidence that at times has threatened to form itself into some theory about Life, or Fate, or Women in general. At some periods of existence, indeed, it has seemed as though every woman I knew and a good proportion of those I had ever loved had been in love with Hunter. The desire to explain this coincidental phenomenon has at some periods been obsessive with me. Did it mean that, in spite of all appearances to the contrary, there are in any individual life only a handful, perhaps a hundred women who are really available? It looks at first as though the field is infinite. Then you start to exclude all those who, at the time of your seeking, are tied up with someone else and you realise that the floating population is actually small. It therefore becomes inevitable, if you take an interest in this population, that you will come across the comparatively few other men fishing in the same waters. For various temperamental reasons, Hunter was incapable of monogamy. So, for a long period, was I.

This is the common-sense view. It is the one to which at present I incline. But for long periods in my life I have veered towards two much more exotic explanations of the fact that my path would keep crossing Hunter's, his mine. Both of these theories, for the time that they possessed my mind, have seemed not merely attractive, but compelling explanations for the coincidental extent to which Hunter and I have almost tripped over one another in pursuit of the same women.

The first explanation is that Hunter is a Don Giovanni who has tasted every fruit and broken every heart in the world. According to this theory, there is nothing surprising in the fact that most of the women I have known at all well seem, at some stage or another, to have been in love with Hunter. The paltry dozen or so women who have been important to him (I am not just speaking of mistresses or wives, but of friends, too) are just the tip of the iceberg. Supposing, for the sake of experiment, I had known well a completely different selection of twelve or twenty women. The same high proportion of them would turn out to have undergone the Hunter experience.

I have usually entertained this theory at periods when I was angry with and hostile to Hunter. Nevertheless, it always filled me with a certain wistful admiration, not least for the sheer levels of physical concentration which such wide-ranging exploits must have demanded. Michelangelo is not to everyone's taste. Nor is Balzac. No one, however, can fail to admire the simple energy, imaginative and physical, required to complete the decoration of the Sistine Chapel or the penning of *La Comédie Humaine*.

It is not as if Hunter has been casual or slapdash. It has been no crude matter of notching up a score. In the handful of examples where I have known anything about it, Hunter has devoted not only time but apparent emotional effort to his conquests. To each of his ladies, he has appeared as the first truly sympathetic man they have ever met. Hours have been spent blowing their noses on Hunter's clean handkerchiefs because he *understood*. Hunter was always a great believer in all the little appurtenances of heartbreak: flowers, letters, boxes of chocolates. (The chocolates themselves are worthy of a monograph, as, over the decades, I was to discover. How perfectly he always chose the brand. How intimidating the Bendicks girls were; and how reassuring those waitresses and stenographers who opened his gifts of Cadbury's Milk Tray.) A huge proportion of Hunter's existence, when added altogether, must have been spent in the dispatch of these tokens – of what? his affection? This is to say nothing of the time he spent with the girls themselves. A whole lifetime of telephone calls and assignations; of exciting, secret little meals which both parties felt slightly too nervous to eat; of visits to florists and chemists and hotels; a lifetime of afternoons, zipping and unzipping.

If, as I supposed when I subscribed to the Don Giovanni theory, I only knew the tip of the iceberg, then Hunter's life must rank as something more remarkable than anything he described with his own pen.

Adding up the hours, however, which I myself have spent in florists, etc., I have dallied with a totally different theory, more astrological in tone and which could be called the theory of the Mystic Link. Even allowing for the fact that Hunter was extremely good at organising his time (witness his tireless committee work) it was only possible to fit a finite number of women into a single week, the more so since he liked all his dealings with women to have an extravagant emotional tinge. The love affairs, moreover, represented only the secret, or semi-secret, part of his existence; assuming that he sometimes needed sleep, there must have been some hours each week during which he wrote his enormous books and, more mysteriously, carved out the position of public importance which, from middle age onwards, he began to assume. Certain things followed from this. If Hunter was not a magician, then I knew – anyway at certain phases of life – all about every one of his *amours*. Or so it seemed. I knew, too, that there was an uncanny level of coincidence. I was treading in his footsteps, or he in mine. Miss Beach was the first name in a catalogue. My epiphany, that cricket afternoon, when I saw Hunter's hands running up and down the naked back of the woman I loved, was to be repeated more than once in the years which lay ahead. Very occasionally, the matter would be reversed, and I would discover that Hunter had taken up with someone in my own past. When the Mystic Link theory was in favour, I imagined that Hunter and I had destinies which were conjoined, and that he, like some Fury or some angelic presence, was bound to recur, haunting some of the most painful as well as the most joyous moments of existence.

Into this last category, the joyous, must surely fall the final day of that summer term. The local garage at Timplingham had decreed that the Trojan was no longer equipped for a journey across country. I was therefore spared the supreme embarrassment of my uncle and aunt driving up to the school gates in this vehicle in order to attend the last day of term – always rather an event in the Seaforth Grange calendar. In the morning, as the families of boys arrived, there were various 'displays' arranged for their diversion: some gymnastics on the lawn, a tennis tournament of excruciating incompetence, presided over by Lollipop Lew, a line-up of the more presentable members of the Scout Troop. An exhibition of art and handicrafts, usually a feature of the day, had this year been cancelled.

The morning was rounded off with a service in the little chapel, a sermon by the Binker himself, and a loud rendering of 'Lord Dismiss Us with Thy Blessing'.

So many friends, parents and relations attended this occasion that a marquee was erected on the lawn outside the chapel door, more or less filling the garden of House Two. All boys had to be in their places in chapel half an hour before the service began. The parents then filled up the back rows of the chapel and the overspill sat on chairs in the marquee. It was a claustrophobic arrangement, since the only mode of exit and entrance was the hole at the far end of the tent.

Darnley and I entered the chapel together. His mother had already arrived with her husband. They were standing quite near Hunter and Vanessa, who had something hard and triumphant in their expressions as, rather too dolled up for such an occasion (Vanessa's hair hidden inside a silly hat), they waited with the other grown-ups, but somehow looking like actors pretending to be at Ascot or Henley.

'Do you think they'll really remember?' I asked Darnley. 'What if they just go off with my money?'

'It's worth the gamble. Oh, it's worth it.'

'It's not your money, Darnley!'

He beckoned for me not to talk so freely. Timpson was within earshot. For all his daring, Darnley was as nervous as a bridegroom before his bride arrived at the church. The half-hour that we sat in that chapel was intensely exciting. Some of the time, we tried to ignore one another, gazed about us, tied and untied knots in our handkerchiefs. Then we would have a spell of noughts and crosses. And three minutes were amusingly absorbed when Darnley managed to lean forward with his ballpoint pen (a present that morning from his mother's husband) and write a word on the back of Garforth-Thoms's neck. It would not seem funny if I wrote it down now, on paper. You had to see it on that pink neck to get the full flavour of the joke. In fact (my nerves were doubtless overstrained) I thought that it was so funny that I might actually faint. However much I bit my fingers and stuffed a grey, ink-spattered handkerchief into my mouth, the word kept looking back at me. Blowforth himself simply imagined that Darnley was tickling the nape of his neck and had no idea of the legend that he was now advertising.

Darnley, the anarchic author of all this merriment – for others in our pew were now squirming with glee – looked facially impassive, his vast mouth drooping in a slightly melancholy way. If you had been told that he had just written a word, you might have guessed, from his expression, that it had been *'angst'* or *'penseroso'*. It was this immovably sad expression, combined, when he raised an eyebrow, with an unmistakable haughtiness, which so enraged his masters and superiors, who were now beginning to show parents to their seats.

Mrs Binker had squeezed herself into position behind the harmonium and, before long, the familiar routine of the end-of-term service was under way – the 121st Psalm, the squeaky suggestion by Timpson, from the lectern, that to everything there is a time and a season, the singing of 'Praise, my Soul, the King of Heaven'. Then the Binker was standing there in his MA gown, ready to harangue the troops.

'I want you,' he said, 'to think about John the Baptist.'

It was a curious thing to want. I have sometimes wondered how many of those women in hats or men in their Sunday best, none of whom seemed exactly John the Baptist's type, complied with this desire of the Binker's.

'You see,' he added mysteriously, 'John the Baptist knew that he was born into this world for a purpose.'

How Scotch his voice was then. Borrrn into this worrrruld for a purrrrpose.

'But so were we all! Ah, yes. Each and every one of us was borrrrn into this worrrruld for a purrrrpose. And it is to help us find that purrrrpose that places such as Seaforth Grange exist.'

This last bit of the sentence was less audible than it might have been because of what sounded like a tractor engine revving up at the entrance to the marquee.

'Sometimes,' said the Binker, trying to ignore the noise, but peering with terrified curiosity down the aisle at what was going on in the drive, 'sometimes that purrrrpose is hid from our eyes for a wee while. But we must train ourselves to seek it.'

There was a clanking noise. A cart was being up-ended. There were voices.

Lollipop Lew's ineffectual tones were saying, 'I'm sure it can't be meant to go there!'

'That's what he said.' Mr Heber's voice.

He?

Darnley and I froze. Surely he was not going to betray us? Not after we had paid him five pounds – a king's ransom.

'You got three guineas' worth there and I had to borrow the cart to bring it round.'

'The way,' said the Binker, 'will sometimes be dark and we shall not see the path before us.'

He all too evidently saw the path leading up to the marquee, and the alarm and anger on his face made the temptation to turn round irresistible. Everyone was now far more interested in the conversation happening outside than in the mysterious purrrr-pose for which they had been born. Lollipop Lew, no more capable of asserting himself with Mr Heber than with the third form, had appealed to Greasy Rhysy for moral support. We now heard Greasy's cross, authoritative tones.

'You'll just have to load it up on your cart again, won't you?'

Mr Heber's contemptuous laugh was music to the soul.

'What with? A pitchfork? Load the fucking stuff yourself if you want to. I've got work to do!'

'A purpose,' repeated the Binker, 'a purpose.'

'But,' protested Greasy Rhysy, 'if you leave it all there on the path, people aren't going to be able to get out of the marquee. Besides,' he said, 'there is a service going on and you are disturbing it.'

'Three guineas' worth!' repeated Mr Heber, evidently with some satisfaction. 'He do things in style, your governor.'

'Who did you say ordered this . . . this . . . ?'

'Ordure, ordure,' muttered Darnley.

'Like I say,' replied Mr Heber airily. (The Binker was still talking, but none of us was listening.) 'Mr Fucking Larmer, that's who!'

And then we heard the cart and the tractor being reversed out into the road.

The Binker could see quite clearly what we only glimpsed in snatches, over our shoulders: something the size of a small haystack, heaped at the entrance to the marquee, forbidding all exit. While his wife struck up 'Lord Dismiss Us' on the harmonium, the chapel filled with overpowering farmyard odours. The rest – the opening up of a side flap of the marquee, the mothers in high heels teetering through the flower beds, the inevitable dozen or so people who trod in what Mr Heber had so liberally bestowed – all this, in a way, was an anticlimax. Darnley, perhaps, had no finer hour. It was with an ill grace, I thought, that the Binker was mouthing the words of the hymn.

> Pardon all, their faults confessing,
> Time that's lost may all retrieve . . .

No one ever did confess to the sin, if it was one, of having paid Mr Heber to unload a cart in that time and place. It remained one of the great Seaforth Grange mysteries. We noticed, by the next term, that the Binker had given up claiming that he would solve this mystery if it was the last thing he did. As to that other matter – the retrieving of Time lost – we were far too young to have thought about it, either its undesirability or its impossibility.

Three

It was four years before I actually met Raphael Hunter. By then I was a very different person. My short pink legs, the limbs of an androgynous putto on a Tiepolo ceiling, had been changed within a space of eighteen months to long, monstrous, knobbly things, covered with hair: the legs of a caveman. In a world where such alchemy could take place, anything could happen. The transformations effected by Nature on my body were minor when compared with the eruptive changes in my character. Adolescence had taken me by storm.

'I'm afraid that Julian has developed into rather an intellectual snob,' my housemaster had furiously averred on one end-of-term report. At that stage, I held this nice man, with his fondness for the novels of Galsworthy and Nevil Shute, in low regard.

But it was all much more mixed up than that. Very probably I was an intellectual snob, whatever that is. But that was not the trouble. I was angry with everyone and yet longed to be liked; furiously against the system and yet deeply anxious to be in with it. (The same week which had seen me squatting in a little bathtub, ostentatiously reading *The Communist Manifesto* half an hour after I was meant to have been in bed, had also seen me privately smarting, with genuine bewilderment, because I had not been made into a house prefect.)

Treadmill, the senior English master, was one of the few people who could control me. I don't mean, stop me misbehaving. A number of sergeant-major types could do that. I mean, have some conception of 'the real me'. Harness this being, fill it with enthusiasm, even – though it seems a curious word to use – love it. We were still, perhaps ludicrously, Master and Pupil. There were few stricter disciplinarians in a classroom than Treadmill. (He hardly ever needed to *punish* a boy; the thought of misbehaving in his classes was too terrifying.) I, for my part, like most boys in the school, perfected my Treadmill imitations.

Even nowadays, I sometimes find myself drifting into them. It may be that I am wandering into the bathroom in the light of dawn to run my tub and that a dressing gown draped around my shoulders involuntarily recalls that MA gown, drooping from the shoulders and sometimes suspended as low as the elbows. And, whether I am alone or in company, I will give voice to that curious noise, impossible accurately to transliterate, which we always made to signal the fact that we were 'doing a Treadmill'.

'Eyair.'

The sound was almost inaudible in the real Treadmill, but all Treadmill imitators said it loudly. They all knew how to hold one hand limp-wristedly in the air (though there was never the slightest suggestion that Treadmill loved his own sex) while the other drooped at his side. Many boys, I think, were disappointed, when they finally reached the privileged position of being in Treadmill's set, to find that his 'Oxford' voice was less strangulated, his vowels altogether less mannered and nasal, than their hundreds of imitators. A real imitation would have been quite difficult. Doing a Treadmill, however, was child's play and I prided myself that I could do whole Treadmill sentences, paragraphs; that I could think Treadmill's thoughts, never dreaming until I was hooked that this was the idea and that the success of teachers who are 'characters' depends precisely on luring their pupils into imitation, if not open mockery. The child thinks it is absorbing the teacher, whereas it is the other way around.

Perhaps one of the reasons he appealed so greatly was that there was in itself something adolescent about the paradoxical combination of immiscibles in his overdrawn persona. He was an old boy of the school and a passionate devotee of the public-school system. Yet, as he loved to proclaim, he was a Man of the Left, of the extreme Left, who had fought in Spain and known everyone. This knowing of everyone was something which all his cruder imitators seized upon, trying to make Treadmill into a simple snob. As the nephew of Uncle Roy, I knew that snobbery was not simple and that the essence of Treadmill's name-dropping was that it was inextricably linked, for him, with the romance of literature itself. He was, as I now realise, a failed writer himself, which is why almost anyone who had ever written a book was surrounded for him by a romantic glow, while at the same time being scorned: for no one had a keener eye for the defects of a writer than Treadmill.

In my Treadmill imitations, I always tried to capture these essences of his nature. It is boastful to describe them as upmarket Treadmills, a thousand times truer than the frankly silly Treadmills you might hear down any corridor or dormitory landing. Mine came to me like the visitations of the spirit from some other world.

'Eyair. Will you open *Paradise Lost* at Book Eight?'

One sees again the shredded-wheat moustache, the horn-rimmed glasses, the voluminous Oxford bags, the oatmeal jacket, the black teaching gown, ragged and worn, which had once (said Treadmill) belonged to Louis MacNeice.

'John Milton, as you may know, was a Cambridge man. Eyair. Woe betide any pupil of mine who thinks of going *there*. Nyair. I never actually met Milton, but of course I have had my days, if I may mention such a thing in petty-bourgeois company such as your own, as a Republican soldier. "Today the deliberate increase in the chances of death." '

He would then look up to see if anyone recognised the quotation. In reality, he would have been astonished if anyone had said, ' "Spain", by W. H. Auden'. It would have prevented him from sniffing contemptuously at our ignorance and continuing with his discourse.

'Poor Wystan. How let down we all felt when he went – eyair, to the United States. Though, as he once said to me in a letter, he had never pretended to be brave . . .'

The essence of the parody was that any sentence, however unpromising its beginnings, united an excitement in literature itself with the strange adventure of Treadmill's own personal myth. How very effective this was as a method of teaching, this ceaseless dropping of names and quotations, is shown by the fact that forty years later I can still remember vast amounts of English poetry, not which Treadmill set us to learn by heart but which he merely quoted *en passant*. It was not long, after I started to be taught by him, before I started to search the libraries and identify the source of all his allusions.

'But Wystan, much as we all love and admire him, is a long way from *Paradise Lost*:

"Think onely what concernes thee and thy being,

118

> Dream not of other worlds, what Creatures there
> Live in what state, condition or degree . . .''

Ah! I vividly remember Virginia Woolf, of all people, quoting those lines to me. We were at Garsington. I was an undergraduate at the time; my only meeting with the great lady. I felt suitably rebuked. Frieda Lawrence was there. Now what a beautiful woman *she* was.'

These idiosyncratic glosses on the text of *Paradise Lost* took us through line after line, fixing the poem in my memory more surely than any amount of formal explanation. Treadmill's English classes were lectures. He had the required text open on a lectern. If it was poetry, he read it aloud, interlaced with his own highly personal commentary. If it was prose, he spoke more concisely. There was no question of class discussion, nor of audience participation of any kind. The performance was to be heard in silence. If there was the slightest sign of disturbance (a boy dropping a pen) his face assumed expressions of pained outrage. It could have gone either way. A man who claimed so much for himself could, you would have thought, have been treated mercilessly by boys. But it was not so. No one misbehaved in Treadmill's classes, just as no one ever gave him a nickname; with a surname like that, he did not need one.

His comments on our essays, of which we had to write a large number, were almost invariably withering; but they were flatteringly detailed. If you handed in a piece of work to Treadmill you could be sure of getting it back the very next day, scarlet with his semi-legible annotations and corrections. I can still recapture the sinking feeling in my stomach when I had handed in what I thought was a brilliant essay on *Antony and Cleopatra*. It was handed back next morning with the single question –'Yeair, you have, I take it, *read* the play?' His innumerable marginal notes showed me how utterly ignorant and superficial I was. This was at a time of life when I really resented other grown-ups not minding their own business and judging me by their own infuriating standards. So, the RSM at Corps thought that I did not know how to blanco spats. So what? So what if my housemaster did think it was ill-mannered to slam a door in Matron's face? These observations on my character were intolerable, intrusive, irrelevant. But Treadmill was allowed to make really devastating assaults on my ignorance

119

and poor style. He spoke with authority. With naïve arrogance, I thought that he was allowable because he shared my values without realising that I shared his, had learnt from him avidly, hungrily.

And I learned as much outside the classroom as in. Treadmill was a conscientious schoolmaster. He took games, even bothering to change for the purpose. (The billowing garments draped from his narrow hips to beneath his knees could not with accuracy have been described as shorts, but they were, Treadmill claimed, the legacy of a rugger Blue who, while up at the House, had thrown Harold Acton into Mercury.) He was a house tutor. Rather surprisingly (I tried to overlook this embarrassing detail) he was a Christian, who found the liturgical arrangements in the school chapel lamentably 'low'. None of this actually interested me. I completely lacked, and lack, Treadmill's public-school belief in being a good all-rounder.

It was as the producer of the school plays that Treadmill first came my way and was the greatest inspiration to me. One of the reasons Treadmill chose to produce fairly obscure Renaissance drama was unquestionably because he liked it. He took the sensible view that we should all have plenty of opportunity in later life to see mainstream repertoire on stage in London or Stratford; less chance to see the work of Marston, Massinger, Beaumont and Fletcher. Another, less worthy motive but, I suspect, no less strong was a desire to *épater* the Headmaster who, like most potentates, including the King himself, reserved to himself the right to censor and forbid the production of plays within his domains. When Treadmill asked him if it would be permissible to produce *A New Way to Pay Old Debts* or *A Shoemaker's Holiday*, the Headmaster was never sure whether he was alone in the universe in being unacquainted with these plays and always let the thing through without question, but not without a sense, I suspect, of being put down.

Long before I got into Treadmill's English set, I was Celia in his *Volpone* and enjoyed overacting as Lady Allworth in *A New Way to Pay Old Debts*. My first male role was Jasper in *The Knight of the Burning Pestle*, a melodramatic part ideally suited to a teenage actor. Anne, my first wife, when I used to bore her with Treadmill stories, considered it 'pretentious' to have extended the schoolboy repertoire beyond the usual Shakespeares and Shaws. The stylish thing about it, though, was that there was never the slightest sense that we were posing or doing anything particularly recondite. Once in a blue moon in the army I would (all too rarely) come across some 'kindred spirit' with whom one could discuss books or plays, perhaps a man who had opted to go to university before he did his National Service. He would almost certainly be on his way to work as a clerk or a trainee Intelligence Officer and I would never have more than a few weeks of his companionship. But I often discovered, in such encounters then and later in life, that I knew the works of dramatists who were only names to some of these university men. Then I would feel grateful to Treadmill for giving me something superior to a university education while I trod the boards at New Big School.

The other out-of-school activity which Treadmill organised was a literary club which met once a fortnight in his house after supper – sometimes to read a paper among themselves, but more usually to hear a talk by some visiting speaker. These visits inevitably summoned up those dreams of other worlds, so readily understood at Garsington, so frowned upon by Milton's archangel. However boring the speaker (and some were real crashers) they always brought with them the breath of another atmosphere, usually one which I felt more able to inhale than that of school. This was the sense which I had had to an infinitely slight degree in Debbie Maddock's company long before, that there existed some bohemian society to which all along I had spiritually belonged, some intellectual fellowship from which I had accidentally through birth and upbringing been excluded but to which, once the tyranny of childhood was overpassed, I would return. Our speakers included Shakespearean directors; poets in knitted ties who called Treadmill by his Christian name (Val); lady novelists who had laboured for a quarter of a century to keep the Woolfs from the door; tweedy dons with stammers who laughed conspiratorially when Treadmill mentioned Dr Leavis (he was the enemy now, Treadmill held him in abomination) – all these figures suggested to me a world in which the things I cared about most were valued, a world in which the things I scorned (but which were so vigorously upheld and insisted upon at school) were scorned also.

Treadmill's society was called the Lampitt Club, after one of our more distinguished old boys, James Petworth Lampitt. Lampitt himself had come down to the society's inauguration a few years before he died and Treadmill possessed several Lampitt letters.

It goes without saying that Uncle Roy chose the school because of its Lampitt connections. (A great-uncle of Sargie's and Jimbo's had been headmaster in Victorian times and there were a number of lesser Lampitts connected with the place.) There was even a Lampitt cup for Fives, a fact to which, apparently, Petworth Lampitt had made squeakingly facetious reference on his visit – a facetiousness which was quite misplaced, since all his audience, Treadmill included, were keen Fives players. The distinction between hearties and aesthetes, which was certainly one made naturally in my own mind, was deprecated by Treadmill as inimical to 'everything a school like this stands for'. That was one of my reasons for making it.

Treadmill's attitude to Lampitt was by no means purely adulatory. He had a distaste for 'purple prose' and there was, in his view, a distinction between true satire and mincing malice which Lampitt quite often failed to observe. For two pins, Treadmill could have dismissed Petworth Lampitt as meretricious, Georgian and lightweight. There were two things, however, which redeemed Lampitt in Treadmill's eyes. The first, and much the most important, was that he was an old boy of the school. The second, which spurred Treadmill into action on a number of other occasions, was Dr Leavis's known distaste for Lampitt's works. The gibe about Petworth Lampitt being the worst writer of the century after Humbert Wolfe was not a piece of private knowledge entrusted to Debbie Maddock alone. It had apparently found its way into print and Treadmill had read it. When Lampitt died, his reputation was at its lowest ebb and many of the highbrow papers had apparently written about him in the most slighting possible terms. Treadmill the old boy had simply felt that the honour of the school was threatened and he had devoted a Third Programme talk (one of those discourses given in the intervals of radio concerts) to a restitution of Petworth Lampitt's tarnished name. As he liked to boast, it was the only occasion when a BBC producer had presumed to alter a Treadmill script. Treadmill had written a vituperative paragraph beginning, 'A Dr Leavis . . .' The BBC, doubtless infiltrated with Leavisites, had insisted on the deletion of the insultingly indefinite article. (Treadmill did quite a lot of wireless talks in those days and even had his own poetry programme, something which was to have its bizarre influence on my own later destiny.)

It was a curious chance, however, that in all the meetings of the Lampitt Club which I had so far attended there had been no mention of James Petworth Lampitt. We had had talks on a wide variety of subjects but nothing on the man whose name we immortalised each fortnight by crowding into Treadmill's dining room.

In the spring term, speakers were thin on the ground. We were an inconvenient distance from London. Weather that year was poor. Everyone seemed to have 'flu. I succumbed to the worst bout of it which I had ever had, a week of near delirium, aching joints and writhing about in my own sweat. The doctor insisted on a week's convalescence when the fever left me.

I was sitting in the large dayroom of the san, staring across the frosty, fog-laden gardens to the Victorian crescent beyond the cedars. Gables and turrets were silver-grey against a haze of winter light. Matron came in and interrupted my mindless reverie by announcing a visitor. Since it was mid-morning and everyone was in school, I knew that it could not be another boy, and I wondered with a darting mixture of homesickness and embarrassment whether my aunt had been fetched from Norfolk by exaggerated accounts of the seriousness of my condition. Instead, still wearing his teaching gown, Treadmill drifted into the room.

' "God keep thee – yeair – worshipful Master Roister Doister," ' he said.

' "Come death," ' I said responding with another quotation from the same play, ' "when thou wilt, I am weary of my life." '

'But I heard you were better? I won't come too close. My own susceptibility to influenza is no laughing matter. Indeed, Geoffrey Keynes, one of the nicest men as well as one of the best doctors I ever knew . . . but that's another story. I was on my way home, I thought I'd drop in.'

It is true that Treadmill lived more or less next door to the sanatorium. I didn't at that stage know how appropriate this was, being as yet unaware that, next to the pursuit of literature, the cult of ill health ranked high among Treadmill's list of favourite occupations. It merely struck me as kind that he had bothered to look in, particularly since he at once put my mind at rest about the play which was then in rehearsal.

'You're not to worry about the play. Michael Redgrave – and in my own drawing room indeed – once told me that a bout of illness in rehearsals sharpened the pace at a later stage. We've got six weeks more and it's all going well. As it happens, you're not the only one with 'flu; far worse news is that Margery Mumblecrust's voice sounds perilously as if it is on the point of breaking.'

'I'd hate to let everyone down, sir.'

'It'll be all right and, more important, it'll be fun.'

This turned out to be true. Treadmill's *Ralph Roister Doister*, heavily cut, was one of the high points of my school dramatic career. That and *Gorboduc*.

We spoke desultorily about rehearsal arrangements.

Then he said, 'You'll be fit, I take it, for the Lampitt Society on Sunday evening?'

'I should think so.'

'I've asked down the man who's hoping to edit Lampitt's letters.'

'I hadn't heard that anyone was.'

'My God, the arrogance of the boy! Because he is Hon. Treasurer of the Lampitt Society, he speaks as if he were Petworth Lampitt's literary executor. Editors are apparently obliged to consult you before approaching the shrine!'

'Sir!' This really wasn't fair. I had already told Treadmill of my family reasons for being interested in Lampitt.

'Of course, I was forgetting, your people knew Lampitt's family.'

'We're neighbours of his brother.'

Treadmill did not, on that san visit, think to mention the name of the Lampitt expert who would be addressing the society.

But, before he left, he said, 'By the way, it might be an idea if at least one member of the society apart from your tired old master had actually read a line of the great man's works before Sunday.'

There was no bluffing or fooling with Treadmill. He knew by instinct what one had or had not read. Lampitt had hitherto not appealed to me. Considering the fact that I had been brought up next door to the man's brother, you might have supposed that I was well acquainted with his work. Probably, Uncle Roy's insistence on their virtue had put me off reading Petworth

Lampitt's books. Perhaps, too, I had been put off reading them by that instinctive embarrassment which we all feel when reading the literary productions of those at all close to us. I had not known Jimbo. But what if his prose somehow revealed a self, a world, which in turn cast Sargie and, by implication, Uncle Roy in some funny light? No, that wasn't it. I think it was that I had heard about all the Lampitts so often that I really wanted to think about something else when I had a book in my hand.

Lurking about somewhere in my head, there was, further, the priggish suspicion that Dr Leavis might well have been right. Perhaps Petworth Lampitt was not merely a *bad* writer, but one whom it was somehow discreditable to enioy. In the intellectually snobbish terms which I was cumbrously working out for myself, liking Lampitt might well have been as bad as, by Miss Beach's standards, liking Rowland Hilder's landscapes; or, perhaps a better analogy, the school of Alma-Tadema.

Treadmill, with a limp gesture, fished a small, green volume out of his pocket and threw it down on my lap.

'It's what used to be called fine writing,' he said, in tones which put heavy inverted commas round the words but which allowed you to take them any way you liked. 'And none the worse for that.'

And, without much of a farewell, he was gone.

I opened the book and I can still remember the tingling excitement brought by its opening paragraph. I dare not quote it here. The austerer tastes of my own maturity, to say nothing of those of the reader, would find much in those perfectly made sentences which was arch, much which was sentimental; for, though regarded by his contemporaries and seniors as an iconoclast, James Petworth Lampitt was more than a little in love with the objects of his derision. I had never before felt the smallest interest in the subject of the book, the life of the Prince Consort. The story was well enough told. But what gripped me was the tone of authorial voice. Now, it slightly embarrasses me, that perfect style and manner. But, that afternoon, it all became so much a part of myself that I cannot consider it dispassionately. The ambition to be an artist, awakened in me by Miss Beach, had still not left me. Treadmill had made me yearn to be an actor. Neither of these desires was abandoned, but to them was added the longing, as deep as love, to write like James

Petworth Lampitt. As happens when one is reading a book which is truly absorbing, the world became insubstantial for the next few hours. A domestic brought lunch. I was asked by Matron to rest on my bed for an hour. I returned, dressing-gown-clad, to sit in the convalescent room. Outside the french windows the mists thickened and by five o'clock night had fallen. But I read on, gulping the paragraphs thirstily and feeling them – again, like love – changing me into a different person by the minute, by the second.

I wanted not merely to write like Lampitt but to *be* Lampitt. Hitherto, I had only thought of him as Sargie's brother. He had come to me filtered not merely through the collapsed, sham-bolic figure of Sargie but through the distorting lens of Uncle Roy's Lampitt adoration: a devotion which was unthinkingly applied to Jimbo because he was a Lampitt and could just as extravagantly be bestowed on the Honourable Vernon or Lady Starling. Because Jimbo happened to be a writer, my uncle praised his style, just as he would have praised the expertise of the Lampitts in any field: the delicacy with which a Lampitt surgeon wielded his knife, the astuteness with which a Lampitt broker bought bonds or sold stock at the judicious moment, the eloquence with which a Lampitt Parliamentarian might argue the inadvisability of some piece of legislation. My incapacity to see my uncle as a person, my adolescent inability to be generous, did not allow me to suppose that Uncle Roy might himself have once fallen under Petworth Lampitt's spell, as I did that afternoon in the san and for exactly the same reasons. It did not occur to me that Uncle Roy probably read Lampitt's *Prince Albert* long before he ever went to live in Timplingham or met old Mrs Lampitt or Sargie. It did not occur to me that I was holding in my hands, if not the key, at least the origin of the abiding passion of my uncle's life. Lampitt seemed then purely my own possession. I was ignorant of the fact that a mere thirty years before, he had been an extremely popular writer with a column in the *Saturday Post*, whose vogue swelled the sales of his travelogues and biographies. Rather it seemed, as the light faded, and I read on and on, as if I were the first person in the world to discover this wonderful writer and as if there were only two people in the world with the right attitude to things, what one can best describe as sentimental irony, myself and Lampitt.

I had never before heard the word 'camp' applied to all those things Lampitt's prose reeked of. Pub evenings with William Bloom lay aeons in the future, conversations in which he would put down his glass of beer –'The only straight thing about me' – and with a nod towards some fantastical creature in drainpipes, tiptoeing towards the Gents, interrupt his discourse about politics or the opera with a toneless, 'That young lady has a camp in both feet.'

On the contrary. I thought then of Lampitt as, on National Service (when I discovered him), I thought of Edward Gibbon – urbane, funny, above all in control of his own manner and material, a writer who not only had mastered completely the apparently simple (actually supremely difficult) matter of making sentences mean what the writer wants them to mean; but had further devised or evolved a style which implied a view of the world without the need to state what that view was.

I think if I were to dwell long with Lampitt's prose today, I would find his manner excruciating, the literary equivalent of an unwanted, well-manicured hand on one's elbow, or the fluttering of the author's eyelashes. The tones which then sounded to me like sharp, Voltairean irony would now be in danger of seeming shrill, fluty. The final paragraph of the famous biography, when the corpse of Albert is laid to rest in Frogmore – 'alone, at last – or, for a little while' – struck me as the most eloquent piece of rhetoric which I had ever read. I read the sentences again and again. They moved me in precisely the way Lampitt had wanted to move the more simple-minded of his *Saturday Post* readers; and like those simple souls, I totally missed the arch implications behind his description of that solitary corpse, allowed at last to sleep on its own without female molestation.

By the time of the doctor's rounds next morning, I had reread *Prince Albert* more than once. I was drunk with it, bleary-eyed. I responded to questions about my health with what I felt to be appropriately Lampittian sang-froid, prompting the doctor to say, in slightly aggrieved tones, 'I'm only asking you because I want to see you get better.'

'Ah, but better at what?' I heard myself, rather surprisingly, saying.

'There's not much wrong with you if you can lie there and make jokes,' said Matron crossly, reading into my remark an innuendo which had not been intended.

127

'Doctor, can I take a short walk today?'

'I shouldn't think it would kill you.'

'I need to get to the Reading Room.'

This was a distance of some quarter of a mile.

'Are you asking us to lay on a bath chair?' asked the doctor. He had a murmuring, rather plaintive voice.

So, while the rest of the school was at lessons, I was able to spend the next couple of days convalescing, pottering, swathed thickly in overcoat and muffler, to the Reading Room and returning to the sanatorium for rests and meals.

An almost complete set of James Petworth Lampitt's *oeuvre* was to be found on the shelf. All but his *Lagoon Loungings*. The first two volumes I borrowed were a collection of his essays and his life of Swinburne. The biography of the poet was even better than that of the Prince Consort. I completely entered into Lampitt's schizophrenic ability to admire Swinburne's languorous and over-coloured phrases while making the poet himself a figure of the purest farce. The passages describing his domestic life with Watts-Dunton in Putney remain, by any standards, hilarious. Similar flights of comedy occurred in many of the essays which, if anything then could have done so, deepened my love of Lampitt. Each essay was to my eye so perfectly made. Nearly every one was funny. Yet, even when the laughter was most unfair, there lurked behind the prose a sense that literature itself was something to be taken supremely seriously. Perhaps it was the *only* thing to be taken seriously. I am thinking of his classic essay on Baudelaire; or another, 'The Christ of Gérard de Nerval' (one of the best apologies for the aesthetic point of view extant), or the curiously perceptive essay on the early Ezra Pound.

I do not think that Treadmill had intended to awaken Lampitt mania on anything like this scale. He probably just wanted to guarantee, when the speaker came to address the club in a few days' time, that at least one member of the audience should have known who Lampitt was and, roughly, the kind of thing he wrote.

I found as the evening approached that I was looking forward to it. I felt something akin to jealousy, too, as if, having fallen in love with a woman, I had been compelled to spend an evening with twenty other men, poring over her photograph and hearing why they did or did not find her beautiful. At the same time, I was excited at the prospect of meeting the speaker, whom Treadmill had not named, but described as a friend of Petworth Lampitt's. Although I knew the writer's brother, I wanted to cast the *friend* in an altogether more exotic light than poor old Sargie. I would not have been surprised if the friend had appeared wearing a cloak or a wideawake hat like Lord Tennyson's. I think I pictured him bearded, certainly, with thick, snowy white hair and possibly a large, silken cravat tied at the throat in an extravagant bow.

By Sunday evening, I had come to believe in this figure so completely that, as we all squeezed into Treadmill's dining room, I was looking round for him eagerly. I had decided that he would be slightly rosy in complexion and wearing check trousers of a shepherd's plaid.

At the far end of the room, by the mantelpiece, there stood a figure in a pale grey suit and blue shirt. So youthful were his smooth cheeks, pallid face and mousy hair that it did not occur to me that he was our speaker, still less a friend of Petworth Lampitt. I thought, indeed, that it might be some senior boy from the school on whom for some reason I had never set eyes, or some nephew or godson of Treadmill's, staying for the weekend. My man, the friend of Petworth, was doubtless waiting in the wings. Ever a theatrical old boy (probably with memories of the Café Royal, Beerbohm Tree, Granville Barker), he would make an *entrance*.

I only recognised our pale visitor at the very moment that Treadmill said in his quietly reasonable voice (the histrionics sometimes shown in school or on stage were always switched off for visitors) that it was a great pleasure to welcome Mr Raphael Hunter, who had come to talk to us about 'Petworth Lampitt the Man'.

Though these evenings were partially designed by Treadmill to wean us from childish ways and to edge us towards the manners of highbrow undergraduates, we were still *au fond* a lot of schoolboys. We recognised the convention that in Treadmill's house (his wife would appear at some stage of the evening with a tray of tea or cocoa) one could not actually *rag* the visitor as one would a newly arrived teacher.

But, if a man wanted to hold our attention, it would have to be good. For one of those impenetrable reasons which no boy could ever *explain* to a grown-up, the title 'Petworth Lampitt the Man' struck Garforth-Thoms as one of the best jokes he had ever heard. His rather heavy features, by now very different from when we were together at Seaforth Grange, assumed a look of intense seriousness as he tried to ward off the giggles, but I could see that it was going to be a losing battle. His cheeks, on which some half-hearted whiskers and vigorously suppurating acne fought for space, had changed from their usual spatter of pale scarlet to an even, purplish red. His lips slobbered and shook. Then he let out a loud roar of laughter, causing several other boys to do the same.

Treadmill, quietly furious, said, 'Garforth-Thoms, *please.'*

'Sorry, sir.'

But the apology made him laugh all the more. He ran from the room as if he was going to be sick and we heard him quietening down in the hall. Later on, he crept back into the room, dabbing the corner of his eyes with a handkerchief.

After this, the atmosphere was a bit sticky, but the worst of the embarrassment was over. Hunter looked pained by the outburst. This expression was what separated him off from the rest of us even though he looked young enough to be a boy. No boy, however touchy, would have wanted an explanation for Garforth-Thoms's guffaws. Some things just are funny. Once one person laughed, another person laughed. It was all as simple as that. Hunter, being a grown-up, showed by his puzzled brow that he thought that there must be some explanation for the laughter, some secret meaning in his title which, had he known about it, would have made him avoid using the phrase, 'Petworth Lampitt the Man'.

He spoke to us from notes. Considering the fact that I was by now obsessed with Petworth Lampitt, I was surprised to discover that Hunter's talk was extremely boring. My mind kept wandering off and I could not listen as he said phrases like 'in the context of the Edwardian literary situation and early twentieth-century prose generally' or 'Of course, we are now in the post-Modernist situation – Eliot has written *The Waste Land,* Joyce has written *Ulysses.'* Liberal in his use of the historic present, Hunter attempted to fit Petworth Lampitt into his own simplified version of literary history. As he did so, I was astonished to realise that this 'friend' of Lampitt's, who had chosen to journey all the way from London to talk about him in Treadmill's dining room, did not think much of the great man's work.

'I believe,' he said, 'that Petworth's work has already dated, that it won't last and that it *shouldn't* last.'

At this point, his hand came down rather firmly on Tread-mill's dining table and his essentially weak features assumed a ruthless coldness. We seemed to have moved out of the world of literary debate and into a universe of power in which Hunter would brook no opposition in this matter of Lampitt being no good.

I mischievously wanted to intervene and say that as a matter of fact Lampitt's intimates called him not Petworth but Jimbo. But with his hand now firmly pressed against the table – the gesture implied that there were spiritual forces present who might at any moment lift the table in the air had not Hunter been so unhesitatingly in control – he turned to his subject: Petworth Lampitt the Man.

'One may as well be honest, Petworth in his last years was a sad man, even a pathetic one. The days of his great success as a writer had really been before the First World War . . . flower of English youth . . . great society hostesses . . . The Souls . . . Bloomsbury . . . the increasing *politicisation* of the literary scene in England . . .' Here the hand pressing the table almost recalled the gestures of a Nuremberg Rally.

In none of any of this was *my* Lampitt to be discerned, that distinctive voice and manner with which I was so entranced. Instead, we were given a catalogue of names which at that time meant absolutely nothing to me: house parties and dinners, Lady Elcho, Lady Horner, Lady Ottoline, oh Lady!

'There were other sides to Petworth's nature, darker sides, but this' – Hunter gave a searching stare in the direction of Garforth-Thoms – 'is neither the time nor the place to expose them. We do him no honour to overpraise him.'

This may well have been true, but so far not a word had been spoken which was not calculated to diminish Lampitt in our eyes. Had this work of destruction been done in Lampitt's manner, one could almost have seen the point of it; Hunter's dismissal of his subject, though, entirely lacked satire or sprightliness. It was puddingy and at the same time self-righteous, vaguely high-minded.

'He belonged to that rightly obsolete species, the man of letters. He wrote his books, he made his travels, he formed his friendships. In my opinion, as a much younger friend, speaking from the perspective of the younger generation, we will come in time to see that Petworth Lampitt's chief glory was that he had such friends. That is, he can best be seen as a way of viewing a whole literary and social world, rather than as a man who was himself intrinsically interesting. At the present time, I am collecting up the letters of Petworth Lampitt. I think there should be an edition. Petworth was a prolific letter-writer. His correspondents included all the great literary names of the age – George Bernard Shaw, D. H. Lawrence, T. E. Lawrence . . .'

For those of us who might not believe him, Hunter read out a list of famous people to whom Petworth Lampitt had written letters. It was the sort of list he might have read to a publisher to interest him in the idea of printing a selection of Lampitt's correspondence. Its effect on an audience was curiously deadening. As became evident, this was his peroration. He paused.

'Edith Sitwell,' he said, 'and, of course, Osbert.'

He was free with 'of course', was Hunter.

Treadmill stared at him. I thought he was going to say, 'Is that all?' but instead he murmured, 'Eyair, thank you very much indeed.'

There was no particular convention about what happened at the end of talks. Sometimes we spontaneously clapped but applause was not invariable. No one clapped Hunter. We were all bored.

Treadmill sensed this. After a longish silence he said, 'Perhaps I could pose a question – about whether you have found anything out about Petworth's schooldays.'

'A few letters survive, but not many.'

'What house was he in?' asked one boy.

Hunter blushed. He couldn't remember.

'That's what you should be able to tell me,' he said, which Treadmill then did. I could see from the way in which Treadmill was compressing his lips and pushing his moustache upwards to a diagonal, almost a vertical position beneath his nose, that he thought very little of Hunter either as a scholar or as an orator.

I did not want my tenuous connections with the Lampitt family to be a topic of general conversation but I involuntarily found myself remembering the day of Jimbo's funeral; remembering, too, those few days before it – my uncle saying the requiem for Jimbo's soul and afterwards describing the macabre manner of his death, falling from a balcony into the area beneath his flat.

'Was he alone when he died?' I blurted out.

'Who, Petworth?'

Hunter's prickly attitude to my question revealed that he sensed my hostility. Hunter could not possibly have known that for the past four years he had been an object of jealous fascination and loathing in my eyes – ever since I had seen him holding Miss Beach in his arms. The upshot of his betrayal was unknown to me. That anyone could so ill-use Miss Beach remained incredible to me. My love for her, hitherto the strongest emotional experience in my history, was something which time had done very little to heal. I was easily able to be transported back to that period, the few weeks after Petworth Lampitt's death. That was perhaps why I asked my question, which I did heedlessly; as I did so, I discovered that I was curious to know the answer. I had rather forgotten it until that moment but in Hunter's presence it all returned – that morning when my uncle spoke about it; my aunt deciding that the whole thing was much too hush-hush to be mentionable in the village; Debbie Maddock being coarse enough to have read about it in the newspapers.

'Petworth lived alone in his last days. He had a flat.'

'Hinde Street?' I said automatically. I wasn't showing off. I could recite the London addresses of the Lampitts almost before I knew nursery rhymes – or so it now felt. The Honourable Vernon – Great College Street; his parents – Cavendish Avenue in St John's Wood; Lady Starling – my uncle's voice would always sink reverently at the mention of it and his vowels would become strangely elongated – in Cadogan Square.

'Yes, it was Hinde Street,' said Hunter.

'It wasn't a suicide, was it?'

There was laughter when I asked this. Not that suicide was considered amusing. It was my persistence and my suddenly seeming to know more than the speaker which made people laugh.

When the laughter died down Hunter said something which surprised me very much and which had never been mentioned in the version recited from time to time by Uncle Roy.

'As it happens,' he said, 'I was with Petworth on the afternoon he died. I had called round in the middle of the afternoon as I sometimes did. Just to see that he was all right, you understand. He wandered into the kitchen to make some tea. It was a small kitchen – little more than a box with a sink in it and a little oven. But it had a french window which opened on to the fire escape. On fine days he would open the window and stand on top of the fire escape which caught the afternoon sun. On the day he died – it was a spring day . . .'

I suppose Hunter must have told this story a thousand times – to the police, to coroners and, subsequently, at dinner tables and in 'talks' such as this. Like almost all frequently repeated narratives it was too fluent to be plausible. I didn't know whether he was consciously lying or whether the truth had simply been worn away by the repetition. But I knew that I could not believe Hunter. I felt instinctively that he who had betrayed Miss Beach could deceive and lie to us also.

I am not saying that I suspected what the police call 'foul play', but instinct made me think that Hunter was up to no good, not to be trusted. I disliked extremely the way he managed at one and the same time to claim credit for having known the famous writer, and to be condescending in his attitude to 'poor Petworth' and to the writings themselves. One felt (or was meant to feel) that not only was Hunter at the hub of things, but he was also sufficiently discerning not to get carried away; he could see that the 'importance' (a very Hunter word, I was to discover) of Petworth Lampitt was not in his writings but in the world which he encapsulated. In other words, what was important for Hunter was not the imagination but the will, not the outpourings, however unsatisfactory one might find them, but the social climbing, the gossip, the crusts and shell, as they seemed to me, of a life. Hunter thereby blasphemed against art – this was the sort of pompous way I reacted in my fury – as well as letting down an old chum by revealing his secrets to a lot of schoolkids. There was enough of my uncle in me to be shocked that a *stranger* should presume to talk about Petworth Lampitt in these terms.

'. . . and without meaning to be unkind, Petworth was not always steady on his pins after lunch. I heard him calling out, "Oh, *look* at that sun!", and then there was a clattering noise – no cry – just a noise. I thought perhaps that he had inadvertently knocked a kettle off the stove, or a hot pan. "Are you all right?" I called out. There was silence. I went into the kitchen. The window was open, but Petworth was not there. I went to the window and looked down. Petworth was lying at the bottom of the area by the dustbins. He was quite still. I climbed down the fire escape as quickly as I could. I turned over his body – but he had already died.'

For a boy audience this was almost as exciting as a murder story. A 'literary' evening which culminates in the speaker discovering a corpse could be sure of a success. When Treadmill finally wound up the show and thanked Hunter a second time, everyone clapped enthusiastically. Few, if any of us, had ever seen corpses. To have seen a corpse was on the same level of sophistication as carnal knowledge. Therefore we clapped. Over the next week, the tedium of Hunter's actual talk and the embarrassment of Garforth-Thoms's guffaw at the beginning were forgotten. Hunter was alluded to as 'a great bloke' and his talk was said to be 'stunning'; in subsequent weeks when Treadmill consulted us about the kind of speaker we should like to see invited to the Lampitt, the general consensus was that 'we' – that is they – should like more speakers like Mr Hunter.

When the meeting was breaking up, Hunter, all smiles and geniality, came up and asked me, 'Was there some reason for your being so interested in Petworth?'

'Not really.'

'Only, you seem to know quite a bit about him.'

'Ramsay here has relations who live near Petworth Lampitt's nephew – is that it?' prompted Treadmill.

'No, sir. Brother.'

Hunter's face became at once more ingratiating and yet more steely.

'Not Sargent Lampitt?'

'There are no other brothers living,' I said, as though any fool knew that.

While Hunter was getting my name straight, I had to blink to avoid the steadiness of his gaze.

'I'm trying to persuade Sargent Lampitt to let me go through the material in his possession,' said Hunter slowly, cautiously. 'I feel sure that there is a lot of it' – once again his voice assumed its nasal didacticism – 'which could be important, but I would have to look at it before we knew.'

The importance of the Lampitt papers apparently was something upon which only Hunter could adjudicate.

'I suppose the papers might be rather private,' I said, not really intending to get so quickly to the heart of the matter. Hunter smiled to imply that I was being a tease.

'Anyway,' he said, 'should I come down later this summer, we shall probably see one another.'

'Perhaps,' I said. The others were drifting into the hall, where Mrs Treadmill had put a tray of tea and biscuits. Hunter would soon be drawn into the mêlée. But I could not part from him without picking at an old wound. In spite of my newly born interest in Petworth Lampitt, I was not really very interested in the fate of the Lampitt family papers. Hunter was primarily, for me, the man who had jilted Miss Beach.

Throughout the previous four years, whenever I thought about it, I had assumed that Hunter had honoured his intention of marrying Vanessa Faraday. With what I considered to be tremendous subtlety, I asked:

'When you and your wife come to Timplingham, where will you stay?'

Hunter smiled and gently touched my arm.

'You mustn't *think* of putting me up! Very kind, but there's a pub, surely?'

'Yes. Not much of one.'

'I'll be quite happy there.'

I had not meant to ask Hunter to stay. Uncle Roy and Aunt Deirdre were thrown into enough of a panic when Granny came for a few nights, or when my aunt's old schoolfriend Bunty made one of her rare visits. The idea of Hunter coming to stay would have been unthinkable had he not so anarchically thought it.

'You see, I think I know your wife.'

Here was real subtlety, real worldly insouciance.

'There must be some mistake,' Hunter smiled. 'I'm not married.'

One could not very well contradict a man when he had just spoken this sentence, but I was so surprised that my reply was unstoppable.

'But you were engaged to Vanessa – Vanessa Faraday. You see, I was at Seaforth Grange before I came here and I remember the whole thing. Even the Binker – Mr Larmer – told me that you and Vanessa . . . I mean, I remember seeing you . . .'

Hunter was less ruffled than I was by these appalling

gaucheries, which died on my lips. He smiled and showed two rows of teeth, surprisingly small and discoloured.

'No, no, a bachelor, I'm afraid. Do you still keep up with dear Robbie Larmer?'

This question was incomprehensible to me. Who on earth was dear Robbie Larmer? Before I had composed myself sufficiently to realise that the allusion was to the Binker, Mrs Treadmill was upon us. She obviously found Hunter completely delightful.

'You are being neglected,' she said playfully, allowing herself to touch his elbow, as Hunter had earlier touched mine. She held up a green cup with tea in it and a ginger nut in the saucer.

'Or there *is* something a bit stronger,' murmured Treadmill, with the hesitant tone of a man who did not really know what this something was. Hunter followed Treadmill's gaze to the dusty half decanter – sherry? whisky? a urine sample? – which stood on the sideboard.

'No thanks awfully, I'm fine,' said Hunter. And everyone else seemed to think the same.

We mingled and chatted. It was only as we boys were leaving in a gaggle that Hunter called out to me, 'See you in Norfolk, perhaps!'

'Right ho, sir!'

The exchange made us all laugh. We had no sooner come out on to the foggy pavement than we all began our Treadmill imitations. As it happened, Hunter and I were to overlap that summer, but not in quite the way I imagined and not until I myself had undergone a series of emotional experiences which did something to heal the pains still suffered whenever I thought of Miss Beach.

In the days when it still seemed certain, in my private hopes, that I would be a writer (by which I meant a novelist) I used to assume that I would make good use of Barbara, or rather of the Barbara experience. As life wore on and it began to be clear that, whatever else the Fates had in store, it was not to fashion me into a weaver of yarns, the difficulties of describing sexual intimacy became clearer to me. By the time I had abandoned any hope of depicting Barbara in a novel, I had seen through all the technical problems. It is only failed writers, I have come to think, who are even aware of such difficulties. Real writers somehow confront their material as only they can – head on.

They aren't perfectionists. There are consequently moments of ludicrous failure. Their greatness carries it off. That is what I have come to feel about D. H. Lawrence, for example, whose titanic stature as a writer is not really diminished by the fact that some of the steamier scenes in *Lady Chatterley's Lover* come close to unintentional farce.

This was the least of my difficulties when coming to write that unfinished, unpublishable fragment of a novel about Barbara. While I struggled with it on iron bedsteads or in transit camps during my wasted two years of National Service, I was sex-starved, disgruntled, bored. Contemplating those carefree weeks in Brittany from the barracks in Northampton, or in the awful tedium of Cyprus, I was in no position to do Barbara justice. I quite ignored the fact that writing down the experience was in itself an act of betrayal, undressing Barbara in public and revealing (were Madame de Normandin ever to read the book) what had been a secret. But even apart from this, I was still years away from recognising that any description of oneself indulging in sexual acts is almost bound to seem ridiculous to a third party.

Then again, even if I were to overcome the technical difficulty of recounting those scenes with Barbara, the actual description of what went on which, when I was writing about it, seemed all important, I would still have come up against another difficulty, namely the sheer improbability of it all. The fact that it actually took place – that Barbara and I made love on a number of occasions – was enough to justify writing it up as a piece of narrative. All that seemed necessary was to change some details. Barbara's name, for instance, which *sounded* so French when called through the food hatch by her mother or by Madame de Normandin, did not look French on the page.

The last time I looked at the manuscript, before consigning the exercise books to the flames, I noticed that she had several names – Marie-Celeste, Brigitte, Françoise – I am surprised that I did not call her Albertine and have done with it. I also found, on my final, embarrassed perusal of the thing, that I had changed the *venues* of our strange and fateful interviews. The beach hut has been transposed to somewhere more flattering to my sense of adventure. Bedrooms, bathrooms and even the dining table at Les Mouettes were scribbled in a list of possible settings.

I was under the ancient delusion that the mere fact of something having happened was enough to authenticate any narrative about it. I thought that truth was bound to shine through. God knows what I thought fiction was. But I was sublimely unaware that all plausible narratives, whether historical or fictitious, require art to make them plausible. The Barbara episodes in the beach hut had in reality happened quite arbitrarily, with almost no reference to anything which was going on in the household around us. I *think* that we liked one another, but we really had very little conversation. My contacts with her may have done wonders for my sentimental education, but they did nothing for my French.

'*Que penses-tu, si tranquille?*' she once whispered in my ear. And, on another occasion, '*Une parole, seulement une parole, je t'implore!*'

How could one possibly convey all this with anything approaching verisimilitude, while giving a true picture of the imaginative effect of that month in Brittany – the whole household at Les Mouettes, the other people, the landscape, the weather? My life with Barbara happened offstage to all this, like something in the life of dreams.

Then again, would I ever be honest enough to reconstruct my inconceivably clodhopping and ill-informed attitude to sex itself? It may have been the case that our hut sessions gave some sort of pleasure to Barbara, but it was not a matter to which I devoted any thought at the time. I supposed myself in love with her, though I suffered for her absolutely none of the pangs which had wrung my heart at the very thought of Miss Beach. I should never have predicted that, as the experience receded, Barbara would have left very little impression on my memory, certainly far less than Madame de Normandin herself. As a very young man it just would not have occurred to me that I would retain a clearer recollection of quite commonplace conversations with an old lady than of my first essays in sexual gymnastics. Madame de Normandin remained a far more vivid figure even as a physical entity. Her neat, white hair in its delicate net and her intelligent, hedgehoggy face (an upper-class Mrs Tiggywinkle) remained in my mind perpetually, long after Barbara's features had become a forgotten blur. The fact that partners in bed, or in beach huts, can vanish completely from one's consciousness, so that one forgets not merely salacious details but even ordinary ones like names and faces, is one of the stranger tricks played by time. Barbara's chief importance in my emotional history was, in any case, a negative one. Until that French holiday I had been intensely involved in the world of school. Life as a boarder at a public school is lived at a level of emotional engagement seldom experienced afterwards. You are cooped up with sixty other boys for two-thirds of the year, sharing dormitories, bathrooms, studies and meals. It is, in any case, a period of life when feelings run high. Anger, resentment, admiration, jealousy, infatuation, disgust, all coursed through one's system as a matter of daily experience. No wonder the Renaissance drama was something which made such an appeal. After Barbara, the whole flavour of it was muted. I recognised school for what it was, just another transit camp in the English Gulag, and I could not wait to leave.

Four

Aunt Deirdre was always the one who made any practical arrangements. It was she who discovered Madame de Normandin's advertisement in *The Lady*. I forget the details, but young, paying guests were offered board, lodging and French conversation in a large family house on the northern coast of Brittany. Shortly before the end of term, one of Aunt Deirdre's letters informed me that I was signed up for half the summer holiday *chez* Normandin.

By then, I had become insufferable. It was small wonder that my uncle and aunt wanted me out of the way. Fair enough, they both got on my nerves. But, rather than avoid them or lie low, I was occasionally drawn, quite irresistibly, to take the war into the enemy camp and to offer unprovoked attacks which were specifically designed to be hurtful. At this period, my uncle avoided me whenever possible. Sometimes, however, he took a meal with us, rather than with Sargie up at the Place. Or I might catch him creeping out of the lavatory, or sidling from the front door to his study. Then I could take the opportunity to give him my opinions about the Christian religion in general and his own apparent interpretations of it in particular. It did not really matter what I said on these occasions so long as I inflicted pain; and, on my uncle's soft, pampered features, pain always registered fast and easily.

It is only on those whom I have loved that I have ever knowingly inflicted pain. The guilt of it remains for ever, my words selected with such malice and the startled expression on the victim's face as the effect went home. These are the faces which return during nights of insomnia, forever hurt in my memories, and inconsolably so. It is said that time is a healer, but it is not necessarily so. Memory has the power to encapsulate moments of pain, to freeze them, so that though the person who suffered has drifted on into other worlds and other states of feeling or non-feeling, the remembered moments of pain can stay. Sometimes in spells of profound depression, it is these moments alone which surface in the memory. Everything else is a bland, misty background against which these figures stand out sharp and clear – women in tears, or my uncle, drawing back the corner of his lips and sticking a pipe in his mouth, trying to conceal the extent to which I was hurting him.

Sometimes, I would start from the position that only a dunderhead could believe in the miracles of the New Testament; and, another thing, couldn't Uncle Roy *see* that a loving God and an omnipotent God (that is, a God capable of stopping pain by magic as Jesus was supposed to have done) was a contradiction in terms? If he could heal one blind man, why not all blind men? Then, having knocked down my uncle as an intellectual inadequate for believing in this stuff, I saw nothing inconsequential or unfair in attacking him for hypocrisy. Anyone, I would tell him, could see that he did not believe a thing; he only wanted to be a priest for reasons of snobbery, or because he liked wearing funny clothes, or because he wanted to live in a grand old Georgian rectory. If they were really Christians, they would live in rags and wander round begging like Jains or St Francis of Assisi.

The restraint of my uncle and aunt during these taunts was remarkable. They never once reminded me that it really had been Granny's responsibility to look after me after my parents died. (Of course that possibility was unthinkable, with her feet, her 'heads', her general need to protect herself from any demands from any quarter.) But my uncle and aunt did not *have* to have me. They were not my legal guardians. By now I had simply grown into a disgruntled, loudmouthed lodger in their house, who paid no rent. It never even occurred to me at that period that the trust fund, set up from insurance payments after my parents were killed, nowhere near covered my living expenses. My pocket money, school fees, clothes and food were all provided out of their own resources. In grown-up years, the question of how life is to be paid for has been dominant. Not in my teens. Perhaps they should have made me more aware of this side of things. As it was, I saw my uncle and aunt (more especially my uncle) simply as irritants who set out to annoy me. I quickly nosed out the surely understandable fact that they had only devised the French sojourn because they wanted me out of the house. At one point in that dreadful row, the night before I left, I actually threatened not to go. The panic on their faces was terrible.

'Your aunt's paid now,' said Uncle Roy in exasperation. 'You've *got* to go now.'

'I expect it'll be quite jolly, old thing,' said my aunt. Her line, when I was being obstreperous, was to continue for as long as possible the pretence that the conversation was not departing from her own standards of cold-fish amiability. Then one would go too far and she (the equivalent of yanking the dog on its leash) would suddenly snap, 'Oh *do* shut up,' or some such call to heel.

'You just want to get rid of me!' I stormed.

'I wish I was going to France,' said my uncle.

'Oh yes? If you wanted to go to France, you'd have gone. You haven't been to France since the war. You never go anywhere. You just sit here in your stupid clothes, playing at your stupid, made-up religion and we're all stuck with it, just because you want to mince up and down between here and the Place licking Sargie's . . .'

'Oh, *do* shut up, old thing,' said my aunt.

My speech shocked them both. It shocked me. It seemed to be releasing spurts of hatred I did not really feel. The wounded look came into Uncle Roy's face and I wondered whether he would burst into tears, or whether the worm was about to turn, and he would strike me.

'I think the sooner you go away the better,' he said quietly and got up to tiptoe out of the kitchen.

'Just what I said. You're all trying to get rid of me!' I yelled.

Uncle Roy had reached the kitchen door, but before he could grasp the handle it turned and the door opened. Felicity was standing there. I don't know if she had been listening at the door or whether her quiet reading in another room had been disturbed by my shouts, or whether she had been coming into the kitchen anyway. Tea was on the table.

But she was there and she had become rather terrible.

'Get rid of you? I wouldn't blame them if they did, you selfish little creep!'

'Now, dear,' said Aunt Deirdre.

But Felicity's wrath was up. I had insulted her father just once too often and she was about to give me the rejoinder which *he* should have dished out months earlier. Her freckled face was drained of all colour and one vein stood out, very blue, on her left temple. A big girl, she was really frightening in her anger. I thought she was going to biff me.

'Ma and Pa have had just about enough of you! You moon about in this house – you never offer to help – you never even make your own bloody bed.'

'That's enough,' said my aunt.

Uncle Roy looked as though it was not half enough for him. His eyes gleamed.

'I don't know what you are meant to learn at that school where Ma educates you at great expense but it certainly has not been manners. And don't think it's charm, either, ducky! You've turned into the most charmless little prat . . .'

There was quite a lot in this vein. You get the general idea. It was conveyed to me that I was an ill-mannered oaf who was not worthy of the kindness which her parents had lavished upon me over the years. If I wanted to earn the right – Christ help us – to complain about being given a month's free holiday in France, a privilege for which most boys would have given their eyeteeth, then I should have to do something more constructive than loll about the house moodily, occasionally squeezing my black-heads in the hall mirror.

Every word bit home. Before the end of her speech I had got up to go, shoving past her and slamming the kitchen door. While I belted upstairs, she had opened the door and was yelling something about the truth being too hard for me to take and her parents being saints who had been given more than anyone could be expected to stand.

I went to my room in a burning rage. I would have liked to kill someone – preferably Felicity and then myself. I think I wept a lot. I saw that everything she said was true, but I couldn't do anything about it. I hated myself much more than she could ever hate me and yet I hated her too for seeing so clearly and for being so just in her rebukes. I felt no penitence, only self-horror.

I must have lain on my bed for hours. At one point, my aunt called up in her 'joke posh' voice, sometimes used for smoothing troubles, 'Sup-per'. The imminence of this repast had been heralded by unappetising smells wafting up the back kitchen for about an hour previous. Rather later, her voice at my bedroom door said, 'I've made a cottage pie, old thing.'

Pride would not allow me to answer. I was too overwrought to eat. My mouth filled with brine, my stomach churned, my eyes scalded but, although I yearned to apologise to her, I couldn't.

About an hour later, she opened my bedroom door without knocking and breezed in, as though none of the previous scenes had taken place.

'Have you packed, old thing?'

'More or less.'

'Got enough socks? Got your bathing togs?'

'Did they say they'd provide towels?'

My voice shook as I asked. It was like going through the clothes list for Seaforth Grange, only now, instead of Vanessa and the Binker and Darnley, it was a lot of foreigners that I was about to meet. I had never been abroad.

'It said "big family" in the advert,' said my aunt. 'I should think they can run to a towel. What is the French for towel? Something funny, isn't it, something you wouldn't expect?'

I tried to say *serviette* but, greatly to both our embarrassment, I found myself choking on the words. My aunt was sitting beside me with an arm loosely on my shoulder – for her a supremely demonstrative gesture.

'Come on, old thing.'

Emotions weren't really Aunt Deirdre's thing. She was better when I'd blown my nose and she was breezily making the cocoa in the kitchen. It was surprisingly late. Uncle Roy had gone to bed. Felicity I did not see until I got back from France.

Such is the distorting power of narrative that the reader might well have derived the impression that Felicity had remained totally silent all her life, only to give voice to a vitriolic denunciation of her cousin in the paragraphs which I have just written. This would be to give a quite false impression. At Cambridge, Felicity had blossomed in just the way her parents might have wished. She had made a handful of 'nice' friends, played hockey in the Girton Second XI and got a very creditable degree. She had even been taken to a May ball by a man called Graham, reputed to be writing a thesis on Schopenhauer. Now, she too was writing a thesis, the working title of which was 'Some Epistemological Problems Since Moore'.

When she heard the title, my aunt said, 'Oh, thank goodness I'm not clever like the rest of you!'

Having no particular plans for the long vacation, Felicity had come home. She was going to earn a bit of extra cash by helping

Sargie sort what he called, with ironic portent, 'The Lampitt Papers': that is, the boxes of Jimbo's old junk which had been languishing at Timplingham Place ever since the writer's flat in London had been cleared.

Felicity was Sargie's goddaughter. She felt protective towards him, rather as she did towards her own father.

'We don't want people snooping through all the stuff until we've made sure there's nothing there,' she had said firmly, happily falling in with the suggestion that she should help Sargie with the task. Hunter's proposal to bring out an edition of Petworth Lampitt's letters had been received guardedly by Sargie. He was glad to think of someone keeping Jimbo's memory green, but he was wary of 'publishing scoundrels'. Hunter's arrival for a preliminary snoop, due to occur some time when I was abroad, was something for which the greatest possible caution was needed.

'There aren't going to be any of Jimbo's letters *here*,' Sargie had said. 'I mean, a chap doesn't keep his *own* letters.'

'No, but Mr Hunter will be able to find out who were Jimbo's main correspondents. Then he can bother *their* families.'

A particular look of self-satisfaction had come into Felicity's face when she said these words. She thought she was being so clever.

The words which had passed between me and my cousin were too harsh for us to face each other over breakfast on the morning of my departure. She stayed in bed until I was out of the house. My uncle, back from early church, was wary over his porridge. Well he might have been. Although I had resolved, after my aunt's good-night kiss, to be 'good' for my last few hours in England, I found the sight of Uncle Roy prissily blowing into his silver porringer irresistibly provoking.

My aunt was journeying with me from Norwich to London, seeing me on to the boat train at Victoria and then lunching with her friend Bunty. There was even talk of her buying a new mac at the Army and Navy.

All these plans went smoothly and, although the quarrel of the previous evening made me uncomfortable, it also made me realise the wisdom of the French arrangement. Uncle Roy and I were for the time being immiscibles. This was a fact which simply had to be accepted. My relief in parting from him had been an almost physical thing. There is a strange illusion which I can remember Darnley practising on me at Seaforth Grange. Somebody presses very hard on your head with the flat of their palm for two or three minutes. When the pressure is released, you have the curious sensation that you are floating upwards, levitating like a Hindu mystic. This was what it felt like saying goodbye to Uncle Roy. To a lesser degree it was what it felt like when I kissed Aunt Deirdre at Victoria Station, though in this case, it was not so much that she irritated me, more that, in parting from her, I experienced a delicious sense of complete freedom. I was going to France on my own! It wasn't a school term. I did not have to do what anyone else told me to do. Within the fairly generous limits set by the law, I could do anything. As I looked out of the train window and saw the platform at Victoria recede, watched London turn to suburb and suburb to Kent I had my first realisation that the previous sixteen years had been lived in a sort of cage. There were people out here who were at large, free, unanswerable to anyone. There was life beyond the cage door. So far, everything which I had ever done had been governed and modified by the arbitrary rules of a game made up by other people. At Seaforth Grange, it was the Binker's game, in which almost everything you could think of doing was illegal – putting your hands in your pockets, reading, talking, going for a walk on your own, omitting to defecate after breakfast, going into a shop. My present school was more free and easy but even so the atmosphere was restrictive. Ordinary freedoms enjoyed by most boys of my age – being able to smoke a cigarette or take a girl to the cinema – were regarded there as highly flagitious.

At school, there were actually rule books. Absurd as they were, you at least knew roughly where you stood with them. At home, there was no book – merely a vast, unwritten, suffocating code, in its way quite as restrictive as the Binker's. Here the punishments were subtler. There were no canings, no gatings, no lines to copy. But there were hurt looks and feelings of intense embarrassment if you so much as spoke of stepping out of line.

I was hemmed in by a further invisible fence – my own shyness and awkwardness. I was still paralysed with fear of the village people at Timplingham. I could not have brought myself to hang round the village pub or talk to the two or three females in the village who were under the age of forty. But, even if I had wanted to, I should have been made aware that while not actually forbidden, this sort of behaviour would have been impossible in the eyes of my uncle and aunt.

And now I was moving into a world where – as I then fondly supposed – 'anything goes'. My head was filled with Rousseau-esque misconceptions about freedom as the natural human condition. England scudded past the window. The train was full of holidaymakers with suitcases and merry faces. Very gingerly, and with the sense that I was doing something pretty wicked, I loosened and then removed my tie.

'Put a tie on, I should,' my uncle would say, on the hottest of days, if there was any question of my accompanying him on a visit to the Place. We would get there and find Sargie in a string vest and shorts.

There was no absolute rule in the world that you have to wear a tie. No one in that train was going to come up and say, 'Put a tie on, I should.' No one would have turned a hair if I had lit up a cigarette.

For the first time in my life I was a free agent. A sense of my freedom stole over me – not *like* a sexual experience, it *was* one. I was at large in the universe, a young bull. I stretched up to put my holdall on the rack above my head. Then, since there was room in the carriage and I did not much like my neighbour, I wandered up and down the train. It was about five minutes later that I asked, 'Is this seat taken?' and returned the smile of a blowzy, brown-skinned girl from Brussels.

How much, in advertisements, depends upon punctuation. My aunt had been under the impression that she was dispatching me to spend my summer holidays with a large family, house on the coast of Brittany. Before my arrival, I had managed to reconstruct all the de Normandins in my mind. *Monsieur*, rather like Monsieur Dubois in our French primer at Seaforth Grange, would be a precise figure, suited, moustached and with an amazing interest in pens, ink, desks and exercise books; talking about them all the time. *Madame*, who also liked to say things like 'The exercise book is on the desk', had a tiny waist, which showed no sign of having given birth to the young de Norman-dins, in whose possession these items of stationery and class-room equipment were to be found. Jean, he who wrote in the exercise book with the pencil, would be my age now, a surly brute in all likelihood, perhaps with a taste for the sort of novels still admired by Felicity – Camus, Sartre – and sexually precocious too. His younger sister, Mathilde, would by now, I hoped, have become a nubile creature who had lost her obsessive desire to accompany her mother to the grocer to buy coffee, tea, butter and other comestibles.

'What else did she buy at the grocer, Darnley?'

'De l'encre, monsieur.'

'Don't be ridiculous. You don't buy ink at a grocer's.'

Hands going up all over the class, with evidence of grocers' shops known to supply ink when required.

'What is it now, Darnley?' Lollipop Lew asks bewilderedly.

'Well, sir, supposing there was ink and you wrote a letter, not in English, but in the language we're doing . . . '

'You mean a French letter, Darnley.'

In the riot which followed, things got thrown. A window was broken, I seem to remember.

No wonder my French was appalling. Though I had advanced from the primer and the prosaic activities of the Dubois family, I was still nervous at the prospect of conversing with all the de Normandins.

It was a surprise, when I had settled into Les Mouettes, to discover that there were no de Normandins at all. Madame de Normandin's daughter, who turned out rather grandly to be called the Marquise d'Alifort, arrived when I had been there about ten days. She made periodic sorties to her mother's house, staying for about three days at a time before returning to her house in the South. She was all that was left of Madame's family. Three brothers of the Marquise had been killed in the First World War. Madame de Normandin and her daughter both lost their husbands in the Second.

Les Mouettes had been a family home. A turreted, granite affair, it would have been hard to classify architecturally. Is there such a thing as Seaside Gothic Celtic Twilight Revival? By Sargie Lampitt's snobbish standards, it would have passed muster: it wasn't a bought house. Madame de Normandin's grandmother had built it in the 1880s. It was large enough to house twenty people with ease. Before the war it had been the de Normandins' summer home. Monsieur de Normandin had been a diplomat – the house was scattered with mementoes of his various postings. The tiny circular drawing room with its signed photographs (George V and Queen Mary; the Princess Bibesco; Daisy Fellowes) was crammed with *vietnaméserie* picked up in Saigon. The library upstairs had a lot of Turkish junk, some of it, I now suspect, rather good.

I have never been easily able to ask people direct questions about themselves. If someone tells me their story I am (almost always) interested to hear. Likewise, if, before being introduced to someone for the first time, a third party gives me what diplomatic or military types would call a briefing, I listen with fascinated interest. But I am bad at admitting to their face that I do not know the details of someone's biography, even in circumstances where no disgrace attaches to ignorance and it would be extremely surprising if I *were* to know. I can't bring myself to say, 'I do not know anything about your past life. You mention a husband – to whom were you married? Is he dead? Did you have children?' or 'You mention Cairo – what were you doing there?' Rather, when a total stranger says to me, 'When Johnnie and I were in Cairo,' I tend to nod knowingly, as though it would be bad manners not to have known who Johnnie was and why he went to Egypt.

If all this is true of me now, it was yet truer when I was sixteen. I never once asked about Monsieur de Normandin during my entire month at Les Mouettes, even though I did a lot of sage nodding whenever Madame de Normandin referred to her husband. Years later, when staying with some friends, I happened to find a new biography of de Gaulle left for my bedside reading. It was much more readable than such books usually are and my interest was sufficiently held for me to read, having opened the thing at random, until the Fall of France. It was only in this way that I learned how the Baron de Normandin, at needless personal risk (his diplomatic status could have allowed him to slip out of the country via Vichy and spend the war in the United States or London), had attempted a last-minute resistance to the establishment of Pétain's quisling government. He had remained in Paris after the Occupation and openly challenged the legality of the Vichy regime. Within a week, he had been shot by the Gestapo. Les Mouettes itself, where Madame de Normandin had lived continuously since the Liberation, had been occupied by the Germans: one reason, as she explained, for the bizarre variety of furnishings. The Turkish tables, Chinese screens and garish rugs had for the most part been stowed in cellars or lumber-rooms before the invasion. Much of the nicer furniture had been damaged by the troops billeted there.

I never heard Madame de Normandin, or anyone else at Les Mouettes, refer to the Germans as the *'boches'*. The brutes who had moved into her house in the summer of 1940 and, when they discovered that it belonged to the Baron de Normandin, had thrown some of the nicer furniture over the cliffs, were always referred to as 'our visitors in 'forty'. Indeed, the outrage was described with such gentle irony that I at first missed the point altogether and supposed that some *Lady* readers had answered Madame's advertisement, come to Les Mouettes and, in a fit of high spirits, decided to destroy the furniture.

'The period of Louis Quinze was not, we suspect, altogether to our visitors' taste. They threw my husband's *secrétaire* over the cliffs, and his bed and a writing table. All the same period – made by Riesener. There is one, you know, in your Wallace Collection in London. It was similar.'

I just nodded, as if what she was saying was general knowledge. I regret this now. It would have been better manners to express curiosity about an extraordinary story and to ask for more details. Perhaps I had been partly inhibited by Aunt Deirdre who had told me not to mention the war to any of the de Normandins.

'They'll all have things they would rather forget. It's only because they are ashamed of what happened after Dunkirk.'

The tone had implied that the French nation as a whole had been guilty of some absurd solecism – speaking 'ee bah gum', for example, or calling my aunt by her Christian name – and that she would rather that the family adopted her policy of 'taking no notice'.

In fact, I think that Madame de Normandin enjoyed recalling the war. Memories were a source of pride to her, rather than the reverse.

Madame de Normandin was very myopic and, rather than attempting to get anything into focus, she usually gazed upwards as she spoke, always rapidly and usually bilingually. These mealtime colloquies were designed, as she frequently reminded us, to teach us the art of conversation. Doubtless, this would have been a useful skill to acquire, but during my first week at Les Mouettes I was inhibited, partly by an intense shyness of saying anything at all and partly because I found my fellow guests uncongenial. There was absolutely nothing wrong with them. I was simply frightened of them, being used either to coevals of my own sex at school or to the quiet Rectory routines at Timplingham. Entirely unabashed either by my silences or by the somewhat different gaucheries of the other young people, Madame de Normandin made conversation relentlessly. She spoke, as it were, in subtitles, putting all the difficult words, and many of the easy ones, into our own language.

'*Alors*, now then! *Tout le monde a passé un bon matin à Perros-Guirec. Qu'est-ce qui se passe au club? Le tournoi n'est-ce pas?* The tournament? The tennis tournament?'

'We just knocked a ball about, *madame.*'

'*Français, s'il vous plaît, Atlas.*'

'*Alors, nous avons . . .*'

These syllables were enough to reduce At Birk's two sisters to derision. Madame smiled patiently (one felt that it was an expression which had graced many an embassy dinner) and tried to help At on his way.

'*Je vous en prie, Wilmington! Atlas, continuez!* Go on! *Vous avez dit . . .*'

'*Oui, oui madame* – Wilmie, quit foolin', can't you? – *nous avons* – what's "net"?'

'*Filet.*'

'Anyway, *nous avons joué au tennis.*'

'*Tennis,*' she repeated, correcting At's pronunciation. '*C'est ça.*'

By then the last little mountain of artichoke leaves had assembled before each plate and it was time for Madame to ring the bell.

Barbara came in to clear away the plates. She was about my age and she wore her dark hair in a pigtail. She was not strikingly pretty. More than any obvious perfection of feature, it was her smile which captivated me; and the fact that she did not smile at everyone. Her face was particularly impassive when she took At's plate.

'*Voilà, chérie, seulement pour toi,*' he said with a lewd laugh. My own accent was not up to much but I was already starting to hear the language in my head. At, who could be quite fluent when he chose, seemed not to have noticed the sound of French at all and spoke it with the same nasal drawl with which he spoke his own language.

While Barbara was in the room, Madame de Normandin spoke English. It was a convention dating back to her husband's lifetime that servants did not understand anything but French.

'And this afternoon, you are all to take Julian down to the sailing school at Perros-Guirec. That's right, isn't it?'

'Would you like to do that?' This kind enquiry came from Coral Birk, the eldest of the party.

'Sure he would,' said At.

I nodded, and tried to smile.

'D'you go sailing in England?'

'I haven't done.'

'But you'd like to learn, huh?'

'Oh, yes,' I lied. 'I mean, ah, *oui*.'

It was not at all how I had envisaged the French holiday. It had never occurred to me that there would be other English-speaking guests. I felt that Madame de Normandin had tricked us. For the next few days I was packed off to Perros-Guirec with the Birks and told to enjoy myself. My tennis was hopelessly less good than At's – not a fact in which I take any pride. My sailing skills turned out to be even worse. I acquiesced in the idea of signing up for lessons without beginning to imagine what they would be like. In an open boat with seven other people I would surely not be called upon to *do* anything? While the sails flapped above my head I could sit back and feel the salt on my skin and the sun on my hair; I could stare back across the bright, blue ocean to the strange, pink, porous rocks and cliffs of the coastline, and the little seaside resort with its coloured umbrellas and cafés. The sailing school took the more rigorous view that having paid for instruction I should be instructed. Our instructor was a bossy little woman with short hair, the Gauloise forever dangling on her lips as she yelled at me furiously. I had no idea what she was saying. (Madame de Normandin with subtitles was still barely comprehensible; this sporty loudmouth did not even realise that my French was too poor to understand her elaborate directions.) I only knew that I was doing almost everything wrong. For instance, there is a large wooden pole at the bottom of the sail which swings to and fro across the entire surface of the boat. If you swing this without warning people, they get hit on the head. Whenever it was my turn to hold the pole, I either forgot to shout or, more shaming, felt too shy. What were the right words? It was only good luck which prevented me concussing the rest of the crew whenever I took the boom.

'He's just so stupid,' I overheard At saying one afternoon, as he rubbed the bumps which I had given him on the back of the head.

'And so, like high and mighty, like, you know, he doesn't want even to talk to us,' said Wilmie.

But Coral, who was the eldest and kinder, said, 'I guess it's all a little strange to him and he's a little girl-shy.'

'Like me,' said At.

'Like hell,' said Wilmie.

'Do you think Barbara loves me? You know the way she looks at me when she clears those plates away.'

'At Birk, Barbara thinks you are a shit. Can't you see that?'

I could certainly see it at that moment, as I came round the corner of the clubhouse to where they were eating their ice-cream cones. He was big, he was blond; the fact that he was covered in spots did not detract from his swaggering handsomeness. I hated his ability to be *open* – to make jokes about his own emotional state. I hated his loud voice and his decent, honest smile.

'Hi, Julian, have an ice cream.'

'No, thanks.'

'Hey, come on! Let me buy you an ice cream!'

'No.'

'Leave him alone, At.'

Increasingly – who shall blame them? – they did. I just couldn't enter into their *bonhomie*. I felt paralysed by it. And Coral was dead right to say that I was 'a little girl-shy'. I was disconcerted by her own shorts and T-shirt revealing so much flesh. I did not desire her – not when I was with her, anyway. I was overcome with awkwardness to have to spend time with someone who was so unselfconscious. She took my arm one day when we were walking down the road together. It was a purely sisterly affectionate gesture (her other arm was linked in Wilmie's) but I froze as she did it, instantaneously hating her action and my own involuntary cold-fishery. Besides, I had by then begun my own obsessive preoccupation with Barbara, with the thickness of her brown hair, falling down her back, and

154

with that back itself, as I imagined it beneath the bow of her white apron. I thought too of her legs, of her large, pale hands as they took away my plate at table, of her strangely deep voice. Through all the tedium of sailing and tennis, and through all the badinage of Coral, At and Wilmie, and through all Madame de Normandin's stately meals and through all the long nights, in my remote turret bedroom with its view of the garden, the beech trees, the pines, the cliffs and the sea, I thought of Barbara. That unwavering concentration upon another person whom we hardly know, which we call falling in love, is unlike any other human relationship. It is different in kind from the way we think about those actually known to us – our family and friends – and has more in common with the incantations of witches or the intercession of those who pray than it has with any ordinary rational or sympathetic process. Long before I had touched Barbara, I knew exactly what the small of her back would feel like when pressed by my fingers and what it would be like when my chest was pressed against hers. As soon as a glance told me, quite unambiguously, that she would allow me to kiss her, everything changed. I took the risk that someone would spot us. She was on a landing, taking some sheets and towels out of an ottoman and looked up when I passed. Without saying anything, I put my arms round her waist. There was no resistance. All that remained, after our lips had parted, was to speak to one another, to make an assignation.

'Carbon?' I said, puzzled by her attempt to explain in my own language where we might meet again.

'On the side of the sea.'

'Oh, the cabin. The bathing hut.'

'Yes, the urt.'

After luncheon the next day was the soonest we could get away. As At remarked at the time, it was some meal. It was the last meal which the Birks ate in that house. The train would soon be taking them to Paris and then on to Geneva where their father worked for the United Nations. No one bore the Birks the smallest ill will, least of all Barbara's mother who had been tipped handsomely by Atlas and, in consequence, pulled out all the stops for the last meal she cooked them.

I had never come across proper cooking before I went to Les Mouettes. I did not even know that it existed. The grand meals which Darnley's mother paid for at hotels in Malvern were really only a step up from Aunt Deirdre's cuisine, with plenty of over-boiled vegetables and roast potatoes made out of leather. School food was universally horrible. The only improvement which I noticed after going to public school was that one was allowed to supplement high tea with eggs or tins of one's own. I wonder what Barbara's mother would have made of the food which Mrs Binker, or even Aunt Deirdre, so regularly set before their charges.

That last meal she cooked for the Birks was a triumph. Even by her own impeccable standards this was a series of dishes done to such perfection that one was half aware, even while eating it, that the memory of the meal would remain for ever. Almost all experience is instantaneously forgettable. Most of what we do remember is only fixed in our minds by chance. For another person to place something in our consciousness deliberately, so that we never forget it, that is art. Treadmill as a teacher had it, Thérèse as a cook. The meal began with a spinach soufflé which was like a thing of nature, a puffy light green crust sprouting from its bowl like a bush coming to leaf. And then there was *raie au beurre noire*, the freshest strands of succulent skate as white as snow amid the black butter and the little, dark green capers: once again, one felt that the food was for the first time in its natural habitat: a naked mermaid was suggested, sitting in seaweed. And then there were pieces of roast beef, pink and tender, served with *pommes dauphinoise*. And then there were *haricots verts* from the garden, served separately when we had all finished our meat. And then there was a fresh, very oily, green salad with which to eat the Camembert. And then, to crown it all, *omelettes soufflées aux liqueurs*, frothing, bubbling in their great buttery pans as Thérèse and Barbara ran in, squealing with the excitement of this success, for sweet omelettes never looked lighter or smelt more spirituous than these. Every time the mother and the daughter appeared throughout the meal, there were exclamations of delight at their genius, and no one seemed to notice the smiles and nods which I exchanged with Barbara, since everyone was smiling and nodding too, in happiness at the meal, and perhaps because everyone was fully able to tolerate the departure of the Birks. At, Coral and Wilmie themselves were eager to be back with their parents. Madame, when they had gone, commended their exuberance but deplored their lack of manners. So, the parting was a merry one.

Though, or perhaps because, it was her last meal with the Birks, Madame did her best to keep up a level of what she considered good conversation. It was not a level to which the rest of us aspired.

'Will you be going to Perros all on your own when we're gone?' At asked me. Now that we were about to part, I liked him and I think he rather liked me.

'*Parlez français,* stupid,' said Wilmie.

'So, who's stupid? *Est-ce que vous allez* ... er ... *au* ... er ... *club de tennis quand* ... ?'

It had never occurred to me that I would play any tennis once At was on his way back to Geneva. Horror must have registered in my face because Madame de Normandin came at once to my rescue.

'*Julian est beaucoup plus intellectuel que sportif,*' she said decisively.

I do not think this has ever been true – the intellectual bit anyway – but it was a relief to discover that I would no longer have to pretend to be *sportif.* Madame said there were plenty of things to do, down on the little beach, at the bottom of the cliffs below her garden. I said that I had thought of spending the afternoon there.

'So, you see, Atlas, Julian will be able to occupy himself,' she said kindly, while Barbara brought in the beans.

'I know who I'm gonna miss,' said At, putting his arm round Barbara's waist. It was hard to know whether Madame, with her faded eyes fixed on the ceiling, noticed this little moment of endearment.

'So Julian'll be all alone,' said Coral.

'*Jusqu'à l'arrivée des Mount-Smiths,*' said Madame. 'Until the Mount-Smiths arrive. They are my very good friends. The grandfather of these boys was a close friend of my husband.'

I had not dared to hope that I would have the place completely to myself when the Birks had gone. But the idea of the Mount-Smiths was, to me, lowering. I felt instantaneously jealous of them for knowing Madame de Normandin so well.

We had finished our beans and their consumption seemed to have cast Madame into a contemplative mood. She clasped her hands together and closed her eyes. She was going to make one last attempt to draw some coherent sentences from her young

157

female guests and on a subject of what might be supposed to be of general interest.

'*Alors, Wilmington! dites-moi, s'il vous plaît, qui est votre auteur préféré?* You see, we are having some intellectual conversation for Julian.'

'Excuse me?'

'Your favourite author, dum-dum' (this prompting from Wilmie's brother).

Atlas Birk's sister flicked him with the last of her green beans. One got the feeling, from the giggles which followed, that Wilmie was under the impression that reading, books, literature, were invariably obscene, or at least vaguely improper.

'*Et vous, Atlas,*' persisted Madame de Normandin. 'Who is your favourite? Mark Twain, or perhaps someone more modern? Jack London, perhaps.'

'I read a little Hemingway.'

Coral confessed to a fondness for Margaret Mitchell. The conversation was getting nowhere.

Madame de Normandin announced that she chiefly liked to read authors for their excellent style. I have never met anyone else with this rigorous ability to distinguish between style and content. Nevertheless, I did not believe that Madame was being pretentious. Coral asked Madame who were the greatest stylists.

'In French – *Pascal et Voltaire*. In English – I believe Agatha Christie and Winston Churchill.'

This led easily into an anecdote which Madame de Normandin recited regularly every few days about coming out into the Champs-Elysées just before the Liberation and seeing a solitary Union Jack. What could it signify, this flag? Was the King coming to Paris (he whose signed photograph she kept with the others in her drawing room)? No, no! It was not the King. It was Churchill.

The climax of the story, as she rehearsed the familiar scene of de Gaulle and Churchill walking together down the Champs-Elysées to the tumultuous acclaim of the crowds, was that the great prose stylist's lapels were wet with tears.

This recitation took us as far as the cheese.

'*Mais, nous n'avons pas demandé qui est l'écrivain préféré de Julian!*'

The Birks assumed a worried air, as if the whole of their remaining time at Les Mouettes might be devoted to a discussion of my literary preferences. I muttered my reply and, rather to my surprise, Madame de Normandin had heard of him.

'*Mais oui, Promenades à Venise* – what is this in English? *C'est un livre qui m'intéresse beaucoup.*'

'*Lagoon Loungings.*'

This was the one I had not read. Madame spoke of Venice, one of her passions. Petworth Lampitt, whose private correspondence was at that minute being revealed to the gaze of Hunter, passed swiftly out of the conversation. The name meant nothing to the Birks and, in spite of her polite interest, next to nothing to Madame. The excitement of the sweet omelette was enough to bring all talk of the Lampitts to an end.

Not long after that, I suppose I must have said goodbye to the Birks. Coral and Wilmie both said it had been good to know me. It was kind of them to say so, because I do not think they knew me at my best. At, with a big amiable smile and a clasp of my shoulder, expressed the hope that we would meet again. There was even talk of my looking them up in Geneva. But I have no real memory of their departing. The rest of the afternoon was spent on the beach. When I emerged from the little wooden cabin there, I had had an experience more memorable even than Thérèse's cooking; an experience after which the whole of life was different.

Some days later, I left Barbara on the beach and returned to the house towards half-past five in the afternoon.

From the first days at Les Mouettes, it had been a pleasant walk – a steep, sandy path with high banks and hedges on either side thick with the flowers of summer. It was almost like a subterranean tunnel, particularly when one passed the spot about halfway along which was overhung with wind-blown pines. By now the path between the house and the beach was associated with a pleasure more intense than anything in previous experience. When I trod the path, even if it was only for a bathe and there was no assignation arranged, I involuntarily felt stimulated. My climbs back up the hill, such as the one that afternoon, were suffused with deep happiness, only marred on that occasion by the knowledge that the Mount-Smiths would be arriving, a pair of brothers at present being educated at Downside.

Madame de Normandin had repeated several times since the

Birks left that it would be nicer if there were some other guests of my own age and sex. The truth is that with very few delightful exceptions I have never got on especially well with persons who fell into this category and the other indications given off by the word 'Downside' were far from reassuring. Downside was a Roman Catholic monastery. Now, I knew that Madame de Normandin kept a missal wrapped in a black lace mantilla in the glove compartment of her Deux Chevaux and attended Mass several times a week; but I did not think of her as RC. I was used to grown-ups spending a lot of time in church. Though I thought of my own life as largely shaped as a reaction against Uncle Roy, I had in fact imbibed many of his prejudices and I had a gloomy sense that Romans, as he called them, were not really the thing. Never knowingly having met an English Roman Catholic, I had no idea what, particularly, was wrong with them. But I knew that Downside boys would be awful.

Emerging from the cliff path, one crossed a patch of rough ground, entered a small gate into a shrubbery and then emerged into the garden of Les Mouettes. Passionate anglophile that she was, Madame believed that she had created, with her few flower beds and abundant bushes of hydrangeas, a veritable English garden. But there were no borders, no roses. There was none of the abundance of the Rectory garden at Timplingham. It would have astonished Madame de Normandin to know that a woman like my aunt spent hours of every day digging and weeding, and dead-heading and transplanting, and trundling wheelbarrows down muddy paths. She frequently spoke of the wonders of British gardens and obviously thought that her own was comparable with them. But *why* English gardens were so green and colourful and abundant was probably a mystery. If she had known how much time the English spend on their gardens, I am fairly sure that she would have thought it was an absurd waste of time, just as my aunt, who prided herself on what she called 'good, plain cooking' would have been scandalised by the artistry, the day-long kitchen toil, of Thérèse.

When one had crossed the garden, it was possible either to turn the corner by the large hydrangea bush and enter the house by the front door, or to weave one's way behind a hedge into a yard and enter through the back kitchens. This was what I did, so that I could hang the key of the beach hut on its hook by the dresser. My heart was full of the questions which Barbara had whispered in my ear. Did I love her? Really? Yes, yes, I had insisted. 'But if you love me, why do you not talk? Why is it – just *this*?' It *was* just 'this'. I had an almost painful awareness of the fact that, though fascinated and delighted by her, I was not after all in love. And this had been clear to me from my first emergence from the hut.

When I came into the back kitchen, I encountered a woman smartly dressed in black, whose neat hair was a shade too blonde to be credible. She both was and wasn't looking at me intently, for one of her eyes met mine and the other, over which there appeared to be no control, stared in all directions. The disconcerting thing about the eyes was that I did not know from second to second which one was wandering and which was staying still. If I withdrew my attention for an instant, the stable eye had started to wander, and I would find that the glide had now come to rest its observant and ironical gaze on me.

Having been in France a little while, I was beginning to feel like a native. It was slightly humiliating to be addressed in English before I had even opened my mouth.

'Good afternoon. My mother is still having a little rest. Let me introduce myself. I am Madame d'Alifort. You must be Julian Ramsay, yes?'

'Yes.'

When we had exchanged civilities, she said, 'I had no sooner arrived this afternoon than we had the most terrible news, my mother and I.'

'Oh, dear.'

'Oh, yes. The boys, the young men, who were to have been your companions for the rest of this fortnight, Dominic and Gerard Mount-Smith, have sent a telegram to say that they have had a death in the family.'

'How awful.'

'It really is. Their mother apparently has died, most unexpectedly, in hospital.'

From the way she squinted I could guess that Madame d'Alifort was puzzled by the grin which I was unable to prevent stealing over my face.

'It is very, very sad, isn't it?'

'Oh, terribly.'

Almost no event is objectively sad. Only sympathy can make it so. A minute's reflection on what the Mount-Smiths would actually be suffering sobered me up and stopped me smiling. But it could not make me *feel* sad. I had so little wanted the Mount-Smiths to be there, so convinced myself that they would be ghastly, that all I was capable of feeling was relief at their non-appearance.

Madame de Normandin and Madame d'Alifort might have had their own reasons for private distress at Mrs Mount-Smith's death. They were family friends of a sort. They were also going to lose a fortnight's money for the two Mount-Smith boys. I had the impression that the quite modest sums charged for board and lodging made an appreciable difference to Madame de Normandin, quite possibly that she needed the money. But there was another problem, perhaps more glaring, and it was me. Madame de Normandin, who was nearing seventy years of age, had her own distinctive manner of dealing with young houseguests. The only times when she felt personally respons-ible for them was during meals and for about an hour after dinner, when her conversations would continue over coffee in the library.

'Dites-nous, Wilmington ma chérie, quel est votre paysage – landscape or scenery, is it not – *votre paysage préféré?* What is your favourite scenery?'

'Excuse me?'

'Just say Swiss, Wilmie.'

More often than not, in the previous week, there had been sudden but semi-plausible announcements, before the end of dinner, that Wilmie, Coral and At were going to the cinema, a fly-blown little establishment which they had discovered in Perros-Guirec. I saw *Stage Coach* there, with subtitles, but full concentration on the film was impossible, what with Coral's knees pressed against my trouser legs and the generally overpowering smell of the lavatories, which seemed to domi-nate, however much the audience tried to drown it with Gauloises.

Into the gap left by the Birks the Mount-Smiths had been destined to step. It never occurred to me for a single moment during my time at Les Mouettes that my own presence there constituted a potential nightmare. How many grown-ups of their age (I suppose Madame d'Alifort was about forty-five) would relish the prospect of three weeks spent in the company of a moody, foreign adolescent who could not properly speak their language? The fact that I so visibly brightened at the prospect of having Les Mouettes to myself must have made it all the harder to tolerate. Had I not been there, Madame de Normandin could perhaps have gone away herself, gone back to stay with her daughter in the South, where there was more company and comfort. Yet never, by the flickering of an eyelash, did Madame de Normandin betray any such feelings to me. Perhaps she realised that things could have been worse. She could have been walled up for a month with At. (But perhaps she would have preferred that.) The only thing to be said in my favour was that years of living with Uncle Roy and Aunt Deirdre had given me plenty of practice at adapting myself to the routines of a quiet, elderly household.

Les Mouettes had all the advantages of the Rectory at Timplingham, with none of its drawbacks. It had beauty and seclusion but I had no sense here, as in Norfolk, of being trapped miles from anywhere in a household of persons intensely uncongenial to myself. For Aunt Deirdre's cottage pies, I had all the abundance of Thérèse's ingenuity and invention. Instead of Mrs Batterbee, waddling about the Rectory with a carpet sweeper and dispensing an odour of self-righteousness and armpits, there was Barbara.

Our clandestine meetings in the beach hut played such a large part of my own picture of how the days were to be spent that it was almost surprising to find Madame de Normandin anxious that, without some plan, I should be unable to occupy myself. Neither she nor her daughter could have had any conception of how thoroughly practised I was at solitude. Indeed, it may be said that I learned it too well at Timplingham and have never entirely shaken off the sense that time spent in anyone else's company, however pleasant, is a departure from the norm, to which one only returns when alone.

Clearly, the hour or two between the arrival of the Mount-Smiths' telegram and the serving of dinner was devoted by Madame de Normandin and the Marquise d'Alifort to a discussion of policy. They did not know anything about me. Supposing, for all his good nature, they *had* been stranded for a month with Atlas Birk? Over the soup, the Marquise, squinting this way and that, explained to me that, since I was now their solitary guest, some routine, some timetable, some *horaire* – she was so desperate that the synonyms poured from her – must be maintained. She wanted to protect her mother, I see that now. Madame de Normandin interrupted with many a delicate apology, as though my solitude, the death of Mrs Mount-Smith, the absence of the young scholars of Downside School, were all calamities so insupportable that it would require in me the patience of a saint to endure them.

'My mother's eyesight is failing,' said Madame d'Alifort insistently, in English.

'Such a nuisance for everyone,' said her mother.

'She must not be strained. But perhaps you could, for example, read her the newspaper after breakfast. This would be useful for your own study of the French language and be of great help to her.'

I readily agreed.

'But she cannot supervise your activities later each day.'

'I wouldn't expect . . .'

'He would find it too boring!' exclaimed the mother.

'You can of course always take the *autobus* into Ploumanach or Perros. Then again, there is the little beach.'

'Our poor little beach!' exclaimed Madame de Normandin. 'Julian is loyal to it, I think. He seems just as happy there as at the, how would one say, *pleasure* beaches. He takes a book. Absolutely *anything* satisfies him!'

Barbara's English was not good enough to appreciate any comedy in all this as she brought in the next course.

'You are always most welcome to luncheon here with my mother,' continued the Marquise.

'And in the afternoons,' said her mother, 'when you are not sitting with a book on our poor little *plage*, I shall drive you for expeditions.'

'My mother is not meant to drive,' said the Marquise.

'I can show you Brittany,' said Madame de Normandin.

I think that the next three and a half weeks were the happiest of my life, a selfish confession since, in spite of my moments on the poor little *plage*, it was a month of delicious uninvolvement. I never came to know Madame de Normandin or the Marquise d'Alifort any better in the space of those three weeks. The same polite level of conversation was maintained. The same amiability was displayed and, I believe, felt. Madame's impeccable manners towards myself actually made me into easier company. She civilised me, just a little. There must have been moments, during that time, of awkwardness, or loneliness, or at least of minor depression or sorrow. No other period of life has been without them, so they must have been there at Les Mouettes, those spells, lasting anything from a few hours to several days, in which life seemed miserable, boring, oppressive. But I have no recollection of any such time at Les Mouettes. Memory paints a purely sunny canvas. I remember waking, morning after morning (in memory it all seems much longer than a month – it is a whole phase of life which has left a stronger imprint on my imagination than many longer spells such as my two years in the army) and feeling happy to be alive. That joyous sense of total independence which I had felt in the boat train at Victoria never left me, all the time I was away.

And then again the place itself, Les Mouettes, had such magic. One was always woken by the cawing of rooks in the beech trees which grew close to the house. Rising, I would open the little window of my tower bedroom, and look across the slope of the garden and down to the flat-topped pines which blackened the view of the sea. Everything at that hour was usually grey with the pallor of a sea mist – *la brume*. Sometimes it would lift and a day of bright sunshine would follow. Equally beautiful to me were the days when the mist never lifted, and when the air was damp and salty all day. It was particularly good to bathe in this weather. Sometimes the beach was so white with fog that Barbara and I could emerge from our hut as naked as Adam and Eve to bathe in the sea, with no chance of being seen from a distance of five yards away. Or again, on misty afternoons, my wrists might be busy with the hand-operated windscreen wipers as Madame de Normandin rattled her Citroën down the high-hedged lanes at a daring twenty miles per hour. Her daughter's claim that Madame de Normandin's eyesight was failing was no exaggeration. I sometimes wondered whether it was worth wiping the haze of the dew from the windscreen. She saw everything, I imagine, through a perpetual *brume*. She sat behind the wheel, as she did at the dinner table, with her head held back. She did not appear to be looking at anything in particular. She knew the roads so well that she appeared to be driving by instinct.

In her company, I came to love the world of the Celtic. Every few miles, we scrunched to a halt beside some primitive granite church. She always remembered exactly what there was to see in each place – here a standing stone or an old cross, fantastically carved with serpents or Scriptural scenes; there a particular piece of old glass or an unusual font. It was all much more primitive than anything I was used to from the splendid Norfolk churches in the environs of Timplingham (and which, when seen with Uncle Roy, were nothing but a bore). The squat Breton saints who looked down from their niches seemed like children's dolls. Moreover, they were saints peculiar to the Celts – St Chattan, St Enedoque, St Ystyple, St Poran, St Brian, St Tugdual. The female figure with a child might be the Blessed Virgin, but she could equally easily turn out to be St Eboubibane. The lawgiver in these parts was neither St Paul nor Moses, but St Yvo.

Madame de Normandin apparently held this Celtic pantheon in the same affectionate regard as she did her neighbours.

'Cher petit saint!' she would exclaim as she surveyed one of these wobbly old wooden dolls in its place of honour. The tone of voice was identical if, on driving through some nearby village, she might say, 'Why – there's Madame de Lanfrancourt.' Then the Citroën might judder to a halt, and Madame would climb out to exchange civilities with some old lady walking out of a drive or hobbling into a grocer's shop.

Comparing her behaviour and that of her neighbours with the way we behaved at home, I concluded that Bretons had better manners than Norfolk types. There was no hint of condescension when Madame called the postman or the gardener *'monsieur'*, nor of servility in their address to her. Between Aunt Deirdre and the villagers in Timplingham there was a carefully graded hierarchy of attitudes and relations, with nothing so liberating as the convention of *'m'sieur'* and *'madame'* as a mode of addressing just about everyone. If Aunt Deirdre had addressed the postman as 'sir', he would rightly have concluded that something was amiss.

There were perfect manners, too, in the fact that, although we visited lots of churches together and although Madame told me many of the legendary stories about the Celtic saints and shrines, there was absolutely no awkwardness from a religious point of view: certainly no sense that I should accompany her on her frequent visits to Mass. She cannot have been a bigot, for one of our happiest outings together was to Tréguier, where I was enchanted by the crooked little cathedral, the steep, winding, cobbled streets leading down to the water's edge and the estuary.

We went to Renan's house, open to the public as a museum. Ernest Renan had left the Roman Church in the same year, 1845, that John Henry Newman had joined it. English readers of his *Vie de Jésus* have mostly regarded it as a romantic, even a sympathetic portrait of its subject. Renan's inability to believe in the miraculous elements in the Gospel could scarcely shock a nation many of whose clergy were honest doubters. In France, in the nineteenth century, things were very different. The divisions between those who believed and those who did not were more sharply accentuated, both religiously and politically. Madame de Normandin, who had been in her teens when Captain Dreyfus was sent to Devil's Island, was in many ways a highly nineteenth-century figure, patriotic, Catholic and Gaullist, with distinct monarchist sympathies. One might have expected her to sympathise with those nineteenth-century clerics who, scandalised when the people of Tréguier erected a statue of their most famous literary son, retaliated by shoving up an enormous (and hideous) Calvary by the railway station, in reparation for Renan's supposed blasphemies. The occasion had been attended by Madame de Normandin's mother, who remembered the huge crowds and some mitred bishop blessing this gruesome memorial to *odium theologicum*.

Madame de Normandin herself, however, like many pious people, regarded the clergy of her Church with a distant sort of derision. As far as she was concerned, they were functionaries whose task was to dispense the sacraments; there was no more need to interest herself in their opinions than in those of others on whom she relied for some particular professional expertise – her dentist, for example, or her plumber.

So – without guilt or apology – we went to Renan's house and inspected the relics which such places always contain – his old coat, stray bits of manuscript, photographs. Renan was a passionate Hellenist. Sepia photographs of Athens adorned the walls. We were shown his famous invocation to the goddess Athena. It was impossible, Madame de Normandin said, not to feel affection for Renan's intellectual honesty and for his love of beauty. He had come from a poor family. His career in the Church had 'made' him. When he had confided his religious doubts to an academic superior, he had received a cynical smile which had shown that, whatever he believed in the secrets of his heart, he could easily have carried on functioning as a professor of theology.

This was the level of Renan's inner heroism. What accounted for his local popularity, however, was that he remained so thoroughly a Breton. Indeed, when one looked at the photographs of his tubby little figure or surveyed the controversial statue which stood between his house and the cathedral, Renan looked simply like the last in a line of fat little Celtic saints, another Tugdual or Samson whose dumpy body had been framed by nature in the manner of the primitive Breton sculptors.

Even had Madame de Normandin and her daughter never cropped up again in my life, I would still think it was worth recording our visit to Renan's house. For, said she, Renan had never really written better than when recalling his own childhood and youth. It was a common enough thing, in all generations since Rousseau, to try to recall the most significant scenes of our early life. But, said she, Renan's *Souvenirs d'Enfance et de la Jeunesse* was an admirable example of the genre. As we were leaving the house, she bought me a copy. That evening after dinner in the library, she handed me a paper-knife to cut its porous, smudgy pages and asked me to read it aloud to her, an exercise altogether more restful than her carefully constructed conversations and one which was in itself delightful. I saw at once why she admired the book and considered it worthy of comparison with Churchill's *My Early Life*.

For myself, the book articulated what it was I had fallen in love with when I became captivated by the land of the Celtic. Renan's love of early Breton lore and history were all of a piece with what I myself was nebulously in love with – the standing stones and menhirs in rough grassland and heather, the pink, rocky coastline, the windswept hedges, the primitive churches, the faces of the villagers round and brown as leather beneath peaked caps or white lace coifs. The world evoked by Renan was one which, with the necessary nostalgia of the memoirist, he believed to have vanished for ever; and much, by the time I came to know Brittany, had changed. The idiots from the asylum, for instance, no longer wandered the streets of Tréguier. But in many ways the Brittany of Renan survived until the decade after the Second World War. The extraordinary, elaborate costumes, for example, worn by the old women, high lace constructions quite as ingenious as the Gothic spires at Treguier or Quimper, were not affected for the benefit of trippers. They were a genuine survival.

So was their piety, apparent at a village *pardon* on 15 August, when Madame de Normandin and her household all followed the *curé* and his acolytes as they carried the statue of Mary out of the village church and down to a ruin of a small chapel on the cliff tops, singing hymns which mingled a sentimental devotion to the Mother of God with a shrewd hope that the sea harvest for the coming year would be abundant. There were no hymnbooks, as in a Protestant service, and the accents of the worshippers were thick – that is, when they sang in French at all, some of the ditties being in Breton. But the general impression conveyed was a profound veneration for virginal purity and a very strong desire for lobsters. Even with my cynical Rectory upbringing (and I took part in the procession partly with the gleeful certainty – I wonder if I was right – that Uncle Roy would consider it silly) I approached it with a residual Manichean respectfulness which was quite inapposite. I thought, because it was 'religious', that it ought to be solemn. When I made out some of the words, I was all prepared to be scandalised by the jarring blend of excruciating superstition and commercial self-interest. And sometimes the jabbering crones were telling their beads and sometimes they were gossiping among themselves, which initially struck me as wrong – surely if they were 'really religious' they would have been unable to gossip at such a solemn moment? I do not know where these ideas came from. Perhaps they weren't ideas, so much as attitudes acquired 'Sunday after Sunday', having to put on a smart suit to go to church, day after day at school of being told that one did not talk in chapel. Religion, which I did not even begin to understand, was something connected in my mind with being on someone else's idea of good behaviour. And there I was, walking along, side by side with Barbara! It was with myself that I felt most priggishly uneasy.

But, as the procession continued, these feelings of awkwardness wore off. Barbara and her mother sang the hymns quite unselfconsciously. I have no idea what their religious beliefs were, where they stood on the probability of the Virgin Birth or the moral allowability of sex before marriage. Nothing, I gradually came to feel, could be less relevant to what we were doing as we followed the *curé* and the lace-draped doll, carried on two poles and a sort of stretcher by an old man with earrings and a miscellaneous gaggle of altar boys.

The whole point of what I felt on that occasion is that I cannot put it into words. There was this strange collection of people, among whom I walked as a total stranger. What they were doing was inexplicable, alien. Yet, for about five minutes of the procession, it stopped being alien. The doll went on ahead. Behind followed the old women in their coifs and then the rest, taking up the rear – a crowd of a few hundred. Our voices were out of harmony, out of tune, out of time. We left behind us the tarmacadamed road and followed a rutty track down the lane which led to the cliffs. Beyond the Madonna, which swayed from side to side on the shoulders of the boys, was a clear blue sky and the sea. For a very short space of time – I have called it five minutes, but it may have been less – I was caught up in it all. At first, to my great embarrassment, I thought it was all going to make me cry; not merely water at the eyes, but really blub as I used to do when I was a little boy. There was a feeling of tears about it.

Since that day, I have tried on a number of occasions to articulate what it was that the procession began in me. It certainly did begin something which has continued to this day. And sometimes I have wanted to explain this as some sort of spiritual quest. And sometimes I have told myself that the procession was an example of natural religion – it worked, because the people took it all for granted. Religion, I have tried to say, is only possible in a world where most people take it for granted. Once you start analysing it and saying how much of it you believe, then it gets lost. But that isn't really quite what I felt or began to feel at the actual time of the procession. It was all much more nebulous than that. The *sort* of feeling it was followed the lines of 'At last I can see what religion *is*'.

This thought subsequently got rationalised into negatives. 'It isn't a matter of theology; it isn't a matter of the Sarum Rite; it isn't even a matter of good behaviour.' I got even hazier when I dropped the negatives and started trying to say what it was. Hazier still trying to remember it and disentangle this from subsequent 'spiritual experiences'. Perhaps it would have been better not to mention it. But it wouldn't be truthful to censor it. I remember it as just about the last thing I did on my holiday at Les Mouettes. Probably that is a false memory. I do know that, after the procession, there were no more secret meetings with Barbara. She said goodbye to me, perfectly demurely, in front of her mother and of Madame de Normandin in the dining room at Les Mouettes. We did not kiss or anything. Nor did Madame de Normandin kiss me when she left me at the railway station.

'*Au revoir*, Julian,' she said.

But a quarter of a century was to pass before this wish was fulfilled.

Five

The sense of our own identity is fluid and tolerant, whereas our sense of the identity of others is always more fixed and quite often edges towards caricature. We know within ourselves that we can be twenty different persons in a single day and that the attempt to explain our personality is doomed to become a falsehood after only a few words. To every remark made about our own personal characteristics we would want, in the interest of truth, quite disregarding vanity, to say, 'Yes, but . . .' Or, 'That may have been true once but it is true no longer.' And yet, although we know this to be the case about ourselves, we can go on devouring works of literature, novels and biographies, which depend for their aesthetic success precisely on this insensitive ability to simplify, to describe, to draw lines around another person and say, 'This is she' or 'This is he.'

James Petworth Lampitt achieved his effects as a literary caricaturist by sketching in the boldest of outlines. His Prince Albert is a figure whom we could recognise at a hundred yards, a two-dimensional creation made up of a handful of supposedly Germanic traits – efficiency, courage, soulful musicality, etc.: an Enlightenment polymath born out of time and trapped in the purely decorative world of tartan linoleum and antlers made into loving-seats which all Lampitt's admirers took to be the authentic Balmoral or Osborne. His Albert was a man who could have been Frederick the Great but who was trapped like a German doll in a musical box compelled to do the bidding of his diminutive female owner, the victim of a domestic tyranny which hovered, like so many other domestic dramas, in the borderlands between tragedy and farce.

Taught by Hunter's *Life* we have probably all by now supplied reasons for Petworth Lampitt's particular obsession with the Prince Consort and his ability to have drawn a portrait at once so convincing and so misleading. Lampitt's misogyny and his well-

172

manicured political radicalism supposedly go back to his experiences in Timplingham Place with his parents. Hunter's way of doing a biography is as different as possible from that of his most successful subject. Whereas Lampitt's portraits were self-confessedly imaginative (he was, indeed, halfway to the novelist's belief that we reach the truth about people only by inventing them) Hunter provided his readers with a superabundance of detail and what he himself like to call 'material'. Every notebook or postcard which Lampitt wrote has been gone through, its significance sifted. We feel that Hunter is being as fair as an experienced advocate who will if necessary (or even if unnecessary) take days to lay his evidence before the court, rather than influence the jury by distortion or paraphrase. And yet how often a defendant on trial, listening to just such a catalogue of his alleged deeds or misdeeds, must have thought that the mere length and detail of the evidence did nothing to diminish the unreality of the proceedings. If anything, the reverse. 'Yes, it is true,' he will think, 'that I did thus and thus, but no account of the matter can ever convey to a jury what it was like to do it: the thoughts passing through my head, the moods then possessing me. When I committed these crimes I was for all serious purposes a different person. Quite a different person from the man you see standing before you. The recitation of dates and facts by the barrister, as if he were the recording angel, is not real as I now am real.'

Hunter's *Life of Lampitt* was praised on all sides when first published for its accuracy and its subtlety. It was only those who had *known* Jimbo Lampitt who thought that this enormous, patiently assembled portrait, constructed from all the 'material' on which Hunter could lay his hands, bore no relation whatsoever to the man they had actually known and was actually less truthful than one of Lampitt's own historical caricatures.

It is only in relations of the deepest intimacy that we can allow to another person the same complexity of nature which we know to be our own. That is, with such individuals, we can stop making presuppositions and merely accept, as we do with our own selves, that there is no need to define them, no need to seek for patterns or shapes, no need to say that she or he is such and such a type.

Even more rigid than biographers in their desire to classify and depict, families impose on their own members the characters which they expect of them. The simplest way to respond to tyranny is to submit. Women whose sons and husbands have decided that they are shrews need never, at home, be anything else. The friends she meets when she is out of the house perhaps find all manner of qualities in a woman which her family have never seen and would not really want to see. If her churlish son or husband were to see her laughing with a friend, good-humouredly and without (as is her domestic wont) flying off the handle, they would murmur suspiciously that this was 'not what she was really like'. The pleasant, likeable, varied character enjoyed by her friends would be, by this judgement, merely a front, put up to conceal the 'real' self, a figure who is either crying over the washing-up or shouting at Dad.

So it is that teenage sons whose fathers know them as mindless rudesbies are found in other contexts to be ingenious workers, clubbable companions, affectionate lovers. By contrast, men suited by temperament to the few, simple modes which make 'perfect husbands' can present very different figures to the world, figures who are little short of odious. The man who is happy to sit on a sofa at nine o'clock in the evening, holding the same hand on to which he placed a ring a quarter of a century before and watching the televison set, can be transformed by nine in the morning into an office bully, free with his amorous attentions to stenographers and his withering unkindness to subordinates.

When we say 'It isn't like him,' we betray not so much our imperception about an individual (as though we might have spotted that the domestic mouse could also be a sergeant-major in a typing pool) as our general incomprehension of human personality. Pronouns are themselves just shorthand, since when we say 'I' or 'you' we really mean only that part of ourselves revealed for the time being to the other and seen through the other's eyes. We speak of the mad as people who aren't all there. But none of us is all there all of the time, that is, there is present in none of us at each moment of the day all the different modes of personality which might occasionally overtake us or be, for the time being, the most convenient mode of expressing ourselves. If we are not all there to ourselves, still less are we all there to others, presenting to the other every disparate particle of our consciousness, as it were, as fixed and artificially moulded as a 'character' in fiction or biography.

This series of rough and ready perceptions about human character, however, cannot quench our natural interest in the lives of those around us. For investigative purposes, we do carry around a rudimentary idea of what certain people are like. This is not because we think that Dickens in his crudest caricatures was nearer to the truth about human nature than masters of the ambiguous like Proust and Henry James. Rather, it is because, if human intercourse is to continue at all, we have to start somewhere and these ideas of other people which we carry about in our heads have some of the serviceability of maps. We know that the red line isn't a road, that the splodge of brown isn't a range of hills. We know the limits of the map's usability but we would rather have it in our pockets when out walking than leave it at home.

My ideas about Felicity, partly because I had lived with her at such close quarters for so long, were of this simple, maplike kind. I do not think they were all wrong, any more than her unsympathetic vision of myself, however little it took account of my inner life, could be dismissed as bearing no relation to the figure I cut in the day-to-day life of the Rectory.

Making my way back to England after a month at Les Mouettes, I knew that I was a quite different person. It vexed me that I should soon be treated as the self I had outgrown and discarded. I also feared that this vexation itself would turn me back into the figure that Uncle Roy and Felicity had (as it seemed at the time) somehow forced me into being.

I attributed my changed personality not to the obviously civilising influence of Madame de Normandin, but to my visits to the beach hut with Barbara. It was therefore quite out of the question that I could *announce* that I was a different person, even if it were possible without awkwardness to say anything so weird.

In fact, though I lecherously savoured my experiences on the little *plage* as I remembered them in the train, their memory was already dim by the time I pulled out of Liverpool Street. As far as memory goes, sex is not different from anything else. A few episodes, not necessarily those which appeared remarkable at the time, form arbitrary tableaux in the mind. For the rest, one is aware that such and such a thing took place, but it is only as it were as a third person narrative in one's brain that one believes in it. The reality of the thing itself fades into insignificance. This is as true of Eros as it is of meals, conversations, places and nearly all the people we ever meet. That, incidentally, is another reason for viewing with enormous distrust the archaeological endeavours of men like Hunter. In actual lives – lives, that is to say, which are lived rather than constructed by biographers – the past recedes and becomes a barely noticeable haze in the background. Things which seemed important in one particular week are shown, by the mere fact of their being forgotten, to be ultimately insignificant. Faces drift in and out of focus. The effect of a biography such as Hunter's *magnum opus* is to paint all these scenes and figures in the same tones. The mountains twenty miles away are as strongly coloured as the sitter's gown in the foreground. Everything, by virtue of being printed on the page in the same typeface, is given the same weight – friendships of enduring importance, encounters which strictly speaking made no imaginative impact at all, social chit-chat scribbled on a postcard, hasty judgements of another person scribbled in a secret diary. In Hunter's defence it has to be said that this method of composition, denying what the painters call aerial perspective and hurling all the material at the reader with no sense of its unimportance, may in its own clumsy fashion be less distorting than some right-minded attempt to view a human life 'seriously'; for then the criterion of selection sets the focus and the picture becomes like one of those strange productions of artistic photographers where everything in the foreground is out of focus and all attention is fixed on some small detail in the middle distance. In the case of a poet's life, for example, the earnest chronicler might wish to single out from the correspondence or journals of the subject only those details which were of a piece with his perhaps modest verse productions; whereas a truer picture might have been that the poetry only ever came from a small part of the individual concerned and that for most of the time, most of the personality was dominated by domestic trivia or alcohol.

But while, as I have said, such adjustments and allowances are made on our own behalf without thinking, it is an almost impossible leap of the imagination to make them for other people. In the train back to Norwich, I glowed with the knowledge of how different I had become in France. Why, the very words in my head were different: I was even dreaming in the strange, bilingual language which I had adopted from my kind old hostess. But although I had witnessed this change in myself, I had not realised that change is a condition of human life which applies to other people as well. I assumed that when I got back to the Rectory it would be a different me meeting the same old them, as though Uncle Roy, Aunt Deirdre and Felicity were as unchanging as the surpliced wooden figures carved on the beam ends of the parish church. How untrue this was, I had all the evidence of my senses to tell me. Felicity, in particular, had been many different persons in the time that I had been living with her. The wholly silent, probably disapproving adolescent turned into the homesick undergraduate in her first year at Girton.

'She's spoken more on the telephone this week than in the whole of her last year at home,' Aunt Deirdre remarked at the time.

And then Felicity had settled down at Cambridge. The fact that she had made several friends suggested a diversity of sympathy not always apparent, nor looked for, in the circle of the family. Nevertheless, the word 'Felicity' still conjured up for me something lumpish and static, and I was in the habit, hard to shake, of selecting only such details about her life as corresponded with the pre-existent caricature of her formed in my brain.

Thus, although there was nothing particularly funny about Felicity's friends, to my mind they were all exquisitely ridiculous, the mere fact of their having chosen to spend time in Felicity's company being enough to suggest that they were at best undiscriminating, at worst desperate for society, even a little crazy. Other girls went to dances and nobody laughed. The fact that Graham had taken Felicity to a May ball wrote him down (as far as I was concerned) as a figure of pure comedy. Photographs of the occasion proved that Felicity looked rather sweet, with a tightly waisted evening dress worn off the shoulders. Felicity was neither plain nor a frump, even though I chose to believe that she was both. The photographic evidence that she had shapely arms, shoulders and breasts made no impression on me at all. When I looked at the picture of her in her ball gown, I just imagined her delicately mottled skin turning to gooseflesh in the wet evening air. I seem to remember wondering, too, whether she had been able to abandon the sandals and ankle socks which at that date were her daily wear and which, for some reason, I found particularly annoying.

This belief, that Felicity was a frump, a joke, an irritant, had allowed me to reach the age of sixteen without ever considering that Felicity had emotions comparable with my own, emotions which had to be taken seriously. Therefore when Aunt Deirdre, having met me at the station at Norwich, broke the news about Felicity, I burst out laughing. It was the inevitable, the only, reaction.

My aunt was at the wheel of the Trojan as we chuntered out of town on the Newmarket Road. During my absence, she had rather severely cropped her hair so that in her simple open-necked white blouse she more than ever resembled a slightly overweight Boy Scout. For the ten minutes or so that it had taken her to negotiate her way out of the station car park and queue at the traffic lights, she had been giving me a rundown of things which had happened in my absence. A Mr Hunter had been up at the Place going through boxes of Jimbo's letters and papers – or as many as Sargie had let him see. Mr Hunter said that there was so much interesting material that they really ought to have a full-scale biography of Jimbo, but Sargie was not sure. He had asked Uncle Roy's advice, who thought there should be a book not just about Jimbo but about all the Lampitts – a history of the family. Sargie had tried this one on Mr Hunter and it had not gone down so well. Oh, and the carpet sweeper at the Rectory finally gave out, but mercifully Mrs Grocott was going to let Aunt Deirdre have hers secondhand because Dr Grocott was buying her a new vacuum cleaner, lucky thing. Uncle Roy – a great event – had got his smart, new summer suit from the tailor. Oh, and that wretched woman *said* she had written a novel, but people did not know whether to believe her and no publisher in their right mind would buy it.

'She was bragging about it in the post office yesterday when poor old Mr Jameson – you know, from the cottages – was standing there waiting for his pension.'

'Do you think we'll all be in the novel?' I asked.

'Shouldn't be surprised. Bet I'm the murderer!'

My aunt always spoke as if every novel contained a murder, which was true in the case of the ones she read.

For the moment I was more interested in the work that was

going on at the Place: the sorting of Jimbo Lampitt's papers. Even more, I wanted to know what Hunter was really like. I still minded terribly about Miss Beach. I think in a way I still do. But I can't pretend that I am still in love with her, whereas, a mere four years after I had seen Hunter's silky hands caressing her back, I think I was still then in love with Miss Beach, a fact which Barbara and France had really done nothing to dispel.

'You know, Granny and I once saw Mr Hunter in Worcester,' I said. 'Having lunch in Bobby's with one of the school matrons.'

'The Mr Hunter who's working on the papers?'

'Yes.'

'How did you know it was him?'

'I didn't. But when he came to give a talk to the Lampitt Society last term I recognised him.'

This version of events was one which I found it easier to give than the truth. Miss Beach was not a subject to bring up with my aunt.

'Extraordinary things you do remember. Actually,' she added, going very red and putting on a poor show of nonchalance, 'something rather exciting has happened with your Mr Hunter.'

'Oh?'

'Don't say I mentioned it – in fact, don't talk about it at all, certainly not to Felicity.'

'Don't mention *what* to Felicity?'

'You see, we think she's developed a bit of a pash on Mr Hunter.'

And it was at this point that I ungallantly roared with laughter.

'You're *not* to tease her about it, Julian, you really mustn't. It's . . .'

But my aunt changed gear and stared ahead at the great Norfolk sky, unable to say, quite, what 'it' was. Had she ever felt 'it' herself, this most extraordinary feeling? During my teens it was unimaginable to me that Aunt Deirdre and Uncle Roy had ever been in love. The very language they used about it – they talked of people being keen on one another, or having pashes – seemed to rule out the possibility of their having any experience of the phenomenon themselves. I did not realise that brisk talk could very readily betoken not ignorance but a whole range of sadder, subtler things: the disappointment of passion fading into the fuddy-duddy boringness and mutual dislike of a middle-aged marriage or, quite simply, the embarrassment which sensible people quite often feel when they look back on themselves in love.

When we got back to the Rectory it was time for luncheon. Spam, beetroot and cold potatoes were in readiness. We ate them, just the three of us, Uncle Roy, Aunt Deirdre and I. Felicity was out.

'You've told him . . .' my uncle ventured.

'Something may come of it, who knows, but we aren't saying a *thing*,' was Aunt Deirdre's reply.

Since, in general, their policy was to treat everything as classified information, I was not surprised that the Felicity–Hunter thing was being kept so firmly under wraps. I wondered how successful they were being in keeping the liaison from the village.

'You're wrong to think I'd joke about it,' I said, by way of an announcement that, since going to France, I had changed.

Getting the message, Uncle Roy merely raised sceptical eyebrows.

'London must have been packed.'

'It was rather.'

'All those *people*! And going to the Festival thingummy!' He raised both hands with a gesture identical to the one he used for praying at the eucharistic altar. 'They must be *barmy*!'

'Quite mad,' said my aunt, firmly dissecting a baby beetroot and putting half in her mouth. She munched crossly, with sharp little movements of the jaw which looked as though they were designed to teach the beetroot some sort of lesson.

The possibility of seeing the Festival of Britain Exhibition at Battersea had crossed my mind some time before the boat train pulled into Victoria. Most of the tourists with whom I was travelling were talking of it. I still wanted to see it. My uncle's and aunt's shared conviction that anyone who wanted to see it (or indeed go anywhere, do anything) must be insane only quickened my wish. But I was 'good' and suppressed any word of dissent from the Rectory line. Of course anyone who wanted to see the most exciting exhibition held in London for a hundred years was off their heads.

'Needless to say,' said my aunt, who had taken a sip of water to swill the chastened beetroot on its passage, 'that wretched Maddock woman took her children. She will call them kids.'

'Well,' said Uncle Roy with a smile. And then, before allowing the witticism to fall from his delicate lips, he dabbed them gently with his napkin. 'We all know that kids are the offspring of nanny-goats.'

It was not the first time he had given utterance to this particular drollerie, but it made my aunt whoop with almost savage amusement.

'We were all delayed for a good ten minutes in the shop the other week when she gave Mrs Beynon – you know, Jill – a blow-by-blow account of how they got to Liverpool Street and how they got to Battersea. And she will call Mrs Beynon Jill.'

My aunt called Mrs Beynon Jill but this was different.

'You could see,' she continued, 'that everyone thought her a complete fool for taking the twins at their age.'

'I should think it would make very little impression,' said Uncle Roy. 'Babies remember nothing. I was two or three before I started to have memories.'

'The twins are five,' said my aunt.

'Even so,' said Uncle Roy.

'Oh, quite' – for this was a moment of Rectory solidarity against the Wretched Woman, rather than an occasion for marital point-scoring – 'and think of the crowds. Think of two five-year-olds getting lost! And of course there are always funny people about in a crowded place, not to mention all the bugs you are bound to pick up.'

'To my recollection those children have never been baptised,' said my uncle, who seemed quite unconcerned to have got their ages wrong. Six months, five years, what was the difference in a mere non-Lampitt?

'And then she said in that "ee bah gum" voice of hers,' and here my aunt adopted her prissy 'imitations' voice which was not in the least 'ee bah gum', ' "Oh, Jill, there's a village post office and stores in my novel but you mustn't think it's *all* based on yours." As if,' continued my aunt in her normal voice, 'anyone would want to read it.'

'Oh, I want to read it,' I confessed. 'What's the title?'

'They do say that it is all about people in the village,' said my uncle. 'But I expect it's mainly about . . .' The hands went up again in a gesture of prayer. The sentence was obviously unfinishable by lips which could not mention sex or any other kind of marital intrigue.

'There've been tremendous dramas on that front while you've been away,' said my aunt; and I wondered whether she would have gone so far before my holiday. Perhaps she sensed that going to France had been emotionally educative.

'The husband always seemed very pleasant whenever I met him,' said Uncle Roy.

'You speak of him in the past tense,' I remarked.

'He was the one who gave you all those books for the fête the year before last,' said Aunt Deirdre, playing for time.

'Not all of them suitable,' added Uncle Roy.

'He may come back anyway,' said my aunt. 'People in the village are saying they don't blame him, but of course we can't take that line so we just say nothing.'

'What's Mr Maddock supposed to have done?' I asked.

It was foolish of me to think they'd say. They all found out about three years later anyhow when her first novel, *The Melon Garden*, reached the mobile library van.

'Catching up on all the gossip since you went away?' said Felicity's voice behind my head.

I turned, and there she was. I hardly recognised her. She looked – beautiful! Really! She had lost some weight, but it wasn't just that. Her face glowed with an almost ethereal joy.

'You've done something to your hair,' I said.

'Isn't it good?' said Aunt Deirdre. 'Now, darling, lunch is here if you want it – we started without you because we thought you might not be home.'

'Oh, I'm exhausted!' she exclaimed. 'Raphael and I have been through fifteen trunkfuls of stuff this morning. Imagine! No, I shan't eat here, thanks, Ma. I've left him down at the White Hart and said I'll go back and join him there. I just nipped home to say he'd love to come to tea this afternoon.'

'Oh, *terrific*!' said her mother.

'So,' said Felicity turning to me, 'what was France like?'

I made some reply or other but she wasn't interested. She was in a daze of happiness, almost mad with it. I don't think I had ever seen her happy before. Not *really* happy. There were moments like when she got her first and she said she was 'chuffed'. Chuffedness and happiness were visibly different. It was almost frightening.

'Raphael says not to make anything special for tea because he's got to have dinner with Sargie,' said Felicity.

'Yes, but he's got to eat.'

'I've hardly seen Sargie since Mr Hunter arrived,' said my uncle in a funny sort of tone.

'Yes,' said my aunt with assumed gaiety, 'we see your uncle much more often now Mr Hunter's around.'

When Felicity had trotted out again like an excited child to meet its first playmate, there was an embarrassed sort of pause. It was broken by Uncle Roy.

'Sargie says he can't find out anything about Mr Hunter's people.'

'Did you know he was with Jimbo on the day he died?' I asked.

'Mr Hunter?'

'He gave this talk to us at school.'

'It doesn't sound quite suitable,' said Aunt Deirdre.

'It baffles Sargie. Apparently Jimbo never mentioned this young man to anyone and yet Mr Hunter speaks as if he and Petworth, as he will keep on calling him, were the best of friends. And yes he was with Jimbo when he died.'

'You never said that before!' Aunt Deirdre shot him an accusing glance.

'You didn't ask.' The putdown was smiling, smug. 'No, Mr Hunter was a witness at the inquest. There is no secret about *that*. The funny thing is that *no one* seems to have heard of him before. Sibs had never heard of him and she saw Jimbo most *days* by the end.'

'You see why we aren't entirely happy?' my aunt said to me.

I felt as you did at school when the teacher finished explaining something and you realised that you hadn't been paying attention for the crucial part of the lesson. Only, on this occasion, I had been paying close attention to what they had been saying about Hunter and still their message, if there was one, had eluded me. They were obviously worried in a general way that Felicity had fallen in with – not to say fallen in love with – a mystery man whom no one knew anything about. But I felt vaguely at the time and much more sharply now that they had a specific worry: one which in Rectory terms was entirely unmentionable. If it was the worry I now think it was, I rather admire their prescience. It never crossed my mind at the time.

Not long after four o'clock, Hunter and Felicity appeared, openly holding hands as they walked up the drive in the sunshine. Felicity was staring at Hunter with an expression which made me see why schoolboys and others said love was 'soppy'. At the same time there was something moving about the pair of them, even though I now believe that, had I known more, I should have seen something spurious in Hunter's smile. With my uncle and aunt, he was all charm. I think the secret of this, which did not occur to me at the time because it was too staringly obvious, was that he genuinely found them charming themselves. It had never occurred to me that anyone, still less anyone from the outside world, would actually *like* my uncle and aunt. But then I had very little experience of seeing them together with strangers.

Neither of them was in the least used to entertaining. 'Village people' came to a garden party once a year. Sargie very occasionally staggered in and out of the house but he seldom ate with us. For the rest, the only regular visitors to the Rectory were old school friends of my aunt's, such as Bunty, and their visits were few and far between.

Even without the drama of Felicity's pash, therefore, Hunter's visit would have been something of an event. My uncle had been upstairs to change several times before the young man's arrival, wondering what gear would be suitable for tea with a possible son-in-law. A whole range of clobber had been got out of the wardrobe, ranging from his cassock, which my aunt very properly shouted at him to remove, to the bright green Harris tweed golfing trousers. A compromise was reached when he finally settled for the jacket which went with these controversial items of clothing and a pair of grey flannel trousers.

It was evident, when we were all in our places, with plates on our knees in the drawing room, that Uncle Roy did not trust his wife to keep us properly nourished.

'See if Mr Hunter would like more tea,' he said sharply at several moments.

In spite of Mr Hunter's 'I'm quite all right really,' Uncle Roy kept jumping up to peer at the contents of his guest's cup with a curiosity which would have been excessive if water lilies had begun to sprout on its surface. Similarly, Hunter had no sooner put the last of a biscuit or a sandwich or a piece of cake in his mouth than my uncle and aunt would leap up and vie with each other to make him eat more. Radishes, spring onions, a freshly baked Victoria sponge were all on offer and there was the implication that offence would be taken if he did not sample some of everything.

'Please, Ma, I *told* you Raphael's having dinner tonight,' said Felicity.

Hunter thrived on all the attention and ate obediently. Even more than this – for anyone, after all, can eat a cress sandwich – he displayed a masterly ability to parry any enquiry concerning his background, family, avocation, or present mode of employment. I suppose that my uncle and aunt chiefly wanted to find out whether Hunter was rich, and whether there was madness in his family, but they skirted round both subjects with what must have seemed to them like subtlety.

'I suppose this interest of yours in Mr Lampitt's documents is all part of your work,' said Aunt Deirdre.

'I'm hoping to make it so,' said Hunter.

'Is it what they call research? I'm hazy about these things.'

'That's more science,' said my uncle hastily trying to cover up what he took to be a gaffe by his wife.

Hunter, however, conceded that research was one word for it.

'I think we've all tended to get Petworth Lampitt quite wrong,' he drawled. I knew the line. But my uncle, who had not had the benefit of having heard Hunter's talk to the Lampitt Society, picked up the wrong end of the stick with alacrity.

'I agree with you there!' He filled his pipe and fiddled with matches. He looked at last as if he would stop offering Hunter things to eat and settle down to some really good talk. 'What fools they'll all look, the moderns, in a few years' time.'

Hunter's face did not betray any pleasure at the moderns, whoever they were, being made to look fools. He moved his head from side to side like a stage Frenchman.

'Sargie always maintains that Jimbo is one of our great *stylists*,' said Uncle Roy. 'Mind you, Sargie himself is a very good writer. Did you ever read his book about the House of Lords?'

Hunter smiled. 'I'm afraid . . .'

'Lady Starling – his sister.' There was a faintly interrogatory tone when my uncle supplied this gloss; it really was scarcely conceivable that anyone should not know who Lady Starling was, but he wanted to be sure.

'Rather a severe lady?' asked Hunter.

'Severe! Sibs?' Uncle Roy laughed indulgently. 'She is famous in the family for being a complete doormat.'

'I only met her briefly at Petworth's funeral.'

'Anyway, Lady Starling says that Mr Sargent – Sargie, that is – is almost a revolutionary. A good example of her famous overstatements. Really, I could write a book about the Lampitts. Wonderful lot. Sibs is married, as you know, to Sir Rupert Starling. Working in the Treasury as he does, he is bound to take an equivocal line about some of Sargie's theories. I'm not really sure what line Sargie *does* take these days about reforming the Upper House.'

'I'm sure Mr Hunter thinks the moderns . . .' My aunt was trying to clear up what she saw was a failure of understanding on both sides, but my uncle shut her up, rather crossly.

'He was just hearing about Sibs. As I say, Lady Starling lets people walk all over her. An extraordinarily sweet person. She lives,' he added with the unspoken implication that this made her even sweeter, 'in Cadogan Square.'

My aunt, determined not to be frustrated in her pursuit of the particular, changed tack and decided that she might at least get some clue as to Hunter's address.

'Do you live near Cadogan Square, Mr Hunter?'

'Not really. But with undergrounds, buses and things – one gets about.'

'Of course. I just wondered with your work – I mean, whether you had to live . . .'

It was five o'clock and still my aunt had been unable to persuade Hunter to admit that he lived anywhere or did anything.

'It's such a frightful bore getting about in London, don't you find?' she said in despair. 'And with this Festival!'

I guessed that Hunter admired the Festival and all it stood for, but he was hedging his bets. He began a sentence and left it tactfully in the air, to be finished by anyone who chose.

'Isn't it . . . ?'

'I want to go,' said Felicity earnestly.

'Darling, think of the crowds!' said her mother.

'Would you have missed the Great Exhibition of 1851, Pa?'

It was a good question. Uncle Roy's pipe was now alight and he allowed himself the luxury of a quotation.

' "From Timbuctoo and Tooting Bec they came, from the Lancashire mills and the villas of Lahore . . ." '

Hunter looked quite blank.

'Surely you remember that bit?' asked my uncle.

I did. It was one of the best set-pieces in *Prince Albert*. It was said that Yeats had considered including it in the *Oxford Book of Modern Verse*, as he had done Pater's passage of purple prose about the Mona Lisa.

'Marvellous stuff,' said my uncle.

'And yet,' said Hunter, 'I think we shall find that Petworth's importance lay less in the books than in the *man*. In fact, I think we shall find that Petworth's true significance only emerges when we have been through all that mountain of stuff at Timplingham Place.'

Like Mrs Maddock, Hunter pronounced the name as it was spelt, rather than 'Timming'em'. He took Felicity's hand and stared into her eyes as he spoke. His desire to get his hands on the papers sounded like a love-song to her, which perhaps in its way it was. Without her help he would not be able to see any of it. Sargie had made that clear from the outset.

'It isn't always wise to rake over the past like that,' said Aunt Deirdre. 'I mean, in your case, you'll behave responsibly. But one does sometimes feel, "Let Sleeping Dogs Lie".'

'Oh quite,' said Hunter, with a very mysterious smile indeed.

As he sat there, young, handsome, refusing a piece of cake, he might, for all they knew about him, have been an angel whom they were entertaining unawares.

The silence which ensued allowed Aunt Deirdre to put a direct question.

'Were you at Cambridge too, Mr Hunter?'

'Cambridge as well as . . . ?' He leaned forward, seeming anxious to get the meaning of my aunt's enquiry absolutely straight.

'As well as Felicity. I thought perhaps . . . I mean, it would be nice.'

Everyone blushed at this for some reason.

Felicity, through her teeth, said, *'Ma!'*

'No,' said Hunter, 'I wasn't at Cambridge.'

'I'm an Oxford man, too,' said my uncle, warming to his young friend. 'Exeter was my college. Which was yours?'

'Sorry,' said Hunter, 'I misunderstood. I didn't in fact go to a university.'

'Oh!' My uncle looked astonished. He could not have looked more surprised if Hunter had confessed to never cleaning his teeth.

'It must have been difficult to get . . . well, to become a . . .' My aunt stared at Hunter. Become a what? Surely he would help her out now? What was he, or what did he hope to become?

I was still innocent enough to suppose that everyone eventually became something. I did not realise that most lives flit by before the person, strictly speaking, has become anything. But, even at this unformed level of understanding, I think I was beginning to guess that Hunter intended to become something and that he had seen in the unlikely quarry of the Lampitt Papers the means towards his mysterious end. Given the extraordinarily unpromising nature of his material – an outmoded author whom he did not even admire, a bundle of 'stuff' which was almost surely rubbish, Sargie and his 'impossible' temperament – there was a touch of genius in all this.

Seeing that the others were getting nowhere in their attempts to pluck out Hunter's mystery, I decided to play a certain card.

'You and I were both at Seaforth Grange. Do you remember, we talked about it when you came down to address the Lampitt Club.'

'That's right,' he said with a smile. I could write a whole book on the way that Hunter has smiled at me. His smiles were different with different people. When directed at me, there was always the implication that I was taking the mickey out of him, but that he was indulgent enough to put up with the tease.

'Have you seen Robbie lately?' he asked. 'I'm sorry to say that Margot has not been at all well – phlebitis in her left leg.'

'How awful,' said my aunt. 'Who are we talking about?'

'The Larmers,' said Hunter softly. 'You know, from Seaforth Grange.'

I could not believe my ears. That a human being, someone who could smile and eat cake and hold hands with girls, was prepared to be on terms with the Binker and his wife was astonishing enough. Yet weirder was referring to the Binker as Robbie, as though he actually liked the man. But to be sorry when Mrs Binker was in pain; this was going too far.

'I try to see them whenever I go back to visit my parents in Malvern,' said Hunter. 'A wonderful pair. Such a shame in a way that they did not have children; and yet, as Margot is always saying, the school is their family. We're all their children in a way, aren't we, Julian?'

The truth was that any child born to the Binkers would, in a decent society, have been taken away immediately and put into the hands of the state. The thought that, by their system of tyranny, persecution and sexual perversion, the Binkers were models of how good parents should behave beggared belief. It silenced me.

'I don't think Julian got on awfully well with Mr Larmer, did you, old thing?' asked my aunt.

'Ah,' said Hunter. Once more, the indulgent smile to conciliate a difficult customer. 'A pity. Most Old Grangers retain quite an affection for Robbie. He was a great friend of both my parents before I ever went to the school.'

'What does your father *do* in Malvern?' A match point, to judge from her expression of triumph. But Hunter lobbed it back across the net with nonchalance.

'My father's retired. He has been for a very long time.'

But it wasn't singles. It was mixed doubles.

'What *did* he do?' asked my uncle. That surely won them the match?

Not so. Felicity, waiting by the net, slammed her father's ball back into the other court.

'What on earth does it matter what people's fathers do?' she asked crossly. 'Anyway, we're off now. We thought we'd have another hour with the boxes before Raphael changes for dinner.'

The mystery of what Hunter *père* did for a living was never revealed. Years afterwards, someone told me that he had been something big in chocolate. I don't know if that was true.

For the next couple of weeks, Felicity and Hunter continued to work together on the Lampitt Papers. I did not see much more of them together but, from her absences, it was safe to infer that Felicity was getting deeper and deeper *in* to whatever it was she and Hunter were in together. Her parents began to speak openly about the possibility that she and Hunter might get married. Then, from something Sargie had said to Uncle Roy, the imminent announcement of their engagement seemed certain.

I don't know exactly what he'd said to Uncle Roy, but it was a prediction to the effect that we should be hearing wedding bells before long; and, since the prediction fell from the lips of a Lampitt, we all took it as infallible. I even began to wonder what it would be like when Hunter was – as I thought of it – a member of the family.

But this was not to be.

One morning, Sargie appeared at the Rectory. On his sporadic visits to my uncle's house, he never bothered to ring the doorbell. He always walked into the front hall and yelled 'Roy!' in the tone other people would reserve for addressing dogs.

'That's Sargie,' said Uncle Roy, putting down his porringer.

It being the hour of breakfast, he was still wearing his cassock and bands, having come over to the house directly from church. He hurtled to his Master's call and the rest of us – Felicity, Aunt Deirdre, me – sat in the kitchen and heard the two men talking.

'I've told you. Just buggered off.'

'But he'll be back.'

'Didn't say so.'

'He can't just have *gone*,' said Uncle Roy.

'It doesn't worry me. I'm in two minds about his nosing through all Jimbo's things and I think the idea of writing a biography of Jimbo is simply crackers. Told him so. No, the worst of it all is, he'd promised to drive me into Norwich this morning, and now he isn't here . . . '

'I can always drive you.'

'Could you, my dear? It would help.'

Realising from this exchange that Hunter was being discussed, Felicity jumped to her feet. Now it was just Aunt Deirdre and I, sitting alone in the kitchen and listening to the three voices echoing tragically round the hall.

'Raphael's not gone away today, surely?' Felicity's voice.

'That's why I came round, darling girl.'

'But he'll be back? When did he say he'd be back?' Felicity sounded not so much angry or incredulous as frightened.

An expression of tenderness came into Sargie's voice as he said, 'He did ask me to come and tell you that he was going.'

'But we haven't nearly finished the work on the papers and he never said anything to me. He wouldn't just go off and *leave* like that.'

By now Aunt Deirdre and I had come out to join the party, and we all stood round Felicity in a circle.

'Oh, there's no need for you all to *stare!*' she exclaimed. Making a poor concealment of her distress, she hurried upstairs.

'Oh dear,' said Aunt Deirdre.

'He'll be back, you see,' said Uncle Roy. 'They probably had a very slight tiff.'

'That's what I came to say, my dear.' There was a look of real sorrow in Sargie's long, lugubrious face. 'He may come back, but something tells me it won't be soon.'

Aunt Deirdre and Uncle Roy both spoke at once. He said, 'But Felicity and he were more or less . . .' And she said, 'Oh, this is the *limit!*'

Sargie shrugged. How much he had been taken into Hunter's confidence, it was impossible to say. How much, indeed, was there to confide?

'It puts *me* in the most frightful spot.'

'*You*, Sargie? Oh, *really* – what about poor Felicity?'

'You see, he's made me promise not to give the poor girl his address for the next six months. And I am her godfather.'

Hunter's departure had an appalling effect on Felicity. The simple way of describing it would be to say that she went back to the beginning and became as morose and taciturn as she had been at the age of fourteen. But whereas her former silences were just grumpy and annoying, there was now something definitely tragic about her. She was hugging to herself an awful, private grief.

'He'll be back – I'm sure he'll be back,' said her father.

'Oh, you just don't *understand.*'

She did not eat. She had endless baths. By the look of her, she did not seem to be sleeping.

'Are you quite sure you're OK, old thing?' asked her mother on Felicity's last morning at home. 'I'm sure you shouldn't be going back to Cambridge on your own.'

It was obvious that Felicity was the reverse of OK, but her unhappiness was so terrible, so heartbreaking to witness, that I guessed that her parents almost welcomed her departure. Some days later, I myself went back to boarding school.

Aunt Deirdre said, 'We should never have let her go.'

This remark was made some months later, towards the end of

October. When she said it, Uncle Roy looked more pained and sheepish than I have ever seen a man look. I was home for half-term, when we had a week off school. By then, the Felicity drama, which had begun for me as a farce when I had roared with laughter at the very idea of her being in love, had plunged into tragedy and sordidity.

Felicity was home again but staying in bed all the time. I had absolutely no idea what was wrong with her. Given her parents' habitual policy of treating everything as a secret, their silence in the matter did not strike me as particularly suspicious. They would have been just as 'hush-hush' about a minor gastric upset or a bout of 'flu and enjoined me not to mention it in the village.

Even so, on this occasion, they were pretty pressing about the need for discretion.

'You're not to mention Felicity is in the house. Not to anyone in the village,' said my aunt.

'We're not even telling your Uncle Sargie. It would only upset him,' said Uncle Roy.

'It's rather upset *us*,' snapped my aunt. She clearly thought this was no moment to be considering Sargie's feelings. 'It's upset poor old Fliss.'

This childhood abbreviation of Felicity's name was hardly ever used now. It betokened a feeling of great tenderness in my aunt. But still I did not twig what was going on.

'It's not catching, is it, what Felicity's got?'

'Well . . .' My uncle seemed doubtful.

'Only I've got the lead role in the school play this term and I don't want to . . .'

'Of course you can go in and see her,' said Aunt Deirdre. 'But be gentle. She's not up to much.'

Just before I put my head round her bedroom door, it occurred to me that something really awful might have happened to her – like having burns all over her face. That was just the sort of thing her parents would not be able to bring themselves to mention.

But she looked reasonably normal. The flushed ethereal beauty which had momentarily possessed her when she believed herself to be loved by Hunter had vanished. She had gone back to being slightly plain and now, for the first time, she was inclining to be scrawny. All the pudge which she used to share with her mother had gone. Her skin was waxy and shone in the gloom of her bedroom. The dark rings under her eyes looked like becoming a permanent feature. She was flopped against the pillows. In one hand there was a *Daily Telegraph* but she was not reading it.

'I wondered if there was anything you needed?' I began gingerly.

Felicity's face made it obvious, even to a sixteen-year-old cousin, that there were many things she needed – things like love, different parents, a happy temperament: all things I was helpless to supply.

'Hallo,' she said, slightly as if there was a shared joke between us. 'What's happening outside?'

'Nothing much.'

There was an achingly long pause.

'I've hurt them so much, Ma and Pa. I mean, apart from all the pain it's caused me, I don't think they'll ever recover.' She spoke slowly, bleakly.

'They're just worried – hoping you'll soon be better.'

She opened her eyes very wide at the idiocy, the sheer ignorance, displayed by this remark.

'I'll never really get over this.'

'Nonsense. You will.'

'I just feel . . .' She looked away.

'What?'

'Oh, it doesn't matter any more what I feel.'

Years later, Felicity herself told me that she had been found by a fellow graduate student in her lodgings in Cambridge. She had been bleeding badly and was rushed at once to Addenbrookes Hospital. A week or so later, she was rescued by her parents. She had tried to keep it all from them, but the college had found out. They had behaved humanely. At that period, they could so easily have dismissed her from the college and brought her academic career to an end.

'The Principal's been very good. They're letting me stay – Ma told you that?'

Since at that time I was unable to guess why my cousin had been taken ill, I was equally unable to guess why the college authorities should have been anything but 'good'. I did not realise that Felicity had broken the law of the land.

When one takes into account how inward and shy Felicity was, how she needed to summon up reserves of bravery to ask for a cup of tea in a café or a ticket from a railway booking clerk, it is almost unimaginable how she was brave enough to procure this treatment for herself. Just saying the words would have been an achievement of extraordinary courage. Having sold her few War Loan bonds and cleared out her account at the post office, she had obviously been able, just, to get the services of some low-level incompetent. She never revealed to me how this person, who lived in London, had been introduced to her.

At sixteen, I hardly knew what an abortion was. Knitting needles and back kitchens were something boys did not talk about at a boarding school. For almost all of us, sex was a thing of pure fantasy. Its realities and consequences never had to be dwelt upon. I am fairly sure that, after my summer with Barbara, I was the only boy in my house who had even the most rudimentary experience with a girl.

I think that, at some stage of our awkward little conversation, Felicity realised that I was completely ignorant of her reasons for being in bed.

'What about you, anyway?' she said.

'School's awful except for the drama.'

'What's that Mr Treadmill putting on this time?'

'It's a play by John Ford.'

'Oh yes?'

All at once, it was I who became shy.

'Hope you've got a good part,' she said.

'The lead.'

I laughed nervously. I hoped she was not going to press me to say the title of the play. She lay there looking so terrible; it was as if the Hunter experience had tortured her physically, as well as in spirit.

'You do the obscurest plays,' she said. 'What was it last time? *Ralph Roister* something?'

'Treadmill says this one's tremendously hackneyed but it's a wonderful play with great poetry,' I said.

'Oh, *Hamlet*?' There was almost sprightliness in her voice as she made the suggestion.

'No,' I said, '*The Broken Heart*.'

Six

It seems as if it is going on for ever, childhood. Then, like a bad dream, it is over. With the arrival of morning, you lie there. All the monstrousness which has possessed your mind during the hours of darkness is stilled and tamed. Whatever horrors the coming day will bring, there will be nothing so garish, nothing so raw. This is not because life's external events get better as the years pass; nor, conversely, because the outward events of childhood are necessarily miserable. It is because the dreamlike self-concern and self-absorption of childhood can never be recaptured during adulthood except in cases of extreme mental disturbance. Henceforward, other people and events not directly relevant to oneself take on sharper outlines.

Belonging to my own particular generation, I had a last staging post to serve in the English Gulag: two years of National Service. No one ever supposed it pleasant. But it was far worse for the boys who had enjoyed 'normal' childhoods, with parents, homes and all. Most of the men I met during my basic training had never slept a night away from their mother's house. For me, the discomfort of army life, the rudeness of the NCOs, the pointless discipline, the blancoing of things which did not need to be white, the hurrying to do in five minutes things which could easily have taken an hour (if they were worth doing at all), were all just an extension of the insane patterns of life which had begun when I first met the Binker.

At school, it was hard not to fall for the con trick that it actually mattered whether you did 'well' or 'badly'. By the system of marks, exams, reports and so forth, it was instilled into us that if we did not do 'well' at school we would not do 'well' when we left. The army, transparently, was not like that. I had no wish to become a professional soldier. I decided just to get by. The system was designed to break young men, but I had been broken years before beyond hope of repair. I joined the Norfolk

Regiment and did my basic training somewhere near North-ampton. The huge sprawling camp was a sort of hell: hundreds of Nissen huts stretched line upon line in a bleak bit of hunting country, where it never stopped drizzling for six weeks and where the sergeant-majors never stopped shouting their idiot instructions. At the earliest possible opportunity I renounced my status as a potential officer and took the slithery course of not-really-trying. This was a mistake since, in the army (perhaps in other areas, too?), not-really-trying is just as much effort as trying-really-hard. The only difference between the two modes of activity is that not-really-trying receives no reward. After a while, it gets depressing, too – but then so does just about everything. Shoddy equipment. Lazy drill. It was not long before the RSM announced in front of all the others that I was a 'nasty-lowdown-piece-of-shit-what-did-I-say-that-you-are?'

One of my greatest good fortunes in life, never having made up my mind what sort of person I am, is that I am usually ready to go along with other people's opinions of me. Not because I think they are necessarily right, but because in any area so nebulous as psychological portraiture one person's guess is likely to be as good as another's; or, if not, anyway of interest. The willingness with which I accepted the sergeant-major's assessment of my personal character was written down as insubordination. You couldn't win.

But there was far more leave from the army than you got from school. We had every weekend off during the six weeks of basic training. I returned regularly and thankfully to the Rectory at Timplingham, refreshed above everything else (though it sounds a ridiculously priggish thing to say) by the fact that my uncle and aunt were not in the habit of swearing. The unimaginative use of bad language in every sentence by just about everyone I met in the army had a tremendously lowering effect on the spirits.

'Martin – my cousin who fought at Ypres – said the worst thing about the trenches was the way the men peed in their boots,' said Sargie, fairly far gone on dry martinis. Uncle Roy and I were lunching at the Place and Sargie's sister was there, Sibs Starling.

She was a surprisingly tall woman. I do not know how the legend began that she was a 'complete doormat'. It is not a phrase which would seem immediately appropriate to anyone who had actually met Lady Starling. My uncle, however, had thus described her so frequently that I was unable to disentangle her from the phrase. It clung to her like an Homeric epithet and had made me envisage her as tiny, cowering.

I should think she was five-foot-nine. Once, she must have been dazzlingly beautiful. She had a much rounder face than Sargie's, with deep-set eyes and a cupid's bow of a mouth. Like her brother, she smoked her cigarettes through a holder. Though she was, perhaps, nearing sixty, she retained the mannerisms of a much younger woman, even of a teenage girl.

'Sargie, don't talk about pee just before we eat.'

'Night after night they did it, apparently.'

'We've heard it fifty times before.'

'But in their boots. Can you imagine? That's the dear old human race for you. They deserve Vernon and his Labour Party.'

'Sargie, you are awful.'

She evidently enjoyed the awfulness, but whether for its own sake, or because it threw into relief her own cool good manners, who could say?

Much later on, when we had gone into the meal and were eating chops and mashed potatoes, Sargie still reverted to the subject of urination in boots.

'I mean, just imagine, putting your shoes on in the morning. It's the great difference between the working classes and everyone else. They won't see ahead. That's why kindly people like Vernon – and myself in the old days – felt we had to do all their planning for them.'

The lunch was memorable to me not just because it was the first time I'd met the doormat, but because it represented a sort of watershed in Sargie's relationship with Uncle Roy. In a way, it was the beginning of the end. Given Sargie's deviousness, my uncle's secretiveness, the wonder is that I followed anything of what was going on.

What had happened was this. Some time after running away from Felicity, Hunter had resumed contact with Sargie and, little by little, wormed his way into the older man's confidence. None of us knew anything about it at the time, but Hunter had started to persuade Sargie that it was not really safe to keep Jimbo's trunks and boxes lying around in Timplingham. The damp was beginning to get at them. It was agreed that Hunter should take the more 'significant' of the boxes into safe-keeping.

By the time I had begun my National Service, I suppose Hunter had probably purloined about three-quarters of the Lampitt Papers. None of us knew about it, because Sargie had chosen to keep his friendship with Hunter a secret. With the whole sad episode of Felicity in the background, he could not very well have talked about it to Uncle Roy. Merely to have *seen* Hunter after that would have seemed, and perhaps was, a species of betrayal.

I was away from home so much that all subsequent developments – of how, in effect, Sargie let Hunter take him over – were unknown to me. I never did discover how much Uncle Roy knew. Very little, I suspect. Even if he had known that Sargie had admitted Hunter into his confidence, my uncle would never have spoken about it. The whole thing was too wounding on too many levels.

Sargie started to say that he found the countryside unutterably depressing, always had, that he wanted a little place in London, couldn't afford one. There was no one of any interest in Timplingham and he had spent his entire life there doing nothing except watch rain drip down window-panes.

It was against this background, some of which was known and most of which was unknown, that the luncheon happened. Talk was undirected. Sargie, becoming increasingly inaudible, commiserated with me for being in khaki. His sister and Uncle Roy talked about Lampitts. Sibs had three children. The two Starling boys were by now in their early thirties. One of them had done frightfully well in the war and another – or perhaps the same one – had done equally well in the City. There was a much younger sister – Anne – who was a student. Presumably she was doing well too – that seemed to be the way with the Starlings.

Like Sargie, Sibs mumbled. The quiet voice was partly, perhaps, responsible for the doormat idea. There was nothing submissive in her general demeanour. Quite suddenly, when most of the meal was over, she turned to me and said, with a smile, 'Do tell Sargie he's being a complete idiot.'

'Oh, shut up, Sibs.'

'No, tell him,' said Lady Starling.

I looked at her glass. Then at her face. We had been drinking water. Before the meal she had had, at most, two glasses of sherry.

'Why?' I ventured.

'This mad idea of getting rid of this place.'

'What!' Uncle Roy almost shouted. 'What's this? Getting rid of the Place? Sargie! Honest*lee*! This can't be true!'

'Suppose you have to know. Tell them, Sibs. Too bloody sad. I can't talk about it.'

'No,' said Sargie's sister, firmly refusing to let him off the hook. 'You have got to tell them. They will tell you what a crazy, wicked idea it is. Just think of what Mother would say.'

At the mention of their mother, Sargie winced.

'Always said . . . only a bought house.'

I had the idea that Sargie might be pretending to be more plastered than he actually was, to let him off having to share with us his plans for Timplingham Place. After all, it was his house, to do with as he chose. But the idea of Timplingham without Lampitts was, from Uncle Roy's point of view, unthinkable. Although it had always been obvious and I had laughed about it, it only then became abundantly clear to me that the Lampitts, and Sargie in particular, represented the emotional centre of my uncle's life. If someone had threatened to shoot his wife and daughter – I am not saying that he would have reacted to the news with indifference, but the effect could not have been more cruel than the possibility of the Lampitts clearing out.

'Thing is, place very expensive.' It was only just possible to hear Sargie's tiny little voice. 'Builder's been. Dry rot. Floors, the lot.'

'You're making no kind of sense,' said Sibs sharply. 'All this started just because a ceiling fell down – when was it?'

'Six weeks ago,' said Uncle Roy. 'And then there were those burst pipes last winter, weren't there, Sargie? But look, you always get things going wrong with old houses. Half our ceilings are on the point of collapse at the Rectory.'

'Exactly!' said Sibs. 'You see, Sargie, you can patch up here and there.'

'You don't have to pay for it, live here, feeling bloody miserable all the time, whole place falling into ruins.'

The semi-coherence and near-inaudibility of Sargie's remarks were the more disconcerting because he did not look drunk. Sitting at the head of the table in that nice old dining room, he looked positively distinguished. He might have been a judge presiding over a rather grand private meal at a club, or the Master of a Cambridge college conducting a meeting of his governing body. He never went red or dribbled at the lips. Alcohol made his voice quieter and gradually obliterated his sense of humour. It also tended to have a poor effect on his legs but at present he was not trying anything so ambitious as standing. I realised, looking at his tumbler, that he had been filling up with Gordon's while the rest of us drank water.

The dining room at the Place was panelled and more beautifully proportioned than any room I can remember. It had been rather spoilt, forty years earlier, by old Mrs Lampitt who had painted it a powdery shade of flat, pale blue. The paint had been slapped on thick on all available surfaces. Now, just as thick, it was coming off. Flakes the size of cabbage leaves curled in the middle of panels to reveal scrubs of whiteish wood or, further up, blackened expanses of mushroomy wall. The pictures, mainly of Mrs Lampitt's side of the family (they had been Bainbridges), were blackened and matted with years of exposure to damp and cigar smoke.

'All right for you, Sibs. Lovely house in Chelsea. You don't have to live here all the year round.'

'Nor do you.'

'Do.'

'You don't.'

A nursery squabble.

His sister continued, 'You could come up to London if you wanted. Jimbo always wondered why you came up so seldom. And that's the *other* silly thing.'

Once more, Lady Starling had turned in my direction and appeared to be appealing for my help against Sargie. This was just a conversational mannerism. She would have enlisted the alliance of the sideboard if she had been alone with her brother. She raised her eyebrows at his folly.

'What's that?' I asked.

It made Sargie sober up fast.

'We're not going into all *that* now, Sibs, so just shut up for once, can't you?'

Sibs cast a glance at Uncle Roy and appeared to get the message. It was lost on me at the time. Sargie meant that she was not to talk about Jimbo and therefore the Lampitt Papers, and therefore Hunter, in front of Uncle Roy.

But I did get a *frisson* of unpleasantness, the first sign that everything between the two friends was about to change. That wonderful double act – Sargie and Roy – which had been playing in the background of my life for as long as I could remember, was about to be wound up. Timplingham Place was threatened. Things fell apart; the centre could not hold.

A little more light was shed on the matter in the car going to Norwich. Since she was driving away in any case, Lady Starling offered me a lift to the station and I cut short my weekend leave in order to go with her.

'My brother is a very selfish man,' she said to me, drawing in her cheeks as she spoke. Against the engine noise of the Princess I was not sure that I was catching every word. Her beautiful lips hovered around the words, sucked them like boiled sweets.

'Everything in our family has always had to revolve round him. Always. He was Mother's favourite, of course. You know that. Spoilt him, absolutely. I think it is because there was such a gap between him and Vivian. Sargie and I were the babies. And now he's doing this to Mother – to us.'

It seemed coarse to remind Lady Starling that their mother was dead and beyond minding what happened to Timplingham.

'What's Sargie up to exactly?'

'Selling the Place, I suppose. There's nothing we can do to stop him unfortunately. I wish Roy would stop him. He used to have such an influence. We even thought Sargie might have become – you know, religious. Are you religious, Mr Ramsay?'

'No.'

I had never been called 'Mister' before by anyone. Instead of taking it as a compliment, I took it as a rebuke for referring to her brother just as 'Sargie'. But I could hardly say 'Uncle Sargie' to her – when he wasn't my uncle; and having known him for so long as 'Uncle Sargie' I could hardly have called him 'Mr Lampitt'.

'No, Roy's lost his influence over my brother, I am afraid. Sargie was so . . . well, you know, after Felicity. I don't myself believe that that was my brother's fault.'

'I'm sure not.'

I was amazed that anyone could have suggested such a thing, but also appalled that Felicity's troubles, which I had considered

201

so secret, should be a matter of general knowledge and discussion.

'He might' – she really sucked at the next few words – 'have kept more of an eye on them. A man and a girl in a library.'

With the last syllables of 'library', her voice sank to silence and her lips became so pursed as to disappear momentarily altogether, before opening out again into their wide selves. I thought there was something predatory about her face: a hawk, not a starling. I stored the joke up, instinct telling me that the truth it contained would be useful to me in the future.

'I don't like the sound of Mr Hunter one bit,' she said, shoving the Princess into second in order to overtake a tractor. When we were past it and on a straight bit of road again, she said, 'You know all about my brother Jimbo, I suppose?'

'I have read his books. I knew that Raphael Hunter wanted to write about him.'

'I mean about Jimbo himself. His weakness.'

'No, no. I never met . . .' After the 'Sargie' solecism, I could hardly say 'Jimbo'. But it would seem equally absurd to say, to his own sister, 'I never met Petworth Lampitt.'

She obviously thought better of any more talk on the subject of Jimbo's weakness, whatever it was. At first I guessed it was drink. Then she said, 'You can never trust them. Horrid little men.'

'Who?'

'People like Mr Hunter. Ugh!'

She shrugged and shivered theatrically, a schoolgirl down whose gymslip someone had just put a slug.

'Really, Lady Starling, there's no need to drive me all the way into the station.'

'I had no intention of doing so.'

'I can walk from here.'

'I know.'

She spoke as if we were coevals and that she could afford to be rude to me. Older people, I've found, are usually polite to the young. Sibs spoke as if she *was* young.

She switched off the engine for a minute.

'It's nice we've met,' she said. 'I need allies. Perhaps you'll be an ally in the future. Being the youngest member of the Lampitt family isn't easy.'

She gave me a weak smile. There was something very like

sexual attraction between us which, in spite of her words, bred instant distrust. I realised that she did not like me and that I found her terrifying. It seemed nothing to do with the present, but rather to be bred in us by instinct as the preparation for some future stage of the journey.

On my way back to Brentwood in the train, I reflected that there were probably at least forty first cousins who could be described, more or less accurately, as members of the Lampitt tribe and who were a good deal younger than Sibs Starling. But she regarded herself as the youngest of the Lampitts.

I thought it was crude of her to hint that Hunter and Jimbo had had some sort of queer relationship – if that was what she *was* implying. I was curiously innocent about such matters. English boarding schools are supposed to be hotbeds of all that kind of thing, but it was not until I joined the army that I came across the phenomenon in any very vigorous form. Bloom was the first thoroughgoing homosexual I ever got to know; and at that stage I had no means of knowing whether or not he, or anyone else I had ever met, was 'typical'. Certainly, his exploits made anything I had ever heard about at school seem pretty tame. I am not just talking about achievements in the flesh. It was amazing to me, for example, that someone of only my age could be so culturally well informed. He knew all about opera, which was something of which I was totally ignorant. I had simply had no opportunity to find out about it. I had never seen an opera. My uncle did not possess a gramophone.

I came across Bloom after my basic training was over and I had been transferred to a camp at Brentwood to await my next posting. He and I were in rather similar positions, being men of allegedly officer material who had elected to stay in the ranks.

Most of my memories of Brentwood are of peeling potatoes and listening to Bloom's extraordinary reflections on the universe, interlaced with accounts of his erotic adventures. Clearly, he was preparing to become a flamboyant undergraduate. Educated at one of the big old London day-schools (Haberdashers, I think), Bloom had got a scholarship to the university which was waiting for him when his two years in khaki were up. I envied him this pretty acutely, having nothing arranged for myself. His company certainly made a change from the amiable, but on the whole somewhat neanderthal, members of my own platoon. By way of small talk, many of my fellow soldiers were capable only of grunts, usually mouthing a very few synonyms for sexual intercourse. Basic training with them had been what is called an 'experience', but I did not feel that I was making friends for life. Then, spud-bashing in Brentwood, I found myself sitting next to the dark, sharp-featured and slight figure of William Bloom. After two months in which conversation had been, to put it mildly, limited, it was a startling change to hear someone say in the tones of a fluty dowager, 'This kitchen is positively Stygian!'

All my reactions to Bloom in the first instance were hostile: what he would have called predictably provincial. I was embarrassed by his willingness to show off in front of the men, by his refusal to adapt himself to his surroundings. Most of them would have had no trouble with the word 'kitchen', so long as no one asked them to write it down. But to use a word like 'Stygian' in their presence was to emphasise the gulfs which lay between us.

I had found it was perfectly possible to get on with the other men in the ranks. At various points I even tried to persuade myself that, despite differences of speech and background, we were all the same really. We all wanted to get through army life unscathed. We were all frightened by the experience, all mildly resentful of it. Nearly all of us responded in the classic fashion of youth by false irony and humour. That was what my first few months in the army were like. Some of them mocked the posh way I talked, but there was no nastiness.

Bloom was something different. A number of them hated him from the start, under the impression, which I think was totally misplaced, that he was trying all the time to make them feel small.

I first became aware of him during some absurd piece of drill.

'Squ—aaaad! Move to the left in twos!'

The corporal gave this order in the rhythmical, exaggerated tone which NCOs all adopted when giving commands. Bloom, a strikingly handsome, small, dark man, looked much older than the rest of us, though he was only my age. He was standing beside an amiable farmhand from the depths of Suffolk, ruddy-faced, muscular and stupid as hell. It was interesting to study this boy's face as Bloom said, perfectly audibly to everyone, 'Here we go, dear, with our *pas de deux.*' On another occasion, to a similarly uncomprehending listener, he said as we moved into quick march, 'Isn't this sheer *Aïda?'*

These outbursts cost him rebuke, sometimes even punishments, from the NCOs. From his fellow soldiers such observations earned him ostracism and sometimes actual physical violence. He was not trying to be 'grand' and, in fact, as I learned when I got to know him, Bloom was largely without social snobbery, if by that is meant a reverence for rank and title. The truth was that Bloom could not stop himself talking to his fellow soldiers in this way. He genuinely made no distinction between persons, which is why almost everyone found his company disconcerting.

At first, I thought it was not just silly, but offensive. When I later met up with him in the kitchens and began those conversations over the spud-bashing, I added to my distaste for his silliness a profound, physical revulsion from the seamier details of his erotic conquests. Like all great imaginations, Bloom's was one which found riches where the rest of us would have seen nothing at all. Many of his lovers, seen purely on the level of imaginative *trouvailles*, had a sort of brilliance. But I was so unused to the tastes he displayed that I was merely revolted and found myself hating Bloom as much as the other men did.

Then I told myself not to be such a stupid little prig and I began to concede, inwardly to myself, that Bloom was the first, the only, interesting thing to happen to me since I joined the army. The sexual talk was actually fascinating. When someone of roughly your own sexual persuasion is confiding in you, there is strictly speaking no interest in the talk at all. There may be collusion, but no *interest.* You understand what they are talking about before they say anything. As far as it extends their sympathy, the talk between two likeminded people on these levels is about as interesting as the song which some of the men at Brentwood liked to sing in the showers:

> I like eggs and bacon
> I like eggs and bacon.
> But if you think I'll tell you why
> You're fucking well mistaken.

What Bloom liked was altogether more imaginative and surprising.

'That little corporal from E Barracks squealed like a weasel when I got inside him last night. I said to him, "When on earth did you last go to the toilet?" '

'What did he say?' I chucked a finished spud into the huge vat of salted water which divided us.

'Talk about cleansing the Augean stables or dear David Herbert Lawrence' (he pronounced the name for some reason as if it were German, with an accent on the last syllable) 'purging the whatever it was.'

'He is like a weasel, Harker, now you mention it.'

'Never again, anyway.'

'I just can't understand what you see in them all. To me he is just a boring little man in spectacles. You presumably . . . I don't know . . .'

'Hear Mahler's Eighth Symphony in my head whenever I see him approach? No. I like to taste what talent there is going, that's all. You should try it – broaden your horizons.'

'There were one or two one-night stands in Northampton before we came here,' I said.

'But they were girls, I expect.'

'Yes.'

'You're like the most boring type of provincial Englishman who'd rather starve when he goes abroad than eat any of the local dishes. Meat and two veg or nothing.'

I admitted that I was a person of very marked emotional limitations.

It wasn't all smut or opera, Bloom's talk. He had an admirable capacity for gossip. He seemed to know everything which was going on in the camp and, because he found it interesting, he was able to make it interesting: which NCOs had got women into trouble, what was for lunch the next day, where we were likely to be sent on our foreign posting (Cyprus and Germany were the likeliest possibilities), everything. He also maintained an astounding capacity to keep in touch with what was going on in the outside world. He read theatre criticism and book reviews. He was the first person I ever met, incidentally, who had read Debbie Maddock's novel. First he talked about the reviews. 'A new star in the firmament apparently. One Deborah Arnott. I must read her when I next return to civilisation.'

After he had returned from his next weekend leave, he had indeed read *The Melon Garden*. It was only when I heard the title that I realised that Deborah Arnott was the same as our Debbie, the Wretched Woman of village-shop fame. From Bloom's description, I gathered that *The Melon Garden* was the story of a sexually attractive and highly imaginative young woman immured in a Norfolk village with a tediously mousy little schoolmaster husband.

'One identified with the more sub-Lawrence moments,' said Bloom. 'There is a memorable scene in a barn with a dairyman; but on the whole the quality of the prose was too painful.'

I had thought it would be a tremendous feather in my cap to claim acquaintance with the author, but Bloom seemed disappointingly unimpressed by my knowing her. He sniffed and said something quite non-committal, as though we all knew novelists.

It was not Deborah Arnott, however, but Proust, in the Scott-Moncrieff translation, that Bloom was reading when I returned to the camp that afternoon, having parted with Lady Starling some hours before. In my recollection, soldiers spend most of their time, when they aren't doing soldierly things like drill, just lying on their beds. I suppose in the army you are tired most of the time – and, for those of us who weren't officers, there were no armchairs or comfortable mess where we could loll and smoke.

Bloom was arranged on his bed wearing a short-sleeved vest and some blue, checked overall-trousers, a memento of an afternoon in the stores with a member of the catering corps. He had stockinged feet. His serpentine posture was reminiscent of the Rokeby Venus. He threw down the little blue volume – *The Cities of the Plain* – and said:

'Oh, it's all too hideously true!'

'Proust? I've never managed to get started with him somehow. Sargie Lampitt reads him, I think.'

I had told Bloom all about the set-up at home. By now we were quite good friends. Funnily enough, he knew some distant Lampitt cousin. I began to tell him about meeting Sibs Starling. It was hardly headline news. I did not blame him for the look of abstraction which passed over his face. He responded to none of my Lampitt prattle. Straightening out from the Rokeby posture and lying flat on the bed, he said between puffs of his cigarette, 'I'm in love.'

'Another weasel?'

'No, no.' He was perfectly serious. I almost wondered if he wasn't close to tears. 'I said in love. With weasels it's just like eating. One just fucks anything which happens to be there. I'm talking about love. The real thing. Shakespeare's *Sonnets, Tristan und Isolde, La Prisonnière*, the whole horror story. Has it ever happened to you?'

'I think it did when I was very young.'

I began to talk about Miss Beach. What I had felt for her, and in a way still felt, was on a much more exalted scale than anything which I had felt for Barbara, or for the one-night stands in Northampton. I thought that I understood the distinction he was drawing between the 'real thing' and the merely available. He wasn't listening to anything I said. He interrupted my discourse with a loud moan.

'Oh, my *God*!'

For the first time in our conversations, he was totally serious. For a moment of sheer egotistical horror, I thought that he was going to say that he was in love with me. We were alone in the dormitory. It was hours before most of the men would be back from their weekends. But the next few sentences dispelled any such anxieties.

'You know the way love makes you frightened? I'm terrified of him. Terrified I'll say or do something which will put him *off* me.'

'You still haven't said who he is.'

'I spotted him the first day I arrived here. Our eyes met. Has that ever happened to you? I *knew*. And yet I didn't know. That's the awful thing about being queer. You can never be sure. He's only spoken to me once.'

'He's a soldier, yes?'

'I thought and thought of ways we might meet. I've written him letters, but of course posted none. Then we just happened to bump into each other in a pub down the road.'

'Oh yeah?'

'It wasn't *like* that, fuck you. He asked me what regiment I was in and we started to say what hell army life is. He's applied to do this Russian course. It's a cinch. They send you off and teach you Russian – it's really almost like being at university, he said, only without the awful people.'

'Has he been to university?'

'No. He's like me. He's got a place when he's finished with all this nonsense.'

'So you have a rosy future together?'

'Don't even say it, not as a joke! Julian, he's just so *beautiful.*'

I wondered, rather crudely, how far intimacy with this Adonis had progressed, but it did not seem an appropriate line of enquiry. There was a quality of reverence and sadness about the way Bloom described his new friend which made it obvious that things were still at a romantically nebulous stage.

'The thing is, I'm frightened that, if I show him how much I mind, it will scare him off.'

'He doesn't feel the same about you?'

'I don't know. I mean, he wouldn't have started to talk to me in the bar if he hadn't – well, *liked* me. On the other hand . . . Normally I hate intensity. God, I'd run a mile if I thought some silly little queen had got serious about *me.*'

'You would?'

'Of course. *Hate* it. The trouble is, I can't tell if he's bent. I can't even tell if he realises that is what I'm trying to tell. Do you see what I mean?'

'It sounds complicated. You hope he is – bent?'

'Well, everyone is really,' he said.

'I don't agree.'

'It's just that some men, most perhaps, have been conned by their mothers into thinking that they actually *need* women. Half the babies' – he made a gesture towards the row of empty beds in the dormitory – 'think they can't open a tin of peas or iron a shirt, so they fuck a woman and she in return acts as their servant.'

'If you think that, you're barmy. People really do fall in love with girls, *fancy* them, William. Most people aged twenty aren't thinking about ironing.'

'You only look on the surface of things.'

'That's where most of life happens.'

'You're so wrong,' he said, dangling one stockinged foot over his raised knee. Then he said, 'I'd do *his* ironing for the rest of his life.'

'When are you seeing him again?' I asked.

'That's just it. He said he might be around in the same bar at about seven o'clock this evening. The thing is, Julian, it wasn't really an arrangement. He just said it casually. I can't tell whether he really wants to see me again, or whether he was just being polite.'

'Would you like me to come along with you?' I asked. 'If he stands you up, we can just get drunk together. If he does turn up, I can make a tactful exit.'

Bloom looked slavishly grateful for this offer which was made, I regret to say, less in a spirit of altruism than one of pure curiosity. I was fascinated to see the beauty which had been able to transform my loftily cynical, world-weary friend into a spoony teenager.

At about six we were dressed and ready. A few minutes later we walked out of the camp and down the bleak, arterial road which led into Brentwood. The pub where the assignation had been made turned out to be one of those featureless buildings, vaguely neo-Georgian in inspiration, which were put up during the 1930s all over greater London. The lounge bar was carpeted and panelled. The windows were too high for looking out of. It was hard to see why anyone chose to go there, but there were some customers. At one table, two men and two women, all aged about fifty, drank shorts and took it in turns to tell smutty jokes. The women appeared to be married to the men, which made their presence in that place all the more mysterious. After all, they had homes to go to. There were a couple of loners at the bar – a man in a mackintosh drinking his way slowly through a pint of bitter and a seedier figure, more bottle-nosed, who was getting through a lot of whisky.

Since I now believed that Bloom's preferences could extend in just about any direction, I looked at each of these figures interrogatively, wondering which of them had inspired this besotted devotion of his.

'Oh, no,' he said, reading my looks, 'none of these.'

'How did you come to find this place?'

'It's so near the camp. I just dropped in here one evening. Most of the men avoid it for some reason.'

'For quite a lot of reasons that I could think of. What'll you have?'

'Half, please.'

'Bitter?'

'Yah. I want to stay sober in case . . . Christ this is him.'

The door of the lounge opened and a tall, languorous figure wearing the uniform of a lieutenant in the Middlesex Regiment

210

entered. His face was conspicuous for its overhanging eyelids, great ovals over each eye, and for his huge mouth. As he approached, I looked at him purely from the point of view of curiosity, to see what constituted (in Bloom's eyes) the ideal of beauty. But, by the time he had reached us and said, 'Ramsay, what on earth are you doing here?', I had recognised him as Darnley.

He had grown about six inches since we last met and he no longer wore specs. I knew that time had made analogously dramatic adaptations to my own appearance.

'Clever of you to recognise me.'

'You've met *before*?' Bloom asked.

He glared at me with angry suspicion. It was several weeks before I could get him to believe that Darnley and I had not somehow set the whole thing up as some kind of prank. Also, never having himself attended an English boarding school, Bloom assumed that promiscuity in these places was so universal that Darnley and I must be ex-lovers. He was unshakeable on the question. Not that it mattered. The whole moment in the pub was jarring and unfortunate, calling in all three of us for instant readjustments of what we had previously thought about one another. It certainly changed my picture of Darnley to think that he might hang about in bars in order to meet 'a man like Bloom'. He for his part, as he confided in me years later, assumed that I had been brought along as Bloom's 'fancy-boy'.

'Bloom's having half of bitter, I'm having a pint. What'll it be for you?' I asked.

'Mackeson's if I may.'

He smiled nervously and we all found ourselves a table in the corner. When I came back with the drinks, Bloom was grinning.

'Heard the news?' he said. 'Miles has just told me.'

'What?'

'Stalin's dead, horrible old shit.'

I had never heard anyone rejoice in another person's death before and I was shocked by it.

'It just came on the news before I came out,' said Darnley. 'You surely aren't upset by it?'

'Well,' I laughed nervously and raised a glass, 'here's to Uncle Joe.'

I knew absolutely nothing about Stalin. Being with the other two, who were both somehow more sophisticated than I was, I wondered whether I knew anything about anything. Perhaps I should just clear off back to the camp and leave them to spend the evening together as they chose. But, out of politeness, I asked Darnley for his news. Since Seaforth Grange, he had been to Westminster, won a scholarship to Oxford and somehow ended up with a commission. He was now on the point of doing this Russian course, a mild bout of pneumonia having prevented him from starting sooner. For all I knew, he still had a sense of humour, but the anarchic little figure whom I had liked so much at Seaforth Grange had sobered up a bit.

'How about you?'

I found that my biography could be contained in about three sentences.

'Wants to go on the stage!' trumpeted Bloom.

I remembered Mrs Webb and Granny saying that this would be Darnley's destiny.

'Oh, yes?' he asked. It somehow seemed to fit in with my being with Bloom and, as he drained his glass slowly, I felt he was reassessing me, reconsidering all our years together.

'It's only one idea,' I said. 'I did quite a bit of acting at school. I know I'm good at it.'

'Curious thing,' said Bloom, 'is that he has hardly ever been to the theatre. Knows nothing about it. Now, dears – drinks!'

When Bloom went to the bar to buy his round, there was a gleam of the old Darnley. As soon as Bloom's back was turned, Darnley, without standing up, put one hand on his waist and managed, simply by squirming from side to side in his seat, to convey the mincing manner with which our friend walked. As a final flourish he lifted a limp hand and waved it about like a handkerchief.

I roared with laughter. There was some reassuring complicity in this. By the time Bloom brought the drinks back we were feeling more friendly towards each other, but sadly there seemed nothing to talk about. It was inevitable that we should fall back on memories of Seaforth Grange.

Our memories were slightly different. We both remembered the big things, like Darnley ordering a cartload of manure to be dumped outside the chapel on Speech-Day. But he had forgotten some of his more engaging little jokes.

'Do you remember "Fielding's quite a different boy"?'

'I remember Fielding,' he said.

Oddly enough, I didn't. I just remembered the joke. The boy Fielding was of no interest to me.

'His sister's a friend of one of my sisters.'

'I forgot you had sisters.'

'Two – and a stepsister.'

There was no point in explaining to him his own joke about Fielding. What made the memory sweet was the thought of Darnley and me as twelve-year-olds, sitting far out near the boundary of the cricket pitch while the umpire shouted at us.

'Do you remember that pathetic man Lollipop Lew?' I asked.

'The one who married the art mistress,' said Darnley.

'I don't know about that.'

'You know,' said Darnley. 'The one you were dotty about, or pretended to be.'

'I was.' I almost added, 'I am,' because the idea of Miss Beach marrying Lollipop Lew was surprisingly painful.

'Not Miss Beach?' I said. 'He didn't marry Miss Beach?'

'Is that what she was called? We called her Beryl, don't you remember? The plain one with glasses. I never knew whether you actually liked her or whether it was one of your teases.'

He smiled at Bloom conspiratorially, as though he too must have noticed my habit of saying things which I didn't mean.

'How do you know she married the French master?'

'Do you remember those awful lessons?' He laughed and put on his Lollipop Lew voice. ' "Gee swiss, tew ayse . . ." I remember them together. We all collected money for the wedding present. Surely you were there? No, of course, you left a term earlier than I did for some reason, didn't you?'

'I think I did.'

'She ran off before the end of the summer term, but by the next term she was back with Lollipop Lew. Probably there are lots of little Lollipops scampering all over the Malvern Hills by now. It was what? Five years ago? Six?'

That was a long time in our time-scale.

'She was going to marry a man called Hunter,' I said. 'Then he went off with Vanessa, the matron.'

'My dears,' said Bloom, 'your school sounds so infinitely more exciting than mine.'

'I vaguely remember the Vanessa business.' He turned to Bloom by way of explanation. 'We had this rather marvellous matron who came and gave us good-night kisses in the dormitory. Really cuddled us. I suppose she was a bit of a nympho.'

'Like one,' said Bloom.

'Do you remember, we saw her with Mr Hunter when we went out to lunch together in Worcester? There was a tremendous fuss.'

'Oh, was there?'

He laughed and, seeing our glasses empty, went to buy his round at the bar. Obviously some memory of that day in Worcester had remained with him, because when he came back with our beer, he said, 'I hope your grandmother's all right?'

'She's fine. I saw her the other week.'

'Ramsay's got this marvellous granny,' said Darnley.

Now that I was almost grown up I was embarrassed by the hint of condescension here. I even nervously interpreted 'marvellous' to mean that Darnley recalled my grandmother's slightly accented London voice. Was he even confusing her with her much more Cockneyfied friend, Mrs Webb? Still, it was nice of him to ask.

'She liked you a lot,' I said.

'We had fish and chips together. You probably won't remember.'

'Of course I do,' I said. 'You know, Hunter – the man we saw with Vanessa – has cropped up since.'

'Who's Hunter?' said Darnley. I could tell he didn't give a damn. 'Oh yes, the chap who married the matron. No, I never really followed that. But the art mistress and Lollipop Lew. Look, let's stop calling each other by such damn silly names. I'm Miles, you're Julian.'

'And I'm William,' said Bloom.

'Yes,' said Darnley, 'of course you are.'

Since we were by now quits and had each bought a round, I rose tactfully after my third pint and said that I would leave them to it, get back to the camp. They wouldn't hear of it. However Bloom and Darnley had intended to pass the evening, my presence changed it. That was the first evening I got really drunk. One of them generously substituted whisky for beer when it was their turn to buy the drinks and after that the dingy little lounge bar began to sway like a stormy ocean. I can remember the swaying movements of the bar changing to swift revolutions, so that the coarse quartet at the next table began to

214

spin round and round my head like whirling dervishes. And I can remember getting out to a grass verge more or less in time and being sick, partly on the grass, partly on my boots. I don't know exactly how I got to bed.

About a week later, Darnley left that camp and started his Russian course, and we did not meet up again until we were both in civvy street.

All love dies, except perhaps the love which parents feel for their children. When it is gone, a bit of oneself is left behind, irrecoverably lost. We *know* that we loved such and such a person; but the sensation itself and the being who actually did the loving, these cannot be brought back. Often, it is imaginatively impossible even to remember what it was that we loved about a particular person. In affairs of the heart, where Eros plays an obvious role, the switches can be violent, terrible, destructive. With friendship it is otherwise. Though some friendships last, sort of, for life, most don't and what the friends once had in common diminishes to something which exists only in memory or which atrophies into habit.

Poets like to tell us that love is everlasting and that 'what will survive of us is love'. But, even in the span of our earthly lives, we discover that love is the least permanent of things, the most subject to change and death. As I sobered up in the showers next morning, with a churning head and traces of vomit still discernible in my nostrils, the shocks of the previous night came back. First, meeting Darnley at all and wondering if he was queer. But worse than this was the thought of Miss Beach married and my feelings for Miles himself cooled. It was as sure a whiff of mortality as a death in the flesh.

It was a time of disruption and severance. In Timplingham, too, between Sargie and my uncle, the estrangement was becoming more pronounced. It had begun with the painfully delicate matter of Felicity and Hunter, but perhaps it was on the cards anyway that Sargie would eventually tire of Uncle Roy, or that my uncle would decide that his friend had for once gone too far.

I was stuck in the camp at Brentwood for longer than scheduled. There was some sort of hitch. We were all meant to have been flown out to Germany. We had our last weekend of leave and bade a fond farewell to our families. Then there followed three anticlimactic months in which we did nothing.

Rumours started to fly about that we weren't going to Germany after all. Aden was mentioned. Cyprus. Africa. I hated the idea of any of these places. Some of the other boys were excited at the prospect of travel. I am often beguiled by the promise of future happiness, but on this occasion I wasn't. It was obvious to me that, wherever we went with the army, it would be identical to Brentwood. Only, abroad, it would be Brentwood with sunstroke, diarrhoea and the likelihood of getting shot added as tempting extras on the menu.

Throughout this more than usually dull period of waiting about, my aunt wrote me her weekly letter, as she had done throughout my days at school. They looked the same, the Brentwood letters – the same, small Basildon Bond paper and envelopes bought at the village shop. But by her standards these letters became painfully frank. The cause of all the anguish was what was happening up at the Place.

Sargie had decided to buy a small flat in London. Sibs had found him one off Kensington High Street. He was not thinking of leaving the village altogether, but henceforward he would only be there occasionally. There was talk of putting Timplingham Place up for sale. Then it seemed that, in its present condition, the house would attract no buyers. My Uncle Roy and Sibs got together, and made Sargie promise never to sell the Place.

A little routine began to establish itself. Sargie, carrying Joynson-Hicks in a basket, set off for London each Monday or Tuesday and returned to Timplingham at weekends. Before long, predictably, he was saying that he missed the dear old village, hated the constrictions of the little flat, didn't know anyone in London any more.

It all began to look rather hopeful. My Uncle Roy even went to spend the odd night in Kensington to keep Sargie company and it seemed as if their friendship was on the mend. Then Joynson-Hicks took it into his head to wander off. Unfortunately, it was while Uncle Roy was in the flat and he was blamed. The whole neighbourhood was scoured, the Metropolitan Police informed. But Joynson-Hicks was lost in London and he never came back.

The incident precipitated an intense depression in Sargie. He returned to Timplingham with his grief and, just at the blackest period of this emotional decline, another ceiling collapsed at the Place. The builder was called and he proposed the final solution.

Why not level Timplingham Place to the ground and replace it with a lovely new bungalow? Sargie could have central heating, toilets which flushed easily, all the trimmings.

My aunt told me of this proposal with many underlinings and exclamation marks. I assumed that no one in their right mind would demolish a beautiful, eighteenth-century mansion in order to construct a hideous bungalow: a fair assumption to make. I forgot that Sargie was not in his right mind – that he had never been in a worse mental condition since the original breakdown thirty or more years before.

Because of the delay over my next posting, I was allowed one last weekend leave. I returned to Norfolk at the height of summer, when the village was always at its most beautiful. The elms near the church were in full leaf, and all the parkland round the Place was lush and abundant – a canvas by Constable.

I could not have returned at a more dramatic moment. Even as my aunt and I came in at the Rectory front door, we found Sargie and my uncle in the middle of an acrimonious conversation. My first thought was one of pleasure that the worm had turned, because my uncle was showing real anger with Sargie. In my simple-minded way I had always seen the friendship as a matter of Sargie exploiting Uncle Roy. But Sargie needed Roy just as much as he was himself needed by my uncle. The dispute which I now witnessed was rather terrible. Both men were in pain and too much hung upon the outcome of their quarrel.

'I've said you were right all along, Roy.' Sargie was crestfallen, apologetic.

'I don't need telling. Anyone could see that it was a crazy idea, pulling down the Place. Sibs told you so. I told you. We all told you.'

'Please, Roy. Just this once.'

'Why *should* I be the one who makes all the decisions for you? I rang up Jackson last week and told him not to demolish the Place. That was because you asked me.'

'I wanted you to, Roy. You're better at telephoning than I am.'

Sargie still looked a highly distinguished, if rather grotesque old gentleman in a double-breasted suit of expensive cut and a large, silk bow tie concluding his long, lugubrious face. His tone of pleading, however, was that of a child.

'You rang the builder,' said Uncle Roy, 'and flatly contradicted

217

my message. You said you wanted the house pulled down after all.'

'I've told you, Roy. He rang me. He talked me into it. He even implied that I would be breaking a contract if I didn't have this ruddy bungalow built.'

'For God's *sake*, Sargie!' My uncle bellowed this. 'It's your house, not Mr Jackson's. Let him sue you. Just let him try!'

'Trouble is, I do want the bungalow. In a way. Don't think my health would stand another winter in that place.'

'Now you're just being silly.'

'Please, Roy. Ring Jackson, Roy. Please.'

'And then you'll ring him back and cancel all my instructions.'

'I'll kill myself if you don't ring Jackson.'

'Oh, you're *ridiculous!*'

'I see.' Sargie was by now hamming it up. 'Your oldest friend kills himself and it's just ridiculous. Something to laugh about. Ha, ha. You're all right, of course. You've got your family, you've got Deirdre.' He turned and looked at us. I don't know how long he had been aware of our presence. 'You've got your beastly religion to keep you going. I don't have anything, Roy. Nothing. And you won't even lift the telephone, not once, to save my Mummy's house.'

His lower lip was trembling.

'But why on earth can't *you* ring the builders?' asked my uncle. 'You can use my telephone, if you'd like.'

'But I only spoke to them an hour ago and confirmed that the demolition work will start tomorrow. I can't ring them back and cancel it all again. They'll think I'm barmy.'

'Suppose I did ring them,' said Uncle Roy. 'Then you would change your mind again in five minutes and want the opposite.'

'You could ring and say you were the Rector.'

'I am the Rector.'

'But you could sort of say – oh, that the demolition was forbidden. Say it was an historic building.'

'It is an historic building.'

'Oh, please, Roy. Please ring the builders.'

'I'm sorry, Sargie. I'm fed up with it all. I've had enough.'

There was a silence.

Then Sargie said, 'I see.'

It was one of the most painful exchanges I had ever witnessed. Sargie turned round, walked past my aunt and out into the

Rectory drive. When he passed me, I saw that his eyes were full of tears. He shambled down the drive. I don't think he walked so unsteadily because he was tight. He was reeling from a blow. My uncle too looked as though he had been hit. Without either of them wanting it, they had just talked out of existence the two things they cared most about – Timplingham Place and their own friendship.

I saw my uncle's point of view. He had, apparently, already rung Mr Jackson four times, with four contradictory sets of instructions from Sargie. He was unable to make a fifth call. Now, unless Sargie made the call himself the Place would be demolished. The furniture had been moved out. Most of it was in store, but the larger pieces had been given to Vernon Lampitt, who had succeeded to his father's title and now lived twenty miles away at Mallington Hall.

When Sargie had disappeared down the drive, my uncle shut himself up in his study and smoked a great deal until evensong.

At supper, he said, 'I just hope he'll have been shaken into making a decision for himself.'

'A decision! Sargie!' My aunt's derision was understandable.

'I think we'll find he'll have rung up the builder.'

'You mean, they won't be pulling down the Place after all?' I asked.

'Good old Sargie,' said Uncle Roy.

The next morning, the suspense of the situation woke me early. I was alone in the Rectory with my uncle and aunt, Felicity (by now a university teacher) being away doing her job.

When I came downstairs fully dressed at half-past seven, I found Aunt Deirdre sitting at the kitchen table anxiously drinking a cup of very strong tea.

'There's plenty in the pot if you want some.'

'No thanks.'

'You're not going over to the church are you?'

'No.'

'Your uncle has already gone.'

She herself, I noted, had more or less stopped going, except on Sundays. I wondered if Uncle Roy was alone over there, reciting the Ten Commandments to an empty building.

'Sargie won't let them pull down the house, will he?' I asked. I was very nearly nineteen. Still, this was one of those situations where one instinctively looked towards a grown-up for reassurance.

Aunt Deirdre just shrugged and pulled a face. I had always been aware that she did not really like Sargie. That morning, I got the distasteful impression that she almost hoped the Place would be destroyed, just so that everyone would blame its unfortunate owner for ever and ever.

'I always remember old Mrs Lampitt saying, "Sargie's a babe." He lets other people make all the difficult decisions for him. He's battened on to your uncle for twenty-five years. Now we are going to see what it's like when Sargie makes up his own mind for a change.'

'Isn't that a bit hard? Sargie's a sick man.'

'Who have you been talking to?'

'No one. It's just obvious that he is – well, weak.'

'All that psychology is a load of twaddle. Weak and sick are two very different things. No, I can remember his mother saying, "I'm afraid we've let Sargie have things too easy." How right she was – but whose fault was that?' Aunt Deirdre sipped from her breakfast cup furiously. 'And he was such a clever person, too,' she said. 'He could have been brilliant but it was all wasted.'

'I thought he was brilliant.'

'Was or is?'

'Perhaps I will have some tea after all.'

While I poured tea into a cup, Aunt Deirdre continued.

'He's just let life go by. He's wasted it! And that's the worst of sins. And he's dragged your uncle into all his time-wasting too.' She gave an enormous sigh. 'Oh, do you think we should still be *here* if . . . if . . . ?'

When she said 'He's just let life go by,' there was the strong implication that, faced with time's tendency to pass, there was something else one could do with it, if one only had the guts or the enterprise. I was silenced by this. Would life, anyway, have been different in another place? What was she thinking? That my uncle might have become a bishop? Surely not. Or that they might have been happy? Ah, that was a difficult one to answer.

Uncle Roy himself appeared not long after our silence began. He was wearing the cassock and cloak which he wore on early morning trips to the church.

'It's started,' he said quietly.

220

'You don't mean it's going ahead?'

He went out again immediately. Neither my aunt nor I needed verbal prompting to follow him. We walked down the lane opposite the church until we reached the point where the Place came into view – the house framed by the beech avenue which led up to it and the clumps of elm behind. A light mist hung over the scene. No one could doubt that there was some machinery being driven about up at the house. Sargie, as we learned afterwards, had got himself taken up to London by car immediately after the quarrel of the night before.

After a short silence, there was a bang and then a second, much deeper booming noise. The house was lost in smoke which mingled in the morning mists. When these smokes dispersed, we could still see the old Place. We stood, the three of us, and saw the roof and the walls of the house shake as if they were made of cloth. Then another explosion and more smoke, dust, rubble. Then a silence. Above our heads, birds flapped their wings and there was a great cawing of rooks. A few days later I was sent abroad and I did not return to the village for fifteen months.

Seven

'You got a nice tan on you, where you been then?'

'Cyprus.'

'In the army?'

'Not any more, thank God.'

'That's my soldier-boy.'

In any professional life there can reach the point where the practitioner, however expert in a chosen field, starts to lose interest. The surgeon's hand has not lost its cunning, but he is bored and the success rate of his operations begins to decline. The tireless criminal advocate begins to lose cases not because he is no longer clever, but because he no longer cares whether or not his clients are acquitted. The imparting of knowledge which, to the young teacher, had been a matter of consuming zeal, has turned into a mere routine. His lessons, once legendary for their intellectual fireworks, now send the children to sleep. To give her the benefit of the doubt, something of the kind might very well have happened to Cindy (or whatever her real name was) who concluded our business together in a manner so perfunctory that, had it not been in England, one would have thought it deliberately insulting.

She got off the bed immediately and for a moment I admired her plump silhouette against the dingy Nottingham lace curtains. She had a top flat in Craven Street off the Strand. It is a part of town of which I am very fond. That day, the proximity of the river seemed to give a particular quality to the light in the drizzly sky.

I had not planned to spend my first hour in London in this fashion. Having left luggage at Charing Cross, I had merely intended to wander about the streets and taste freedom, knowing with a sense of incredulous happiness that the independent existence was about to begin. Cindy had engaged me in conversation almost as soon as I set foot outside the station and the next half-hour was the result of impulse. It was not that I grudged her the thirty shillings. I just felt vaguely cheapened by the experience itself. I had never paid for it before. To have done so was a blow to vanity.

'Well then, darling,' she said, 'see you again.'

'Hope so,' I said.

I was back in the country where nobody means anything they say to one another. Had I met her an hour later, Cindy would probably not have had the slightest recollection of having met me before. The drizzle had turned to quite heavy rain by the time I was outside in the street again. Nevertheless, a walk seemed the obvious way of clearing the head. I crossed the Strand, and wove my way in the direction of Leicester Square and Piccadilly. Sometimes I stopped and looked about me with disbelief. It really was true. I was out of the army. I wasn't at school. I was very nearly twenty-one years old. I was free! Free! As I passed the theatre at the bottom of Charing Cross Road I stood and looked at the photographs of the actors displayed outside. It seemed only a matter of time before my own face would be looking down with theirs. The legend would be posted up outside: 'ANOTHER BRILLIANT PERFORMANCE BY JULIAN RAMSAY.' Or 'I LAUGHED TILL I CRIED.' Where to start? That was the only question.

I crossed Leicester Square and walked down Piccadilly, half wondering, in a grand manner, whether to buy my aunt a little present of something at Fortnum and Mason. Before I reached that emporium, however, I paused by the window of Hatchards bookshop. The whole of one window was filled by a pyramid of stout duodecimo volumes, each bearing the title, in yellow capitals against a green background: *Petworth Lampitt: the Hidden Years, 1881–1910, by Raphael Hunter.*

Since Felicity's misfortune, now nearly five years in the past, Hunter had been an unmentionable word at the Rectory. I had therefore no means of knowing what progress, if any, had been made with the sorting of Jimbo's stuff. Sargie, since the demolition of the Place, spent more and more time in London. My aunt's letters hardly made mention of him and my uncle never wrote to me. The whole Lampitt family and its concerns had been pushed out of my mind by the experiences of the previous twelve or fifteen months. I had hardly given any thought at all, since joining the army, to the question of whether Hunter would one day persuade Sargie to let him edit some of

Jimbo's letters. The idea of a huge biography of the man was not something which I remembered being on the cards, though doubtless it had always been Hunter's ambition. I recalled the funny look which had come over Miss Beach's face at the name of Lampitt. Had Hunter even then disclosed to her his ambition to become 'the greatest English biographer since Boswell' (the words were not mine but those of a reviewer in the *Sunday Times)?* Did Hunter, all those years earlier, sense the extraordinary *potential* of the man Petworth Lampitt? Potential, that is to say, in the nebulous area of what makes a successful book?

'Petworth Lampitt was the archetypal Edwardian man of letters, but, as this fascinating new study shows, he was something much more . . .'

The blurb of the new jacket which I soon found myself reading inside the shop went on to hint that Lampitt was chiefly of interest because of his enormous range of acquaintances. 'Here was a man who grew to manhood in the aftermath of the Wilde trial and who knew a complete cross-section of English society. . . . We meet here many famous names in surprising settings. . . . The first volume of Mr Hunter's enthralling study is a reassessment not only of a much-neglected writer but also of English society itself . . .'

These were big claims. Perhaps the publishers were bound to make them, since they were charging a guinea for the book. I had been out of the country too long. I did not know that this biography of the first thirty-five years of Petworth Lampitt's life was already a best-seller. Its huge popularity was partly owing to the fact that there had been talk, which the judicious publishers had done nothing to quell, of a prosecution for obscenity. As it was, Hunter's second volume appeared after the triumph of *Lady Chatterley*, so that he was free to write more or less what he chose. The activities themselves, in this volume, were never described in Lampitt's diary entries, but rather in Hunter's own cotton-wool prose. Opening the book at random, my eye fell on the sentence 'Petworth had found in Dr Hastings [evidently some schoolmaster] the father-figure he lacked in his own ineffectual parent . . .' Hunter's subject was 'Petworth' throughout, never 'Lampitt'. It gave a peculiar quality of coy intimacy to the book which was somehow unthinkable with the majority of male subjects (other than monarchs or popes) of whom biographies had ever been written. Could one read a life of Johnson which referred habitually to 'Samuel'? A life of Osip rather than one of Stalin?

I flicked to another page. 'No one can ever say with any certainty whether, after the incident in the punt, Petworth and Oscar Browning were ever lovers in the accepted sense. But a deep bond had been formed . . .' Another flicking revealed, 'It was probably Hugh Walpole who introduced Petworth to Turkish baths as a way of life . . .' And then another page, quite near the end: 'Petworth's tragedy, like that of many of his kind, was that he was doomed to form attachments with men who were wholly heterosexual in temperament. It was a tribute to his charm that he succeeded with so many and on so many occasions. The incident with Lloyd George was typical: the herald of hundreds of such episodes in the years which lay ahead . . .'

Lloyd George? I looked up the name in the index and found the appropriate page. Petworth Lampitt, when in his late twenties, was taken by an uncle to luncheon in the House of Commons. They shared a table with David Lloyd George, then Chancellor of the Exchequer. The 'incident' – perhaps the lawyers insisted on vagueness, or perhaps Hunter preferred it that way – appeared to have been a case of fellatio, or at least some intimate embrace, in the corner of the library. Nor were they alone in the room. Sir Henry Campbell-Bannerman was sitting by the fire (admittedly fast asleep) while, in another alcove, Hilaire Belloc and George Wyndham were shouting out lines of French poetry. This carefully contrived tale was given reference notes (P.L.P. 2487: this stood for Petworth Lampitt Papers; the obscure style of numbering was devised by Hunter himself). As I turned the pages I discovered the pattern of the tale very clearly and saw at once why the book had been given a prominent place in the shop window. It is not quite true to say that Lampitt, in Hunter's account, had it off with every man you ever heard of. But the catalogue was decidedly impressive. Cardinal Manning – a guest of Petworth's grandmother in Rutland Gate – had allowed his archiepiscopal hand to stray over the child Petworth's sailor-suited person. I thought of William Bloom. Here was his vision of the world: or, come to that, Proust's. It was a world teeming with inverts, most of whom were cleverly posing as 'straights' or celibates. The psychological (not to mention circumstantial) improbability of the narrative did not stop it being compulsive reading. Was Petworth Lampitt a supreme fantasist whose surviving journals and memoirs had hoodwinked Hunter? Or was it actually possible that a young man of supreme personal attractions might succeed in captivating a person who, in any other circumstances, would have no interest whatsoever in their own sex or indeed in anyone else's? Women, it would appear, fell for Petworth Lampitt quite as readily as men, but he was incapable of giving them what they so indecorously implored.

'I am not ambivalent myself, but the cause of that ambivalence is in others,' as Lampitt once quipped to George Bernard Shaw, just about the only man in Hunter's book who did not at some stage or another take off his trousers for 'Petworth''s amusement.

I had paid my guinea and caught my train, and settled in a compartment with Hunter's book before I began to see how much he was the master of innuendo and suggestion. The first time you glanced at the tea party with Manning, it seemed as though Hunter was sparing the reader's blushes and forbearing to state an obscenity. The next time you read it through, it was obvious that no evidence whatsoever existed to convict the Cardinal of child-molesting. All that existed was a number – P.L.P. 913 – which might have referred to some inaccurate memory of Petworth Lampitt himself or which equally might not. When closely perused, all we saw was the fact that Manning once had tea with old Lady Lampitt and that Petworth, aged seven, was allegedly present. It is Hunter who says, with a clever use of negatives, that 'it is not for us to say whether this incident was what inspired Petworth's Firbankian short story "Watered Silk" . . .' which was evidently some unpublished and vaguely improper *jeu d'esprit* about a bishop misbehaving himself.

The day when I read Hunter's book through, beginning at the beginning, lay in the future. My train-perusal was a matter of turning here and there, collecting impressions.

For me, the biography was doubly absorbing. On the one hand it was the story of a writer whom I admired and whose inner life appeared to have been, to say the least, highly coloured. On the other, it seemed like the confirmation in print of an extraordinary, private fantasy – not mine, not Hunter's, but Uncle Roy's. For the eroticism of the story only took up a tiny proportion of the pages. Here was an index bulging with

Lampitts, the whole tribe of them. And yet it all had a curious unreality for me, precisely because I had been taught to lisp their names since early childhood. Needless to say, the Lampitts in Hunter's pages were shadowy figures when compared with the characters who peopled my uncle's narratives. Where other children were told fairy stories or folktales, I had been reared on Lampitt legends. My dragons and demons were all cousins or uncles or aunts of Sargie's. It was inevitable that Hunter's approach should have been duller than that of Uncle Roy. Whatever his motive for writing this enormous book, Hunter had none of the obsessive love which had dominated my uncle's grown-up life. And then again, my uncle's method of retelling the old tales was vividly oral whereas Hunter existed behind a cloak of the flattest prose imaginable. If my uncle was Homer then Hunter was a classical dictionary. It seemed strange to read of all these characters stripped naked of epithet or anecdote. Sibs Lampitt merely appeared as 'Petworth's youngest sister Sibyl, who married Rupert Starling, a Permanent Secretary at the Treasury'. There was nothing about Lady Starling's famed resemblance to a certain item of floor-covering. Bobby, who went out to be a farmer in Rhodesia, was alluded to, but without any of the stories inseparable from his name. For a moment in the train, I put down Hunter's book and thought of Uncle Roy, convulsed with mirth, as he tried to repeat what Bobby had said to that waiter in Brighton. It was the day he proposed to Slish, of course. It would not have been funny if written down. It needed Uncle Roy going pink at the gills and shaking as if he would suffer from apoplexy.

'In my book, a duckling is a young duck and not an old horse.'

This was the celebrated putdown with which their food had been sent back to the kitchen. The proposal of marriage was slipped in while the waiter was remonstrating with the cook. But none of it was funny or interesting unless it was told in my uncle's voice, enlivened by my uncle's love. As he dabbed the corners of his eyes with a silk handkerchief, he would say, 'Extraordinarily witty man, old Bobby.' And then, growing quiet, he would murmur, 'Typical Lampitt story, that. An old horse.'

In half an hour, I would be met by my uncle at Norwich station – our first meeting for well over a year. As I prepared for the encounter, the full force of his personality came before me.

For years, my complex feelings about Uncle Roy had forced me into making simple judgements of him, nearly all hostile. During my year away, I had not really missed him; but I had been homesick and I had missed the whole Rectory set-up. And now, just before we met again, I enjoyed a sort of revelation about him. I do not know whether it was an accurate vision, but I suspect that I never came nearer to the truth about him. For years, the chief thing which embarrassed me about Uncle Roy was his relationship with the Lampitts and with Sargie in particular. It all seemed humiliatingly toadyish. In this view, Uncle Roy appeared as a pure snob, making obeisance to a lot of people who 'in fact' (whatever that was supposed to mean) 'were no better than we were'.

But, with Hunter's book in my hand, I realised that the Lampitts with whose exploits I had been brought up were all creatures of Uncle Roy's fertile imagination. He was an artist, a novelist *manqué,* a natural one who did not realise his vocation or his gift. He possessed the one thing needful. Doubtless the figures with whose stories he regaled me, or anyone else who would listen, were in some sense real people, whose births and deaths had been recorded by a registrar. But it was my uncle's vision which breathed life into them and – as I had discovered for myself when I met Lady Starling – these 'real' people often bore no relation to the characters teeming in my uncle's brain.

Of Uncle Roy, needless to say, Hunter had written not a word. There was, however, a certain amount about Sargie who, although twelve years Jimbo's junior, had shared the same house, the same nurse and the same extraordinary parents. Much of the 'material' unearthed by Hunter was certainly new to me. My aunt had admitted that Mrs Lampitt was 'a strange old girl', but she had never explained how. Some of her eccentricities (for example, her insistence for the first six years of his life that Petworth was a girl called Petronella) doubtless helped to explain the sad story which Hunter felt constrained to tell. I don't know what it explained about Sargie, but it made one rather less surprised that he had turned out so rum.

Rather unimaginatively, I assumed that the publication of a book entirely devoted to the Lampitts would naturally be the first subject which my uncle would wish to discuss. I was beginning to look forward to my aunt's euphemisms for Petworth's amorous adventures. At the same time, I quite genuinely rejoiced in Hunter's book, because I thought that, for the first time in my life, I would be able to discuss something with my uncle as a fellow adult, without adolescent sensations of annoyance. What better than a book about his favourite subject? Hunter's flat prose would surely unleash a whole torrent of stories and corrections – memories of old Mrs Lampitt and of Timplingham Place in the old days.

By the time the train arrived, I was really looking forward to the reunion with Uncle Roy. It was a tremendous shock, therefore, as the train pulled in at the station and I glimpsed him on the platform, to find within me all the old childhood irritation and embarrassment welling up, as if I were a thirteen-year-old. I tried, in the few seconds which remained before greeting him, to take a grip on myself and to tell myself that he was a perfectly amiable man, who had only my best interests at heart and who had absolutely no desire to provoke in me either embarrassment or rage. But both were there, bubbling away inside me, as I stepped down on to the platform.

Uncle Roy was wearing his bright green Norfolk jacket and matching tweed knickerbockers. A pipe was between his teeth and, as often on stations, he was so deep in conversation with a porter that at first he did not notice my approach. When he did see me, he hurried up and took my hand. It was not the gesture of an uncle greeting a relation whom he had not seen for a long time; much more that of the host at a party who has found just the right person to lead up to a favoured guest.

'This man's father was a gardener at Mallington Hall,' were Uncle Roy's words of greetings.

'That's right, sir,' grinned the porter.

'Now,' said Uncle Roy, looking around, 'you have some luggage.' I allowed the porter to carry what there was – a large suitcase and a holdall.

'No,' said Uncle Roy, though I hadn't as yet opened my mouth, 'we were just saying before you arrived that we were *afraid* that *old* Lord Lampitt – that's the present Lord Lampitt's father – was a tiny little bit of a humbug.'

My uncle's shoulders were shaking. I could see an anecdote coming on. It was the one about old Lord Lampitt (Dickie) making a speech in 1914 against food hoarding, while in fact he had a sack of flour and another of sugar in the boot of his Rolls. His heir (who, as the Honourable Vernon Lampitt, had sat in

Attlee's Cabinet) was, in Uncle Roy's judgement 'an immensely able economist'. I found myself asking silently and furiously what Uncle Roy ever knew about economics.

'Oh, Mr Vernon's clever – His Lordship I should say now,' said the porter.

'There was always the hope, you know, that he would succeed Sir Stafford Cripps as Chancellor of the Exchequer. Instead it went to Gaitskell. But he is an immensely able economist.'

'Maybe,' said the porter, who wisely took nothing on trust, least of all when it was spoken by Uncle Roy.

He followed us to the car park and looked askance at the coin which Uncle Roy had placed in his hand as a reward for struggling with my bags. I thought there might be a danger of his cursing us, or even of offering a show of physical violence.

'It's been very enjoyable talking to you,' said Uncle Roy with a lordly smile. When the man was gone, my uncle added, 'What an extraordinarily nice man. And how nice to see you. I'm afraid to say that the Trojan finally conked.'

He opened the door of a dilapidated Rover, which it was unkind of someone to have sold him.

'Your aunt prefers this car,' he added as we jerked forward, 'but I miss the old one.'

It was just my luck to have come across a porter with Lampitt connections.

'I was telling that man about Bobby going out to Rhodesia. He didn't really know much about our branch of the Lampitt family.'

'I've just bought Mr Hunter's book,' I said. 'But perhaps you've already got it.'

My uncle concentrated purposefully on the road.

'Your Granny's looking forward to seeing you,' he said. 'I warn you, she's grown a bit older in the last year. Nothing to worry about, but she's deafer.'

'Aunt Deirdre wrote that Granny's come to live with us.'

'Did she say that her great friend had died?'

'No! Not Mrs Webb?'

'Extraordinary memory you have. We thought it was better not to write it. You never know with a letter. It might fall into the wrong hands. No, poor Mrs Webb had a stroke at Easter. She didn't recover. Your grandmother has been staying at the

Rectory ever since. We never meant to have her, but – she can't really manage on her own, you see.'

'Without Mrs Webb, she'll be lost,' I said.

And this death, this passing, made me forget the essentially frivolous subject of Petworth Lampitt's love-life. We were more or less silent for the remaining few miles of the journey.

One notices the smallest changes in the scenes of childhood memory. Timplingham without the Place was bad enough. But now there was a horrible petrol station on the edge of the village and more bungalows where green fields had been. The post office had been painted a different colour. Jill, who no longer ran it, but lived in one of the new bungalows, thought yellow was a 'ridiculous colour in a village', a judgement entirely endorsed by my aunt. In the next couple of weeks, Aunt Deirdre was to fill me in on most of the village news, including the fact that the Wretched Woman had another novel on the stocks, but had gone to live in Hampstead with her 'kids'. For the moment, though, Aunt Deirdre's concerns were more immediate. The Mulberrys were blaring as we entered the house – perhaps a symptom of Granny's increased deafness. Tinker was yapping in the kitchen. Aunt Deirdre came forward to kiss me.

'Brown as a berry!' she exclaimed. Then, in quite a serious voice, 'I made a cottage pie because I didn't know when you'd be getting in.'

I didn't have words for the death of Mrs Webb, so I just hugged Granny and kissed her powdery old cheeks. And Felicity was there too. I think the peck we gave one another that early summer evening was our first kiss.

'She's frightfully grand!' said Aunt Deirdre as I kissed her daughter. 'Junior Dean, no less.'

'It doesn't mean anything,' said the philosopher, adding, 'How are you, anyway?'

'I'm OK.'

Felicity followed me upstairs. Her parents stood in the hall and shouted after us.

'Your room's had a face-lift,' yelled Aunt Deirdre.

'Yes,' said Uncle Roy. 'The diocese has at last offered to give the place a lick of paint.'

Felicity helped me with my holdall. Instinctively, when we were alone in my bedroom, I opened it and took out Hunter's book.

'We'll need to have a talk about that,' she said, putting her hand on the book. 'But there's no need to have it now.'

'Uncle Roy didn't want to talk about it in the car.' While I spoke, I was taking in the effect of the 'face-lift'. An alarmingly jaunty, floral wallpaper danced its way all over the room, waging war not only on the books and the furniture, but also on the view from the window, the subdued colours of a Norfolk evening, the village rooftops, the octagonal, flint tower of the church, the narrow River Timp running muddily through the paddock beyond our vegetable garden.

'It doesn't exist, of course,' she said.

'I'm sorry?'

'As far as Ma and Pa are concerned, that book does not exist. They won't talk about it.'

'Isn't that a bit silly?'

'It's hurt everyone very, very much,' she said, quietly.

This, the most obvious thing about Hunter's book, that it was bound to be hurtful to all who knew and loved the Lampitts, was something which had just not occurred to me.

'Sargie's in pretty poor odour with the rest of the family, needless to say, for letting that man anywhere near the stuff.'

'Raphael Hunter, you mean.'

'God, I hate him,' said Felicity.

This exchange made me burn for more news about the whole story of Hunter and the Lampitts, but there was a cottage pie to be eaten and news to be exchanged. I had thought that they would want to know all about my year in Cyprus, but all we heard about that was Granny's observation that she didn't like Archbishop Makarios and that Mrs Webb had never been able to abide a man with a beard.

What they all wanted to know were my plans for the future. I was astonished by the speed with which they got on to the subject. I murmured something about acting. I had hoped that this ambition would be something which was obvious to them, but that they would be patient while I thought of ways in which I might start on the career of my choice.

'I wondered whether you would think of following your father,' said Granny. 'I know it's thirteen years since he passed away, but there will be those at Tempest and Holmes who remember him. In fact, I know there are, since I still get a card at

Christmas from Mr Pilbright who was in Accounts with your father.'

I looked at Granny's face to see if she was being serious, as of course she was. It was a horrible moment.

What was wrong with thinking that I should live as my parents had lived? My father had been an assistant manager in a shirt factory. Had he lived, he might have ended up as a director; anyway, a full manager. He would have exchanged his semi-detached house in Fulham for something a little bit further out of London, perhaps in Ewell. But, for me, this way of life was not something which I had even contemplated. There was no *reason* why I should not become one of those thousands of people who had a job which bored them, and a mortgage and a suit to wear to the office.

'You'll have to settle for something,' said my aunt firmly.

'Mr Pilbright was ever so kind after David's funeral,' said Granny. 'Do you remember him, dear?'

'Vaguely,' said Uncle Roy.

The subject of my father's death was excruciating to him. It was hardly ever mentioned.

'He said, "If there's *anything* I can do to help." And he really meant it,' said Granny. 'As I say, he still sends a card at Christmastime.'

'I'm not sure that I'm cut out for that sort of work,' I said.

'There's no money for a university,' snapped my aunt. 'I mean, even if you *had* passed those exams.'

'I wasn't thinking of a university,' I said.

'What were your ideas?'

The women were persistent.

'It takes a bit of time,' said Uncle Roy gently. 'I expect you've had several thoughts.'

Seeing him at the end of the table, dreamily smoking his pipe, I realised that my uncle had hardly done anything for the previous quarter of a century. Oh, he had driven Sargie to Cromer and he had read the Prayer Book services and he had worn clothes. But he had never been obliged to go to an office or tolerate the condescension of Mr Pilbright in Accounts.

I genuinely don't know and it would be impertinent to speculate whether Uncle Roy felt a true sense of religious vocation. But during that conversation I had a very clear vision of how *silly* I had been, during all those terrible quarrels of my teenage years, when I had tried to catch my uncle out in some theological argument or accused him openly of hypocrisy. Certainly the clerical life was not for me. But it had rescued Uncle Roy from suits off the peg, and semi-detached houses in Ewell and Mr Pilbright of Accounts. I had other dreams. I wanted to write a great book; act a great Hamlet; have a great and complicated love affair. None of these things could be accomplished unless I could persuade my family that I did not need to take a job. And how could someone who was penniless do that?

These were now huge, urgent considerations. I had to find a plausible alternative to my grandmother's suggestion. Otherwise the shirt factory beckoned. My only objections to it were snobbish or aesthetic. They weren't *rational*. The sensations of freedom which I had tasted in London that morning and which had helped to drive me so impulsively into the arms of Cindy were quickly evaporating. None of the ideas about the future which existed in my mind could be voiced without embarrassment. I could not, in that company and at that moment, say, 'I'm hoping to write a book,' or 'I rather want to go on the stage.'

Instead, I said, 'I thought of living in London for a bit.'

'What on?' asked my aunt mercilessly. 'You have no money.'

'We could probably find you accommodation,' said Uncle Roy. 'Sibs would help, I'm sure.'

'That would be very kind.'

'Just to start with.'

'We had a charming letter from Sibs the other day. It looked at one point as if Gavin was going to follow in Father's footsteps and become a civil servant. But instead he has gone into banking, like young Michael, Anne is studying art – the history thereof.'

'Who's this?' asked Granny.

'Lady Starling, Mother,' her son shouted. 'No,' he added in a quieter voice, 'Sibs has been absolutely wonderful lately about keeping in touch, with Sargie being so barmy.'

'Barmy?'

But no explanation was offered. For the moment the subject of my career was dropped. The twin beacons of Lady Starling's boys had been held up to light my way. Even Lampitts had jobs. It was a woeful thought. The question of whether Sargie had in fact lost his wits or whether the phrase merely suggested that he was still being tiresome would have to wait until I was alone with Felicity.

It was still light after supper, so Felicity and I took a walk together in the midgy evening air. Barminess, Sargie's or anyone else's, was a good enough subject for laughter. I chuckled as I asked about it.

Taking the road out of Timplingham, the very slight incline actually increases one's sense of the infinite sky which stretched above us. The drizzle had cleared. Wind blew. That familiar soughing for which I had so often and so painfully been homesick in the Mediterranean moved the trees.

A few years of giving tutorials (at Oxford now) had made Felicity much more coherent. Perhaps unhappiness, perhaps the austerity of the meals in a women's college, explained the fact that she had lost so much weight. She was much more handsome: tall, lean, intensely serious, a being quite other from the adolescent, silent girl whom I had frightened with a toad.

'Pa's been through hell,' she said.

'With Sargie? Has he actually been certified?'

'You've been away so much, it's hard to know where to begin,' she said, stopping to light a cigarette. She was now smoking a lot. 'That man Hunter has a lot to answer for.'

'From you, certainly.'

'I don't care about him any more personally. It's as though none of that happened between him and me. Honestly. It's not a question of "hell hath no fury". Though I do see now the way he treated me was all of a piece with his totally ruthless desire to exploit everyone who crosses his path. Look at what happened. First, years ago, he latched on to Jimbo Lampitt. I don't know whether that was a simple case of what it looked like. Perhaps we shall have to wait for Hunter Vol. II or even Hunter Vol. III to find the answer to that one.'

'You're surely not suggesting that Hunter and Petworth Lampitt . . .'

She offered me a cigarette and I took one.

'I don't understand Raphael,' she said, 'and I don't really want to understand him. God knows why he wanted to write this foul book in the first place. It isn't as if poor old Jimbo was even a very good writer.'

'Oh, I disagree with you there.'

'Well, he wasn't Gibbon.'

'Isn't it legitimate to write the life of a writer even if he wasn't Gibbon?'

'Not if it hurts people,' she said.

'Who's it hurt?'

'Oh, just about everyone, that's all. Everyone who matters. Sargie is absolutely devastated. It's his own fault in a way, but not in another. Raphael simply took him over. I know how that can happen. It was starting that summer when he first came to the Place and I was working with him. But after Sargie moved to London, the takeover was complete. Now, of course, Sibs and the rest are saying that Raphael should never have been given the Lampitt Papers. But he just *took* them. What could old Sargie do?'

'Did you know all this racy stuff about Jimbo? Is that what you and Hunter were reading that summer five years ago?'

'You know, the funny thing is, I went through an awful lot of the old boy's papers that summer, even before Raphael descended on the Place, and I never found anything remotely interesting in them. Oh, there were some letters from famous people . . .'

'Which famous people?'

'Oh, I don't know. Hugh Walpole. Lascelles Abercrombie. There were one or two from Henry James. But nothing to suggest that he was leading this rampaging, alleycat sort of life.'

'You have to admit it was clever of Hunter to find out about it.'

'Clever?' She stopped to light up again. 'That's one word for it. I did not go through everything, of course. Jimbo left so much. I don't think the Lampitts realise how much there was. It's all very well for Sibs to say that Sargie should have read the papers before he gave them to Raphael. But I'd like to see *her* go through it all. There were at least fifteen large trunks all bursting with papers.'

'And Hunter just appropriated them?'

'They really were getting mouldy at the Place, I believe. Just look at it now!'

We leaned on a wall and looked across the fields. In the old days, this would have provided a view of the splendid old stables behind the Place. Now there was nothing except Sargie's bungalow, where a light was burning. The fading sky did very little to disguise its uncompromising brashness; as if the new bricks were not bad enough, Sargie had yielded to the builder's suggestion of a royal blue front door, frosted glass and a carriage lamp.

'Raphael just took Sargie over,' she said. 'Poor Pa was edged out. They would never have quarrelled if it had not been for Raphael. I am convinced of that.'

'There have been phases before when they were off one another,' I said. 'I think they'll come round to one another again.'

'The old things were tiffs. This was a real rift. And it was deliberately created. I feel certain of that. I am sure that Raphael wanted to stop Sargie seeing the people who loved him. He wanted me out of the way and he dispatched me in the most efficient possible manner.'

'Isn't that going a bit far?' I asked.

'He did not want me to know the contents of those papers. I'm sure of that. And I'm absolutely sure that his desire to keep me out was stronger than . . . his desire for me.'

'But this is to make him into some kind of . . . *devil!*'

'Julian. Either he *knew* that those trunks contained the most awful secrets of Jimbo's sex life; or – which is what I suspect – he knew they didn't. Either way, he did not want a witness spoiling his story. He knew that an innocent galumphing girl would just never go away from her godfather's house, unless she *had* to go away in disgrace.'

'You're not serious?'

'It's all right. I haven't gone round the bend, though sometimes I've thought that I would, just thinking about it all . . . The point is, we'll never know. We'll never get our hands on the Lampitt Papers. Raphael will make sure of that. In my opinion, the biography is equally disgraceful whether it is a pack of lies or a deliberate, if truthful, betrayal of trust. It has to be one or the other.'

'But why – what are the motives?'

'You know, in the last few years, it has become clear that it wasn't just that Raphael wanted the papers for his wretched book. He had a compelling need to make Sargie betray those who loved him best. Sibs was a victim, you know. She thought she was in control, but she just let Raphael walk all over her.'

'A complete doormat, in fact.'

'Why do you say that?'

'Nothing.'

'She even rang Pa to ask if Sargie was still *alive*. She'd written to him three times, asking him to meals and things, and he simply wouldn't reply. She tried ringing his flat, and whenever she did so Raphael answered and said that Sargie wasn't available. Hunter moved into the flat. He's living there now, I believe – which is why Sargie is sitting over there in the bungalow drinking himself silly, poor old boy.'

'Couldn't you all have done something to rescue him? Get a doctor or something?'

'Well, there you are,' said Felicity. 'Paranoia creates what it fears. For years Sargie has been imagining that all the Lampitts had been holding councils of war and talking about him behind his back. Now they really did.'

'Lady Starling summoned a council of war?'

'Sibs had the whole gang of them round to Cadogan Square to decide what to do. Vernon wanted them to get a power of attorney over Sargie – have him certified – anything to get the papers out of his hands.'

'So they had begun to suspect what sort of beans Hunter's biography was going to spill?'

'There'd been rumours. In a highly calculated way, the little slug had gone round London feeding people with titbits. The news certainly reached Oxford. I was dining in New College one day – Sargie's old college – and my host, not knowing that I knew anything about the Lampitts, raised Jimbo's name. The usual thing. "Does anyone nowadays read James Petworth Lampitt? My bookseller advised – buy in while he's still at the bottom of the market. First editions of *Prince Albert* are still purchasable for a few shillings. When the world gets to know of his liaisons with all and sundry, my business sense tells me that he will *appreciate*. Nothing like a little sex for improving an author's standing with the book-buying public." I naïvely said that I thought Jimbo had been a bit of an old woman, but hardly a Lothario. Upon which, my genial philosopher said, "I'll spare your blushes, Felicity, but how many old women of your acquaintance give blowjobs to the Prime Minister of the day? This throws an altogether new light on the women's colleges." '

'Quite good.'

'As may be. But, you see, if my philosopher friend's appetite had been whetted, that meant that a key five hundred people knew about Raphael's so-called research. And they were the five hundred people who determine, in the end, whether a book will be successful or not.'

'The public determines that – the public alone.'

She merely laughed at my simplicity. I took another of her cigarettes.

She said, 'Apart from anything else, it threw the most appalling light on Raphael's own relationship with Sargie. It has tarred Sargie with Jimbo's brush, this making out that Jimbo was a sort of Oscar Wilde.'

'Good Lord. You don't mean that anyone thinks that Sargie and Uncle Roy . . .'

'It has tainted *everything*.'

From the grass where we walked – not ten feet ahead – a pair of larks rose almost vertically into the air. Our eyes followed them until the brightness of the yellow sky made it impossible to stare further. There was no visible sun, but the clouds were full of light.

Obviously – if anything was now obvious – the very thought of Uncle Roy having some sort of inverted association with Sargie was totally preposterous. It would have been impossible to find a friendship which on its own terms was more innocent. Yet the meaning of Felicity's words was perfectly clear. Hunter's biography was bound to sully the atmosphere. Perhaps – this was what she seemed to be saying – that was why he wrote it.

'He's like some horrible parasite crawling its way into the system,' she said. 'He could beguile anyone.'

I could not answer this without raking up her own affair with Hunter. I need not have been so delicate.

'He got me,' she said. 'I was *so* in love with that man, Julian.'

'I know.'

I wondered if there had been other men since. Felicity and I were not used to sharing confidences. She knew nothing of my inner history. I would have known nothing of hers, had she not been made ill by it.

'I still don't really understand why it was so important to batten on to Jimbo,' she said. 'Why write a biography of him, of all people?'

'Oh, that I think I do understand,' I said. Although it was an evening for confidences, I still felt too shy to admit that I understood what it was to have a literary ambition. 'I dare say he wanted to get started, in a literary way. To write a book about anything. Jimbo was to hand.'

'Was he?'

'Oh, it looks to us like some inexplicable conspiracy. First, Hunter intrudes himself into Jimbo's life, then he steals the papers. But don't you think that from his point of view, it might all look different?'

'How do you mean?'

'Suppose he was in love with the idea of himself as a writer. It would mean that anyone who fitted in with this idea of his would become an object of fascination to him. So he was in love with Jimbo's memory. In love with the girl who helped him sort the papers.'

'That's your explanation for what happened between me and Raphael?'

'It might explain why he became infatuated with Sargie.'

'I never thought of Sargie as a queer,' she said.

'I don't suppose he is. There are ways and ways of taking people over. Hunter's way of taking *you* over would be different from his taking over Sargie.'

We walked along the path at the side of the field and back again into the road. The walk was more than halfway over and now we were turned for home. The evening light was fading and the rooks were noisy in the sky.

'It's broken Pa's heart, all this,' she said.

'I don't quite see why, or how.'

'You know how paranoid Sargie is.'

'Yes.'

'Well, when Sibs and the others became really frightened about Raphael they came to Pa and begged him to do something. So he went down to London and took Sargie out to lunch. There was the most frightful row. Sargie said that Pa had been paid, all these years, to spy on him for the other Lampitts. They really are estranged now. I don't mean they will never meet or never speak again. But Pa never goes near that bungalow and Sargie never comes down to us. In terms of Pa's life, it's sadder than anything. Much sadder than the ending of a love affair.'

'He's got your mother,' I said, realising, as I said it, that this cut both ways.

We walked back to the house in silence. Something rather deep had happened during our walk and it would take time to absorb. Among other things, for the first time in my life, I had been compelled to take Uncle Roy seriously. I had been able to perceive him as a sentient being like myself, capable of hopes which could be dashed and feelings which could be hurt. I had no idea how much consolation could be derived from his religion. But, as I lay in my bath after the walk, it was of those early morning rituals in church which I began to think: my scuttling across to serve his altar on winter mornings before the light appeared. I thought of the very morning when Jimbo Lampitt had died and of my uncle in his funereal Mass vestments: a vaguely frightening figure at that moment, indulging in something which was on the edge of being magic.

Descending in my dressing gown, I found Uncle Roy in the hall, staring through the glazed front door at the night sky. He was swaddled in his own mannerisms to such a degree that I felt unable to penetrate to him and offer the sympathy which I now so acutely felt. I noticed that, since I went to Cyprus, he like Felicity had lost quite a bit of weight. The white collar and the bow tie hung loosely from a neck which had become scrawny and birdlike. The Oxford bags into which he had changed were not merely voluminous. They now seemed tragi-comic, like trousers in a farce or a mental ward, waiting at any moment to fall to his ankles. He was only in his mid-fifties, but he had started to look old.

'I think it's going to be a nice day tomorrow,' he said.

'The weather forecast has just said the opposite.'

I hated myself for saying this, but my instinct to point out that almost everything he said was wrong was unstoppable.

'We'll see.' He smiled, unperturbed by anything so modern as a report emanating from the wireless. 'I think you'll find it's fine in the morning.'

'Do you still have an early service on Thursdays?'

I asked the question hesitantly. He was no fool. He must have known that I had not undergone a religious conversion in the previous year. My desire to present myself at the altar was potentially embarrassing to us both. At that moment, however, I could think of no other way of showing my uncle that, in spite of all our difficulties together, I actually loved him. If I'd been a girl, I could just have gone up and given him a big kiss.

'Yes – yes – we still have the seven-thirty on Thursdays. But really, there's no need . . .'

'I was wondering if you'd like a server?'

I suppose by pious standards I was suggesting a blasphemy. I wasn't a believer. I was in a state of mortal sin. But I did not think much of a God who would damn me for what I was proposing and I prayed inwardly to this God who did not exist to make Uncle Roy accept my offer.

He repeated his unfinished sentence about there being no need. But he was touched and he read the signals right. He said he would be most grateful if I could serve his altar in the morning.

I set my alarm clock for six forty-five and woke earlier, my mind churning not so much with thoughts as with a whole jumble of images past and present – girls I'd been in love with, chaps I'd known, things which had happened in the army, things from much further back. School. Mummy. The train pulling out of the station and Mummy standing there, surrounded by men in uniform, and waving goodbye for ever.

Woven into all this undirected collection of feelings, there was my memory of the previous evening's conversation with Felicity. As I dressed, I opened Hunter's *Life of Lampitt* and looked at the photographs – Petworth with Lytton Strachey and Duncan Grant at Charleston. Petworth with Cynthia Asquith. Petworth, Arthur Machen and Yeats. These disparate moments of *their* lives had all been gathered together, artificially made into an historical whole, which they had never been at the time, by the painstaking but surely uninspired pen of Raphael Hunter. I could not believe in Felicity's theory that he had invented Jimbo's emotional life, because I could not believe that anyone capable of writing such flat prose could be so imaginative.

As I tied my tie and put on my shoes, I thought of Hunter. What motivated him? In Felicity's vision, he was a purely manipulative figure who had intruded himself into the life of the Lampitt family – and thus into our life – for the purposes of some obscure form of self-advancement. To me, as I looked back over the years, Hunter began to seem different.

There he had been at the beginning, embracing Miss Beach. And would his curiously youthful, fascinatingly dull smile be there to greet me when I tottered towards the end? I half wondered whether he was not some sort of magician, capable not only of the spuriously fictitious art of biography, forcing outlines which had not been there on the haphazard existence of old Jimbo, but also an occult master capable of controlling and shaping the lives of the living, perhaps even pulling the strings of my own existence. Such a fantasy would seem, in the light of future developments, to have been not wholly wide of the mark. At the very least, if not a controller, Raphael was some kind of recording angel, a figure who arbitrarily connected with some of the most intimate moments of my emotional history far too frequently for it simply to be a coincidence. Hunter's destiny and mine appeared to be mysteriously linked. At times, as with the experience of watching him embrace Miss Beach, I was compelled to have my experience filtered through Hunter. At other times, as with our very different perceptions of the Binker, or our quite different relationships with Felicity, we were destined, like figures in Oriental religion, to represent two sides of the same phenomenon, the dark and the light, the positive and the negative. My heart was already preparing itself unconsciously for the idea that Hunter was not just a figure who would keep cropping up but, much more strangely, that he was a figure without whom my own life was not quite imaginable.

Perhaps the whole concept of imagining one's own existence, seeing it as a finished entity, is a misguided one. Whether or not this is the case, I had the sense of Hunter's presence that morning, either as a fellow actor or as a master of ceremonies, but always a figure on the stage with me, or waiting in the wings, one whose exact role in the drama had yet to be disclosed.

My dressing was complete. The whole palaver of getting up for the early service – tiptoeing on landings so as not to wake the rest of the household – inevitably made me a twelve-year-old once more. I even experienced a particular kind of early-morning collywobbles in my stomach which I had forgotten existed.

Outside, it was pelting with rain. Monsoon conditions. As I squelched my way through the churchyard, I could see a light on in the vestry. My uncle was there. He had already lit the candles on the altar, and placed the bread and wine on the credence table. The church felt extremely damp and cold. It was as empty as ever.

I walked up the aisle, staring into the shadowy roof at the rows of carved, surpliced figures on the beam ends. And there she was, looking down over the pulpit, baring the incomparable

Timplingham Titties as she had done for the previous five hundred years. Perhaps, rather than being the aberration of some lecherous carver, this curious piece of sculpture hid some profounder theological purpose. As the prospect of serving the altar drew nearer, I thought sheepishly (with embarrassment more than with guilt) of Cindy and of some of the other erotic moments in life. Quite involuntarily, I remembered the extraordinary excitement (with the one-night stand in Northampton) of discovering that they too could *come*. It was a revelation which filled me with guilt in relation to Barbara. Her *'lentement, chéri'* and her *'ici, ici'* now had meaning for me. These images flashed through the mind when I should have been praying. And then I thought of another moment with Barbara, walking along with her in that religious procession and thinking I might blub. It wasn't guilt, it wasn't morbid eroticism which prompted those tears. It was something much odder, something which I had not got round to thinking about and which probably should never be approached by the medium of *thought*.

Waiting in church for the service to start, though, I did have a thought. If there was a God of love, I thought, then presumably an indulgent and even an amused eye was turned to the bizarre ways in which we tried to make ourselves happy. The naked wooden breasts exposed so flagrantly over the pulpit were perhaps not so out of place. Instinct told me that Aunt Deirdre was wrong to think them 'a pity'.

I bowed to the altar, not because I believed that there was any magic there, but not just to please Uncle Roy, either. I don't know why I bowed. Uncle Roy was kneeling at the back of the Lady Chapel with his face in his hands.

I went into the vestry where his green chasuble was spread out on the vestment chest. At seven twenty-five he came backstage and threw this item of attire over his head. At seven twenty-seven he put the maniple over his left wrist, and I led him out of the vestry and up the north aisle to his altar. Rather surprisingly, there were about five village people kneeling there for Mass. My aunt wasn't among them.

The Prayer Book service was the same as ever I remembered it. The Lord's Prayer in my uncle's monotone began at the very moment that the little clock over the north door struck the half-hour. After the Collect for Purity, the Ten Commandments.

'Thou shalt not commit adultery,' said Uncle Roy.

244

In response, I said the words which were printed in the book, but with absolutely no confidence that my heart, in the years to come, would be inclined to keep this law.

A BOTTLE
IN THE SMOKE

One

Killing Time. One spends more and more time doing it, I find. Sleep used to account for at least one-third of each twenty-four hours. Now I'm lucky if I get five hours of oblivion without a Mogadon. And I turn up early for everything. A luncheon date in Westminster at twelve forty-five found me, not long ago, pacing about on the Embankment at eleven in the morning, and deciding to revisit old favourites at the Tate. I often go there, particularly to look at the Blake Room, and the modern sculpture, for which I have a weakness, and the Turners. Somehow, on that particular day, the minutes dragged past and I found that I had seen everything I wanted to see within three-quarters of an hour.

Coming down into the main hall, I decided to visit their special exhibition, and only then noticed that it was called 'Mr Pilbright At Home'. Nothing could have been more calculated to bring before me Time's strange trick of long holding secrets in its bosom which are then, years later, trumpeted forth. Letters written in secret command high sums from the Sunday newspapers a generation later. Love affairs become a mere matter of serialisation rights. Spies who have handled information which, if disclosed, could ruin the lives of thousands are prepared, in time, to put the whole thing down on paper for in-flight entertainment.

Uncle Roy had a word for it in one of his church services – 'when the secrets of all hearts shall be disclosed'. Biographers like Hunter make such disclosures their stock in trade. Mr Pilbright probably had no dramatic secrets to conceal except his genius – or his whatever it was, if it wasn't quite genius. If he had written any love letters they certainly did not survive. He appeared to have had no close relationships with women except that with his mother. The mysterious girl, variously called his 'angel' or his 'Magdalene', who appears so often in his pictures was thought by critics to have been a creature of his imagination, purely. She was not a model at any of the life classes he (to me surprisingly) turned out to have attended in the 1920s and 1930s. Yet again and again, she crops up in his work: as the angel telling the Fulham bus queue 'He is not here – He is risen!' or as the canvas nicknamed *The Woolworth Magdalene*, one of the Tate's finest Pilbrights, a moonfaced girl with her dark hair cut short, her skirt tight against her thighs as she kneels to empty a bottle of 4711 over the sandals of the slightly schoolmasterly, bearded figure, sitting in the pub with His friends. Critics admire the way she has kicked off one of her peep-toe stilettos to reveal malformed feet with toe-nails, exuberant splashes of his vermilion brushwork.

The religious element in Mr Pilbright's pictures does not always speak to me, and most of the comparisons with Blake seem pretty wide of the mark. There are paintings of his which I can enjoy – though not those with too overt a message. The enormous number of sketches and watercolours of people at work or simply going about their ordinary business in wartime or just post-wartime suburbia are the things to which I return. There's a lovely one called *Spring Comes to Balham* which I found once in the art gallery at Aberdeen. He seems to redeem the triviality of things by looking at them so lovingly. Plant pots. A woman walking her Scottie. Tulips in a window-box.

Some of the pictures of work recapture my own brief period of being his colleague at Tempest and Holmes during the year after I finished National Service. I have sometimes wondered whether I wasn't the model for *Boy in Accounts*, one in that series of sketches done in the mid-1950s which he worked up into that showy canvas, now in the Pompidou Centre, *Matthew Forsakes the Inland Revenue to Follow Christ*. Mr Pilbright never sketched at work, of course. It was all done from memory. His existence as a painter was entirely unknown to me or to any of his colleagues at the time.

The special exhibition was extremely well done. You walked behind a large screen and immediately you were gazing into two perfectly constructed interiors, exact reproductions of the ground floor of Mr Pilbright's Balham semi-detached. The front room (so designated, apparently by Mr Pilbright himself, though I wondered whether he wouldn't have been a 'lounge' man) was a perfectly respectable neat little interior, whose varnished oak furnishings dated mainly from the Edwardian period. The two-seater settee and the armchair were draped with antimacassars. The windows were concealed by lace curtains. On the vaguely 1909 neo-Tudor sideboard was a Bakelite wireless set. A small bookcase contained sentimental novels – one noted the names of Mrs Henry Wood and Marie Corelli on the spines, but Day Muckley's *The Calderdale Saga* was also there. The gas fire was the old-fashioned sort, where the elements resemble false teeth. The pictures on the walls gave little clue to any artistic interest on the part of the inhabitant. There was a portrait of Mr Gladstone, a couple of Arundel Society prints, and a large photograph of Mr Pilbright's mother, hung up, it was conjectured, some time after that lady's demise during the Second World War.

The back room was in the greatest possible contrast. The orderliness, the bourgeois ordinariness of the front room was anonymous. If you thought long about it, perhaps there would have seemed something self-consciously old-fashioned about it; but there must be many people, particularly the unmarried residing with parents, who live with inherited furniture and never bother to express their own taste by the purchase of contemporary fittings.

The back room was a chaos. A catalogue which I bought on my way out of the exhibition assured the visitor that the two rooms had been reconstructed with complete faithfulness. Certainly the difference between the two rooms fitted well with what I knew and did not know about Mr Pilbright all those years ago. At the front he was the bourgeois suburban man, anonymous in his tedious, orderly acceptance of the conventions. Behind all this rioted his hidden artistic obsession.

The window of the back room had been boarded up. This had apparently been done long before the blackout. Mr Pilbright preferred to work by the same even and unsatisfactory light dangling from the 60-watt bulb (no shade) in the middle of the ceiling. The reason for this became clear as soon as you thought about it. Nearly all his work had to be done at night. He reached home by about six, ate a high tea, and then retreated to the studio for four or six hours' work. On Saturday and Sunday he would work a more or less full day in the back room. He was scarcely out of the place, a fact which accounted for that pasty prison complexion which I so well remember.

One wall of the back room was covered with his striking mural: *The Great Draught of Fishes at Kew Bridge*. Not one of his best. On the other hand, one saw his real merits, as an observer of the human scene if not exactly as a great artist, in the many half-finished paintings and drawings which littered this room. There were studies for *Morning 'Bus Ride*, and some of those memorable pen-and-ink sketches of ARP wardens after a raid. The room was crammed with these pictures, dozens of them – oils, charcoal sketches, watercolour studies. The room was carpeted, strewn with them. Palettes, jars of turps with brushes, paint tubes with no tops, were scattered all over the place, evidence that he worked in a frenzy, giving himself no time to tidy up afterwards, when exhausted after a solid spell of creativity, he would clamber into bed. A 'voice-over' – instantly recognisable as a replay of Raphael Hunter's television Arts programme, 'Perspectives' – informed us that Pilbright worked each evening until he was so tired that the brush fell from his hand. Then he would remove his paint-stained overalls, go upstairs and sleep until the time came, a few hours later, to resume the persona of a manager in Accounts at Tempest and Holmes.

At this point in Hunter's narrative, Mr Pilbright's own voice was heard. The content of what he had to say was not, when analysed, exactly interesting. I've often thought that, about the utterances of painters, sculptors, or other non-verbal communicators; when they try to put into words what they have been up to in their art, it's not particularly impressive. But it was, from a personal point of view, truly extraordinary to hear that voice after nearly forty years, and in such a context. I had missed the original television programme, transmitted in the early 1960s, which had 'made' Pilbright's reputation. Hearing it for the first time in the gallery, it was almost as if Hunter and Pilbright, both in their different ways haunting figures, had been summoned up from the vasty deep. Hunter had just said to Pilbright that he enjoyed his canvases because of their sympathetic evocation of the lives of ordinary people.

'But there are no ordinary people!' said Pilbright. 'Never heard of such a being! Ordinary! Jesus Christ was an ordinary person, if you are going to take that line. . . . No, in all my work, I've just tried to . . .'

252

'And religion has always been an important part of your inspiration?'

'Inspiration? Religion. Oh, dear, oh, dear!' In the cross scepticism and the cockneyfied twang of this retort I heard again *my* Mr Pilbright. 'Our watches must be set to different time-scales,' I remember his saying to me sarcastically when I arrived for work at ten past nine. 'Mine's Greenwich Mean Time, what's yours?' 'No,' he was now saying to Hunter. 'I've worked hard. Inspiration! I've lived by rule.'

'You worked for many years in a shirt factory, I believe,' wheedled Hunter.

'Look, I told you before you switched on all this equipment that I would only talk about art, about my work.' Crossly, firmly, grandly, Mr Pilbright's voice put Hunter down.

I couldn't blame him for not wishing to reminisce about life at Tempest and Holmes, which was tedious enough. There was probably nothing, imaginatively speaking, for him to remember. Life, properly defined, probably only happened for Pilbright in that back room in Balham beneath the naked 60-watt bulb. Hunter, in his obvious way, discerning the fact that Pilbright's best pictures captured the qualities of workaday life, probably supposed that Pilbright would have something to say about it – as though painting were a substitute for talk. He might as well have assumed that Titian would have had more interesting things to say than the next man about classical mythology, or Winterhalter about Queen Victoria, or Picasso about women.

What really astonished me, though, was how mistaken, how utterly mistaken, I had myself been about old Pilbright. I had known this for years. Pilbright became famous in the 1960s, decades before I chanced upon this special exhibition at the Tate. But 'Mr Pilbright At Home' brought home to me the sheer crassness of a younger self, the crudity of my judgements, the simplicity of distinctions which I allowed to form in my mind between what was and wasn't boring, what did or didn't matter.

In the office, Pilbright had embodied everything which I considered uninspiring and unimportant. I despised him because I was so certain that he belonged to a world where art, literature, the theatre, music (my own imagined spheres) did not figure. If I had been more honest I should probably have admitted that social snobbery came into play, too. It usually does in England. My years with Aunt Deirdre and Uncle Roy had left their mark. I might wince at their talk of people being of 'good' family or out of such and such a 'drawer', but in fact with a large part of myself I had come to accept that the upper social reaches, or at least the cultivated classes, were inherently more estimable than the suburban sort of families from which we ourselves sprang, and to which Mr Pilbright, all his life, unpretentiously belonged.

'Of course, I'm fond of Wagner,' his cross voice, disembodied but now immortal, was saying through the loudspeakers, as visitors drifted through and peered at his reconstructed rooms, which were sealed off by plate glass. 'Debussy, yes. Mainly composers who were working at the time my parents were married, I suppose you would say. Yes. César Franck, yes, yes. Did you say Elgar?'

Hunter, in the original interview, had apparently said Elgar.

'The choral music, are you trying to say?' said Pilbright's voice accusingly.

As he painted in the back room at Balham, Pilbright was apparently accustomed to play these composers on 78 recordings. Though at the period when I knew him, or didn't know him, I was almost completely ignorant of music, I would have been surprised that Pilbright knew these composers' names, let alone their work. If he had listened to anything, I should have conjectured that he would have been a Gilbert and Sullivan fan, or fond of 'Music While You Work' on the wireless.

I don't exactly blame myself for failing to recognise at less than twenty-five years old that people seldom reveal much of themselves at their place of employment. Pilbright was a studiedly dark horse. If the exhibition catalogue is right, he had been bitterly disappointed, during his own young manhood, by his failure to sell so much as one picture. It would seem as though he had doggedly, and in a spirit of self-immolation, thrown himself into the boring work at Tempest and Holmes. I now see that there was a strong element of self-parody in the way that he arrived each morning at two minutes to nine and left on the stroke of five. No one seemed to know where he lived. Since he never missed a day of work, it did not matter; there was no call to get in touch with him at home. Some of the typists giggled occasionally about the mystery of where he spent his dinner hour, always taken from half-past twelve until half-past one. What lay behind their fantasies was the shared assumption that Pilbright was so colourless that even the idea of his drinking half a pint of bitter in a pub, let alone seeing a woman, was so *risqué* as to be laughable. There is probably no bit of work done by Pilbright for Tempest and Holmes which could not nowadays be accomplished by a computer. His knowledge of the contents of the various ledgers and order books was encyclopaedic. He knew, for years back, all the transactions in which the firm had been involved, he knew the names of all the reps, all the retailers.

'Now let us *see*,' he would say, with apparent relish; I now think there was irony, almost laughter, in this 'enjoyment' taken in work. At the time, I thought that shirts were Pilbright's be all and end all. 'Merrick and Son. Leicester. Yes, of course.' First the town where the particular draper or men's outfitter was located. Having recited that, Mr Pilbright liked to rehearse how many of a particular type of shirt they had, over the years, been able to sell. 'Strangely enough, they've always been rather advanced in Leicester. What you would call avant-garde, young Ramsay.'

This showed that he had sized me up as a person who would use the phrase and admire what it denoted. 'Merricks were the first of our retailers to plump in a big way for collar-attacheds. Well, they all buy them now, of course, confounded inventions. You want to change your collar every day, I can see that, and your cuffs if you have that kind of work. But phew! A clean shirt every day!'

This was obviously out of the question. He seemed positively to relish being this sort of person, the sort who had a 'bath night' – once a week? – and changed his sheets by rote once a fortnight. He did not belong, and still less wished to pretend to belong, to any world where the expression 'avant-garde' could be used except in a humorous context.

It was entirely Mr Pilbright's fault that I was working at Tempest and Holmes. My father had worked with him in Accounts there before the war. When Mummy and Daddy were killed in the air raid, Mr Pilbright wrote a purely formulaic letter of condolence which touched my grandmother deeply. Subsequent communication had been limited to Christmas cards. Pilbright was quite a bit older than Daddy. I have no reason to suppose that my father was any closer to him than any of Pilbright's other colleagues had been. Granny, however, had for long had it in mind that I should follow in my father's footsteps. It was a joke proposition as far as I was concerned. But when National Service ended, and I was able to provide the family with no plausible alternative, events took their inevitable course.

There was naturally no question that Granny herself could write a letter. Apart from her eyes – suitable for reading, jaunts to the cinema in Norwich, and observing the passing scene but too frail for *writing* – there was all the 'botheration', her word, of finding the wherewithal to write a letter. And then the further difficulty of posting the letter when it was complete. It must have been my aunt who was delegated to write the actual letters, one to Mr Pilbright and another to the managing director. Much to my chagrin, I found myself not merely being interviewed, but offered a job. It is easy enough to say that I was not suited to the work, but since I had no money, and no 'contacts' who could get me into drama school, or journalism, or any other exotic area, I found myself submitting. For the larger part of a year I did very little except study ledgers. I copied figures from one ledger into another ledger. I sorted certain bundles of the morning mail, and divided incoming settlements from the invoices. No wonder I remember no detail of the work. It was of a kind which did not occupy my imagination at all. One just did it, like a machine. Life was not enhanced by the fact that Aunt Deirdre had fixed me up with some 'very suitable accommodation', as the lodger of a highly uncongenial family (friends of Aunt Deirdre's friend Bunty). For about six months, I was simply crushed by the experience and felt too unhappy and disappointed to shake myself out of it. Until looking at those reconstructed rooms in the Tate and hearing again the voice of Mr Pilbright, I had forgotten that feeling of desolation, the thought that life was never going to happen. It would simply be swallowed in work which I did not enjoy, meals which I did not like eating, company which afforded no kind of diversion. With the returning gloom, I felt a great envy of Mr Pilbright. I remember telling one of my fellow clerks (whose name now escapes me) that I did not intend to be a drudge for ever. I wanted to write – was indeed at work on a novel – and I wanted to act. Pilbright, coming along the row of desks at the moment when these ambitions were being aired, paused and looked into my face. How vividly I recall his expression; the sky-blue eyes behind steel-rimmed spectacles were laughing at me, I see that now. Was there not a clue in his curious hairstyle – the silver hair *en brosse* cut so short as almost to be a crew-cut – that he was not quite the office automaton we all supposed? 'Artistic ambitions, Ramsay? Wouldn't it be better to leave that as a hobby? Something to do with yourself in your spare time. Nice to have a hobby.'

When he had gone, somebody spluttered an obscene suggestion as to Pilbright's chosen method of filling leisure hours. We all sniggered. Memory of that laughter increased my envy now. This was the right way round for fame and fortune to smile. The life which inspired that sniggering in Accounts had ended in a triumph – Hunter's 'discovery' of Pilbright on 'Perspectives' articles in the national press, exhibitions, interest from collectors, a belated ARA. For all his years of pure artistic activity he had the satisfaction of being able to work without the distractions of fame. To be a neglected genius (or whatever he was) for years and to be discovered at nearly sixty was a fairy-tale piece of good fortune which a true artist, in any sphere, would envy. Day Muckley's contrary fate – the Best-Seller, as we so cruelly dubbed him in the Black Bottle – was much worse. He was prodigiously famous before the war for writing one book, *The Calderdale Saga*. The success could not be repeated. By middle age, however hard he tried to write books which would attract his old public, they resolutely refused to be interested. By the time I knew Muckley, he had sunk into an obscurity which was total.

Or seemed so. The television serialisation of *The Calderdale Saga* came too late for the Best-Seller himself to enjoy it, but it showed that fame offers its bearers strange fortunes. Was it better to enjoy some posthumous fame, such as Muckley's, than to have none at all – to be like Fenella, dreaming all the time of the Big Break which would make her a celebrated actress, but having to live not only without recognition, but also without much money or, surely, without any confidence that she was really any good? The enviable, maddening thing about Pilbright is that he must have known that he was good – or good in his own way. Self-confidence sustained him for forty years of absolute obscurity. The house when he died was full of pictures, hundreds of them, many of which now hang in the most prestigious galleries and collections in the world. I do not suppose that Pilbright ever left London, unless for a day out by the sea at Brighton or Ramsgate. He had probably barely heard of the Museum of Modern Art in New York. He died before they built the Pompidou Centre in Paris. It probably did not give him any particular pleasure to read critics who said that he was better than Lowry or Stanley Spencer, a figure who lifted English art out of its provincial confines, or that he deserved to be considered in the same league as Picasso and Pollock – a man who had recovered, as they had not, a new way forward for representational art. Whether or not he was a genius, he had the complete self-confidence which always accompanies genius. That was what sustained him for over forty years at Tempest and Holmes, that and the knowledge, when they presented him with his gold watch, at the time of his first 'retrospective', that he had used up most of his waking hours in a pointless job, faultlessly executed. Not long after he retired, the factory itself closed down. Its few remaining buildings have since been transformed. On one floor there is a dance studio. On another, strangely enough, one of Vernon Lampitt's granddaughters runs a thriving business which makes loose covers, festoon blinds, and huge profits out of upwardly mobile people uncertain of their own taste in interior design.

Probably Pilbright would have agreed with my grandmother's merciless assertion when insisting that I took the job that 'you've got to do something with your life'.

Unashamedly old-fashioned in her attitudes to the sexes, Granny appeared to think that this applied only to men. She could not be said to have done much herself, though the vehement tones in which she described her wholly passive role in things made it sound as though existence had been a constant drain on her reserves of energy. There was always the implication that having endured what she had done, it was unreasonable to expect any more of her.

'I did live through the 1930s,' she'd say. 'Ooh, they were a worry. You never knew whether you were coming or going. First it was the Abdication, and then it was whether they were going to have a war. I ask you!'

Uncle Roy would flinch if she embarked on these sentiments, not because he disagreed, but because of the (to him) excruciating hints of a glottal stop when she said a word like 'thirties', the threat that the Abdication would become the Abdic-ie-shun. It is perfectly true that not everyone survived the 1930s. Granny's boast that she had done so, however, implied that after such a feat of endurance it was hardly feasible two decades later to expect her to go shopping or to help with the washing-up. 'I brought *two* boys into the world *and* I brought them up.' The sentence was often on her lips, reminding hearers of the alarming fact that mothers do not necessarily do much for the care of their offspring. '*And* I brought them up.' When she repeated the phrase, Granny would shut her eyes (a habitual gesture when on the verge of crossness) and her lips would close so firmly as to disappear altogether. Her expression announced that anyone wishing to hear more on that particular subject was going to be disappointed.

I had never questioned that, having brought Daddy and Uncle Roy into the world, Granny could not be expected to look after me when my parents were killed. Until I grew up, and she came to live with Uncle Roy and Aunt Deirdre, I only saw Granny at carefully spaced intervals. It was decreed by her protectress and close friend Mrs Webb that you could hardly expect Thora to look after a child, not after what she'd been through. The phrase suggested something more ominous than existence itself. It made all the odder Granny's assertion (which she must have borrowed from the hyperactive Mrs Webb) that 'you've got to do something with life'. Granny knew what I have discovered in later years, that it is possible to do absolutely nothing with life, simply let it go. 'The things Thora has been *through*,' Mrs Webb would assert, with vehement shakings of the iron-hard perm. True, no doubt, just as Pilbright might have seemed, by those with more actively adventurous standards, to have had no life at all, but had, in his pictures, absorbed into his imagination a whole range of experience to which that artificial persona, Mr Pilbright of Accounts, would have been a stranger.

I think I shared this idea – whether it came from Granny or from Mrs Webb – not merely that one should do something with life, but that this doing was a matter of option or will. I thought that a series of infinitely extensible choices stretched ahead. All that was required was to try hard or to wait long enough. I was too young to know that very few wishes are ever fulfilled, or by the time they are, you have often stopped wishing them. I knew nothing about the strange part played in everything by chance. All I foresaw in the way of difficulty was the notorious trouble many creative people encounter in getting started. Thereafter, I should be able to fashion events. My ill-defined ambitions, and my only sporadically realistic sense of myself – a self which in any case was changing all the time – kept the perceptions of late middle age curtained from view. How trivial and empty and shapeless life for the most part is. I did not know that lives defined in terms of something durable (lives, as it turned out like Pilbright's) are very rare. The rest of us, crowds flowing over London Bridge into oblivion, leave no trace behind on this earth except offspring. Granny was right, perhaps, to make so much of her having brought two sons into the world. By some infinitesimal degree, evolutionary history had been changed by her. I was here, for example. And I must have inherited much of her passivity, else why should I have stayed so long in the routines imposed by my employment at Tempest and Holmes? If memory serves correctly, I worked truculently, but quite acceptingly. I rose early, and went to bed early, I travelled on a crowded bus at the beginning and end of each tedious day. I knew that the majority of Londoners lived like this, but I also knew that it was not what I regarded as 'doing something with life'. In fact, I saw Pilbright as the embodiment of what was wrong with this living death, his clean anonymous clothes, his grey suits and white shirts, his polite, industrious manner and his apparent non-existence after office hours. Even when the office routine began to wear me down with depression, I still did not fully believe myself to be a free agent. Held back by sheer lack of funds, my imagination did not allow itself to realise that I did not have to work at Tempest and Holmes. If I left there, no RSM would put me on a charge, no housemaster would gate me. I was to this extent free. It needed a friend to point this out to me, and for most of the time that I was working at Tempest and Holmes, I made no effort to keep in touch with the few friends I had. Then, completely by chance one Saturday, I met William Bloom, an old friend of army days, now a publisher. It was lunchtime and we were both looking round the same second-hand bookshop in the Charing Cross Road. It was only a matter of minutes before we were catching up on each other's lives, negotiating the trafffic of the Soho streets, and settling ourselves in the saloon bar of the Black Bottle, my first visit to that pub.

No less simian, Bloom looked smarter, more prosperous, than when last seen in a demob suit. His thick hair, cut short, was greying at the temples, though he was only my age. His blue corduroy jacket spoke of a literary world, light years away from Pilbright.

'You're sure we want to go here?' I asked incredulously, as he pushed open the door of the Black Bottle. 'It doesn't look much of a place to me.' Later in the conversation, when I had bought the first round and explained my predicament, my hatred of Tempest and Holmes, my despondency about getting any sort of congenial work, it was Bloom's 'Don't be so bloody wet!' which first stirred me to realise that my destiny in the short term was perfectly controllable.

'Live dangerously, my dear! Leave the awful job, carry on with the novel, go to auditions, act in the evenings.'

'What do I do for money?'

I had the rather bitter belief, indefensible probably, that everyone I had met was much richer than I was. It was all right for Bloom, with his cosmopolitan background, to suggest giving up my job. What would I live on?

'You could get a part-time job in a bar. Pubs always take on extra staff. You could write your novel between the intervals of serving drinks. Thank God for the licensing hours. And you'd be in Soho – think of all the fascinating creatures who would come your way.'

I looked through the cigarette haze of the saloon bar in the Black Bottle. Two old women were at a table drinking brandy and eating a packet of potato crisps. At the bar there was a blond young man with an iron contraption on one foot, and a man clad all in black, with a bowler hat on the back of his head. In that moment the place seemed a sort of Paradise from which work and Pilbrightery were excluding me. The Bottle was never by the wildest stretch of the imagination a fashionable pub, and it was hard to see any creatures who by Bloom's standards, or by mine, could be described as fascinating. Soho was Soho, though.

'And where are you living, for heaven's sake?'

When I explained about Bunty's friends the Murrays, Bloom exclaimed, 'Darling, this really won't *do*! I can find you something so much more fun.'

'I know what that would be like. No thanks.'

'I assure you, Julian, your reputation would be quite unsullied. They're out-of-work actors, a man and his wife, and they're rather short of lodgers just now. It would be miles more amusing than where you're living at present.'

'That wouldn't be difficult.'

'Why not tell old Pillprick or whatever he's called that you are just going?'

'William, he's so awful, he's – oh, I suppose it's pathetic really, but he's a non-person.'

'My dear, I can't bear it for you.'

It was William's turn to buy drinks and he made his way to the bar. For a moment I had the extraordinary sensation of seeing T. S. Eliot dispense the drinks, in William's case a Bloody Mary, in mine a Winter Warmer in a straight glass. Of course, I had only seen photographs of Eliot, but it was quite unmistakable. Not only the features of clerical cut, but the dark suit, the charming smile, the stoop. Mr Eliot and Bloom seemed to be in conversation for some time before my friend returned with the drinks.

'He's persuadable,' said William.

'Of what?'

'Of taking extra staff, part-time.'

'Does it strike you that he looks like . . .'

'Yes – it's the only thing to be said for this pub. Surely you know about Cyril? He's one of the sights of London.'

'I've not had time to go out much.'

I don't remember whether it was on that very first occasion at the Bottle or whether it came later that Cyril offered me work there. The resemblance to St Louis's most piously fastidious exile did not go beyond appearance. Neither in voice nor language was he markedly Eliotic.

'You a bum-boy? Not that I mind, see, only I don't want you bringing them all in here.'

After a disavowal of any such inclinations and an acceptance of pitifully small wages, I was taken on as a barman.

Whether it was then or another time, Bloom raised his glass and drank to 'Pillballs!'

'To Pillock!' I said.

My dislike of old Pilbright began before I ever went to Tempest and Holmes. Had it not been for his bloody Christmas cards my grandmother might have devised some other idea for how I should earn a living. Upon arrival at the offfice I had expected him at least to be friendly. He wasn't particularly. Beyond calling me 'young Ramsay' with a bit of a smile which was half a leer, Pilbright showed me absolutely no preferential treatment. Being young, I was vain and I assumed that the almost-leer was suggestive of concealed sexual interest in myself. Did he get a bit too close, I wondered, when he said, 'Oh dear, oh dear, oh *dear*! Can't you draw a straighter line than *that*, young Ramsay?' And then he would lean over and take the metal rule from my hand and draw a straight line in my ledger for me. Yes, I have seen the hand of Pilbright clutch a pencil and draw, though it was only a straight line in my ledger. Was that the reason for his smile? Did he know that one day his secret would be out, and we would try to recall any detail which hinted at his talent? I can remember his large pink hands, clumsy hands in appearance, controlling the pencil and the rule. I remember the smell of his breath, too, oddly pleasing, like milk.

Looking round the 'Mr Pilbright At Home' exhibition, I realised that I still rather disliked the old man, perhaps disliked him more than ever. One of the secretaries – until that moment I had forgotten her existence; what was she called? May? June? A name redolent of summer or weather; her voice was immediately familiar – was now speaking. Her voice rang out to the visitors at the exhibition as it had once pealed down the row of desks in the Accounts department, talking in those days of commonplace things, the price of clothes, the latest dance steps.

'We all knew he was an artist at heart. Oh, yes. Well, he had the real artistic temperament, like you might say. Oh, yes! You'd see him looking out of a window sometimes. For inspiration, I suppose you'd say. He was always looking, Mr Pilbright was, you could see it in his eyes.'

Hunter's voice took up the refrain. 'He was always looking. Pilbright's eyes were open, all the time, the artist's eye, looking at the world. Even colleagues at work like Dawn Simmonds saw it . . .'

Dawn, that was it! She and Hunter were so wrong. We didn't know Pilbright was an artist, no one did; that was the point of Pilbright. I even believe now that after the initial disappointment of his early years, Pilbright came to enjoy his work at Tempest and Holmes. Work consoles. The more boring, the more pointless, the better. It removes us from all the things which cause pain – families, lovers, dreams. Pilbright knew it because he was of an age to know it. I was too young then. I wanted the relationships and the dreams to be front stage. I had not yet come to feel that life (if painfully short from some viewpoints) goes on the hell of a time, and you need something to fill it up. Granny was right. You need something to *do*. Aunt Deirdre had chosen the best, the most archetypally time-consuming occupation of them all: gardening. 'Always something to do in a garden,' she would rightly say. Only I didn't want to do it.

I wanted at that stage to cut a dash: writing, acting, anything would serve. Nor was perpetual, only occasionally fulfilled lust quite enough, either. I wanted to define existence in terms of some big relationship with a woman. Presumably, once I had left Tempest and Holmes, that was why everything happened so quickly, going to live with Rikko and Fenella, meeting Anne, getting married, writing that nondescript book – all the things which I crammed into that short period. Hearing Pilbright's voice brought it all back with painful vividness. I remembered the morning I told him that I was going to start a new way of life.

'What's the matter? Aren't we arty enough for you in Accounts?'

Dawn Simmonds, fat, toothy, cackled with mirth.

'Wants to write a book, apparently,' pursued Mr Pilbright mercilessly. 'Or a play.'

'If it's a nice comedy I'll come and see it,' said Dawn. 'Like Ben Travers. I like him.'

Why was this funny? But we all laughed. It would have been rude not to.

'Got a part lined up? In a play?' Pilbright asked.

He had been through all these things in his own mind when he was a young man. He had opted for safety, anonymity, for keeping his art to himself. I now see how vulgar my choices must have seemed to him. At the time, I was determined not to admit to him the haphazard nature of the arrangements – half-board and lodging, arranged by Bloom, at Rikko's and Fenella's, a part-time job as barman at the Black Bottle, time enough to write my novel and look about for theatrical work, perhaps attend some classes and think about drama school.

'There are quite a lot of possibilities,' I said.

He looked at me closely.

'I just hope it won't be a decision you regret,' he said. 'Your father, now, he *liked* working here. We got on very well.'

'He was lovely, your dad,' said Dawn.

They had never spoken about Daddy before. It made the conversation all the more painful. As well as rejecting them and their harmless way of life, I appeared to be spitting on a dearly loved parent, setting myself above him.

So embarrassing did I find this conversation, which took place just before the dinner break, that I went straight out to a nearby pub and never returned to the Accounts department. Presumably my cards were posted on to me at a later date, perhaps by Mr Pilbright himself? I forget. How differently I view it all now. Mixed as my feelings about Pilbright and his pictures must remain, I think he was right. It is not an accident that human beings provide for themselves the narcotic of drudgery. Those of us who have opted out must pay the consequences.

At some turn of the painful conversation, he had said, 'You need something to keep you going – I'm not just talking about money, of course.'

The obviousness of this remark was not obvious to me then. I thought that just being me would keep me going, not realising that for much of the time this is precisely the thing one most needs to escape.

'I suppose painting's just a hobby,' he said in one of those too-frequent newspaper interviews he gave. 'Very rewarding, very satisfying, no doubt, but I don't regret having had a normal life like everyone else. What would I have had to paint, I wonder, if I'd just been an *artist*, and hung around in – what do you call it – a *coterie?*'

When one thought of the huge retrospective which set the seal on Pilbright's reputation – room after room at the Hayward Gallery, filled with his work, exhibiting, whatever one's doubts about it all, a confident exuberance, an ease with the medium, a sense of colour and dash, which were all highly unusual – one felt he must have been lying when he said that it was just his hobby.

But it was only later that I saw the wisdom of his positive distaste for a way of life which was self-consciously artistic. Hanging around, being a bohemian, accepting a carefully fashioned, *rive gauche* manner of living was just what I wanted, in so far as such a thing could be achieved in London. Much good it did me.

But to see Pilbright's rooms! To hear his voice again in this strange, sanitised setting! He had become a bit of history. By extension, so had I, in so far as I could claim, for a very brief spell, to have known him. This exhibition, though, as a milestone in my own inner history was one of those deadening reminders of how much of life had gone, of how little I'd ever done with it, the advice of Pilbright and my grandmother notwithstanding. It had just *gone*. Inevitably, thoughts of Pilbright and that last conversation I'd had with him awoke a whole flood of other memories of that time. I thought of Anne's ponytail of lustrous brown hair, and her pale, slightly freckled face and her way of laughing which lit up not only her features, but the whole world around her.

In such a frame of mind, it was not quite possible to return to the outside world. Nor was the Pilbright Special Exhibition the right place to clear the head, wipe the memory clean, return to the present day with the painful old images of the past expunged. I wandered aimlessly through the ground-floor rooms, looking at the larger abstract paintings, and then back to the modern sculpture. But even there, reminders of the past were to be found. Among the Moores and the Frinks there was that stunning, swooping shape, reminiscent of a bird in flight, by Beryl Lewis.

How much I had been in love with her when I was a schoolboy, and she the art mistress at my private school. When love is completely unrequited (and in this case, undeclared, even) it never quite dies. I do not mean you go on feeling it at the same pitch; you'd go off your head if you did. Once reminded of it, though, as by the Beryl Lewis piece in the Tate, one recaptures the agonies and delights with much of their old intensity. Standing beside her work, I would hear her voice again, as it had been when I was just 'Ramsay' and she was 'Miss Beach'. No Christian names. The recollection, happening inside my head, was more vivid than any reconstructed scene, such as the faked-up rooms of 'Mr Pilbright At Home'. And to think of Miss Beach was to think of Hunter and that dreadful afternoon, the first time I ever set eyes upon him, when I looked up at the window of her room and saw her in his arms.

Memory itself is a form of necromancy. Indulge it consciously and I find that strange things start to happen. The painful associations of Hunter and my marriage, and that whole year after I parted from Pilbright, might well have been triggered by some telepathic knowledge that Anne, not met for ages, was in fact nearby.

In younger days I should have caught sight of her sooner, but total concentration on the Beryl Lewis sculpture made all the middle distance of my vision into a fuzz. It was hearing her voice, older but unmistakable, which made me blink and focus on the other side of the gallery, where, with another woman of about her – our – age, she was staring at and holding forth on a Brancusi bronze.

It was the tone of Anne's voice which, during my brief and terrible period of hatred for her, had most annoyed me. It was pompous. About matters other than art, Anne was not in the least pompous. Get her talking about painting or sculpture though, and she could have been – even at twenty-five – Dame Ursula Lampitt, thirty-five years older than herself, lecturing to undergraduates at Oxford. There was free use of phrases like 'as it were' and 'one feels' and 'it seems to me'.

She was saying to her companion, 'One feels as if Brancusi, as it were, has outsoared matter, and this, it seems to me, is a particularly successful piece. . . .'

Anne could not help being instructive when she talked about these things. Even when I was crazy about her, her art talk bored me, not because I was indifferent to the subject, but because of the way she . . . *spoilt* it. About all other matters, she could be as larky and as frivolous as everyone else known in those days.

'It's a pity we have no time,' said Anne. 'There's so much else I want to show you. We must spend half an hour with the Turners. I mustn't prejudge your reactions but it seems to me, as it were, that they've hung them in a manner – well, you'll see.'

She had developed a nervous giggle. It had grown out of that infectious girlish laugh which first made me love her.

The friend said nothing at all. She seemed wonderfully patient. Perhaps she had asked Anne to show her the gallery.

I hid behind a large Henry Moore.

Feelings for those whom I had hardly known, Pilbright or Miss Beach, could be momentarily recaptured in something like their old forms. At least I could remember the feelings, even if they, like everything else, had been muted by Time's decay. With Anne, to whom I had been married, it was otherwise. I had known such a wide variety of feelings for her – an overexcited crush of much the same childish intensity I had felt for Miss

267

Beach was the first thing. I had also found in her a hilarious friendship. We laughed so much in the early days; we found everything funny. Early, too, I had found that without any complications or guilt we seemed made for one another in bed, and this at the same time seemed like a joyous extension of the crush and the friendship and the laughter. When the other feelings entered in later on, the marital day-to-day irritation, the terrible feeling of disillusionment when I realised that she was not in love with me, my own guilt when I betrayed her, the hatred which flared up during our quarrels and our silences – when all these things had come upon us, I told myself that I had never really been in love with Anne at all, it had just been a juvenile mistake. But this wasn't true. I was in love with her certainly. Though silly and green, our younger self is worthy of our respect, deserves our truth-telling, as much as soberer phases of existence.

This seemed hard to remember, looking at the sixty-year-old woman in the gallery. At that moment, I felt nothing for her, nothing. Just an embarrassed hope that she would not look up and see me and greet me in that perfectly poised manner which she adopted whenever we met. I knew her well enough still to know that this poise concealed feelings of awkwardness, probably as acute as my own. There was no bitterness or enmity between us any more, just a sad blank.

Why should feelings matter so much? Why have I spent such a very high proportion of my life considering what I feel about other people, or what they feel about me? Temperamentally, Anne and I should have been able to knock along together when the first difficulties had died down. We shared many of the same friends and interests. There was no physical incompatibility; the opposite right to the end. It was just this wretched matter of feelings which came between us. We no longer felt the same about each other. Anne felt, as she had never apparently felt about me, for Another. So we had to part. Would it not be better to cultivate indifference to feelings? Wouldn't life be more endurable, more civilised, if we decided to eschew feelings as we can, with enough effort, resist nicotine? Certainly it would be less painful. In a few rare individuals I have met such detachment. Like those many people devoid of aesthetic sense the non-feelers, or almost non-feelers, are probably likely to cause little emotional nuisance; perhaps on balance they are happier than the rest of us.

I remember a don at Oxford, a colleague of my cousin Felicity's, remarking in a slow voice after dinner one night, 'I try not to make a distinction between liking and disliking people. In practice I find that I don't go in for liking or disliking. Does one have to?'

Shakespeare was impressed by such cold-fishery, by those

> Who, moving others, are themselves as stone,
> Unmoved, cold, and to temptation slow.

The years have made me suspect 'feelings'. In their name, we seem to be able to inflict so much hurt on one another. But the chance sighting of Anne in the Tate made me recognise that even this suspicion itself took me no nearer the possession of wisdom. My acquired cold-fishery of late years was not a willed acquisition of detachment, but an atrophy of heart, a kind of death, like the failure of eyesight or trouble with teeth.

If I could choose, I should prefer to be that earlier self – impulsively able to feel, capable of foolish emotional adventures. The capacity to hurt, and to be hurt, does not depart when the capacity to love has been forgotten. In the end one returns gratefully to obvious truths, like Keats's 'I am certain of nothing but of the holiness of the heart's affections.' Treadmill, my old English master, had quoted the words to us in class long since. None of us had known who wrote them but I knew at once that this was my creed.

Anne looked dreadful. Her hair was short, grey, lank, swept back from the forehead defiantly as if she did not care any longer what she looked like. She was fat now. When I had been in love with her, she had the body of a lithe athletic boy. Her legs had now become a funny shape, the result, I suppose, of varicose veins. There were bulges where there shouldn't have been and one ankle had a bandage beneath the stocking.

I managed to get out of her line of vision and hide in the Gents until she and her companion had moved on. The face that looked back at me when I stared into the glass over the wash basins would probably have excited her embarrassed pity, just as she had done in me. She had gone to fat, I to scrawn. At some point, just past fifty, the whites of my eyes had turned yellowish and they were often, as today, rather bloodshot. The bony skull – how recognisably work for an undertaker now – was half bald and when I grinned, the teeth were appalling. I've no idea how I managed to develop so many lines on my face. If, like so many people I have known, I am doomed to go on until eighty, then the work of dilapidation is only three-quarters done.

'I am certain of nothing but of the holiness of the heart's affections.'

A young man's words. Good words. If we did not accept that love was ennobling and even in some cases durable, what else could redeem death of its horror, and before death, this relentless destruction of the flesh? Perhaps, in seeking redemption, we were seeking sham consolations.

Children would change everything; I see that now. One's own collapse into nothingness, the blotting-out of all memory and desire by the sheer process of bodily decay, ending in oblivion a non-being which rendered every second of being itself trivial, all this would be quite different with children and grandchildren; for through them, people defy time, and their own death. Then one would view in a different light the horrible mystery tour down the Senility Line (stopping posts at Bad Breath Halt, Incontinence Junction and Amnesia Whatsit; Arthritis served throughout the journey). It would be different with children. I have no children.

Another way, granted only to the few, was the artist's life. To write or paint or compose something which would endure – this surely would be a blow against the Enemy? Was my ego always rebelliously conscious of the enemy, long before I became conscious of him myself? Was it that which prompted my rash decision to be, in Pilbright's word, 'arty'? In leaving Tempest and Holmes, I was only aware of reacting against precisely such a death-in-life as Pilbright of Accounts appeared to represent. But he had been deceiving us, and he was now at one with the Immortals.

As I left the gallery and came down the steps into Millbank, there was a rainbow over the other side of the Thames reminiscent of Pilbright's *God Gives a Token at Battersea that He Will Bring No More Destruction upon the Earth*. (Another broken promise?) In Pilbright's big self-confident canvas the sky was a thick splashy mass of greys but sun shone through light rain and the bow was naïvely bright. The real rainbow at which I now looked was even brighter, and the whole arc was visible, casting an implausible nimbus over the former Power Station. The waters of the river were high, like boiling gravy. Old Pilbright had won immortality, all right. Who would have thought it? Well, well.

Two

I met Anne a few months after the final parting with Pilbright. Cutting loose from the office routine had all been perfectly easy. I had half imagined that someone might come running after me, compel me to go back, make me get up early in the mornings and wear a suit and tie. But who in the world cared?

Aunt Deirdre in one of her regular letters said that she thought it was a 'bit of a pity' that I no longer had regular work. In my shamefully rare letters to her and Uncle Roy I had rather played down, in fact, to the extent of not mentioning it at all, my job at the Bottle. I had emphasised the literary side of things, and the fact that I was doing a tremendous amount of acting and theatre work – a number of temporary stagehand jobs at small West End theatres, drama classes, and some amateur work. The chance of a Part had begun to seem real to me. Neither in life nor in my professional aspirations had I the smallest inkling of what the great Casting Director had in mind for me – the smallest of walk-on parts, little more than an extra in the 'crowd flows over London Bridge' sequence. If we knew these things, perhaps we wouldn't attend the auditions.

Aunt Deirdre and Uncle Roy were snobbishly quite pleased that I had extricated myself from the world of sale and manufacture. From my uncle's point of view, the desire to be a writer placed me (in an infinitely junior capacity) in the good company of the various Lampitts who had found their way into print. Not everyone reads Sargie Lampitt's book on the House of Lords, nor his cousin Ursula's *Anglo-Norman Literature: The First Decade*. James Petworth Lampitt is in a different league. His books have made a comeback ever since Hunter's first scandalous volume of biography of the man appeared. There was even a TV series (fronted by Hunter) based on Lampitt's Victorian sketches. Uncle Roy never mentioned Hunter, nor would he have stooped to the purchase of a television. But such was his general obsession with the whole tribe of Lampitts that he could only be pleased that the paperback-buying public were now enjoying such classics by Jimbo (as he was always known in the family) as *Prince Albert* and *Swinburne*.

'I always said Jimbo would last,' my uncle had remarked when we last met.

Perfectly true. Anything my uncle said about the Lampitts was something which he 'always said'. Since Roy's disastrous quarrel with Sargie, Jimbo's brother, one might have supposed that he would have found another family to talk about, but this was not the case. The less he saw of any member of the Lampitt family the more he apparently needed to talk about them, rehearse their names and deeds and dates. Blessed are those who have not seen and yet have believed.

My aunt, who had had a surfeit of Lampitt talk, seldom responded when he was in full flood, but occasionally even she was prepared to allude to my uncle's enthusiasm, particularly if, as on some rare occasion, he found something new to say.

'Talking of Lampitts,' she had written in her last, 'your uncle' – When had he done anything else? My childhood was the story of my uncle talking of Lampitts. – 'wonders if you'll come across Orlando Lampitt. Rather a black sheep, we gather!!! A cousin of Jimbo's and Sargie's who went on the *stage* in 1928 . . .'

My uncle did not often write me a letter, but he sometimes added marginalia to my aunt's small blue leaves of Basildon Bond. In his thick, florid italic, the ink blacker than I have ever seen, he had added at the bottom of my aunt's letter, 'I must ask Sibs about Orlando. Do call on Sibs, by the way. I'll let you have the address if you have forgotten it.'

Since my first going to live with Uncle Roy I had heard him recite the names and addresses of the Lampitts – Jimbo, 19 Hinde House, Manchester Square; Sargie (when in town, which I now gathered he was all the time), 14 Kensington Square, W8; Vernon, 11 Lord North Street; Ursula, The Principal's Lodgings, Rawlinson College, Oxford. How could I ever forget the address of Sargie's youngest sibling? *108 Cadogan Square*.

I had no desire to visit Lady Starling, none whatever. If there was anything which I wished to escape more than the world of Pilbright and Accounts, it was the Lampitts and all their breed, who had obsessed my uncle and dominated all my childhood and adolescence, not by their physical presence, but by the fact that we talked about them at almost every meal. Besides, Lady

Starling, though a magnificent-looking person, and in her way an amusing talker, was not someone with whom I had exactly hit it off in the past. It would have been impossible to drop in on her in Cadogan Square without in some infinitesimal degree reconstructing the obsequious spirit in which my uncle had called on the Lampitts at Timplingham Place in our village. The very idea of calling suggested a hint of deference. I much preferred the squalor of Wetherby Gardens, the house full of lodgers, myself now one, the stench of dogs and Camels, the raffish hours, the overpowering sense that one was in a house where Art mattered more than Life.

Bloom had fixed it that I should have a room *chez* Rikko and Fenella. In spite of a successful life as a young publisher Bloom always had time to boss about his friends, and he took a benign interest in Rikko and Fenella, who had been his landlords once upon a time. Most of their income derived from the rooms, rather than their art. One paid cash. All transactions with Fenella were for cash. It was some years since her last bust-up with a bank manager. No clearing-bank could be found who would allow either of them a cheque-book – not since the last time, when Rikko, with less than nine pounds in the current account, had impulsively bought a yacht from a man in a pub.

'He didn't realise who we *were*,' croaked Fenella, flicking Camel ash into the gas fire as she recalled the incident. 'I told him, we're theatrical.'

This – by some definitions – was self-evident.

'The fact that I don't put "The Lady Fenella Kempe" on my cheque-book doesn't mean a thing. You don't go crowing about titles. I don't have it on my Equity card either.'

The fact that she did not put 'The Lady Fenella' on her cheques, in the days when she had cheques, was best explained by her not being entitled to do so. In spite of frequent hints that she was the daughter of some ancient and distinguished lineage, there was in fact no evidence for this at all. If anyone were cruel enough to suggest that they had been unable to find a reference to Fenella in any of the usual books she would rumble, 'Irish peerages are a bit different, darling,' as though anyone with the slightest social pretensions would not have been seen dead in *Debrett*.

Her voice was deeper than most men's and sounded as though

she were suffering from appallingly painful laryngitis. Emaciated to the point of being stringy, she made gallant efforts to recall her prime with scarlet lipstick and a blonde hair dye which hinted of a less subtle, more innocent era than our own. Her very even dentures, slightly smeared with lipstick usually, gave the winsome smiles a ghoulish air, which she tempered by holding her head on one side and shaking her marigold tresses first on to one shoulder and then on to another.

'I told him,' she would say, of the man who had sold Rikko the yacht, watched the cheque bounce, come round to remonstrate, 'it's only *middle*-class people who keep money in current accounts. People like us have trusts, we have *land*.'

When her claims, either to former triumphs on stage or screen, or to high birth, became too fantastical, Rikko would take his thumb and forefinger and squeeze the flesh of his brow just above the bridge of his nose. He would close his eyes and wait until the worst of the embarrassment was over. If Fenella persisted . . .

('I told him, my father was a marquess, I've acted in Hollywood, I'm a friend of Lauren Bacall's and I'd no more think of paying his cheque than I'd think of saying *toilet* . . .')

. . . then Rikko, in his precise and well-modulated voice would say, 'Shut up Fenella, shut up, shut up.'

If it got worse, her boasting, he would arise, still clutching his brow, and announce that he could bear it no longer.

'I'm taking Irving and Terry down the Gloucester Road.'

Zipping his windjammer and muttering something about how he didn't know how he could stand living with Fenella, he would mince off, an Afghan hound pulling at each gloved and beautifully manicured hand.

How anyone survives life with anyone else is a bit of a mystery – not one to which, at that age, I'd given much thought. Bloom used to say that Fenella and Rikko had nothing in common except their hair dye. Certainly it was hard to understand why such a handsome (if mildly overweight) man, not much more than forty, should have chosen to make his hair the same violent yellow as his wife's. But perhaps there all mystery ended. Perhaps instead of trying to explain Fenella as a mother-substitute for Rikko (she must have been a good twenty years older than he) one should have accepted the fact that for some, perhaps much, of the time they simply liked each other.

The household, with its ever-changing population of lodgers, provided both of them with doubtless necessary variants to their sole companionship. The actors (in and out of work), painters (ditto), students and layabouts who stayed in Wetherby Gardens, some for a few nights and some, on and off, for years, provided Rikko and Fenella with something to love, beyond each other and the Afghans. I never heard of either of them being *in love* with any of the lodgers though that might have happened. They had an extraordinary capacity, though (in this respect like parents who love their children), to see virtues and talents in their lodgers which were far from apparent to anyone else.

'What people never see about Donald,' Fenella would say about the morose unshaven young man in her attic, seldom up before two in the afternoon, by no means unsmelly, 'is that he is multi-talented. He can *act*, he can *paint*, he can *sing*.'

It was true; people never saw it.

'He's got a beautiful voice,' Rikko agreed.

For some reason, casting directors, theatrical agents, art schools, all failed to spot it. The Royal School of Ballet had been similarly myopic about redheaded Briony and her flat feet. If you had believed Fenella's version of things, it would have been incomprehensible that Melissa (a near genius by the sound of it, and an Honourable) kept failing her A-levels.

This was the sort of person who crowded into that house, paid the quite modest rents and ate Fenella's meals, which were hit-and-miss affairs depending for their palatability on how sober she was when meat or vegetables found their way into the oven. She served what I would think of as being Good English Food – lots of roasts – but always spoke of it as if it were traditional French cooking.

If by some aberration of a casting director Fenella had ever found herself in what she called work, I think she would have missed being a landlady. Bloom said, rather cruelly, that her career had been destroyed by the coming of the talkies.

'She really was in the movies once. But sound did for her, my dear. Not only was she far too stupid to learn the lines but her voice was so deep! People would assume she was just some old drag queen. Rikko, now! He could have done a nice falsetto and acted Marilyn Monroe off the screen.'

As so often when Bloom made these remarks, he opened his

mouth wide and almost put out his tongue as he guffawed at his own jokes.

Without resorting to female impersonation, Rikko had managed in a very minor way to keep afloat. Though most of his tiny trickles of money had been earned as a waiter or a teacher of English to foreigners, it was still not a complete mockery of the truth to put 'actor' on his passport. He usually found several weeks' work a year in rep, and there was now the exciting new outlet of television. That, indeed, was why we were all huddled around the set in the drawing room on that particular evening.

Their drawing room told its own story. It was a Noël Coward set in the midst of which a furniture remover had apparently left a load of old junk for a few days before consigning it to the knacker's yard. There was a large white grand piano. On either side of the fireplace a gilded putto supported a lamp. All the lampshades, stools, marble ashtrays and festoons made gallant efforts to give off a 1930s rococo air of the gin-and-ostrich-feather school. But amid what Bloom called the all-too-predictable splendour of white and gold ('Ionian, darling? It's Edgware Road!') there were such objects as the lumpy old boarding-house sofa, bursting springs and stuffing from its floral loose covers. A wobbly standard lamp, vaguely Chinese, gave you a slight electric shock every time you tried to switch it on. A heavy chintz armchair. This mingled assemblage of rubbish mingled oddly with the Louis Seize piano stools (*circa* 1934) or the tiger-skin rug near the hearth.

Several inches of dust resting over all the furniture gave a Sleeping Beauty air to many parts of the house. Fenella only intermittently employed charwomen and never herself cleaned the place up even if, as sometimes happened, Irving or Terry, unable to resist the calls of nature, had deposited turds on the frayed Oriental carpets.

It was on such a carpet that most of us sat round that evening, Fenella, Rikko and a handful of lodgers. We were all squeezed in to watch the wooden-framed set which was plugged in on the other side of the fireplace. Television in those days was enough of a novelty for one to be willing to watch absolutely anything which appeared on the screen. I forget what particular gibberish was being churned out on that occasion. It stopped eventually. And it was then, with her concentration so fixed on the screen that an inch of ash grew on the end of her Camel without being flicked, that Fenella said, 'Now hush, darlings, this is Rikko.'

Sure enough, there on the screen he was. First, you saw him smartly dressed in a suit, seated at a large office desk. Then his face was contorted with agony. A voice then said, 'Acid indigestion, it can catch you unawares, anywhere.' The screen was then filled with a diagram depicting a human silhouette. Rays of pain throbbed around the intestinal regions. A pill of the kind recommended made its swift passage through the lips of the silhouette down to the trouble spot. We then cut once more to Rikko, whose painstruck features relaxed and became wreathed in a smile. Within seconds, the thing was over, to be followed by one for washing powder.

It wasn't *Hamlet*, but I suppose it was work. I was disappointed that Rikko was not able actually to speak in the course of his film. The man recommending the washing powder in the ad which followed was given quite a lot to say about its detersive properties. All Rikko had to do was to look as though he was being tortured, and then act an expression of profound relief.

He was a good actor – made for television, really, since he had such a variety of facial expressions. The relief of the man with acid indigestion was in its way a masterpiece.

'Pity they made you wear that tie.'

'Fenella!' He pursed his lips and wriggled his shoulders. He had obviously been proud of his performance.

'Probably they give you a tie to wear,' I said.

'Of course,' said Rikko.

'I wanted you to wear that Old Harrovian one that Hamish' – some lodger who may or may not have been to Harrow – 'left behind in his drawer before he buggered off.'

'I did wear it, since you made such a thing of it. The advertising people said it looked greasy.'

'But the tie they gave you was all wrong for the part.' Fenella was settling down to a thorough post-mortem on the piece. There were frequent reshowings throughout the season so she had plenty of time over the next few months to analyse the shortcomings of producer, wardrobe mistress and cameraman.

'You see, darling, they never understand upper-class people.'

'I'm not upper class,' said Rikko.

At this Fenella grinned coquettishly. Her smile suggested a

278

conspiracy with her company not to take any such disavowal seriously.

'And anyway,' said Rikko, 'there was no need for the man with the bellyache to be upper class. They needed someone with whom the viewers could identify.'

'Nonsense, he was a company director.'

'That's not upper class!'

During this conversation, one sensed Rikko and Fenella becoming really angry with each other, one of those marital exchanges where the apparent subject under discussion could not possibly explain the heatedness with which it was being conducted. Most of the other young people were milling about, talking, hugging the dogs. The television pursued its own silly life in the corner. The adverts were over and I switched channels for 'Perspectives', an arts programme set up to rival a similar one broadcast by ITV and compered on this channel by Raphael Hunter.

He was already a familiar face on the television screen, so it was no longer a shock to me to see his bland, apparently ageless features smiling out from the cathode-ray tube. The impenetrable questions posed by that face were just the same on screen as off. Was he as insipid as he seemed? If so, how had he managed to advance himself so forcefully in his career, break the hearts of so many women, achieve that enviable combination of admiration and notoriety which Volume 1 of his *Petwort Lampitt* had brought on all sides? (Those who deprecated the indiscretions of the book were often those who were most in awe of Hunter's perspicacity, his detective work and his sheer industry in producing a volume so large.) The TV persona was just another string to Hunter's bow. This 'Perspectives' programme was wide-ranging, consisting mainly of studio interviews, conducted by Hunter himself, with various practitioners of the arts. It was on this programme, about five or six years after the time I am describing, that Pilbright's reputation was made. As it happened, another of Hunter's more famous interviews was in progress that very evening, but hardly anyone in Fenella's room was watching. My eyes, naturally enough, were glued to the set. I felt I had been looking at Hunter's face all my life; now it had a power to hypnotise me, recalling already so many phases of existence that he had become a sort of Guardian Angel, witnessing, if not presiding over, some of the key moments in my life. But I was also watching so intently because the second face on the screen – that of the man being interviewed – was also familiar to me, though I could not place it at first. Working in a pub, you see any number of faces, some of them on a regular basis, without ever putting a name to them. It slowly dawned on me that the man being interviewed by Hunter was a 'regular' at the Black Bottle, and I then realised who it was.

He usually sat on his own on a bar-stool drinking beer in pints. He had a huge white fleshy face. Horn-rimmed specs depended from elephantine ears and bridged a wide nose. A bruiser's face, but a highly intelligent bruiser. The lips, in the pub, were always wet, blubbery almost. He was accustomed to slurp as he drank, and as he did so he liked to talk. Cyril, my employer, nicknamed him the Best-Seller, but I had hitherto taken the sobriquet in the scornful spirit in which it was meant.

My very first day at the Black Bottle, the Best-Seller had surprised me, before ordering his pint, by speaking his name, something I never knew any other customer to do.

'Day Muckley,' he said firmly, raspingly, almost threateningly.

The name meant almost nothing to me. The books for which, before the war, he had been famous – *Valley of Folk, That Tender Last Farewell*, but above all, *The Calderdale Saga* – were precisely of the kind I never read, broadly speaking, family sagas and love stories set in the district of Yorkshire where Muckley had grown up. Granny and Mrs Webb had been very fond of *The Calderdale Saga*, but until I met him, I should have been hard-pressed to remember the name of the author. No wonder my blank expression when the Best-Seller announced his name caused such a slyly belligerent look to pass over his face. He smiled contemptuously as though not to know the name was a mark of complete idiocy. When I knew him better I came to feel that the smile concealed a great hurt. He was always saying his name to people, bartenders, shopkeepers, waiters, barbers, bookies; and if they were under the age of fifty, he always got the same blank response. On first meeting, and on the few other subsequent occasions before the television programme, I thought of him as just another 'character' of the sort you might expect to meet in a pub in central London.

Inviting Muckley on to the programme was entirely typical

behaviour on Hunter's part. One of the many things which made Hunter widely liked was his desire to rehabilitate lost reputations, set up new ones. It must in part have been simple kindness which motivated him; in part, power mania must have come into it, the thought that he could control Fame itself, and determine that unknown names should suddenly become household words.

Just when everyone had forgotten Jimbo's books, Hunter published *Petworth Lampitt: the Hidden Years*. In the entirely unknown Pilbright he discovered one of the most interesting representational painters of the century. The interview with the Best-Seller was obviously designed to be just such a refurbishment job. It was always noticeable to my unsympathetic eye that Hunter's tastes were conservative and middlebrow. He liked the sort of art of which the Binker, headmaster of the private school which Hunter and I at very different stages had attended, would have approved.

In his effort to make Day Muckley into a Best-Seller indeed, Hunter had not reckoned on the dangers of attempting a conversation with him after six in the evening. I myself tended to do lunchtime stints at the Bottle and I had not quite realised until the broadcast (which like most broadcasting then was live) Day's pattern of drinking; nor had I quite realised that his three or four pints put away between eleven in the morning and two in the afternoon, only intermittently fortified with whisky chasers, were merely his way of dealing with the hangover of the night before. It was some time after five that the spirit-drinking began in earnest. It was now perhaps half past eight or nine in the evening. I didn't hear Raphael Hunter's opening *spiel*. Rikko and Fenella were talking too loud. But I caught the odd phrase: 'not ashamed to tell a good story . . . that much undervalued quality characterisation . . . literary reputations have their ups and downs . . .'

The camera now began to focus on the Best-Seller, who looked at first sight his usual smiling froglike self. It was only when Muckley attempted speech that the flickerings of anxiety in Hunter's face became explicable.

'The point is . . . Raphael . . . the point is this.' Muckley spoke as if he had all the time in the world to make his point. You could almost hear the cameras turning over in the long pause which followed. He fumbled. He lit up one of his cigarettes – he smoked an Irish brand called Sweet Afton – and then he smiled, the first part of his sentence forgotten.

'Your novels stand very much in the realist tradition,' Hunter said. 'Names like Galsworthy, Priestley, Hugh Walpole.'

'Sod Hugh Walpole,' said Day Muckley.

'Sod', except as a way of defining a piece of turf, was not a word which was used on British television in those days. The actual phrase uttered was all the less acceptable because it had a kind of biographical plausibility; just some such conjunction had indeed been hinted at by Hunter himself between Walpole and Petworth Lampitt, an incident alleged to have occurred in a Turkish bath near the Elephant and Castle.

'No, Raphael, the point is, the point is this.'

Whatever the point was, the Best-Seller was the devil of a time coming to it. The extremely broad Yorkshire accent, though I'm sure genuine, was almost comically emphasised as if he were afraid that anyone would forget the northernness on which his literary reputation had been built.

'No, the point about a writer . . .'

'Arnold Bennett is another writer who has been mentioned,' said Hunter briskly, trying to retrieve a hopeless situation by giving the TV audience a boring lecture on the realist tradition. 'We might call it the English branch of the Balzacian –'

'Let me finish, Raph, Raphael, will you.' The Best-Seller lurched angrily in his chair and gestured jerkily with the cigarette. 'I'm asking a serious question. The point is . . . this. Is a writer . . . *readable*? That's all the, sorry, that's all the book-buying public, that's all they want to know. When they pick up a book . . .'

'Your readability,' said Hunter, 'has always been one of your most –'

'They don't want to know is it modern, is it avant-garde, for Christ's sakes . . .' (That again! Echoes of Pilbrightery.) 'Or is it exist–exis . . .'

'Existentialist.' Hunter was mopping his brow.

'Sarter.'

As I discovered when I knew him, the Best-Seller always anglicised foreign names. The Joe Blunt manner on which he prided himself did not prevent him from being familiar with a wide range of foreign literature. In fact, I think it quite likely that he had never read Bennett, Galsworthy, or any of the other

English authors named by Hunter. But he had read Dostoyevsky, Proust, Flaubert . . .

'I mean, *La Nausée*. They want something wholesome. People. Wholesome. They want something for Christ's sakes that is *readable*. They don't need to be existentialised, bloody cheek. I mean *La Nausée*, to my mind, Raphael, does literally –'

At that moment a girl burst into the room and screamed with laughter.

'My God! There's a man . . . I can't believe it, *look*! There's a man on the television, being sick!'

Everybody turned to the set. What she said was undeniably true. The whole scene was momentarily obscured by a smudge of liquid, grey to our sight, which hit the lens of the camera as Muckley looked towards his public. I cannot say for certain what this grey smudge was, but if it was a normal day the mixture might well have included some fish and chips, some brown sauce, beer, cheese sandwiches, chutney, possibly a few pickled onions and, by nine in the evening, the best part of a bottle of whisky.

One heard the Best-Seller's voice, saying, 'I'm very, very, sorry, feeling slightly off colour today' before the scene switched to the next item of the programme. Hunter, considerably ruffled, his suit a bit stained, announced that we would have a few minutes while a classical guitarist, visiting London from Madrid, displayed his soothing skills. By the time this performance was over Day Muckley had been trundled out of sight.

'Did you ever *see* such a thing?' said the girl. When she spoke her voice rose to a squeal which made everyone who heard it join in the laughter. I immediately started to laugh, laughter which lasted on and off for about a year.

'This is Robin,' said my old school friend Darnley, whom I saw there for the first time.

I'd written to Darnley, telling him my new address, suggesting he drop in on me one evening and tell me his news. We'd been rather out of touch. When last heard of he was still an undergraduate. The melancholy of his grown-up appearance, lank floppy hair, heavy eyelids, thick sad lips, was increased by being muffled up in a dark, hooded duffel coat, Black Watch tartan scarf, black trousers. His features, as he watched the scene of Hunter trying to cope with being puked at on live television, recalled to me the miraculous way in which, during side-splitting episodes at school, Darnley always managed to keep a completely straight face, particularly when he himself was responsible for the chaos or comedy being enacted.

Not so his companions. They were two girls, guffawing with uncontrollable amusement. One of them, who looked a bit like Darnley, only pretty, I rightly took to be his sister. The other one, the one he called Robin, was Anne, the girl I was destined to marry. I assumed she was Darnley's girlfriend, and felt immediate envy of them both.

I introduced my friends to each other.

'Miles, this is Rikko, Rikko and Fenella, Fenella Kempe.'

'This is Elizabeth, my sister. I forget if you've met before.'

'Miles, I told you I'd never met Julian,' said Elizabeth. For some reason this was so funny that she could hardly say it without laughing.

'This is Robin,' said Darnley, almost as if showing Anne off.

Robin apparently lacked a surname. One was not mentioned, anyway. She looked as if the sight of Fenella might set her off again, unless she was very carefully handled.

'Darling!' Fenella instructed her husband with an imperious gesture, sending Camel ash everywhere. 'Open a bottle of really good Burgundy.' (Her usual way of describing the Algerian red of which she kept a modest supply in her kitchen.)

'We can't stay,' said Darnley. 'We've come to take Julian out.'

'Well, at least you can take your coat off,' wheedled Fenella.

Why was this so funny? Both Darnley's companions positively whooped.

'That's what I can't do, remove my coat,' said Darnley.

' 'Course you can,' said Fenella.

It was perfectly warm in that room. Darnley nevertheless continued to hold the scarf to his throat and clutch the duffel to his person. I began to wonder if he had no shirt on.

'Go on!' Robin spoke, her face absolutely full of mischief. 'Take your coat off. I'm going to powder my nose.'

'Up the stairs and turn right on to the half-landing,' recommended Fenella. Rikko came back with a corkscrew, a bottle and some glasses. While these things were happening, Fenella did manage to divest Darnley of his duffel.

His attire underneath the coat came as a great shock to me, but it confirmed something which I had long begun to fear about Darnley, ever since, after a gap, we met up during army days:

that is, that he had his serious side. As a young child, when we were closest to each other, he had shown no seriousness at all. I looked at him now.

A high Roman collar, of the kind Uncle Roy never wore, encircled Darnley's throat. He wore a jet-black jacket and black corduroy trousers. We had been out of touch too long. It occurred to me that in our last few communications, he had been vague about what he was going to do with himself when studies were complete. Now all was revealed. In spite of growing up in a rectory (more likely, because of that fact), I belong to that huge proportion of the English population who are embarrassed by the clergy, unable to suppress in their presence the feeling that something unwholesome, not quite right, has prompted this individual to take the cloth. Usually if pressed for an explanation of this reaction, one would fall back on the individual's semi-successful attempt at repression of some not necessarily homo-erotic proclivity which was 'coming out in other ways'. Such cheap explanations probably fail to explain the shivers one gets down the spine with parsons. Much more obviously, the sight of the clerical collar arouses the embarrassing sense that the individual concerned has been prepared to subscribe to a number of metaphysical propositions which it does not seem quite sane to think about, still less to believe. If the clergyman is also, as in this case, a friend, there is the further embarrassment of wondering how could *they* have swallowed all *that*? Or, if we suspect them of having swallowed less than they should have done, how could they be so cynical as to pretend?

Rikko's and Fenella's attitude to the whole thing was much more practical; an immediate fear that they would be asked to do something, attend a religious ceremony, part with some money, or provide 'jumble'.

'You're a Catholic?' croaked Fenella.

'Just C of E,' said Darnley sanctimoniously.

'Only, we're Catholics,' said Fenella.

Rikko, dispensing drinks, twitched as he could not help doing when Fenella told one of her whoppers. Afterwards, she explained it as a matter of policy. Not only was Fenella one of those people who imagine (for reasons which have always been lost on me) that Roman Catholicism had more chic than other forms of Christianity, but she had discovered that to claim membership of the largest Christian church had a sobering effect on paid-up members of what our sergeant-major in the army called the AODs, whether a vicar begging money for the church roof, or a Jehovah's Witness talking gibberish on your doorstep. Apparently, if you were only prepared to say that you were a Catholic, these different individuals knew that they were beaten and made a polite retreat.

'You do drink, though?' said Fenella.

'Just a very little.' Darnley never in fact drank much. Since his ordination, his voice had become ostentatiously parsonical. And he had been such an amusing person when we were boys. No doubt he would be one of those witty clergymen you read about, but he would still be a clergyman, damn it, with all the creepy things which that implied.

'When we lived in Paris, I always liked to go into the Sacré Coeur to light candles for friends on their first nights. You know. One always wants it to be a success for them, and believe me, first nights are hell. I've had enough of them in my time.'

'Do you mean honeymoons?' asked Darnley with a solemn sniff. 'I hope you don't approve of premarital relations between the sexes.'

'First *nights*, darling. We're theatrical,' said Fenella.

When Anne came back from the loo and saw Darnley revealed in all his clerical clobber, her face instantly told me that I'd been a complete fool, and that he had no more right to be wearing such a collar than I did.

The premature unveiling of his fancy dress had now plunged him into the awkward position of having fooled Fenella. Never quick on the uptake, she would find it hard to grasp that Darnley had adopted this rig as a joke. It would be hard to reveal that he had done so without implying that he had deliberately set out to gull her. Rikko, I could see, had already begun to smell a rat, but when you meet someone for the first time dressed as Darnley was that night, you cannot easily accuse them of being an impostor.

Wine in hand, cigarette alight, however, and pleased to have a new audience, Fenella was perfectly happy to dream her dreams aloud into Darnley's ears. Though on one level it was bad manners to allow her to continue thinking that he was a clergyman, on the other it did not really matter. With Fenella, it hardly made sense to distinguish between reality and falsehood.

'If I hadn't come from a very old Catholic family, there's no knowing who I might have married!'

Rikko's thumb and forefinger automatically went up to his brow when he heard these words, and he took a pinch of agonised flesh while the rest of us sipped our plonk.

'Of course it's just ridiculous,' said Fenella, 'that Catholics can't marry a member of the Royal Family.' She switched on a flirtatious flash of the dentures and kittenishly hung her head sideways. 'Now I've gone and blurted it out,' she said.

With his eyes shut and his lips taut, Rikko said, 'You never knew any member of the Royal Family.'

'Darling, you don't know what you're *talking* about! I knew David Windsor terribly well in those days, long before Wallis Simpson came on the scene. If they don't keep up with me any more, that's hardly surprising.'

Fenella did not quite state that were it not for her religious affiliations, she might have been the Queen of England. Instead, she launched into one of her favourite anecdotes. It concerned an incident when she was working as an usherette at one of the larger cinemas in Leicester Square. The world première of some film was being shown; naturally, she knew all the stars. The Duke and Duchess of Gloucester were in attendance. Rikko squirmed in his seat, swigged his wine, swore at the bottle for being empty, turned it absolutely upside-down and shook it over his glass, as if it concealed hidden reserves of alcohol. We were all drinking fast, anxious not to be hearing any more of this stuff.

Glasses were all more or less empty by the time the Duke of Gloucester was saying, 'Fenella, darling! What the hell are you holding that torch for as if you were a bloody usherette.'

'I told him, "Harry, we've all got to live." '

' "Well, at least come and have dinner with us afterwards." '

'I think the dogs need a walk,' Rikko announced.

'Did you go and have the dinner?' Anne asked. She was always, and I am sure still is, wholly literal in her approach to things.

There being no more wine, Darnley proposed that he take me off to the pub, with 'Robin' and his sister. 'Robin' surprised me, as we were going down the stairs, by saying, 'I've heard so much about you. I want to hear all about the old days.'

I, too, had a duffel, only camel-coloured, not dark like

287

Darnley's. 'About me?' I asked her the question as I put on my coat in the hall. Rikko and Fenella, standing on the landing, were having such a row about the untruth of her Duke-in-the-cinema story that they did not say goodbye.

'No one is denying you were an usherette . . . All right, in the bloody Gaumont. Did I deny that? You might even have been there during some royal première . . .'

'That woman still thinks I'm the vicar,' said Darnley gloomily.

'We were going to surprise you,' said Robin. 'Miles was going to take his coat off in the pub quite casually and you were meant to think.'

'It would never have worked,' said Darnley. 'Julian has known me too long.'

'I was fooled for a minute,' I confessed. 'It wasn't such a strange idea as you think. . . .'

'What!' exclaimed his sister. 'Miles, a priest?'

'Is this pub all right?' I asked. 'It's not spectacular, but it's near.'

The Strathcona, just off Hereford Square, was a solid Edwardian place, with fine engraved glass and oak panelling around the bar. There were still booths to sit in if you wanted to be private in the public bar, though there was a saloon with a few semi-upholstered chairs, and button-backed benches in red velvet. Though the furnishing and look of the place suggested an era of self-confident pleasure-loving people of the sort who might have been painted by Sickert, the clientèle of the Strathcona was nondescript. Rather than kept women, moustachioed military types, or red-faced roués in bookmaker's tweeds, the customers were chiefly drawn from the bedsit brigade, who had come to the pub not because they wished to drink or be convivial but just as an alternative to putting another shilling in the meter.

I got the first round while the others found somewhere to sit. Standing at the bar waiting for drinks, all kinds of thoughts raced through my head, most of them prompted by the fact that, more or less instantly, I had fallen in love with 'Robin'. Was she Darnley's girlfriend? If so, one had to rule out the idea of becoming involved.

From whom had she 'heard so much about me'? From Darnley, presumably. What old days? I came back to their table with the cider, which was what we were all having. By the time I reached them, I could see that Darnley's collar was having a satisfying effect on a group at the next table, some perky young men, about five years older than us, who might have been commercial travellers.

'You can't fool me, vicar! Choir outing is it? And two lovely birds in tow!'

'Don't mind him, vic,' said a friend, attempting to pour oil. 'Nice to see a gentleman of the cloth.'

'Nice to see one who likes girls for a change.'

'Cut it out, Len.'

'The first time he wore that thing,' 'Robin' said as I put the glasses down, 'was coming to see Mummy. Can you imagine? He took his coat off in our hall, and I *just* didn't know what to *do*. As you can imagine, she was totally fooled, and as you can also imagine, she was completely furious when she found out that she had been tricked.'

Gigglingly, 'Robin' lit up a Woodbine.

'Mummy sends you her regards by the way,' she said between puffs.

Darnley and his sister began to have a boring conversation about the Morris they apparently shared; something to do with one of them having to take it to the garage in the morning.

'Your *mother* sent me her regards?' I was completely puzzled that this angel from another planet to whom I already felt my destiny linked should turn out in some sense to know me. I was under the impression that I did not know anyone, and certainly did not know their mothers. Could she be some relation of Bunty or her awful friends the Murrays?

'She wondered if you and I might go and see Sargie, who, as usual, is feeling sorry for himself. Mummy says you are good with Sargie.'

'I haven't seen him for ages.'

'Mummy wants him and your uncle to patch up this quarrel they've had.'

Do call on Sibs by the way – my uncle's postscript.

This girl's mother was Sybil Starling. It came as a shock to discover that such a pretty, animated being had not, as I supposed, burst into my life by accident, but had come as an emissary of the Lampitts. Uncle Roy had almost certainly written to Sibs and told her I was lonely and would value a visit. I felt a yank on the strings; I was a marionette after all. My sense of independence which had built up since leaving Tempest and Holmes now felt illusory.

'Robin was at school with Elizabeth. We were round at their place the other day and they were all talking about, would it be your uncle?'

'Roy sounds so *sweet*!' said 'Robin'.

I admitted that there were those who found him so, myself included really.

'It wasn't long after you'd written. I was coming to see you anyway, and then Lady Vulture said we ought to take you in hand and send you on errands.'

'Roy writes Lady Vulture such super letters,' said Robin. 'And he really knows more about the family than we do, it's incredible.'

'I know.'

'Julian's uncle and my uncle were really, really close friends,' Robin explained to Darnley and his sister.

Like a good catechumen I rehearsed in my mind Lady Starling's relationship with all the other Lampitts. She was the youngest sister of Sargie, Jimbo (James Petworth) and the other 'Timplingham' Lampitts, a cousin to the Labour peer Vernon Lampitt, and also a cousin, in a way I momentarily forgot, to such worthies as Dame Ursula Lampitt, the Principal of Rawlinson College, Oxford, or Sir Antony Lampitt, our man in Abu Dhabi.

Lady Starling was married to a man who was an *éminence grise* at the Treasury. She had three children – two sons, Gavin and Michael, both in the city and both I should guess already in their thirties, and a much younger daughter, Anne, whom I remembered, not quite accurately, to be an art student.

'I've just finished at the Courtauld,' she said. 'I want to do a thesis.' Even at that moment the disappointingly solemn, incipiently pompous tone came upon her, and I felt my mind drifting as she said that she wanted to write about the iconography of Winterhalter.

It was one of those moments in life when any sense of freedom which you might have been entertaining gets abandoned. Existence seems instead to be a foreordained drama in which your part has already been written. My feeling that I was striking out on my own was completely removed by the discovery that Darnley's friend 'Robin' was in fact Anne Starling, whose name I had heard so often on Uncle Roy's lips.

'Extraordinarily sweet child.'

'How do you know – you've hardly met her.'

'She came to old Mrs Lampitt's eightieth.'

'When she was about three.'

'Everyone says she has come on *extraordinarily well*.'

'Robin' was a school nickname based on an obvious free flow of ornithological association. Darnley had picked it up from Elizabeth who had known Anne and been having her to stay in the Darnley household since she was about fourteen. The further extensions of bird names – Lady Vulture, or, for Robin's brothers, the Storks – were Darnley's own elaborations. It was typical of him that he should hold on to Anne's school name when everyone else had abandoned it. (Elizabeth called her Annie.) Darnley's acts of rebellion were seemingly anarchic but in fact they were reassuring and conservative. The desire to dress as a clergyman, for example, suggested a world in which people took the clergy seriously – else what would be the point of the joke? These were all aspects of Darnley's character which I pieced together later over the years rather than being things which I considered that evening in the pub.

I more thought then of my Uncle Roy and his interest in (His interest? His consuming obsession and love for) the Lampitts. In childhood, this was something which had seemed like a joke. When going to stay at the Rectory one Christmas, when I was about six, I can remember Mummy saying, 'I do hope we don't have too much of the Lampitt family.'

Daddy, leaning forward in the railway carriage, had done a meanly accurate imitation of his brother Roy saying, 'Lady Starling – Sibs to the family – is an extraoooooordinarily nice woman.' When meditating anything truly serious like the Lampitts, Uncle Roy's vowels became deliberately elongated; perhaps the pleasure of uttering Lampitt names and addresses was so intense that he could not bear to allow the sounds to escape his larynx without caressing them. The syllables 'Cadogan Square' in the lady's address were always enunciated with a solemnity which would not have been out of place when celebrating the Eucharist.

But then Mummy and Daddy died, and I grew up with Uncle Roy, and Lampitt mania shaped my days, my mind. I now saw

291

that this was no mere episode of childhood. Act I was over. What was about to begin? Not, as I supposed, a new play, but Act II. My days and days and days of listening to Uncle Roy recount his conversations and outings with Sargent Lampitt had just been prep for life with Anne. The difference between falling in love with Anne and any previous attachment resided in this strange inner certainty, which might not have dawned at once, but which had certainly established itself in the pub by the time that Darnley was buying more cider, that our fortunes had already been forged.

At children's parties your partner in a game is allotted to you by the hostess or master of ceremonies. It's just pot luck whom you get. A similar feeling came over me as we sat there in the Strathcona on the window seat. Although Darnley and Elizabeth were there, and over at the other table the perky travellers were drinking beer and eating peanuts, and around us there must have been sixty people in varying stages of intoxication, it felt as if Anne and I were quite alone together. And it was not, as on other occasions when feeling suddenly keen on a girl, a case of 'Will she have me?' but much more, 'Here is my partner, who has been assigned to me.' At the same time, I felt that simply by being there I was betraying Darnley.

What was the partner like, who had been assigned to me in this particular round of party games? I could not believe my luck. Not only was she extremely pretty – she had such a nice face. I could never imagine, then or now, her ever saying a truly mean thing, even though she found so much in the human scene absurd.

'How is Sargie these days?' I asked.

'Well, when did you last see him?'

'And when did you last see your Lampitt? As I say, it's been a long time. More like years than months.'

'Mummy says she never quite worked out what the row with your uncle was about. Partly Sargie pulling down Timplingham Place; partly that really ghastly book the man wrote about Uncle Jimbo.'

'The ghastly book, by the way, was written by the man we've just seen on television.'

'Not the one who threw up? God, that was funny.'

She started to laugh again and – a gesture which I found

instantly captivating – she tried to suppress the laughter coyly with the back of her hand, as though keeping back a cough.

'Not that one, the other one,' I said.

'Oh, the really handsome interviewer-person. Mummy saw a lot of him when he was writing the book. Said he had a specious sort of charm. See what she means, now.'

From that very early moment onwards, it became one of our shared jokes that Anne was crazy about Raphael Hunter, found him irresistible, slept with his photograph under her pillow. It was a bit of banter which surfaced several times a week in all our time together.

When Darnley came back from the bar with more cider, he asked me, 'How did you manage to find yourself such a very distinctive landlady?'

'I thought she was a man!' said Elizabeth Darnley.

'I didn't find her,' I said. 'William Bloom did.'

'Not the pansy you used to hang around with in the army?'

'Guilty secrets!' Anne laughed.

She wasn't one of those Englishwomen who positively prefer their men to be homosexual, but she assumed (not surprisingly, considering her Lampitt inheritance) that there would always be a fair spoonful of this sort of thing in the mixture.

'Not at all,' said Darnley. 'You think everyone's queer. This is just one of Julian's unsuitable friends. I entirely see now that he would go for your landlady, and even more for Mr Afghan Hound.'

'Bloom's rather a successful publisher already,' I interrupted. 'Odd isn't it? His having grown up, settled down, whatever the word would be, before the rest of us have got started?'

We talked a bit about our lives. Darnley did not want to do any of the normal jobs. He was eating dinners at some Inn of Court, but had no intention of becoming a barrister. Journalism in some form tempted him.

Anne's sense of her own career was much more determined. She was going to be, already considered that she was, an art historian. It all seemed reassuringly far from the world of Pilbright, the world where people may convincingly be said to earn their livings. When closing time came, the four of us walked once or twice round Hereford Square before saying goodbye. Darnley and Elizabeth walked ahead, I was paired with Anne. Then, without much ceremony, I parted from the three of them and let myself into the house in Wetherby Gardens.

That evening changed my life. Up to that point, my solitariness in London had been nearly crushing. I knew a tiny handful of people, none of them precisely my cup, but I clung to them with a kind of desperation for fear of having nothing and no one. The resurfacing of Darnley in my life changed all that. It was not so much that all of a sudden I made new friends. Rather, I now felt as if I were part of a group, however loosely constituted that group may have been. This resulted almost immediately from falling in love with Anne. I was no longer alone in the world. It seemed then that I had been lonely not merely since coming to live in London, but all my life, since that horrible day when a train pulled out of Paddington station and for the last time I saw my mother standing there, waving. From that moment of goodbye to the moment when I met Anne had been an era, an interregnum. It was over now, finished, as I thought, for ever.

I could not make out, still, in what sense Anne and Darnley were together. Was he just an old family friend? Or was it more complicated? Did he love her, and she not love him? I was in the state of mind where it was not really imaginable that anyone could know Anne and not be in love with her. I wanted her so much, and yet I so little wanted to behave like a shit to my oldest friend.

These thoughts, and the indigestible mixture of Fenella's Algerian red with the pub cider, guaranteed that I should not sleep much that night. A new life was beginning. But Anne's appearance, and all the talk about her family, had summoned up remembrance of things past with such poignancy that, even if I were not so riotously in love, I think I might still have lain sleepless, and haunted by a thousand scenes which had gone by for ever.

Arising at three thirty a.m. to make extensive use of the toilet on the half-landing not far from Rikko's and Fenella's bedroom, I could not avoid hearing the rhythmic groan of bedsprings in their old four-poster, and the rumbling bass tones of Fenella. She sounded very happy. It was embarrassing to overhear it, yet in a strange way reassuring, a harbinger of existence determined by marriage and its funny old routines.

Three

'Take my word for it.' The man drinking gin-and-lime was called Peter. 'It happens bloody faster than you'd think possible.'

'Don't you have any say in the matter at all?' I was polishing glasses as he spoke.

He was usually the first in. I had noticed him on my very first visit to the Black Bottle. Short blond hair, swept back from a smooth brow, a well-formed strong-boned face: in features, he could easily have been one of those Battle of Britain heroes or cricketers who used to appear on cigarette cards. In fact he had been a jockey, and promised well, until that calamitous Cesarovich when his horse Pride and Joy collapsed beneath him in their final furlong, and destroyed Peter's left foot. No one knew if the iron which he still wore was medically necessary, or whether he put it on as a painful sort of talisman, a visible token of why he had nothing better to do than sit around all day in the Bottle.

He usually wore a blazer, and I don't suppose he was much more than forty, if that. His most striking features were the bright blue eyes whose whites at this hour of the day were a faint pink. His hands shook violently as he fumbled for a Park Drive.

'Women,' he pronounced when the fag was alight, 'make all the choices in life. Don't fool yourself about that. They choose when you get laid, they choose when to tie the wedding knot, they choose when to throw you out which, if they've got any sense, they do quite early on. Mercifully, almost no women have any sense.'

'You married, then?' I asked as casually as possible. I genuinely wanted to know, but I did not want to ask questions which, in my employer's ears, would sound ridiculous or naïf.

Unfortunately, Cyril heard my enquiry.

'Him? What d'you think, cod's cunt? Peter's been married more often than you've been sick.'

'Eating your hot dinners, I suppose,' retorted Peter.

'You boring little arsehole,' said Cyril, I think to Peter rather than to myself.

Cyril's way of addressing colleagues and customers came as a sharp surprise, given his appearance. There was nothing of T. S. Eliot in his manner, except in so far as he was a good judge of a bit of cheese. Cyril's rudeness had something to do with Style. He had his style all worked out; perhaps he had been born with it. Mine was still at the planning stage.

Peter ignored the landlord, and continued talking to me.

'You want to watch out,' he said. 'Along she'll come, some nice girl who's decided for her own stupid reasons that you're Mr Right and that'll be it. You'll have no say in the matter at all.'

'Three times, he's been married, stupid cunt,' Cyril, not to be ignored, put in.

'Doesn't it take two to tango?' I asked.

Silently, Pete held out his glass and I refilled it from the upside-down bottle with the Gilbey's label. Pushing the tumbler against the teat of the bottle to get a double measure felt as if one were milking some cow which gave out gin, not milk.

('Plenty of those, dear, in the pubs I like to go to,' Bloom would have to chip in.)

It was eleven twenty-five a.m.

'A bit more lime as well?' I asked.

'Not so much as you gave me last time.'

By the time he stubbed out the Park Drive, his hand was shaking less.

'It might take two to tango,' he said. 'It takes less than two to arrange a wedding. You just wouldn't believe the sheer fucking speed with which they operate.'

'Why?' I asked. 'What's in it for them? Particularly if they're going to throw you out again.'

Cyril put his hand on my shoulder and smiled seraphically at Pete.

'Take this baby in hand, shortie. Educate him a bit.'

'We do our best,' said Pete.

By midday the bar had filled up. The old man who never spoke to anyone and who could make half a pint of bitter last over an hour was occupying his accustomed seat by the dusty grey window. His trilby-hatted head was a silhouette against the pane, framed by the semi-circular letters ɴooⱯⱯɐꙅ. Peter had turned aside to talk about racing (never a subject on which I have been able to concentrate) to a man with a very red face who looked like an old-fashioned lawyer's clerk – a black bowler hat on the back of his scarlet nut, an old black fustian coat and waistcoat, a winged collar. Known to Cyril as Mr Porn, he made his living by composing scrofulous tales, obtainable from some shop in Frith Street where he also worked as an assistant.

Most of the tables (Cyril was a passable cook) were now full. The Kempes were there. Rikko was anxiously consulting the gold watch buried in hair on his left wrist. There was a decided contrast between the dark hair on his arms and the arresting blond on the top of his head. He wore blue corduroy trousers, yachting shoes and the sort of jumper then denominated a Sloppy Joe. The sleeves of this garment were pulled up to the elbow. One forearm was held in mid-air.

'They're a couple,' said Cyril. 'Go and see what he wants to eat or we'll have Special Branch down on us. You can't have blokes waving their arms like that; looks as if he's soliciting.'

'Cyril wondered if you were ready to order,' I said to them when I got to their table.

'This man from the BBC's over half an hour late,' said Rikko, holding up the watch and the decoratively furry forearm to emphasise the point. An arrangement had been made to meet a wireless producer in the pub. 'A really big part in radio drama,' was how Fenella envisaged the possible outcome of the interview.

'It just could be Rikko's break,' she said.

Her hair had been redyed for the occasion, the lips were brighter than ever. In spite of these superficial touches of glamour, the two of them sitting there put you in mind of a mother and son on the child's first day at school. Rikko obviously wanted her to be there. Her bright lips, yellow hair and jangling bracelets probably seemed as beautiful to him as his did to her. Fenella's fur coat, which to a dispassionate eye might have seemed like a suitable prop for Flanagan and Allan's 'Underneath the Arches' routine, to Rikko probably seemed as glamorous as a new one in Hollywood.

Was their marriage to be explained in the simple terms outlined an hour earlier by Peter? Had Fenella just decided to swoop down on Rikko and take him over? Or was life more complex than Peter supposed? Or, not more complex. Rather, were Peter's matrimonial failures based on his absolute refusal to live with saving illusions? Were happy marriages (Rikko's and Fenella's, for all their interminable bickering, could surely be so described) based on shared fantasy? These weren't questions I'd been sent over by Cyril to answer.

'Do you want lamb chops?' I asked.

They agreed that they did.

'We mustn't drink too much,' said Rikko.

'Two cutlets!' I called back to Cyril.

'I'm not fucking deaf,' he replied from behind the bar. This was simply Cyrilese for 'message understood'. He went backstage to prepare the grill and his wife, Brenda, came to help me serve behind the bar. By the time the chops were done, I could see Rikko and Fenella making contact with the wireless producer who had come down that morning from Birmingham. When I carried over their chops, they introduced me to the man briefly. He was in the middle of a long, unconvincing-sounding rigmarole about why he was so late. He had hoped to bring down one of the temporary scriptwriters – Val – to discuss the part with Rikko. At the last minute, Val had been overpowered by some digestive disorder, a suspected appendicitis, and the producer, whose name was Rodney Jones, had caught a later train. By the time I came back and gave him his sausages with fried potatoes, and a glass of ginger beer shandy, it seemed as though the interview with Fenella and Rikko was proceeding amicably.

Between serving other customers I was keeping half an ear open to the Best-Seller who, perched on a stool at the end of the bar opposite to Peter and Mr Porn, was talking relentlessly to anyone who cared to listen and continued to talk even when his audience got up and walked away.

I had been far too embarrassed to allude to his misfortune on the television, now several weeks in the past. Nevertheless, in the course of not discussing it, we had somehow or another become friends. I can't quite explain how, but I now felt an affection for the old blighter even though there was little in his speech or manners which one would single out as obviously congenial. Liking and disliking, quite as much as more reckless forms of love, are totally arbitrary in my experience. Niceness (where could you find a nicer man than Hunter?) was not always lovable.

'No, Julian,' said the Best-Seller as I took the money for other people's beer and continued to fill their glasses. 'The thing about England today is this. It's *decadent*. Look at those two.' With a nod of his head he indicated Pete and Porn. 'They're both intelligent men, or anyway not positively moronic, for Christ's sakes. And they've nothing better to do with their time than sit around in the middle of the day drinking.'

I handed him the second pint of the morning and he smiled his froglike grin.

'Discipline is what they need, lad.'

'What are you gassing about – hanging, I shouldn't wonder.' It was the pornographer who shouted this, adding a jest, which he was not quite articulate enough to make neat, about being well hung. It would probably have been funnier before his third glass of whisky and ginger. It was true that it took very little to start Day Muckley off on the matter of capital punishment. The execution of Ruth Ellis, the last woman to be hanged for murder in England, had particularly captured his imagination.

'Why do people suppose I'm such a cruel bugger?' he asked.

'Because you are,' said Peter, coming down the bar and jabbing the air crossly with his Park Drive. 'It was downright uncivilised, hanging a kid like that. Twenty-eight years of age she was.'

I was familiar with the feelings on each side of the argument. Peter was an out-and-out abolitionist who considered that the death penalty was on a level with murder. The Best-Seller was a law-and-order man; but more than that, he derived an obvious delight from baiting people, and had learned that the expression of reactionary views in a public place was as good a way as any of making people like Peter get overexcited.

'What in Christ's name does her age matter or, come to that' – he paused to spit out a bit of loose tobacco which had stuck to his lips from the Sweet Afton – 'come to that, her sex. She gunned down a man in cold blood. On Good Friday, I might add.'

'I suppose you think that makes it worse.' By Peter's third or fourth large gimlet of the day he was capable of quite passionate fury, though for some reason he did not usually get violent until the evenings.

'As a matter of fact,' said Day Muckley, 'I do think it makes it worse. A lot worse.'

'Jesus was hanged,' said Peter intensely. 'Jesus was a victim of capital punishment. You're on the side of the people who murdered Jesus, I suppose.'

'That sort of argument is beneath contempt,' said the Best-Seller, trying to keep his dignity in spite of rather an audible fart which he let out at this juncture. 'Quite despicable, as a matter of fact.'

'Why is everything a matter of fact,' asked Peter, 'and why can't you answer me? I asked you a question about your religion. You're supposed to be on the same side as Jesus, aren't you?'

'Tell you one thing,' said Cyril, who clearly thought the conversation nasty and needed a change of direction. 'That pub where she did in her man – the Magnolia in Hampstead.'

'The Magnolia,' repeated the Best-Seller, in a tone which suggested that Cyril had said otherwise and needed correction. 'I've had more than one drink in the Magnolia, lad. It's not far from where my mistress lives.'

'Well, that's just it,' said Cyril.

'If I was your mistress,' said Peter to the BS, 'and I had a shotgun . . .'

Ever since Ruth shot her man outside that place,' said Cyril, 'the place has been packed to the doors. Good for business see, murder.'

'Ghouls,' said Peter with complete seriousness, all irony gone from his tone. 'People disgust me sometimes.'

'You want to watch out I don't have one of you monkey's pricks shot on your way out of here one day,' said Cyril. 'Multiply my trade by ten that would.'

While these interesting matters were being aired, I looked across the smoky saloon and saw that Rikko was leaving with the producer chap, Rodney. Fenella, smiling triumphantly, advanced towards the bar and informed me, 'They're off to BH! He's going to have a voice test.'

'Just so long as he doesn't have to have a hormone test,' said Cyril.

'What's BH?' I asked.

'Broadcasting House, catshit, and serve some customers, please. I don't pay you money for asking fucking ignorant questions.'

'I'm going to have a gin-and-tonic to celebrate,' said Fenella.

300

'They're obviously desperate to get someone for the part and it looks as if at last that agent of ours has found Rikko his break.'

'He hasn't got the part yet,' I said, putting ice and lemon into a glass before squeezing on the Gilbey teat.

'What part is it anyway?' asked Cyril, who took an interest in most aspects of the drama. Fenella put her head on one side and grinned.

'It's one of the main parts in "The Mulberrys", actually.'

'Oh, yeah?'

For a moment, Cyril was stuck for an insult. I could tell he was quite impressed. Like about half the population of the British Isles he was addicted to this wireless serial, broadcast in daily episodes, claiming to be a realistic glimpse into the life of a small village of indeterminate region. I'd been 'brought up' on 'The Mulberrys'. Aunt Deirdre was another addict. In later years, I had got out of the way of listening.

'It's not to replace Stan, is it?' asked Cyril.

'Well, it is, as a matter of fact,' Fenella simpered modestly. It was as though Rikko had inherited a dukedom, but we were all to continue calling her by her first name.

'Well, well,' said Cyril, and he began to whistle the 'Mulberrys' theme tune. Now he really *was* impressed.

Out of touch as I might have been, I could yet remember that Stan Mulberry, heir to the largest farm in Barleybrook and son of Dick and Elsie, played a major role in the drama. Having been a bit of a lad, Stan had recently settled down and married. I now remembered having seen some item in a newspaper about the actor playing Stan. He had died, but the producer of the series had decided to replace the actor, rather than 'phase out' the character of Stan. Hence, presumably, the hurry for a new Stan.

'Fancy that,' said Cyril. 'To think I've been selling Babychams to Stan Mulberry.'

'He's always been brilliant at accents,' said Fenella, quite truthfully. 'It was obvious that Rodney was terribly impressed. Who knows? We might *all* get parts in the series now.'

I hoped Cyril would hold his tongue, and luckily he did. I had begun to feel protective towards Fenella, as though she were some tiresome but much loved relative. If she really imagined that she might get a part in radio drama, it was obvious that she did not realise what her voice sounded like. All kinds of Cyrilese answers were imaginable. 'You? A part? What as? A fucking corncrake?' But he said nothing. Heart of gold, that man.

By the time she left the pub, Fenella was cock-a-hoop. She said she was going to the Italian butchers in Old Compton Street, promising a sumptuous dinner of osso bucco, Rikko's favourite, later that evening.

The bar was beginning to empty. The scene with its empty glasses and its almost numinous nicotine haze resembled a picture I had not yet seen, but was to admire in later years, Pilbright's *Marriage Feast at Canonbury*, now hanging in the National Gallery in Washington, DC.

The little old man by the window had drunk his second half pint and tiptoed in and out of the Gents. Mr Porn, too, had departed. He said that he had one of his 'swish and bond' romances to complete before the afternoon was out. Evidently his literary productions flowed from the pen with much greater ease than my own novel, which obstinately refused to get to its conclusion. Peter, who had simmered down, was apologising to the Best-Seller.

'I shouldn't have attacked your religion, Day. Actually I have a great respect for Catholics, in spite of the fact that my second wife became one, silly cow.'

'It's a rock, lad,' the Best-Seller asserted, 'something to hold on to when all the rest of life is pulling you down the bloody sink. Anyway, that's the way I'm made. My mistress, she doesn't understand it any better than you do. "Look at you, you hypocritical old sod!" She really will say that to me, Julian.'

'I can believe it,' said Peter, who was holding out his glass for more medicine.

'But I always make an act of perfect contrition, you know, every time I make love, in case I have a bloody heart attack at the moment of climax.'

He paused so that we could all take in his capability in this regard. I'd already begun to observe that older people (the Best-Seller at around sixty struck me as positively antique) liked to keep you informed of their continued genital interests and attainments, though not everyone did so as blatantly as he did.

'Oh, yes,' said Day Muckley, 'I love it every single time. But I always make an :ct of perfect contrition before getting into bed to have my wicked way with her, Julian. Come to that, I make an act of perfect contrition if I'm getting into bed on my own, which I do from time to time, and if I'm just so bloody tired, for Christ's sakes, that all I want to do is sleep.'

'Do you really suppose God gets upset when you've been having it away?' asked Peter. 'That's one of the things I don't understand about religion. Why should God worry Himself about people having a spot of How's Our Father? I'm perfectly happy, sitting down here and downing the occasional glass of the Gilbey's, to know that all around us, in knocking shops all over Soho, they are playing the beast with two backs. It is even a positively cheering thought to me. It keeps them out of mischief. It momentarily stops them being unkind to one another.'

'Except for the swish and bond merchants,' said Cyril.

'Even they are only doing it for pleasure, and pleasure is in short supply in this world which God has so graciously filled with tears and disease. But God. He's different from me. He gets so angry every time you so much as toss off that He needs to be placated with these acts of perfect something or other. That's what finished religion for me at school. Once I'd had my first bird, that was it as far as God was concerned. I said to God, "If you're so fucking jealous, or inquisitive or intolerant that you mind me having some crumpet, then you needn't expect me to turn up and sing you to sleep every Sunday morning." Never thought about religion since, not seriously, not for myself.'

'What you don't understand about God, Peter, is this.' The Best-Seller spoke with absolute authority on the matter. 'God is a dictator. As a matter of fact He is very like old Stalin used to be. He doesn't really like cringers and whingers. He has a lot of rough rules, but He really prefers the rogues. He has a very soft spot for rogues. I'd even go so far as to say He has His favourites. Look at the Bible if you don't believe me. There's King David behaving like a complete and utter shit and God rewards him, even though he has stolen another man's wife, and sent that man off to certain death in battle. But along come the virtuous bloody characters and they say, "O Lord, we worship Thee, we have kept thy statutes, O Lord." And what does He do? He smites the buggers with plague and murrain and exile and makes their temple a smouldering ruin.'

Day Muckley sipped his beer and smiled. This wholesale programme of destruction obviously seemed to him quite reasonable, all in a day's work as far as the Deity was concerned.

'No,' he repeated, 'God has his favourites just as old Joe Stalin used to have. You might have some perfectly virtuous man, who never smoked, a teetotaller from birth perhaps, never fornicated – and what happens to him? He gets smitten down with cancer. And then you get one of God's favourites, like King David – or like me. Take me. I smoke. I drink. I fornicate. And God looks down and He laughs. "Eee, it's only old Day Muckley, having his little bit of fun." '

God, in this version of theology, spoke with a Yorkshire accent even more pronounced than Day Muckley's itself. The Best-Seller smiled seraphically as he contemplated his intimacy with the Mind behind the Universe.

For myself there was something hard to puzzle out about the Best-Seller. I couldn't catch his tone. If this God-as-Stalin theory was a joke, it was surely, from the RC point of view, profane and possibly blasphemous. But if he genuinely believed this cosmic horror story, it was a puzzle to me how he could derive such evident comfort from the practice of his faith. He was forever lurching into St Patrick's Church in Soho Square to catch the tail end of a Mass or to light, with the same fumbling fingers which ignited his forty a day, a candle to the Sacred Heart or to the Little Flower.

Perhaps because I was self-confident enough to disapprove of the Best-Seller's attitudes, he was the first person whose religion I positively envied. Having been brought up in a parsonage, Anglicanism was in my blood. Whole chunks of the Book of Common Prayer and Coverdale's Psalter have remained in my head and provided me with a sort of mental furniture. But the C of E, as hitherto encountered, was relentlessly respectable. I was not looking for a religion to believe in. What I envied the Best-Seller in his (wholly incredible) religion was the possession of a place, an institution, an inner world, where he could take himself and relate his own messy character to a universe of values outside himself.

'Within that household,' as he liked to quote from a favourite author, 'the human spirit has roof and hearth. Outside it, is the night.'

'That's perfectly true, the last bit,' Peter had replied from his neighbouring bar-stool. And then, after a long silence, 'What you don't seem to realise is that inside, it is the night as well. What you call the night is just the condition of things.'

'I go to Mass to lay down my burdens,' said Muckley, shifting tack. 'Not to be made better, for Christ's sakes.' He must have regarded moral improvement as something like piles or influenza; it might, in the ordinary course of things, happen to anyone, but only a lunatic would seek it out.

Although Anglicanism provided an analogous 'roof and hearth' for me, I found that it could not possibly provide what the Best-Seller got from St Patrick's. The thought of shuffling into, say, choral matins at Westminster Abbey half tight and then staying for only ten minutes of the service would have embarrassed me. Muckley was somehow able to behave in church as if he were at home. By paradox, my inability to do so had to do less with some innate Anglican stuffiness than with the fact that church was indelibly connected in my mind with childhood, with growing up in the Rectory at Timplingham, with Uncle Roy and Aunt Deirdre. Though religious belief had been abandoned, church doggedly remained; not 'church' in any nebulous sense, certainly not a theological concept, but as an actual place, Timplingham Parish Church, its cold Perpendicular aisles, its vast rood screen. Beyond the screen stood the high altar, the riddel posts introduced by Uncle Roy and paid for by Sargie, who never went near the place. And before you reached the altar was the choir, with misericords carved with bucolic representations of late medieval life, and hidden by garish hassocks gros-pointed by the Mothers' Union. And above were the carved beams of the aisle, each boss supporting a figure: twenty-three Carmelite friars, and one maiden with a naked chest.

It was not just as a piece of architecture that I thought of Timplingham Church, as I might think of Timplingham Place, the handsome Palladian manor-house, now demolished, where Sargie and my Uncle Roy had spent so many evenings together. When I thought of the church, it was of a phenomenon with which I had not yet been able to come to terms. At that period of life, when working at the Bottle, I should have said it was a phenomenon which was neither interesting nor important to me. Inside myself, I knew it to be both, in fact. Five hundred years earlier, the smaller priory church of Timplingham had been rebuilt, like so many others in East Anglia. Wool money had provided an airy, spindly house of light with tall clear windows and narrow fluted columns. And it was not quite enough to say that this beautiful building had been put up in the middle of a field in Norfolk to appease the guilt of some wool merchant. For all over the world they have been building shrines for time out of mind. It merely happens that Timplingham Church is the one I know and to which I will always continue to make an emotional response.

What one *thinks* about such places, rather than how one feels, perhaps doesn't matter very much. But I knew, even in my early twenties, that an England without its churches is unimaginable, even if everyone stopped believing. A life, to me, is unimaginable without recognising that impulse which led to churches first being built. Ultra-orthodox churchmen would probably say that the churches were built just to embody rituals and doctrines, to house the Mass; but this is not true, for very often the first churches were built on the sites of older shrines and groves and altars to the 'false' gods of paganism. Nor do I really like the superior humanist's idea that churches are only important because we have brought to them so many grave or serious moments of our lives, such as the funerals of those we love, or baptisms and weddings. In an awkward clumsy way, whether signing the visitors' book at the back of the building or making gros-point, or arranging flowers, those who enter these buildings are doing much more than wishing to solemnise their own experiences. At the heart of experience is a bottomless hole of irrationality. Any attempts to explain it, or to explain it away, will always fail. Any language which tries to tell us why there is no God, or why there is one and what He is like, is bound to fail; just as any system of psychological theory which thinks it can plumb our crazy and impulsive natures is bound to fail. The caveman who instinctively turned towards the rising sun and sacrificed his wild beast, the Druid who erected a ring of stones, the Christian founders who placed stone on stone in Timplingham, were not guided by any such cerebral considerations. They followed impulse, not argument; what we respond to in such buildings we respond to imaginatively, and not intellectually.

Our ancestors had the half-articulated belief that material existence only makes sense when seen in an eternal glass, and that humankind cannot be defined or understood other than as children of God. But this was something which we lost, entirely, a hundred years ago or more, when Matthew Arnold heard the sea of faith withdrawing from Dover Beach, so that though we are homesick for our shrines and know that we need them, we are afraid of saying things which are untrue or indulging in nonsense. So we stay away, which is a pity, and leave the churches to those who have narrower ideas but probably have no more reason or right to be there than we do.

Even if it had not been for Matthew Arnold, and Doubt and all of that, I think I should have had to boot out religion from my life at that point, as a way of coming to terms with Aunt Deirdre and Uncle Roy. They were intimately connected in my mind with God; so much so that now, as Day Muckley talked nonsense about religion, I was instinctively conscious of Uncle Roy, two hundred miles away in Norfolk, smoking his pipe in his study and writing short letters to far-flung members of the Lampitt family, or reading the newspaper. ('Don't disturb your uncle, he's very busy in the study.' How often that sentence of Aunt Deirdre's was repeated during my boyhood.) And now I thought of Aunt Deirdre herself, working for six or eight hours a day in the garden and returning to the house at intervals to concoct execrably dull meals, or to comment on the usually no less dull 'news' of village life, gathered that morning in the queue at the post office.

I suppose that ever since I had been to live with them, I had walked a knife-edge, feeling that almost any course of action would earn the disapproval of my uncle and aunt. There was no particular justification for this theory. When their daughter Felicity got into a scrape, for example, they were remarkably free of moralism. But neither did they radiate, in their daily conversation, much of that easy warmth and toleration of human weakness which would normally be associated with the forgiveness of sins. I could not explain why *my* religion failed to provide me with the sort of hearth and home which the Best-Seller's gave to him. But if I were forced to explain it, or at least to realise it imaginatively, I only had to imagine an unthinkable meeting, Day Muckley and Aunt Deirdre herself. Instead of seeing him, as I had so often done in real life, staggering into St Patrick's, Soho Square, I had to place him in my mind's eye making the same tottering and uncertain steps up the aisles of the parish church at Timplingham, and finding my aunt crossly arranging cotoneasters and foliage beneath her husband's pulpit. 'Yes?' she would say, and as she looked at the Best-Seller, she would draw in her breath. By those short, almost violent inhalations my aunt indicated disapproval of almost any form of human behaviour which she deemed 'silly'; and this was a wide category.

Certainly the Black Bottle at any hour of day contained a high proportion of individuals who were by Aunt Deirdre's severe definitions very silly indeed. Soho, by Aunt Deirdre's view of things, was altogether a very silly place; she would have seen no point in it whatsoever.

I think he was still talking about God, old Day Muckley, when Cyril rang the bell for time. When we finally locked him out, the Best-Seller would presumably go for a snooze at the back of St Patrick's. The only alternatives were an afternoon with his mistress (he looked a little far gone for that, and did she in any case exist?) or the option of a total anaesthetic – two or three hours drinking spirits at the Concord Club, a dingy pair of rooms up a staircase in Dean Street, which somehow managed to get round the licensing laws and was able to dispense alcohol throughout the afternoon. I polished glasses and watched the Best-Seller's face. The question of where he was to pass the next few hours did not look as if it were troubling him. Somewhere between the fourth and fifth drink, his features lost their animation and his eyes began to stare without focusing. His huge fleshy face, still quite pale, looked terribly, terribly sad. Peter on his nearby stool had managed to buy one more snort of gin-and-lime before Cyril called last orders, and he also looked sad. He did not have the unfocused look, though. His face had turned red, and he had an expression of passion; his red eyes looked downwards and sideways with alarming fury. What he appeared to be looking at were the rows of fruit juices, bottled stouts and 'mixers' which we kept on a lower shelf behind the bar, but from his face you might have guessed that Peter had seen his worst enemy and was planning a karate chop. Perhaps he too was thinking of God, and imagining what he would say to Him if they ever met.

There weren't many people left in the saloon, when Cyril shouted in the direction of the door (paradoxically, since it was opening), 'We're fucking closed, can't you read a watch or something?'

But it was Anne, who was already perfectly used to Cyril's conversational mode. Taking no notice, she came up to see me at the bar. Most days now, she came to see me when work was finishing. Sometimes we'd see a film or 'do something with the afternoon'. As often as not, though, we'd just loaf about, smoking or talking, or going for walks arm in arm. It was strange, the speed with which we had 'clicked', the way it seemed we were meant for each other.

Catching sight of the Best-Seller at the bar, Anne brought out a wild shriek of laughter, and said, by way of introducing herself, 'You're the man who was sick on the telly-box!'

This was the one sentence which no one, not even Cyril, had been able to utter to Day Muckley. It was too humiliating. Reference to his television appearance had been minimal even among the regulars in the Bottle, most of whom never watched TV anyway. The fact that Fenella and Rikko had their 8-inch set was a sign of their extraordinary extravagance and rather vulgar desire to be up to the minute.

Muckley blinked, his face at that moment recalling some old seal floating just above the surface of the ocean.

'Who's this delectably nubile young beauty?'

I introduced them.

'And do you' – he assumed a mock-lecherous leer – 'do you, you decadent young . . . have your evil way, you . . .'

'You were though,' insisted Anne, 'the man who was sick?'

The Best-Seller sobered up by about four drinks at this call to order (disconcertingly reminiscent of Sibs's way of speaking).

'Oh, you mean that television programme?'

'That's what I said. It must have been terribly embarrassing. I was sick during a chemistry lesson at school once. It went everywhere. You feel so ashamed.'

He smiled.

'I did hear that the *other* Day Muckley was up to his tricks again that night.'

In time I came to think that this was one of the Best-Seller's heavier jokes. Later still, as so often when thinking about my friends, I came radically to revise the judgement and to believe that he was a genuinely divided self, the right hand which wrote *The Calderdale Saga* and defended simple old-fashioned 'morality' in occasional contributions to the *Yorkshire Post* scarcely aware of how much booze the left hand was pouring down Day's throat, or of the anarchic views of God and man thereby stimulated.

'I keep hearing about old Day Muckley, lass,' he said. 'That night you mention when, as usual, I was tucked up in bed at half-past nine with my mug of Horlicks and my Dorothy L. Sayers mystery . . .' He paused. This was obviously an image of a perfect evening for him, an image which night after night the other Day Muckley smashed up and destroyed.

'Of course, I don't have a television set. For one thing I could never afford it. For another, I consider it to be decadent bloody rubbish. American rubbish, too, which is worse. But I gather old Day had no such scruples. He went on the television, and made a bit of a nuisance of himself as usual.'

'You were sick all over the camera,' said Anne. No trace of fantasy, no desire or need to lie, existed for her.

'Could you give me just, just a . . .' Being confronted with himself in this uncompromising manner diminished the Best-Seller's ability to be articulate. 'Just a little more . . . another drop of . . .'

'You heard me call time,' said Cyril. 'You've had your lot.'

Peter, still perched on his bar-stool, was staring at his empty glass with the air of a man who could not imagine what had happened to its contents. He shook an empty packet of Park Drive and leaned over the bar.

'And does the law forbid the sale of cigarettes after two thirty p.m.?' He spat out the words.

'The law doesn't. I do. I'm fed up with you piss artists. Can't you sod off for a few hours and give us all a rest?'

In some moods Peter would have started a row at this point, but he merely turned to Day Muckley and said, 'Let's go to the Concord.'

'Well, Peter, I think that's a very, very . . .'

By the time Day had repeated 'very' and negotiated the words 'good idea', Cyril had taken pity on Pete and slapped down a packet of Park Drive on the bar.

'Here you are, dog dirt, and don't come back till we open again.'

'Thanks.'

Peter handed over the one-and-six.

When he and the Best-Seller had swayed off to Dean Street Cyril turned to me with a quiet smile, removed his spectacles, huffed and puffed on the lenses and began to polish them with an immaculate white handkerchief.

'You've done enough work,' he said with the quiet tones of

310

the bank manager. 'Why don't you both go and leave me in peace? Eh? Go on. Scram. Sod off.'

Hand in hand, Anne and I walked through the afternoon sunshine of Soho, I in my not-quite-winklepickers, tight blue jeans and sloppy jersey, she in a tight-waisted pleated skirt and a blouse. There was a coffee bar we both liked in Greek Street. Lonnie Donnegan was emitting his nasal, jerky noises from the juke-box. I carried the frothy coffees to the Formica-topped table where she already had two Woodbines alight, one for herself, one for me.

'Sargie's broken his toe,' she said. 'He's in some little hospital he's discovered in Bryanston Square. Mummy said he'd like a visit.'

'OK.'

It was certainly not how I'd planned to spend the afternoon. Though I now felt fairly certain that Anne and I would be married, I had not allowed my mind to concentrate on her Lampitt connections. There had been one rather tricky dinner with her family during which I'd confirmed the impression made many years earlier that Lady Vulture didn't much like me. I still wanted to hold at arm's length any notion that in marrying Anne, I might in fact be doing the one thing that Uncle Roy most desired. Accompanying her to Sargie's hospital bed would bring together the two worlds of childhood and manhood with uncomfortable violence. Though it was only a few years since I had seen Sargie, it was, imaginatively speaking, a whole lifetime.

'I'm nearly seventy, my dear,' he told me that afternoon in his small private hospital room. Sargie would have been nauseated by the Black Bottle, but he got through life with the same sustenance as Pete, Day Muckley and Mr Porn. A Gold Flake was alight in Sargie's bone cigarette-holder and the tooth mug in his right hand contained a dry martini, with gin, replenished from time to time from a cocktail shaker on his bedside locker. His foot, in plaster, was suspended from a pulley which he said was the sort of farcical arrangement which put one in mind of the Marx Brothers.

'At any moment, I expect the bed to roll away while I'm left here screaming in agony,' he laughed. 'Perhaps in the arms of Margaret Dumont. Harpo playing a serenade perhaps. Ha!'

He was in a beneficent mood. Being hospitalised suited him. It guaranteed not only that he was the centre of attention, but also the centre of sympathy. Ever since I knew of Sargie's existence, he had been trying to persuade someone, usually Uncle Roy, that he needed special treatment. His whole life, indeed, had been dominated by the need to make people feel sorry for him. The broken toe (consequence of an unwise attempt to lift a crate of gin which had been delivered to his flat off Kensington High Street) had cheered him up. He laughed a lot as Anne told him about her encounter with the Best-Seller.

'Didn't he write something rather good before the war?'

'*The Calderdale Saga.*'

'Something about these mill-owners in Yorkshire who'd been Catholics ever since penal times. Mama read it and thought it was rather good, I seem to remember.'

'That's the man.'

'Not my kind of thing. I can never believe in novels – can you? Still, my dears. You are moving in literary worlds. Such a pity Jimbo's dead. How he'd have liked hearing about it all. Not to go, there, of course, not this pub of yours. Don't suppose that Jimbo ever darkened the doors of a pub. Rather a prude in many ways. You never really knew him well, did you, Julian?'

'Sargie, he died when we were tiny!' Anne said.

'No, I was twelve when he died,' I said. 'I never actually met him, though he did call on Uncle Roy once to talk about the Archbishop Benson book.'

I introduced this reference to my uncle as a measure of how the land lay. I might have been mentioning the name of Trotsky to Stalin's Politburo. Sargie showed no awareness in his features that the previous nineteen syllables had been voiced.

'I can actually just remember him,' said Anne. 'He gave me lovely presents when I was a little girl. My Arthur Rackham's Hans Andersen one Christmas and another time, that musical box in the shape of a gondola – you know,' she said to me, 'the one I showed you the other evening.'

'Lor! I remember buying that with him before the war,' said Sargie. 'We had a jaunt to Venice. Not a very happy one. The place is bloody depressing – ever been there? And we stayed at an absolutely godforsaken hotel.'

'You should have stayed at one of the grand ones like the Gritti.' Anne spoke with the authority of one who had written undergraduate essays on Titian, Tintoretto, Ruskin.

'Gritti! That's the place. God Almighty! My room overlooked this dreary sludge of water . . .'

'The Grand Canal,' said Anne.

'I hate looking at water from a bedroom. And the stink. It made me ill. I had to get them to change my room, of course. Couldn't look out on that brown sludge. Like being in the back streets of Manchester or some God-awful place. And damp sheets, and boring food. All macaroni kind of stuff and fried fish galore. Thought I might actually die of constipation. They don't eat proper Italian food at all there, you know. You never so much as see a tomato.'

'Your brother's Venice book is surely due for some kind of revival,' I said.

'Have you been talking to Lover Boy? I notice that no publisher has actually reprinted the bloody thing.'

'Who's Lover Boy?' asked Anne.

'Jimbo's biographer. Wows all the girls. Working like billy-o to get all Jimbo's books back into print. Can't tell what he has to gain from it – perhaps nothing; perhaps it's just altruism.'

I had never asked Sargie's opinion of Hunter's book about his brother Jimbo. The publication had caused fury in the Lampitt family by its implied disclosures of a promiscuous homosexual life on the part of its subject.

'Your darling mother, Annie, thought we should have stopped Lover Boy writing the bloody book.'

'Anne's one of Lover Boy's conquests,' I chipped in. 'Mad about him since seeing him on television. Careful what you say about him, Sargie.'

'You wouldn't be the first, my dear.' He drew on his bone holder and was silent a space. 'No – but – family solicitor, threats, I said, "Sibs, you *can't* stop a man writing a book." We could, I suppose, have withheld permission to quote from Jimbo's work, but it would only have tempted Lover Boy to write a book, which was even more exciting for the Great British Public – the IP, as I call them. To think of the *time* we've wasted in our dear old Party trying to better the lot of the IP and look at them now, all guzzling like hogs, earning more money than I do, most of them, all with inside *topos* and these bloody television things.'

'I suppose Lady Starling thought Hunter's book would hurt people,' I said.

'Well, it did. Of course it hurt people. But the only alternative is censorship, and that isn't an alternative.'

'I don't know.'

'Oh, for God's sake, Julian! Grow up! Read some Milton or something! If a man wants to publish a book saying Jimbo was queer, then you've got to let him do so. The only redress you would ever have lies in your own freedom to write a book saying he wasn't. Funny thing is, I don't think he was exactly, not old Jimbo. I never got the slightest whiff of it in his company. And of course he was terribly fastidious, a real old woman, you know. That Venice trip we made together – it was like going abroad with a maiden aunt. Smelling salts, Malvern water. It is simply unimaginable to me that Jimbo would ever have wandered off down some stinking alley and dropped his pants for a gondolier. Totally unthinkable. But young people think everyone's having sex all the time. They aren't, you know, my dears, they just aren't. I know that families get things wrong but I just don't think that Jimbo had a sexual nature.'

'What about this diary he kept?' I asked. 'It seems to have implied that he went to bed with almost everyone.'

'Hardly bed. There seem to have been a lot of visits to the *topos* and other larks in the most unlikely places. Do you remember that supposed incident with the Duke of Albany in the tea tent during a Buckingham Palace garden party? I mean, I ask you! No, Julian, the operative words in your question are "seems" and "implied". Lover Boy very seldom gives a direct quote from those diaries of Jimbo's. Now it may have been as an insurance in case Sibs or I served a writ on him and prevented direct quotation – there's hardly any direct quotation in his book. The other explanation is that the diaries are not so specific as Lover Boy says.'

'Are you saying' – I remembered a theory of my cousin Felicity, who had done a bit of work on the Lampitt Papers when they were still deposited at Timplingham Place – 'that your brother wrote the diary as a sort of fiction, a fantasy?'

'You mean wrote things down which weren't true?' Anne asked with a puzzled tone. 'Why would anyone wish to do that?'

'Most of us live in fantasy of one sort or another,' I puddingly advanced. 'A writer such as your uncle might have decided to lead a vicarious fantasy life which he had just made up.'

'Yes, but if it isn't true and you know it isn't true,' said Anne,

314

'how could it possibly be consoling?' Darling Anne, how unlike the majority of the human race she was, and indubitably still is.

'As a matter of fact, my dears,' said Sargie, who reached up and heaved himself into a more comfortable position in the bed by means of a winch, 'I shouldn't mind your advice about Lover Boy. You see, he's still sitting on all Jimbo's papers and I'm vaguely worried about it. Foolish of me to lend them to him, I suppose, but I did.' I wondered at this point if Sargie would allude to Uncle Roy, who had been delegated by Sibs to 'disentangle Sargie from that horrible little man' – meaning Hunter. But nothing was said about Roy. Their friendship had been not merely important, but all-important to my uncle. I am sure that he thought of Sargie all the time. Perhaps Sargie was so solely occupied with his own concerns, and for much of the time with purely bodily sensations, that he did not think about it at all. Who could tell?

'Is Hunter ever going to write the second volume of your brother's life?' I asked.

'Well, that's what I shouldn't mind finding out,' said Sargie. 'Easier for you than for me – you're both more his sort of age.' (Hunter was, at this date, what? Forty-odd? I was in my early to mid-twenties.) 'Besides, I've got this wretched toe.'

'Poor Sargie.' Anne got up from her canvas chair and planted a kiss on her uncle's brow.

'You see,' I joked relentlessly, 'she's desperate to meet Lover Boy.'

'It was a bit off, don't you think – putting it around that Jimbo was some sort of Oscar Wilde or Tom What's'isname?'

Anne reminded him of the name of the Labour MP whose adventures, always mysteriously kept out of the newspapers, were a bit of a byword.

'I've met him once or twice with Vernon, who likes him a lot. You know my cousin Vernon, don't you?'

'Heard a lot about him,' I said. 'Never actually met him.'

'You must get Anne to introduce you.'

'Mummy's so silly about Vernon. Says he's a red.'

'Is now, practically,' said Sargie. 'There's been a real lurch to the left since Gaitskell beat him to the Chancellorship. Inheriting his father's title and all that money didn't help either. If you're of leftish persuasion, the richer you become the redder you get. Don't know why it should be, but it's an infallible rule.'

'Mummy says that Vernon's the only serious Lampitt left,' said Anne. 'A couple of generations ago they were all serious.'

Old Joseph Lampitt, who made money brewing in the 1760s, had been a serious man; a philosopher by bent, Unitarian, republican, pro-American. He had come William Blake's way, and once promised to buy some engravings from Blake's *America*. His large progeny had risen in the intellectual and political world. The eldest son Jo married an Isleworth heiress. Another son, a friend of the Godwins, had been a pioneer feminist. Most of that generation had married well. Thence had sprung that tribe of Lampitts who became professors of science and philosophy, social reformers, and pillars of the *bien-pensant* Victorian intellectual hierarchy, intermarried with Sidgwicks, Wedgwoods, Stracheys, Potters, Bensons and Darwins, as well as with landed money.

'Old Joseph' – always Sargie's way of referring to the founding father of this dynasty – 'is mentioned in Gilchrist, you know.'

'Gilchrist?'

'Don't you know Gilchrist's *Life of Blake*? Oh, you're missing out.' I made a mental note to look for the book when next in a secondhand bookshop.

It was not the first time that I had admired Sargie's method of getting his own way. In the midst of an apparently incoherent ramble about his family, he had had a very clear objective. We were to be delegated ambassadors to Hunter. We were to find out if he was contemplating writing any more of his biography of James Petworth Lampitt; we were to broach with him the extremely embarrassing question of the diaries, and if possible, get them back into Sargie's possession.

'Thing is,' said Sargie, 'I think it would be better coming from someone of Lover Boy's kind of age. You could be so much more casual about it all. But you remember all that hullaballoo when the first volume appeared. We don't want that all over again – your mother having the Dalalie Taps.'

We all agreed that almost anything was preferable to an emotional disturbance in the bosom of Lady Vulture.

'He seemed really cheered up by our visit,' said Anne, squeezing me as we came out again into Bryanston Square.

'Yes.'

'Well, that's a good thing, isn't it?' She shook my arm, sensing my reservations.

I said, 'I just wonder what we've let ourselves in for, that's all.'

Four

The question of whether Hunter was making progress with the biography of James Petworth Lampitt was completely peripheral to my interests and concerns. Uppermost in my mind was the question of what I was going to do with life, or life with me. Would the novel ever be finished, and if finished, published? Would the theatrical ambitions, instead, take over? A thousand times more important than either question, would Anne and I be married? Only later would I come to see that the Hunter question was closely linked to all the others, a good example of how seldom life gives any clue as to what is or isn't going to be important.

Hunter had first come my way as an object of sexual jealousy, then as a sort of predator making havoc, chiefly among Anne's Lampitt relations, but also among my own. The passage of a number of years, while not obliterating these images of Hunter from my mind, has allowed me, in common with most television viewers and readers of the highbrow Sunday newspapers, to be aware of Hunter the public man. I remember a sermon of Uncle Roy's in which St Augustine was quoted, describing his own career as a rhetorician as 'so much smoke and wind'. Hunter, in terms of tangible achievement at this date, was exhaling prodigious evanescent signals that he was there: a regular reviewing slot in some Sunday paper, frequent appearances on television (though none so memorable as the attempted conversation with Day Muckley); as well as all the usual appurtenances of such literary celebrity – membership of committees, a judge of various prestigious literary prizes. Giving out such quantities of smoke and wind must have been a very satisfying substitute for the rigours of literary composition, and it was not surprising that Volume II of *Petworth Lampitt* had so far not made its appearance in the bookshops.

I know that it was around this point that I bumped into Hunter; but here is a good instance of how unreliable a narrative account of things can be. There were at this stage so many things going on. Had I, for example, already been auditioned for a fortnight's rep in King's Lynn? I think I had. I assume the novel was done, or knocked into some sort of shape. Was I still working at the Bottle regularly, or had it become a more casual arrangement? I simply can't remember, and since my diary of the period was not a daily chronicle so much as a sporadic outburst of thoughts – sometimes about reading, sometimes about life in general – I have no clues about the more mundane but interesting questions which now haunt me.

I know that Anne and I had by now taken to visiting Sargie fairly regularly. The toe had long healed and he was cheerfully installed at home with a newish cat, a bad-tempered Siamese called Eden with the habit of running up the curtains if you tried to stroke it. Frequent exposure to Sargie's concerns prompted me, when quite by chance I met Hunter in St James's Square, to bring up the subject of the Lampitt Papers.

'Sargie was asking after you the other day,' I said.

A grin passed over Hunter's face. It was a flirtatious parody of 'sheepish'. It seemed to say, 'You and I know more than the rest of the world about what lies behind that remark; we both like each other so much that we regard it as rather a joke.' The odd thing, which I am sure most readers of this narrative would find it hard to believe, is that I did actually quite like Hunter. In that conspiratorial moment in the square I liked him very much. I felt as though he were drawing me into a very friendly conspiracy.

'I'm sure it's the same for you,' he remarked, and for a moment the smile deserted his boyish face. 'One takes on too much. Sargie is probably anxiously wondering what has happened to Volume II.'

'On the contrary, I think he was wondering what had happened to the Lampitt Papers.'

This looks rather a threatening remark when written down. I said it smilingly, however, in a manner which fitted Hunter's own, and as soon as the words were out of my mouth, we both laughed.

'I promised Madge' – his publisher – 'that I'd submit last Christmas.' (Raised eyebrows said, 'Aren't I awful?') I quite understood what he meant by 'submit' – that is, 'submit a typescript of my next book'. He was sufficiently confident of himself not to need to supply such nouns. It was taken for granted by all who crossed Hunter's path that he was uppermost in their minds – his books, his career, the meetings he had to attend. It was probably a condescending awareness of this which inspired his kindness to writers less successful than himself; it was perhaps analogous to Sargie's theory that the richer left-wing people become, the redder in politics.

'But what are *you* writing?' he asked.

I began the usual mock-modest remarks about my novel's defects.

'I suppose you wouldn't let me read it?' he said. 'If it's . . .' He paused for a split second and I could see him finding a polite synonym for 'no bloody good'. 'If it's Madge Cruden's kind of book – she's my publisher, you know Madge, I expect, and she's always only too glad to have good stuff pushed in her direction.'

'That would be awfully . . .'

I had not shown my book to Bloom, who was the only publisher I knew. He told me not to, said that however much I thought I wouldn't mind if he rejected it, I *would* mind. Instinct presumably told him at a hundred yards that the book was no good. Hunter's offer seemed all the more welcome.

'Not a bit,' he said. 'Look, we ought to have lunch one day.'

Before I had time to return to the question of the Lampitt Papers or to pay homage to Hunter's increasing skill as a televisionary, he was consulting his wrist-watch.

'Good heavens! And I'm having lunch with the great man before this afternoon's meeting of the London Library Committee.'

'Which great man?'

As so often when I have asked Hunter a straight question, he smiled, as if one's only motive in asking must have been some frivolous and unexplained desire to tease. The syllables 'Tom Eliot' were murmured. I have since wondered whether he did not intend to write Eliot's biography. The knowledge that there was an embargo on such an enterprise would no doubt act as a stimulus to Hunter's pen.

I was not lunching with T. S. Eliot's double at the Black Bottle, though it would have been neat if I had been. In fact I had agreed to meet Anne and her mother at Simpson's in the Strand. On arrival, I blurted out a version of my conversation with Hunter, partly to explain my own lateness at the restaurant.

'He just wanted to get you off the subject of Jimbo's diaries,' said Sibs.

She looked no older than when I had first met her a decade or so earlier; the long Lampitt face, the hooded eyes and strong bones in cheek and nose, all of which gave something comic to Sargie's appearance, were in his sister elegant and beautiful. She had lovely, soft, very pale skin and terrifyingly sharp eyes. I never did know how my uncle had formed the unshakeable impression that Sibs was the downtrodden member of the Lampitt family. It is *just* possible that during her childhood at Timplingham Place when Mrs Lampitt had much favoured the older boys, had taken little interest in the longed-for daughter when she had been born, that my uncle had heard of some scene in which little Sybil had been made to know her place, as the youngest member of a family of egoists. Conceivably, he had even seen her, as a young woman, demonstrating her unquestioned domestic skills about the Place, perhaps by tidying up after Sargie or another brother. To the end of his days, Uncle Roy would refer to Sibs as 'a complete doormat'. It meant that on the occasions when he met anyone else who knew Sibs there would be a moment of confusion, while the other speaker felt it necessary to protest that if a doormat were under discussion this could not possibly be *their* Lady Starling. My uncle, for whom all Lampitts existed more as imaginative projections than people he saw much of, would take no notice of such contradictions and usually repeat the metaphor, or add, 'Extraordinarily nice woman, Sibs.'

Spirited, strong-willed and – I have to confess it, though she was thirty years older than me and I was in love with her daughter – sexually attractive to me, was Sibs, nice, either ordinarily, or extraordinarily?

'Really, Julian, you are a twerp,' she said when she heard all she wanted to hear of my Hunter story. 'You really had your opportunity there. You should have made a specific date with Mr Hunter to go to his flat and pick up Jimbo's diaries.'

'I don't know where he lives. He's a bit of a mystery man.'

'Instead of which you let yourself be flattered by his remarks about this story you've written.'

'Poor Julian! Mummy, leave him alone!'

Anne's voice rose an octave when arguing with her mother.

'How could he have got hold of Jimbo's silly old diaries? Anyway, you have to admit that Mr Hunter is a bit of a dish.'

Sibs stared across the table at me. For some reason the moisture of someone's eyes is one of the first things I notice when I find them physically appealing. Sibs's eyes were large, turquoise, as bright with moisture as could have been without actually weeping.

'Don't be silly, darling,' she said. 'Ah, at last!'

She immediately transferred her commanding-officer manner to the waiter who had arrived with the meat trolley. At his side another young man in a tall white hat sharpened and brandished the carving irons.

The two young men, who smiled at Anne as a pretty girl and largely ignored me, danced attendance on Sibs. She enchanted them. The boy carving the meat in particular was affected by her. He put down his knife on the trolley and made a little bow to her, raising his chef's hat to reveal a Brylcreemed ted's coif. She did not in the least object to this little bit of obeisance.

'The veal is always good,' she asserted.

'It's what I would have chosen for you myself, madam,' said the carver, who had a pronounced squint.

When we all had meat set before us – I dithered about the possibility of choosing lamb, but Sibs flatly vetoed any such idea ('Much easier for this young man to give us all the same!') – she fell to reminiscing about Jimbo, and her other brothers, and life in Timplingham before they were all scattered.

'I am a survivor, really. Oh, those Timplingham Christmases when Mama was alive! You can't quite imagine what family life was like in those days, a whole table full of interesting grown-up people, and all one's brothers and lots of cousins. We just didn't need the world outside us. I think that was Jimbo's trouble in some ways, and Sargie's now. They have never got used to living without that large supportive, innocent society of which we were all members as of right, and for which there is no substitute in the world. Yes, you know, that's what's so wicked about Mr Hunter's book. It doesn't matter that he gets all the social details wrong; you'd expect that from someone like that.'

'Mummy!' protested egalitarian Anne.

'You know what I *mean*, darling.'

'Yes, and I don't like it!'

322

'You're forgetting Anne's crush on Mr Hunter, Sibs,' I prompted.

Her mother lifted a forefinger towards her daughter.

'Don't you *dare*,' she said with great fierceness. 'Don't you *dare*! As I say, you would expect him to get everything wrong. Whenever I appear in the book, which mercifully isn't often, I'm called Lady Sybil Starling.'

'Mummy, people don't mind about those things any more.'

'And he's so horrid about Mama, who wasn't a dragon a bit in the way he suggests. It is true that early on she very much wanted a daughter and Jimbo had to wear girls' clothes for a bit.'

'Till he was ten,' I said.

'I think many boys did in those days.'

The squint-eyed one appeared again, offering us second helpings, which we all accepted.

'But of all the men I ever knew, Jimbo was in some ways the most innocent. He was kind, too – and you don't get any of that in the Hunter book. He was *so* kind to us when we first got married. He lent us his flat in Manchester Square because our house was all haywire with decorators, and he really was a very good uncle to your brothers. I'm only sorry you were too young to know him well, darling.'

'But I *can* remember him,' said Anne. 'I came to some of the readings.'

'After early supper in our house, Jimbo would often read aloud to the children. *Great Expectations* and *David Copperfield*, we had both those, and *Huckleberry Finn* and *Vice Versa*.'

'One of my favourite novels,' I said. 'Perhaps the truest novel ever written about what it is like to go away to school.'

Sibs had no interest in what I thought of books. She continued with memories of Jimbo and her other brothers. It interested me as a purely academic issue that Hunter's *Petworth Lampitt*, which at the time I took to be a lifeless but authoritative version of the man's life, should bear so little resemblance to Jimbo Lampitt as he was actually remembered by his family. I saw this, I can't remember why, as an inevitability: that Sargie and Sibs could not bear to read 'the truth' about Jimbo. The notion that their actual memories of a real man might be authentic, possibly more so than Hunter's written narrative, did not strike me as even worth considering, until that luncheon. As Sibs spoke I began to have a glimmering awareness that things might be otherwise. Part of the difficulty was that the Lampitts were, for me, already semi-fictionalised beings before they began to cross my path in person. As a child I had heard of little else. They were Uncle Roy's obsessive theme, creeping into his conversation however unlikely the beginning of a sentence might appear. Did Aunt Deirdre's friend Bunty, on a rare visit, allude to the petunias in the front garden? Before his wife had a chance to reply, Uncle Roy would have interjected with the one about Ursula Lampitt and the geraniums in her window-boxes. ('I thought we were going to have another War of the Roses on our hands' was how she concluded her debate with the Fellows of Rawlinson upon the matter.)

The world itself was divided in Uncle Roy's consciousness not as atlases divide it, into political regions or physical areas of mountain, sea, plain, or river. It was a Lampitt world, in which other creatures, trees, elephants, Atlantic breakers, Australian deserts, served as a mere backdrop to Lampitt anecdotes. Mention the Grand Canyon and you would (of course) get old Grandfather Lampitt's visit to the United States in the late 1880s, or Angelica's 'famous' misadventures with those railways shares. Speak of kangaroos, and that would be but a short step to Melbourne, and in Melbourne, naturally, you think of Richard Lampitt's ill-fated attempt to set up business there and his no less ill-fated Australian marriage, not a 'suitable' subject for mentioning in front of a child, had it not been for the fact that Richard's father-in-law was destined to become the governor of Queensland. Africa? Well, you have an *embarras de richesses*. Vivian's phlebitis in Mombasa, Jimbo's unlikely and hilarious visit to Kenya ('Which way round do you point a gun, Fanshawe?'), or, for variety, what of Mary, who married that banker in Cape Town?

As the saying goes, I had had them until they were coming out of my ears; and if I had said that to Uncle Roy, he would only have been prompted to remember that time Sargie thought he was going deaf in that hotel in Torquay and summoned the doctor to syringe his ears – not once, but three times.

That is why when Volume I was published I almost liked Hunter. The book itself came as a relief to me: at last, a vision of the Lampitts so different from that of Uncle Roy that I assumed it must be true. This silly family (as I by then thought them) were at last going to get their comeuppance. I was not rational about it; I did not consider the fact, for example, that they had not *asked* Uncle Roy to develop this obsession, any more than they had asked Hunter to write his book. At last, I felt, the record could be set straight. My uncle's Lampitt mania, born as I cruelly supposed from sycophantic snobbery and hardly relieved by his so often making the Lampitts the subject of unamusing 'funny stories', was at last going to be counter-balanced by the irrefutable printed word.

It was only after the publication of Hunter's book that other lines of thought opened up. I had not begun to question the whole morality of biography, its intrusiveness, its know-all claims, its essential vulgarity. I was immediately conscious, however, that Hunter's biography had hurt people, not least Uncle Roy himself. In its peculiar way, it had led to the severance of the most important thing in his life, his friendship with Sargie. The thought that I might become involved with a member of Sargie's family, that Uncle Roy might himself become a Lampitt in-law was heady stuff, and I was not sure how to break it to him, not least because the overwhelming Sibs obviously rather liked my uncle and because Anne was so irrepressibly anxious to make his acquaintance. The first meeting did not occur until several months after that lunch at Simpson's. Anne and I met Darnley one Friday morning in London, and we all travelled eastwards together as far as Cambridge. I forget if it was his last term there, or whether he was just hanging about.

All my worries about what Darnley felt about me and Anne had been put on one side – not because I had received any reassurances from him, but because I was drunk with happiness, so delirious in my love for Anne that other people had very largely ceased to exist as real beings for me. I certainly would not have considered placing their feelings above my own in importance. How I felt – how Anne felt or how I imagined she felt – that was all that mattered. We were intoxicated by an *égoïsme à deux*. It is hard to behave unselfishly in such circumstances. I did notice that the larky side of Darnley's nature seemed quiescent, and that he was low in spirits by the time we reached Cambridge. Given the environment, this seemed all too understandable – the grey brick courts, the howling winds, the ill-shaven dons in tweeds pursuing their mad way by splay foot or punctured tricycle through mean narrow streets. Thus

Cambridge to a London eye. We were there to borrow Darnley's car, the Morris he shared with his sister. He kept it concealed down a side street off the Huntingdon Road. Perhaps he had rooms there. I remember his strange smile as he waved and we jolted off towards Norfolk. For Anne insisted that we should go and see my uncle and aunt.

Probably more than a year had passed since I had been back to Timplingham, but in a way all homecomings there were the same, the same sense that it was and wasn't home, the same unworthy feeling, born I suppose from my inability to recover from the loss of my parents, that the Rectory was a joke, a mockery of home. These things were buried deep – too deep for me to understand them as a young man. I was always puzzled by my reactions to Timplingham. Like a child I would look forward to seeing my uncle and aunt, but by the time I had arrived, often within a matter of minutes, uncontrollably negative feelings would surface. Both of them, but particularly Uncle Roy, had a power to enrage me unrivalled by anyone else I ever met. 'More coffee?' Uncle Roy always said this just before he finished his own breakfast. I have sometimes thought that he was actually risking his life by saying these three syllables. What was annoying in that? Any reader who needs to ask that question has never belonged to a family. The 'causes' of why the remark was excruciatingly, sometimes heartrendingly annoying, were quite unanalysable.

On this particular visit everything would be different because Anne would be there. I did not quite know how my family would react to this new development in my life. At first I assumed Uncle Roy would be pleased. Then I wondered whether he would not be vaguely peeved, on the grounds that the Lampitts were his department, not mine. Would my bringing Anne to Timplingham stir up sorrowful old memories of his quarrel with Sargie? And, a different consideration, would he bore Anne to death? I never sufficiently took account of what a charming man my uncle was. Because he had this secret, familial power to irritate me and embarrass me, which by no means meant that I did not love him, I was in a poor position to see him as others saw him. When they said they found him charming and delightful (which in so many ways he obviously was), I always thought they were 'just saying it' rather than meaning it.

The large Norfolk sky brooded ominously over our heads and the great elms which bordered the road were in bud. Momentarily there was a gap in the trees and hedgerows, and across flat fields and meadowland one would make out the flinty octagonal tower of the parish church.

'That's it,' I said.

Anne, who was driving, drew up by the side of the road. She leaned over and very delicately kissed me on the lips. She had a look of her mother when she said, with good humour, but firmness (the school matron who had just slapped iodine and plaster on one's cut knee), 'Don't worry! It will be all right.'

I held her for a moment. Had we seen the thing through, as the Prayer Book says one must, till death, we should doubtless have known a whole range of physical feelings for each other. Because our marriage was of such short duration, this was not so. I always felt her to be almost painfully attractive. Her large laughing turquoise eyes, her big mouth and her chest touching mine had their usual effect.

'What?' she laughed. 'Here? Now?'

'Why not?'

'What if someone came along?' In a rustic accent (certainly not of Norfolk) which was quite bad enough to have got her a part on 'The Mulberrys', Anne said, 'Oi were cyclin' paarst Top Meadow moindin' me own business an' what should oi spoi but paarson's nephew cavortin' wiv 'is laars in fiel' yonder.'

But even in this comic voice the prospect which she summoned up was irresistible. We were soon lying in the fresh spring grass behind the hedge. One can't write about such things – or, I can't. Yet how well I understand the desire of other writers to celebrate such joys, and to explore their meaning.

Returning to normal consciousness after such an experience, dressing again, and wandering back to the car, dazed and hand in hand, we found that Timplingham was the same old place, and yet never quite the same again.

'We're going to be late for lunch,' Anne said.

'There's Uncle Roy now,' I replied, as the Morris scrunched up the rectory drive.

He was wearing his green golfing trousers and a tweed Norfolk jacket to match, a high, rather soft white collar (I wonder if Pilbright would have approved?) and a floppy white bow tie. Our lateness was bound to have disrupted that clockwork-run household. I thought it possible that he had been sent out by Aunt Deirdre to see 'what on earth has happened to them'. If so, he was endeavouring to be nonchalant, inspecting the jasmine near the front door rather as if he were a stranger to the place and had never seen it before. He turned with an actorly display of surprise and delight when we opened the doors of the car.

'Well, well!'

'We're frightfully late!' This was Anne, plunging straight in as always.

'Not at *all*,' insisted Uncle Roy. 'Not in the slightest degree. Though you remember lateness.'

We both paused, puzzled by this superficially surreal question.

'Martin and the meetings of the railway board! He was a *byword* for being late, so much so that the secretary always told him that meetings were before lunch, in the hope that he would turn up to take the chair by half-past two!'

'Is that my great-uncle Martin?'

'Uncle, uncle. But you are too young to remember him. Charming man. You, if I may say so, have grown since we last met, but since you were only two at the time that is hardly surprising.'

He began to reminisce about the time when she and Sibs had come to Timplingham Place – 'the last time poor Sibs saw her mother alive, I am sorry to say.'

'I hardly remember my Lampitt granny.'

'A great lady,' said Uncle Roy, 'a great lady.'

As he led the way into the house, I realised that, beyond one short, airy wave in my direction, he had barely greeted me. He was not going to waste a second of precious Lampitt time spent with Anne.

'As a matter of fact, we nearly met some three years later before you started at that school.'

'Greencoats?'

'No.'

'Frances Holland?'

My uncle smiled indulgently.

'Before Greencoats they tried you at a place called St Werbergh's.'

'So they did – we wore lovely little straw hats. But fancy you knowing, or remembering.'

I had warned Anne of my uncle's interest in her family, but even so, his grasp of detail surprised and impressed her.

'Your grandmother, who was an exceptionally wise person, did warn your dear mama. I remember it so well at the time.'

He held back a chuckle.

Uncle Roy could have performed such feats of memory with any member of Anne's family who had happened to turn up at his front door. Where they had been to prep school, early trouble with their teeth, no detail of their early biography (assuming it to be repeatable) would have gone unrepeated.

He led the way through the hall and then called out – the stage laird calling to the stage parlour-maid – 'They're here!'

'Well, bring them through' came my aunt's voice, and a merry 'Hallo!' from Granny.

With a shrug and rather a disloyal little smile ('The wife!' was what it said) he pushed through the kitchen door. As he did so he was still trying to clear up what seemed from his tone to be urgent matters: the exact date when he had narrowly missed meeting Anne the second time during her childhood; and her grandmother's exact views of the apparently dud Knightsbridge school which Anne had attended for a term or two. My aunt's coming forward to greet us (a peck on the cheek for me, a handshake for Anne) and Granny's lazy old wave from her chair seemed to annoy Uncle Roy. They were irrelevant intrusions into the urgent settling of Lampitt business.

Aunt Deirdre was shy with new people and blushed crimson when Anne took her hand. Granny, who was already seated at the table, laughed as she said, 'What on earth have you been up to? You're *very* late!'

'I said they would arrive any old time,' said Aunt Deirdre briskly. 'That's why I did a shepherd's pie, doesn't spoil, hope that's all right.' She added, by way of explanation to Anne, 'We go in for plain food, you'll find.'

Certainly no other impression could be derived from the steaming Pyrex bowl, which she transferred almost immediately from the Aga to the cork table mat.

'Roy,' Granny persisted tactlessly, 'was like a cat on hot bricks before you came; running in and out of the kitchen and wondering where you'd got to.'

'I did nothing of the kind,' he said genially.

'We are very late, I'm afraid,' said Anne. 'Julian said you liked to eat at a quarter to one.'

It was now ten to two.

'Your Uncle Jimbo used to madden his mother, I remember, by saying that the proper time for luncheon was half-past one. Said it ate into the day if he had it any earlier. "Yes," your grandmother used to say . . .' My uncle Roy slowed down, signal that a Lampitt *mot* was to be enunciated.

'Whose day, we know,' snapped Aunt Deirdre, to get the anecdote over as soon as possible. She had begun to scoop spoonfuls of grey mince and mashed potato on to our plates. 'Now, Anne, do start as soon as you get your food. Don't stand on ceremony.'

'Whose day,' my uncle repeated. You could not hurry these things, any more than you could hurry a good wine. His face was wreathed in delight at the prospect of old Mrs Lampitt's sharp words.

It was all new to Anne, like most of the Lampitt lore which he unfolded to her that weekend. To say that she was 'good' with them would imply that she made some kind of effort, which I don't think she did. She liked them and they immediately liked her.

After lunch, we washed up, and my aunt showed Anne to her room upstairs. There was a choice between the spare bedroom, occupied about once a year by Bunty, or my cousin Felicity's bedroom, which was very slightly more comfortable and a few yards nearer the bathroom.

By the time Anne had unpacked a small holdall on to Felicity's bed my aunt had emerged on the landing in her 'gardening rig': thus designated, but to all outward appearance identical to what she had been wearing in the morning: blouse and tweed costume. We followed her into the back kitchen, where she assumed a sacking apron and rubber overshoes, and took down the trug from its hook on the wall. It contained thick gardening gloves, secateurs, twine and other necessaries of her craft. We followed automatically as she left the back door. It was the only moment of the day, in my recollection, when she lost the look of disgruntlement which otherwise played over her features.

Uncle Roy had begun to age; not so his wife. She still seemed the slightly overweight Girl Guide, no hint of grey in her mousy cropped hair, no lines on her large pink face.

'There's an awful lot to do,' she said, leading the way into the garden.'Particularly since poor Mr Gillard had his stroke.'

Having delivered this information in the no-nonsense tone of her ordinary speech, she then broke into a quite different voice.

'Trot-ter! Trot, trot, trot-ter!'

This aria was addressed to a bouncy little wirehaired dachshund, a replacement for Tinker, who, as a sad letter had told me some fifteen months earlier, had been called to his eternal reward. When I last visited them, my uncle and aunt were dogless, for them an unnatural condition. Trotter had arrived in the meantime. My aunt never allowed such a playful, semi-flirtatious note into her voice when addressing a human being as when she said, 'What are you *not* going to do today, Trotter? What are you? No, you're not going to chew canes. No, you're not. No.' She suddenly switched to a serious human tone again. 'If you could help with a bit of the digging I should be so grateful. As you can see, it's all a bit of a mess.'

I never saw a garden more orderly. The mess was all inside Aunt Deirdre's head. The lawn, which had already been mown twice that year, sloped away to a sea of daffodils and narcissi under the huge copper beech. A wall of brick and flint, part of the old medieval priory in Uncle Roy's opinion, provided the background for the big herbaceous border.

'Everything's a bit dull at the moment, you see. If you came in six weeks, things would be much more interesting . . .'

She walked along the border slowly, every now and then bending her knees and sitting on her haunches, either to remove a weed or to inspect the condition of a plant.

'I'm so fed up with universal pansies,' she said; a remark I could have imagined on Bloom's lips in different circumstances. 'That *Camellia japonica* at the back there provides a nice touch of colour, doesn't it? Funnily enough, I thought it had died in January.'

'What are these dear little purple ones?' asked Anne.

'D'you mean the primula? Oh, that! It *is* nice, isn't it? It's a saxifrage – *Saxifraga oppositifolia*. Again I thought I'd lost that one in the frosts, but it's doing well. Oh! Will the weeds never stop coming up!' She took out a fistful.

'But the rhodos are good, aren't they,' she said. With a

sweeping gesture, she indicated the great expanses of colour on the other side of the lawn, trees from the brush of Samuel Palmer, full of mystic light. 'I'm glad I cut them back so firmly last year,' she said. 'Mr Gillard said I was being too ruthless, but I knew what I was up to.'

And she did, she did. I have seen and delighted in many marvellous gardens, but none have given me so much pleasure as hers.

'It's the vegetables which are going to be the real worry. If we can't get a replacement for Mr Gillard – I'm not quite sure . . .' Her voice trailed off.

The flinty brick wall was not the end of the garden, but a division within it. The path encircled the border to a small door which opened on to the walled kitchen garden, a scene which made one expect to see Peter Rabbit or Mr McGregor stooped over his cucumber frames.

'Potatoes have done very well, and I'm pleased with my spring greens; but look at this – a wilderness! I suppose if one does a bit each day.'

There was absolutely no sign of a wilderness. Already she had peas, sweet peas and two sorts of bean planted out in neat rows with arches above them. Beyond, in net cages, the gooseberry and currant bushes, having recovered from the vigorous short back and sides to which my aunt had subjected them at the end of the previous year, were putting forth their shoots. It was only in the comparatively small area of the garden where my aunt intended to plant out cabbages, carrots and lettuces that the supposed wilderness existed, a few scrubs of sorrel and the occasional dandelion disturbing the even brown surface of the earth, which she had evidently raked and sieved for weeks.

'I want to dig some compost into it before I plant it,' she said. And then, desperately trying not to look as if she was saying something important, and looking away from us both, she said, 'No, I'm only sorry that Felicity couldn't have come back this weekend to meet Anne.'

She said it too casually. It was the sentence she had been planning to say ever since we left the back kitchen. She stomped off to hoe another part of the garden, leaving us with our forks. She had twigged that Anne was now to be part of our family. She wished that her only daughter had been here to welcome her.

332

'I think we should *tell* them,' said Anne, when we were left alone with our digging.

'Leave it to me, though.' I didn't want one of her frank outbursts. Mine wasn't a family for a lot of candid talk or discussions of 'relationships' around the kitchen table. When such conferences had been attempted they had ended in quarrels. I didn't want Anne's happiness marred by a quarrel, by Granny telling us we were being rash, for example, or Aunt Deirdre asking practical questions about how we supposed we could live. It was typical of the unjust way I couldn't trust any of them. It seems extraordinarily cruel, from this perspective of time, not to have kept them better informed. There was absolutely no reason to suppose that they would have been other than kind to Anne. But I allowed the whole weekend to pass, hoping that the right moment would emerge and never actually finding it. As a family we were not great talkers. Certainly we were not given to the sort of talk which occupies people in great novels or plays. Whether, or with whom, we are in love, what, if anything, we believed about God or politics – these were matters which were never for one moment discussed at the rectory. The jabber which filled our silences was anodyne. In Aunt Deirdre's case it was largely concerned with the village or the garden. Uncle Roy only abandoned his pet theme if some item of ecclesiastical life was preoccupying him.

'I don't at *all* like the look of South India,' he remarked that evening at supper. 'No proper bishops.' His facial expression would have been more appropriate if he had just told us that Indian bishops dropped their aitches. My aunt, conspicuously more and more fed up with church as years passed, looked quite aggressively bored.

'I'm jolly grateful to you both, anyway,' she said. 'That kitchen garden's almost respectable at last.'

We were eating slices of corned beef, unadorned boiled potatoes and some of her early spring greens.

'I feel so glowing and tired,' said Anne.

I felt worse than this, positively knocked up. My hands and back were aching and my neck muscles felt as if they might seize up. I realised that I had not done any work, real work, or exerted myself physically, since Aunt Deirdre last asked me to 'help' in the garden. Life in the Bottle, and other pubs, and a heavy increase in the number of cigarettes smoked each day, were beginning to make a difference.

Was Aunt Deirdre trying to help us out, Anne and me, with the revelation about ourselves which she must have guessed we wished to make? Again, she reverted to Felicity, who had by now, between my aunt, Anne and myself, become a sort of code word for 'Anne is about to become a member of the family and it is a pity that Felicity can't be here'.

'Fliss is kept pretty busy,' said Aunt Deirdre.

Uncle Roy repeated the name of Felicity's college at Oxford, in case Anne had been slow to recognise the significance of the word.

Granny who was moving into a phase of life where all manifestations of human behaviour were amusing, guffawed at the idea of Felicity being 'busy'.

'I asked her the last time she was home what philosophy *is*,' she declared. 'It isn't what I thought at all. I'd always thought it was your ideas about life, how to be – you know, a better sort of person.'

She ate her corned beef hungrily; we all did.

'It's some years since I saw Ursula,' said Roy, by now puzzled that Anne had failed to pick up his drift. Surely anyone hearing that Felicity taught at Rawlinson College, Oxford, would immediately think of the Principal, Dame Ursula Lampitt?

'Mind you,' said Granny, 'it's all money, isn't it? Fliss gets paid for giving these what-d'you-call-'ems.'

'Tutorials,' snapped my aunt, who was clearly angered by her mother-in-law's implied contempt for the way Felicity spent her days. 'She's very clever.'

'Oh, we all know that.'

'Only sometimes people don't always give her credit for it,' said Aunt Deirdre, going very red. 'Poor old Fliss.'

I wondered if, like so many people in jokes and films, Aunt Deirdre hated her mother-in-law. Because I had always loved Granny it had never crossed my mind that anyone could find her any other than lovable. Now I could see that she was being almost deliberately provoking. On the other hand I could see the point of her deliberate unseriousness, whether or not it was valid. One couldn't imagine her common-sense friend Mrs Webb having much time for such questions as the problems of knowledge.

'Dame Ursula – Felicity's principal,' said my uncle heavily, giving Anne one last chance to knock the ball back over the net. She did just manage it, though it was hardly an impressive volley.

'Do you mean Dr Lampitt? She's some sort of relation of mine.'

'Second cousin once removed,' said my uncle briskly. This established, he could proceed with his fund of Ursula talk at the leisurely pace it deserved. 'I went back to Oxford some years ago for a college gaudy. The place is much changed, I'm afraid, since the war. I called in on Ursula for tea one afternoon. You will know her well enough to realise that this is a typical Ursula story.'

Surrendering Anne to my uncle, the rest of us talked among ourselves until the punchline of this particular saga was accomplished.

'What about you, anyway?' said Granny, who had finished meditating on the strange fact that people *paid* Felicity for having her 'weird ideas'. 'Been writing stories? And acting?' For some reason this was supposed to be funny; anyway, she laughed.

'It really looks as if the novel has been accepted,' I said. The only reason for my sheepishness in that company was that the book was all about them. Nor could I talk about it much without revealing how extremely kind Hunter had been, more or less acting as unpaid literary agent, pushing the book Madge Cruden's way, securing a promise from her that she would at least send the typescript to one of their better readers, and, when the report was not wholly unfavourable, chivvying the firm to accept it. None of this could be told because Hunter was an unmentionable name at the Rectory, since his love affair with Felicity.

I was prepared to let bygones be bygones. Hunter was becoming my enabler, an almost priestly figure in my life, if not a guardian angel, effecting my transition from one stage of existence to the next, from layabout and barman to someone whose existence could plausibly be defined as an artist, a writer. Bloom had begun the transition by getting me installed at Rikko's and Fenella's. Hunter was to complete it. But I knew there was something disloyal in being so willing to entrust my destiny to Jimbo's detractor, Felicity's seducer.

My aunt said, as though putting Granny down, 'If that's what Julian really wants to *do*. Different people are different.' Then with a girlish blush, she added, 'And to think you really know Stan Mulberry. Is the actor at all like the real thing?'

This was how Aunt Deirdre phrased the question.

Stan Mulberry, a flimsy creation of radio drama, was, as far as she was concerned, far more real than Rikko Kempe. How far did Rikko measure up to the reality of Stan Mulberry? It was difficult to answer. Not the least of my difficulties was to know how far it was possible to tell the truth about Rikko (his hair, his mannerisms) without being malicious.

'I think he got the part because he's good at accents,' I said.

'I'd assumed the "ee bah gum" was natural,' she said, with some disappointment. 'But I love Stan. He's such a decent sort. Take the way he helped out old Mrs Humberbach with those hospital visits to her mother. That was Stan all over, even though it was in the middle of lambing.'

There was something completely innocent about my aunt's fondness for 'The Mulberrys', innocent about the programme itself, come to that. I felt rather sorry for her when Granny scoffingly remarked, 'It's all rubbish.' Then, after a pause, she said to me, 'You should think of getting a part in it yourself one of these days.'

'I think it would spoil it, hearing Julian pretending to be someone at Barleybrook,' said my aunt.

'It's a good idea,' said Anne. She would have seen nothing insulting in my grandmother's observation. She had none of my capacity for nosing out offence; and she was pathetically ready to believe in my talents. 'Now he's got this agent, I'm sure parts will come along.'

It was true that I had been taken on by an agent and that several small parts sounded as if they might be in the offing. The trouble was, I had begun to doubt whether I was cut out to be an actor. My sense that life's possibilities were infinite was receding. I no longer thought that I could act Hamlet, paint as well as Cézanne and write a literary masterpiece.

Granny, like Sibs, was scornful of the artistic ambitions because they did not seem very likely to make me much money. As I sat at the table wiping shreds of corned beef from my plate with a slice of bread, I felt rising within me some of the irrational furies of adolescence. The anger, doubtless, was partly prompted by guilt. I simply would not allow myself to see why Granny felt so strongly about my having left Tempest and Holmes. Her eldest son had worked there from the age of twenty until he joined the RAF. Had he lived, he would probably have returned, and would still be making his daily and dutiful way to the Accounts department. Why not? Wasn't this the way in which most people earned their living? What was so special about me? In rejecting Tempest and Holmes, I was rejecting Daddy; but at the same time I was too insensitive to see that it was this which hurt and angered Granny. Tempest and Holmes were hallowed names for her. I wonder if she had so much as seen the place. For me, the shirt factory had no glamour at all. When I heard its name, I thought not of Daddy, whom I had never seen there, but of the tedium of my own routines. I heard again the clatter of the typewriters in the office pool, or saw again the huge workshops at the back where rows of women impassively supervised the passage of the shirts, in various stages of composition, into the sewing machines. I conceded that men wore shirts, so someone had to make them and sell them, and presumably some poor person in the middle had to enter the details of the transactions between the factory and the retailer into the company accounts. I wasn't proposing a shirtless universe, merely one where my contact with shirts was limited to buttoning and unbuttoning the things on my chest twice a day, and making sure that they were periodically washed and ironed. Let others do the rest.

'That Mr Pilbright who worked with your father was such a nice man,' said Granny. She turned to her daughter-in-law. 'I remember him at David's funeral . . .'

She always said 'David's funeral', though I believe that my parents had a joint service.

I could tell that Aunt Deirdre wanted to get the conversation back to 'The Mulberrys'. Uncle Roy, who found any mention of his brother's death excruciating, had taken a sudden interest in Trotter's bodily functions.

'Yes, yes,' he said to the little dog, who scurried about the stone floor of the kitchen much as Tinker had done in the old days, 'after supper, I'll take you for a walk after supper.'

'Mr Pilbright, who worked with him, was so kind. I remember Mrs Webb saying, "Now, Thora, I call that a really kind gentleman." You know, he said, "If there's *anything* we can do"

. . . and unlike some people, he really meant it. And he's always sent a card. Every Christmas since . . .'

'Just as soon as we've done the washing-up,' said Uncle Roy.

'Well,' said Aunt Deirdre crossly, 'if it wasn't Julian's line.'

The strain of life with her mother-in-law had led to a transformation in my aunt's views since I was last home; she was now a defender of my way of life for as long as Granny disapproved of it.

Only Anne gave Granny her complete sympathy and attention. The rest of us had heard Granny's views of Mr Pilbright a thousand times. For Anne it was all new; and, with each unfolding detail, Mrs Webb's remarks at my parents' funeral, Mr Pilbright's formulaic offers of help on Christmas cards, the punctiliousness with which he always sent out these cherished objects 'nice and early', Anne's large and infinitely kind eyes became more and more liquid. By the time Granny was saying, 'Well, naturally I thought it would be nice if Julian followed in his father's footsteps,' large tears were rolling in profusion down Anne's face. This, in Aunt Deirdre's book, would be another black mark against her mother-in-law; my aunt deplored displays of emotion, and no doubt thought that Granny was getting Anne 'worked up', something she was often accused of doing to me as a child.

'It's like what Mrs Webb often said when we were out in the country together, looking for, you know, a nice place to have a bit of lunch. "Thora," she'd say, "we could go further and fare worse." Well, it may be that Tempest and Holmes aren't exciting, but I think Julian could have gone further and fared worse.'

Throughout this speech Granny, without stirring from her chair, was turning this way and that, forcing her body to make gyrations of nearly 180 degrees. I knew the action well: it meant she was searching for cigarettes and matches. The more they eluded her gaze, the more she turned her head and shoulders. Anne, as much an addict of nicotine as my grandmother, offered her a Woodbine.

'Aren't they workmen's cigarettes?'

'Are they? I don't know.'

'They'll be much stronger than my Craven A.'

'I don't think so.'

They lit up.

'Oh, you're a funny lot,' said Granny, blowing her smoke in two very straight lines from her nostrils.

It was true. I knew that she had appreciated with embarrassing clarity, and without anything needing to be said, that my reasons for not continuing my work at Tempest and Holmes were almost purely snobbish. Without my wishing to do so, I had become the creature of Aunt Deirdre and Uncle Roy. There sat Uncle Roy, in his tweed knickerbockers, about to start another hour or two of Lampitt talk. His fantasies were different from my own, but they were contrived with equal certainty of success to remove him from the taints of suburbia.

I lay awake most of the night. Partly, we had all gone to bed too early. I listened to the sounds of the house, so very familiar to me from early boyhood, the wind in the elm trees down the lane, soughing and rustling. The wind in the chimney, making a sibilant murmur to itself, reminiscent of that *sotto voce* musical accompaniment supplied at no extra charge by Mr Sykes, the village barber, while he cut one's hair. And there were the sounds of the house itself. Quite of their own accord, floor boards would creak, though no visible step trod upon them. Water pipes gurgled and groaned. Through all the hours of darkness there were very few moments of silence. Lying there in the blackness I didn't like myself much. I was beginning to see how harmless and amiable my family were; yet I still reacted inwardly to them as if they were fiends.

All Granny's talk about my career was upsetting. I was actually despondent about getting anywhere with the writing. The black shadows of night brought only regret for the past, uncertainty about the future. I was totally sleepless, but my waking was unlike the waking condition of daylight when one moves, and is upright. Lying in inky dark, unable to see more than hints of shadow within shade on the ceiling, caused by the flapping of the curtains against faint moonlight outside the windows, I could have been anywhere. But the whole feel of the place was entirely unmistakable. Though I was able to see almost nothing, I would have had no doubts about where I was, even if someone had taken me there blindfold and put me to bed without telling me my whereabouts. It was not only the unmistakable sounds of the house; the whole feel of the place was tangible. I think it was the fact that I lay there seeing nothing, but feeling so much – a curious sensation – which lifted me from the present and carried me with such ease into earlier phases of being. In this very bed I had screamed and cried for Mummy to come and sit with me, night after night before I lost consciousness. I remembered it so clearly that it was almost as if she had returned that night, a silhouetted figure, stroking my forehead and singing 'Golden Slumbers'. These painful recollections passed into a time of darkness, of unknown duration, in which the mind went blank. Then, involuntarily, another phase of life would return, summer nights during adolescence, tormented by sexual frustration, or angry occasions when I had run to be alone in this room during some dreadful row in which things had been said, usually by me, sometimes by my cousin Felicity, which would have been better left unsaid. And then again, these images were supplanted by other periods of darkness, perhaps the most satisfying periods of the mind's life, when one is conscious of being awake but not thinking of anything at all. Then, the mind feels cleansed, emptied.

It was not long, however, before the emptiness filled with another image. Things returned to me that night which I had wholly forgotten. I remembered that at one period, perhaps when I was about fifteen, I was perfectly happy as Uncle Roy's companion. In all my conscious spoken memories of my uncle, there were tensions and difficulties. I found him embarrassing or boring or uncomfortable. Not here. As if somebody were showing me an old film of myself, I was conscious of a phase (I suppose it was only one four-week holiday from boarding school) when I positively rejoiced in Uncle Roy's company. I felt myself (a condition of mind wholly forgotten) exquisitely amused by Lampitt tales. I felt no awkwardness about religion either, so it must have been when I was still quite young. This memory shocked and pained me more than any of the others because until that moment it had passed out of mind; and yet it should have been an important memory to which I had often returned. Relations with Uncle Roy had once been harmonious; the frictions and distances which had since grown up felt in that dark moment as if they had all been of my own cruel making. I felt that I had been offered love by my uncle and spurned it either for no reason, or for reasons which were unworthy.

This chilling thought made me need Anne all the more. I hated being alone in bed. Anne and I were at a stage where it seemed natural not merely to touch and hold each other but to be entwined in each other's arms all the time. In the company of others, we kept our distance from each other; one did not want to be silly in front of Aunt Deirdre. But when we were alone together we flew into each other's arms.

I rose and walked out into the blackness towards my cousin Felicity's room. The creaking noise on the landing when I trod on a loose board must have been loud enough to wake the household; but there were innocent reasons why I might have been pacing the landing in the small hours, and I had no fear. Instinct led me to Felicity's room. I did not even have to fumble for the handle. Then, when I did so, the oddest sensation came over me, lasting no more than a split second, but memorable thereafter. For that tiny fraction of time, I imagined that it was Felicity that I was going to visit, and found the prospect intensely exciting. Felicity and I, who had grown up together, had had our ups and downs. It cannot have been easy for her, an only child, to accept my arrival on the scene, as a permanency, when she was about ten or twelve. Never for a minute in all the time we lived together had I lusted after her or even thought of her in sexual terms. Now was different. The split second passed. I remembered that it was Anne and not Felicity to whom I ardently wished to make love. I turned the handle of the door.

Every movement which Anne and I made during the next half-hour produced such creaking of the headboard, such *boing-boing* of bedsprings, that we might as well have called out to Aunt Deirdre and told her what had happened. Afterwards we drew back the curtains, and the moon, which had climbed higher in the sky and grown brighter, shed enough light for me to be able to see Anne's pale thin shoulders in front of me. I stood with my chin on one of her shoulders, and put my arm around her breasts.

'I think you must tell them,' she whispered.

'I will, tomorrow.'

She giggled quietly.

'It is tomorrow. It was tomorrow ages ago.'

'Anne.'

'What?'

'I thought I was going to be one of those people who was never happy – I thought I'd never know what happiness was. I thought . . .'

341

'There's no need to say it.' She kissed and then stroked my hand which lay across her breast.

'I know,' I said. 'There's no need to say anything.'

In those strange moments of silence we watched the clouds racing across the sky. We stayed there until the last hour of night when there was a hint of sunlight dawning.

'But we must tell them,' she repeated.

I knew that what she said was true, but Speaking Out had never been something we much went in for in our family, and Sunday was not the best of days for it. Uncle Roy and Aunt Deirdre both went to church at eight a.m. and returned to the rectory to cook Granny's breakfast. It never even occurred to me to attend church later in the morning, though afterwards Anne said that we should have. Instead, at the time of the sung service, we stayed in the kitchen and watched Aunt Deirdre prepare the treat luncheon in Anne's honour, boiled fowl. Aunt Deirdre obviously welcomed company, but she did not want us to talk. The wireless was tuned in to the hour-long extended version of 'The Mulberrys', to which she could listen without the irritating presence of her husband or the scornful commentary of her mother-in-law.

It was strange to hear Rikko Kempe's voice, transmogrified into that of Stan Mulberry, talking of the milk yield and the fecundity of sows; not normally Rikko's kind of thing. Odder still was the look on Aunt Deirdre's face, while Rikko was reading his lines. In all practical respects, for all it mattered, she believed completely in 'Stan Mulberry'. During an altercation with a recalcitrant farm labourer, she entirely took 'Stan's' side.

'Oi caarn't shift all them bales on me own, Maaarser Stan.'

'I wasn't asking you to shift them on your own,' said Rikko, who managed to suggest, with his understated Herefordshire burr, a deep dependability and common sense.

' 'Course he wasn't,' said my aunt, crossly holding a potato under the cold tap.

'Only with moi baark, Maaarser Stan . . .'

'Get off with your bother,' said my aunt. 'Your back's as healthy as mine.'

'I'm sorry, Jos, but those bales have got to be shifted,' said Rikko, with none of the agitation which came over his voice during real disputes.

'Good old Stan,' murmured my aunt. 'Don't let Jos get away with it, he's been playing on your better nature for too long.'

And so on, for an hour.

By the time 'The Mulberrys' theme tune had announced the conclusion of that week's visit to Barleybrook, my uncle and his mother were returning from church. It was a new thing, churchgoing, in Granny's life. I never recall her having gone to church in London during the lifetime of Mrs Webb.

'Funny psalm,' she remarked firmly, lighting her Craven A as soon as she had taken her accustomed place in the armchair by the kitchen range. '*I am become like a bottle in the smoke*. Whatever would that mean?'

My uncle, still in his cassock, was untroubled by the enquiry.

'Old Mrs Lampitt, bless her, was full of such difficulties. She was not a churchwoman, as you know.'

'Never darkened the doors of the church,' said Aunt Deirdre.

'Church is not the Lampitt thing. She did *occasionally* come – to harvest Festival, for example. But I can remember her saying – he nearly guffawed – ' "Roy, I'm not like a pelican in the wilderness, why should I say that I am one?" Typical!'

The skin round his eyes creased up as he laughed affectionately.

'You were cross at the time,' said my aunt.

'And you haven't answered my question,' said Granny. ' "I am become like a bottle in the smoke." '

'It means you're browned off,' said my aunt quickly. No doubt she wished to cut short any further reminiscences about the Lampitts, but I also strongly sensed that the Psalter was not to her taste. Its extravagant expressions of despair, elation, moral triumphalism, abject guilt, unspecified depression, spiritual ecstasy were not at all in Aunt Deirdre's mode. By all means get browned off, her tone implied, but why on earth go on about it?

'It wouldn't have been a glass bottle,' added my uncle, at last stirring himself to respond to his mother's exegetical enquiry. 'You've got to think of yourself shrivelling up like an old leather pouch too near the fire.'

Granny laughed so much at this that she nearly choked on her cigarette.

'Thank you, I'm sure.'

Her facial expression reminded me of the day when she and Mrs Webb had taken me and Darnley out from school. Scarcely a dozen years had passed since that day, and yet, here I was with Anne. . . .

As we drove away down the old road out of the village in Darnley's car, Anne said, 'You are a fool. That was the whole point of our visit, to tell them.'

'You could have told them.'

'Julian, they're *your* family.'

'You don't think they sort of guessed?'

'Wouldn't they have said anything?' she asked.

'Not necessarily.'

'Mummy will certainly have something to say when she sort of guesses.'

This alarming prospect was all too believable.

But it was interesting that even Anne, who in most company was naïvely outspoken, had been reduced to diffidence by the Rectory.

'I'll write them a letter,' I said.

'They'll be hurt you didn't tell them in person. Particularly your grandmother.'

'Oh, God, I *know*.'

They were hurt, too. And it hurts to remember. At this distance of time I just can't remember why I found it so difficult to tell them that the day before our visit to the rectory, with Darnley and his sister as the only witnesses, Anne and I had been married at the Chelsea register office.

Five

'Joys impregnate,' as the great man said; 'sorrows bring forth.' The next year was one of impregnation, and is a blur in my memory. I can't even remember the order in which things happened. It was a time of transition in my working life, but I no longer know which event preceded another. None of it matters much, or so it seems to me. Since reading Gilchrist (on Sargie's advice) I have always followed Blake's view that 'the inner world is all-important; that each man has a world within, greater than the external'.

The history of this world within, which I now shared with Anne, is distorted by too great clarity. The outer things, I can hardly recall: the bar work at the Bottle, the novel being accepted by Madge Cruden, amateur theatre work leading to a couple of tiny bits of work. But the story of me and Anne, though now it only returns to me in the occasional vividly recalled episode, was life-changing.

It was a year of blessedness.

Sometimes, when I was working behind the bar at the Bottle, Day Muckley would lean forward and say, 'Don't let it spoil you, lad, don't let it spoil you.' I now see that I must have been glowingly, transparently happy. There was tremendous wisdom in Day's advice.

'What do you know about happiness, toad's pus?' Cyril had genially enquired.

'I don't, I don't . . .' He drank from his beer glass and faltered.

'None of us is fucking happy or we wouldn't be drinking in your shit-hole of a pub,' said Peter, addressing the remark to his favourite landlord but speaking into his gin-and-lime, like a priest speaking over the chalice at Mass.

As far as I was concerned, there were no lessons to be learned from the fact that everyone hanging about the place had made a mess of life, or alternatively, like Cyril or Fenella, had been born into the world as comic turns, 'characters', whom I could enjoy like puppets in a show. I did not see the pathos of being a 'character', of having a life no part of which anyone was prepared to take seriously. All I knew was that my life was to be different. I took its present blessedness completely for granted. I had been, on and off, abjectly miserable ever since Mummy died. Now I was acquainted with joy, and I did know the difference. There was so little excuse for throwing it all away.

Loving Anne transfigured existence, it changed everything. I found that all bodily sensations were quickened by loving her. Memory distorts, but I was so surprised and fascinated by this phenomenon that I jotted down very rough diary notes at the time. My eyesight, for example, became more acute than it was before. I don't mean that I was able to read farther down the optician's test card than in the days before I met Anne. But my appreciation of the way things looked was so profoundly enhanced that I felt in many respects that I had only begun to 'see' since knowing her. Colours were perceptibly brighter. Sometimes when I left her in the morning and cycled into Soho, I would find myself dismounting and staring with wonder at quite 'ordinary' sights, a tree, a bird on a window ledge, sunlight on a building which I had seen a thousand times but suddenly saw for the first time. It is hard to put what I experienced into words which do not sound as though I were experiencing some hallucinatory 'high' of the kind which others have achieved through drugs. I certainly was not conscious of these experiences as metaphysical phenomena. They were deeply natural. I was not seeing a bird or a tree transformed into something else, but I was seeing trees and birds as if for the first time, and seeing 'through' the eye, seeing into the life of things, so that the act of vision became a Vision, and a morning bike-ride an occasion for alleluias.

Unquestionably, all this was bound up with the energy and passion of my love for Anne. I have written that I left her each morning (and sometimes, even if the parting was only for a few hours, it would be almost intolerable); but it would be truer to say that we were never parted. When we were not together physically, we went on being together in an almost literal way. Not only did I carry about a powerful physical sense of her – we smelt of each other – but underlying all my thoughts and actions throughout a day apart from her, she was *there*. She had come to inhabit my mind as well as my body. We often, during our delighted evening reunions, would find that we had been in touch telepathically, thinking the same thoughts during our hours of separation.

That makes it sound solemn. At the time, it was all high spirits, laughter. Never for a moment did we seem 'serious'. Looking back from my present perspective, I now think that this was in fact the first truly serious, non-trivial thing which had ever happened to me. And it is this which makes it so hard for me to acknowledge that I did, in Day Muckley's phrase, 'let it spoil me'.

I think I must have assumed that this was just what it was like the first time you fell in love with someone 'properly'. I'm sure that's what I felt. Maybe I'm being too hard on myself, but I think I behaved as though these wholly unlooked-for sensations of well-being were my due. They were the reward for being young. I was aware that the world was now a different place. My love was quickened, not just for the world of nature, but for animals and people. Language, even William Blake's, is soppy when it tries to describe the unsoppy way in which love sees all creatures as lovable, all creatures and all people.

William Blake certainly played a part in my love story. Not only had Gilchrist's life of the poet been recommended to me by Anne's uncle – and I had carried it frequently in my pocket during our courtship; I actually seemed, with Anne, to be experiencing many of the things which Blake wrote about:

> And we are put on earth a little space,
> That we may learn to bear the beams of love.

It was certainly reading Gilchrist, and Blake himself, which made me aware that one way of describing the universe is not inherently more rational than any other. What enables us to see the truth is the exercise of the Imagination, and not submission to some supposedly dispassionate or 'scientific' version of things. Imagination in this context I take to be the same as love. Uncle Roy's version of the Lampitt story is infinitely richer, and probably truer, than Hunter's.

Hunter, who became a friend of mine at this date, once pointed out that Gilchrist's *Blake* stood in the greatest possible contrast to one of James Petworth Lampitt's mannered little biographies. It was different, too, I could have added (but didn't) from Hunter's own godlike poses in his biographical work, and his apparent belief that, having accumulated a lot of spurious 'material', he had 'understood'. As a work of art, Gilchrist's book is non-existent. It was not even completed by Gilchrist, but cobbled together by friends after he had died. The central figure, Blake himself, is always more important than the author. If James Petworth Lampitt had been writing the book, how sniggeringly anxious he would have been to cut Blake down to size. How easy it would have been to make a guy out of the son of a small shopkeeper who believed himself to be having regular visits from Julius Caesar or the Archangel Gabriel.

Doubtless, too, there was something inherently ludicrous, viewed from a worldly angle, in Blake's inability to make a success of things, to choose worthy patrons or tap the supplies of cash which are always available to artists who know how to compromise themselves. Hunter would certainly have despised that side of Blake's life. He would manage to popularise Mr Pilbright through the medium of television. Blake, however ardently he had desired that the world would take seriously his sublime engravings, poems and paintings, could not really have done himself justice on that essentially two-dimensional medium. Though he was abstemious, his attempt to sell himself on TV would have been as unsuccessful as Day Muckley's. Hunter, if he had taken Blake on as a subject of biography, would have wanted to establish at the outset that Blake couldn't draw (untrue) or that his prophecies were gibberish. Hunter would then have devoted three or four times Gilchrist's 300 pages to a dissection of Blake's psychosexual nature. Was there not something odd about a man who could sit naked with his wife in their arbour, imagining themselves in the Garden of Paradise, but being unable to produce babies? What happened – or, if Hunter were asking the question on television, *just* what happened – between the Blakes in bed?

The fact that no one knows, no one could know, would not prevent Hunter from the dark suggestion that *he* knew. To sell the book, there would be a 'new line' or what publishers sometimes call a 'new angle'. If no new 'material' was forthcoming (and it almost certainly would not be there to be discovered), this would not prevent Hunter hinting at sensational discoveries. Copious extracts from Boswell's *London Journal* or the *Memoirs of Casanova* would provide a readable gloss on Blake's ability to hear 'the harlot's cry from street to street'. Or lengthy disquisitions from some psychologist would persuade Hunter, and his readers, of an indissoluble connection between visionary experiences and precocious exercises in masturbation.

And yet neither of these approaches, neither the neat Petworth Lampitt satire nor the ponderous know-all manner of Hunter, would have allowed Blake, as Gilchrist does, simply to be himself. There he was, in his black hat, simple breeches and stockings, short of stature, bright of eye, presumably cockney-fied of voice. Though he had been dead for a century before my time, when I became addicted to the book, Blake was as real to me as any of the other Soho characters who came to prop up the bar of the Bottle. I would come out into Poland Street and think of his five years' residence there, and of the wonderful things which he had produced while living in mean lodgings with his wife, a mere stone's throw from the spot where Cyril and I now dispensed their medicine to the Best-Seller, Mr Porn, Pete and the rest. 'The now dingy demi-rep street,' Gilchrist informs us, 'one in which Shelley lodged in 1811 after his expulsion from Oxford, had witnessed the production of the *Songs of Innocence* and other poetry and design of a genius unknown before or since to that permanently foggy district.' In addition to his incomparable lyrics, Blake had also produced some of his 'Prophecies' here, and the 'Proverbs of Hell', not irrelevant to my clients as they became hourly more imprisoned in the caricatures of themselves which drink had made.

Day Muckley had asked me where I had been.

'Where's he been?' Cyril answered for me. 'Southend-on-Turd.'

This was true: a fortnight in an execrable comedy during which Anne and I had lived as the guests of a seaside landlady.

'I once took a woman to Southend,' said Peter.

'The thing about the English seaside is this,' said Day Muckley, dewy-eyed with a whisky chaser. 'It is fun, but it is fundamentally innocent, for Christ's sake.'

'This one wasn't innocent. Next time I saw her, I said, "It's just as well I'm not allergic to penicillin." No subtlety, that cow, she didn't understand me. But she must have known what she'd given me.'

Day Muckley was not interested in these consulting-room

details. His monologue had half-congealed into one of those occasional *causeries* which he wrote for the *Yorkshire Post*.

'I still maintain, and never mind "what the butler saw", what I still say is never mind a bit of sauce. If it's still inno – it's still what I say.'

'I've got a customer in Southend,' said Mr Porn. 'A plain brown parcel goes off to him once a month. Anything with a bit of anal torture and he's happy.'

'Really,' said Bloom. 'This pub gets more and more disreputable, with soliciting tarts in the saloon, and probably tarty solicitors in the Loo-loo Bar, one doesn't know where to turn.'

'If forced to a decision, surely you wouldn't find it difficult,' I said. 'Besides, that isn't a tart, soliciting or otherwise. It's Fenella. She's just had her hair done, that's all.'

The road of excess leads to the palace of wisdom.

I rather doubt whether William Blake would have got on with some of my friends in the Black Bottle. But certainly his proverbs were much in my mind during that first year of my marriage. *The lust of the goat is the bounty of God. . . . The nakedness of woman is the work of God. . . . The tygers of wrath are wiser than the horses of instruction. . . . Enough! or too much!*

Anne and I initially lived in two rented rooms a good way down the King's Road, more or less at Parson's Green. We were so far from what my mother-in-law regarded as the 'centre of things' (i.e. Peter Jones in Sloane Square) that we were within perilously close hailing distance of Tempest and Holmes. Once I actually caught sight of Pilbright from the top of a bus going down the Fulham Road.

Anne was incapable of the subterfuge which was second nature to me, with my upbringing in the Rectory, where everything was kept secret, from one another and from the village. As soon as she saw her mother again – it was about a week after our marriage – she told her the truth.

There was the predictable explosion, and the next time we saw her father he said in his tight-lipped manner, 'Nothing wrong with your being married. There are ways and ways, that's all.'

'Unpleasantness' of any kind was to be avoided at all costs as far as Sir Rupert Starling was concerned. Given this fact, there was something paradoxical in his having chosen (if that was what he had done) to marry Sibs. Perhaps marriage had changed them, made her more aggressive, and him more determined to be a high-ranking civil servant, both in and out of office hours. Thus, while wishing to avoid any sort of altercation about Anne's marriage to myself, he saw no harm in pointing out where procedural solecisms had been perpetrated. Two of his children, sons, had followed conventional paths and turned, by Sir Rupert's standards, into satisfyingly dull dogs. Anne, much the youngest child, interested in art, visibly a throwback to her Lampitt forebears, was acknowledged by her father to be something different. Fair enough, his manner implied; just so long as we all knew where we stood. The register office wedding with no guests was in order. One felt that almost any form of nuptial ceremony would have been acceptable – a naked wood dance conducted by witches during the summer solstice – so long as Sir Rupert were not obliged to take part, and so long as he had been duly minuted and kept informed.

All he actually said when he heard that we were married was 'Oh.'

Some months later, Anne and I crept nearer the centre of civilisation as a result of her father increasing her allowance. We could afford three rooms in Lamont Road, several bus stops nearer the Starling family in Cadogan Square.

Sir Rupert was a tall, balding, red-faced man in his mid- to late fifties when Anne and I got married. Although his face was round and shiny, and seemed like the face of a fat man, the rest of his body was elongated and thin. His rather well-made dark suits hung from bony shoulders to bony ankles as though draped from wire coat-hangers rather than worn. He always looked down when he spoke, unwilling to set eyes on his company. When I was in the room, this was understandable enough. He must have hated my guts. In so far as I was aware of this at the time, I put it down to his being lamentably 'conventional' in outlook, rather than because it might be reasonable, given his obvious love for Anne, to be hurt that she had married without telling her parents, and chosen as her man a juvenile layabout with no prospects.

'Not there, darling,' said his wife, watching him put down a very small glass of very dry sherry on the wine table by his plushly upholstered chair. 'And not on the carpet either!'

Sibs in that moment appeared to possess absolute power. She was not remotely interested in where her husband put down his glass, but she could not resist pulling at the puppet string from time to time, simply in order to amuse herself and to remind Sir Rupert, as if he could ever forget, who was in control.

'But this is lovely,' she said to us. 'You're both getting on with things at last.'

Anne had just been told by her supervisor that a chapter of her dissertation about Winterhalter was so original that she should think about publishing it. I, in addition to getting a novel accepted (and I didn't tell Sibs that it was through Hunter's influence), had various small acting roles half promised me. Moreover Hunter by some process had become our marital friend, though we never said anything about it to Sibs. All the strands of life seemed to be reaching a satisfying resolution. Sibs, a cigarette in one hand and an ice-cold dry martini in the other, stood by the fireplace pulling the invisible strings which made the whole puppet theatre spring to life. Her full but not fat legs supported her magnificent body with complete confidence. Her superb figure filled the dark blue cocktail dress. Her red lips stained the Du Maurier which she inhaled. Her eyes glistened with the excitement of so much activity. Although there was grey in her straight, well-washed hair she still seemed like a young person; certainly she seemed much younger than Sir Rupert, though they must in fact have been about the same age.

'If I can organise *you*, Julian, to pick up these boxes from Little Rat Hunter . . .'

'Don't be silly, Mummy.'

'Anne, I can call Little Rat what I like. (Oh, dar-*ling* – don't put your glass on the floor . . . no, and not on the hearth either!) That really would be magnificent, because we can get the whole lot to the solicitor's office. I'm just so glad that I've made Sargie see sense at last.'

'But Sargie isn't going to refuse Mr Hunter the chance of quoting from the papers in his next volume.'

'There won't *be* another volume!' she said triumphantly. 'Everything's working out satisfactorily. I've got you your flat.'

(She had, it is true, recommended the name of an estate agent.)

'Yes, Mummy.'

'There's your being a success at last, Julian, and there's your thesis. (Darling, don't balance the glass on your knee, there's a pet. It'll stain his trousers.) Yes, there's your thesis, Anne, and now at last Sargie seeing sense about Jimbo's stuff.'

Everything – my ability to write, Anne's knowledge of nineteenth-century art, Sargie's mood swings – was of course directly attributable to Lady Starling's force of character. One of her sons, Gavin, had reason to make fairly frequent business visits to the United States and it was he who had found out about the Everett Foundation, a curious institution in Manhattan. The chairman of a small oil company, one Virgil D. Everett Jnr, had decided to invest in a collection of literary manuscripts and rare early printed editions. He specialised in the late nineteenth and early twentieth centuries. Already, he had built up a consider-able collection of Wilde letters (including one of the lost typescripts of *De Profundis* with marginalia in an unknown hand); he had a good Lionel Johnson archive, a certain amount of Yeats material, some Arthur Machen.

Gavin Starling had made the right enquiries and it transpired that Virgil D. Everett Jnr was very interested in the diaries and literary manuscripts of James Petworth Lampitt. By the terms of Jimbo's will, all these papers belonged to Sargie, who could be relied upon to welcome the rather generous terms being mentioned by the Everett Foundation, while changing his mind at least twenty times about the advisability of the deal. Hunter had no claims on the papers and would have to surrender them. It was only because of Sargie's casualness that Jimbo's biogra-pher should have been sitting on the papers for so long. Since Hunter was now our friend, Anne's and mine, the scheme to sell the papers would involve, on our part, an inescapable clash of loyalties. On the one hand, family was family. On the other, one questioned the wisdom of allowing Sibs absolute power in this or any area, not because she would necessarily behave with incaution or foolishness, but because of some natural instinct which makes us resist tyrants and their need to assert absolute control.

This scheme, to spirit the papers from Hunter's reach and into the hands of a private collector on the other side of the Atlantic, had been vaguely discussed for months now. Anne had even hinted to Hunter himself that something of the sort was in the offing. He had merely shrugged. No one would suppose from his smile that the Lampitt family were about to deprive him of his life's work; there seemed at the time something noble and magnanimous in the slight curl of his lip. I came to feel that sexual jealousy must be the most distorting of all lenses through which to view our fellow creatures. When I first saw Hunter, he was embracing the art teacher, Miss Beach, with whom I happened to be in love. It meant that the next time I saw him, in Treadmill's dining room at my later school, I was prepared to invest with sinister meaning the smiling geniality of Hunter's face. But surely the truth was that he was quite a pleasant fellow? And was he not taking this business of the Lampitt Papers, in so far as he yet knew anything, extraordinarily well?

There remained the possibility, which I now began to consider, that Hunter had in fact lost interest in the Lampitt Papers. He had other fish to fry: television, journalism, his wide range of important committees. Certainly, however, if he wished to continue his researches into the life of James Petworth Lampitt it sounded from what Sibs was saying as though access to the papers would be extremely difficult. Virgil D. Everett Jnr was known to be stingy in his attitude to scholars; he did not allow material from his collection to be published on the sane commercial grounds that unpublished manuscripts were more valuable than those whose contents had seen print. There would be no chance for any mere literary sleuth to rifle through Jimbo's diaries once they had been encased in the well-padded air-conditioned strong-room in East Sixty-third Street.

'Mr Everett is coming over in a few months and you must come to dinner to meet him,' Sibs declared.

'So long as I'm not away, acting somewhere. There is a small chance that I might get a fortnight at the King's Lynn rep later this summer.'

'Well, you must cancel it if you do. (Oh, darling, not on my *Times* – you'll put stains all over the Births, Deaths and Marriages.)'

'No,' said Sir Rupert.

Was the worm about to turn? Was he going to tell his wife that he would put his sherry glass where he damn well liked? Was it anger or dry sherry which brought the crimson to his weird spherical face?

'It seems' – he twiddled the glass in his hand awkwardly – 'a very sensible provision, particularly since we gather that Mr Everett is averse to the – er – publication of any papers in his possession.'

'Oh, there could never be a published version of Jimbo's diaries now!' Sibs was exultant. 'We'll just have to make sure that Sargie isn't an ass again.'

The silent movement of Sir Rupert's shoulders and the faint suggestion of a smile which played about his lips indicated the equivalent in other human beings of a guffaw. Meanwhile, he stared at his sherry glass as others would have looked at an insoluble crossword puzzle. Clearly, he could not put it down, but nor, as his wife was now saying, was he meant to 'fiddle about with it, there's a pet'.

Perhaps the answer would be to put it in his pocket handkerchief, hammer it into small pieces, using the poker in the hearth . . . But then, what? Put the handkerchief in his pocket? Stir the powdered glass into his wife's next martini?

'We mustn't stay,' said Anne firmly. 'We've promised some friends we'd meet them before the play.'

We were going to see Hubert Power's *Uncle Vanya*.

'I've heard it's superb,' said Sibs. She spoke in tones which implied she had somehow been responsible for the play's success.

'Never got on with Chekhov,' said Sir Rupert.

'Yes, but darling, you remember Hubert Power in *The Doctor's Dilemma* last year.'

'I never remember actors' names,' said her husband.

'If you are thinking of putting more sherry in that glass, don't. I don't want you upsetting your liver, and if you aren't going to fill it up again, do put it down, there's a pet.'

She turned on me a sly grin, delighted to display to a young man how easy it was to tie a member of my sex up in knots.

Her husband was asking, 'But isn't that by Shaw?' as she ushered us out.

Anne and I held hands on the Number 19 which took us from Sloane Street to Shaftesbury Avenue and on the way I talked about myself, how I couldn't make up my mind whether to be a great actor or a great writer; and I talked, too, about Jimbo Lampitt, and Hunter's biography of the man, and my increasing fondness for Hunter and how kind he was being, at that juncture, to both of us. Anne was silent, but I did not register her silence and sometimes she squeezed my hand, not as a lover would do, but as a mother might squeeze her child's hand in a dentist's waiting room.

It was only a short walk from the bus stop in Shaftesbury Avenue to the Bottle, and arriving there a little after seven, we pushed open the frosted glass door (emblazoned SALOON – LADIES ONLY) to see the familiar scene of greys and browns, overlaid at the top of the canvas by a smudgy haze of silver tobacco smoke and greasy yellow ceiling. Fenella and Rikko were standing at the bar talking with the Best-Seller; or, as I framed it in my mind, they had 'got waylaid' by him. For once, there seemed ample justice in Rikko's anxious consultations of his wristwatch, for breaking away from Muckley in mid-sentence was not always an easy thing to do and the curtain of the nearby theatre went up in half an hour.

Rikko was wearing a blazer, white trousers and what could have been a cricketing tie. It was not possible to guess why he (or more probably, why Fenella) had deemed this a suitable outfit for an evening at the theatre. It contrasted oddly with the gold lamé of Fenella's tight stocking-dress, a garment which unflatteringly revealed how extremely thin she was.

I felt that Fenella's fixed grin on this occasion was meant to display an aristocratic disdain for any bourgeois witness to the scene crass enough to suppose that she objected to Muckley's strong accent and evidently proletarian origins. The smile did equally well, however, to gloss over a probable ignorance of the literary matters under discussion.

'There's a limpidity in Chekhov,' said the Best-Seller. 'It's all so sodding clear. You read something like the seduction scene in *The Lady with the Dog*, or the opening scene of *Uncle Vanya*, come to that, and you think, by Christ, life is this – it isn't like this, it *is* this.'

He prodded some imagined opponent of the viewpoint with an ignited Sweet Afton.

'And at the same time,' said Rikko, 'as well as being so specific, I dunno. One gets this sense of a whole *society* behind the bleak lives he depicts. English writers can't write about societies. They can only write about families. Whereas almost every individual in Chekhov or Dostoyevsky seems able to suggest a world behind them. I dunno.'

Day Muckley, one of the chief pre-war exponents of the English family 'saga', looked at Rikko with considered belligerence. No doubt he was aware of his failure to match the Russian giants. At the same time, you got the feeling from looking at him

356

that this would not necessarily restrain him from punching Rikko's face, if, as appeared to have happened, need arose.

'Don't give me all that sodding rubbish about *The Cherry Orchard*,' he said. This must have related to another conversation, held with someone else perhaps, years earlier, about another of Chekhov's masterpieces. It was vain to speculate what the rubbish was, but Rikko obediently kept silent about it.

He hastily offered us all drinks. Mine was a gin-and-tonic, Anne's a grapefruit juice. Fenella relaxed her grin and said, 'We want to see Hubie tonight anyway – he's very special to us.'

Muckley emptied his straight glass of beer and mused on this desire.

'No,' he said, 'I wouldn't want to see Hubie Power or any other bum-boy pretending to be Vanya, for Christ's sakes.'

'Doesn't that rather rule out any theatrical experience?' I asked. 'Isn't that what going to see plays *is* – watching bum-boys pretending to be someone else?'

'Cheers,' said Muckley, taking most of his double whisky in one gulp.

'As a matter of fact, and I'm not sure why I'm telling you – it must be the drink talking.' Fenella's coy smile heralded a true whopper. 'My grandmother was practically a lady-in-waiting to the last Tsarina.'

Rikko still had his back to us, since he was collecting his change from Cyril, but with one free hand he was able to pinch his forehead, and as he turned, I think he was muttering, '*Shut up, Fenella, just shut up, will you.*' But the Best-Seller responded to the discourse. She might have hoped that he would be impressed that she was only a step away from the court life of old St Petersburg, but Muckley's face showed no more excitement than if she had said that her grandmother once visited Morecambe Bay in the holiday season.

'I have no sympathy whatsoever, with the . . . no sympathy with the Tsar.'

And that was the end of his chaser.

'And how's life down on the farm, then?' Cyril was proud to have a star of 'The Mulberrys' propping up his bar.

I had begun to notice a certain smile creep over Rikko's face when people spoke of his radio work. It was the look of a man who was trapped. Rikko was doing the part really well, so well, in fact, that some radio critics were beginning to write about the programme in the same column as serious radio drama. But Rikko knew that he had opted for something safe, he had ceased to stretch up to the inaccessible, and, in so doing, he had killed something in himself. There was more pathos in his 'success' as Stan Mulberry than there had ever been in his failure to get the big roles. While he was being a waiter or advertising indigestion tablets, Rikko's Hamlet, or Rikko's Vanya were still imaginable dreams. Stan Mulberry was somehow stronger than they. One knew that Rikko would never quite take himself seriously again.

'You should keep that drunken brother of yours in order,' said Cyril. In spite of his totally cynical attitude to life, he clearly shared Aunt Deirdre's willingness to make an exception in the case of 'The Mulberrys'.

'They were so cruel,' said Day Muckley, 'and so fucking stupid, that they deserved it. They had it coming to them.'

While Cyril topped up his Teacher's and gave him another pint of Courage, Day Muckley spoke of the imbecile credulity of anyone who could trust Rasputin.

All kinds of conversational hazards loomed up. Peter and Mr Porn had put down their racing papers and looked ready for a major set-to on the old religious question. On a more mundane level, I knew we should be late for the play if we waited for the Best-Seller, in his present state of sobriety, to make up his mind how to pronounce the word 'haemophiliac'. We stepped out into the summer evening. The plane trees near St Anne's Church were in leaf, I saw when we came into Dean Street. Anne was on my arm, and such a variety of impressions assailed me that I did not notice, still less interpret, her silence. I took her love for granted, just as, in that moment of quiet but intense happiness, I took everything for granted. I can remember an insane conceited grin which involuntarily stole over my features in those days. No doubt it came over my face as we all walked down Dean Street, as though I were the master of ceremonies and had organised all the things which at that moment gave me pleasure: my friends being so much themselves, whether in Cadogan Square or the Bottle; the anticipation of the play (I would never have admitted it during the conversation in the bar, but I had not read or seen any Chekhov and my smiles and nods concealed an ignorance deeper than Fenella's); even the physical conditions of the evening filled me with a conceited glee. I had more than a little of Sibs's egoism, the ability to behave, when things went well, as though I was partly responsible. I would not have thought it unreasonable if Anne had at that moment thanked me for the sunlight on the great branches which once again had come to life by the side of the little bombed church; for the Hogarthian ribaldry which the law still in those days permitted to the girls of Soho who called out to us from doorways and windows as we walked along, and who themselves cruised the pavements or hovered by lamp-posts in exaggerated poses; the crowds who outnumbered and largely ignored them, intent in some more generalised way on 'an evening out'; the charabancs in Shaftesbury Avenue debouching the parties of old people and schoolchildren who had been driven up to town for an evening at the theatre. The whole happy world of London preparing for an evening of pleasure was so much part of my mood that I could almost have believed that I had created it.

We were only just in our seats by the time the curtain went up, and at first I did not settle. The evening outside was too bright and warm to be conducive to an evening enclosed in the dark fantasy-box of theatre. But, as everyone knows who saw or read about that production, it was one of the very great examples in theatre which do not merely redefine a work of art, but which stretch and enhance the human experience itself. No one who saw it will ever believe again in any other actor's Vanya. They will merely judge new performances by the extent to which the actor in question falls short of Hubert Power's interpretation. Likewise, any actress one sees attempting Sonya will merely remind one of Isabella Marno's definitive interpre-tation. I was electrified by the play. It was an evening which, as will become clear, began to change my life in more senses than one; but in spite of all its personal emotional dramas, it taught me for the first time what theatre *was*, what was the point of it all. Hitherto, either in my own feeble efforts to act or in the more or less competent theatre which I had witnessed, one never ceased to be aware of the fact that people were acting. The more I came to be interested in the theatre, the more expertly I felt myself able to judge the quality of delivery, stagecraft, timing; but I had more or less lost sight of the notion that theatre has a much greater power than a mere technical ability to pretend. If the alchemy is effective . . . Even to finish the sentence is to utter a commonplace, that the stage becomes a new world, the actors different people. But it is supremely rare for it to happen and that evening at *Uncle Vanya* was the first time it had happened in my presence.

As often happens to me in the presence of truly great art, my reaction was at the immediate level completely trivial. Without willing it, I allowed my own preoccupations to be interwoven with the realities of the play. Though the whole situation of the play was entirely different from anything which I had known, I allowed the dreary Russian farmhouse to become the Rectory at Timplingham. The professor Serebrakov, most unfairly, was identified at this level of half-consciousness with Uncle Roy, and I, ever the hero of my own tale, was Vanya who shot him. All impure responses to art bring our own lives into the play, poem, picture under contemplation, and this is not because we are only half attending to it; rather because we are focusing our entire attention upon it, and are therefore unable to divest ourselves of our lives and feed solely on art with ear or eye or mind. By the end of the play, however, these crude levels of half-identification had fallen away, and the existence of those miserable people, miles from anywhere in a vanished Russian world, was more real to any of us than our own lives, and in the simplicity of Sonya there was something indescribably ennobling and touching. The last scene certainly had me in tears. In the actress playing Sonya, there was such transparent moral simplicity. She was so obviously an innocent, so completely a sexual and emotional virgin, so strong in her faith that 'we shall rest'. Her face, Isabella Marno's, was almost too real to have been put on the stage. There was nothing pretty, nothing actressy, about it. And the simplicity with which she played the role of Sonya brought out the rugged manliness and the bitterness and brokenness of Vanya himself. Vanya, one felt, had he ever come to London, would have found a welcome at the Black Bottle.

I see why those (my cousin Felicity among them) who dislike the theatre do so with such intensity. The combined genius of Chekhov and Hubert Power, with Isabella Marno's superb Sonya, had persuaded a packed theatre full of people that what we were watching was more real than our own lives. For a moment, those actors had held absolute sway over a thousand people. One could say that was all for the good, but Felicity the Platonist would probably have wanted to say that it could not be truly good because it was of its essence false. The tumultuous applause, the thousand hearts beating as one, the emergence from one's seat feeling that a truly important emotional landmark had been passed, all this could have been evil, not good. Crowd emotion, mass emotion, must always be suspect. It was for this that Shakespeare had given his life, out of this he had made his fortune, aware of the folly, and perhaps of the moral dubiety of making himself a motley to the view, conscious that a purer life would be possible only when the revels were ended and Prospero's staff thrown away.

These thoughts, if present in my mind at all that evening, were embryonic, the conscious emotion being a vast negative epiphany, a discovery that the theatre was not really for me. It took me a long time to act on this piece of negative information, but 'information' is what it felt like, an absolutely certain diagnosis of my life and position. Without any humility, I knew I could never be an actor of Hubert Power's stature. The qualities which enable a good, even a great actor, to strip self of self and put on another being were ones with which I had been fascinated as a schoolboy actor and Treadmill my master had filled me with a literary interest in the drama as a literary form. But there was no longer quite room in my life for this psychological game. I more and more wanted to live in the world of the Imagination, less and less in the world of Let's Pretend.

Fenella's Let's Pretend was completely out of control that night. Over drinks in the interval, she had insisted on the importance of congratulating the performers in their dressing rooms after the show.

'It does so much for their morale,' she honked. 'We simply must go back and tell Hubie how much we enjoyed it. He'd never forgive us if he knew we'd been to the play and not come back.'

It is true that such a convention exists, though I suspect that Hubert Power could have lived with the knowledge that we had been in the house without calling on him. To judge from the tumultuous applause which followed the final curtain, lasting for at least a quarter of an hour, it was unlikely on that particular occasion that he positively needed Fenella's assurance that his performance had been satisfactory. However, I was quite anxious to meet him, and I believed he had been at the RADA with Rikko. The Kempes' claim to acquaintance with him was surely much less fantastical than Fenella's assertion of intimacy with the royal families of Europe. I noticed that Rikko could tolerate mention of Hubert Power without pinching his forehead.

While the audience were dispersing, we fought our way through the back of the house. Theatres (even modern, well-appointed ones, which the old Duchess of Kent's certainly wasn't) are almost rudely scruffy and uncomfortable once you step behind the façade of plush stalls and well-lit stage. Narrow corridors, peeling gloss paint, bare light bulbs, fire-buckets full of sand, induce an immediate sense of letdown. The place seems to crow over someone who has been credulous enough to believe in, or even to have enjoyed, the spectacle. It hurls your enjoyment and belief back in your face. It is like the postcoital sensations a man might feel when he had half persuaded himself, in the previous quarter of an hour, that a prostitute really loved him. The immediacy with which she breaks away from him when the deed is performed, the harshness of her smile, remind him that he has been tricked by a fantastic illusion. The knowledge that the illusion was all inside your head, purely self-inflicted, that the theatre never pretended to be other than a theatre, or the street-walker anything other than a sensation for sale, only adds to the sense of disillusion and feeling of self-reproach.

We were not alone backstage in these corridors, Rikko, Fenella, Anne, I. Actors, theatre staff and visitors jostled about us.

'I don't want to be here,' said Anne, rather desperately.

'We shan't stay long.'

I tried to squeeze her hand, but she did not want to be touched. I merely thought she must be moved, as I was by the extraordinary last speech of Sonya. It was a moment for silence, aloneness, not for Fenella's charging forward saying, 'I'm sure it must be down here!' in her deepest Camel-throated bass.

'Looking for the Gents?' asked a bright young spark, presumably a stage-hand.

'Hubie's dressing room actually,' said Fenella. 'We're very close friends.'

When we'd moved off in the direction indicated by this boy, I heard him saying to someone else, 'Wonder where Hube picked up that old faggot, real drag queen.'

By now I had grown so used to Fenella's voice and appearance that I had forgotten how on my own first meeting with her (in spite of thorough preparation by Bloom) I had found it hard to believe she was truly of the female sex. Now, hearing the boys laugh at her, I felt protective towards her and sorry for Rikko, who had tried not to notice their talk.

'Now, Fenella, promise not to gush over Hubie,' said Rikko.

'Hubie knows me too well for that,' she said.

There were already a number of people in Hubert Power's dressing room when we burst in. I'm not sure who they were. It certainly did not feel as though there was room for four more.

Anne repeated her anguished, 'Oh, do let's *go*,' as soon as Fenella strode ahead.

Fenella actually spoke the line 'Darling, you were marvellous.' She put such peculiar emphasis on the words, however (like Edith Evans wanting to make the handbag line her own in *The Importance of Being Earnest*), that she managed to deprive the cliché of any meaning, stressing the word *were*. The oddness of the stress emanated from her croaking larynx with great gusts of Camel smoke, as from the nose of some Wagnerian dragon. Hubert Power, rubbing his face with cotton wool and vanishing cream, looked up at the reflection in the glass. The only visitors whom he could see were Fenella and myself. His face became tautened by fear.

'I don't think . . . ,' he said.

Like the stage-hand whom we had just met in the corridor, Hubert Power must have supposed Fenella to be a man, perhaps myself her sexual companion, or merely her fellow-blackmailer who had cruelly selected an evening of particular triumph in the theatre to enact the vengeance of nemesis.

'Oh, darling!' Fenella repeated. 'It's only *us*.'

His first moment of shock over, Power was able to compose his features. He said, a little primly, 'I'm afraid that you have the advantage of me.'

Unabashed, Fenella continued, 'I told them you wouldn't *forgive* us if we didn't drop in to say how absolutely brilliant you were, darling.'

Conversation which had been in progress while we burst into the room had now stopped. The three or four other people there stared and faltered, and for a few terrible seconds one could see them wondering whether Fenella was actually a criminal or merely one of those poor deranged characters who are found wandering at large in any city, their minds possessed by some sort of nonsense or another, in this case the belief that she and Hubert Power were the best of friends. The moment was saved by Rikko, who had been hanging back in the corridor and who now pressed past Fenella.

'Hubie, we should never have come, we'll just shake hands and bugger off.'

'Rickie, darling!'

Recognition between the two men was instantaneous. Greasy with remover, and with one hand still clutching a dirty piece of cotton wool, Power arose from his stool and enfolded Rikko in his arms.

'You've met Fenella – my wife,' said Rikko.

'Dear boy, of *course* it is.' Whatever he quite thought Rikko to have said, he had slightly misheard or chosen by this tiny piece of non sequitur to distance himself from the fact of Fenella's existence.

'And this is Anne and Julian,' said Rikko.

'Not your babies? Not already?' Power's lips pursed. 'Hers, then?'

'No, no, just friends,' said Rikko.

'Well, do come in, and spread yourselves, dears, spread yourselves.' He had resumed his seat and his rubbing with the cotton wool. 'There's some bubbly. And darling Rikkie, I want all your news.'

This was obviously not true – the part about wanting the news – because before Rikko could say Mulberry, a very rapid staccato post-mortem of the evening's performance poured from the actor's lips. The magic, felt at the front of the house, was now being analysed trick by breathless trick. He examined each scene in technical terms from the point of view of how some other member of the cast had succeeded or failed in helping him to achieve some of the evening's more stunning effects.

'Billy' – that was William Landaw, playing Astrov – 'comes in too fast, damn him, in the first act. It must be me saying, "See him! Stalking across the earth like a demigod!" And then, *pause*, *pause* while Astrov thinks. But Willie never thinks, hasn't got a thought in his prick of a head, just bursts in with "I believe you envy him!'' and ruins my effect. I still hate the way Hayho' – Henry Mackenzie, the director – 'is making us play that final bit of the first act, too. The placing on the stage is all wrong. I'm a mile backstage. "How can I look at you otherwise when I love you?" – I have to bellow the fucking lines. And God knows Jan' – Janice Brunner, playing Helena – 'is beautiful but the audience don't need to have her absolutely front stage, I mean, my dears, practically in the footlights while I'm languishing by the bloody french window.'

It was strange that only two hours before, these words, when Vanya admitted his love for Helena, had struck me as deeply moving, more real than emotions which I had experienced myself. Now they had no more reality than puppets whose strings had been laid aside after a performance.

I found myself standing by Power at this moment, Anne having hung back by the door, shyly accepting a glass from someone else present. Rikko and Fenella likewise hung back so that I bore the full glare of Hubert Power's penetrating eyes. As he spoke of stagecraft (his face was clean now, and he had spun round on his stool to face the company) his hands fluttered like butterflies and his glance darted from me to Rikko and then back again.

His eyes strayed quite shamelessly up and down my person, as if the clothes I was wearing, possibly the limbs which inhabited them, were for sale. Feeling that it was probably the only chance I should ever get to be in the presence of one who was obviously destined for a great career on the stage, I lost my self-consciousness and felt that only simplicity could match the hour. Power's sheer disappointingness of personality when met without the greasepaint didn't really diminish the achievement of his Uncle Vanya, in fact the reverse. When one saw what a very unprepossessing figure he cut, small and (Uncle Roy would have perhaps wished to add) very much not the gentleman, the alchemy by which he transformed himself into the despondent, maddening but wholly sympathetic figure of Chekhov's Vanya was all the more remarkable. Sycophantic as it sounds when written down, I simply blurted out the truth, that I had never heard or read the play before but that tonight had been easily the most moving and interesting evening which I had ever spent in the theatre, and that this had much to do with his own performance, and – of course – with Sonya's final speech.

He seemed quite genuinely touched by my essentially juvenile sincerity. He stroked my wrist and murmured, 'Dear . . . *dear!*' as I spoke, and his eyes continued to dart up and down my body and occasionally across to Rikko.

When, as it clearly seemed to him, I had diluted my praise of his Vanya with kind words about Isabella Marno's performance, his happy smile momentarily vanished (it was only the matter of a split second) and was replaced by a much firmer, totally artificial one, a chimpanzee's grin.

'You're *so* right, you're *so* right. Bella was fucking marvellous. But then it's a marvellous speech, a fucking gift to an actress, my dear. Where *is* Bella, by the way? Let's' – his hand tightened on my wrist – 'go and find her.'

I attributed Anne's grumpy expression to an uncharacteristic resentment at the fact that I was momentarily the centre of attention. I must say that it crossed my mind that Hubert Power was only asking me into the corridor to attempt some sort of grope, but the idea that this posed a serious threat to my wife was ludicrous. What had happened to her sense of humour? She held up her own wrist and made signals that it was time to leave.

'We're just going to see if we can find Isabella Marno,' I said. 'Oh, come on, Anne, don't look like that. Surely you'd like to meet her?'

Anne's face was not merely angry, it was positively murderous. I knew that I had said or done something to annoy her but I could not imagine what it was. There was little enough time to consider the question since Power was bustling me out into the corridor.

'My dear,' he hissed *sotto voce* as soon as we had closed the door, 'is that really Rikko's wife?'

I said it was, if he meant Fenella.

'But it's grotesque. What's it supposed to be, my dear? It's seventy-five if it's a day. I'd always heard that Rikko had made a mistake, and we've seen each other now and again over the years, but really! This is a very great shock. It's too much.'

I felt a great wave of loyalty to Fenella as these quite unnecessarily merciless words were spoken. Her quite simple kindliness and goodness of heart to dozens of lodgers over the years, and above all her kindness to me, cancelled out, as far as I was concerned, any absurdity of which she might be accused.

'She's a friend of mine,' I said.

'Of course, my dear, of course, but . . .' His voice trailed away. 'Now where is *fucking* Bella?'

I regretted provoking this petulance, and the repetition of this disagreeable epithet. I could have no idea how accurate it was until he kicked open Isabella Marno's dressing-room door, without knocking, to reveal the actress on her dressing table, sitting in a petticoat, her legs wide apart, with a visitor standing between them with his back to us.

'Not now!' she said over his shoulder, I think to us rather than to him. Then, seeing Hubert, she said, 'What is it, Hubie, darling?'

It was an intimate moment, though as it happened not quite so intimate as at first appeared. The visitor at least was fully clothed. Indeed, the light grey suit which he wore was entirely familiar to me. Even before he turned I realised that it was Hunter who held Isabella Marno in his arms, the scene oddly recalling the important moment in my boyhood when I had seen him kissing Miss Beach. His expression on this occasion was noticeable for its complete lack of embarrassment and I took this to be the way that sophisticated people are supposed to behave when caught in positions which would make lesser figures blush. There was more to it than that, but I could not see what this *more* was. He was positively pleased that we had found him there, that was evident.

'Lordings!' exclaimed Hubert Power. 'You were both invited to drinks with me. Now, come on! Do your duty!'

'Hallo, Julian,' said Hunter.

'Ah, so you know each other.'

'Bad luck, Hubie,' said Isabella with, as I thought, real malevolence.

Hunter introduced me to the actress. I could not repeat to her the speech I had made to Hubert Power about the production; my version of 'Darling, you were marvellous' therefore sounded a bit flat. She looked cross to be interrupted and in no mood to join the party in Power's dressing room, but he was insistent, and as he led them off down the corridor he began to explain in a deafening stage whisper that I had been brought along by his sweet friend Rickie, who, poor boy, had married his landlady long ago.

'No one thought it would last five minutes, but my dears, he has been landed – well, you'll see, you'll see, my dears!'

Fenella's croaky enthusiastic greeting when we returned to Power's dressing room implied that it was her own place.

'And to think!' I heard her exclaiming, 'these people' – she gestured to Rikko, myself, Anne – 'were against coming backstage at all.'

It was clear that she was preparing to have a whale of a time.

Hunter came forward and kissed Anne on the cheek. She gave him a funny look as she did so and then peered at Isabella Marno with an expression which I could not characterise; it seemed, unaccountably, like terror.

'Julian, you said we could *go*,' she said.

'We won't stay long.'

'Julian, *please*.'

'It's not like you to be a party pooper.'

In making this remark, perhaps a trifle irritably, I intended absolutely no rebuke. I didn't think of it as a serious comment. Probably my attitude to the whole scene was like Fenella's. I was looking forward to extracting every ounce of amusement and entertainment from it. At the same time in an egotistical way I was quite glad to find Hunter there because there were a number of small details concerning the publishers he had helped to find for me, about which I would have welcomed his advice. That he had been kissing an actress was quite unsurprising, given his 'reputation', and it was no more than a source of mild amusement to me that traces of her red lipstick were now discernible on Hunter's own smooth, thin upper lip, giving his mouth an aspect of full-bloodedness and generosity which it was sometimes without.

I stood between Hunter and Isabella Marno. I felt absolute well-being. If you had said that I had left behind Tempest and Holmes solely in order to make such moments possible, it would not have been far from the truth. It gave quite disproportionate pleasure to contemplate Isabella Marno's fame as an actress, Hunter's as a man of letters. Whatever the snobbish implication of the word, I could not have been better described than as a parvenu. For I had arrived somewhere, in a place which I had ardently sought, without knowing its name or its whereabouts. In fact, I was merely standing in a small, overcrowded room talking to a lot of people whom I did not know, and most of whom I would never see again. The prattle was meaningless. Yet I felt an intense glow of happiness akin to the pleasure of love. I did not exactly feel that the pilgrimage was over, but I had reached the gates of the holy city and stood on the threshold of its shrines. It was therefore all the more astounding to me when Anne moved to the door and said quietly, 'I'm off.'

Hunter tried to exchange a sentence with her, but she pushed past him. The speed with which she did so made me, at first, misinterpret her action. It only made sense to leave a room in such a way if you needed a lavatory. Then I saw that she had her coat and bag with her and she was evidently intending to leave the room without saying goodbye to anyone. I felt embarrassment on her behalf and an equally engrossing rage. As soon as I twigged what she was doing, I followed her down the corridor. She was almost running.

'No need to follow me,' she said without turning round. 'Stay with them, if you'd rather.'

Her words were angry and bitter in tone. One understood at once that staying would be about the least sensitive thing one had ever done. But why?

Once out in the street, she lolloped along at a pace where I could barely keep up with her, making herself the cross mother and me the child who had done something naughty, screamed or been sick in a shop. Her long Lampitt features which I had found so instantly irresistible when first met – and those large staring eyes – seemed for the first time lofty, mad and unreasonable. And her insufferable behaviour did not so much *remind* me of Sargie's absurd 'leading Roy a dance' in my boyhood. It actually became the same infuriating farce. For me to kow-tow and to put up with it was to place myself in the same toadyish position which Uncle Roy had, all those years, accepted vis-à-vis Sargie. This was just what Sargie would have done if he had not been enjoying a party – walk out, and give off powerful indications that his own unhappy whim was somehow everyone else's fault.

She stalked down Shaftesbury Avenue and crossed roads when she reached Piccadilly Circus without looking to left or right. It was pure luck that she was not mown down by traffic. At the bus stop in Piccadilly she had to pause and I had time to catch up with her, but I only saw her tail of dark hair, since she stared away from me in the direction of Burlington House. I tried to offer her one final excuse.

'If you're ill,' I said.

She made a tutting, clicking noise with her tongue as though this imputation were simply moronic.

A Number 19 came. There were plenty of empty seats for two, but she sat down next to a woman in a headscarf, making it impossible for me to sit beside her. So I sat looking at the back of her neck, wanting very badly to take hold of it and strangle her. It was partly pity which inspired this desire. Pity and hatred are terribly close in my emotional barometer. I could not bear her misery, it made me angry. Also, I felt that my love for her which had begun as something so fresh and new was now doomed, for ever, to be a mere reiteration of the Lampitt tragi-farce. By implication, my own life itself, which I had pathetically imagined to be full of new and interesting freedoms, was programmed, it seemed, to follow genetically ordained patterns. I was Roy without the knickerbockers. She was Sargie without the moustache.

She managed to get off the bus before I did, and we walked home separately; but she was still waiting on the doorstep of the house in Lamont Road when I arrived. I had half expected her to go inside, climb the stairs to our flat and slam the door in my face.

'Julian, I'd really rather be alone.' I was silent. She added, 'Without you hovering there.'

'I live here. Perhaps you'd forgotten.'

'Oh, *shit!*'

It was clear – again, it could be Sargie himself! – that she had lost her latchkey, come out without it. She was hopeless with keys and left spares with her mother, with Mrs Wiley who did for us twice a week, and with Darnley's sister Elizabeth.

'Let us in.' I sadistically enjoyed the moment. I intended to make her confess that she had forgotten the key. I had no intention of reaching into my own pocket and opening the door for her.

'I've lost my bloody key.'

I had half a mind to open the door, walk through it myself and slam it in her face. Instead, I relented, and said, 'Just as well I brought mine.'

My hand felt in my jacket pocket where it should have been. Then with self-disgust I remembered changing into a suit just before we left the flat for drinks with her parents. What had I done with the jacket in whose pocket I normally kept the keys?

Thrown it over a chair? Had I taken out the pocket book? Yes, I checked and felt it there just over my heart. But – in the right-hand pocket, where I normally kept keys . . . nothing.

'Get on with it, it's cold.' She hugged herself and still refused me even the turning of her head in my direction. Certainly she was not going to offer me anything so polite as a look.

I was speechless with babyish shame. It now appeared that to admit that I had been as absent-minded as she would be some kind of defeat in the great marital war which had apparently started. Strangely, as far as I was aware, the evening had begun quite well. She had been in a bit of a mood, but, without counting things out on my fingers, I guessed it was the wrong time of the month. Besides, seeing her mother always put Anne in a funny mood, and I knew she didn't like Fenella. A mood was to be expected, but this was like lunacy, her present condition.

'You've come out without your key, too.'

It was the old, literal Anne, seeing the truth and stating it. I, less at home with truth, and badly needing to get my own back for the pain I now felt, wanted to construct a ludicrous fiction.

'I had it until we got to the theatre. Then, if you remember, I gave it to you. You had it. You surely remember?'

By now I was the husband in *Gaslight* wanting to drive his wife mad by pretending her memory was going. 'You had my key as well as your own and you bloody go and lose them both.'

'We could ring Mummy,' she said, obviously deciding that my lies deserved no proper answer.

'Oh, that's right, ring bloody Mummy.'

'Julian, it's nearly midnight. It would be better than ringing Mrs Wiley, and I don't intend to spend the whole night pacing the streets. If you hadn't insisted on going backstage with that grotesque gang of people we wouldn't have been so late.'

'It's your fault if it's anyone's,' I said. 'Don't go blaming me. As I said, I gave you . . .'

'Oh, God!'

She burst into tears and for the first time since leaving the theatre she turned her face towards mine. I still felt furious with her, but at that moment all I wanted to do was make love to her. This, I supposed, would solve everything. And yet something about her, something which I had not observed before, repelled my advance. I was to watch her unhappiness but I could not

371

touch it. This instinct was confirmed when I reached out to put my arms around her and she stepped back to avoid me.

'It's all your stupid fault,' I spat back at her. Seeing her face crumple yet more with tears, I renewed my attack. 'You've behaved like a spoilt bitch this evening. Why couldn't you at least pretend to enjoy yourself? Do you think I *enjoy* some of the places you take me to? Do you think I *enjoyed* having sherry with your father? Christ!'

I railed and railed in this vein. At first, she moaned and through her streaming eyes she wore an expression of complete incredulity that someone whom she had loved and trusted could so wilfully inflict pain on her when she was already in a state of misery. Then, perhaps, her unhappiness entered further depths. She tried to say a sentence such as 'I can't . . . stay here and listen to any more of this.' But it all came out in jerky sobs, and then quite suddenly she turned and ran down to the King's Road where as it happened a taxi was free. She hailed it and before I had time to stop her, she went off. I learned later that she had gone to spend the night with Elizabeth, who had never much liked me, and I think thereafter had good cause to hate me. At the time, standing on the kerb watching Anne's taxi hurtle off towards Sloane Square I felt as close to despair as I ever felt in my life. I thought she was going for ever, and perhaps it would have been better if she had done so. 'Thought' is the wrong word for the whole jumble of totally irrational impressions which thundered and galumphed through my consciousness: fear that she would commit suicide, hope that she would, embarrassment that (as I was also certain) she had 'run home to Mummy', heartbreak that she did not love me any more, anger and fear, lacerating remorse for all the things I had thought, done or said since leaving the theatre.

I still hate myself for that evening. Not long ago it all came back with surprising vividness. I had been to dinner with some (rather smart, how things change) young people who lived in Lamont Road, and afterwards I stood on the kerb of the King's Road waiting for a taxi to trundle past. The dinner, where I had eaten well, met a number of old friends, been happy, evaporated at once into nothingness, as I found myself standing in what must have been almost the very spot where Anne and I had parted that night. Once again, I confronted that offensive and angry young man who stared after Anne's cab. Until that moment, I had forgotten the manic need which I had felt to press home an advantage in a non-existent battle, to fight Anne, though there was nothing to fight about. Nothing can ever quite cancel out these ghastly moments of truth about ourselves: not the passage of time, which in this case merely anaesthetised the pain for some thirty-five years, and then revived it with a pity for both of us, pity for our youth. It astounds me now how recklessly I risked and inflicted pain when I was in my twenties. The avoidance of pain, from middle age onwards, has been an obsession with me.

When Anne's taxi had gone, I realised that I wasn't quite drunk enough to be oblivious to all the tedious incidentals of the situation – seven or eight hours to be got through until breakfast, the flat locked up, the wife gone. Nor was I quite sober enough to reflect sensibly on what to do. Blundering up the road, I stopped in the first telephone kiosk which I reached, and dialled Sir Rupert Starling's number. He was an abstemious, regular man in his habits; I am sure he was in bed by eleven o'clock most nights, and probably asleep by the present hour of half-past twelve. After a few trills of his telephone, I heard his voice, alarmed and at the same time deferential. Who did he suppose might be ringing at such an hour? The Prime Minister? It was not an impossible thought.

I pressed Button A and for a moment his voice was lost. Then I heard the deferential tone become crisper before being blotted out by the dialling tone. I had forgotten to put in a penny. I took out a few coins and felt, as I did so, the desire to smoke.

The next time I dialled, with fag alight, I had the coins ready and did everything in the right order. Complete certainty that Anne was with her parents possessed my mind until the very second when I actually got through to her father. It then occurred to me, not by any process of reasoning but by instinct, that his tone of surprise, and of just having woken up, would not have been right if Anne were with him, sobbing her eyes out. I realised that Anne would never have exposed her parents to the scene which had just ensued; she was too proud, too distant from them, too considerate.

'Hallo,' said Sir Rupert's voice sternly.

I paused.

'Look, if this is some kind of practical joke,' he added.

All at once, his disapproving tones brought back the world of school, of larks, of everything being a huge practical joke played against the grown-ups.

'You may not realise that you are breaking the law,' he said with some pomp, but also with a tremble in his voice.

Quite near him, I could hear his wife speaking.

'Oh, Rupert, don't be such an ass.'

Then there was a noise as of some great Atlantic roller bursting into a cave as she dragged the receiver across her linen sheets and then said into it, quite calmly, 'Whoever you are, just bugger off.'

The line went dead. The incident, momentarily hilarious, was of the kind which Darnley, or Anne in happier days, would have split their sides over. Having no one to share the joke with – indeed as cold air and increasing sobriety reminded me, it not being a joke – brought with it a bleak loneliness. I left the kiosk and walked. A bus came along, and I sat on it until I reached Victoria. I didn't sleep much in the cheap hotel near the station where I had found a room. Next morning, unshaven and with bad breath, I retrieved the contents of my trouser pockets which – incurable habit – I had scattered on the chest of drawers before undressing for bed. Coins, a matchbox, and inevitably, a front door key.

Six

'Have we taken sufficient account,' asked Anne's brother Gavin, 'of the capital appreciation factor?'

'Rather difficult to do without the figures.'

His father sniffed, and all eyes turned down the table towards Sargie.

Such a gathering of Lampitts would have kept Uncle Roy happy for weeks, savouring the memory of each 'typical' utterance of every figure at the table.

They had assembled in Sibs's dining room to hear the details of how Sargie intended to dispose of Jimbo's papers to the Everett Foundation, and we had all been given the printed brochure, drawn up by the Everett, listing its present holdings, and its ambition to become one of the 'primary manuscript collections of Dowson, Pater, Wilde, two Douglases – Alfred and Norman – and Arthur Machen'. The miscellaneous names collected suggested a very distinctive area of taste on someone's part, presumably that of Virgil D. Everett Jnr himself.

One of the odd things which had emerged over lunch was that Gavin Starling had not in fact been the initiator of the deal, even though the Starlings knew the Everetts slightly and the phrase 'World Bank' had been murmured to suggest a plausible link between Sir Rupert and the great American financier. The final approaches had been made by the firm of attorneys in New York to the Lampitt family solicitors, Denniston and Denniston of Lincoln's Inn Fields. Things had gone further than Sibs had realised, which was why she had convened this tribal pow-pow for the purpose, as she phrased it of 'putting Sargie on the spot'. Aware from early childhood of Sargie's congenital nervous imbalance, his inability to make up his mind, his capacity to be fussed by more or less anything, I felt sorry for him in his approaching ordeal. A Sunday luncheon had to be got through first to which Sibs had asked her cousin Vernon, the former Labour cabinet minister, and Ursula Lampitt, another cousin,

Principal of Rawlinson College, Oxford. Gavin Starling was there, a figure comically similar to his father in manner and appearance, only thirty years younger; Anne and I had been asked along, and Sargie had brought the elder of the two Denniston brothers. The implication behind this impressive moot was that they were all responsible for Jimbo's literary remains. As they now turned to Sargie, there was the strong sense that he was on trial, and needed to justify himself, or at least to explain how much of Virgil D. Everett Jnr's money he had taken, or intended to take, in exchange for the Lampitt Papers.

One of Sargie's 'famous sayings', endlessly repeated by Uncle Roy (it was the trivial sort of thing which no one else would have remembered), was that he liked to have a piece of dry toast on his side plate at every meal. 'Not to eat, just to comfort me.' 'Typical Sargie,' my uncle would add, and although he laughed at the saying, he treasured it. I thought of this 'famous saying' at that moment, when I saw that Sargie had placed himself next to the solicitor. Sargie was not going to consult this dandruffy bespectacled figure, as it happened; but it was clear that the silent presence of Andrew Denniston would, like a piece of dry toast, bring its own mysterious strength. Something did.

I can remember, during the worst period of Sargie's depressions, that it had required in him, merely to decide whether or not he wanted to drive into Norwich, depths of heroic resolve which would have enabled other men to besiege towns or conduct *coups d'état*. Even nowadays, if one asked him over for the evening, one could expect six or seven telephone calls to alter, cancel, reconfirm arrangements. Psychosomatic symptoms would bombard him by the half-hour, making it hard for him to know whether he could trust himself to go out without the descent of a migraine, muscular seizures, nausea, or simply overpowering, debilitating gloom. The present semi-formal assembly of his relations, not one of whom I had the slightest reason to suppose Sargie liked, was a sadistic idea of Sibs's who cooingly reiterated, when the dishes had been cleared away and we all sat with wine, brandy, or in Sargie's case watered gin, that we had only come together to help him.

Any sympathy which I had been reserving for Sargie was, however, completely wasted. He was sitting more upright than usual and the alcohol seemed only to strengthen resolution rather than make him vague. The smouldering Senior Service in his bone holder was held between his lips as he began to speak and occasionally removed for the chance of flicking ash in the vague general direction of Sibs's ugly Elkington epergne. Uncle Roy had often remarked incredulously that Sargie had been a member of several government committees, and a powerful and effective figure on them. When my uncle spoke of this fact, none of us could quite picture the shambolic Sargie of Timplingham impressing his will on men of power and influence. But now one saw how it was done. Whether it was the money he was getting for the papers which thus emboldened him, or just the right amount to drink, or some feeling of atavistic rivalry with cousins and siblings, it was impossible to say.

Sargie ignored his nephew's overt enquiry about the price being offered by the Everett Foundation for the papers. With the sort of voice which might have been suitable for a public lecture, he began to speak.

'I think we have to recognise that there was no option here of standing still. At some time, and somewhere or another, these papers of my brother were going to pass out of my hands. That is a fact of mortality.'

'You could have entrusted them to one of the children,' said Sibs.

'But darling Sibs,' said Sargie with a triumphant smile (and he obviously loved denying his nephews and nieces the ownership of the Lampitt Papers), 'that raises all kinds of questions. I mean, I'm sure Andrew would bear me out . . .'

The Piece of Dry Toast (as I now thought of Mr Denniston) lowered his head in assent. Clearly his readiness to bear Sargie out was unconditional, since he did so before Sargie had finished his sentence.

'. . . when I say that once you get into that area you open up a whole lot of irrelevant questions. Obviously I should have to choose one member of the family to be the custodian of the papers. One can't have a lot of people deciding these things.'

'Why not?' Lord Lampitt and Dame Ursula both asked at once.

'And if it went to the next of kin, I think it would almost certainly turn out to be one of Vivian's grandchildren in Nairobi or whatever flea-hole it is they live in.'

'Mombasa,' I chipped in automatically, unable, when these questions arose, to forget my childhood catechism.

'Then there are Rachel, and Michael, and there's all Ivo's brood, most of whom I haven't even met.'

'Put the ashtray nearer him, someone,' said his sister wearily as the incinerated fragments of his Senior Service flew about the area of his chair. It was not avarice which was making her so cross. It was the knowledge that she could not exercise control over either Sargie or the papers.

'No,' said Dame Ursula, 'once we started offering the papers round the family, the situation would become completely chaotic.'

She was a figure of whom I had heard much, but never met until that day. She had such a recognisably Lampitt face – a long beaky nose, a prominent chin, the Punchinello aspect of Sargie himself – that it was hard to think she was quite real, rather than being Sargie dressed up. A nervous laugh, totally devoid of mirth, revealed her false teeth to the company every time she spoke. She wore a funny old chintzy dress which could have been (and perhaps was) run up from a pair of drawing-room curtains. Over her shoulders she draped a lumpy maroon cardie.

'A library's the place for it.' Giggle. 'No doubt at all about this.' Giggle.

'I agree with yer, Ursula, I agree with yer,' said Lord Lampitt, leaning forward on the table with one elbow, flicking on a lighter over the bowl of his pipe with another. Vernon must have been by then between fifty and sixty. He had inherited his father's Lloyd George peerage 'under protest' and abandoned his seat in the House of Commons.

As if to emphasise what he hoped we would all agree was the farcical inappropriateness of coronets or ermine in his own case, determined man of the people that he was, he had devised a curiously demotic pronunciation for himself bearing no relation to any discovered regional accent but differentiating him as strongly as possible from his own class, however that might be defined. He had a stupid but very amiable face, protuberant eyes, oval pink cheeks, reassuringly crooked teeth. A very few Lampitt genes seemed to have gone to his composition.

'If stuff's going to be preserved, let it be kept where yer ordinary bloke, yer researcher, maybe, or just yer interested enquirer can see it.'

'But why should we want people to see Jimbo's diaries?' asked Sibs.

'Me old dad used ter say' – Vernon sucked on his pipe, and then came out with the *mot* – 'it'll all come out in the wash.'

I had heard this catch-phrase before, but never known that it originated with the first Baron Lampitt. The thought occurred to me that if Vernon with his funny voice failed to get any further with politics there would probably always be a part waiting for him on 'The Mulberrys'. Barleybrook as yet lacked, for example, anyone directly classifiable as the Village Idiot.

'You can always' (giggle) 'limit the access to papers,' said Ursula. 'There are many archives in the' (giggle) 'Bodleian which the' (giggle) 'public aren't allowed to read.'

'But yer see, Ursula, with great respect I don't happen ter believe that's right.' Vernon's manner was that of a patient teacher explaining something obvious to a backward child.

Sargie smiled at the chaos of views already presented by his kinsfolk. Then he continued.

'I think we all see the point of putting these documents in a library,' he said. 'I don't want a whole bloody archive in my flat. None of us live in places big enough to house such collections, except the very rich like Vernon.'

Lord Lampitt shook his head as though his undeniably huge capital were a figment of our imagination, and Mallington Hall (like his other large house in Lord North Street) quite a modest little place really.

'The question remains "Which library?" ' (Giggle.) Ursula couldn't stop. 'And a library like the' (giggle) 'Bodleian . . .'

'Of course,' Sargie conceded, 'we could put all Jimbo's stuff in some library like the Bodleian or the British Museum and place an embargo on it. Of course we *could*.'

'But yer don't understand me point about the free availability of *information* for yer ordinary bloke.'

'It would have to be a pretty *extraordinary* bloke who wanted to read Jimbo's diaries,' said Sibs.

Sir Rupert loyally made a harrumphing noise which I took to mean that he had found his wife's intervention witty.

Anne and Gavin alone among the Lampitts seemed capable of sitting quietly and hearing Sargie out. Their elders, like naughty schoolchildren, had the compulsion to express dissent, amusement, agreement, quite instantaneously, and were unable to wait until Sargie had explained himself. Rather than being put off his stroke by this, Sargie seemed to appreciate it, and offer it as the very reason for the course of action which he expounded.

'And some of us wouldn't be happy to think of every Tom, Dick and Harry peering into them.'

'Dear-a-dear,' sighed his lordship. 'Whatever happened to those socialist principles of yours, Sargie?'

'No, we don't want people peering at them the moment they're put on deposit. But this place in New York isn't a public library. Even scholars have no right of access to it unless they can persuade the chairman of the company, Virgil D. Junior himself, that they are *bona fide* investigators. I'm sure we'll come to a good agreement with old Virgil.'

The Piece of Dry Toast once more inclined his head in assent.

'Ask again, Gavin,' said Sibs.

'If the remuneration . . . ,' my brother-in-law began.

But Sir Rupert silenced him with another harrumph.

'I suppose,' said Rupert, 'that the question exercising some of us is how much this would affect the biography.'

'That again, Rupert, my dear, is what is so ingenious and pleasing about the present scheme. I know you all blamed me for letting Lover Boy get his hands on the papers.'

General murmurs of ' 'Course not, Sargie', 'Good heavens, no'. Ursula began a little lecture on the subject of Hunter's book. 'The trouble with Mr Hunter's biography is that it starts from a completely false premise . . .'

While she was speaking, perhaps to some imaginary audience of undergraduates, Sargie continued, 'On Jimbo's stuff, that is. No, you all blamed me. But here, you see, is old Virgil, and we've no reason to suppose that Hunter even knows who he is. Now if it's all locked up in New York, Lover Boy isn't going to be able to read it. And old Virgil D. Junior has given us assurances.'

Again the Piece of Dry Toast inclined his head. He seemed to bow his head whenever Virgil D. Everett's name was mentioned, as some High Church people bow at the mention of Our Lord.

'. . . absolute assurances that no one will have access to the Jimbo Archive without the personal permission of Virgil D. He very much doesn't share your views, Vernon.'

Vernon had taken his pipe from his mouth, and with its spitty stem he was counting off the fingers of his left hand.

'Multimillion dollar oil conglomerates in California, one of the biggest law practices on the East Coast, then there's 'iz art collection – don't forget the Everett Dalis – and that's not to mention all 'iz directorships of the big multinationals. No, 'course 'a don't approve, Sargie, nor would you uv done if he hadn't offered you a thumping great cheque.'

'Harrumph, which is really . . . ,' said Sir Rupert.

'Come on, Sarge.' Sibs was a little girl in the nursery once again. 'How much is he offering?'

'Well, they were mine, those papers,' said Sargie.

Having delivered the facts of the case rather clearly, he was now quite prepared to switch on the pathos. He became the Sargie remembered from my boyhood, a figure who seemed that he might burst into tears if you tried to 'fuss' him.

'You always blame me,' he said, with a sweeping gesture which sent his gin glass and its contents flying down the table. It was an 'accident', not a tantrum, but it was hard to believe that it was not staged. In the ensuing muddle everyone got up from the table. Dame Ursula made things worse by shaking her sodden lap in the direction of Vernon, and the hostility between them, a theme on which my Uncle Roy had often discoursed, became undisguised.

'Mind where yer going. Yuv sprinkled me best trousers, now, Ursula, yer clumsy . . .'

Giggle, giggle.

'And I suppose yer think it's funny.'

The spilt gin glass provided the punctuation which we all required. There was no point in further engagements that day. The battle had gone to Sargie and the Starlings had been foiled. None of us knew at the time that Sargie had in fact, even as we discussed the matter, signed all the papers, handing over to Virgil D. Everett Jnr the ownership and rights in all Jimbo's stuff. Sargie told Anne and me a bit about it, as we drove him home. Anne had bought an Austin Seven, so there was no room for the Piece of Dry Toast, who bowed his way into a taxi in Sloane Street not long after we drove out of Cadagon Square.

'I say, Robin, slow down unless you want to kill us,' Sargie said automatically, as soon as she got into third gear. And while she was saying that we were only doing twenty, Sargie added, 'Thank goodness we got through all that, though. I don't think your mother will bother us again. What is it your friend calls poor old Sibs? Lady Vulture?'

'You're sure you want to go through with this sale?' Anne asked.

'The thing is – look, darling Robin, I know I said slow down, but I didn't mean a funeral pace – left, left bugger you, here.'

'I can't turn left here now, Sargie. Not since they made it one way.'

'Bugger one way.'

By now it suited his purposes to appear pretty sozzled; perhaps he actually was in this condition. Before we got him back to his flat in Kensington Square he had persuaded us to promise to do the final stages for him. This no doubt had been his object when he accepted a lift in Anne's car.

'My only difficulty is how to get the papers out of Lover Boy,' he said. 'They really ought to be in Andrew Denniston's office in a week or two. Thing is, I can't specifically remember how much there was.'

'Surely Mr Everett has not bought the whole archive without looking at it?' said Anne.

'Trusting fella.'

'There's something funny there,' said Anne.

We never did quite find out how, in the first place, Hunter had come to be looking after the Lampitt Papers. At one stage he and Sargie had been thick as thieves. Then later, for reasons which never became clear, Hunter fell from grace and Sargie began to share Sibs's unflattering views of the man. Sargie never bothered to explain any of this to us. Perhaps there was nothing to explain; he had always been capricious, and changes of mood about Jimbo's biographer were an inevitability. He had started out as one of that huge category of people who found Hunter charming. Like all members of the family, though, he was horrified by Hunter's biography of his brother. It was not that he had any of Sibs's humbug. He was not in favour of suppressing evidence if it was there. He simply failed to believe that Jimbo had led the life of a promiscuous and indiscriminate homosexual.

All this was awkward now that Anne and I had befriended Hunter. I wouldn't want to exaggerate the number of times he had been to our flat, but he was by now a fairly regular visitor. He always came at my invitation; he was not one to drop in. As it happened, Hunter was supping with us that very night, so, having left Sargie in Kensington Square, we had time to discuss the matter in the car as we returned to Lamont Road.

We had not had any major row since the terrible Night of the Lost Keys, but we were very much under strain. I was tormented by the thought that she had fallen out of love with me, and I couldn't imagine why. I still loved her, but there was so much hurt in my mind that I might as well have hated her. The eating and the living together and even the sex went on much as before. What had once been ecstatic now seemed merely routine, enjoyable on its own terms but almost impersonal. A deep, dark gulf had come to divide us.

We no longer held hands in the theatre or walking down the street. The expression 'something has come between us' felt almost literally true. It was as if there was something which I could not see forcing us apart. I had thought that we were Nature's exceptions. We had broken all the rules and some kind angel or deity had, it seemed, spared us the sort of crabby non-relationship which appeared to be what most married couples of my acquaintance settled down to. Now, all Day Muckley's or Peter's bar-stool wisdom about marriage had a hideous plausibility. Both Anne and I had ceased to be happy. Before, our own company had been the source of the most ecstatic, semi-mystical happiness; now we did not really want to be alone together. When it was just the two of us, the misery was inescapable. Partings, such as saying goodbye to Sargie that Sunday afternoon, became painful little leaps from the world of friendliness back to one of gloom and togetherness. It was not that either of us planned to be in a particular mood once we were left alone together. It was more like entering a haunted house and not knowing what we should find there.

It puzzled me now that I failed so completely to read aright the signals of Anne's strange behaviour. Only a few weeks before the disastrous Night of the Lost Keys, we had seemed to be getting on as well as we had ever done. Or was that true? I now began to reassess the past and to admit to myself, or invent, the fact that Anne's breeziness had always caused me misgivings. It now appeared to me that she had never truly taken me seriously, whatever that was supposed to mean. It felt as if I had given her my besotted and whole-hearted devotion, but that she had only been able to respond with laughter. Sexual experiences which seemed at the time like journeys to a new stratosphere had perhaps for her been no more than jolly schoolgirl romps. Now, a spoilt youngest child and every inch her mother's daughter, she was bored, and she was not kind enough to conceal it. This was the sort of assessment I made of Anne's character and her changing relationship with myself. The chilling thing was the belief that on her side not much had changed, that she never had minded about me in the way that I so devotedly cared about her. Presumably it was because I felt so hurt and so frightened by her behaviour that I protected myself from any intelligent analysis of its causes. When contemplating the Night of the Lost Keys, I did not ask quite simple questions: What had that evening been like for Anne? Why had she been so unhappy in the first place? What was it about our visit to the theatre, and in particular our going backstage, which had caused her such pain? Was she not by nature a killjoy? Anyone outside the situation would have asked these questions and found what I now see to be the obvious answers: but marital unhappiness has the capacity to stupefy, to stun to the point where right judgement is impossible. All that mattered during this particular phase of horror was that we should not be left too much alone together. This was, paradoxically, one of the only things which united us. We therefore spent so much of the time out. I was glad of my job at the Bottle, and even in periods when I was not being paid by Cyril to dispense drinks to the others, I spent more and more time in the place, on one side of the bar or the other.

Anne was often at the Courtauld. We never lunched together any more. In the evening there was still the rigid convention that we met up. Sometimes we would visit Sargie or her parents or go to a restaurant with a third or fourth party. If at home, we nearly always tried to have someone to eat with us. We had the most miscellaneous string of people to suppers – never in large numbers since our table could not really seat more than five. Fellow research students of Anne's from the Courtauld, Darnley and his sisters, William Bloom were regulars. Sometimes there was the social equivalent of a one-night stand, somebody we happened to have met in the course of the day and whom, in desperation, we had asked back so as not to have to dine à deux. There would have been plenty of such takers in the Bottle, but, understandably, Anne drew the line at my pub friends. Day

Muckley had, on a number of occasions, said he would like to bring his mistress round to see us. I should have been pleased if he had done so because I did not quite believe in this person and was embarrassed that he should so frequently refer to her; but Anne, whose first glimpse of him had been on television, thought of him solely as 'the man who puked'; she did not wish to risk the awkwardness of an encore on our rented carpet.

We ate almost entirely picnic food bought at delicatessens, which in those days seemed exotic. French or Italian cheeses, ditto bread, salamis, taramasalata, cole slaw – stuff which any English person can now go and buy in a supermarket – was something to be sought out in Soho.

Our entertaining of Hunter must be seen against this background. His visits belong to the period when we first started to get on really badly. It has to be said, however, that his visits were unlike those of the others. For one thing, we did not supply him with a picnic in which a piece of Dolcelatte or a Spanish sausage might be brought to the table in a brown paper bag. For Hunter, an effort was made. I polished our few glasses. Anne cooked simply, but always well.

It is painful to admit that we made so much effort simply because Hunter was now 'famous'. Speaking solely for myself, this had an extraordinary effect upon me. There was really no reason, on past form, why I should much like Hunter, though he had always tried hard enough to be charming when we met. The fact that he was now a face on the television screen, and a famous man of letters, worked on me, I am sorry to admit, like a drug. I hugged to myself, with delicious sensations of superiority to the rest of mankind, the knowledge that Raphael Hunter knew me, ate my wife's lamb chops, lolled in our rented armchair, drinking a glass or two (Hunter was always abstemious) of the best cheap wine we could afford.

My snobbery about Hunter was what blinded me to the situation and I blush for that. On the other hand, he had also become a sort of friend and over the matter of my novel he had been quite needlessly generous. Many people in his position might have put in a good word with their own publisher on behalf of a struggling young writer. But he seemed to have gone much further than that, talked Madge Cruden into accepting my novella for her list at Rosen and Starmer. Here again, I knew nothing at the time of the extent to which Madge doted on

Hunter. She would probably have been prepared to publish any rubbish with which he presented her if thereby she could increase in his esteem. I believed the many stories about Madge being a powerfully formidable woman, nobody's fool, and it did not occur to me that so famously tough an individual might have taken on my book merely because she loved Hunter. On the contrary, I thought that it was my book and its brilliance which had broken through even Madge's iron resolve. Though I had decided that the stylish thing was to be modest about it, I inwardly believed that my novel was quite on a level with *David Copperfield* and Proust's recreation of Combray. I do not even possess a copy today but even if I did I know that I should be unable to read it. Something tells me that this barely fictionalised account of my childhood with Uncle Roy and Aunt Deirdre and their preferring their dog to myself was not in fact quite the masterpiece which I had supposed.

'Madge is very pleased with it indeed, anxious to see your next,' said Hunter at supper. He was sitting in the cane armchair and sipping Chianti. By his side was a lamp which had been made out of a wine bottle. It had a red raffia shade.

Emboldened by the thought that I, a soon-to-be-published author, would soon be hobnobbing with all kinds of famous people, I said, 'I'm sorry it's just the three of us again. We should really have asked someone with you. Isabella, perhaps.'

I was becoming as bad as Fenella. The idea that we might actually entertain a famous actress like Isabella Marno, whom I had met for about ten seconds, was a preposterous one. Hunter and I, luckily, were alone together when I said it, though to judge from a louder-than-average clatter of saucepans in the kitchen it is possible that Anne overheard the remark.

'I like coming alone, really,' said Hunter. He made no attempt to pick up my cheeky allusion to Miss Marno. I even wondered whether he really knew her all that well. Perhaps he had gone backstage and met her that evening for the first time? Such a thing was by no means impossible. (Though as it happens, I should add as a footnote, untrue. Hunter had at this date been Isabella Marno's lover for about six months. They remained together, on and off, I understand, for about another year.)

My excitement at the imminent publication of the book, only a few months in the future, was intense and it must have revealed itself in every muscle of my face. For some reason, however, I thought it would be disgraceful for any pleasure to show. In consequence, I lolled with my Chianti and made some most injudiciously blasé remarks about the hideous dust-jackets used on Rosen and Starmer books, and then moved on to some very unwise jokes about Madge.

Everyone who knew about Madge made jokes about her. Like Fenella or Day Muckley, she was one of those people who had decided to become a caricature of themselves. Perhaps it is wrong to say that they decided on it. One naïvely wondered whether there was ever a time when they were less 'themselves', when the persona so garishly thrust at the world had been rather less violently Technicolored. This is a question which I still have not resolved in my mind about those who set out to be 'characters' and end as the prisoners of their own act. Madge was a byword, not just among publishers but in London generally, for being a 'battle-axe'. Bawling out secretaries, throwing books around the office, spitting insults at literary agents down the telephone: these, legend had it, were her favourite games. If you wanted to appear discerning, it was usual to add, after some account of Boadicea-like office ferocity, that Madge had extraordinary literary discernment, a wonderful eye for a book. If my own case was anything to go by, she was not one of the world's great editors. I had spent an afternoon in her office while she chain-smoked Gauloises over my poor little quarto-leaved typescript, turning each page with rapidity and with no sign whatsoever of any enjoyment. It felt like taking work up to teacher's desk. The only things for which she seemed to be on the lookout were errors of spelling or punctuation.

Until that afternoon, I had sincerely believed that it was impossible to read my account of Uncle Roy (Uncle Hector in the book) getting tangled up in Tinker's (Smudge's) lead without laughter. Indeed, any normal person would, I considered, be in hysterics over this passage, as over the invented scene of Aunt Dolly (Deirdre) holding a meeting of the Mothers' Union at the Rectory and the Lady Novelist, loosely based on Deborah Maddock, who used to live in our village, introducing a frank discussion of sexual morals.

Madge read through these superb pieces of burlesque without the smallest flicker of amusement on her face. Her only comment on the Mothers' Union scene was to squiggle her pen twice through the word *ciotus* and add the symbol TRS in the margin.

'You've made that mistake twice, Mr Ramsay.'

'I thought it was funnier if Mrs Sidebotham believed it was pronounced like that. It's a sort of malapropism.'

'But it isn't the right spelling. *Coitus* is what you meant.' She showed real impatience as she explained this to me.

'I did mean to spell it like that.'

'Well, it was wrong.'

She read on for some time, making innumerable tiny adjustments to the page with her blue pencil. At length she sighed and said, 'Mr Ramsay, where did you go to school?'

I told her.

'And did they teach you nothing about punctuation?'

'I think they did.'

'One day you and I must have a word about commas.'

I was saved by the bell on this occasion because the telephone rang and she was soon upping the decibels on account of the late departure of a recent title from the warehouse.

'I don't care what the shop steward says. . . . So am I a member of the Labour Party. . . . That doesn't excuse pure, bone idleness. . . . Look, I want those books in the shops, tomorrow!'

In Hunter's company I made the supreme blunder of supposing that no one took Madge quite seriously. The fact that she had really made his career by zealous promotion of *Petworth Lampitt* did not touch my imagination. Nor at that time had I heard any gossip about her and Hunter which might have warned me of the fact that she found Hunter heartbreakingly attractive. But Anne was clearly aware of this.

'I'm not sure,' I was saying, 'that Madge is really any good. Are you, Raphael?'

He sat forward earnestly in his chair, Rodin's thinker or a man at stool.

'Madge is very . . .' He went red.

'She's publishing your book, damn it,' Anne snapped out, adding, 'Raphael, come and help me with the washing-up.'

'Quite unnecessary,' I said.

But he went.

This was part of the little routine. Hunter established his essential ordinariness, the humility of the man behind the famous face, by clearing away the dishes and spending some time in the kitchen with Anne while the coffee was being prepared rather than enjoying the conversation in the sitting room with myself. It mildly annoyed me that he did not wish to sit with me for the whole evening; but great men must be allowed their whims and I imagined that it meant a lot for Anne that he could perform this little gesture of condescension. I always left them to it on these occasions. There wasn't much room in the kitchen and I was idle about all domestic tasks. While the coffee percolated (and our percolator took a very long time) I pottered about, refilling my glass, or putting a record on the gramophone, or did something Anne hated me doing, lifted up the tablecloth with all its crumbs and fragments and shook it on to the carpet. By the time they emerged from the kitchen, I was hoping that she wasn't boring him with talk about her research. I had been planning the conversation which Sargie in his cowardice had shuffled on to us, breaking to Hunter the news of the Everett Foundation's latest purchase.

'Raphael,' I said, as Anne poured the coffee, 'I'm afraid to say that something's cropped up.'

'It's all right,' said Anne, 'I told him.'

'You might have left it to me,' I said.

'You had all evening to say something about it.'

She now seemed incapable of concealing, even from an outsider whom we wanted to impress, that we were getting on badly. Instead of being able to smooth over this unpleasantness I was angered by it.

'I just hope you got all the details right,' I said.

'Look,' said Hunter cooingly. He suddenly seemed, though looking remarkably youthful and handsome, to be much wiser and saner than either of us. 'It's very kind of you to have told me about all this.'

'It isn't kind,' said Anne. 'Not if it's going to make your work totally impossible.'

'You see,' I said, 'Sargie has actually asked us to . . .'

'I know, I know.' Hunter sighed. Sympathy for us in our embarrassing plight seemed the dominant emotion on display. 'Of course you must come and collect the papers whenever you like.'

'Sargie doesn't always realise how busy other people are,' I said testily. 'I have my book coming out . . .'

'We *know*,' said Anne.

389

'I just don't know when I am going to find time to come to your flat and help you move all those boxes to the solicitor's office. I still have a part-time job in this weird pub, you see.'

'You mustn't think of doing anything,' said Hunter.

'I've said I'll do it all,' said Anne quietly and swiftly. 'There's no need for you to be involved.'

Although I protested great business, I in fact had almost nothing to do, and for some reason it had seemed obvious to me that I should be the one who supervised the transfer of the Lampitt Papers.

Talk was desultory after that. Anne did start boring him with thesis talk, and when I tried to stop her, he said he was finding it interesting.

I was jealous that Anne had been the one chosen to help. I should have valued the opportunity of seeing Hunter's flat: I should have liked to feel myself getting to know him better; for it was a curious feature of our relationship that though he had now called on us frequently, there was never any question of his returning our hospitality. This simply never crossed our minds as a possibility.

Anne's ability to persuade Hunter to part with Jimbo's diaries without fuss made me jealous of those powers of social competence which she so alarmingly shared with her mother. She was always able to get things done and to persuade people to do things for her: tradesmen who claimed not to deliver their wares were always willing in Anne's case to make an exception. Plumbers or electricians, if I implored their services, would refuse to come and mend overflowing cisterns or smouldering fuse boxes. But they changed their minds the moment she seized the receiver and said, 'Let me talk to them.' In the first year of marriage this superb efficiency had been one of the things which I loved about her. Now I rather hated it and I even allowed myself to wonder whether it was quite ethical. Hunter could scarcely have been aware of the family pow-wow, of the strength of feeling against him among Anne's relations. He seemed so calm and smiling that I wondered whether he realised the implications of Anne's effectual confiscation of her late uncle's papers. Had she been quite straight with Hunter? Was he aware that they were going to be locked up in some strong-room in Manhattan? It would surely spell the end of his career as Jimbo's biographer; and yet he was smiling. There was something almost pathetic about it.

'I'm afraid that the papers are in a state of some confusion,' said Hunter. 'It might require several visits.'

'I'll come as often as it takes,' said Anne.

'She'll enjoy hanging round your neck,' I said.

Since I was cross with her for getting the assignment and so impressed by Hunter's sang-froid, I could only take refuge in the tired old banter of Anne being in love with him. This was a joke which we had never until that moment shared with Hunter. I helped him on with his coat and saw his features pucker as I said the words. I was then sober enough to remember that we had never told Hunter of my fantasy that he was Anne's 'pin-up'; no more did he know of Sargie's nickname for him. His slightly puzzled frown soon vanished and by the time he turned, his blandly vapid smile was restored, an expression which was now so familiar on the television that one wondered whether in some strange way the face was not the invention of television lights and cameras, whether the smile, like that of the Cheshire Cat, was not disembodied from the smiler, hoicked out of the props department in the television centre and imposed upon him as a badge of his trade like the old masks of tragedy and comedy in Graeco-Roman theatre. It was not the first time that I had imagined Hunter's bland waxy face as a mask. The pained expression which I had glimpsed in the hall glass, infinitely brief and slight, hinted that if the mask of comedy were removed, a quite different countenance, perhaps a different character, would be found underneath.

Anne for her part looked mortified, furious, at my resurrecting this antique piece of marital banter. Hers was the kind of fury a child might have at school or at a party if a parent carelessly blurted out his secret family nickname. In the early days of our love she used to scream with laughter at the idea of having fallen in love with Hunter at the minute he was splattered by Day Muckley. Now, it appeared, jokes were out of order.

'As always,' said Hunter, 'it's been lovely.'

He patted my arm and smiled. He had the air of one man encouraging another man. It was one *littérateur* to another. We saw together the obstacles which lay ahead: Madge perhaps being difficult, reviewers failing to see the point of the book. Together we would overcome, but there was nothing in his little gesture of patting my arm to suggest that this was what he meant. Touching someone's elbow is scarcely code for how to get on in the literary world, but at the time I was so certain that I knew Hunter's mind that his clasping my arm might have been a ritualised and universally (if secretly) recognised sign such as the Freemasons share with one another. I noticed with a certain childish glee that for all Anne's offer to help him with the papers he was really more interested in his friendship with me. He even forgot to give her the little peck on the cheek which he sometimes bestowed before leaving our flat. Indeed, I do not remember his even saying goodbye to her, whereas his farewells to me were on the verge of being effusive.

As soon as the front door closed I felt ourselves once more entrapped by the old sensations of intense unhappiness. Our feet crunched on the cream crackers which I had shaken on to the carpet.

'Oh, I've told you not to throw food on the floor,' she said.

I felt a surge of rage against her for saying this. Keeping the flat clean was not my job. I was not her skivvy. What was Mrs Wiley for? I wanted to clout Anne, but she moved out of range and lit a cigarette.

'I don't see why I should always be held responsible for keeping this place tidy,' I said. 'If it weren't for Mrs Wiley the place would be a refuse heap.'

She murmured something. It might have been 'Oh, shut up.' It was quiet, incoherent. With pompous slowness, an investigating magistrate's tones, I said, 'You said? I didn't quite catch what you said.'

I opened the bottle of cheap Scotch on the mantelpiece and poured myself some.

'Are you sure you aren't having too much of that stuff?' she asked, moving swiftly into the advantageous position of herself as prosecutor. The remark stung me. I was at the stage of being pleasantly blotto, but knew that one more glass would change this state into one of unpleasantness; and thereafter if I carried on drinking, I would be on the way to becoming blind drunk with all the dangers of the room spinning round, stomach and bowels emptying themselves, not necessarily at convenient time or place. These physical awarenesses arrived in the brain simultaneously with a hot, confused need to assert myself over Anne. Her arrogance was insufferable as she stood there on the other side of the fireplace, combing her hair with her fingers, pulling back her fringe to reveal her big pale brow. The gesture filled me with lust. I looked down at her legs. The sight of her calves in black stockings made me want to rip them off, her truculent fury with me only adding to her allure.

'Are you saying I'm drunk?'

'Don't be boring, Julian.'

'Answer me.'

She sighed a long sigh, blowing out smoke through lips and nostrils. Then, as she stubbed her cig she said, 'I'm going to bed.'

Gulping my whisky, pausing to refill the glass, I took this as the signal that I was meant to rape her. Perhaps I paused to refill the refill, because by the time I reached the bedroom she had already undressed and got in between the sheets. I noticed as I blundered into the room that my feet were not quite touching the ground. I sort of swayed about, not quite able to reach the carpet with my shoes; funny feeling. We had never gone in for pyjamas, so I knew she would be naked. She had turned off her bedside lamp and was lying on her side. Her eyes were closed.

I pulled back the bedclothes and saw that she was wearing a petticoat. What did she want me to do? Rip it off?

'I'm trying to go to sleep,' she said. She did not open her eyes but her lower lip was trembling and she was on the edge of tears. I put down my drink on the dressing table and started to take off my own clothes, kicking shoes anywhere as I tore at shirt buttons. Had anyone observed me (and Anne, the only possible witness, had her eyes shut) they would have seen an almost infinitely derisory figure: the oldest joke in the world, a man with his trousers falling down to his ankles dancing like a clown to remove these cumbersome leggings. Within, by contrast, I was Blake's Tyger, tyger, burning bright. The violence but also the cosmic beauty of what I had to offer Anne made me feel like an embodiment of energy. Or so it seemed.

Without turning, Anne spoke through gritted teeth.

'*No*, Julian.'

It was the first time in eighteen months that these words had ever been spoken between us and I refused to believe my ears. I leaned over the bed and took her by the shoulders.

'No!' she repeated.

Though in distress she was still in full command.

'Come here, will you.' I grabbed her roughly. She sat up at

once and clobbered me – hit out at my face with a fist. In spite of the violent fantasies which had flitted through my consciousness earlier, this was not a game I wished to play. I never wanted fighting to be part of the act of love, nor was it possible to mistake Anne's words or gestures as being anything remotely playful. She did not want me. That was clear; and the knowledge was sobering, painful, like being stabbed between the ribs with an icicle.

She sat up in bed, open-eyed. She looked at me with simple dislike. The course of action which I had been so brutally proposing some minutes before had been, throughout the last year, the central thing of my existence. All our spare time had been devoted to it; it coloured and made joyful the whole of life. We had done it everywhere, in open fields, on the bathroom floor, on hearth rugs, in bed, by night, by day. With this rapturously enjoyable accompaniment one felt that any pain life offered was superfluous, bearable. With this action 'all losses are restored and sorrows end'. There had never been any question before, even when we were quarrelling, that we were lovers, waiting sometimes with intolerable impatience to be left alone together so that we could resume the dance. It was against this background that my shock has to be registered. Anne was looking at me as if she had just received an improper advance from a stranger, as it were the window-cleaner.

'What the hell's going on?' I asked.

She burst into tears. She had pulled her knees towards her face and she hugged them desperately as she sobbed and moaned.

This sobered me up even more. I felt humiliated, cheated, deceived, and didn't know why. At the same time my heart was wrung by her misery and I too began to weep at the sheer pitiableness of it all. Instinct made me want to comfort her, to take her in my arms. I no longer wanted to force myself upon her; rather to cling to her myself for comfort. But even as I advanced and touched her, I felt her shoulder blades freeze and she shook me away. This rebuttal was worse than the first. I assumed that she had read all my unspoken signals exactly as I felt them. A small particle of unselfish common sense might have allowed me to see that there might have been some quite simple physiological explanation why she did not feel equal to the gymnastic rigours proposed. Now, however, she had rejected even simple kindness and sympathy. Her little shrug hurt and angered me terribly. Once more, I felt cheated. The clever, funny frivolous Anne with whom I had been in love had been a chimerical illusion concealing this, the real Anne, a congenitally moody, self-obsessed madwoman.

'Sargie, like many of the Lampitts, is very mildly barmy,' Uncle Roy used to say. 'And there was Angelica, of course.'

'Oh, Christ,' I said.

I got up and went over to the chest of drawers where I had left my whisky glass. After a swig, I asked, 'It would help if you could tell me what I'm supposed to have done wrong.'

She sniffed, a long, disgusting sniff.

'Oh, Julian, let's try to get some sleep.'

'Why – that's all I want to know.'

'I'm tired.'

'I'm married to you – remember?'

'Good night, Julian.'

The glass which had been in my hand hurtled through the air and smashed against the wall over the bed, its fragments flying everywhere. Splinters of glass were lodged like sequins in Anne's hair.

I wasn't in control. Any observer would have agreed with Anne's statement, repeated at various junctures in after-time, that I had thrown the glass at her, and by any strict standards this was true. But it no longer felt as if I were doing things. My body was doing things in response to a wild pain which surged up inside me.

'Julian, put that chair down.'

Her tear-stained face was now wide awake, and serious. She spoke slowly as to an animal. My eyes met hers, those great blue eyes which still had a complete and hypnotic power over me.

'Put it down, Julian.'

Her head swayed about, momentarily becoming two heads. I was sober enough to realise that I was about to enter a phase of uncontrolled drunkenness. This little part of me which was still sober wanted to reach out to Anne's stern, calm voice and to look into her eyes for pardon. The chair was thrown aside. There was a terrible bang as this happened, but at least I did not throw it at *her*. Collecting myself with what felt like magisterial *gravitas*, I made for the door and on the second attempt I got through it.

Cold woke me, and the glimmerings of the grey dawn, which

made the curtains of the sitting room, hitherto an inchoate darkness, a discernible shape. I could make out the window between them. There was still a bit of spin left in my vision, whisky was still in the veins. The terrible physical sensations woke me. The back of my skull was pounding as I lay there on the carpet, my mouth and nostrils ached and reeked with too much smoking, a feeling which burnt its way all down my oesophagus into the stomach. Even in this faint pre-light my eyes were terribly sore. I felt very cold underneath the blanket. It wasn't for an hour or more that I made sense of the blanket and realised that in all her anger and fear and grief, Anne must have tiptoed out of the bedroom to cover my naked and recumbent form as it lay stretched out on the sitting-room floor. Somehow this action, when I was awake enough to deduce what had happened, seemed the most heartbreaking thing of all.

Seven

It hurts to remember how much pain I caused. Some of this pain was inflicted wilfully, some of it was because I was young. Being in pain myself, I lashed out, heedless of where the blows would fall. But almost the most painful thing to recall is how stupid I was. The evidence was staring me in the face that Anne was in love with someone else; it was evidence which I was slow to piece together, slower to accept. The idea that she was really in love with Raphael Hunter was one which never crossed my mind. Even if I had recognised this staringly obvious fact, I still was not in a position to guess that he would exploit this situation.

But it was obvious that something was wrong, terribly wrong. Anne had changed. She was no longer the person with whom I had been so ecstatically in love. A great coldness had descended. Drunken quarrels of the kind which flared up after the supper with Hunter were rare. The anger which became habitual between us was without passion. It was dead and dull. Childishly hurt by her, I never asked myself why she was in this strange mood. The fact that she was different changed and destroyed me, but I saw the transformation as something which she was doing, or not doing, to me. There seemed no need to look for explanations outside the prison house of our own poisoned relations with each other. She was sullen and morose. I blamed her for being so unloving towards me, but I assumed that she had begun to find something amiss in myself, and therefore attributed all her stoniness to a puritanical distaste of my drinking, or a simple jealousy of my having had a novel accepted. Now, if I came into the room, she hardly looked up or she would make an excuse to get up and walk out. She did not always refuse me my 'marital rights'. In a ghoulish way she seemed actually amused by the continuance of this desire on my part, sometimes lighting a cigarette or even on occasion reading a book (*The Calderdale Saga*, as it happened) while the activity lasted.

'God, your friend writes badly' was her only comment at this supposedly ecstatic moment. The hungry, giggling little monkey-Anne of our earlier supremely happy conjunctions had become this blasée indifferent figure who, although lying there, seemed to be taking no part in the proceedings. All these were pretty definite signals, but of what, I would not allow myself to see. Anne is not a fundamentally unkind person. Perhaps she wanted me to dislike her, to make the sense of letdown easier. If so, she failed. I had come to hate her, but I remained passionately in love with her. Had I loved her less, had she been more of a friend and less of a mistress, I might have been able to sympathise with her, to guess at her predicament. If from the first I had known the cause of Anne's sorrow, I have sometimes wondered whether I should not have been able to 'save the marriage'. Since, in moments of terrible repining, I have supposed that I would have been able to set matters to rights. Time heals most things, but especially the wounds from which she suffered then. But I was far too hurt by her sudden withdrawal of affection to be able to see her as she was. I began to attribute it to some supposed small-mindedness which had been inherent in her character from the beginning but to which love had blinded me. The only new ingredient in our relationship, as I saw things, was the fact of my literary success. Therefore Anne minded my having befriended Hunter, made a success with Madge. She was prepared to love me when I was a pathetic figure, a part-time barman, the nephew of the village parson. Now I had become someone in my own right, and it was a different story. Incoherent rage with Anne, and through Anne with all the tribe of Lampitts, welled up from atavistic depths. 'They' had always despised 'us'. Anne had had her mind poisoned against me by her mother, perhaps even Sargie's lordly manner towards me had begun to brush off. They disliked me for knowing too much, that was it. Since childhood, I had had my eye unwillingly trained on the Lampitts by Uncle Roy and it made them uneasy. They wanted to send me back 'where I belonged'. The shirt factory was my proper place, following my father's footsteps. What had the likes of me to do with Cadogan Square? These thoughts were all totally preposterous. Even as they fixed themselves in my brain I did not quite believe them, but I said them to myself as we sat in silence on either side of the fire. Anne had given up reading at home. Sometimes she would have a newspaper on her lap, but more often she just sat, evening after evening, staring at the eiectric bars, smoking a lot, her once animated face transformed into a mask of sorrow. We gave up asking people to supper and little by little friends stopped calling. We must have been wretched company. Only Fenella was kind or stupid enough not to take account of this, but her visits were generally early in the evening, before Anne got back from the Courtauld.

Suppers with Hunter had fizzled out with the rest of social life. This fact puzzled me as much as the fact that Anne, who had now been weeks sorting and arranging the transfer of the Lampitt Papers from Hunter's flat to the solicitor's office, found so little to say about it all. Normally, she was a good gossip, and would have found plenty to relate. If I pressed her about it, she was snappy.

But I wanted to talk to someone, and it was with half an idea of unburdening myself to an older man that I telephoned Hunter some weeks before the novel was published and suggested that we lunch together.

We had never had a social engagement *à deux* before, and on the telephone he sounded a bit harassed.

'Nothing special, is there, that you wanted to talk about?' His voice was nasal, conciliatory, his committee voice.

'Yes and no.'

The truth was that after two or three very unhappy days with Anne I was desperate to talk to someone, someone sober, that is. Peter and the Best-Seller were the obvious recipients of such marital confidences. That is one of the functions of pubs, the secular person's confessionals, the poor man's couch of analysis. I was frightened, though, of finding in Peter's unhappy experiences of marriage too many humiliating parallels with my own. If his vision of the universe was true, men and women were essentially enemies, and alcohol was the only way out. I was not strong enough to take such a view as my own. My unwillingness to sound out Day Muckley was based on a different delicacy, the fear of shocking him. He spoke habitually of the decadence of the age and deplored his own inability, blamed entirely on the outrageous behaviour of his wife, to lead a life of domestic rectitude – 'as you do, Julian, lad, but then you are very happily married.' The Best-Seller used to say this so often to me that I simply felt unable to confront him with the reality of the case. He spoke eagerly of Anne and me spending an evening in a restaurant with himself and his mistress. I had not the heart to tell him that home life was miserable. An evening with him and Anne was anyway unthinkable. In the days when she liked me, Anne would have been in a perpetual state of schoolgirlish giggles because Day was the man who had puked. Latterly, she would have been truculent, as on the evening when I 'made' her go backstage and see 'a lot of grotesques'. I could not begin to guess that the real cause of her unhappiness on that evening was that she had known of Hunter's liaison with Isabella Marno, hated watching her rival's triumphant performance on the stage, and hated even more being brought backstage to confront, with her own eyes, the intolerable knowledge that Hunter was, as gossip had related, hovering about the actress.

He was edgy, as I said, on the telephone.

'I thought you might ring, actually,' he admitted.

'You did?'

There was such a silence that I thought we had been cut off. 'Hallo?'

'Let's talk in the restaurant,' he said.

We ate at a Greek place in Charlotte Street, and for the first part of the luncheon he talked obsessively about his own professional affairs. The success of 'Perspectives' was all very gratifying, but it made serious inroads into other equally important and weighty concerns. 'Tom' and 'Rupert' (not Starling, I think) had been marvellous in securing the future of the London Library, but Hunter somehow implied that it would have been too much to expect them to do so without his taking a much more active role on the committee. There was, he added with a ruthless glint in his eye, *dead wood* on any committee and it was part of a good committee man's function to get rid of it.

Then Madge had asked him . . .

'Oh, talking of Madge,' I said. I was anxious to get on to the subject of my book, but Hunter was full of a major new literary prize which he and Madge were going to set up for a work of 'literary' fiction. Then, as always, there were reviews to be written. There were some big international literary events which really demanded Hunter's presence. Yevtushenko had been over to England.

'I only managed to see him once. I feel bad about that.'

I began to feel really sorry for Hunter that his television success was absorbing so much valuable time.

'Cyril should write an extra chapter of *Enemies of Promise*,' said Hunter. The only Cyril I knew was the landlord of the Black Bottle, so this sentiment caught me momentarily by surprise until I grasped Hunter's drift.

'Television is a worse enemy than the pram in the hall,' he added.

'And on top of all that,' I said, 'you've got to deal with the Lampitt Papers.'

I never did know for certain how long it would take to transfer the papers from Hunter's flat to the lawyer's offices in Lincoln's Inn Fields. At a generous estimate, it must have taken the best part of one afternoon. At the time, I entirely accepted that this task was absorbing weeks of Anne's time, necessitating frequent visits to Hunter's flat. From the way that his face darkened at the mention of the Lampitt Papers, I now discern the fear of a showdown from the wronged husband; though I also realise that, even if this had been a card in my hand, Hunter, who must have met with variations of this problem before, would have handled things adeptly. During lunch itself, I interpreted his frown, his slight hesitancy, as irritation with Anne. Blood will out, I supposed. In her thoroughness with the papers, Anne was getting her revenge for the wrong that Hunter had done her family as well as showing herself to be the conscientious scholar who knew how archival material should be treated and preserved.

I now ask myself how it was possible for me not to see things as they were. I am tempted to think, because of what I subsequently knew about Hunter, that, during this lunch with him, I was mistaken to act towards him as I did. Yet, while obviously true in one way, it is surely false to suggest that people can be got right or wrong, like mathematical puzzles, rather than being entities in a state of endless flux who react so differently to each separate combination of circumstances or relationships that it makes no sense to define them. It is upon the fallacy of fixed personalities that biographers have made their trade, either by reinforcing caricature in Jimbo's dated manner or more often, like Hunter, parading themselves as fearless iconoclasts who are demythologising the 'character'

401

concerned. The exercise perhaps has a certain literary charm so long as no one supposes that it relates to the real, felt life of the individual under discussion. What shocks now in my surprise that I should have tried to unburden myself to Hunter, and share with him my marital difficulties, is the surprise itself. It is a clue to me that memory has hardened and ossified my picture of Hunter, and to a lesser degree of my earlier self. I am making them into stereotypes, which is why my vision of how they behaved is capable of surprising me. The real me, and the real Hunter, as opposed to these mythological projections, were figures of infinite fluidity, and even as they sat together in the restaurant in Charlotte Street they were many persons, possessed of many thoughts and aims. I have no way of knowing what a mixture of embarrassment and guilt Hunter felt, sitting with the husband of one of his current areas of female interest; nor whether his relations with women, which so obsessed me, had ever at any time played a large part in his consciousness; or whether they were always, if not a means to an end, at least subservient to his true aims.

Years later, during an indiscreet luncheon with Isabella Marno, I was astonished to learn, from the actress's own lips, the sort of details which lovers should never decently reveal to a third party. A general lack of interest on Hunter's side was what was conveyed. Throughout her period of most besotted devotion to Hunter, their secret afternoons and very few, very occasional weekends, he had been cold and languid. When in her company, his face had never been lit up, until he parted with her, to chair a committee or be interviewed by a journalist. I felt instinctively that Bella Marno's experience had been typical. Hunter's indifference to sex, while 'allowing himself' to be involved with it (and this apparently was how it had felt to Bella), was part of the secret. It drove her wild, and it must have been what drove the others wild, too – the thought that if they loved him with sufficiently hysterical abandonment, he might begin to match with deeds the passionate colouring of his first, verbal overtures. So, perhaps, even as I sat there in Charlotte Street, unable to eat, and thinking that Hunter might be able to shed light upon the problem of Anne's unhappiness, his mind was really occupied with the edition of 'Perspectives'. And if this was the case, and if, as I now believe, he had only half wanted Anne to be his lover (and that for mixed motives, such as we all might have), it is perhaps not surprising that I did not during that meal sense him as a rival. This is not to say that he was not my rival, nor that, only shortly after that meal, I came to hate him quite violently. But at that juncture, I saw him only as a friend, and also, ludicrously, as an expert on the Lampitts. It was in that capacity that I had sought him out; it was in that capacity, therefore, that I saw him.

From the many comments on his work already passed by Sibs, Sargie and the other Lampitts, it is a little surprising that I still thought of Hunter as the great Lampittologist.

'He just gets us wrong,' giggled Ursula mirthlessly to me during a later phase of existence, dining at her austere high table. 'The whole feel of us is wrong. We don't *smell* like Lampitts in his pages. And that sense that he gives off of Jimbo being the malicious sort of' – giggle – 'bachelor, if you know what I mean. But it wasn't fair; Jimbo could be the kindest man in the world. Of course you only have to read his descriptions of Angelica to see that Mr Hunter didn't have a clue! "True blue" – for Angelica, who was almost as communistic as Vernon! And as for the suggestion that Angelica might have married Rupert Brooke! Well, one day you must get me to tell you the story of her and Hilda Bean.'

But most of us are slow, I certainly am, to dispute self-confessed expertise. I still believed in Hunter's knowledge and understanding of the Lampitts, and valued him precisely because he had considered the family from a dispassionate, academic viewpoint. He had an encyclopaedic knowledge of all Anne's relations. I myself had grown up with firsthand knowledge of what Sargie could be like if – in the surely unfair Rectory phrase – 'he chose' to be difficult. Choice was probably the last thing which came into play on these occasions; Anne's sudden mood swing against me could surely be put down to what Uncle Roy called 'the very mildly barmy strain in the Lampitts'.

On the other side of the table, Hunter disposed of a plateful of moussaka with clean, systematic forkwork. I had no appetite at all, and however much I played with my heaps of food they did not seem to diminish in size, or in nauseating unpalatability. 'If in doubt give them mince': one of Aunt Deirdre's 'mottos' appeared to be the view of the Greeks, if the limited menus of their nastier restaurants were anything to go on. I preferred my aunt's grey, rather watery shepherd's pies to this oily pile of cheese and gristle.

'I'm only sorry,' said Hunter, 'that I shan't be there for your party.' He was reverting to the publication day of my novel. 'Madge, as I'm sure you realise, likes any opportunity for a little gathering.'

'I'd assumed you'd be there.'

'I'd love to, but it's a "Perspectives" night.'

'Of course.'

I had rather hoped that Hunter would invite me on to 'Perspectives' to publicise the book, but presumably the decisions about whom to have on such programmes was left in the hands of organisers other than Hunter himself. Now, rather than allow myself to nurse feelings of resentment at my non-inclusion, I began to feel that it was somehow clumsy of me to publish a book on a 'Perspectives' night. I started to apologise, and say how much I owed him. Then I went on to say how much I had always enjoyed his visits to our flat, what a good friend he had always been to both of us, to Anne as well as myself.

Hunter ceased to look at me straight. His eyes, which were rather small for that round, pasty face, developed a narrow, weasely expression which at the time I read as telepathic concern for my marital problems.

'I'm a bit worried about Anne actually,' I added. 'She doesn't seem quite herself these days.'

Hunter pursed his lips.

'You've no idea why?' he asked. Here his sidelong glance became so oblique that he stopped looking at me altogether; in fact, he turned and looked out of the window. The moment of possible intimacy passed by. From an intense desire to confide I suddenly felt embarrassed at myself and drew back from the abyss. Instincts of marital decency reasserted themselves. One doesn't speak of such secrets, even to a very close friend like Hunter.

'I think it may be that she finds it hard to be married' – there was a pause before I dared to finish the sentence with ponderous self-conceit – 'to a novelist.'

Visible relief had passed over Hunter's face when he swung round, faced me once more and laughed.

It stings me to contemplate what lay behind Hunter's laugh. There was something in it of whooping, almost obscene relief.

He must have come to the restaurant with near certainty that he would be confronted by the young man he was cuckolding. At the very least, the man would expose him as a liar; but perhaps worse would follow – scenes of violence. These were still the days when such an incident could conceivably have cost Hunter his job at the BBC, an organisation which at that date resembled a large Victorian family, prepared to turn a blind eye to its children's lapses from propriety so long as they weren't found out. Had Hunter been cited as a co-respondent in a divorce case, it is not impossible that his future as the presenter of 'Perspectives' would have been jeopardised. These and perhaps a dozen other fears explained Hunter's anxious looks. When my words made it clear that I was completely ignorant of his relations with Anne, it is hardly surprising that his mouth opened with such triumph. When it did so, I had a few seconds of surprise that his rat-like little teeth had gone quite black since I last noticed them. Then I realised that their sharp yellowish surface was coated with particles of the spinach which he had eaten as an accompaniment to his minced lamb. Recovering himself, dabbing his lips with a napkin, he was able to pontificate in general terms.

'I do believe that husbands and wives find it difficult to come to terms with their partners writing fiction, but then I am hardly in a position to say, never having written a novel, and of course' – he rubbed his plate with a piece of pitta bread which he put into his mouth and chewed. When the bread had gone down, he finished his sentence: 'I am a bachelor.'

During his laughter, my desire to unburden myself to Hunter of my private sorrows left me for ever. Hunter, instinct at least told me, was not that sort of friend. It was something of a relief to both of us, I think, when a man whom I did not know came over from some other table in the restaurant and spoke to Hunter while he was signing the bill.

'Well, I've got a very full week, Dick,' said Hunter.

'I know,' said the man called Dick. 'I know. I shouldn't bother you if I did not think it was important but if we could meet for half an hour before the meeting . . .'

Evidently they were fellow members of a committee. Hunter's eyes had lit up at the prospect of some behind-the-scenes manoeuvring. Needless to say I remember very little of his conversation with the man Dick, but for the first time then since the beginning of our grown-up phase of friendship, I felt the difference between our ages. This committee chat was real grown-up stuff. I could not imagine a condition, nor a state of mind, when I might be interested in such things.

'I think it might be as well,' said Hunter, 'if I rang her *before* the meeting, actually, Dick. I'm sure she'll vote our way, but I don't want her to be influenced by all that emotional blackmail that Jonquil can produce at times.'

He was too remote from my juvenile difficulties to understand them. Perhaps, though, I had begun once more to be wary of him; the spell of enchantment which he had cast over me, really ever since I saw him on television, that night I fell in love with Anne, was beginning to evaporate; once more I became mindful of those occasions when he had been unscrupulous or manipulative.

'No, no, Dick,' he was saying. 'Don't whatever you do, do that! We don't want this as a named item on the agenda. It is the sort of thing we should spring on them during Any Other Business.'

In a brief flickering one saw how he loved to exercise power, and instinct made me shy from allowing him to exercise power over us. Later, when I told Anne that I had lunched with Hunter, she received the information stonily.

'I thought you'd envy me,' I said, never tiring of the worn-out banter. 'Lunch with Raphael – what greater bliss?'

There were two minutes of absolute silence broken only by the scratch and hiss of Anne's match against the side of its box as she lit up a cigarette. She had lately switched to Du Maurier, her mother's preferred brand.

'You're smoking too much,' I said.

She curled her stockinged feet beneath her haunches on the chair and opened a German grammar. Her only response to my observation about her smoking habits was to flick a bit of ash on to the carpet. I began another tack, and spoke of the publication of my novel, whether or not I should offer Madge dinner after the 'small gathering' in her office about six o'clock on the day the book came out. In my mind, I had no doubt what one of Madge's 'small gatherings' would be like. I had built up the party in my mind so much that my feelings of excitement and anxiety relating to this social event overshadowed my feelings about the book. Madge 'knew everyone'. This fact excited me, but it was also terrifying that she might have included among her guest list figures of such fame, or eminence, that I should be overwhelmed by embarrassment. I wanted a touch of chic on my great day, but I was anxious that Madge would wheel out the really big guns. At the same time, I secretly yearned for the greatest guns of all, and wondered, if she invited some of the luminaries with whom Hunter spent his time, whether or not I should soon be dwelling in unapproachable light, not merely in the literary world, but among such social divinities as Mrs Eggscliffe or Lady Mary Spennymoor.

At the same time I was aware of this change in myself, the substitution of pure snobbery for artistic ambition. When I walked out of Tempest and Holmes, I had wanted life to contain more than pay slips and ledgers. I had wanted time on my own, not time doled out to me by an employer. I had been led on in part by a sense of life's sacredness, that it was too good to waste. These feelings had not been defeated by a half-fearful longing for social advancement; but there was the danger that, like Uncle Roy, I was going to use what imaginative gifts I possessed in building up a hierarchical vision of the human race fed by fantasy. In such a state of mind, the Lampitts themselves, and my marital connection with them, seemed to be a mere resting-ground before I pressed on to the higher reaches. And there was much less innocence in this than in Uncle Roy's highly localised and particular devotion to the Lampitts themselves. He genuinely believed that they were the most interesting beings in the universe. Mr Attlee had been of interest not because he was the Prime Minister but because he had enjoyed the inestimable privilege of having Vernon in his Cabinet. Had he been on terms with the Queen herself, Uncle Roy would have found the fact exciting only in so far as Lampitt connections could have been forced; Majesty, no less than any other individual, would have been treated to 'appropriate' Lampitt tales, the extraordinarily amusing occasion when Vernon's father had been to the palace to collect his peerage from her grandfather George V, or the good fortune enjoyed by that monarch and Queen Mary to reside for some of the year at Sandringham, not three-quarters of an hour by car from Mrs Lampitt of Timplingham, and nearer still to Lord Lampitt's residence at Mallington Hall.

But my mind was possessed of something less pure. It wasn't, or I told myself that it wasn't, respect for rank or blood for their own sake. It was the world of literate and intelligent London which with my baser self I dreamed of conquering; but the yearning itself, like some unwholesome erotic impulse, brought with it a sense of self-loathing so strong that I looked about for another person to blame, rather as an unhappy homosexual might blame the individual who first opened his eyes to the existence of the underworld where his tastes might be indulged. I had not been like this before I met Anne. That was a new stick to beat her with. She had corrupted me. Since, by now, we were barely on speaking terms, I could not choose to enter into the matter with her, but the case for the prosecution built itself up, silently, inside my head. Nothing could have been less fair. I don't believe that Anne ever cared 'who' anyone was. As far as that circle of the heavens was concerned in which Hunter was a bright star, I do not think she even realised that it was meant to be important or impressive. When I first met her, she read little modern literature and I am sure that it had never occurred to her that one might be excited to meet the authors of books one admired. She found the newspapers and politics a bore, so that those hostesses who, like Lady Mary Spennymoor, had married newspaper proprietors and liked to entertain the more presentable members of the House of Commons, together with writers, musicians, or actors, would have carried no weight at all with Anne. That Sibs was a contemporary, and even a bit of a friend, of Lady Mary's (less friendly with Mrs Eggscliffe) was hardly Anne's fault; nor was the fact that, all along, I had been more excited by these facts than I cared to admit.

The approaching 'gathering' was supposed to precipitate me into these worlds by my own steam, or, indirectly, by Hunter's smoke and wind. The very fact that I could, if I had been less shy of doing so, easily have asked Sibs herself to introduce me to these ladies gave me the savage wish to do it all on my own.

Can that really be right? I write these words, but the strange thing is, I can't really remember what I felt. Now, all these figures have passed into history. I never did belong to this world, which I found at that time so alluring, though many members of it came my way, and sometimes younger people will ask for my memories of the 'famous'. Newspaper articles and books have been written about the 'circles' of Mrs Eggscliffe and Lady Mary Spennymoor. Certainly as a young man I believed these circles to exist. If someone, such as Hunter, would take me by the hand, like Virgil leading Dante through the purgatorial regions, it would have been possible in my belief to know that you had arrived in a particular trough or domain of fixed beings. And what modern researchers into the period find so hard to recognise is that it was not truly like that; no world was ever as fixed as a Dantean circle; and even when these hostesses wished to make their drawing rooms into *salons* along a continental pattern, few of their friends, one is almost tempted to write 'their clients', took such ambitions seriously. Anyhow, it seems upon looking back and trying to remember the rare occasions when I was entertained by such figures that they introduced me to the very least interesting people I ever knew, not one of whom was as much fun as the Best-Seller, or Pete or Cyril or Fenella and Rikko, still less interesting than Darnley, Bloom, or Aunt Deirdre and Uncle Roy.

But I was different then. I can write that, but it is hard for me to recapture the reasons, the inner promptings which awakened this rather unworthy set of social aspirations. They mean nothing to me now, just as my love for Anne means nothing. All those feelings have gone. This narrative, this framing of the actions and sensations of an earlier self, has been for me a rediscovery of Blake's view that 'the inner world is all-important . . . each man has a world within, greater than the external'. If I had ever done anything which had merited someone writing the story of my life, the biographer would perhaps be able to tell my story at this juncture quite neatly. A short chapter would suffice to describe how, having left the shirt factory, I tried my hand at literature and drama. My novel and the date of its publication could be chronicled. As for acting, few enough roles came my way, and had it not been for Nicholas Gore (my agent) getting me a little work in radio drama I would not have been employed at all. The Black Bottle was still my main source of income. I now worked there two evenings a week as well as most lunchtimes. Such were the external facts. A more probing biographer might have been able to discover that this was the period when Anne was so in love with Hunter, and such a writer could weigh the pros and cons of whether the pair ever actually slept together. I can't make up my mind about that. When I found out about them, it was the thought of their lovemaking which obsessed me to the point of actual nausea. Visions of Anne, ecstatic as she had once been with me, her bare legs clasped behind Hunter's back, would send me retching to the nearest bathroom. But this lay a little in the future. What my biographer would never be able to convey (since there is no written evidence for it) is the fact that those particular weeks were dominated not by any outer shape of what was happening so much as by the feeling of interior desolation which gnawed at my heart.

'They change completely as soon as you get them back from the registry office and untie the gift wrapping,' Pete used to say, stabbing an ashtray with his Park Lane butt.

'My wife is the most selfish, the most voraciously cruel person I know,' the Best-Seller would say. 'Old Karamazov' – pronounced 'Carrer-marzoff' – 'had nothing on her for naked, bestial unkindness.'

'Why do you think they are all queuing up for punishment?' Mr Porn would spit out. 'So many happily married men – who would have thought it? It's because they are all bloody masochists. Believe me, there's no torture they could devise for you down at our place at Frith Street which could rival the horrors of an ordinary suburban marriage. Barbed wire? Chains? Dildos? Golden showers? It's nothing to the day-to-day, hour-by-hour knowledge that you're stuck with them, the bitches, with all their moods and their bloody relations and their . . .'

'They reveal sides of themselves' – Peter again – 'you never saw until the marriage lines have been scribbled on. "I hate the smell of cigarettes." That's what Helen said to me.'

'Wife number three,' Cyril glossed.

'The very hour, the very fucking minute, we got back from the registry office, I lit up in the hotel where we were having the party and she told me she didn't like the smell of cigarettes. I told her, you've known me six weeks, you silly cow, and you wait till now to say you wish I didn't smoke. She told me she'd hoped I'd change.'

'What I will never forgive my wife for is this' – with automatic hand the Best-Seller held out his whisky glass for replenishment while with his other hand he raised the beer to his lips – 'humiliating me, quite deliberately, in front of my children.'

All the faces on the other side of the bar at the Bottle were telling the same story, whether it was the regulars or other lonely characters who came in just once to echo the chorus.

410

During all our spell of courtship and early marriage, it had never once occurred to me that these stereotypical expressions of disillusionment were anything more than a sort of comedy, produced like ribald jokes or salted peanuts as an inevitable accompaniment to pub drinking, but in no way relevant either to the human condition in general or to myself in particular. The discovery, now that I had myself belatedly removed the gift wrapping, that Anne had changed completely was by far the most important thing which had yet happened to me, and I listened to the old soaks at the bar with a growing sense of horror that they spoke from the heart. What they said corresponded to what I had suffered. When she was her old self, I had been totally incredulous that anyone could speak in this unenlightened way of women. Had they never been friends with a woman? Anne and I were the best of friends and surely always would be. I could not conceive of speaking about her in the way that Pete or Day Muckley described their spouses. That was before Anne became the truculent, cruelly silent chain-smoking companion of latter days. Day after day it went on. She was usually out when I got home. In the mornings she would leave early to go to the library or the Courtauld, her mind supposedly engaged with thoughts about Winterhalter. What went on, now always in darkness, in our bedroom, had started to become horrible, leaving feelings of unfathomable gloom. In daylight hours, our eyes hardly ever met. She was sadly remote, even a little mad. Already I began to understand the bar-stool confessions. In my early months at the Bottle it was a source of wonder to me that anyone could be so disloyal as to describe their most intimate relationships to strangers. Now, the impulse to tell someone, to find a sympathetic ear, simply to get help, was very strong. If help could by the nature of the case not be found, then at least I might find an ear. Hunter, in the restaurant, had obviously been the wrong choice of confidant.

Sometimes, when surfacing from the very worst pain of the problem and seeing that it was, must be, Anne's sorrow as well as mine, I thought of airing it with the family. As well as disliking Sibs and knowing that she disliked me, I also got on with her quite well, if the contradiction can be understood. I had more in common with her, in some ways, than I did with Anne. In retrospect I have come to share Uncle Roy's admiration for Sibs, even if his idea that she was of a submissive temperament remains unaccountable. If Anne had developed swollen legs, or glaucoma, or the symptoms of a duodenal ulcer, it would have been entirely unnatural not to mention the matter to her mother in the hope that the best medical advice could be procured. Might it not be that this slamming of doors, these long silences, this alternation of irrational anger and tearful frigidity, constituted a problem that was in essence medical? No mother would relish being told by a son-in-law that her daughter was round the twist, and one risked the retort, if the diagnosis were accepted, 'Whose fault is that?' But wasn't this an obvious source of help – even in Sibs's brisk way of comfort?

The trouble was, as I remembered on one of Sibs's impromptu visits to our flat, that none of her offspring had any defects whatsoever. Where their characters showed variations from the normal which in others might have been a cause of disapproval, Lady Starling pursued one of two vigorous courses. The first, and simpler, way was to deny that the alleged fault existed. But her more usual tactic was to pounce on anyone (her husband included) who dared to see fault in her children. She would not deny, when in this mood, that they had the characteristics described; she would merely deny that there was anything wrong with the quality complained of. It is true that her son Michael (always called Youngmichael, as if one word, by Uncle Roy to distinguish him from his uncle Michael, who had been 'one of the kindest men I ever knew') was notoriously stingy. Sibs's response to this would be to ask: 'If a young man in the city with a jolly good job and a jolly good income can't be careful with his money, where does that leave the spendthrifts?' This aggressively expressed viewpoint sounded almost like logic when Sibs said it, and certainly had the tendency to silence opposition if only by making your head spin. The ability of her other son, Gavin, to reduce dinner tables to silence, either by his own silences or by the unvarying tedium of his few chosen utterances, was hailed by Sibs as a positive social attraction. Hostesses should, his mother implied, be falling over themselves to get Gavin as a spare man at their table. 'He didn't say one word all evening to the boring woman on his left, who should blame him, and to that absurd Amanda Harding he spoke only of stocks and shares. Mary was furious, but I think it was just a scream!' That was the last time Gavin was ever entertained by Lady Mary Spennymoor, and it was to be hoped that Mrs

Harding did not take his advice about the shares. When he gave detailed advice to Ursula about her college portfolio she involved her Fellows in a considerable financial loss. 'I think it did those dons no harm at *all* to pull in their horns,' said Sibs at the time. In short, we were living in a world where the moral absolutes had been abandoned, or in some cases actually reversed, for the benefit of Lady Starling's children. Logic did not come into the question, since Sibs felt perfectly free to criticise her children mercilessly and without stopping. But it was quite a different thing for another person to detect their faults. It was difficult then to raise the matter of Anne's near-lunatic manifestations of depression without implied criticism, and sentences beginning 'I'm worried about Anne' died inside my head.

Sibs looked as ever rather magnificent when she called round. She wore a tweed suit with a little dark blue velvet collar and very good black patent leather shoes tied with ribbons in bows.

'She's never at home, that girl,' she remarked of her daughter.

'Not often.'

'Isn't that marvellous – doesn't do a bit of housework!' Lady Starling gestured to the brimming ashtrays and unfolded newspapers, clues that Mrs Wiley was with her brother in Bridport, 'and always at work on this thesis or whatever it's called.'

'It is called a thesis.'

'It's pure Lampitt, my dear, like Gavin working late at the office. Do you know the cleaners can't get in to do his carpet until nine o'clock at night sometimes? They wanted to knock off and go home without cleaning his office but he wasn't standing for that, lazy brutes. Then they had the cheek to ask him if he could just move out for half an hour while they did it. People's *cheek* since the war! Anne's a bit the same. Very single-minded.'

This new explanation for Anne's behaviour, a purely genetic tendency to work at unsocial hours, became momentarily attractive, and my mind briefly seized on it as possible. I felt a few seconds of exaltation and relief, followed by worse sorrow than before when I realised that Sibs was talking nonsense.

The real reason for Sibs's visit was to announce the triumphant conclusion of her master plan. It had somehow become hers, even though she had had nothing to do with finding Virgil D. Everett Jnr; no one had exactly asked how the contact had

413

first been made, and all subsequent negotiations had in fact been orchestrated by Sargie and the Piece of Dry Toast. This did not prevent Sibs from seeing herself as solely responsible for the coup by which Jimbo's papers were delivered out of Hunter's flat and into the offices of Denniston and Denniston, as the first stopping post on their irrevocable journey to the United States.

'I think that's the last we'll see of that little man!' she said triumphantly, a Boadicea exultant over the Roman slain. Sibs took the not unreasonable view that Hunter's meteoric rise to fame was owing entirely to his having filched Jimbo's papers from Sargie and made out of his essentially innocuous life the scurrilous fantasy entitled *Petworth Lampitt: the Hidden Years*. At the moment of her visit to the flat, her opinion would have embarrassed me since I still thought that I admired Hunter; but I never specifically disbelieved Sibs's version of things. Nor did the fact that Hunter's ambitions were puny and dull change the force of her argument. He had wanted to *get on*. No doubt, ambition should be made of sterner stuff than to be president of the PEN Club, or a spokesman for the arts on the less entertaining television programmes. But if that is the chosen field, then, however odd the choice, it is probably as good as any other in which to exercise power. Nor were Sibs's destructive views modified by the view taken by Sargie, and by myself, that if it had not been Jimbo's diary, it would have been something else which gave Hunter his leg up in the world.

'He'd have used someone else, my dear, if he hadn't used me, old Lover Boy would.' Thus Sargie, and his sister would snap back, 'Sargie, that isn't the point.'

She was right. It wasn't. It was understandable, now that she had heard that the Lampitt Papers were in the hands of the lawyers, that she should rejoice.

'Mr Everett is coming over to London in a few weeks' time,' she said. 'Mary Spennymoor knows him a bit and says he's an absolute sweetie, not at all the brash sort of American, quite nice suits, she says, and soft-spoken. We'll have a private dinner and you and Anne must come. We might even lure Roy to the capital. He'd like a real gathering of Lampitts.'

'He'd love to come. Only wouldn't it be awkward if Sargie were there?'

'Feuds are so silly. I'm often wanting to ask Cecily to things and then can't because Sargie refuses to see her. He just walks out of the room if she's there. And now there's an embargo on Roy. Oh, I had the most divine letter from Roy the other day, and he really does know more about my family than I do myself. It's too extraordinary. I've got these cousins in Mombasa, haven't ever met most of them, and it's years since I saw Pam – when she was over in London before the war. My mother knew them all, of course, and since she died your Roy writes to them all. Well, he'd heard from Stephen – you know, Pam's eldest – the other day and it appears that Jimbo went to Africa. I never knew that. I bet Mr Hunter never knew it.' She really hissed the last sentence.

'I think I'd heard before from my uncle,' I said. 'There was a story about his not knowing which way to point a gun.'

'Oh, and guess!' she said. 'Rumours have reached Roy from Mallington that Vernon of all dotties wants to drop his peerage and go back to the House of Commons. Gavin says it's totally impossible, if you inherit a title you're stuck with it, and I'm sure he's right but apparently there are a number of the more Bolshie peers wanting to do it.'

'Has Uncle Roy been over to Mallington?'

'Apparently. Vernon had a lunch for the Red Dean – well, you know he doesn't know any clergy, church was never the Lampitt thing. Rupert says that Vernon really wants to be the leader of the party. Our house'll become a commune. No harm in that, I suppose, but Vernon is extreme. And Sargie's as bad.'

'I thought he'd given it up.'

'Oh, he *says* frightful things about the Idiot People, but deep down he's the same as Comrade Vernon. Well, we *all* support the Labour Party, always have, always will.'

I don't know why, but this came as a surprise to me. I knew that old Lord Lampitt was a Labour peer, and from Uncle Roy I had imbibed the view that uncomplicated Toryism of Aunt Deirdre's kind was vaguely common. At the same time, I had never supposed that Sibs had seen herself as a supporter of the movement. A house in Cadogan Square, sons in the City, a husband like Rupert, did not to me suggest a particularly radical political standpoint. It was all the more surprising when she added, 'Rupert's the reddest of the lot if the truth were known – which of course it can't be, because he's a civil servant.'

This indiscretion had the appearance of being blurted out accidentally: but Sibs was an odd mixture of schoolgirl frankness and Machiavellian guile. One never knew, with what Rupert Starling called her gaffes, whether the information apparently conveyed by mistake had not been planted in one's mind quite deliberately; though it was hard to see then why she should have wanted me to know her husband's economic or political views, or indeed anything else about him.

'Isn't it marvellous, though, the way Roy keeps up with us all,' she resumed her earlier theme, 'hardly ever straying from Norfolk, but knowing everything. It's made all the difference since Mama died.'

Mention of Uncle Roy occasioned pangs of guilt. It was months since I had written to him and Aunt Deirdre. If Sibs herself had not insisted upon it, the week after our wedding, I wonder if I would ever have got round to telling them that I was married. My guilt about not telling them during the weekend that Anne and I went down to stay should have spurred me into keeping in closer touch. Instead, it distanced me from them. It is so silly when I look back on it. I don't suppose that Uncle Roy or Aunt Deirdre would have wanted to see much of me. A regular letter and a visit every month or so would have been very easy to keep going. As it was, unable to aspire to some ideal of family intimacy inside my own brain, and full of self-reproach whenever I thought about them, I had more or less cut my uncle and aunt altogether. I also formed the view, based on nothing at all, that they violently disapproved of my marriage, thought it hasty, precipitate, juvenile. They had never said that was their opinion. Had Anne and I continued to be happy, perhaps we should have developed a regular routine of visits to Norfolk. As things turned out, I was anxious to keep secret the misery in which Anne and I were now engulfed. It was quite unmentionable by rectory codes. I had been brought up by them to keep things to myself, to play my cards close to the chest.

'There are some things we just don't talk about,' Aunt Deirdre had said once. She was explaining, or not explaining, why she disliked the Wretched Woman, that is to say the novelist Deborah Arnott, who had for a while lived in our village and exercised no such conversational restraints. Politics or the secrets of emotional life (her own and other people's) were merrily and openly discussed by the Wretched Woman, in the course of shopping or queuing at the post office. For years, I accepted my aunt's belief that everyone in the village, the

416

butcher, the subpostmistress, the fishmonger, the man in the fruit and vegetable van, all disliked the intrusion of Deborah Arnott (Debbie Maddock in those days) into those areas about which One Didn't Talk. In retrospect I could find no evidence of this universal disapproval. Debbie was an open-hearted, intelligent young woman whom everyone liked and no one (that I could see) shared my aunt's ill-defined but sharply held sense of conversational boundaries beyond which it was improper to stray. The 'things' not talked about included all the aspects of life which for most of the time occupy our thoughts – sex, religion, friendship, the behaviour of immediate neighbours, politics. It may have been one of the reasons why Uncle Roy developed his habit of making all conversations concern the Lampitts since this was a way of talking about forbidden subjects in a cipher. Over the Suez crisis, for example, I am sure that my uncle and aunt were divided. Aunt Deirdre had once blushingly agreed with Felicity when she said that she thought Anthony Eden the handsomest man in the world. This was years before the Egyptian crisis blew up, but I guessed that she vigorously supported British intervention in North Africa. When our troops set out for Egypt, she remarked that 'the Yanks are always unreliable – look at all the girls in this neighbourhood who got led a dance by GIs'. This seemed to suggest that the campaign should proceed in Egypt, regardless of international disapproval. And, more evidence, once when hearing Nasser's name on a wireless bulletin, a few minutes before 'The Mulberrys' started, she had uttered the word 'twerp'.

Uncle Roy was really a pacifist and as a true Lampittite he was to the left of the political spectrum. He certainly viewed the Suez affair with dismay, but it was not quite safe to say so when sharing his house with so convinced a patriot as my aunt. The formula of the Lampitt anecdote here came into its own. Instead of saying 'I think such and such' (and any sentence which began *I think* was in danger of entering the conversational Out of Bounds), he could recount Vernon's view that Nasser was 'in his way a perfectly good chap'. The late Mrs Lampitt's watercolours of the Pyramids provided their own oblique commentary on the international crisis, as did Sargie's knowledge of international law. On the worst night of the crisis, when it really looked as if world war might begin, I had come home for the weekend; it was when I was still working at Tempest and Holmes.

'What people always forget about the Canal,' Uncle Roy said, 'is that when Disraeli built it, one of the chief engineers they consulted was Roland Brown. Absolutely brilliant man.'

I had not long since been discharged from the army and was dreading what seemed like the certainty, now that war had come again, that I should have to go back into uniform. I did not quite understand why Roland Brown's name was being raised. I had never heard of him; nor, I think, had Aunt Deirdre, nor Granny, nor Felicity, as we sat round listening to the set. Brown's brilliance, with that of others, had provided a shorter trade route to the Indian Ocean from the Mediterranean. The wealth of Empire had grown up on it. Now, as we all came to terms with the fact that there was no Empire, it made a sort of emblematic sense that the Canal should be closed again by the Egyptians to show us our place in the world. But that wasn't what Uncle Roy had meant. Even as the excited news-reader tried to tell us that Britain and France were in danger of fighting a war without the support of their other allies, my uncle's mind was fixed on more important things. There was a greater providence which brought to pass more wonderful happenings than the waxing and waning of empires, or the moving of great ships beneath a foreign sky. We did not during that bulletin catch the crucial bit of news about the failure of the campaign, because Uncle Roy was talking.

'Roland Brown. Brilliant man. I hardly need say that he married Hypatia, Sargie's great-aunt.'

Sibs's great-aunt, too. I thought of the incident, a couple of years later, as Sibs stood there in my sitting room.

'Well,' she said, 'I don't know what you're smirking at. There's nothing funny about the Labour Party.'

'Oh, I don't know about that, Sibs.'

'Well, if Anne's not here, I must love you and leave you.'

Since I had become a member of her family, Sibs had taken to giving me dry little pecks on the cheek.

'I'll tell Anne you called.'

'So I'd expect. Funny thing to say. You're not on No Speaks or anything are you? *Don't* be.'

I resented her ability to get to the heart of the matter. I still hoped, assuming that our deep unhappiness, Anne's and mine, would blow over. The idea of it being known in the family became suddenly horrifying, not because it was embarrassing but because it made it all so much more real.

'She'll be thrilled to know that Mr Everett is finally coming to collect Jimbo's junk,' said Sibs in valediction. 'No, I'll let myself out at the front door, don't bother to come down. All stacked and stored in nice Mr Denniston's office.'

She was still talking about the safe storage of the Lampitt Papers as she walked down the stairs. The fate of Jimbo's junk was of indifference to me, but it was not without importance in the short remaining history of my marriage. Later that evening, when Anne came home, I broke the silence by telling her that her mother had called and that Virgil D. Jnr would soon be in London.

'I wouldn't mind seeing his art collection,' she said. 'He collects pictures as well as manuscripts. He's got Renaissance stuff (a Filippo Lippi), as well as nineteenth- and twentieth-century: some Henry Wallises, two Winterhalters, and a large number of Tukes.'

'How d'you know what he's got?'

This provoked more silence. It was not a restful silence, but a jarring space in which one felt that terrible things could have been said, but were being held back for reasons yet more terrible. These sessions of non-saying caused such pain in the mind that they drove one's power of thought awry. The natural thing would have been to repeat Sibs's expression of delight that all the diaries were now safe with the lawyer. The Piece of Dry Toast had assured her of this. I certainly did not withhold the information from Anne. Considering the pain it caused in the next half-hour, I should have done anything to spare myself the lie which then fell from her lips.

To my eyes she was looking more beautiful than ever before as she sat there on the uncomfortable sofa, her stockinged feet curled up beneath her haunches. Her eyes were always averted from me so that one saw her face in new three-quarter profiles which had not been visible so often in the days of our happiness when she looked me in the eye. Her mouth was perfect as it jutted out and said, crossly but calmly, 'I've still got weeks of work on those diaries before I can move them from Raphael's flat.'

A ghastly blush spread over her face as she said these words. I suspect that they were the first lie she had ever told in her life.

She is so intelligent that I wonder whether she did not tell this easily penetrable untruth in order to be discovered. That was not how it felt, however, in the instant of her speaking. One talks of being stunned by information and it is assumed that mere metaphor is intended. On this occasion the experience of being lied to was almost like a physical blow. An instant before and I should have said that Anne was incapable of untruth. Now she was deceiving me. I knew that Jimbo's diaries were in Lincoln's Inn Fields. She told me that she would be occupied for weeks ahead, sorting them in Hunter's flat. The exact truth, so staringly obvious when one recalls it, did not dawn. I still did not realise that she was spending her time with Hunter. All I knew was that she had lied; she was providing herself with an excuse to be out of our flat for limitless hours. That could only mean that she was seeing another man. It makes sense to say that I was stunned because it really felt as if I had been hit. In one blow, Anne's mysterious behaviour all made sense, her distance, her bad temper, her dreaminess, the sense that she obviously did not love me any more. She was having an affair.

I ran from the room and just reached the bathroom in time to kneel, abject and reeling, with my head in the lavatory pan. When I emerged, Anne was still sitting there in the same position on the sofa. Her hair was loose these days, she no longer had the ponytail. The lamplight behind it made it seem as though her head was haloed. She was sucking a pencil and concentrating on German grammar. It was all the same scene which I had left, but now I looked out at it all from a cage of pain. The dull depression which had hung over me in previous months was nothing to this lacerating horror.

She looked up and said, 'You look terrible. Have you been sick?'

I nodded some sort of assent.

'Julian, it's just *silly* drinking so much.'

It is not quite possible to put into words what I felt for her then. It was because I loved her so much that she had such power to hurt; it was because she hurt me so much that I so hated her. My sense of rejection and humiliation was total.

'Where are you going?' she called after me; and, important afterthought, 'Have you got a key?'

It was a good question, where I was going, and I can't answer it now. For the next few days I wandered about London and drank too much. Some of the time I returned to the flat to sleep. I don't think I ever slept rough, but I wasn't really bothered where I was. I did not contemplate suicide but I was in a state of mind where I was quite uninterested in self-preservation. When I began to sober up, the thing which caused most pain was having to admit to myself my complete ignorance. I had married a stranger, whom, it now appeared, I did not know in the least. It was now quite obvious to me that she loved someone else, but who that was I couldn't guess. Someone at the Courtauld, presumably, whom I'd never seen. I tortured myself by going back in time and adding up all the evenings and afternoons which Anne and I had spent apart, all the times when she had said that she had to be in the library or, latterly, sorting boxes with Hunter. I had never questioned any of these assertions. Now I questioned them all. Oh, why the shit had she married me if she did not love me? How could someone who seemed so nice, so tomboyishly decent, have been prepared to unleash pain on such a scale? From the perspective from which I now survey it all, there seem many answers to these questions, many ways of exonerating Anne, most of them covered by the simple fact that she was young. She probably intended none of it to happen. She, as much as I, was a victim. She could not help being in love with Hunter, given the circumstances. If she could have avoided torturing me, she would have. But it did not seem like that at the time. I felt shock and fear. I developed feverish symptoms, I couldn't stop shivering and I began to think that I might become really ill. These symptoms never developed into influenza or pneumonia, any more than alcohol could numb my sense that everything, my whole life, was torture.

I spent a couple of nights during this very bad patch sleeping at Rikko's and Fenella's house. Its noisy and over-populated routines helped to swallow up my silent, miserable self-preoc-cupation. Rikko was away in Birmingham recording episodes of 'The Mulberrys', but there were never fewer than eight at meals. The floating population of Fenella's lodgers, friends, ex-lodgers, jabbered comfortingly about their own areas of gossip. The friend of a friend, a member of this group, I forget names, I was drunk half the time that week, brought Elizabeth Darnley to a meal one night. As a particular friend of Anne's, Elizabeth was rather icy with me, but she told me that her brother was living in London permanently now, working on a weekly paper; Darnley

421

had apparently remarked not long before that he had not seen me in ages.

It was a saving remark, this of Elizabeth's, the first thing in over a week of pure mental agony which lifted me out of myself. I felt the genuine curiosity and affection of a friend, wanted to know how Darnley was, what he was up to. Struck by my interest, the next night Elizabeth came back to Fenella's table, bringing Darnley himself, and it was as convivial as could be. For a couple of hours I forgot my sorrows. He was very funny about all his colleagues on the *Rambler*, the weekly where he had landed a job, he was funny about the old days, affectionate about my grandmother. The only point of the evening where satire strayed into malice was when Darnley recalled Bloom in the army. Evidently, the two men were still on quite good terms, but saw each other as rarely as Darnley now saw me. This was one of the sad things which marriage had done, blowing old friendships, as well as happiness itself, sky-high.

The renewal of love for an old friend is one of the most – I should say *the* most – consoling of compensations for the rest of the dud cards which arrive in one's hand with such regularity as the game reaches its dull end. Why had I ever allowed my friendship with Darnley to lapse? 'With thee conversing, I forget all time.' With Darnley I did not want or need to get drunk. The morning after he had been to Fenella's was the first for weeks when I had not woken up with a hangover. I rang Darnley at his office and proposed meeting again that night. He suggested the French pub in Dean Street.

I suppose I'd decided in advance to unburden myself of marital troubles. After all, Darnley had been a witness at our wedding. Week had followed week and we had not seen him. In the first happy year, it was easy to let time pass without friends. By the time nearly a year had gone by, we had got out of the habit of meeting. But Darnley was my oldest friend, and he was the appropriate ear into which to tell my doleful tale.

I got to the pub first, having put in an hour dispensing their medicine to my clients at the Bottle. Darnley turned up at the French about nine, wearing that dark blue gaberdine which seemed almost a conscious allusion to the world of school, and a large brown trilby hat. Beneath the gaberdine were visible rather crumpled grey flannel trousers (again a schoolboyish touch) hitched too short, and revealing pale grey socks which could have been on the Clothes List which had to accompany our return, three times a year, to Seaforth Grange.

'Ginger beer, please,' was his answer to what was he having. The previous night I had seen he drank water. The teetotalism, like the school clothes, was to be a constant feature of Darnley's life and personality from now onwards. Not feeling much like ginger beer myself I ordered a half of bitter.

When we'd found a table, never easy in that overcrowded pub, he produced from his pocket a battered Everyman which he put beside the ashtray.

'Ever read this?' he asked. 'I found it quite by chance the other day on a barrow in the Farringdon Road. Don't know why I bought it really, never been very interested in poetry or anything. But it's one of the most extraordinary books I ever read.'

It was Gilchrist's *Blake*.

It is not a book so obscure that this coincidence demanded explanation in psychic terms. This book which had meant so much to me, and been my companion during the previous twelve months, had become a sort of lifeline to sanity. When plunged into drunken self-pity, or tempted by various manifestations of *snobisme*, the figure of Blake rose up in my imagination like a sort of prophet or redeemer. When I had read some pages of Gilchrist, it was like having a long, relaxing bath. Friendship with Darnley had, over the years, been like this, too. When one's footsteps seemed to be turning badly astray, he seemed capable of redirecting them, not by advice but by what he was. The sort of thing which Hunter, say, or in a different way Sibs took seriously never for an instant tempted Darnley. Though he might have had momentary sympathy with the Devil (as Blake did), he never had any time at all for the world or the flesh, which was why, I suppose, on the one hand he could be so hilariously funny, and on the other suggest disconcerting areas of seriousness. The clergyman's rig in which he had been dressed that night at Fenella's house was not quite as inappropriate as his sister supposed.

We spoke of Blake for about an hour, and found that we liked many of the same things, though Darnley was quite sharp in his distinction between what he called 'the decent stuff and the absolute balls'. I rather enjoyed some of the absolute balls, by which he meant the prophecies, but Darnley liked only the epigrams and the lyrics; yet we were agreed in liking Gilchrist and considering it perhaps the ideal biography. We also, and above all, liked Blake himself, and considered his supposed unworldliness, his lack of interest in anything which smacked of a good career or commercial success, as estimable and something to imitate.

The subject came to a natural conclusion when Darnley fought his way to the bar for drinks. When he came back, I plunged in at once.

'Miles, I'm in a jam.'

'Move around, then, to my side of the table. It's more comfortable than perching on one of those little stools.'

'No, I mean I'm in trouble. We're in trouble. Anne and I.'

He looked down into his ginger beer, visibly embarrassed by this line of talk. Even as schoolboys, we had not gone in for 'confidences'. Anecdotes, yes; if a story about your private life would make the other person laugh, then it was worth telling; but not 'soppy' stuff. I remembered him teasing me for being in love with the art mistress. 'I hate love,' he had remarked at a similar period. Perhaps this was still his position.

'You don't mean money worries?' he said, still peering into the ginger beer. 'I mean, God, I'll give you a cheque.'

Anything, it seemed, to get this embarrassing part of the conversation over.

'Anne's completely changed,' I pressed on. 'It's as if she's gone off her rocker. Do you remember that first evening, the evening you and Elizabeth brought her round to Fenella's house?'

For a split second, a look of sadness flickered over Darnley's features, which then creased into laughter. 'Your friend the great novelist expressed himself rather vividly over that shit Hunter.'

'Why d'you call him a shit?'

'Isn't he one?'

'Anne was so exuberant that evening, so bubbly. So happy. And now we've been married over a year, and she just sits there, staring into space. She's so miserable, Miles.'

'Oh, Hunter's a shit all right,' said Darnley.

I can't guess whether we would have got any further with our conversation had we not been interrupted. I was just about to have another go at telling him of Anne's dishonesty when my eyes became aware, at chair level, of a pair of black moleskin trousers and a little navy blue donkey jacket.

'My darlings,' said Bloom, 'a Cézanne, the pair of you hunched over the tavern table like that. All that is lacking is a clay pipe.'

Had we needed to be private, Darnley and I could have chosen a less popular pub. It was foolish to be angry, as I was, at Bloom's appearance. He and Darnley did not really get on; and Bloom's determinedly frivolous attitude to everything would render impossible a serious unburdening of myself. Somewhat to my surprise, Darnley greeted Bloom with something like rapture, the ship passing the horizon after hours of standing on the beach of the desert island waving his shirt.

'What will you have, William?' he asked.

'Oh, he's in a mood to offer me things,' Bloom cackled. 'No, it's all right, darling, Mother's OK.' He held up a glass of Campari to prove it.

'What a day. What' pause 'a' pause 'day.' Whether we liked it or not, we were going to hear about it, as he settled himself down on the stool beside me. 'I've had sales reps all day, and not in the sense you might think.' His eyes flew aloft and down again. 'On top of which, Mother gets home and finds that Brucie' – his current, I seem to remember fairly temporary, attachment – 'has one of her stomachs. I said to her, darling, you can stay at home with a rice pudding. I'm going out. Just once in a while, Mother's going to enjoy herself. I say, did you ever see such a decorative creature?'

The figure indicated by William's sidelong nod was a rather clumsy-looking labouring man, unshaven for about forty-eight hours, leaning against the bar with a pint of beer in his hand. Blue overalls were spattered with dust and plaster. He was flabby, much addicted, if the double chin and the protuberant gut were reliable guides, to beer and fried potatoes.

'Gorgeous, isn't it,' sighed Bloom, 'but not looking my way, of course. But I say' – he touched Darnley's arm, and dropped the camp voice – 'has Julian told you his news?'

'Well . . .'

'A book about to be published, even though it is with that bitch Madge Cruden. Oh, she's a bitch.' He laughed, his tongue-out laugh. 'And then you've had one or two little acting roles.'

'One, and it was some weeks ago.'

Darnley looked relieved that my 'news' was limited to professional areas of interest.

'It's his real break,' said Bloom in a too-perfect imitation of Fenella. He actually seemed to turn into her. Not only did he capture the timbre of her rumbling cigarettey bass; his face seemed animated by her spirit, and although they did not resemble each other in the least, he was able to suggest her winsome smile.

'Julian's multi-talented. It's just like what David Windsor said to me once when I was staying at the Fort . . .'

'Shut up, Fenella, shut up.'

By now, William was both the Kempes, his finger and thumb rising to his brow in embarrassment, conjuring up Rikko with the same eerie exactitude with which he was able to be Fenella.

'I tell you I knew David *terribly* well, long before . . .'

And we all joined in the chorus of 'Wallis Simpson came on the scene'.

In my wretched condition there was consolation in this childishness. Darnley took no chances, and he rose to his feet while we were laughing in case the conversation swooped once more into a serious mode. He was gone, with a wave of the hand, before I had time to notice he was leaving.

Bloom had bought me some whisky, and almost at once I started to tell him of my marital difficulties. The whole tale poured out of me, Anne's silences and sulks, my feeling that she was no longer all there. I expect Bloom was as embarrassed as Darnley had been, and at first he tried to laugh me out of it.

'Now you know what I go through with Brucie when he gets his bilious turns. Come on, more whisky.'

I laughed at the mention of Brucie because, of course, Bloom's life was comic whereas mine was totally serious. This was quite an achievement of Bloom's, to make his complicated and in some ways sad life an unending melodrama which the rest of the world accepted precisely on the terms presented to them. Viewed neutrally, Bloom's troubles with a difficult partner were no less sad than mine. Even if it had occurred to me to be sympathetic, however, Bloom would not have wanted my sympathy. This did not stop him being extremely sympathetic to me. I had always known instinctively that he was much more grown-up than I was.

'Anne's well, physically?'

'She hasn't said. How should I know?'

'You haven't asked her?'

'We're no longer quite able to speak to each other.'

'It's not Miles, is it?'

'What's not Miles?'

'I don't mean she's necessarily in love with him. She probably never was. He's probably still mad about her, but if people won't say, how's Mother to know what's on their little minds.'

'William, what is this nonsense?'

'Oh, has Mother put her big foot in it again?'

'I'll be back in a minute,' I said.

Standing in the urinals, I tried to meditate on what Bloom was saying. I'd put out of my mind, a year or so ago, the idea of Darnley being in love with Anne. Now I began to contemplate the possibility that they were having an affair. Surely he was too decent for that? I never did quite know what Darnley felt for Anne. Subsequently, it became quite clear to me that they had never been lovers. At the time, though, Bloom's gossipy, heedless remarks opened up new areas of discomfort in my mind which already throbbed with alcohol and terror.

When I emerged from the Gents, Bloom had left our table and was talking to the portly labouring man at the bar.

'Look, dear,' he said to me, 'would you think it frightfully rude of me if I abandon you. You see, Eric and I' – he touched the elbow of his new friend – 'have things to talk about.'

'I was on my way in any case,' I said.

Stepping out into Dean Street, I felt hurt by Bloom's chumming up with the man in overalls. I saw it less as a harmless and inoffensive compulsion and more as a deliberate desire to shake me off. Unhappy marriage had made me into a bore.

The pavements of Dean Street were crowded with people, all pursuing pleasure and none of them caring about me. The lights of the restaurants, the smiles of the prostitutes, the gleam of street-lamps on the wet paving slabs all seemed callous and hard. I wanted love, only love, and that hard-hearted street and the black night sky above my head were cruelly indifferent to my sorrow. It was raining gently. I stood for a while and looked at the tower of the ruined church, St Anne's. The clock on the tower revealed that there were twenty minutes before closing time. With the air of a man turning for home, I retraced my steps

427

to the last refuge of Soho's bores. They were all there when I pushed open the door of the Bottle, Day Muckley, Peter, Mr Porn. Cyril was behind the bar. The saloon wasn't crowded like the French pub.

'You back, cunt face?'

'A large Teacher's, please, Cyril.'

'You're getting to be as much of a piss artist as this lot.'

'The marriage laws, as a matter of fact . . . the marriage laws of the Catholic Church are irrev, irrel, bloody irrelevant,' said Day Muckley.

'They didn't stop you getting a divorce, though,' said Mr Porn.

'Why do we promise for life?' asked Peter, pushing his empty glass towards Cyril and igniting his fiftieth Park Lane of the day. 'If you make friends with a man, you don't promise it's for life. When you both get pissed off with one another, that's it.'

'I got pissed off with you years ago,' said Cyril, handing back the umpteenth gimlet, 'but I'm still stuck with you week in, week out.'

Day Muckley turned on me one of his genuinely beneficent smiles. It felt like the first real kindness I had received in months.

'I don't know what you're doing here with us, lad, I don't really. You're young. You're happily married, very happily married, as a matter of fact. You've got all your life before you. This place is meant for the likes of him and me – yes, you, you drunken bastard,' he said to Mr Porn.

'Not . . . pissed . . . as you,' Mr Porn tried to say.

'No, Julian,' continued the Best-Seller, 'the thing about me is this. I've buggered up absolutely everything. My marriage, my writing, my life. Everything. I've buggered up the whole lot.'

Peter looked across at us and smiled.

'That's very easily done,' he said.

Eight

I can remember that when, years after this particular phase of life was over, Granny lay dying, one was conscious of moving into a different time-scale. The last phase, the deathbed, lasted about a fortnight, but we who sat with her, watching, waiting, no longer measured time by the rising and setting of the sun. Her life was over, and we knew that; but we were far from adapting ourselves to her non-existence. We still instinctively believed that there would be another time when she broke out into laughter at someone's tactlessness to her. ('He said, "You sit there, love, your feet look as though they can't hardly bear the weight." ') Yet, in reality, we knew that she would never again shut her book using her folded reading glasses as a bookmark and then, two minutes later, ask, 'Would some *clever* person find my glasses?' Never again would she shut her eyes and inhale a Craven A as she listened to 'The Mulberrys', her taut, intelligent features concentrating so intensely that she might have been a musicologist determining the rival merits of two interpretations of an intricate violin sonata. (And then, when the programme was over, 'What a lot of rubbish!') We had seen the end of all that made her distinctively herself, but it took two weeks of slow, stupefying resignation to accept this reality. We knew she would die, as we knew that we should all die; but this did not prevent the death, when it occurred, being shocking and almost as surprising as if she had been killed suddenly in the middle of an active life.

Granny's dying, which took place a decade after Anne and I split up, is the best analogy I can find for the stage our marriage had reached in that week of Madge's 'little gathering' for my book. Hindsight makes it obvious by that stage that the marriage was over. At the time it was far from obvious. With the slow but strangely timeless acceptance of a watcher at a deathbed I came to accept, as presumably Anne did, too, that things would never be the same again. Life has such a vivid power to create routines, however, that we adapted to the new regime. We hadn't talked about The Situation. Anne wouldn't and I found that when I tried, I couldn't do so. It was a dark, lonely time for us both. I became acutely conscious (more so, I suspect, than Anne, who is far less vain than I, less interested in the figure she cuts in the world) of how it would all seem to others if they knew the extent of our severance and misery. Our families in particular haunted my fears. How could we break it to Sibs? To Uncle Roy? And, yet more chilling thought, what was it that we would be breaking? Was the marriage truly over? How did we not know that this was just what marriage was like? Plain sailing for the first year or so, and then unmitigated hell, covered up by various wheezes such as friendship with outsiders, or a shared interest in property and children. Maybe what we were going through was what they had all felt, Fenella and Rikko, Sibs and Rupert, Uncle Roy and Aunt Deirdre, only keeping it a secret because they chose not to make a display of it, as my friends down at the Black Bottle liked to do. Just as the figure on a deathbed continues to digest, to function at a minimal physical level, so did we carry on with life. There were a few, often cross, words at breakfast; most of each day we spent apart. If we could avoid doing so, we did not dine together, but it often chanced, still, that we did. Anne was often in a mood, tearful or cross. Largely because there was nowhere else in a small flat for us to sleep, we still shared a bed. Just as by holding the sick person's hand, saying his name, smoothing his brow, the watchers by the bedside half hope that they can bring the dying person back to life, I more than half believed that it would be possible to save the marriage so long as it did not quite cease to exist in carnal terms. Now, when I think of those two young naked figures lying together in the dark, she so unwilling, and he so wounded in his pride, so emotionally stupid, I feel an almost intolerable pity for them both. They do not seem to me like me and Anne but two figures quite separate from ourselves, strangers or even emblems of life's dreadful sadness.

Our daylight selves cannot be recalled without embarrassment. We were both behaving fairly badly, and if unhappiness explains this phenomenon it does not make it any less excruciating to summon to mind. I blush to remember how angry I was with Anne for not taking seriously the publication of the novel. At the time it was for me the most important event in the universe. The day when my six complimentary copies of the book were sent round by the publisher caused in me a frenzy of pride and pleasure.

'Not very big, is it?' Anne said when she saw it. The observation could not have been more humiliating if the organs of regeneration had been under scrutiny.

'Nor is *Candide*, nor is *Rasselas*.'

'A hundred and thirteen pages,' she said literally, turning to the back.

This was no way to judge a work of art. When she went on to say that it was a boring dust-jacket, I could have murdered her. Rosen and Starmer had a policy, congenial to the austere pre-war ambience in which they came to birth, leftist, functionalist, economic, that they had no fancy jackets for their books. All Rosen and Starmer books looked the same, rather as I assumed (quite wrongly) that all books in the USSR looked the same. The same pale green paper, the same Roman lettering in yellow picked out with black, the title, in this case *The Vicar's Nephew*, and underneath, the name of the author. The egalitarian and mean spirit in which this scheme had been drawn up meant that no Rosen and Starmer author was treated above the rest. My name, utterly unheard of, was printed in the same chaste characters as that of their more illustrious authors. For example, they had managed to lure away Bertrand Russell from his usual publishers for a short monograph entitled *Why Civilised Man Rejects the Atom Bomb*. This was produced in exactly the same format as the highly popular Duncan O'Rorke detective stories, or the first volume of Professor Wimbish's *History of the Labour Party*. There was a volume of essays by Lord Lampitt called *I Will Not Cease*, a Blakean promise which Vernon seemed intent on keeping.

There was no doubt that I had joined a pantheon, and I was certain that the little gathering in the offices in Coptic Street would project me into the stratosphere.

> Dream not of other worlds, what creatures there
> Live in what state, condition or degree.

My old schoolmaster Treadmill had more than once quoted these words of the Archangel in Milton's epic, and ever since I had heard them I had known that, like Adam in the poem, I would disobey the advice.

Madge, my editor, whom I admired but could not quite like, had rung about a week before the 'gathering' to enquire if there was anyone I especially wanted to invite. It struck me as rather short notice to put this question since the list of names I had in mind contained those who presumably filled up their engagement books weeks in advance. About the younger stars I was candidly uncertain.

'I don't want people just classifying me as another Angry Young Man,' I said. 'On the other hand, I suppose if you could get John Braine, Kingsley Amis, Colin Wilson . . . '

'You don't understand,' said Madge. I could hear her sighing into the telephone, the schoolma'am exhausted by the attempt to expound Latin syntax to illiterates. 'Is there anyone you know whom you'd like to invite. Your family.'

'I don't think so.'

'Wouldn't they like to come and have a drink in my office?'

Madge, as I was to learn, had strong family feelings. My casual desire to exclude what family I had from the celebrations probably shocked her. Rightly, I now think. I could at least have asked my cousin Felicity down from Oxford. Uncle Roy and Aunt Deirdre had no reason to like the book but even they might have been less hurt by it had I asked them to the 'gathering'. They probably would not have come, but if they had, they could have stayed in a hotel, supped with Aunt Deirdre's friend Bunty, or seen a show. Sensing Madge's disapproval, I tried to read her meaning differently.

'It isn't that they wouldn't *like* your office.'

'I didn't for a moment suppose they'd have an opinion on the matter.' She sounded even crosser now. 'I'd buy you both dinner afterwards but I have to get home to cook for a child. Still it will be nice to meet your wife.'

I was silent.

'Your wife will be coming?'

'Probably.'

There was an icy silence.

'Don't you know whether she's coming?'

'Sort of.'

'We publish her cousin Lord Lampitt. Vernon and I have been

432

friends ever since Spain. His volume of essays has just got a stinking review in the *New Statesman*, you probably saw it.'

'No, no, I didn't. I'm so sorry.'

'That rat Muggeridge.'

'Oh, dear.'

'There's no "Oh, dear" about it, Mr Ramsay. It's the best publicity the book's had.'

It had been foolish of me not to realise that author and publisher could not have hoped for anything nicer than a 'stinking' review.

'I hope I don't get a stinker,' I said.

'We'll have a review here or there if we're lucky.'

When she had hung up, the implications of this dispiriting forecast began to dawn on me. Until Madge said this, I had assumed that all the literary pages would be buzzing with excitement about *The Vicar's Nephew*. I had steeled myself for a few lukewarm comments from hasty reviewers who did not appreciate what I was up to. But if, let us say for the sake of argument, Harold Nicolson or Philip Hope-Wallace did not like the book, there would always have been Cyril Connolly, Philip Toynbee, or Jack Lambert to sing its praises. I was hoping for a notice from Evelyn Waugh in the *Spectator*. Madge's prediction that getting any review coverage at all would be a piece of good fortune must have been intended as comic irony. I had no comprehension of how many dozens of novels poured into a literary editor's office each week; no idea that it was perfectly possible for books to be published and received in blank silence from the critics.

Certainly, on the day of publication, it was a disappointment that none of the newspapers carried notices; I was not at that point to guess that the novel would in fact receive only two reviews. The *Church Times*, towards the end of that year, had a round-up of fiction. It described my biting little satire as 'a quiet comedy of rural life, set in a country rectory'. It conceded that there was a certain 'Old World charm' in my portrait of the eccentric parson and his crosspatch wife but wondered whether there was much originality in my 'reworking of the tired old theme of English middle-class childhood'. There was a more favourable notice in the *Rambler*. It was about two hundred words long and was signed with the initials S.K.C. For some weeks I persuaded myself that this was a dispassionate stranger who had found me 'readable and funny'. Though he never admitted it, I soon guessed that the review was written by Darnley.

On the day of the 'gathering' I had no idea that this would not be the reception of a devastatingly incisive novella, which, in spite of the conventional setting, was in fact disturbingly 'modern'. Old World charm and vicarage comedy were not at all the effects at which I had been aiming; nor had it occurred to me until reading the *Rambler* piece that 'one of the more pleasant aspects of the comedy is the way it rebounds on the narrator. He sets out to guy his clerical relations and only succeeds in writing himself down as an ass.'

'Are you sure you aren't coming?' I asked Anne, one last time, before leaving the flat.

Silence.

'Anne – please?'

'I've said I'm not coming. I hate parties.'

'Oh, *be* like that.'

I slammed the door and walked – since there was so much time – all the way to Knightsbridge tube, taking a Piccadilly line train to Russell Square. There were plenty of minutes during the journey, in which to regret my *be like that*. It was so childish. Each time I expressed anger like that I was farther, as I knew in my deepest heart, from reconciliation. By now I felt that marriage had spoilt everything in my life; not just Anne, but marriage itself was to blame.

'Hebden Bridge is in a valley. You've got steep wooded hillside rising up all around you and if people come along there on a nice day in summer they say, "Eee, isn't it luvly." And what they don't realise, lad, is that Hebden Bridge for ninety-nine per cent of the year is swathed in wet fog. Living there is like being trapped under a bit of wet sack.'

The Best-Seller had once so described his hometown. Marriage cast a similarly dispiriting canopy over my skies. Every experience, however potentially pleasurable in itself, such as this publishing party, had to be snatched from a diurnal pattern of misery. Instead of walking calmly down to the offices of Rosen and Starmer, the literary man coming to meet his colleagues and admirers, I stomped along in a fury with myself for having lost my temper and a fury with Anne for having provoked it. '*She spoils everything'* was the phrase which kept recurring in my mind like a mantra.

I was early for the party. Madge had said to look in at about quarter to six and it was only half-past five. I occupied myself by walking round the block, past the railings of the British Museum and into Bloomsbury Square. It was a muggy summer night with more than a hint of thunder in the air. The large leaves of plane and horse-chestnut rustled menacingly over my head. Then I stopped walking, and I stood still beneath that iron grey sky and bright green foliage, intending merely to notice, from a clock glimpsed through trees on the other side of the square, whether it was time to go in to the party. I was visited by a moment of great strangeness and stillness. It lasted only a few seconds, but it had power. In this brief period, as in a vision, I saw my own life. It is hard to put into words the absolute clarity with which I saw my existence as a contained, visible thing, a career or course on which I was running. Some people under anaesthetic and close to death on the operating table have experiences out of the body when they have felt themselves looking down upon the surgeon and their own prostrate forms and known themselves to be detached from their physical presence. This moment in Bloomsbury Square was analogous. In this vision, I saw myself, not as still, but as running, scurrying, after goals, such as fame and success, which did not in the least engage my emotions. As I surveyed my life I saw myself scurrying like this for ever, in a hurry to move from experience to experience without considering whether or not it was what I wished to do. Something different lay at the core of what I truly needed and desired. I felt a tremendous sadness, like homesickness, but it was not an empty sadness. It felt populated, and my mother was there, reaching out to me to lead me home. When the split second of this odd sensation passed, I saw things only as a set of negatives. I did not really want to be an actor; I did not want to be married; I no longer cared about this book, though I felt the beginnings of a deeper desire to write fully, and honestly, not with the brittle surface of my mind, and not humorously or cruelly. This was the beginning of a simple, positive desire to record experience in prose as a homage to life itself, born from the certainty that I myself, before I was forgotten, would pass into forgetting, and owed it to experience, trivial or important, sad or joyful, to set down something of

435

what I had felt. There would have been more wisdom to kiss the joy as it flies and live in Eternity's sunrise. But I had never felt sure about Eternity, nor about Art for its own sake, and I now began to wonder, in the middle of all my confusion about love and life, whether my only task would be to record; to see whether it was not possible, against the unknown chaos of nature, to map out a truthful picture of where I had been myself, and what I had seen, not with the aim of finding or imposing a shape as some stylish biographer might do with a more distinguished life, but merely in a spirit of reverence for the only thing given to me, life and existence itself. These thoughts came like a visitation, and although I have described the 'homesick' sensation as a sad one, there was also a feeling of joy which, again, lasted only a few seconds. It was a joy with which I wanted to be alone, and the last thing I wanted was to go to Madge's party. The thought of that room, full of glittery and fashionable people, famed chiefly as columnists in Sunday newspapers, filled me with despondency. And yet it took almost no time at all for the purer vision to fade; and I realised that if I did not go to the party I should regret it. Seeing that it was nineteen minutes to six, I retraced my steps into Great Russell Street, and by the time I reached Coptic Street I had begun to form in my brain fantasy conversations with the famous people I was about to encounter, and to calculate which, or how many, Sitwells would be standing at the top of the stairs when I went in.

The offices of Rosen and Starmer were crammed into a small house between a shoe shop and a secondhand bookseller who specialised in Oriental languages. In those days, London front doors were left open during office hours. I pushed my way in and announced myself to the receptionist.

'Go on up,' said the girl, who was painting her finger nails while reading the evening paper, and therefore couldn't look up. 'Madge said someone might be looking in before we locked up for the night.'

'There's a party,' I said.

'Don't think there *is*,' said the girl, with her eyes still fixed on the cartoon strip towards the end of the *Evening Standard*. I could not really see her face, just a fuzz of back-combed reddish-blonde hair. 'But I know she's expecting someone.'

Madge sat in her office, a small square panelled room which

overlooked the street, heavy with cigarette smoke, and piled high with proof copies and typescripts kept together with rubber bands. She had had her hair done. It was grey, hard and curly, more like an elaborate pewter helmet than hair. She was tiny, sharp, bespectacled.

'Come in, come in!' She removed her cigarette to say the words in festive tone. 'Isn't it *hot*? Just wait a moment while I finish this page.'

I stood there in the stifling little office and watched her peruse the typewritten page in front of her. To do so, she put her face very close to the desk. She did not look like a woman who was on the point of throwing a large party. I wondered if I had got the day wrong.

'I wonder if I'll ever meet an author who can punctuate.' With fierce strokes of the diminutive blue pencil she attacked, rather than read, what was set before her.

'A difficult art.'

'Not difficult in the least. I have quite enough trouble wading through the appalling prose of these individuals without having to put in all their commas and semi-colons for them. If I did not do so, however, they would be unintelligible.'

Having established that she had a universally low opinion of her authors' accomplishments, she added, 'Even dear Raphael isn't what you would call a stylist.'

'Not what I would call a stylist, no.'

Crossly, she raised one eyebrow; the expression appeared to ask if I were trying to be funny.

'Is that . . . '

'His book?' She smiled bitterly. 'No, I wonder if we'll ever see that. I'm sorry he won't be coming. He's so busy, the poor dear boy, I'll say this to you, Mr Ramsay, though I would not admit so much to Silas, but it is entirely because of Raphael that I bought your book. Entirely. Left to myself I should have said that you needed time. It is not necessarily a good idea to publish the first thing that comes into your head. People nearly always regret their early attempts, things perhaps which were of no great quality but which they wanted to get off their chests.'

This was entirely typical of Madge's blunt way of expressing herself. I felt stung, almost tearfully angry that she could be saying such things, partly because I knew them to be true.

'Still, we shall say nothing of that to Silas. He has always taken the line and in my view it is an admirable one, that a publishing house should stand by its authors; that means standing by its mistakes as well as its successes.'

She stood up. She was wearing a neat little blue dress with a ruby brooch just above her left breast. She was probably only in her mid-forties, but I reacted to her as if she were much older, and it astonished me that she had a child young enough to require its supper cooked for it.

'You haven't met Silas, I think?'

'No, I haven't.'

'Come on, then.'

She led me up the stairs to the room above her own which was twice the size, having been knocked together with the room at the back. It was furnished like a small library, as neat and comfortable as Madge's office was chaotic and austere. The walls were lined with books. There was a small eighteenth-century knee-hole desk, and a couple of leather armchairs on either side of the fireplace. Silas Rosen stood at the window, a small silver-haired man, bearded. His tininess matched that of his colleague. Indeed, everything seemed to be on a Lilliputian scale, and I felt clumsily large, standing between the two of them, neither of whom came up to my shoulder in height. He wore a bottle-green smoking jacket, grey trousers and slippers, said by some to have been embroidered by Madge herself, who was known to be a keen needlewoman.

'Come in, darling,' he said to Madge in a quiet German accent.

'Silas, this is Mr Ramsay,' she said.

'What delayed you this morning?' he enquired sharply. 'I waited until eleven thirty, twelve, I think, what does this man think I am, with all morning to waste?'

'No, Silas,' said Madge, 'that was the young man coming about the job. Would you believe it, Mr Ramsay, we said we'd interview this young man, he was sent over with a recommendation from another publisher whom it would be indiscreet to name . . .'

'A very old friend,' said Silas Rosen. 'You can guess who it was, I'm sure.'

I did not then, as he assumed, have any idea who his friends were; nor did I know anything about the publishing scene.

'And he simply failed to turn up,' said Madge. 'Not that we

need any more editorial staff. No, dear, Mr Ramsay's written a book.'

'Really? Well, show it to Madge. If she likes it, who knows – we may, I only say *may*, want to publish it.'

'You did,' I said. 'This morning.'

'I mentioned that novella to you,' said Madge. *'Scenes from Clerical Life.'*

'The Vicar's Nephew,' I said.

'This calls for a little celebration, I think,' said Silas Rosen.

His voice never rose above the low monotone in which he spoke English. He had the fluent idiomatic speech of one who has learnt English as his second or third language. It was this, more than the very slight accent, which betrayed his foreign beginnings. Not that these were anything of a secret; he spoke of them at once.

'How long have I been in London, Madge?' he asked as he opened the bottle of ice-cold hock which stood on a table in an ice bucket. Had it been placed there for my benefit, or did they always conclude the office day by drinking together?

'Twenty years,' she said.

'Madge has been a tower of strength. I arrived in London as a penniless refugee. Penniless.'

The story was a dramatic one and it put any sorrows or adventures which I have supposed myself to have had into a humbling perspective: the decision to leave Berlin, the anxiety of abandoning relations and friends whose maltreatment and ultimate murder at the hands of the authorities were matters of certainty, the financial ruin, the decision to set up a publishing house attacking fascism, the prosperity of the list, the making of a small fortune, the decision to buy old Gareth Starmer's backlist of respectable middle-brow novels, the birth of the firm of Rosen and Starmer, the death of Gareth Starmer, the rise of Madge from her position as Starmer's secretary to being Rosen's help-mate, colleague, sister, friend: all this was poured out in Rosen's well-modulated educated tones. He must have told the tale, Ancient Mariner-like, to everyone who ever stepped into his office, but it came out that evening with all the freshness of a tale told for the first time. The last thing, evidently, which they wanted to discuss, was my book.

'I've asked one or two people to look in,' Madge said to me. This was all that she had promised when the idea of a small gathering had formed itself inside my head. She had just said that she would ask a few people for a drink. It was I who had translated this into a full-blown reception. As soon as Silas had finished his summarised autobiography, Madge began to speak of the receptionist in the hall.

'I told her that if I saw that nail varnish in the building again, she would have to go.'

'She was painting her *nails*?' He could not have sounded more incredulous if the girl had been daubing obscene graffiti on the office walls.

'And she doesn't answer the telephone correctly. *Rosena-Stormer.*' Madge was a good mimic and this was a plausible rendering of the way the girl spoke. 'I told her, you must simply pick up the receiver and say, "Good morning," and perhaps the number, "This is Rosen and Starmer," quite distinctly. She should then ask the person concerned if they wish to speak to me or to you, Silas, dear. But then, not to go putting through every Tom, Dick, or Harry who might wish to disturb our morning's work.'

While Madge was demonstrating the difficult art of using a telephone, two figures entered the office. One was Day Muckley, who had had his hair cut. He wore a blazer and clean grey flannels and I snobbishly thought that he looked like a man on his way to a bowls championship. He was accompanied by a figure from my childhood, Debbie Maddock, now better known as the novelist Deborah Arnott. When she was first married and lived in Timplingham, married to a schoolmaster, Debbie had (probably unwittingly) occupied the unenviable role of my aunt Deirdre's *bête noire*. That Wretched Woman, my aunt's phrase for her, was how I still thought of her. She was no less handsome than I remembered her, and she did not seem to have aged. Being in her thirties suited her better than being a harassed young mother in her early twenties. Perhaps the skill of a London dentist, or perhaps my own vision of things, made the teeth straighter now than in my memory of her earlier incarnation. They were very sexy teeth. They seemed to compel her to hold open her full cherry lips, giving her a film star's pout. Her mass of blonde hair was thick and springy round her oval, intelligent brow. Her brown eyes were eager and alert. The low-necked blue-and-white-spotted blouse revealed that she had lost her slight tendency to scrawniness which I remembered

440

from East Anglian days. I wondered why on earth she was accompanying Day Muckley.

He grinned amiably, and he was the first person that day to say the sentence which I had been expecting to hear a thousand times.

'A big moment, lad. And I wish you every success with the book, I do really.' This was said with an affectingly transparent sincerity.

'Raphael said he thought you two were friends,' said Madge. 'The old writer comes to salute the young.'

'Not so much of the old, thanks very much, Madge,' said Debbie.

'I merely meant a well-established writer in an old tradition,' said Madge self-importantly.

'You know,' said Day, 'when I was a very young man, Arnold Bennett said to me, "They'll tell you a lot about how English you are because you speak with a regional accent." ' He certainly was doing so that evening, with inflexions which would have sounded exaggerated on the stage. 'So they'll want to make you into a provincial genius.'

'*A Man from the North*, in short,' said Madge.

'I am from the North as it happens,' said Day, who, if he had remembered the Bennett title, did not intend to show that he did so. 'I've never denied coming from Hebden Bridge. But I'm forgetting my manners. Madge, I hope you don't mind my bringing a friend of mine, Deborah Arnott, to salute the man of the moment.'

'You'll never remember me,' said Debbie.

'Of course I do,' I said.

'How's your auntie and uncle?'

I had never thought of Aunt Deirdre as an auntie, pronounced *anti*.

'They're fine.'

'The auntie in your book is wickedly accurate,' said Debbie.

'Thanks.' She took her tiny glass of wine from Silas.

It was embarrassing in some ways that my portrait of 'Aunt Dolly' should be so transparent. But here was someone who had read my book! She was saying all the right things about it; and, moreover, she was herself a well-established writer.

'But he said to me, Arnold Bennett did, as a matter fact, there is no such thing as an English tradition. And if you want to write

441

good, realistic and above all *readable* fiction don't bother with English writers. Everyone says English writers have this tradition of realism, but all the best English writers have been fantasists – Swift, Defoe, Dickens even, in his way. Lewis Carroll.'

'How's Isaac?' Silas Rosen asked Debbie. Isaac Zimmerman had been a (fairly friendly) professional rival to Rosen back in Berlin days, before they made their separate escapes to England. Zimmerman had brought out the last six or seven of Debbie's books, and she immediately began to tell Rosen about Zimmerman's latest dinner party, when Mrs Eggscliffe had smacked the face of the Belgian ambassador.

'No, Bennett said read the French novelists if you want to see how it's done. Read Balzac. Read old Balzac, for God's sake. Read Floor-Butt.'

He began to expound the merits of *Un Coeur Simple*, but it was evident that in a publisher's office such a literary line of talk simply would not do. Madge began examining the face of her wrist-watch and Silas, having shared the bottle of hock among the five of us, showed no sign of opening another.

Madge was snapping open and shut her handbag, checking that she had her car keys and powder compact.

'It has been very nice to meet you all,' said Silas Rosen. 'Darling, we shall have to talk some more about the painted-nails lady.'

'He's too kind,' said Madge. 'What is there to talk about? She will just have to go.'

For a moment it seemed that the five of us had been assembled in order to discuss the incompetent receptionist. Madge was extremely friendly as she shook me by the hand, but there was no ambiguity about the valediction.

'Goodbye, Mr Ramsay,' she said firmly.

She beamed at me, and I understood. I was not to come back unless I could write a better book than *The Vicar's Nephew*. It was eventually remaindered, and I don't think even those copies sold. Presumably they were pulped.

Outside, in the streets of Bloomsbury, it was hotter and muggier than ever. Clothes stuck to the body. The faces of Day and Debbie were glistening. I had now put two and two together and concluded that she was the person to whom he referred as his mistress. One tends when young to assume that people plan

442

their lives or do things for reasons, rather than finding that in the right company or with the right amount to drink they have done things which they do not quite have the heart to unscramble. I therefore searched my mind for an explanation. Why should a beautiful, charming and successful woman have chosen to have anything to do with my collapsed old friend?

I did not know if they were trying to shake me off, or mutually wondering what to do with me.

'You'll be going to meet your wife now, lad, for a slap-up supper?' Day Muckley inhaled deeply, as if with energy he could make the air less torrid.

'No, actually . . . ' It was hard not to allow an edge of pathos in the confession that, on this night of nights, I was entirely alone.

'Haven't you made any arrangements?' Debbie touched my forearm and the pressure of her hot fingers was more than sisterly.

'You'd think that bitch Madge Cruden would have the decency to take you out to dinner,' said Day. 'It disgusts me. A young lad publishes his first book, for Christ's sakes.'

'Anything to save money,' said Debbie. 'Come on, we'll buy you your dinner.'

And she took my arm as we walked westwards where the sky over Oxford Street was an ominous gunmetal grey. The next hour, during which we made our way to Greek Street and sat at a table by the open window of the restaurant, was devoted to initiating me into the one shared emotion which binds together the majority of writers, a detestation of publishers. I discovered that Hunter's fondness for, even friendship with, Silas and Madge was highly unusual. The majority of authors, however successful in the eyes of the world, and however much on the surface they appear to like those who publish their books, in fact carry around a whole bundle of resentments against their publishers which it takes almost no more than a glass of wine to reveal. Rich or poor, best-sellers or failures, they nearly all have a story to tell, each one as tedious as the last, about mistaken royalty statements, shoddy proof correction, hideous dust-jackets or simple failure on the editor's part to behave as if they were dealing with a genius. These compulsive and hate-filled tales occupied us until another bottle of wine had been consumed and some smoked fish had been toyed with on our plates.

'Mind you,' said Day, 'mind you, I will say this. Madge is in some ways very, very pathetic. She's never going to get Raphael Hunter, she's never going to get Raphael Hunter to drop, to drop his mistresses, for Christ's sakes.'

'Let alone his trousers.'

The wine must have been doing its work because this remark of Debbie's was enough to make us laugh loud and long. After about five goes, we even managed to remember, or think we remembered, Dorothy Parker's one about men making passes at girls who wore glasses. We made a terrific noise honing the quotation which Debbie had misremembered as 'Men don't want sex with girls who wear specs'.

'He's made a pass at one or two, any road,' said the Best-Seller, reverting to Hunter. It was news to me that even Madge was numbered with the elect, one of those adorers who found Hunter attractive.

'They don't, I mean you're not,' I said. 'Hunter and Madge aren't?'

'We never really know what Mr Hunter wants in bed, do we, love?' said the Best-Seller. He held hands with Debbie across the table, but the focus of his eyes was becoming indistinct. I did not know what he meant by this which, on one level, might have implied that Hunter had some curious *ménage à trois* with the pair of them. Day Muckley sat opposite us, holding Debbie's hand, while she and I were pressed close together on our chairs. Our thighs and calves touched. Far from being displeased by this I nestled up closer to her as the meal progressed. Since Day did not seem to notice or mind, my hand occasionally strayed beneath the tablecloth to meet her own moist palm which lay in the warmth of her lap.

'We know what Madge wants though, don't we, poor bitch,' said Debbie.

'Isn't she married?'

'If you can call it being married. She never divorced Cruden.'

'The poet?'

'It lasted about a fortnight, or so they say. Long enough to give her a kid and a chip on her shoulder. Can you imagine being married to Madge?'

I wanted to avoid a general discussion about marriage of the kind which dominated each evening at the Bottle, but inevitably as the main courses were dished up, Muckley began a rambling autobiography, most of which I had heard several times before,

444

a wife who never appreciated his work, her extravagant ways, her need, after the success of *The Calderdale Saga*, to keep two servants, her prudish attitude to the physical aspects of matrimony. Eventually, after some row he had been thrown out and lived thereafter in rented diggings in North London.

'Of course, Julian, you knew me when I was first married,' said Debbie. 'Innocent days really.'

'Apart from the fact that . . . apart husband, apart from the fact that you were married to a complete and utter bastard of a husband.'

'Go easy, love'; she stroked his hand. We were on our third bottle.

'Complete bastard, the way he treated you.'

'Oh, marriage makes the nicest people into bastards,' she said. 'That's why I'll only have occasional lovers from now on. I mean, what a crazy thing to do, to promise yourself to someone for ever, to the exclusion of your friends, your profession, OK and your lovers. We all fall in love more than once in our lives.'

She pushed her beef olives to the side of her plate and lit up a cigarette. It was too hot to eat.

'I shall never . . .' Day Muckley's big froglike eyes filled with tears. 'I shall never be in love with anyone but you,' he said simply.

I felt almost as moved as he looked by this testimony. I edged away from Debbie's thigh. As soon, however, as she removed her hand from his, as it lay there on the tabletop, it was evident that in some senses she had been holding him up. His weepy eyes were glazed, lifeless as marbles, as his thickset head cascaded towards the tablecloth and was cushioned by the picked-over remains of a bread roll and a very melted pat of butter.

'Oh, God,' said Debbie Arnott, 'here we go again.'

A waiter came to ask if everything was all right. With some difficulty we pushed the Best-Seller into an upright position, and Debbie solicitously wiped the butter and breadcrumbs from his cheeks. We forwent coffee, not because some stimulant at that stage of the evening might not have been welcome, but because such a request seemed to offer too many risks – heads in broken cups, stains on tablecloths. To my amazement and horror, the meal cost nearly eight pounds. Very generously,

Debbie paid, with cash from her purse, in spite of my offering a pound note of my own.

'No, love, it's your treat tonight. And now I suppose we must get this old man home.'

'You must let me help you.'

She looked at me, her large brown eyes seeming in that moment very sad and very wise and very appealing. In that first glance I read many of the things which were to characterise our relationship, strong physical attraction, but also a desire shared by us both to behave well towards Day. We both knew that if I helped her get him home, it would not end there.

'If you're sure,' she said.

In the compulsive bursts of marital autobiography during the coherent part of the meal, we had said nothing about my own marriage. When Debbie asked me if I was sure, I thought of Anne and momentarily missed her, felt homesick for her as I had felt so often homesick for my mother. But I wanted an Anne who no longer existed, an Anne who loved me as she had appeared to love me in the early months together. I knew that if I went home, I should either find it empty or full of Anne's new frigidity and anger and silence, full of her love for someone else whom I could not identify, but had begun to fear was Darnley. And I lusted after Debbie.

' 'Course I'm sure,' I said. 'You can't get him home on your own.'

'I've done it often enough before,' she said.

There is a knack to standing on a pavement with a man who is too drunk to stay upright on his own. We found a lamppost and took it in turns to hold underneath Day Muckley's arms while the other scanned the street for a taxi.

'Perfectly all right, all right really . . .' he muttered as we shovelled him into the back of the cab. At several points of the journey, he murmured, 'Sorry, love. Sorry, lad . . . wanted it to be so . . . nice this evening.'

'It's all right, pet, it doesn't matter.' She had one arm on his shoulder and stroked his head as she spoke, a mother comforting a sad child. Her other hand was clasped in mine. I did not quite know by this stage to whom her words were addressed.

There was something inherently squalid about the three-quarters of an hour which followed, but Debbie's kindness deprived the scene of much of its indignity. Mercifully, he more or less woke up as we got him out of the taxi, and with both of us holding an armpit we got him through the front door of the house. We were in Pooter-land, spiritually if not in fact: Leighton Road in Kentish Town. Nowadays only members of the middle class could afford such a residence. In the 1950s it seemed pathetic that a man who had once written *The Calderdale Saga* should be in such reduced circumstances. He occupied two small rooms on the ground floor. It was to the back room that we propelled him. As we did so, he began to chant, a phlegmy, gurgling,

> 'I am sick o' wastin' leather on these gritty
> pavin'-stones
> An' the blasted English drizzle wakes the fever
> in my bones . . .'

No song could have been less meteorologically appropriate. The heat in Kentish Town was positively tropical and heaving Muckley made us even hotter. But in the song's melancholy longing for escape from life's ordinariness, he had perhaps hit on an appropriate ending to our revels.

'Shush, love, shush.'

'Is that door open?' I asked.

'Just push it,' she said. She was obviously an old hand at this exercise.

> 'Though I walks with fifty housemaids outer
> Chelsea to the Strand
> An' they talks a lot o' lovin', but wot do they
> understand?'

A door opened on the landing above us and a female voice, disembodied as far as I could see, said sharply, 'Would you mind being a little quieter?'

'Very sorry,' said Debbie.

'Is that a young woman down there? You know I won't have young women visiting after ten.'

'We're just seeing Mr Muckley home,' I said.

'*On the road to Mandalay!*'

'Shush, shush, my baby.'

We did get him on to the bed, and as we pulled at trousers and

447

shoelaces, he was quieter, but not asleep. He lay now with his
eyes open, staring at the ceiling. It was a room of heart-rending
dinginess. The bed took up most of the space, an ugly Edwardian
thing with mahogany headboards. There was a towel-rail from
which depended a few grey rags which might once have been
towels and a number of damp items which, earlier in the day,
the Best-Seller must have been attempting to wash: some odd
socks, a string vest. Three or four metal ashtrays, purloined from
pubs, were dotted about the room, balanced on the chipped
white chest of drawers and the wobbly bedside table, and on the
washstand in the corner, which was ingrained with dry shaving
soap, some of it black with filth and a hundred semi-successful
attempts to shave. The only adornment in the room hung above
the bed: a picture of Christ, revealing his Sacred Heart.
Underneath the picture was the legend SACRED HEART OF JESUS
HAVE MERCY UPON US.

There was an absolute simplicity about the way Day Muckley
gave himself up to being undressed and prepared for bed. He did
not resist. He was like a baby, or a man who had never known
the use of his limbs. His lips were moving. At first I thought he
was cursing or continuing to quote Kipling.

'Oh, my God . . . Oh, my God,' he said. And then his prayer
came fluently from his lips: 'I love Thee with my whole heart
and above all things and am heartily sorry that I have offended
Thee. May I never offend Thee any more. O, may I love Thee
without ceasing and make it my delight to do in all things Thy
most holy will.'

'Come on, pet.'

He was down to vest, socks, pants, and by lifting him we were
able to get him under the appalling sheets.

'You'll be too hot with a blanket,' she said, stroking his head.

'Stay with me, my darling girl, stay with me.'

'Not now, love, it's after ten and Miss Whatsit's getting angry.'

'Sod Miss Whatsit.'

'Good night, love.'

It didn't feel right to be the witness to such a scene of intimacy
and tenderness. I tried to creep from the room unobserved, but
he said, 'See her home, lad. I'm very, very.'

'Good night, Day,' I said.

'I'm tired,' he said. 'I'm very pleased for . . . '

In that moment I vainly wondered whether he was not saying

that he was pleased to have reintroduced me to Debbie. Or was he pleased for me on the day of my supposed publishing success? Or was it something else which pleased him?

As we crept out of the door he was muttering, 'Pray for us sinners now and at the hour of our death.'

The unseen woman on the landing above was still hovering there. One could sense her and see the light from her door which was ajar, and which opened farther as we came out into the hall. In every sense I felt a trespasser. As soon as we were out on the pavement I took Debbie in my arms. In later months I ungallantly told myself that I had never really been in love with Debbie, as though the word 'really' in such a sentence meant anything. We waited for a taxi, but when one failed to appear we walked home to her house in Dartmouth Park Avenue. We did not sleep that night. Compared with the absolute harmony of my lovemaking with Anne, it was all very fumbled, but at a moment which could not have been more fitting the bedroom was illuminated with lightning and an almost instantaneous thunder clap. We were still tight in each other's arms, silent with the strangeness and beauty of the moment as rain began to beat hard against the windows.

'You really made the sky move,' she murmured, though I knew that I had given her almost no pleasure at all.

Then began the conversation which we had in various forms over and over again throughout our affair. Because it was a ritualised conversation we took it in turns to take an opposite viewpoint. One would argue that what we were doing was crazy, that we were playing with fire, that it would desolate Day if he ever found out about it. The other participant in the debate would assert that it did no harm so long as no one knew, so long as we had something to give to each other, that life was short, that we wished Day no ill, that we did not want to upset Debbie's children, nor Anne if she was capable of being more upset than she was already.

Peter one day at the pub had said, 'It's when you go off and screw someone else that a marriage has finished. It's such a fucking stupid thing to do. It ruins it. Once you've done it, you never make love without looking over your shoulder. Don't give me all that cobblers about affairs enhancing your marriage. I know. I've had three of the fucking things.'

One never listens to advice.

Lying there in the thunderstorm it was not of our folly that I thought. In that particular moment, Debbie and I simply needed each other. She told me 'all about' her love affair with Muckley, and I tried to tell her about myself and Anne.

I must have said that I thought Debbie was kind to Day.

'Don't be such a patronising sod. I love him.'

That was the real reason why our affair had no future.

'Some people probably think I spend my two days a week with him because I'm sorry for him. Just because he gets pissed – well, I admit, that's boring. But they think, because he's an old wreck and he hasn't got any money . . . '

I was also on the point of adding that Day Muckley could be quite thunderingly boring, but I'm glad I didn't. She was squeezing my hand as she said, 'I love him because he's a real man. We first met at some awful party and he was half plastered, not so bad as tonight, but pretty far gone. I remember Bridget Hewlings' – another novelist – 'saying, "Day Muckley's here, drunk as usual, hands wandering over every skirt in sight," and what Bridget said was true and of course when we met he tried to grope me within about ten seconds. He probably would have done it to absolutely any girl, but I just felt ten feet tall.'

'But there must have been other men . . . since your husband?'

'You mean I'd go to bed with anyone.'

'You know what I mean.'

'Oh, there were other men, yes, with poncey southern accents, or wives, or problems with bisexuality, or all three. Sorry, love.' She squeezed my hand again. 'But with Day I knew I'd met a real man.'

Since I had no right to be in her bed, I had no right to be jealous, which I was. I knew, though, that she spoke with absolute sincerity when she said that she loved Day Muckley and explained to me the rather curiously rigid regime which she and the old man had devised, never meeting for more than two days in each week.

'But Debbie, if you love him – why me?'

'Don't ask, love, don't ask. I don't know. I could ask you, if you love your wife . . . '

I went very quiet.

'Do you love her? Anne? You must.'

I did in that moment very much miss Anne. At this point,

lying with Debbie was like spending Christmas Day with the kindest family in the world, and realising that though they offered me turkey and presents and pudding, they weren't *my* family.

'Let's be honest with each other, Julian, always. Don't let's pretend anything. The worst thing about what we're doing would be if it made us think we had to pretend to hate Day and Anne. That's what so many insecure people do when they have affairs; to justify it all to themselves, they pretend they have been more unhappy than they really were with their regular partners. You don't need to pretend to me, love.'

And the rain fell against the windows and we made love again. After the silence which followed, she leaned over to the bedside table and lit two cigarettes, putting one between my lips, as she asked, 'Are you happy?'

With my hand on her stomach, I said, 'What do you think?'

'I don't mean now, here, silly. But perhaps you don't want to talk about it.'

I did want to talk about it. I had been wanting to talk about it for weeks, months, but unable to find the right person, the person with whom it did not seem disloyal to reveal the depth and extent of my marital wretchedness. The moral paradox of the situation was that having committed the ultimate act of infidelity with Debbie, it was only with her that such conversational infidelity lost its wickedness. I no longer felt it was a betrayal of Anne to describe what had happened between us in recent months. By talking about it, Debbie was helping me regain my lost respect for Anne, or so I was believing until she dropped her bombshell.

'I know it's hard for you, love. I remember how shattered I felt when Derek had his first affair. And he felt so guilty he had to take it out on me and the kids.'

'You married very young.'

'So did you. Julian, I know it won't make it hurt any less, but it won't last, you know, Anne's affair. They never do.'

Starting at the base of my spine and rising to the back of my head, I had the chilling knowledge that Debbie knew more than I did, and that perhaps everyone knew more than I did. Perhaps Anne's emotional life was the subject of gossip – but how had it reached the 'literary world' which Debbie Arnott inhabited?

'They never last.'

451

'Derek's affair lasted. He married her, didn't he?'

'That was different.'

'How do you know?'

'Because she was pregnant. And Mr Clever never gets his girls pregnant. That poor cow Bella Marno thought she'd got him, but he was two-timing her all along with Anne. Or so it seems.'

I had the strange sense of something popping inside my ears, and with the pain, which was so strong that from its first inception I did not know how it was to be borne there came a grim relief at last to have arrived at the truth. Such puzzles as why Anne had been so furious that night at the theatre now became explicable.

I now realise that Hunter and Anne probably drifted into whatever it was they had drifted into. At the time I imputed to them motives of pure villainy. Hunter must have planned every stage of my betrayal, softening me up by getting Madge to publish my rotten book. He had only wanted Anne as a notch on his totem pole, a name in his catalogue of conquests. The mind raced back with horror to the first evening of my meeting Anne, and her jokey little comments about Hunter's handsomeness. Had the *whole thing* been a falsehood, all my love for her, all her professions of love for me, all our happiness and trust – all false, all meaningless?

'What are you saying?' I asked quiveringly. I had to be sure, now, even though I knew what she was saying, and it all made sense – her frequent visits to his flat to sort the Lampitt Papers, his preparedness to eat supper with us. Oh, damned, smiling, villain. 'You're not saying that Raphael Hunter . . . '

'Oh, darling . . . ' Debbie propped herself up on the pillow and looked down into my face. 'I thought you knew. I thought that was what we were talking about.'

'No . . . no . . . no . . . '

'Oh, poor pet. It's always the one who's most affected who's last to know. Oh, my poor boy. It does you good to cry, pet, it does you good to cry.'

Debbie's kindness to me then probably explains why I was still able to look on her as a friend long after our short affair came to an end. Not since childhood had I so given myself up to grief. Probably the weeping only lasted half an hour, but it felt as if we lay there like that for half the night, me sobbing, Debbie comforting me. When morning came, she said, 'Hey! You've got to go, love.'

'No, Debbie, don't kick me out.'

'I've got to, love. The kids will be awake soon.' Brisk, no-nonsense talk now. 'If this is going to be more than a one-night stand you've got to realise that the kids come first. I'm not putting any man first in my heart again. So long as you understand that I love the kids and I love Day.'

Weeping for a long time is a bit like heavy drinking. It works you into a kind of frenzy which you need shaking out of. This line of common sense shook me out of my tears. So did the sight of her nakedness in the dawn light.

'Hey, *gerroff*!'

'You're irresistible.'

'No, I'm throwing you out.'

Which she did. As I left the house, one of the twins was shouting to her that he could not find any clean socks. The twins were in their early teens and needed to be got up early for the journey across North London to their school. I walked down towards Kentish Town, retracing our steps of the previous night, and then sat on top of a bus which wove its slow way southwards into London. To the east, the sky was a blaze of gold. The thunder of the previous night seemed to have washed the air itself and I thought of Blake's famous remark about those who saw the sun as a golden disc in the sky the shape of a golden guinea. No doubt, in the previous twelve hours, my life had become more complicated, sadder. But it had also been retouched by a glimpse of glory. I thought with great tenderness of Debbie during that bus journey and of Day Muckley, who would soon be awakening to the rays of the sun, and of Anne and of Hunter and of myself. For months I had been angry with Anne, without understanding the reason; and now that she had broken my heart, I was not angry with her. I breakfasted at a café patronised by those who had to be at work by eight o'clock. It was the sort of scene well evoked by Mr Pilbright. In one Pilbright it is through the roof of just such a café, with Formica-topped tables, sauce bottles, ashtrays and plates of baked beans, where customers wore overalls and headscarves, that his friends were lowering the paralytic man to the feet of Christ.

'He was completely paralytic,' the Best-Seller was to tell me, the next time we met, complaining that the 'other Day Muckley had been up to his tricks again' on the night of my 'publication party'.

I ate black pudding, eggs, bread, the complete fry-up, and drank mug after mug of tea. It helped to counter the effects of having been awake all night. When I was fairly sure that Anne would have left the flat, I turned for home.

Nine

'Really,' said Anne, 'you do like the most awful people.'

It was true. I had begun to notice it myself. No explanation occurring to me, I pretended to be puzzled.

'Do I?'

'The Kempes and their filthy dogs.'

'I don't really like the dogs.'

'And there are all those slobs from the Black Bottle. And now Day Muckley's girlfriend. They say she's the last word in awfulness. All the same, she *is* becoming rather famous.'

'Not so you'd notice, surely.'

'*The Melon Garden, My Mother Said, Man About the House.*'

I was silenced by this display of knowledge. She had never been aware of modern literature before, nor responded with the faintest interest when I had tried to speak about it. I concluded that Hunter had been initiating her into the somehow guilty knowledge of who was who. When she had first seen Hunter on Fenella's television set, Anne had regarded his encounter with Day Muckley as a purely comic turn. Later, when she first met Hunter, and, come to that, Muckley, she had shown no more excitement than would a child who had been shown the Punch-and-Judy puppets after a show. Now a version of her mother's beady-eyed snobbery seemed to be at work in her. She had picked up all the right opinions about everyone in the literary world. I am sorry to say — and I set it down without malice — she is still lumbered with them. Long after she was done with Hunter, I found, on the occasions when we met, that she had been permanently affected by his habit of viewing contemporary art as a variety of London-based fashion parade. Instead of thinking about new books, films, or plays, she seemed only capable, when we discussed them, of sniffing out the prevailing view of them; the view prevailing, that is to say, among the comparatively small number of people whom Hunter and his kind esteem. I do not think she was ever a great reader; such people seldom are. But she always knew what to say about the latest books. Manifestly boring or ill-constructed novels always earned her highest praise if they had been well reviewed in the Sunday newspapers. She even spoke in reviewers' clichés. How I blushed for her when, at some family obsequies long after our marriage was over, she told me that she thought Debbie Arnott's latest (*A View of England*) was 'a *tour de force*'. As it happened, that was the book which marked Debbie's transition from the warm-hearted, if gushing, chronicler of young married women and their emotional problems to being the rather pompous narrator of her later books. 'Undoubtedly a great step forward,' Anne added.

Even in her own field of expertise, painting, she never again showed anything which one could distinguish as taste. About her nineteenth-century subjects – Winterhalter in particular, Landseer to a smaller degree – she became more and more of an 'expert', though I seldom heard her explain the merits of these painters, merely the facts which, in copious profusion, she had established about them. When it came to judgement of what was happening among contemporary painters, however, she spoke like any old colour-supplement reader. Her statements about modern art were no more than echoes of that dull, parochially English way of looking at things which has dogged most of the London critics in our lifetime. She was tepid in her praise of anything happening in Europe or the United States and was happy to speak as if L. S. Lowry, Pilbright and, in after days, Hockney represented the *dernier cri*. She would probably have been astonished to think that anyone judged her opinions as unoriginal, because they were always expressed with great conviction, just as a pious person, taking the church catechism for his own, might say the Creed as though he alone had thought of it. She would have been even more astonished to hear that anyone attributed this dogged conventionalism to Hunter's corrupting influence.

Her pleasure in my new friendship with Debbie Arnott was the first sign of this tendency. It crossed my mind that she guessed what was happening between us, and even felt some relief, as if this somehow let her off the hook with regard to Hunter. Years afterwards, I discovered that this was a false deduction and that she had known nothing of my affair with Debbie. I told her that we had met at Madge's 'party', taken Day

Muckley home, drunk too much. I allowed Anne to believe, without saying so, that the Best-Seller and Debbie had been with me all the time, and I omitted a description of our putting him to bed in his lodgings.

'You want to watch Debbie,' she said. 'They do say she's rather a one for men.'

Again, 'they', in this sentence, could have meant only one person, since neither Anne nor I moved in circles where Debbie Arnott had been heard of, let alone discussed. (The fact that she was a 'famous' novelist only meant 'famous' to the circle of people who esteem such novels. She was not famous as Agatha Christie or Somerset Maugham were famous.) When Anne dropped these hints that she had been absorbing all Hunter's dispiriting views of the world, I suppose I should have challenged her, and accused her of betraying me. Since, however, I was anxious not to reveal all the secrets of my own heart during that period, there seemed no point in a 'showdown'.

I have spoken of an 'affair' between myself and Debbie, but this is rather a big word for something which occupied only a very short interlude in my life. In the next fortnight I met her a number of times. I visited her house during the middle hours of the day. We were both deceiving Muckley, and my wife, but the association was strangely consoling. As far as relations with Anne were concerned, I suppose that my going to bed with Debbie was decisive in finishing the marriage. I am not naturally monogamous but, like the weighing machine speaking to the fat man in the joke, I want only 'one at a time, please'. Since Anne had shown no willingness of late in the bedroom, this seemed the moment to bring that side of things to a close. Nothing was said, but after Debbie, things were over between Anne and me. In the short term, however, I felt buoyant. I went through a shortsighted phase of believing that the affair with Debbie would enhance, or even heal, my relations with Anne. Certainly I was better humoured during those weeks. Some of Debbie's volubility and desire to be amiable had perhaps been absorbed.

Amiability was certainly required of me at that period, since, *faute de mieux*, I had been adopted by Sargie as the man who drove him about, provided companionship at luncheons, kept him supplied with cat food and library books, or met him for 'snifters', when the mood took him, at his club in Mayfair. This

457

had all happened gradually, so that I did not notice it creeping up on me. He asked no questions about me and Anne, but since he had himself been estranged from his wife, Cecily, for years, I hoped that it would not scandalise him to know that I was fast approaching an analogous position. In fact, if it left me freer to be involved with his needs, all the better as far as he was concerned. He was cunning enough to spread the duties around, and since the breaking of his friendship with Uncle Roy, he never relied upon one individual to be his sole companion and slave of his whims. But now I took it for granted that, whatever happened between me and Anne, I would somehow be stuck with the legacy of looking after Sargie, at least for some of the time.

At the approach of Virgil D. Everett Jnr's visit to London, to meet the family and celebrate his purchase of the Lampitt Papers, Sargie became more and more excited, and summoned me one day to his club at twelve to hear about the final arrangements. The habit of very early luncheons, I remembered from childhood, was one of Sargie's ways of breaking up his mornings, and the mornings of anyone else whose time he wanted to waste. The selection of this particular venue had its own appropriateness in my mind since it was outside the Savile Club that I had parted from Sargie on the very day of Jimbo's funeral, not long after my twelfth birthday. Uncle Roy had conveyed me to Paddington station, where a train waited to take me back to another boarding school term, though not, as it happened, any old term, since I was then on the threshold of a new life; I was about to fall in love with Miss Beach and to experience all the torments of jealousy when I saw her in the arms of Raphael Hunter: my first glimpse of the man. The story, in some ways, had begun on the steps of that club.

Few of these associations could have been present in Sargie's mind. He must have known as little of my inner life as I of his, though I did wonder whether he remembered that he and Uncle Roy had lunched at the Savile on the day of Jimbo's funeral, and whether, if so, he thought it was a setting fit to celebrate, as he saw it, the salvation of the Lampitt Papers, and with them, the salvation of the Lampitt name. The sale was final, complete. A sum, undisclosed to the rest of us but said to be absurdly generous, had been paid, via Denniston and Denniston, into Sargie's bank account. It only remained for Virgil D. to arrange for their final transport to the Everett Foundation in East Sixty-third Street, and the ultimate triumph would be complete.

'You see, the beauty of the scheme is that Virgil D. Junior has bought the whole collection *and* the copyright. Rather unusual, that,' said Sargie with a gleam. 'In fact, Andrew Denniston had never heard of such a thing!'

'Why does he need the copyright? Surely he's not going to publish the Lampitt Papers?'

Sargie laughed aside the very idea.

'I wondered, but Andrew has put my mind at rest. Let's be bloody frank about this, Julie, my dear, Jimbo's old boxes of junk are completely valueless as far as we are concerned. Virgil D. has bought a pup, an absolute bloody pup!'

I laughed because Sargie laughed, and because we had already put away an unwisely generous dry martini apiece. All the same, I could not help asking:

'How d'you know, Sargie, if you never read them?'

'What's that, dear boy?'

'Well, when your brother died, Hunter almost immediately homed in and took away the papers, didn't he?'

'Not quite right. I hung on to them for a couple of years.'

'And you read them?'

'Turned over the odd notebook. Quite amusing some of it – old Jimbo met everyone, you know, in that early phase of his success after the *Prince Albert* was published. Conrad, dinner with Joseph Conrad. He even went down a few times to see old Henry James, in what's the name of the bloody place?'

'Rye.'

'That's the boy. But none of this filth that Lover Boy dug out. Don't know where he got it – made it all up, Sibs thinks, bless her. I mean, can you imagine Jimbo, aged twenty-something, same age as you are now, and Henry James, who never laid a finger on anyone else as far as we know. . . . Look, let's have another drink.'

'I still don't see how Virgil Everett buying the copyright will help you.'

Sargie ordered more drinks and then he lapsed into a little doodle which was so familiar to me that it almost antedated memory. I can remember perching on a tiny beaded footstool at Timplingham Place – Mummy must have been present, and Uncle Roy as ever would have been in attendance, and Sargie would suddenly relapse into a semi-nonsensical fashion of speech. When I was a little boy, and instructed to call him 'Uncle Sargie' by my actual uncle, we had called this particular gabble 'talking Chinese'. It wasn't a sign of drunkenness, it was deliberately done, and it involved muddling all the consonants in a word and blowing raspberries between each syllable.

'Ben-er-lubber-lubber-ph-phpston-Dennis-blubber-lubber-velly clebber-phph-st-velly clebber fella.'

I believe that the habit of talking Chinese went back to Sargie's childhood, and was something which he used to do with his brothers.

'I do wish that Sargie wouldn't do that silly kind of talking,' Aunt Deirdre once said crossly one afternoon during the war, when we were all on our knees lifting a row of carrots which she had patriotically intruded into the herbaceous border.

'Oh, but it's *funny*,' Mummy remonstrated, 'and it makes Julian laugh.'

'And then before we know where we are, he'll be talking like that all the time,' said Aunte Deirdre. 'Now how did that get there?' She yanked furiously at a fistful of greenery, and then surveyed its roots. 'Thank goodness. For a moment, I thought it was hogweed back again.'

'How has Denniston been clever, Sargie?' I asked, to break the reverie, and destroy the memory of my mother in the garden on that perfect summer day. Sometimes even nowadays, the longing to be with my mother is so intense that I feel it will kill me, and it comes at just such inconsequential moments – sitting in a club with Sargie, or in the middle of a meal when all around me are quite unaware of the mental agony which has suddenly descended, the panic, the sheer childish need to be in her arms, a longing which can never be satisfied.

'Well, apparently these collectors aren't so interested in owning a manuscript if it's already been published.'

'So the manuscript of Keats's "Ode to a Nightingale" would interest them less than a letter from, say, F. Locker Lampson?'

'Point taken, clever clogs. But on the whole, collectors of literary manuscripts like unpublished stuff. If we'd only sold Virgil D. the manuscripts themselves, but retained the copyright, we could technically have allowed someone like Lover Boy to quote from them, you see, publish great chunks.'

'In his first volume, he hardly quotes at all. He *refers* to the papers, but his narrative is chiefly based on paraphrase.'

'Sibs said we should have sued him, but you're right. He'd done his work very cleverly. All innuendo and hints and very little, if any, quotation, for which he would have needed our permission, legally. I think we were powerless. But, you see, now that Virgil D.'s got the stuff we are actually in a much stronger position. That's what Andrew Denniston thinks. We won't have any control over the family papers, true. That's been handed over, lock, stock and thingummybob, to Virgil D.'

'Do the others realise this?'

'What others?'

'Sibs? Vernon? Ursula?'

'Virgil D.'s a wily old bird by all accounts,' said Sargie. He looked shifty. 'He's not going to let the likes of Lover Boy into his strong-room.'

'Well, let's hope not.'

'I say, drink up, my dear. If you sit there dawdling, we're not going to get any lunch.'

The abrupt transition from the leisurely, lolling self slumped in a leather chair in the bar into a panicky figure who was being delayed by my own procrastination summoned back many incidents in Uncle Roy's word-hoard of Sargie stories. Sargie's desire to speed up or to slow down the pace of things was sudden and irrational, always an occasion for blaming whoever he happened to be with. He pulled himself quickly out of his chair, looked at his watch and flicked ash off his waistcoat with petulant gestures. Then he led the way upstairs to the dining room. It was by no means late – only about quarter past one – but by some chance the place was packed. It soon became clear, when Sargie buttonholed the head waiter, that he had failed to reserve a table.

'I'm sorry, sir. If you'd like to wait in the bar, there might be a table for you in half an hour. Rather a lot of members have . . .'

'Oh, this is hopeless.'

Sargie looked angry and crestfallen at the same time. All his exuberant excitement at the sale of the Lampitt Papers had deserted him. I could see that it was vexing – he had hoped to give me lunch at the Savile, and now he would be unable to do so. But this was not the end of the world. His manner suggested no such sang-froid.

461

'I'm sorry,' said the waiter.

'I don't mind waiting,' I put in feebly.

'Well, I *do*,' said Sargie. 'The *buggers*! It's a disgrace. I'm going to write to the committee.'

Presumably those referred to, whether or not sexual inverts, were those members of the club who had had the cheek to lunch at the place on the day when Sargie wished to entertain me there.

'I am sorry, sir.'

'Don't keep saying you're sorry. Anyway, you're not sorry.' We had moved into a near-tearful nursery bate. 'What are we going to do? Look, what about that table? Here's a free table, Julie.'

'I'm afraid that table is reserved, sir. Reserved for a member who booked.'

'Oh, death!'

'Come on, Sargie,' I said. Heads were starting to turn in our direction.

'It amounts to turning a chap out of his own club.'

'I'm happy waiting,' I said. 'Truly. Or we could go somewhere else.'

'I'm not waiting about here for this man.' Sargie was glaring at the waiter with almost murderous hatred in his face. His tone suggested that the word 'man' was the deadliest insult which could be imposed. None of Cyril's inventive rudery at the Bottle ever sounded more devastating. He turned his back on the *man* while the waiter was repeating the profusest apologies.

'I don't have to stay here,' said Sargie. 'We'll go to Claridge's and eat oysters.'

It was hard to see how this was supposed to be skin off the waiter's nose, but a look of childish triumph illumined Sargie's face as he had come up with the idea.

'That'll show *him*,' he said, as he led the way downstairs once more. 'We'll go to Claridge's and see how he likes *that*. This club has become horrible anyway. Full of shits.'

This last was said not to me but to two club members who were just climbing the staircase as we came down it. I followed at a discreet distance, hoping that it might not necessarily be assumed that I was with Sargie. He could see their faces, which were impassive as they walked past him, as though they had not heard. Because I was several paces behind Sargie I could see that as soon as he was past them they smiled in a resigned, conspiratorial way which suggested that these little tirades were a regular feature of Sargie's club life.

In the hall, he was an excited child.

'We'll go and have oysters at Claridge's,' he repeated. 'That ought to show them.'

It was certainly a relief to be out in the street. Not until that moment had I ever fully appreciated the nobility of Uncle Roy's character. Extreme nobility, or an intense fondness for Sargie, would have been required to put up with this sort of thing over repeated occasions over so many years. It would not have taken much for this Saga of the Luncheon to be worked up into one of Uncle Roy's anecdotes. And as he finished telling it, and wiping away the tears of laughter, he would add, 'Good old Sargie.'

That was the saddest thing about the estrangement between the two of them. Others in future might be kind to Sargie, and keep him company as I was doing at the moment. When the 'moods' darkened to the point where medical attention was deemed appropriate, there was no question that his family would stand by him and do all the right, humane things. But no one except my uncle Roy would say 'Good old Sargie.' No one would positively love in Sargie the very things which made him annoying, which is perhaps a way of saying that no one else, quite, would love him. To be able to love other people as they are, rather than as we wish them to be, is rare. Perhaps this was what prompted me to take Sargie's arm as we teetered down Davies Street to our palatial destination.

Claridge's had always been used by Sargie as a place of healing. I don't think he was much in the habit of staying there, but discreet luncheons in the dining room had often been his way of molly-coddling himself when the rest of the world seemed indifferent or positively hostile. The waiter recognised him as he shuffled in.

'Good afternoon, Mr Lampitt. A table for two, yes?'

'If it doesn't mean waiting all bloody day.'

'But of course not. This way, sir.'

'See?' said Sargie to me defiantly. Some point had been scored against the head waiter at the Savile.

As soon as we were seated at our table, he called for oysters and his own particular favourite Chablis. Sargie was not a sybarite. So long as he could be half tight during waking hours, and so long as he had something to smoke, I do not think he thought much about food. The 'treat foods' with which on such occasions he wanted to supply himself and his friends had a purely emotional function and status. Lobsters. Salmon. Oysters. *Crème brûlée*. I have no reason to suppose that he liked to eat these things more than cottage pie, but they were ordered as gestures of defiance, kindly lights amid the encircling gloom.

'*En mangeant les huîtres, toujours on soupire la mer* – the sea air itself seems to come out of them.' It was one of Mme de Normandin's phrases.

There is that strange moment just before the oyster goes into your mouth when you inhale what seems to be the very essence of the sea, followed by the sensual experience of putting the oyster into your mouth. The soft moisture of this creature on the tongue could almost be another tongue, fishy but willing, so that even as one is about to swallow one has the sensation of kissing, perhaps kissing a mermaid or a siren.

Mme de Normandin had a passion for oysters, and they were often at her table. I had not eaten them much since, *huîtres* for some reason hardly ever being featured on the menu at school, or in the NAAFI, or at the cafés where, in Tempest and Holmes days, I had exchanged my luncheon vouchers, or at the Black Bottle. 'It's a mistake,' Aunt Deirdre liked to say, 'to give people food that's too rich.' It was a mistake she was studious to avoid in her own cuisine and I am certain that an oyster never passed her lips. It is hardly surprising, then, that the gleaming porcelain plate, with its dozen grey coracles of shell whose touch recalled the rocky purlieus of our *petite plage* at Les Mouettes and whose very aroma reminded me of the Atlantic Ocean pounding against the shingle, should have summoned up an earlier phase of life which now seemed very innocent. All that guzzling, and those secret assignations on the beach with Barbara, Mme de Normandin's maid. Since then, what compromises, what acceptance of the unacceptable, what bleak discoveries about one's own lack of single-mindedness. When pain cannot be avoided, it must be accepted. It is only when we think we have found a remedy or a cushion for unavoidable pain that we diminish ourselves. Pain can be embraced without morbidity. Its sting does not always bind us. Pain is not the worst thing in life. But I did not know that then. I looked for consolation in a situation where there was no consolation, and succeeded in making more unhappiness, not less.

The only good thing to emerge from this is that it deprived me of the temptation to play the role of the 'wronged' husband when, as eventually and inevitably happened, our marriage came to an end. (Though even being deprived of the temptation did not stop me on occasion from yielding to it.) The first time I had been to bed with Debbie it had seemed like a blessing, a balm sent to heal a broken heart. After half a dozen times, it threatened to become a habit, and I found myself becoming coarsened by the experience. In moods when I wanted to disguise this fact from myself, I expressed it in a cliché – I had joined the human race. By this phrase I meant that life is punctuated by emotional calamity. If your wife falls in love with someone else, hard luck; but maybe she will fall out of love, or maybe you, too, can find consolation. I assumed that it had begun from Debbie's point of view as a piece of harmless sensuality, or simple kindness. For me, it represented a fall. Secret bedroom assignations in the middle of the afternoon. Returns to the bar where Debbie's lover sat getting drunk, or to my flat where my wife had perhaps been working or perhaps spending the day in a fashion similar to my own. This is the stuff which makes us cease to believe in life.

Sargie, it may be said, was only a more privileged version of what I encountered on a bar-stool every hour in the Black Bottle. His nervous disorders were peculiarly his own. In his attitude towards Cecily he could have been Pete or the Best-Seller.

'It'll be good to know that Cecily will never get her hands on Jimbo's diaries,' he said between mouthfuls of brown bread and butter. His manner was genial once more, with food inside him.

I had never met his wife, who was still quite a friend of Sibs's.

'Did she want them?'

'Lord, yes. Cecily even tried to make out that Jimbo would have wanted *her* to inherit the papers. They were thick as thieves, you know. Ganged up against me all the time.'

'How?'

'Tales out of school to Mama – naughty Sargie is in debt or drunk, or failed to give one of his lectures. I was a don then, when I was married to Cecily. Norham Road. Oh, Christ.'

I had never visited Oxford. I did not know whether Norham

Road had any significance beyond the fact that it had been Sargie's marital address.

'Two years of absolute bloody hell I had with Cecily,' he said, repairing to his glass of Chablis. I now half wanted to join in with his marriage talk. Sooner or later the Lampitts were going to have to know that Anne and I were estranged. Sargie might have been a sympathetic ear. On the other hand, it was by no means safe to take this for granted. Those who have felt no obligation themselves to struggle on with matrimonial difficulties are capable of violent disapproval of the comparable misfortunes of others, particularly when their own flesh and blood have been slighted. Experiences which for themselves have been harrowing, pathetic, even tragic, become immediately disgraceful in their minds if undergone by other people. Sargie had walked out on Cecily because, as he told everyone, he no longer liked her. There was no certainty that he would forgive me for doing the same to Anne. Nor could I be sure, were she eventually to be the one who did the walking, that the Lampitts would regard me in any more sympathetic perspective. In such a case, they might reasonably wonder why she had walked out and conclude that I was simply impossible to live with.

'Some people aren't strong enough to be married,' he added. 'Now you are. I can see you are, my dear.'

He dabbed his moustaches with a napkin and smiled at me. There was something a little cruel about the smile. If I told the truth I should have denied this assertion. It felt as if he were taunting me to deny it. If I accepted it, however, this was to consent to be placed in the crudely insensitive class of those who did not get on one another's nerves. But I didn't reply because Sargie's head had gone out of focus. Drink was not responsible so much as an involuntary concentration of the optic nerve towards a table on the other side of the dining room which now came clear into view as I allowed Sargie to become a fuzzy shape beside me, a colourless blob eating the last of its bread and butter and feeling sorry for itself.

There were three figures at the table I was staring at. Anne's was the first to arrest my attention. Anne had a way of wearing quite simple clothes and looking dazzlingly smart. A black skirt and a striped-black-and-white blouse could have been the

clothes of a school prefect; but on her the effect was sophisticated. She was her mother's daughter. A great self-confidence
lit up her appearance. She was animated, smiling, gay as she had
been when I first met her. I had begun to assume that she was
now incapable of gaiety, but here she was keeping her company
in high spirits.

The two men with her were Hunter and a man in a large
double-breasted suit of pale grey. The suit was large for the very
necessary reason that the man was large – fleshy but also huge.
Hair of a similar silvery grey to that of the suit was swept back
from a big brow. The hair was much thicker than in most men of
his age, which must have been between sixty and seventy, and
much longer than was fashionable in those days.

The vision was interrupted while a waiter took away the
oyster shells and prepared to bring tournedos. Another waiter
was asking Sargie if he would care to taste the Margaux. It must
have been years since Sargie's palate, perpetually overlaid with
gin and cigarettes, had tasted anything, but he sipped the wine
and declared, probably truthfully, that it was very nice.

The meal progressed. Sargie's mood of good cheer was
restored. He began talking Chinese again – 'Clabbages vebby
clebber men' – as he packed away the forkfuls of meat, mounds
of broccoli, sprouts, potatoes. I suppose he wasn't properly
speaking an alcoholic because he hardly ever abandoned the
habit of eating. When out, and eating food for which he was
paying – that rather mean strain in the Lampitts – he ate greedily
to get his money's worth. Sibs was much the same. I ate, too –
you couldn't not, it was so good – but without much relish. I felt
I'd spent a lifetime looking across restaurants to see Hunter with
women he had no right to be with. In fact it had only happened
once before, but it was one of the moments where my dealings
with Hunter seemed fixed, almost destined.

The certainty that he was my wife's lover had of course
changed my attitude to him completely. I wondered how I could
possibly have been taken in by him. One now had the sense that
behind his seemingly expressionless and almost boring face,
there lay depth upon depth of hidden motivation. He had been
nice to me in order to seduce Anne, that much was clear. But
one also got the impression, though it was impossible to prove,
that he had seduced Anne (I was sure that he had done so) for
some further ulterior purpose. But what? And why did we all let

467

ourselves be used in this way? Presumably, none of us would have known much about Hunter had he not been able to practise his wiles on old Jimbo, for it was as a Lampitt expert ('Petworth Lampitt's close friend and personal assistant', it said on the blurb of the paperback) that Hunter rose to fame. In so far as he had crossed my path, I had watched him use people and then discard them with complete ruthlessness. My cousin Felicity had first helped him sort the Lampitt Papers. Sargie had fallen under his spell and in the aftermath of that, we had all been changed. This was just the Hunter *we* knew. It was hard to suppose that there were not dozens of such sad stories of exploitation lurking behind his pasty countenance. (There was, for example, the whole pathetic story of Madge's unrequited passion for him.)

None of these considerations, however, weighed so heavily as the desire to get out of Claridge's without actually encountering the trio at the other side of the dining room. Sargie's mood had been restored to an acceptable level of good cheer. He was not embarrassing me in front of the waiters. After the histrionics at the club, I could not face any sort of public showdown between Sargie and Hunter; nor could I quite work out how I would behave during such an encounter. I had not set eyes on Hunter since Debbie had given me an explanation for all Anne's strange behaviour. The fact that Debbie had told me in bed might be thought to have deprived me of all right to hold a view, but I was not rational on the subject: not even rational enough to reflect that Debbie could not possibly have known, not exactly, what went on between Anne and Hunter. I was convinced that Anne spent all her available spare time in acts of fornication. Such thoughts, when entertained of a spouse, induce something like lunacy. I now consider it on balance unlikely that Anne slept with Hunter. She was obviously in love with him. But from what I know of him, he could achieve his effects without the trouble of undressing, and he would have been happy to leave it at that. Besides, her miserably inarticulate 'It's not what you think', spoken to me at a slightly later date, hinted at her innocence if I had only allowed her to finish the sentence. One of the Rothschilds in the early days of the family fortune is supposed to have remarked that any fool can make a million but it takes genius to keep a million. I suspect this truth (if it is one) has its parallels in the emotional life.

At various stages since my marriage ended my old love for Anne has flared up again. My self-reproach has taken the form of incredulity. How could I have been so stupid as not to cherish her? How can I have not seen that her fundamental niceness, decency, honesty, would have helped me through if only I had been more patient? The passion for Hunter might have lasted for months, or for at most a year or two. Instead of waiting, I had to walk away and blow it all. Without seeking it I had landed a million, and within a year it was spent; the account was empty. That in sentimental terms was what had happened.

'I call that a jolly good lunch,' said Sargie to the waiter. It must have been, for with rather surprising moderation, he waved away the idea of pudding, port, brandy or liqueurs. 'We don't want too much of a good thing.'

'And actually, Sargie, I've got to go.'

'Not absolutely at once.'

'Fairly at once.'

'Not ill, my dear?'

'No, no.'

'What do you think of my having a little dinner for Virgil D. *here*? It might be rather nice, don't you think? Americans like this sort of thing. He probably stays at the Connaught. Sibs wants to have him to Cadogan Square, but I don't want to put her through all that. Rupert's always making her entertain. Walks all over her, poor little Sibs.'

This was the closest I ever came to hearing Sibs described, except by Uncle Roy, as 'a complete doormat'. I was silent.

'Do you like Rupert?' Sargie asked baldly. Seeing my discomfiture, his smirk changed to a laugh. Then he lit up yet another cigarette in his bone holder. 'Dynamic Rupert. Do you know what Jimbo used to say about him? "Rupert makes Stafford Cripps seem like a ball of fire!" '

Rupert Starling's dullness was so extreme as to be almost interesting. On another occasion, I should have been happy to mull it over, debate what it was about the man which had attracted Sibs who, as Sargie was perhaps right to say, 'could have had any man she wanted'.

Was the sobersides manner a carapace beneath which a quite different Rupert Starling lurked? Was he laughing at us all for taking his act seriously? There was no evidence for this in his manner but there was the extraordinary detail, if true, which

Anne had once told me, that Rupert's favourite author was Richmal Crompton. He always had a *William* story by the bed, and sometimes read them aloud to Sibs. All this would have been a matter for a seminar in Sargie's best academic manner, but not there, not then.

'He's quite extreme politically, you know.' Sargie's eyes narrowed. 'Far to the left of Vernon.'

'I thought civil servants had no political views.'

Sargie made a sound like *'Pah!'* so loud that it could be heard all over the dining room. It attracted the attention of the very group I had wanted to avoid. Anne saw us first. Our eyes met as she looked across the room. At that moment, Hunter and his silver-haired companion were rising to their feet. Sargie, too, was standing up, his back towards Anne and her friends. I did not need to judge from Anne's glance, since marital telepathy was telling me that she was as anxious as I was to avoid an encounter. I decided to speed Sargie out of the dining room before they got to the door, thereby giving Anne the chance to hang back and delay her exit for a few minutes. I hadn't reckoned on the old gentleman by her side who now strode ahead, a faster walker than Sargie, and reached the wide vestibule at almost exactly the same time. This was no accident, as became almost immediately clear, as immediately, that is, as his manner of speech allowed. He spoke with long pauses and hesitation between carefully chosen words.

'You'll forgive me – er, er – sir – for – er – intruding upon you with no introduction, but I could not allow this opportunity to pass without – er, er – saluting you. When I told your – er – niece that I had instantaneously recognised you from photographs in the Lampitt family albums in the offices of Denniston and – er . . .' He paused for a really long time, as though, having remembered the name of the first Denniston, it was difficult to recall the second. 'Denniston,' he said at last.

He exuded good-humoured affability. His voice was soft, low, gentle.

'Julie, who is this?' asked Sargie, with typical rudeness, not even looking at the large smiling man who addressed us.

'Forgive me, sir,' said the man. He extended a banana bunch of a hand on the little finger of which sat a large glinting ruby set stubbily in good old gold.

'Virgil D. Everett Junior, sir, it's a pleasure to meet you,' he said.

'But we were just talking about you,' said Sargie, 'wondering if you'd like this place. I thought you were going to stay at the Connaught.'

'I am.'

'Next week, you said.'

'I'm around in London next week. I had things to do here this week also.'

By now there was no disguising who his companions were. Sargie first saw Anne and automatically moved forward to embrace her. It was in the course of doing this that he saw Hunter. It would be wrong to say that Hunter was skulking. In his way I expect he relished his triumph. Others in his position would have sidled away to avoid the awkwardness of a confrontation.

Sargie was silenced. He hoped, I suppose, against all hope, that Hunter was part of some other group and not accompanying Mr Everett. But Virgil D. made any such hope untenable. In Hunter's presence the American seemed as innocent and gullible as the rest of us. Though he spoke slowly, he actually took less time to say Hunter's name than an Englishman would have done because he rendered the syllables as one continuous stream of sound – *Rafflehuntr*.

'When – er – Rafflehuntr suggested to me that you might be prepared to sell all the Lampitt items in your possession, sir, I could hardly believe my good fortune. And I'm sure we're all going to collaborate, that is to say, work together just fine.'

The exact significance of these words did not fall into place until we knew the full story. Hunter had persuaded Virgil D. Everett Jnr that he was some kind of emissary from the family. He whetted his appetite for the cash value and salacious contents of Jimbo's diaries, convinced him of the advisability of a purchase, hinted at the existence of rich and voracious rival buyers, got himself made (as the former 'private secretary' to Jimbo) an honorary curator of the Everett Foundation in New York with the special charge of the Ann-Louise Everett Collection, as it is named in memory of Virgil D.'s mother. None of these details were known on that afternoon in Claridge's, nor the consummate delicacy with which, at the English end, Hunter had kept in the background, appeared to be the man

471

who stood most to lose by the transfer of the papers across the Atlantic. As I learned afterwards, Virgil D. had acted in perfectly good faith, genuinely believing that Hunter was a close family friend of the Lampitts. In the first beautifully printed brochure of the Ann-Louise Everett Collection, Hunter was described as the closest personal friend of James Petworth Lampitt, and his 'companion for many years'. The beauty of Sargie's scheme, as we all thought of it, was that the family papers were going to pass out of Hunter's hands. Now it appeared that Denniston and Denniston had bungled and placed the papers in Hunter's hands exclusively. The one safeguard which the family had possessed, the copyright, had been handed over to Virgil D., who appeared to be eating out of Hunter's hand. All Denniston's assurances that Mr Everett would never publish, or have anything to do with Hunter, looked rather silly.

I suppose that in a novel, the writer would feel that some outward action was required to emphasise in the reader's mind the overpowering significance of this scene. Sargie, perhaps, would make a speech of denunciation. I would have hit Hunter. Anne, or perhaps Mr Everett, would have burst into tears. But in fact nothing had happened. In outward terms, Sargie had made far more fuss, a couple of hours earlier, about not getting a table for lunch at his club than at discovering that his grand scheme had come to nothing. Anne had made far more fuss months ago about losing our front door key than she did in this terrible moment which was, I suspect, when she began to see that Hunter had been playing a double game. Mr Everett's brow wrinkled. You could see that he smelt a rat, though he had no reason yet to guess anything of the family's violent hostility to Hunter. I looked across at Hunter and met his face. He knew, he must have known, that I now suspected his relationship with Anne. He certainly knew that his dishonesty over the papers had now been exposed, because it was I who, months earlier, had tried to warn him of the 'American dealer', as I had wrongly termed Virgil D., who had made approaches to Denniston and Denniston. And yet Hunter smiled at me, not sheepishly but tolerantly, as though I were the one at fault, but that just for old friendship's sake he was going to overlook it. The moment of truth which occurred to all three of us about Hunter perhaps lasted about twenty seconds, and we probably all realised that there was nothing any of us could do to alter a situation of which

Hunter was completely the master. Perhaps it was just the sense of our powerlessness which made us stand there in stupefied silence, broken by Mr Everett expressing his sense of honour at having become the owner of these truly fascinating Lampitt items, and his hope that as many members of the family as possible could be his dinner guests the following week.

'No, no, you must be our guest,' said Sargie. He was almost leaning on Virgil D., patting his arm. They looked like fellow mourners at a funeral.

Hunter advanced on me, shameless at being found in Anne's company, and bared his increasingly brown foxy little teeth by way of substitute for a smile.

'I saw Madge the other day. She's very pleased with the way *The Vicar's Nephew* is going.'

'She's not said so to me.'

Again, his indulgent smile as though I were the one stepping out of line.

'In fact,' I added, 'I don't believe the book has sold at all.'

'*Succès d'estime*,' said Hunter. I got the strong impression that he would like to indulge his patronage further, and perhaps welcome me into his brood of unjustly neglected authors, names he sometimes brought into reviews or broadcasts, reputations for which he laboured with paperback publishers. 'Literary reputation is a matter of luck as much as of merit,' he had once written in a Sunday paper. 'The historians provide us with, as it were, a governing cabinet, but those of us who have read in the by-ways of literature know that there is a shadow cabinet waiting in the wings who could, had things been different, have occupied these seats of power now held by Thomas Hardy, W. B. Yeats, or Joseph Conrad.' It is not really a tenable point of view, but I was struck by it when I read it. There was a generosity of spirit here, and, for Hunter, something almost elegant in its manner of expression. Not until later, doing my own researches in the Ann-Louise Everett Collection, did I find the original sentence almost word for word in a notebook of Jimbo Lampitt's.

'I'm sure Madge is looking forward to your next,' said Hunter. 'Not that I'm one to talk! She's been promised my next for years now.'

'Your next – volume?' I could not quite bring myself to ask, 'Of the Lampitt biography?'

He just shrugged and gestured towards Mr Everett, as if things were all in the hands of the gods. Anne disappeared into the Ladies and re-emerged to collect her coat. When she came out, the men, too, dispersed. She was the one member of this small group with whom I had not exchanged a word.

'See you later,' I said to her as we stepped out into the street.

She just smiled, and waved, as she set off alone in the vague general direction of Piccadilly. It was not long before I had seen Sargie back to his club, where we had left our coats, and where there had been all the kerfuffle. We had somehow said goodbye to Hunter and Mr Everett without noticing it; the moment had simply passed.

Coming out of the club, we managed to hail a cab. I saw Sargie into it and promised to meet him again soon. It was nearly four o'clock. I had had an arrangement to call on Debbie at her house at three. I went for a walk alone in Hyde Park, and across to Kensington Gardens. White clouds flew rapidly across a blue sky. The leaves of all the trees, noisy in the wind, were on the turn, yellowing but not yet brown. By the time I had reached the Round Pond, I had decided that my adulterous liaison with Debbie must come to an end.

Ten

The moment in the park, the moment of the Awakening Conscience, was a bit like the ending of a great Russian novel. The hero walks along beneath the trees and feels at one with the world of Nature, the sunlight and the wild sky. His life is changed, and he no longer wants to live in the old way. He would put away the sins which beset him, in this case afternoons with Deborah Arnott, and aspire after a purer soul. Crestfallen, overbrimming with emotion, the hero will find consolation in loving one good woman and thinking simple thoughts. Amazing how these images appeal to men. My momentary impulse to regard Debbie as a bad habit, something like booze or cigarettes which I was trying to give up, was dignified in my mind as a high moral decision. Just as she was beginning to get a bit fond of me, just as there emerged a reason for me to be gentle, I started to regard her as an obstacle to personal goodness, or perhaps merely as a distraction. Perhaps Hunter felt this when he sailed on to new destinations, leaving another Dido sobbing on the shore.

I just dropped Debbie. Didn't turn up on the agreed afternoon. Didn't write. Didn't ring. In the meantime, I had several amiable encounters with Day Muckley. One day in the Bottle he told me that he had been visited by a strange sense of blessing, a sense of well-being not experienced since the days of his young manhood in Yorkshire.

'We all know the reason for that, you filthy old goat,' said Cyril.

'No, no, though relations with my mistress are as happy as ever. They're neither more carnal, neither *more* nor less.'

'Early senility,' said Cyril and wandered off to the other end of the bar, a sort of *palais de glide* of a walk. Before he delivered an insult to a harmless middle-aged stranger who had made the mistake of coming into the pub for a drink (asked the man if anyone had ever told him he had a face like a badger's bum), he turned to the Best-Seller and shouted, 'Sorry, forget I said *early* senility; just senility.'

'You see, I'm writing again, lad. After about ten bloody years in which I couldn't write at all. People who aren't writers don't understand the torture of that silence. But now I feel like a traveller setting out again, old Ulysses turning again for home. In fact, that is what the novel will be about – after a very long journey, and making an absolute bloody mess of life, a man comes home. You'll have guessed that the man is in fact . . .'

I assumed he was going to say himself. At that point, Pete enquired, 'Don't we get served any more in this place? I mean, why does Cyril still employ you?'

By the time I'd topped up Pete's gimlet, the Best-Seller was expanding on his theme.

'My Ulysses figure is of course Clive Pendlebury.'

My bluff was not quick enough. There were a few seconds during which it must have been abundantly clear that I had not the first idea who Clive Pendlebury was. Since he was the main character in *The Calderdale Saga* it was therefore obvious that I had not read Muckley's masterpiece. He smiled, summing me up. It was the expression of a man who had just come across an uneducated fool – not to know Clive Pendlebury was like not having heard of Ulysses himself. More stomach-churning than this was the thought that Day, as I was, might have been racing back in his mind over the many conversations which we had had in the past year in which the subject of *The Calderdale Saga* had come up. How much, implicitly or explicitly, had I claimed knowledge of the book? I couldn't remember. Because he assumed that everyone knew the book, there would never have been a possibility of admitting that I had not read it. But his nerve was no stronger than my own. He was not prepared, in the silence which followed, to risk my saying anything which would make clear that all my expressions of sympathy for his falling sales, of amazement at his hard-luck stories about obtuse publishers, of admiration for him as an author, had been based on sheer wind. How could I ever say now, without crushing embarrassment on both sides, that it was for himself that I liked him, not his books? (This is as deadly an insult as could be delivered to an author, who, when in the grip of authorial self-conceit, would sacrifice the love of a spouse, family and friends

476

for one flattering sentence, perhaps from someone he did not know or did not like, about his writing.)

'Clive Pendlebury from *The Calderdale Saga* will be the Ulysses, and there will in fact be several figures from the other Calderdale books. Like I say, an Odyssey, a homecoming. A confrontation between this man who has totally wasted his whole life, thrown it away, and his wife, and the wife's suitors who have been betraying him. Oh, ay, lad, they'll have done it in my version. No Penelope's web for Lettice. Lettice Pendlebury. That's Clive Pendlebury's wife.'

'I know who Lettice is,' I said hotly, wondering with sweaty horror, because he smiled at me when I made this confession, whether he hadn't tricked me, whether no such character as Lettice Pendlebury occurred in the Muckley *oeuvre*. I also wondered whether Muckley knew about me and Debbie. If so, I was causing him the same sort of pain that Hunter had caused me.

'The world divides as a matter of fact – no, thank you, I'm all right' – he had made a pint last half an hour and showed no inclination to overdo things – 'no, the world divides between those who think the *Odyssey* is the archetypal story of human life and those for whom it's the *Aeneid*. The Odysseuses wander through all kinds of hazards and adventures entirely by chance, or so it seems when they can't see the gods who guide them. But their journey is always in essence a homecoming. Aeneas, now, he's a very different bugger. He knows where he's going, all right, and he's going to get there however many people he tramples all over. The New Troy, the Roman Empire, is vividly present to his imagination all the time, and that's what motivates all his journeys, all the lives he ruins, all the hearts he breaks. But he's a man of destiny, too.'

'What'll it be for you?' asked Cyril. 'Ulysses or Aeneas?'

'Are they cocktails? How too thrilling, darling.'

It was Fenella, unseen, or so it felt, since the Dawn of Time. She greeted all around her with condescending smiles. She, like Muckley on that particular morning, seemed on the up and up, basking in the regular money brought in by Rikko's impersonations of Stan Mulberry. Rikko joined her in a moment – he had been in the Gents – and so there was no chance of developing the Best-Seller's Odysseus and Aeneas idea. Cyril whistled the 'Mulberrys' theme tune and for a split second (absurd idea) I imagined he was going to stand Rikko a Babycham on the house.

'That'll be two and nine, you ponce.'

'Our producer's joining us here for lunch,' said Rikko, 'and he's bringing along one of the script-writers. You remember Rodney, I expect, Rodney Jones.'

'Terribly important to remember directors' names,' said Fenella.

'He came here for lunch when he offered you that job on "The Mulberrys," ' I said.

'Well, before my audition.'

'I don't really' – the Best-Seller was toping now in earnest and there was a large whisky in his hand – 'I don't as a matter of fact listen to the wireless at all.'

'Alexander said to me – Alexander Korda – "Darling Fenella." '

'Shut up, Fenella, shut up.'

'And anyway,' said Mr Porn, who was there somewhere in the middle of it all, 'this chap comes into the shop and says would I have a use for soiled – soiled, mind you – ladies' knickers.'

It was hardly the most propitious moment for resolving the complications of my life. As it happened, however, life was to be changed in the next few minutes. First Cyril told me – 'Why should slags ring you at fucking work?' – that I was wanted on the telephone.

'Julian, it's me, Debbie, Julian.'

Her voice was all trembly. She had not normally repeated my first name in that manner.

'Hallo.'

'Where have you been?'

'A bit busy.'

'Julian, I've got to see you.'

Long silence.

'Julian, I said . . .'

'I know what you said. It's a bit difficult just now.'

'Julian, just tell me what's happened. Just tell me what I'm supposed to have done. Tell me what's changed, love. That's all I want. Just tell me, and I'll be able to accept it. Really, I will, Julian.'

'I can't talk here. There are people listening.'

'Too fucking right they are. And paying you to serve at the bar, not talk to women.'

'Julian, are you still there?'

'Yes.'

'If it means everything's all right again between you and Anne . . . I just wanted to say that's fine, I'm really glad for you.' She was crying now. From where I stood, way out of earshot, I could see the Best-Seller shaking hands with the men from the BBC, and accepting a drink from Rodney.

'Look,' I said impulsively, not being able to stand the tears and realising in the same instant that instead of behaving sensibly (as I had hitherto believed) my attitude since the park *éclaircissement* had been about as morally admirable as a belch, 'I'll come and see you. I'm sorry, I'm really sorry. I'll come.'

'When, pet?'

'I'll come this afternoon.'

'You're lucky,' called Mr Porn. 'I've not come since the Blitz. You don't in my trade somehow, it's the last thing you want to do.'

'Oh, Julian, will you really? You've made me so happy, pet. Oh, Julian.'

' 'Bye.'

When I came back to the bar I was astonished to see my old schoolmaster Treadmill standing between Rikko and the Best-Seller. The man from the BBC was with them, too. I wondered whether Treadmill had come deliberately to see me or whether he had wandered in by chance.

'Val says he knows you,' said the one called Rodney, the producer.

'My dear Julian.'

At school, while pretending to mock Treadmill, we'd all been in awe of him, his range of acquaintance, his experience of the world, the fact (for example, his left-wing views) that he wasn't like the other masters.

Meeting him in the real world was potentially embarrassing. In fact, the slightly two-dimensional persona which any successful teacher must present to a classroom is not unlike the sort of 'character' which gets built up in pubs. Now I summoned back to memory some of the names dropped by Treadmill at school. Wasn't there some story about Dylan Thomas having cadged money for cigarettes and a taxi? Treadmill had worked it into the lesson in the way he did. The beginning of the sentence probably had to do with Chaucer. Then, by some curious sleight, Treadmill would have told us about Chaucer's known riotous and bawdy behaviour in London taverns, which would have led on quite naturally to our sonorous Swansea bard. Not long after wondering whether he would ever see his ten-shilling note again, Treadmill would have intoned, ' "Do not go gentle into *that* good night!" ' which of course none of us had heard of, though it instantly became one of the many poems, first heard on Treadmill's lips, which passed into the repertoire.

'Dylan said he would willingly come down and read his poetry to the Lampitt Society' – Treadmill's small literary club for older boys – 'but Pamela Hansford Johnson, sitting indeed in that very chair, advised against it.' The significance of this statement was lost on a room full of sixteen-year-olds, though one grasped at once that it contained a significance. Treadmill's, in some ways morally dubious, method of teaching was to whip up a yearning to belong to the in-crowd, as it was always implied that he did himself. Unlike us whom he once dismissed as bourgeois bores, he had fought in Spain for the Republic, been to Oxford, and, now I came to think of it, done a bit of sound broadcasting, mainly talks between concerts on the Third Programme, but also a couple of plays. And there was the ten-shilling note lent to Dylan. As he had declaimed, *Et in Fitzrovia Ego.*

So here he was being introduced as Val, and rather than feeling that Treadmill was diminished or that his schoolmasterly poses made him seem from grown-up perspectives ridiculous, I found that I moved at once to accept this different, new, adult Treadmill on his own terms, and that must have been a tribute to him somehow. Yet I could not forget that he was my teacher, and I was ashamed, after all he had tried to teach me, that I had found nothing better to do with my life than pull pints for Cyril. Something of this must have been said or hinted, I forget the details, before Treadmill was kind enough to say that I had been one of the best schoolboy actors he had ever known.

'That's what we came to see you about actually,' said Rodney, who had a rather unsatisfactory beard. He stroked it, less out of love, one felt, than to see if it was really there, and in some lights it was hard to know whether it was or wasn't.

What was I to call Treadmill? 'Sir' was an absurdity which

could hardly be continued in grown-up life; 'Val' was too matey, even though this was what Rodney and Rikko both called him. I settled for calling him nothing.

'I'd absolutely no idea that you wrote "The Mulberrys",' I said, immediately aware that this was a potentially insulting remark.

'It's not my only source of income or employment – as you may know.'

The last phrase, added with heavy irony, was preceded by an infinitely slight non-verbal vocalisation, a sort of *mm*, little more than a closing of the lips. When as children we all imitated Treadmill, this mannerism was exaggerated into a strangulated *Yeair* sound. So much in memory did I recall the imitations of Treadmill, my own chiefly, that the Real Treadmill's voice seemed almost toneless. For the others, he was just perhaps any shambolic figure of the kind who might drink in Soho bars and do odd bits of work for the BBC. They could have no conception of what this man had been to me, what worlds he had opened up. It was just one of those many instances in life where one is confronted by the mystery of our different views of one another. The extremest case is when we are in love. When I was most in love with Anne, I would be astonished that she could enter a room and not produce in every bosom present some of my own feelings of worship. Had everyone felt as I did, then each time she walked into a pub, library, drawing room, would have been like the Exposition of the Blessed Sacrament to the faithful. Every knee would bow, every tongue confess her. Yet, mysterious fact, she made her effect on so comparatively few. In her case, sexual attractiveness and stunning prettiness made a few heads turn, but that is not what I am talking about. She did not engage the imagination of others as she had engaged my own.

'I'm really an understudy,' said Treadmill. 'When P.J. – you must know P. J. Barnes by name?'

'Not, I'm afraid.'

'Val's wonderful,' said Rodney. 'Whenever P.J. wants a few weeks off, Val is prepared to step into the breach and keep the show going. Quite often, we find that it is during Val's period as – with great respect, Val – caretaker scriptwriter – an awful lot has happened in the series.'

My knowledge of the intricacies of 'Mulberry' politics lay in the future. I did not know that Treadmill's nickname among the regular cast was the Angel of Death. If Rodney did not like actors or actresses, it was often during P.J.'s absence that they were irrevocably removed from the scene. It was Treadmill, for example, who had scripted the episode when Mol Mulberry drowned in Barleybrook Pond, a tragedy not unrelated to the fact that the actress playing Mol had a violent temper and had upset most of the cast by her uncontrolled ego. When another actor had a lover's tiff with Rodney, Treadmill was hired to arrange a family tragedy among the Swills. When two or three other members of the cast said that they would resign if Timmy were got rid of, the dread pen of the Angel of Death ordained that motor accident on the way to Silchester. Len Swill's pig van, originally destined to career into a stone wall, found another target when his 'little friends', as Rodney called them, had rallied to his aid: the vicar's Austin Princess with Nora Tilehurst at the wheel. There were complaints from Equity, but once the characters had been killed, there was not much that Treadmill could do to resurrect them.

'There's a borderline between keeping listeners interested and straying into – melodrama,' he said.

'But we are thinking, aren't we, Val, of a new story-line,' said Rodney.

'When did you last hear "The Mulberrys"?' Treadmill asked me a little sharply.

My truthful reply was that I was now only an occasional listener to the programme, my chief period of addiction having belonged to my teens. Cyril, though, was a devoted 'Mulberry' fan and he came up and leaned on the bar next to me, quite deliberately ignoring all the signals from Rodney, myself, Rikko, that a private conversation was in progress.

'You can't come and join us at a table, I suppose?' Rodney asked.

'He can't, he's serving,' Cyril said, smilingly.

'I don't know' – Treadmill's voice sank to a whisper, and it was clear that what he was muttering was classified information – 'if you've kept up with old Harold Grainger.'

'The silly old blacksmith?'

'It is evidently some time since you listened,' said Treadmill shortly. Apparently this was a less than adequate description of Harold Grainger, the strongest comic character of the drama, and a source of wry wisdom, country lore, old songs and a lot of other things which might in a happier world have been kept under wraps.

'What we're really thinking of,' said Rodney, 'was to give old Harold a bit more depth; add, not tragedy exactly to his life, but well, that other dimension.'

'You want to fucking well leave him as he is.' Cyril volunteered this advice spontaneously and with real vehemence. It was the sort of reaction found in those who feel some beloved monument of their imaginative world threatened by change. New dimensions in the life of Harold Grainger were of the same order of turpitude, I could see as, for analogous devotees, the Ring at Bayreuth in modern dress or updatings of the Book of Common Prayer.

'Look, this is all very private at the moment,' said Rodney.

'Then what are you talking about it for in the middle of a public bar, you stupid blob of snot?'

Ludicrously, Rodney responded as though he had to justify himself.

'This was the only day we could both manage to come to London. Val has to see a specialist at four.'

'Nothing serious, I hope,' I asked.

Treadmill held up a scaly hand, purportedly to forbid any anxiety on the score of his health. The rhetorical effect of the gesture was to suggest stoicism in the face of terrible difficulties.

'I've all my life had duodenal trouble, it's no more serious now than it was when you first knew me, Julian.' And then, perhaps displeased by the expression of relief on my face, he added, 'Not *much* more serious anyway. As Rodney says, we were hoping to do a short voice test and audition before I take myself along to – Devonshire Street.'

'What's this, then?' asked Cyril. 'You cunts offering him a part in "The Mulberrys"? That's the second bloody bit of casting you've done in this bar. I'll set up as a theatrical agent if you carry on at this rate, you arse merchants.'

He was glowing with pride as he walked back to Mr Porn's end of the bar where conversation concerned the dog races at White City that night.

'Have you noticed?' asked Treadmill. 'That extremely rude man, whom I take to be mine host, bears the most extraordinary resemblance . . .'

'He does,' I said.

483

'Resemblance to whom?' Fenella asked.

Cyril had surmised at once what was slow to dawn on me, that Rikko, Treadmill and Rodney had come to the pub to try me out for a job. The bucolic, innocent wiseacre Harold Grainger was getting a bit bland even by the standards of the BBC Home Service. They recognised that he had become a national institution and that hordes of listeners like Cyril would protest if Harold were killed off or worse, revealed to have some unexplored side to his character, such as an interest in art or dishonesty as treasurer of the Parochial Church Council. But it was perfectly legitimate and indeed added a faint touch of tragedy to old Harold's nature if he were to be landed with a relative who was a black sheep. They were still toying with the idea of making this figure a younger brother of Harold's who had been in Australia and now turned up like a bad penny. The alternatives were that the figure should be an East End Cockney woman, foisted on Harold's household as an evacuee during the war and now exploiting his good nature, or, as was finally agreed, the figure should be that of old Harold's son.

Cyril let me off work at the bar as soon as it became clear what was in the offing, and, saying goodbye to Rikko and Fenella, and waving to the Best-Seller, who was by now sitting with the dog fanciers, I turned towards Langham Place and Broadcasting House with Rodney and Treadmill.

The collection of a visitor's pass from the uniformed official at the door, the journey down long subterranean corridors in the bowels of the Corporation, the fiddling with tapes and machines in a recording studio: these seemed to me that afternoon no more than a pleasing diversion from the main business of life itself. I gave very little thought to what I was doing, and when they gave me passages of script to read into the microphone, I felt no nervousness.

'We had thought of making Jason speak in the same accent as his father,' said the producer, 'but – what do you think, Val? I think that supercilious pseudo-posh accent is very good, Julian. Jason has risen above old Harold, left the nest, excellent.'

The supercilious pseudo-posh voice so much admired by Rodney had been, until that moment, the one I regarded as my own. Soon, listeners all over Great Britain would be getting used to it and hating it, hating Jason for all the trouble he was causing his poor old dad. Among the heinous crimes lined up for Jason to commit were conning his father out of his life savings, a little blackmail, and possibly getting the barmaid into trouble.

'But we have to play down those sorts of elements,' murmured Treadmill, 'for obvious reasons.'

'Cards on the table,' said Rodney, 'it's an idea. It might work, it might not work. We'll give Jason eight weeks. If it doesn't come off, well, none of us are losers. P.J. will have come back then as our regular scriptwriter, and we can always force Jason to leave the village, go back to the Smoke, perhaps even get arrested by the police.'

Since the offer of a role in 'The Mulberrys' was made in these very tentative terms, it did not feel like a serious step when I accepted it. I shook hands with Rodney and we parted in the vestibule of Broadcasting House. Treadmill and I walked northwards together, in the direction of Devonshire Street.

'I'm sorry you have this awful stomach trouble,' I said.

'Oh, I've had it ever since Spain. The school doctor, strictly *entre nous*, is an incompetent. He made me drink barium meal, which guaranteed that I should be constipated on the actual day of the Inter House Seven-a-sides. He said the X-rays showed me to be fit. That merely showed that he did not know the truth of something Johnson once said: "Sir, sensation is sensation." '

'Well, we shall probably meet quite often in the next couple of months.'

Treadmill beamed weakly. This was only the first of dozens of conversations I had with him about his health. He raised his hand in that strangely effete limp gesture and disappeared behind the polished mahogany of his specialist's front door.

Human faces – it is one of the things which distinguishes them from supposedly lesser creatures – acquire a particular look of totally concentrated absorption when they are about to indulge themselves without regard to the needs or requirements of others. A glutton peruses the menu in his favourite restaurant. The roué eyes up the girls in a brothel and selects one to his particular taste. The old Breton women in the church near Les Mouettes edged nearer the confessional. Their turn would soon come to bore the priest with an account of their own lives since the previous Friday. Just such a look had come over Treadmill: in prospect, a professional man's undivided attention while Treadmill talked about his digestive processes.

I did not realise it, but Treadmill had just solved for me the

485

problem raised by Granny when I left the army: what was I to do with my life, for the time being at least. Jason Grainger was a figure who was waiting to take me over. In the next month I made two or three visits to Birmingham to record perhaps a month's worth of life in Barleybrook. These improbable rustic adventures were then snipped up by Rodney into ten-minute episodes of 'The Mulberrys'. Having discovered that what acting talent I once possessed had entirely deserted me, I was not prepared for any of this. Nor was I prepared for the powerful magic of broadcasting. I was, wasn't I, acting, when I read the lines apportioned to Jason Grainger? And yet Jason's return to the village, his inability to tear himself away from old Harold, whilst landing his father in any number of scrapes, felt like a fantasy projection of the relations I had had over the years with Uncle Roy. Not for the last time, I wondered whether it was possible to escape the drama of our own childhood and adolescence, whether in fact we only ever relate to our families, whether all subsequent friendships, love affairs and emotional adventures are not programmed repetitions of our infancy, or, which amounts to the same thing, attempts to react against it. All journeyings into the uncharted seas turn out to be a voyage home and the only story we are able to tell is our own story. If Day Muckley's set of contrasts was a plausible one, I was a Ulysses and not an Aeneas.

Doubtless, had I tried out this idea on Aunt Deirdre she would at once have smelt a rat.

'Isn't that psychology?' she would have asked. Shudder. 'A friend of Bunty's had it once. Wouldn't let them near me, electric shocks and a lot of, well, *silly* ideas.'

Yet silliness would keep on bursting through, in my life at least.

'Surely you could spare me a fiver, Dad, to help your own son out of a difficulty?'

'It baint thaart, son. Truly it baint. Only, Constable Brayley 'e bin raarnd askin' 'bout that car you've em said you'd bought. Stolen proputty 'e said it were.'

'Really, Dad. Constable Brayley is a man of very limited sensibilities.'

' 'E mebbe uv limited sensib-whatjuma callems, but the law's the law 'e sez.'

'That itself is debatable,' said Jason snootily.

I hated Jason, almost more than I had hated anyone, as I sat and listened to his pseudo-posh.

' 'Ow much longer is yer goin' ter stay, son? It baint that I don't wantcher, yer knows thaart.'

'Poor old Harold,' said Aunt Deirdre, when the inevitable climax had been reached at the end of the programme (Constable Brayley knocking at the door of Harold Grainger's cottage). 'Pity they had to make you into quite such a villain, old thing.'

'It's to give themselves the option of getting rid of me,' I explained.

'It spoils it for me when you say things like that.'

Tender towards her illusions, Aunt Deirdre was, in the years that followed, a mixture of curiosity and caution whenever we spoke of 'The Mulberrys'. If I had to earn my living by pretending to be someone else (and from the start, I conceded that this was a frivolous thing to do), then there was no drama in the world which would have more occupied my aunt's attention. 'The Mulberrys' had been her favourite programme, almost her vicarious existence, for as long as I had known her. At the same time, precisely because she loved 'The Mulberrys' so much, she wasn't sure that she wanted to be told all the secrets. The idea that Rikko was different in kind from Stan Mulberry was something which she had long ago excluded from her mind and if I attempted to say anything of Rikko and Fenella (a rare enough occurrence because I knew that my uncle and aunt would have disapproved), it was always greeted in silence. Happily at that date there was no bad news to relate about Rikko, but had I told her that some personal calamity had befallen him she would have received the news with unshakeable indifference. She was capable, however, without much whimsy, of a genuine empathy with Stan and would often ask after him. I was not sufficiently a professional 'Mulberry' actor to be able to play up to such enquiries by imagining the world of Stan outside the scripts written for him. Normally I answered these questions with some reference to Rikko himself, Fenella's cough, or Rikko having recently splashed out on new lampshades at Peter Jones, or a possible palliative having been found for the Afghans' bowel troubles. Aunt Deirdre would look bored and say, 'No, Stan works himself too hard, I'm afraid, and Gill isn't all the support she should be. I mean, I ask you, taking her mother to Lyme Regis during harvest week, just when Stan needed her most.'

There was nothing very unusual in Aunt Deirdre's need for vicarious living. Uncle Roy had been doing it for years, only the serial drama was not coming out of a radio loudspeaker but was going on inside his head and was called not 'The Mulberrys' but 'The Lampitts'.

I'd gone back to stay at the Rectory for a few days, and after the customary non-conversations, I felt strongly on my last day that I should say something about me and Anne. The three of us were in the kitchen having washed-up lunch. Granny was upstairs listening to the wireless in her bedroom where she spent more and more time. Uncle Roy, who was to hold a ruri-decanal chapter meeting that afternoon in his study (he was rural dean now) was dressed in his version of clericals, a white bow tie, white shirt and grey flannels.

I had made up my mind to tell them calmly and fully, and not to blame Anne or myself, but simply to say that after an initial period of great happiness we had both come to realise that the marriage had been a mistake. I would go on to say that I fully respected their religious and moral principles and did not expect them to approve, but that I was going to divorce Anne. In trying to frame this difficult narrative in my brain I was preoccupied with my own feelings, to a lesser degree with Anne's. What justified the divorce, made it inevitable and even desirable, was my certainty that there was no virtue in two people making each other unhappy. That my uncle and aunt disapproved of divorce I took for granted, but I had not been home often enough to appreciate what my marriage meant to Uncle Roy.

The fluent and sensible speech did not come out as planned. I blurted out, 'There's something you ought to know,' and then wasn't able to finish the sentence. After a very long silence, I said, 'It's . . .' And then another long silence, at the end of which I said, 'Anne and I.' Then more silence before the single word 'divorce' escaped my lips in a whisper.

'She's asked you for a divorce?' Aunt Deirdre said.

'No, but we just aren't happy.'

'Nothing's happened, has it, old thing?' I think this was Deirdre-ese for wondering if adultery had occurred.

'No, nothing's happened exactly. Just – don't get on.' Long

pause: a pause so long that the world could have ended. 'Miserable, both of us.'

'I often think there's no point in two people staying together if they're miserable,' she said decisively. Often? When did these thoughts come to her? As she was stooped over the flower beds yanking at weeds, presumably. I hadn't expected her to be understanding. She looked very sad, but kind. My uncle's face was a picture of desolation.

'This can't be true,' he said.

'I'm afraid it is.'

'Many people live apart,' he said. 'Sargie and Cecily hardly ever lived with each other. But a divorce is unthinkable.'

'If we don't want to be married . . .' I feebly began.

He was staring away into nothingness.

'Poor Sibs,' he said quietly.

I tried to take in the significance of those two syllables, but I couldn't. Only later did I realise what my brief, careless marriage had done to my uncle. For a little over a year he had enjoyed what he had always dreamed of having, a family connection with the Lampitts.

'It would hit Vernon very hard,' he said, coming to grips with himself. 'The Labour Party can be very prudish about such matters.'

We had re-entered the region of sheer fantasy. That Vernon's 'career' as a Labour peer should have been changed one way or another by the marital status of a first cousin once removed was not to be believed.

'And Ursula. The Ladies' Colleges, again . . .' His voice trailed away. Perhaps Felicity's life had shown him that Ladies' Colleges were occasionally able to accept the ups and downs of an imperfect human condition.

'But poor Sibs,' he repeated.

'And poor old Julian,' said my aunt, patting my shoulder with her fingertips, an extremely demonstrative gesture for her.

My uncle looked up sharply. He was angry.

'I think Julian is being very selfish,' he said. And he left the room without another word. There did not seem much more to say. Not long afterwards I got into the car and roared back towards London. Poor Sibs. Not poor Anne, not poor me, but poor Sibs. I had made the mistake of supposing that life was an occasion for pursuing personal fulfilment and I had forgotten that its true function was the contemplation of the names, doings and sensibilities of the Lampitt family. No wonder that my uncle was shocked. By his standards, the step which I was contemplating was insane. A philatelist watching a child stick a Cape Triangular into a book of Green Shield stamps could not have reacted with more horror than Uncle Roy when he saw me throwing away my Lampitt bride.

I drove the car, Anne's car, dangerously, my mind entirely detached from the driving, focused with obsessive intensity on the drama of my interior life. I felt the need to go back to Anne, to talk, to sort things out once and for ever. One has this sense when very unhappy that a crisis can be resolved by doing or saying one more thing. One loses the sense of life as an idling hilly landscape of long vistas which we get through whatever happens and which will not be altered much by one big conversation, or one big decision. Oddly enough, the certainty that I must see Anne, settle things, talk of lawyers, was accompanied by a great dread of the conversation itself and of its finality. I was not truly certain that I knew what to do and I found, as the traffic got heavier in the streets of the City, that I was continuing westwards with some reluctance. What if her mother were to be in the flat when I returned?

The answer, obviously, was that I would postpone any big conversation until Anne and I were alone together. I did not think of this answer. The thought of 'poor Sibs' was enough to determine the path which the car took, nosing its way down Oxford Street and the familiar left-hand turn into Soho Square. The square was full of people – office girls sitting cautiously on benches; shy men, some in uniform, wondering about a tart before their next engagement; tarts themselves, as well as many people just wandering and enjoying the heat. It was the last day of summer. Autumn weather was on its way. I parked in Poland Street and looked at my watch. It was only about six thirty. Not many would yet have arrived in the Bottle. Indeed, the Best-Seller himself had not yet arrived, for even as I was locking the Morris, he came shambling towards me, a determined smile enlivening his big froglike face.

'Well, Julian, lad, this is a very pleasant surprise.'

'You're looking very pleased with yourself. The writing is still going well?'

'So, so, lad, so, so.' I didn't believe him. There had been no mention of his modern *Odyssey* novel since the first time he had told me about it.

'I thought perhaps you'd won some money on the dogs.'

'The dogs?' His mock outrage, his little attempt to put on a posh voice, did not quite come off. 'Young man, are you implying that I gamble? On the dogs? How very socially . . . inept!'

He was very smart. His hair was smarmed back with bay rum, his collar was stiff and clean, the blazer and trousers were just back from the cleaners. The tie was the Bradford Rotarians'.

'No, as a matter of fact, I've just been to confession,' he said. 'Wiped the slate clean again, lad. It does you good, like a real dose of syrup of figs. Cleanses you. Empties it all out.'

'I get the idea.'

'I feel twice the man.'

'They say it's good for you. What I find difficult to believe is that past deeds could ever be undone.'

'They're not undone, lad, no one believes that. No, the difference between Catholics and the rest of you is this. We all want to forget, we all want to pretend it didn't happen, we all want to put it behind us for Christ's sakes, and we all want forgiveness. But the difference between a Catholic and someone like you, Julian, is that a Catholic knows forgiveness. You could confront the worst sides to your nature, the most horrible things you ever said or did if you knew you had the forgiveness of God.'

'Maybe God has less to forgive than we have. Maybe we hurt Him less than we hurt one another.'

'That's where the crucifix comes in,' said Day Muckley. He said it on the pavement outside the Bottle. He said it as we crossed the saloon and he said it again when we reached the bar and he asked me what I'd have.

'I'd better have a very large Scotch,' he said.

'Glad you got a large something, apart from a mouth,' said our genial landlord.

'I'll stick to beer,' I said.

Hardly anyone was there yet. The little man haloed by a trilby and the two old women smoking and drinking brandy, and Mr Porn who had abandoned his literary endeavours for the day. In spite of the warmth of the evening, he still wore his bowler hat, his black shirt, thick black suit and black tie. Sweat cascaded down his smooth red face as he sipped his gin-and-water.

'I heard you say crucifixes were coming in,' he said. 'Very interesting. I mean, I've known for years in my business about the kinky appeal of all that stuff. What else are all those High Church nancy vicars except transvestites? Convent girls with rosaries knotted around their tits, monks with hard-ons under their habits, group sex on the High Altar, it's all got its market.'

'Shut up,' said Day Muckley. He had gulped down his first large whisky and was holding out his glass for more.

Pete said, 'Jesus, not another religious discussion, if you please. I thought we'd all agreed to keep off the fucking subject. I'll ask you all the question which is a bloody sight more interesting than theology.'

' "All questions are ultimately theological." Cardinal Manning said that,' the Best-Seller informed us.

'Well, he must have been a prat. What's theological about women? And don't let's have another go over the Virgin Mary, please. There was an Irishman in here one day . . .'

'Why don't they go to one of their own fucking pubs?' wondered Mr Porn. 'God knows, there are enough of them.'

'He told that one about the Virgin Mary and the camel,' said Cyril. 'Oh dear, you'll be on to the Jews next. I don't care what religion people are so long as they spend money.'

'I warned you,' said Day Muckley. He had started to sweat and to go red.

'My point is,' said Peter, 'where do we get our ideas about women and sex? Maybe the Virgin Mary does have something to answer for, come to think. I mean, when a man's been unfaithful, he's a shit.'

'You may have been,' said Cyril.

'No, he's a shit. It's all "Where in hell have you been? Get out of my life, you horrible man, you've ruined everything." But when a woman goes and screws a bloke . . .'

'Then it's "You whore, you've ruined everything." ' This viewpoint of Mr Porn seemed at least to strike a balance.

Seeing the Best-Seller subside into his customary evening stupor prompted thoughts of 'poor old Debbie', as she had become in my thoughts. I felt guilty about not seeing her, as I had promised to do, when she had so obviously needed cheering up. I had no intention of reviving or continuing our affair, but I was conscious of owing her at least some kindness, and the image of Day Muckley's inebriated face gave me an acute sense of what she must have suffered. I finished my drink and said I must be getting along.

'It's always "Poor girl, I don't know how she puts up with him," ' said Peter. 'Always them having to put up with us, isn't it? Never a word about what they make us suffer.'

'I'll be going then,' I repeated.

Day Muckley did not even reply. He was just staring, staring, too vacant to contribute to the Marriage Debate which was in perpetual progress at that bar. Driving northwards towards Tufnell Park, I pictured the scene upon which I was to intrude. Debbie would be giving an early supper to the boys, perhaps to some of their teenage friends. It would be a good time to call. Not long thereafter the boys would go to their rooms and Debbie would make coffee. I would apologise for having stayed away and explain that it was the best way of ensuring that neither of us became too fond of each other. She would understand, and then I could go back to Anne. A mood of benevolent optimism overcame me. I was not drunk; indeed, I made a firm resolution not to drink any more that evening. In this new mood, when I thought of Anne, it was not of the truculent Anne of recent months but of the happy, beautiful girl I had married. What if Uncle Roy's reaction was not the right one? Had I been too quick to despair? We were both sensible people. (What on earth allowed this idea into my head?) We might after all work things out happily. Debbie would go on being my friend. Anne might pass through this phase if I could only tell her what she meant to me.

The days were drawing in. It was dark by the time I drove downhill into Dartmouth Park Avenue. Walking up to the house, my feet scrunched on fallen leaves and the shells of horse-chestnuts. I rang the doorbell, rehearsing a pleasantry with Simon or Jon, whichever twin were to open the door. In fact, Debbie stood there alone.

'Hallo, stranger.' It was unmistakably a reproach.

'Hallo, there.'

'Julian, it's been weeks.'

'I know, Debbie, I know.'

'What do you want?'

'Can I come in?'

Her cross expression was mollified by a toothy smile.

'Why do I put up with you? Come on, I'd been looking

493

forward to a quiet evening with my proofs. Day said he'd ring, the sod, and he hasn't.'

'And the boys?'

'It's one of their weekends to be with Derek. They just hate going there, Julian. They have to share a bedroom and there's nothing for them to do . . .'

We walked into the kitchen as she spoke compulsively about the legal arrangements relative to Derek's access to his sons.

'There's a bottle of wine opened. Chianti.'

'No, thanks.'

'What's the matter with you?'

'Oh, all right, then. Just a glass.'

She filled up a big tumbler of the stuff. There was a longish silence after I'd taken my first sip and sat down. Her kitchen was very modern, with red and white fitted units, coated in plastic and Formica, strip lighting in the ceiling, fitted cupboards, and, on top of one of the units, a food mixer.

'I've been busy,' I said. 'I've some work at last.'

'Day told me. You're wasting yourself, Julian, you know that.' Was she drunk or just emboldened by disappointment? 'Acting in crap on the wireless instead of getting down to a proper book.'

'Writing isn't everything.'

'It is to me.'

'Everything?'

'That and the kids. And the few people I can rely on.'

Another punishing silence during which there was nothing to do except drink up my wine in nervous gulps. When my glass was empty, I said, 'Debbie, what we had together, it was fun, it was lovely, but it wouldn't have lasted.'

'I wasn't asking for it to last, Julian. Just for a bit of sympathy, when I needed you.'

Her lower lip trembled and she began to cry. I rose and went over to comfort her. She was not sobbing, just crying quietly with tears coming out of her great brown eyes.

'I wasn't kidding myself you loved me,' she said, responding to my caress by stroking my hands as they lay on her shoulders. 'I just missed you.'

'I missed you, too.'

Why did I say this? It was almost completely untrue. She stood up when I spoke these words and put her arms round my neck.

'Still, you're like all the others, the selfish sods.'

It was just reaching the point where it would be bad manners not to respond to these endearments. Our lips were meeting. Hands were straying up and down each other's backs.

'Debbie, I . . .'

'There's no need to explain, pet, no need to explain.'

Perhaps there wasn't. What harm was being done? At length, having opened another bottle of Chianti, and given me the three-quarters-finished one to carry, she led the way into the sitting room. The lounge was as lavishly modern in style as the kitchen, no expense spared. Three walls of ochre paint were contrasted with the fourth which was covered in a heavy bold wallpaper, midnight blue with splashes of orange to match the contemporary Scandinavian sofa on which we sank down.

'You're just lovely,' I said.

'You're wicked.'

'Just a bit.'

We drank up the first bottle of wine and smoked a bit and then we went on to the second bottle. I took off my jacket before resuming our embrace. She put one hand inside my shirt, and I began to unbutton her blouse, and to undo the awkward straps and hooks which I found inside. While I was thus engaged, she froze, and asked, 'What's that?'

'What?'

'Was that the front door?'

'But the boys are away. You said.'

'Yes, but.' She did not need to explain what she meant because the lounge door opened and Day Muckley lurched in. She had said he might call. My hand was instantly withdrawn from Debbie's chest, hers from my trousers. Evidently, he had a latchkey and came and went as he chose. Was it conceivable that he would suspect nothing, or suppose that there was an innocent explanation for the two of us to be sitting on the sofa, I with tousled hair, she with blouse unbuttoned to the waist? Was it possible that he was too far gone to notice? I dreaded his wrath, but more I dreaded his hurt, and it would have been an impossible insult to them both to suggest that what was taking place on the sofa was entirely without seriousness as far as I was concerned.

She began to button herself decorously and he just stood

there, staring. He was pale, and his eyes were more than ever marbly behind thick lenses.

We were frozen in that terrible scene for some moments. Debbie began to shiver. Then she said, 'Hallo, love. Day!'

He said, 'My God.'

His voice was gravelly, flat, despondent. I do not doubt that he did appreciate what was going on. He could not have failed to put the worst possible interpretation on what he saw.

'Love, it's not what you think,' said Debbie.

I said, 'I'll go.'

I had not thought how to manoeuvre my way round his figure as he stood by the door. Even drunk, his short, stocky body looked massively strong. He could do damage with a punch.

'Day, Day,' said Debbie. Her voice fluttered. She was anxious. Her third 'Day?' was interrogative.

'My God.'

His pale, impassive, masklike face now creased with pain and a huge hand came towards his lips. Was he going to weep, or belch, or repeat his celebrated television performance?

'My God, I love thee with my whole heart . . .'

He was not talking to Debbie, he was talking to God, but his sentence got little further, and became a deep groan. He bent double and clutched his stomach.

'Oh, no, love, not here,' said Debbie.

He did vomit, but what came out of his mouth was a torrent of blood, and he collapsed on to the carpet, dragging a table over as he fell. When we knelt beside him, we saw that blood was dribbling from his nose and continuing to come out of his mouth. His brow was already that of a corpse, white and damp, but he was breathing in bursts. Blood was coming out of his ears.

We tried to lift him and found that he was squelching in blood from behind, and his light mackintosh was crimson and sodden.

'Where's the telephone?'

'Oh, Day, Day, love.' She stroked his head and wept.

'The *telephone*.'

'In the hall. Oh, Day. It'll be all right, love, it'll be all right.'

I dialled 999 on the hall telephone and came back into the room when the ambulance was ordered. Debbie looked up at me. Her face was quite changed. All its innocence was gone.

'Oh, he's not going to, he's not going to, is he?'

'The ambulance will be here soon.'

'Oh, my God.'

Her hands and cheeks were stained with blood. She fell on him, clawing and crying in uncontrolled grief.

We both felt instinctively that our act of casual betrayal had precipitated if not actually caused this terrifying effusion. Certainly in my own case (though all Debbie's feelings must have been proportionately more painful in so far as she loved him) I felt like a murderer. In the discussions we were to have after the funeral, Debbie told me that Day had often been to a doctor complaining of stomach pains. Unlike Treadmill, he had not taken his disorders to a specialist and his doctor had done no more than prescribe an occasional palliative, dismissing the very idea of ulcers. I knew nothing about the condition and in so far as I knew of people suffering from duodenal or gastric complaints I had associated ulcers with hypochondria, or with those who were pushing themselves unattractively hard. Ulcers were for thrusting business executives. If I had had to name anyone of a literary bent who would have been a likely sufferer it would have been Hunter, not Day Muckley. I certainly did not know until I witnessed it what a burst ulcer, a haemorrhage on a gigantic scale, could do. Nor until I watched over Muckley's bloody and recumbent form had I thought how tenuously the human body contains itself. The line in *Macbeth* is so right: who would have thought the old man to have had so much blood in him? And only when the blood starts to come out, and uncontrollably, when all the orifices are opened and the polite arrangement by which we are parcelled in with skin and muscles to contain our liquid constituents breaks down, does one realise what a mess we are physically, and how little it takes to destroy us. He wasn't dead. His eyes were shut, and he was deathly pale and his breathing came very irregularly. When, quite soon, the ambulance arrived, Debbie recovered her composure; and when Day had been lifted on to the stretcher she became aware of the minor practical difficulties of the situation.

'How will you get to the hospital? Oh, look at that carpet . . . If I stay behind and you go in the ambulance . . . Oh, no, look, if you . . .'

It was one of the ambulancemen who resolved things for us. Debbie went with Day in the ambulance. I stayed behind to clear up some of the mess, saying I would come to join her in the hospital, the Royal Free.

When she was gone and I had the house to myself, I wondered how conceivably I could have found myself in a position socially so painful, morally so shabby. In the ordinary course of things, had it gone unwitnessed, what had passed between me and Debbie on the sofa that evening would have been harmless, though it was not what I intended and it certainly muddied the situation between me and Anne. And now Day Muckley was dying under the impression that a friend of his had deceived him with the woman he loved, which would have been bad enough if it was true: but it wasn't really true, or I didn't think it was true, believing at that age that actions took their moral colour from how you felt when committing them rather than from their effect on others. Perhaps this was Hunter's criterion of behaviour, too; and perhaps this was how he was capable of causing so much pain in others while appearing to suffer none himself.

I must have made between ten and twenty journeys between Debbie's sitting room and kitchen with a bucket and mop. The carpet was not merely stained but sodden. No one would ever get rid of the stain but with enough diligent rubbing and sponging I could clear up the worst of the mess and leave it to dry. Having a grim practical task to do was particularly consoling. While I worked I thought of Day Muckley, as I was often to do in the months and years that followed. He was not destined to die immediately. In fact he lingered for several days in a coma before the end, which was, I remember, on Michaelmas Day. I had grown fond of him for reasons which could not be put into words and when in after-years I spoke of him others would be puzzled that I had liked him. All stories about him, or nearly all, made him sound coarse or boring; and he could be these things. But I was fonder of him than I was of Debbie, particularly in the years which followed his death, when her devotion to literature seemed increasingly bound up with a desire to get on in the world. Day Muckley had wanted desperately to get on. He had none of Blake's self-confident otherworldliness. He wanted his books (which I didn't like much, when I read them) to make him rich and famous. But he had helped to develop in me what he held as a genuine creed for himself, the sense that literature was something to be intensely grateful for, almost something worth living for. I doubt whether he would have been much fun before the war, in the brief period of his triumphant success, when he had liked to waste money on showy cars and to mix with the more famous practitioners of his craft. (How he had envied Arnold Bennett's yacht.) My Day Muckley was a collapsed man in a pub, no longer convincing anybody, given to anger and confusion and plausibly, though incomprehensibly, at one with his God.

(At his funeral, we sang a belligerent hymn called 'Faith of Our Fathers', said to be his favourite, whose jaunty trivial tune was at variance with the suffering of the martyrs it described.) If God were like Stalin, as Day had once averred, then there was nothing surprising about the way He had dealt this last blow to His loyal old supporter. ('Did He smile His work to see?') Just such a bloody end awaited those in the USSR who had kidded themselves that they had got on the right side of the Kremlin mountaineer. Yet Muckley's Church taught a different doctrine, that God when He walked the earth had turned His feet to places where He could eat and drink with sinners, places like the Black Bottle, in fact.

When I'd done all I could for Debbie's carpet, I drove to the Royal Free and found her, tearfully waiting in the corridor outside the intensive care unit. His wife had been sent for, and the last piece of torture which Debbie had to suffer during those final few days was to be compelled to make herself scarce while Mrs Muckley brought a priest to her husband's unconscious body. I forget what the doctors did to him, if anything. There was some talk of an operation if he was strong enough, which he wasn't.

Debbie and I sat on a bench together.

'I'll never forgive myself,' she said.

'You shouldn't feel like that.'

'I do, I do.'

'If it was anyone's fault, it was mine.'

'Julian – how could we?'

She blew her nose. Then she said in a determined, brave voice, 'He'll pull through. I know he's going to pull through. And when he does it will all be different. I shan't limit his visits to two days a week. He needn't go on living in those horrible little rooms. He can come and live with me. We'll make a life. Together.'

'Of course.'

'I'd rather be alone now.'

'I see.'

'Can you understand? I want to be alone.'

I touched her hand, got up, and walked away down the corridor. There was no more to say. A clock on the wall said five past twelve and it conveyed nothing to me. I had no idea what sort of time it should have been, and no consciousness of whether it was the middle of the day or the middle of the night. Because it was dark in the car park, I remembered it was night, and that six hours earlier I had been on my way home to see Anne.

London was curiously empty, so that the journey from Hampstead to the far end of Chelsea took barely half an hour. My mind was no longer full of Debbie, or of Anne, or of my work, the things which had haunted so much of the last year. Nor had I framed into any rational cliché the notion that in Muckley's end I had witnessed a horrible version of what we were all journeying towards, whether in a stately genteel manner (the car was passing Cadogan Square) or in the more unvarnished mode of my friends at the Black Bottle. I thought rather of Muckley himself and how sad I was that I'd never see him again, talking nonsense with his pint of bitter in his hand or swaying out into the afternoon light of Poland Street. And I wished I could tell him the truth about what he'd seen on the sofa, wished I'd been able to explain that I had meant no harm by it, certainly no harm to him. But I knew that such wishes would never be fulfilled.

The car sped down the King's Road. Just by the Town Hall where Anne and I were married, I saw Hunter standing alone by a lamppost. He appeared to be doing nothing. He was some way from the nearest bus stop and did not seem to be on the lookout for a taxi. I supposed that he had been at our flat, and the thought made me angry, but I slowed down to check that it was truly Hunter, rather than someone who looked a bit like him. I have a tendency when much preoccupied with a person to 'see' them all over the place and to recognise them in perfect strangers. It was possible that this was some other man, not Hunter at all. As the car slowed down, Hunter looked up and peered through the side window with a strange smile. It infuriated me that he should be trying to ingratiate himself after all that had happened. But when our eyes met, the smile vanished and his face revealed genuine surprise. Who had he supposed it was? Our eyes met only for a second; I had merely slowed, not stopped the car, and I immediately drove off, leaving him there. In the driving mirror, I saw that he had turned and walked briskly up in the direction of Sloane Square.

The lights were all off in the flat when I got in. I switched on one of our raffia lamps in the sitting room and sat on a cane armchair. One last cigarette before bed. As I lit up, Anne appeared at the bedroom door, bleary-eyed. Either she was becoming a good actress or I had woken her up.

She had on an old dressing gown of mine left over from schooldays.

She yawned and asked snappishly, 'Where in hell have you been?'

DAUGHTERS
OF ALBION

It was one of those journeys on which a man
perpetually feels that now at last he must
have come to the end of the universe, and
then finds he has only come to the beginning
of Tufnell Park.

G. K. CHESTERTON

TO
R.

One

Love was in the air.

At one end of the Formica-topped table they spoke of the prostitute, and at the other of the bishop. I was caught between the two colloquies; I sat opposite Darnley who was always exactly halfway down the table, a position from which he could hear as much as possible of what was being said.

'I can't see what difference it makes if a Cabinet minister, like most other healthy individuals in the fucking world . . .'

The speaker, Peter Cornforth, was interrupted by Vernon Lampitt.

'With great respect, Pete, that's not the point.'

'How do you think the world got populated?' asked Peter. 'You got children.'

'That isn't the point. The world is not populated by public figures exploiting the services of young girls. . . .'

'Exploitation!' Peter laughed and ignited a Park Drive. Understandably, he seemed weary of the food placed before him. A school dinner chosen by Darnley. We had eaten our way through steak and kidney, suet, boiled potatoes, cabbage, gravy. Now the rhubarb crumble lay in front of us, poking above the custard, rocky islands in small yellow seas.

Peter Cornforth, a wounded jockey who had made a sporadic living as a freelance hack, contributed a page of racing notes to Darnley's little magazine *The Spark*, which had been running a bit less than a year. It was a strangely miscellaneous publication, reflecting the disjointed nature of Darnley's own personality. The general verdict, when, as inevitably happened, it folded, was that Darnley had not made up his mind what sort of magazine it should be. I don't think this view is altogether correct. Darnley did make up his mind what the paper should be like, but his mind was not the easiest of things to fathom, and the general public evidently did not think, at 6*d*, that it was worth the effort. Those who might have enjoyed Pete Cornforth's gossip about trainers, bookies, or racehorse owners, or the even more scurrilous passages of social and political comment in the 'Diary' at the front of the paper, would not necessarily have wished to wade through the longish articles about literature, politics, or religion in the second half of *The Spark*. Darnley had the idea that if he produced a paper which contained nothing but items of interest to himself, then the public was bound to follow him. He was wrong, even though one now sees that *The Spark* was of its time; little papers were springing up all over London in those days. Some were to turn into national institutions, like *Private Eye;* others, more identifiably political than *The Spark*, would enjoy specific moments of notoriety before running out of cash or being closed down by the law. *The Spark* had something in common with these semi-underground rags, though in other ways it was more a throwback to earlier traditions of journalism, *Night and Day*, *Horizon*, even *GK's Weekly*.

Almost more important to Darnley than the paper itself was the regular lunch which he held for contributors and friends. His zest for the dingy made it inevitable that he should have decided the Black Bottle to be a suitable venue for these symposia. It was a pub where I had worked as a barman and spent more time than was useful in my early twenties. Now that my thirtieth birthday approached, I felt sheepish about going to the place. Cyril, the proprietor, laid aside a small back room, which it would appear was now being used as a store for domestic rubbish, since the dozen or so guests for lunch that day had squeezed past a broken standard lamp and a mangle which were half blocking the door.

Talk of the politician's downfall, and his association with the young woman, was for a moment drowned by the group on my right talking of the bishop. A fat journalist was speaking in gravelly northern tones.

'Either you believe in God or you don't, and if you don't believe in God, you shouldn't be a bishop.'

'Oh, but it's less simple than that!' screamed some woman, whom I have never seen since. Beehive hairstyle and big teeth.

To my left, Vernon Lampitt and Peter Cornforth were now setting to.

'You may be completely virtuous,' said Pete. 'He is.' He

stabbed the air with an ignited Park Drive in the direction of Darnley who sniffed imperiously, and then roared with laughter. If sexual coyness is to be associated with virtue, then I think Darnley was extremely virtuous, though this was one of the many ways in which the adult Darnley was unlike the ten-year-old whom I had first befriended at our private school, Seaforth Grange. In grown-up life, we did not see much of one another for long periods. Then there would be spells when we picked up the threads. I had only the haziest idea of his emotional make-up, beyond having decided that he was one of those people to whom sex, or rather his own sexual nature, was not very important. Other people's tastes in these areas were a different matter, so long as their proclivities led them to behave in a way which Darnley considered risible.

'Look,' said Pete, 'Members of Parliament are away from their wives all week, lucky bastards. Most of them are too horrible to make friends with nice girls.'

Darnley put on his High Court judge voice.

'Are we going to allow that to pass?' he enquired. 'Ernie?'

'No,' said Vernon. 'And yer missing the point, Pete. This is a matter uv national security. We're talking about a minister uv the Crown. . . .'

As often happened when Vernon was enunciating an argument, he began to speak more slowly, as to a classroom of backward schoolchildren. He removed his pipe from his lips and counted out each phrase, holding the pipe in one hand and touching a separate finger of the other with its dottle-wet stem for each separate point he wanted his hearers to understand.

'We're talking about a Cabinet minister responsible for the defence uv the realm, friend uv the Prime Minister and the ruling establishment. . . .'

'What do you think you are if you aren't the ruling establishment?' asked Peter.

'I'm not the establishment. The Lampitts, that's me family, have always bin anti-establishment and I could give yer chapter and verse for that. But let's stick to the issues. . . .'

'So you think he's been muttering military secrets to this girl as he flops back on the pillow. "Was that nice for you, darling, and by the way, I've been meaning to tell you, nearly forgot, we're thinking of sending a tank regiment over to Aden." '

507

'She's bin seein' a man from the Russian Embassy,' said Vernon.

'Friend of yours?' shouted the fat northern journalist.

'Ernie,' said Pete with sudden intensity. 'When did you last do it?'

Pete had moved into a new phase of drunkenness. His brilliant blue eyes were flecked with red, and his cheeks had become scarlet. Vernon hummed and hawed. I wondered if he was seriously trying to retrieve from the cobwebs of memory the information Pete demanded.

'Would you speak about military secrets to a woman?' asked Pete.

'In principle, I don't see why not,' I volunteered.

'Because they're too fucking stupid to understand military secrets, that's why not,' Pete explained.

'It's all a symptom,' said Vernon who with his dottle-drip was preparing to count out another list on his fingers. 'A symptom of moral bankruptcy in the established class, a symptom of the real emptiness of the capitalist system, yes you can laugh.'

Most of them did.

'Pugh will never tell us,' said Darnley, 'how he managed to know about this distressing affair months before the journalists. Will you, Pughie?'

As he gazed down to the end of the table where they were discussing the bishop, a look of something like adoration passed over Darnley's face.

'It was bound to materialise at the last,' said the man to whom we all turned. 'And Lord Lampitt is surely right. . . .'

'Ernie, Ernie!' protested Vernon. 'None of this "lord" rubbish.'

'There is a place for a hierarchy of nobilities, Lord Lampitt, you are wrong to deny it,' said the man whom Darnley called Pugh. 'But you are right to discern that these events have symptomatic reverberations. Here is a portentous conjunction. You meditate upon the Harlot, while we discuss the Episkopos.'

He intoned, more than spoke, in a nasal cockney voice and stared at the ceiling as the strange words passed his grinning lips. Very thick lenses, bottle glass, magnified his dark eyes into bulbous marbles. For the fashion of those days, his hair was unusually long, brownish grey, receding from a Shakespearean brow. He was unbearded but 'clean' would be an inappropriate adjective for the manner in which he was shaven. He wore a crumpled dark blue double-breasted suit. Between the greasy tie and a quarter inch of greyish neck a stud jutted between collar and shirt. Mr Pilbright, my superior in the Accounts department of the shirt factory where I was once employed, would have approved that here was 'no nonsense about collar-attached'. I had no idea who the man was, though I formed the instantaneous impression that it was 'typical' of Darnley to have collected him.

'I've heard of the Bishop and the Actress,' said Pete. 'But this is a new one. The Harlot and the Piss what?'

The portly northern hack, whose name was Godfrey Tucker, and who for years had an 'opinion' column in one of the middle-brow Sunday newspapers, laid an odoriferous miniature cigar in the remains of his rhubarb crumble and repeated, 'Either you believe in God or you don't. As it happens, I am not a believer myself, but for a bishop, a bishop of the *Church* . . .'

'What other sorts of bishop are there?' asked Darnley.

'I could tell you,' said Pugh darkly.

'To say in a public article, in a high-falutin Sunday newspaper, read by all the Hampstead intellectuals, that he doesn't even believe in the Resurrection . . .'

Darnley beamed at Tucker, satisfied, as always when people parodied themselves. From early days together, I had noticed in Darnley what I came to think of as the ringmaster's expression. The poodles were about to stand on their hind legs and teeter through the hoops. 'I think a piece is coming on,' he muttered, pointing to Godfrey Tucker with his thumb.

'The bishops are appointed to give a lead in matters of faith,' grumbled Tucker. 'Not to sow doubts.'

'New para!' shouted Darnley.

I have never been much interested in 'the news', and I shared none of Darnley's fascination with journalistic ephemera. I had missed the article in which some bishop, famous at the time, had expressed the usual Anglican incredulity about the Christian story. The other matter – the scandal in the Cabinet – I could not avoid knowing about. It was one of those nauseating moments in English life when a sexual débâcle gripped the public mind and, wherever you went, intruded itself into every conversation. There was talk of the Government being brought down by it. Any connection between this semi-comic, if sordid chain of events and the desire of some cleric to make a splash in the newspapers by a declaration of unbelief was not one which I should have made myself but, as I came to feel, it was highly characteristic of 'Pugh', who was never more in his element than when sacred and erotic love were enmeshed or confused.

'The Episkopos, like many Englishmen, is imprisoned in the empiricist fallacy,' he enunciated. 'Either/or – the two falsest words in the English language.'

'You're not saying the bishop's involved in all this other business?' asked Tucker. He had cottoned on to 'Pugh''s ability to form bizarre connections, and also to his genius for esoteric gossip. Tucker was suddenly very interested. If a bishop, albeit a suffragan, could be found to have shared the favours of the young woman with a Soviet Embassy attaché and a Cabinet minister, this was the sort of thing his editor would like to hear.

'Randy Bishop in Sex Romp,' said Pete.

'The Frolics I Mitre Had,' said Darnley.

'The Episkopos is chaste,' said 'Pugh'.

Disappointment was visible on every face round the table, including Vernon's.

'His thought is vapid, impotent,' added our sage.

'Do you mean, he can't get it up?' asked Tucker. 'Now, how would you know a thing like that?'

For the moment, it was evident that everyone in the room had come to believe that 'Pugh' might conceivably know such things; might even be omniscient.

'The Episkopos has lost his vision of the Mystery. The Harlot has her grip on the Cabinet minister for similar reasons. We can't live without believing in Mythos. Belief is not just something which you accept with a part of your mind, it is what you live by. England has lived by a Mythos ever since Dunkirk, the Island Race against the powers of Darkness. Now it has all evaporated. No one believes in the Mother of Parliaments or the new Commonwealth or the Flag. Until another Mythos replaces these old ones, the sludge at the bottom of the collective mind rises up as in dreams, and we have filthy little stories. The Harlot and the Statesman become interchangeable. Secrets are sold like human flesh and the Church has lost its Christ.'

'Why not call a bishop a bishop?' asked Pete. 'Why all this Episkopos crap?'

Vernon spoke. 'Yer right. We have lost touch with something.

But yer see, Mr – er – Mr Pugh, there's always bin another England apart from the privileged little class who are at last being dethroned. Yer right ter think it is appropriate they should be brought down by a prostitute because prostitution is at the core of the capitalist system. It's buying people, and that's what yer factory owners have done, yer mill-owners, yer mine-owners. . . .'

'It isn't buying people,' said Pete, 'it's buying a fuck. Most of the girls do quite well out of it, better than if they were waitresses, or barmaids in this fucking horrible pub. I'd sell my body if anyone would buy it.'

'The Whore & Gambler, by the State
Licenc'd, build that Nation's Fate,'

chanted 'Pugh'.

It wasn't a surprise to hear the words of William Blake on his lips. 'A fuck, as you call it, my friend, unites us to the Sacred Fire,' he said. 'It's not that it shouldn't be paid for, so much as that it can't be paid for.'

'They've been quoting you too high a price,' said Pete.

'It can't be paid for any more than you could pay for Holy Communion or buy a ray of the sun.'

'Pugh' was unable to develop this line because Vernon was in full flight.

'Ever since 1689, a little moneyed class have had it all their own way, they've run the whole show – they've put in their own tame monarchs from Holland and Germany, oh yes, and they've made governments out of their own class to protect their own interests, but it's all over for them now. The people uv England'll see 'em off. That's the true England, the true tradition.' Another finger-counting exercise began. 'Yuv got Wat Tyler, yuv got the Pilgrimage of Grace, yuv got the Diggers and they saw what Landowner Cromwell was up to by Golly, yuv got Wilkes and Liberty, yuv got the Chartists. . . .'

Vernon was running out of fingers in his catalogue of radical high watermarks in English legend.

'People often say ter me, ''Ernie yer some kind a Marxist'' – yer made the same easy joke just now, assumin' I was friends with the Russian Embassy bloke, and I like ter reply, ''Long before Karl Marx, and good luck ter 'im, came and took refuge in the British Museum, and 'e'd uv bin lucky ter do that with this new Immigration Bill comin' up, there was this strong healthy native tradition which saw through the lies uv the ruling class." '

'There has to be a ruling class,' said Tucker. 'All you want to do is to boot out the educated classes, all right and the rich like yourself, and make the proles the ruling class. Instead of having a country run by reasonably civilised individuals with two or three hundred years' practice at it, you'll have it incompetently run by a lot of bullying trade unionists. It's champagne bottles or sauce bottles.'

We all groaned.

'The time of refreshment is past, and toil must resume,' said 'Pugh' consulting a watch which hung from his broad lapel on a leather strap. He rose to his feet. 'No, please, Mr Darnley, I do not wish to disrupt the continuum of the tabula.' He said goodbye to all those around him – 'Lord Lampitt, Mr Cornforth, Mr Tucker,' and when he came to me, 'Mr Grainger.'

Jason Grainger was the character whom I played in the radio drama series 'The Mulberrys'. Darnley habitually called me by the name and must have thus introduced me to his other friends. It did not, however, occur to me to wonder whether 'Pugh' was a real name or another of Darnley's joke sobriquets. I hesitated and wondered whether to correct him. It seemed pompous to do so, and he was in any case wrestling with the detritus of domestic rubbish by the door. It was surprising to see him pick up the broken standard lamp in one hand as if it were a bishop's crosier, and somehow get a grip with the other hand on the mangle.

'Cyril'll give you a hand with those, Pughie,' said Darnley, for the publican was at that moment coming into the room, staring at us all with a contemptuous smile as if he never saw such a collection of cretins in his life.

'Cyril fucking won't,' said Cyril. 'What d'you want to cart all that rubbish round London for anyway?'

'There is an electrical shop near here which will mend the lamp,' said Pugh, in a much more matter-of-fact tone than had informed his conversation at the table, 'and an ironmonger in Berwick Street said he would look at the mangle. I think it's just rusty.'

'It *is* just fucking rusty,' said Cyril. 'You should throw it out.'

'That isn't a possibility,' said Pugh's voice.

He was invisible now, having negotiated his way out of the room, dragging the mangle behind him.

When he was gone, Darnley smiled satirically and whispered, 'Domestic troubles.'

'He was a rum cove,' said Godfrey Tucker. 'Gave me the shivers, actually. Continuum of the tabula? What's that meant to mean when it's at home?'

Professor Cormac, who until this point had been asleep at Tucker's elbow, awoke with a snort. He was deceptively young in appearance in a cherubically Dylan Thomas style. He spoke in a broad Ulster brogue.

'Didn't catch that man's name,' said the professor. Though still far gone in drink, he had not lost his desire, transparent at the beginning of the meal, to tick off in his mind, like a schoolboy spotting trains, the names of potentially famous people he had met on his day-trip to London from Oxford.

'Great man, Pugh,' said Darnley and burst out laughing. You momentarily wondered whether he was joking, and whether he could not see that Pugh was ridiculous. Then he screwed up his eyes and I saw that he meant what he said. Whether or not he was 'great', the man called Pugh was a disturbing figure from the first. His mind seemed full of subjects normally considered serious about which he pronounced with alarming vigour and confidence. He spoke about solemn things not as if they were a joke but with this mildly satanic grin on his face. Such matters as political and social gossip, by contrast, made his face become stern. As I came to learn, he was proud of having his ear to the ground. It was he who contributed much of the gossip to the 'Diary' in *The Spark*. Where did he get his information? Did he overhear it in bars, or invent it? His belief in the importance of Myth is apparent in the pages of his unfinished book about Christ. Perhaps those fragmentary pages were trying to illuminate the interesting question raised at that lunch by 'Pugh' – the myths we live by. My life as a radio actor involved me in a very minor way in a part of national mythology. The popularity of 'The Mulberrys', unabated to this day, must owe something to the way the English view themselves. The bucolically unreal Barleybrook, the village where the Mulberrys farm, where old Harold Grainger was the blacksmith and I, Jason, was his wastrel son, was perhaps a place where all Mulberry fans longed to be. The Mulberrys are not art, but their saga touches a place in the soul similar to those images of England which had been memorably drawn by true artists. We find it in the realism of Constable's skies and landscapes, in the native airs of Elgar and Vaughan Williams, in the novels of Thomas Hardy, all of which appeal to the rural fantasies of a race who for the most part live in towns and suburbs but like to think of themselves as countrydwellers.

The professor, Cormac, was drunk enough not to mind being a bore, but sober enough to be able to brag about his powers of recall: he knew 'who Pugh was'.

'Albion Pugh,' he said, 'those extraordinary novels.'

'Never heard of them,' I said, remembering as I did so that this was not quite true.

'There are four. He wrote them ages ago,' said Darnley. 'He has never done anything in that line since. There's nothing quite like them.'

'There's one about King Arthur,' said the professor. *Towered Camelot*. A couple are staying somewhere in Wales, and there's this classic country-house murder. Only it isn't. It's more than that. Excuse me.' Cormac protruded his very moist lower lip and belched. Looking less dazed, he continued. 'One of the characters turns out to be a witch, and the lost body of King Arthur, sleeping in Avalon until his people need him again, is found in the caves near the house. Anyway, the detective character . . .'

'Pugh's got this way of making the supernatural seem totally real,' said Darnley.

'Like our friend Blake?'

'Very much like Blake, Pugh,' said Darnley. 'Same weird thing of having a vision of England. Similar, too, in the way the sublime stuff goes hand in hand with absolute balls.'

'How did you meet Pugh?'

'Sent a letter, care of his publishers, to say how much I liked the books. I didn't even know if he was still alive. He wrote back, pretty chuffed, said he hadn't had a fan letter since the war. We took it from there. The best of the novels is set in Egypt.'

Memphian Mystery, oh, now that's a *delicious* one,' said Professor Cormac, with the perky air of a child doing well in a quiz. 'A party of travellers, mainly English, some Americans, cruising in the Med. Typical Agatha Christie stuff, you might

514

have thought. One of them is carrying this sacred scarab – he doesn't know what it is, of course. Anyhow . . .'

But Darnley and I turned away. Albion Pugh. *Memphian Mystery, Towered Camelot.* I could place them now, though I could not say that I had ever read them. I remembered the green and white covers of the pre-war Penguins lying about in my uncle's rectory at Timplingham during my childhood. I had a visual memory of my uncle's daughter Felicity, truculently absorbed in *Memphian Mystery* whose plot Professor Cormac was even now rehearsing as he sat at the table in the Black Bottle. He was speaking to himself. All the other guests had risen to their feet and were dispersing.

A few stragglers leaving the pub hovered on the pavement. Vernon Lampitt was there – Ernie, as it now seemed more polite to call him. He was in his early sixties, and his hair had turned quite snowy since our last encounter. My uncle liked to quote a Lampitt family saying that Vernon was very much more a Charles than a Lampitt, Charles being the maiden name of Vernon's mother. It is true that physically Vernon did not have the classic Lampitt features, as my ex-wife Anne had, or her mother Sibs, or her uncle Sargie – that long face with a protuberant chin. Vernon's sister, always referred to by Uncle Roy as the Honourable Penny-lope (as a boy I never realised that this was a joke pronunciation) had these features. So did Dame Ursula Lampitt, the Principal of Rawlinson College, Oxford. Vernon's face was rounder, and softer, with large, popping blue eyes. (Old Mrs Lampitt, Sargie's mother, wondered if Vernon suffered from thyroid trouble, though she would never say so to the boy's father. 'A *wonderful* woman,' Uncle Roy would add.)

Standing outside the pub with Vernon, it occurred to me that his pop-out eyes, often described by journalists as penetrating, were the very opposite of Albion Pugh's. You had the sense in 'Pugh's' presence, in spite or because of his evidently defective vision and thick spectacles, that he could see through you. Vernon's eyes gleamed and stared, but when they fixed on a person, there was no indication that he took in what he saw.

We did not know one another well, and beyond a general recognition of my presence at the lunch table, Vernon did not give me any clue that he remembered who I was. Since Darnley insisted on introducing me to everyone as Jason Grainger, there would have been every reason for a certain vagueness in the matter. I wasn't even sure, having some years earlier split up with his cousin Anne, whether Vernon would regard me in a friendly light. But as we stood there in Poland Street he seized my upper arm in a comradely fashion and squeezed it in a manner suggestive of a boxing trainer anxious about a featherweight's biceps.

'We don't see enough of yer, Julian. We *hear* yer all right. Pat's a great Bilberry fan.'

'Mulberry.'

'I don't have time for it meself unfortunately.'

'Of course not.'

The very idea that Vernon could spare a quarter of an hour in the midst of his political concerns to listen to the Mulberrys was a preposterous one.

'Yer still with us, I hope?'

'Us?'

'Yer've not gone all right wing or anything? I know yer uncle Roy's still *dong le mouvemong*. Saw him not so long ago.'

I was disgracefully lazy about keeping in touch with my uncle, particularly since I now shared a house with Felicity and felt that I kept in touch with her parents vicariously, through her.

'Where did you run across him?'

'That's right.' Vernon seldom gave answers which suggested he had attended to one's questions. Had he not been a professional politician you might have supposed him to be deaf, which, for all I know, he might have been. 'Yah. Yer never met me poor old cousin Bobby.'

'The one who farmed in Rhodesia? Didn't he once make a rather amusing remark about a duckling?'

From earliest times I could remember my uncle hardly able to contain himself at the repetition of this 'famous' *mot*, made to a waiter at the Adelphi Hotel in Brighton. Vernon either had never heard the duckling story or chose to forget it. He showed no surprise at my absolute grasp of his extended and complicated family tree.

'Poor old Bobby was a bit of a fascist really. Came back to London to die – his boys took over the farm. He finally passed on three weeks ur so ago. Yer uncle came up and took the funeral.'

'He didn't tell me.'

I felt unjustifiably aggrieved.

'It was Sibs's idea to have Roy.'

There was that phrase of Jimbo's (i.e. of James Petworth Lampitt) which had so annoyed my uncle: 'Sargie's tame parson'.

'Very appropriate,' I said.

Like all people lacking in social confidence, I respond to unexpected information as if it were somehow designed to trick me, or show me up. Vernon could not possibly have cared whether I knew about my uncle's visit to London, but I felt the need to lie about it.

'Now you mention it,' I said. 'Felicity did say something about her father coming to London to conduct a funeral.'

She had not done so. She spoke about very little except her work, and I formed the impression that Roy's visit to London had been kept a secret even from his daughter; not for any sinister reasons, but simply because he saw the Lampitts all too rarely these days and would want to concentrate on solid joys and lasting treasure without dissipating the experience by exposure to his own flesh and blood.

'You remember Felicity?' I needled Vernon.

'Good *Lord* yes.'

His overemphasis suggested that the reverse was true.

'Foreign Office?' he fished.

'As it happens, Ministry of Works,' I said, 'but she's only been a civil servant a short time. It's an experiment. She got fed up with being a don and they're giving her a few years off from Rawlinson to see how she likes something different.'

'Rawlinson. *Course*. With Ursula. Don't know why I thought Felicity was in the Foreign Office. Anyway, come down to Mallington, both of yer. Do.'

'That would be nice.'

'Ridiculous place, uv course. I long ter be rid uv it. Pat 'n I debate its future all the time. Should be nationalised like all these dirty great houses. A conference centre, or mebbe a place for youngsters, a place fer thum ter come at weekends, mebbe learn a trade.'

Any less likely setting for an apprentice to perfect his skills in, say, electrical maintenance or welding, would have been difficult to devise.

Cyril, mine host of the Bottle, came to the pub door to address Darnley.

'That fat bugger's still in there.'

'The prof?' smiled Darnley.

'Still sitting at the fucking table talking about the fucking pharaohs. I've told him to sod off but he's too heavy to lift. Irish, inne?'

'I'll come and have a word with him,' said Darnley.

'These lunches 'll have to stop if you can't clear out the piss artists after closing time,' explained Cyril.

'It's Professor Cormac,' said Vernon. ' 'E's practically fascist, yer know. Wrote a really foul review uv me friend Tommy Wimbish's history of the party. Did yer see it?'

'No,' I said, though I rather enjoyed Professor Wimbish's books, which were written for people like myself, intelligent 'general' readers, who can't be bothered with footnotes. 'Don't all dons hate one another, as moles are supposed to do?' I asked.

This was certainly the impression I received from conversation with Felicity.

While Darnley tried to shift the recalcitrant professor from his chair, Vernon and I took our leave.

'I'll walk with yer ter the Tube. Got ter get back to the Chamber. We're inter the second reading of this Immigration Bill. Between ourselves, I hope we send it back to the Commons for reconsideration. Our party's got it wrong I'm afraid ter say.'

It slightly surprised me, in view of his principles, that Vernon was prepared to take his seat in the Lords. There was much talk in the family of his renouncing his peerage, but this did not seem to have happened yet. He appeared to me to have a very muddled attitude to the Immigration Bill, on the one hand reacting to the issue like any Little Englander, and on the other seeing it as an opportunity to trounce the Conservatives.

'You can't be for the Bill?' I asked.

'Lord, no. But I think it's scandalous, if we're honest, ter hold out the hope of British citizenship ter folk in Africa und the West Indies when we haven't bothered ter provide indoor toilets for our own people.'

'So, you might vote with the Tories?'

He waved any such absurdity aside.

'No, we'll get rid uv the Bill, we'll get rid uv the Government, we'll get rid uv the Tories and start to rebuild. . . .'

'Jerusalem, in England's green and pleasant land?'

'If yer like, if yer like. If I may, Julian, I'll write ter yer and suggest a date when yer can come down ter Mallington. Perhaps yer could bring Darnley? I see quite a future for this little paper uv his.'

I refrained from mentioning Vernon's own prolix article in the present issue on the nationalism of the clearing banks.

'I don't know who feeds Darnley half his stories for the "Diary",' he said.

'Albion Pugh, it would seem.'

'The funny bloke with glasses?' Vernon laughed. 'I thought he had a bit of a screw loose.'

It takes one to know one. At Tottenham Court Road station we parted, he for an Embankment train, and I for one in the opposition direction, Camden Town.

The encounter with Vernon set off a reverie in my mind which drove away Darnley, Albion Pugh, the harlot and the bishop. Too much execrable wine with the meal, followed by a ride in a stuffy train took me back to the day which I had almost forgotten when I first saw Mallington Hall, and my mind was so full of it that I forgot to get out at Camden Town and sat in a daze until Tufnell Park, where I alighted and walked home southwards thinking of the day God pulled the plug out.

Mrs Webb, my grandmother's close friend, was saying, 'It's not proper sea, not what I would call proper sea. We've walked for miles, and just look at it – it's *still* miles away.'

My tiny legs were certainly tired. I was barely five years old. We had walked and walked, past shining mudflats where oystercatchers, terns and black-headed gulls patterned the wet surface of the empty creeks with their thousands of intricate footprints, and made our way over sandy paths alongside still ditches and dunes where the grass was coarse and thick and springy, and yet the sea was still far off. The small village where we were staying seemed equally distant now. Further off were the clumps of flat-topped pines. Before and behind, the distance stretched with apparent infinitude and in that very clear September light no detail of it was faded; it was all bright as some Dutch landscape painting of the seventeenth century.

'That's Mallington Hall,' said Daddy. 'We might go there tomorrow.'

I was sitting on my father's shoulders. He pointed.

'Look, Julian. Do you see the lovely house?'

The brick and stucco shape was too far away for my eyes to

take in, in any detail, but I could see it, far away, safe in its own inaccessible beauty. We did not go there the next day. Our holiday was to be cut short.

'Come on now, son, try and walk for yourself a bit more. Daddy's shoulders are getting tired.'

He lifted me down, and I ran to hold Mummy's hand.

My grandmother stood still and tried to focus her eyes on Mallington.

'I can't see it,' she said.

'There!' Daddy often laughed at his mother, but in an affectionate rather than satirical way. 'There!'

Before any comment could be made upon the view, Mrs Webb leapt to Granny's defence.

'It's a shame to bring Thora here with her feet,' she announced.

Daddy did not answer. He strode ahead, indicating that the walk, or route march (which was what it felt like), had resumed, regardless of discontent in the ranks. He wore very capacious shorts so that only a little of his pale legs was revealed. His white shirt was rolled up to his elbows, and his forearms were brown.

We traipsed in single file, all of us. I held a small spade, which, while I had been astride his shoulders, Daddy had been afraid would poke his eyes. I also carried a bucket. It was decorated with a transfer of Mickey Mouse. Granny had bought it for me earlier in the summer when she and Mrs Webb had taken me to Westgate, where the sea was unimpeachably proper, fully equipped with bathing huts, toilets (though these had been denounced by the two ladies as 'a disgrace'), a pier, ice-cream stalls, and cafés serving 'nice' cups of tea and the full variety of light meals on toast – beans, roes, eggs, sardines, what not. I myself much preferred Westgate to this new sort of sea.

'Mummy,' I said.

'Not *another* stitch?' she asked.

The reason that my father had consented to carry me on his shoulders was that, a few minutes before, we had all had to stop while I relieved a stitch, touching my toes and gulping with the pain of it. The stitch was indeed returning, but I did not want to admit this, in case Mrs Webb crowed and triumphed too much over my parents. There had been no question of a stitch at Westgate. The whole visit there had been a riotous success, with donkey rides, and an attendance at the Punch and Judy show, followed by a positively delicious plate of egg and chips for tea. It was all too imaginable how Mrs Webb would make use of the present situation. Silly, wearing the boy out before we even reached the sands. Thus she would rail, putting Daddy in the wrong.

'It's gone,' I said, referring to the stitch. 'Only, Mummy . . .'

'What is it now, Julian?'

She wore a straw hat over her thick brown hair and her loose, short-sleeved dress was splashed with a floral print of yellow and green. The skirt was perfectly ironed and stiff and stuck out as a triangle around her pink smooth legs. I wished we weren't walking in single file, because I desperately wanted to hold Mummy's hand. Do I deceive myself? Was this the very same dress which she wore on that terrible day, several years later, when I set eyes on her for the last time on the platform at Paddington station?

'Was it like this when Moses dried up the sea, Mummy?'

'Probably,' she said.

'Not far now,' said Daddy.

We had passed the mudflats and could see the glistening sand, stretching in every direction, a huge expanse. The sea, infinitely beyond, was lower than the shore. It was a vast, brooding, dark blue bath, heaving beneath the sky, but too distant for us to reach.

Behind me, Mrs Webb observed, 'It isn't nice to think of *them* just over the water. Probably *in* the water, with submarines and swastikas stuck all over them. It's disgusting.'

This frightened me. I did not know who 'they' were. If any more of the sea were to disappear, however, there would be a limitless stretch of sand and they, swastikas and all, could merely climb out of their beached submarines and walk up to us, as the children of Israel had walked across the bed of the Sea of Reeds.

'Has God pulled the plug out?' I enquired.

Granny and Mrs Webb were always on the look-out for jokes, and this remark was often repeated in later years. That fateful day in European history became, in our family, 'the day God pulled the plug out'.

'He'll let the water back in again,' said Mummy. 'You'll see.'

I was not so sure that He would. My earliest impression was that He was not necessarily to be trusted, and I had imbibed

521

some of Mrs Webb's distrust of religion. At Westgate, we had given a very wide berth to a beach 'mission', and Granny had given full assent to Mrs Webb's view that there was a time and a place for everything, but that it somehow was not quite nice to be singing songs about Jesus where the kiddies were making sandcastles and trying to enjoy themselves.

We struggled on in silence until we had passed the grass-grown dunes and came to the shore itself and settled ourselves with rugs and two picnic baskets and the old ladies' books, and my bucket and spade. Daddy said that he and I should go in search of sea-shells.

'It's nearly one,' he said with a glance at his wrist-watch. 'They should be here very soon.'

'It'll take them ages in that contraption of theirs,' said Mummy.

This exchange filled me with alarm. First Mrs Webb had let the cat out of the bag with the information that 'they' were hiding in the sea. Now, my parents calmly announced that 'they' would be arriving in a contraption. I did not realise that Mrs Webb was talking about the Germans, and that my parents were discussing the arrival of Aunt Deirdre, Felicity and Uncle Roy, Daddy's brother. Leaving Granny and Mrs Webb with their Warwick Deepings and their Craven As, my parents took me further on to the sand, following a shallow inlet which ran down towards the sea and which Daddy said was good for shells. Mummy collected the most, lifting the hem of her skirt to form a sort of marsupial pouch which I helped her to fill with whelks, scallops, razor-shells, giant mussels, oysters, limpets, cockles and clams.

'Mrs Webb's right, really,' said Daddy, referring to an earlier altercation. 'We should have seen if we couldn't get to a wireless to listen in. There's probably one at the hotel we could have heard.'

Our holiday cottage was primitive. I seem to remember that there was no electricity and that water was drawn from a pump in the back yard. There was certainly no wireless.

Mummy stroked my father's shoulders.

'Maybe it will all blow over,' she said. 'It did last time.'

Daddy sighed. 'Oh, Jill,' he said.

'They can't' – she faltered, and then with the hand which was not holding up her skirt she stretched and gestured towards the wide sand, like Moses stretching forth his rod over the waters. 'They can never bring all this to an end.'

All this: the huge sea-shore and the wide flat land which stretched as far as the eye could strain over staithes and dykes, fields and woods to the squat tower of Mallington church and beyond that, in its well-planted park, to the Hall itself. I do not know why, Londoners, my parents had chosen this particular village as a suitable holiday place. Presumably they liked that strange bit of the north Norfolk coast, unlike anywhere else in the world, and felt it was sufficiently close to Daddy's brother to allow for family visits while being far enough away to maintain a safe distance – an hour in the 'contraption', an extraordinary old car called a Trojan which had solid tyres. I am sure that the proximity of our cottage to Mallington Hall played no part in my parents' fondness for the place. I have no reason to suppose that they were interested in architecture and I know that they did not share my uncle Roy's consuming passion, the genealogy and doings of the Lampitt family, a branch of whom lived in the noble pile which could be glimpsed beyond the flats and pines.

My uncle Roy's parish, Timplingham, was about twenty-five miles inland, to the south, and contained another branch of this, to him, inexhaustibly fascinating family: 'our Lampitts', as I came to think of them: old Mrs Lampitt, her 'hopeless' son Sargie, who was Uncle Roy's best friend, his brother, the writer James Petworth Lampitt (Jimbo) and their sister Sibs (destined for a time to be my mother-in-law). These others, the Lampitts of Mallington, were cousins, leftish politicians by calling.

A quarter of a century after 'God pulled the plug out', I met 'Albion Pugh' and heard expressed the commonplace view that we cannot live without myths. (It sounded impressive on 'Pugh''s lips, not least because he used the word 'mythos' rather than 'myth' and said it in his strange cockney sing-song.) Uncle Roy's saving mythology was the Lampitt family, more interesting, it would seem, than his own, more capable of engaging the imgination and providing life with a shape.

I was too young when Daddy died to be able to form a realistic impression of how well he got on with my uncle Roy. The fact that a man speaks satirically of his brother by no means implies lack of fondness but, with the literalness of a child, I imagined that Daddy did not much like Uncle Roy and that it would be wrong, even disloyal, of me to do so. As I write this down, I see how this fact must have complicated the sometimes painful relationship I had with my uncle when he had taken me to live in his house after my parents were killed in the air raid.

'When they *do* come,' said Mrs Webb, 'I hope we don't have to hear too much about the Lampitts. We'll have Lampitts coming out of our ears, the way Roy talks about them.'

There was a general, laughing assent to this surreal possibility.

'Lord Lampitt' – Daddy put on his cruelly accurate 'Uncle Roy' voice, which was rather posher than his own – 'a charming man, but I'm sorry to say . . .'

Mummy was already laughing and even I, at barely five years old, knew the chorus by heart.

'Just a tiny little bit of a humbug.'

We said it in unison, and it partially resolved my fears. From everything the grown-ups had been saying during the past few days it was obvious that something was about to happen, something big and disastrous which the Prime Minister would tell us on the wireless. 'They' were coming.

I now realised that they were not going to kill me or take my Mummy away. When they had completed the tedious journey across the North Sea in their contraption, 'they' would emerge in their swastikas; but, as I now learnt, all we had to dread was the possibility of Lampitts coming out of our ears. I had never realised before that the Germans shared with my Uncle Roy this Lampitt obsession. For all I knew, everyone in the world was interested in them except us. I had not yet been imprisoned in what Albion Pugh would have termed the empiricist fallacy. I had never knowingly set eyes on a Lampitt, unless perhaps to be given the occasional gin-flavoured kiss on the top of my head by Sargie, and I was not of an age to ask whether stories were true or false. All that mattered was whether stories were interesting, funny, or frightening. If two children came across a house made of gingerbread and candy in the middle of a wood, this was no more improbable than Lord Lampitt being a humbug. I imagined him as part human, part boiled sugar, the sort of figure Tenniel would have drawn well, his cheeks striped and shiny with hard minty surfaces, the pointed corners of the asymmetrical cube serving him for nose and ears.

'They should be here by now,' said Daddy – we had walked back to rejoin Granny and Mrs Webb – 'though I know that Roy has to finish his service thing.'

Granny and Mrs Webb, unwilling to 'wait about all day' had already consumed a quantity of cress sandwiches, hard-boiled eggs and cold chipolatas. Eager eyes were already being cast on the fruit cake. I was desperately hungry and accepted the sandwich which Mrs Webb held out to me.

'Sit up again on Daddy's shoulder,' said my father – has anyone ever explained why so many grown-ups, when addressing children, refer to themselves in the third person? – 'and tell him if you can see Uncle Roy.'

Daddy pretended to be a camel and lolloped up the sand dunes until we had found a good vantage point.

'Someone is coming,' I said uncertainly.

'Is it your uncle Roy?'

Anxious to give an answer which would please, I said 'I think so,' even though I could not in fact see my uncle. I saw Aunt Deirdre, though. Over her fleshy shoulders, the thick canvas straps of a haversack were tightly drawn. She wore a white floppy sunhat, Christopher Robin style. Her white blouse and blue skirt could have been – though in fact were not – uniform. Behind her, in almost identical rig, certainly wearing the same sort of floppy sunhat, came her daughter Felicity. Their ages at this time were, perhaps, twelve and thirty-eight, but in appearance they could have been sisters. Felicity in childhood always seemed old before her time, while Aunt Deirdre, roundfaced and crop-haired, retained an ageless innocence.

Aunt Deirdre waved. As was her wont, she looked slightly cross. I seldom saw this expression vanish from her face, in the course of her entire life, except for those rare occasions when she actually lost her temper and 'let rip'. Very occasionally, when gardening, one would see the disgruntlement vanish from her features, but for the most part, she seemed to be holding back sharp words. Slightly before she reached us, she began her explanation of Uncle Roy's absence from the scene.

'Of course, as soon as he heard the news, Roy felt he had to stay behind and comfort Sargie. He was in a terrible tizz, Sargie I mean.'

It was of Sargent Lampitt she spoke, the humbug's cousin.

'Mrs Lampitt and he heard it on the wireless of course, up at the Place. Sargie came straight down to church, if you please, and that made history in itself. I knew something was up, because I happened to turn round and see him hovering while

Roy was chanting the last of the versicles. When Roy got to the third collect, first Sunday in the month, so it's Mattins which I *much* prefer, Sargie boomed out, "You'd better all know we are finally at war". . . .'

'At war with Germany,' Felicity corrected her mother. 'Uncle Sargie said we were at war with Germany.'

'How many were in church?' asked Mrs Webb, with merciless directness.

'Roy kept his nerve, of course,' continued the messenger. 'No point in doing anything else. He said "Before you all rush off, I think we should . . ."'

'"Hasten away",' said Felicity. 'Pa said "hasten away", not "rush off".'

'Same thing,' said Granny.

'They're not the same words,' said Felicity. 'They're not what Pa actually said.'

'He asked us all to stand,' persisted Aunt Deirdre, 'and sing "Jerusalem". So we did.'

'How many of you, though?' Mrs Webb wanted to know. Family pride or perhaps the dark suspicion that my grand-mother's friend might be chapel or, worse, RC (and therefore with no business to know what went on in proper churches) made my aunt instinctively cagey about revealing the numbers at Mattins at Timplingham that morning.

'Naturally there were fewer than usual,' said Aunt Deirdre. 'People were staying at home to listen in.'

'I can't believe it,' said Mummy. 'I just can't take it in. I thought it would all blow over.'

'There were six of us,' said Felicity, 'if you count Mrs Collins who was playing the organ. Seven for "Jerusalem", because Uncle Sargie joined in.'

'I should have called that more a Women's Institute hymn,' said Mrs Webb. ' "Fight the Good Fight" 's more like it now. Or the National Anthem.'

'Well,' said Aunt Deirdre, choosing to ignore this imperti-nence, 'this time he's gone far enough.' She spoke in the same impatient, cross tone with which she might describe a child whose behaviour had become raucous at a parish tea party and who had been sent to 'cool off' in the corner while the rest of us passed the parcel. 'We gave him Czechoslovakia on a plate and he should have been jolly grateful for that, though Roy and

Sargie both said it was wrong at the time. But he just wants more and more and more. No satisfying some people. Now he's gone and invaded Poland when we *told* him he couldn't, and – well, enough's enough.'

'Always nice weather when a war breaks out,' said Granny. 'Do you remember the last one? Lovely weather then.'

Larks rose vertically from the springy dunes and the gorse was brilliant with flowers. Nothing looked different from five minutes before, in spite of the news my aunt had brought. The wind blew, but by the standards of that coast, it blew gently. The sun continued to shine.

'Only, Roy said at once, we couldn't leave you stranded; you might have been waiting here all day.'

'There's no wireless in the cottage,' said Mummy. 'This was the first we heard of it.'

'I said I'd drive Fliss over, the air would do us good. No good moping, just because there's a war, and I'd already made the potted meat sandwiches. Got to eat, Hitler or no Hitler.'

'Uncle Sargie's upset,' said Felicity. 'He was crying during "Jerusalem". He said it was all bloody nonsense, but it made him blub.'

'It is quite unnecessary to repeat that word,' said my aunt hotly. Felicity went so red that I thought she herself would cry.

'Fliss is right, actually,' said my aunt, perhaps fearing her daughter's tears. 'Sargie was bitterly upset. Roy had to stay with him.'

'Naturally,' said my father. 'A war breaks out, and where is Roy? With his own family? Comforting the troops? Oh, no. He has to stay with Sargent blooming Lampitt.'

An awkward silence followed that observation. When I lived in the Rectory and became acquainted with its routines, I learnt that my aunt also resented the amount of time spent by Uncle Roy in Sargie's company, but marital loyalty would not allow her to admit this to my parents. She merely seemed 'browned off' – that would have been her phrase – with Hitler. The mad dictator should have been more thoughtful. Invading Poland was bound to upset Sargie and, as she often said, 'When Sargie suffers, we all suffer.'

'Roy was really looking forward to coming today,' she said in his defence. 'He had hoped some of us would want to call at Mallington, bless him.'

'That's where the Honourable Vernon Lampitt lives,' said Felicity with intense seriousness. 'Pa says that he is a brilliant economist.'

'Oh bother the Lampitts!' Mummy exclaimed. 'The world is about to be destroyed, and all we can do is to stand here and talk about the Lampitts.'

'They do say,' added Mrs Webb, 'that London will be flattened. Levelled to the ground.'

Her lips were set firm at the prospect. It was not, exactly, a defiant expression: it was not saying, 'Come on, Hitler, do your worst!' It seemed to accept the tragic destiny of London, of its inhabitants, including herself, perhaps the tragic destiny of the entire human race, but to refuse, quite, to bow to its inevitability.

'Well, I do think it's *hard*,' said Granny. 'Hard.'

Aeons pass. With the indifference of a clumsy child, throwing broken toys into a corner, Fate removes characters from the scene. Mummy and Daddy and Mrs Webb had been long since dead when I met Vernon Lampitt round Darnley's lunch table with Albion Pugh, Pete Cornforth and the rest. (The Honourable Vernon was himself Lord Lampitt now, and it remained to be seen whether his party inclined to Uncle Roy's high views of his skills as an economist, or whether they would endorse Sibs's malevolent judgement that Vernon was 'a dimwit – the dimwit of the family, really'.) Hitler himself, and his threats to destroy England, had vanished. Twenty-four years had passed since God pulled the plug out and since Aunt Deirdre, Uncle Roy, Felicity, Sargie and the others had sung Blake's words, speculating about the legend of Christ visiting Britain as a child, and declaring their refusal to cease from mental fight until they had seen Jerusalem built in England's green and pleasant land: all matters of vital interest to Darnley's new friend Albion Pugh. England had passed out of austerity into a phase when we were supposed never to have had it so good.

Certainly, this political cliché implied more than economic prosperity. Perhaps the Harlot and the Episkopos were indeed tokens. The vapid agnosticism of the bishop, surely shared by the majority of churchmen, reminded us of how much had been eroded of the old certainties. The Ten Commandments had been left behind with our ration books. The public threw up its hands at the Cabinet minister's unsuitable choice of companion, but the simple fact was, that people envied him. They too, had they been able to afford it, would have liked to romp naked by the swimming pool at Cliveden, and attend wild parties, and disregard their marriage vows, and put sex before their tedious jobs. The scandal became a signal for a general whoopee which would engulf England for at least a decade.

In this new arrangement of the scenery we all stood poised to play our parts. The brilliant economist (or family dimwit), in his new incarnation as Ernie Lampitt, the people's friend, was quite possibly destined for high office in the new Britain which was waiting to be born. He had managed to laugh aside his inherited barony as 'me dad's little bit o' nonsense'. His large house in Norfolk, to which I had just been invited, was spoken of as a burden. Neither title nor property seemed to deter Vernon's advancement as a working-class hero. Presumably, if the chance of really high political office came his way, he would discard the peerage, and become plain Mr Lampitt. A Lampitt Prime Minister! My uncle had been speaking of the possibility for as long as I could recall. I had never taken him seriously, since in his vision of the universe, only Lampitts fully existed, the other inhabitants of the planet being shadowy, ethereal beings in whom it was eccentric, by the standards of Timpling-ham Rectory, to take very much interest. It was natural that Uncle Roy should have seen Vernon as the next Prime Minister. Now, by an extraordinary chance, the world seemed to be of Uncle Roy's mind.

The Lampitts, who had seemed to be a purely private obsession of my uncle's, did, as I now realised, have some place in the public consciousness. Since Raphael Hunter had published that notorious volume of biography, the world knew more than it needed to know of James Petworth Lampitt, the man of letters. There had been a great revival of interest in his works and even talk of Jimbo's biography of Prince Albert being made into a film. Hunter showed no signs of writing a continuation of the biography, taking it from Jimbo's young manhood to his death, but he had kept the Lampitt flame aglow with several 'spin-offs'. There had been a reissue of some of Jimbo's books with introductions by Hunter, and there was a projected television series, scripted and 'fronted' by Hunter, based on some of Jimbo's sketches from Victorian life. Jimbo himself, in Hunter's version of the story, had become an emblematic figure, though one less tuppence-coloured than the Bishop and the Harlot. If, as Hunter implied, Jimbo had been a promiscuous homosexual, this was all to the good, as far as his current sales and popularity were concerned. At the period when Hunter was researching the book in Sargie's house, the period when he formed his disastrous attachment to my cousin Felicity, homosexuality was, generally speaking, frowned upon except by the enlightened few. Even those of homosexual disposition themselves might well share the general view that having a particular preference somehow constituted a handicap, even a form of spiritual disease from which a cure could or should be sought. Different mythologies were about to burst upon the world and Jimbo's supposedly limitless sexual appetite, his ability to seduce members of his own sex however heterosexual they might have been (the Lloyd George incident is the one most often referred to), made him a potential hero in the age of the Harlot and the Bishop. Whether the real Jimbo bore any resemblance to the Petworth Lampitt in Hunter's biography was a matter of hot dispute. His brother Sargie still denied it vigorously, and doubts had been sown in my own mind by Felicity, the only person I knew, apart from Hunter, who had even cast an eye over the 'Lampitt Papers' now safely housed with a private collector in New York.

These matters occupied my thoughts as I walked southwards to Camden Town. As sometimes happens to me when I am mildly drunk, whole scenes and conversations replayed themselves inside my head, sometimes from long ago (the day on the beach when we heard that war had broken out), sometimes from the most recent past (the lunch, Darnley, his new friend Albion Pugh – sage, prophet, gossip, religious charlatan, failed writer, mystery man).

It was of Pugh that I thought as my feet passed the litter-strewn pavements by Camden Town station: his high brow, not dissimilar, it now seemed, to William Blake's, his long hair awry, his marble eyes distorted by the lenses of those ancient specs.

'Either/or' – his cockney voice sang inside my brain – 'the two falsest words in the English language.' What had he meant by that?

I turned into Parkway. The road where I lived was first on the left past a pub called the Camden Stores. The street was lined by a middling-sized terrace of brick houses built in the 1840s when London was expanding northwards beyond Regent's Park and when those regions were inhabited by just such poor waifs as William Blake had pitied – industrial child-slaves whose Irish parents had been enlisted as navvies on the railway as it extended through Chalk Farm and Primrose Hill, or who worked in the factories dotted around Camden itself. Now, the terrace had a handsome, peeling gentility which I found congenial. Twenty years were to pass before this part of London became in any sense fashionable, though it had, I suppose, a certain bohemian chic. (Dylan Thomas had occupied a house round the corner from my own.)

I say 'my own' but, again, these were the days before anyone of my limited means would contemplate taking out a mortgage. Like the huge majority of Londoners, I paid rent.

After my marriage to Anne broke up, I did not really care where I lived so long as it was not in the area on the edges of Chelsea where we had become so miserable together. Anything with SW in the address was to be avoided. NW seemed as different as possible, and my present address was very convenient for Euston station. I now earned my living, such as it was, as a radio voice. Two or three times a month, I had to make the journey from London to Birmingham, where the Mulberry programmes were recorded. Euston was where I caught my train. My other radio stint was a weekly broadcast from London, at Bush House in the Aldwych, a book programme on the World Service of the BBC. I liked the producer of this programme and he would usually give me work reading aloud extracts from writers under discussion.

The money was not good, and I was poor. I am fortunate enough never to have greatly minded about these things. I did not aspire to live grandly, I dressed like a scruff, and initially, in the first couple of years on my own, I had all that I needed. Little by little, however, an early harbinger of middle age, I found that my domestic needs were becoming marginally more – how shall I phrase it? It was not comfort or luxury which I needed, it was privacy. I had moved from various lodgings and then I found myself sharing a house with two other actors and someone who worked on the technical side of things at Broadcasting House, a sound recordist. We all four kept ourselves to ourselves, had separate bed-sitting rooms, sharing only the bathroom and kitchen. There was a communal sitting room but we seldom all sat in it together. When one of the four left the household to get married, I took his room, not because I needed any extra space, but because I did not want the risk of an uncongenial neighbour on the same landing. I could not really afford the extra rent – if I named the sum here, it would seem ludicrously modest – but it was worth it. The two actors eventually moved on, and I took over the whole house and sublet the top floor to lodgers. It was not a success. The desire to be alone, to be my own master, had taken possession of me, and I was an intolerable landlord, complaining about the noise of their gramophone, seething with rage if 'they' put food in 'my' refrigerator (even though it was part of the agreement that they were allowed to do so) and generally making myself unpleasant. I retained the fourth bedroom as a 'spare', though I had few enough friends to occupy it, a fact which eventually dawned on my cousin Felicity, at that time a lecturer in philosophy at Oxford. She took to coming to stay fairly frequently during the university vacations. Camden Town was conveniently placed for the British Museum where she liked to work in the reading room, and she had various friends, of vaguely intellectual flavouring, who lived within a short bus ride of me. At the height of my trouble with the lodgers, Felicity put to me a scheme which seemed at the time irresistible. She would pay half the rent for the whole house in exchange for being able to come and stay whenever she liked. We would lead separate lives. She would occupy the top half of the house, and I the bottom, and we would continue the arrangement of a shared kitchen and bathroom. The lodgers were dispatched and their rooms were refurnished with objects familiar to me since childhood, since Uncle Roy and Aunt Deirdre had more than enough furniture at the Rectory and were probably despairing of Felicity ever setting up house in a 'conventional' way with a husband.

For some time this arrangement worked very well. For half the year Felicity was in Oxford, and for half the year she occupied the top half of the house in Arlington Road. Then, a year or more before I met Albion Pugh at the Black Bottle, all this changed quite dramatically. I do not think that Felicity was deliberately manipulative or dishonest; I do not think she undertook to share the house with me knowing that she would soon be living there all the time, but I do believe that having a house in London helped her towards the rather precipitate step of changing her career. It was after Christmas dinner at Timplingham that she broached the subject with me. Uncle Roy was reading aloud a Margery Allingham to Granny while Aunt Deirdre pored over gardening catalogues, and Felicity and I were washing-up in the kitchen.

'Julian, there's something I should have told you.'

She blushed. For some reason, I spontaneously recalled the time, so far away emotionally that it might have been in a previous life, when she was recovering from her abortion, the necessary consequence of her entanglement with Hunter. She looked sheepish and vulnerable. Her resemblance to her mother, so strong in childhood, had grown much less marked with the years. Aunt Deirdre still looked like a disgruntled Sea Scout with a round, unchanging jawline. Felicity had her hair cut short too these days, but her cheeks were hollowed and she had become much paler than her mother. As I knew from sharing a house with her, she was an insomniac and her large eyes were shadowed beneath with sleeplessness. Her oval features were very lightly freckled. Her eyes were green, and something about the shape of the brow had come to resemble Uncle Roy, a point of likeness which had never showed itself in earlier times. One of the strangest features of Felicity's face was that her lips had become almost indistinguishable in colour from the flesh of her cheeks. They were full, rather sensual lips, particularly when opened to reveal those big teeth, but no girl ever had less rosy lips. She was several inches taller than Aunt Deirdre, who had once taken grave offence when someone, I think a gym mistress at school, had described Felicity as 'gawky'. In shoes, another fact I had not known until she moved into Arlington Road, she took size eights. As I stood in her mother's kitchen and looked at Felicity, blushing, and looking down with such seriousness, I guessed that she was about to say she was engaged to be married and I at once began to wonder whether her husband was coming to live in London too.

This was not what she had to say.

'I'm giving up philosophy,' she blurted out. There was a long silence, and then she added, 'Perhaps for ever.'

'Do you mean that you want to give up teaching?'

'That as well. I am giving up teaching because I am giving up philosophy.'

'You make it sound like giving up smoking.'

'I know. It would perhaps be as true to say that philosophy has given up me. It's not exactly that I can no longer do it.'

Family loyalty made me rush to her defence. I was sure that old Fliss could 'do it' with the best of them, whatever 'it' was. Like the rest of the family, I had never been too sure what philosophy was, though I more inclined to Aunt Deirdre's opinion that Fliss was jolly clever and should be given all encouragement than to Granny's view, enunciated with heart-less vehemence on those occasions (these days rare) when she was awake, that philosophy was 'a lot of nonsense' – an absurdist definition which would, I suspect, have found an echo in the bosom of the ever-lamented Mrs Webb. Felicity, when rattled once too often by this line of her grandmother's, had snootily pointed out that some Frenchman, himself a philoso-pher, had come to this very conclusion in one of the most interesting books of the century.

'It's not that I can't do it,' she repeated, ignoring my expressions of certainty that she could, 'even though it is the most devilishly difficult thing in the world to do, and it may be that there is a madness in trying.' She paused and was silent for about a minute. 'Not in considering it important, that's not mad, but trying might be mad. The devil of it is, that except in a very limited number of mathematical and scientific statements, we are obliged to use language as the means to discuss the important matters before us.'

'You mean, like whether there's a God or not?'

'That's not often discussed these days.'

She laughed lightly.

I had introduced this question because I did genuinely suppose that it was the sort of thing with which philosophers were occupied. I also, however, felt a gossipy curiosity. That Christmas was the first since childhood at which Felicity had attended her father's Midnight Mass. I always went. As a conscious unbeliever I positively enjoyed the shape of the liturgical year. The Mass, with its gospel story of angelic salutations to the shepherds, its carols, its lights, was for me an essential part of Christmas and I was untroubled by an inability to regard it as anything but folktale. Felicity, for reasons which had never been spoken, but which I took to be ones of intellectual scruple, had stayed away from church altogether.

'Shouldn't philosophers be interested in the existence of God?' I asked her again.

'It depends by what criterion you are using the word *shouldn't.*'

'Surely it is important whether there is a God or not.'

'Yes, but equally important is where you derive your standards of importance, how they may be usefully discussed. . . . But you don't need me to say this. It's common sense. It is the difficulty of what happens when we go beyond common sense which is reducing me to silence.'

'Do we ever need to go beyond common sense?'

'I don't know. We choose to do so often enough, if by "we", you mean the human race. Oh, Julian, I need *time.*' She ran a large white hand through her short hair and raked it back from her waxy brow. 'Time, not to think, but to stop thinking. The brain tires itself out by thinking, it becomes sore with it, and can't go any further. I very much want to go further, but I don't like the directions in which my thoughts – which have stopped being thoughts and have become something else – are appearing to push me. I like common sense as much as you do, dear.'

'So, you're giving up teaching.'

'Most philosophers and mathematicians give up thinking before they reach my age. That doesn't matter. You have to be a genius actually to *do* philosophy, rather than merely being able to see what it is. For the purposes of my job, giving tutorials to young women, that's enough, that's all I need.'

'You mean, you can tell them the gist of what Hegel said, Kant, Plato, the kind of thing you get in Russell's *History of Western Philosophy.*'

'My approach would not be the same as Russell's, but I see what you mean.'

'It is the only philosophical work I have found even remotely readable.'

'It is a silly and unfair book.'

'Oh.'

We continued to bang about in the kitchen but I did not speak. These lofty, snubbing remarks of Felicity's had been putting me in my place since childhood. I still hated it when she went all superior. I wrenched open cupboard doors and piled saucepans and baking trays with a clatter. She showed no conciousness that she had made an offensive remark.

'Who was that one who gave up philosophy because there was no more to be said – it was something like that, wasn't it?' I said. 'You saw him once in Cambridge. He became a village schoolmaster? No?'

'I'm not going to be a great philosopher like him, ' she smiled sadly. I saw how much she would have wished to be in the same league as Wittgenstein. Through most of the years when we had shared our childhood home, I, similarly, had nursed all manner of ambitions: I wanted to be a great actor, a great writer. Perhaps those who achieve greatness in life are not those with the most talent, but those who never lose the childish self-confidence that they can walk on water. Once they question their ability to do so, they sink. Such a moment had evidently occurred in Felicity's life.

'Ursula Lampitt is being terribly good about it,' she said. 'When I told her why I wanted to give up my job, she insisted upon keeping my options open. They've appointed a temporary lecturer for three years. I can go back after that if I want to.'

'And what will you do?'

'I want to do ordinary work which doesn't leave the mind churning in the small hours.'

'A market garden?'

'Anyway, I'm fed up with Oxford.'

'I shall miss hearing all about the Fellows at Rawlinson.'

'I've been there nearly ten years. You have visited me perhaps twice.'

'I didn't want to *meet* your colleagues. I liked hearing about them. Better than the Mulberrys, or your father's stories about the Lampitts.'

'Poor old Pa.'

Felicity had a quiet capacity to bring her colleagues to life. I knew each of the Fellows at Rawlinson so exactly from her verbal portraits that when I did eventually pay one of those rare visits to the college, I had no difficulty in recognising any of them. I knew before being introduced, that I was about to shake hands with Dr Barclay, an expert in the literature of the German Romantic period, who was said never to have crossed the Channel, spoke German with a Roedean accent and had the habit of lifting a cardiganed sleeve to cover the protuberant yellow teeth as she gave utterance. And there was the generously filled sailor's suit of Miss Plumb; pure maths, but vaguely impure, if unrequited, feelings for her pupils. Miss Darke, the pinched, snobbish English don, liked to make the girls cry and had a bee in her bonnet about the numerology of Spenser's *Faerie Queene*. How well, without anything so overt as an imitation, Felicity had conveyed to me Miss Darke's lips; the way, when she had delivered herself of some particularly barbed comment, Miss Darke's lips would implode, so that her mean little mouth would momentarily disappear, leaving nothing but a pencil line between the sharp nose and the triangular chin. With the imminent removal from my life of this gallery of entertaining figures, I felt as the listening public might feel if the Broadcasting Corporation chose to take 'The Mulberrys' off the air.

'What, then,' I asked, 'if not a market garden?'

'I've joined the Civil Service.' She blushed very deeply now. 'I suppose we should have talked about this sooner, because it will mean I'll be living in London all the time.'

Thus it began. Felicity started work at her ministry that January, and since then, she had been a permanent feature of life in Arlington Road. We still nominally led separate lives, ate most of our meals apart, and occupied separate floors of the house, but from that moment, everything was different . . . I was no longer able to tell myself with complete accuracy that I lived alone. Initially, I resented this; I knew that Felicity had every right to spend as much time in the house as she liked; after all, she paid half the rent. But my solitude was threatened. It was an alteration to the original agreement. I was no longer, quite, an independent being in the sense that I had been before. I found myself involuntarily developing irritation with Felicity which was just like my fury with the lodgers; only, it was deeper because it revived ancient childhood hostility between us. The clumsy way she filled a teapot, her large talcum-powdery footprints on the landing linoleum – these annoyed me. Much worse was her intrusive interest in my 'work'. For as long as I was alone, I could hide from myself the fact that I was a professional failure, that I was not doing with my life what I had initially wanted to do, that my 'writing' had come to nothing, that radio work for the most part bored me, and that my private life was pathetically empty. I did not spell these things out to myself, still less to Felicity, but they became starkly obvious as soon as our shared life began. There was too much curiosity in her, too much intrusive sympathy, real but crushing. But the worst feature of her presence at Arlington Road was that, while finding it maddening, I also came to depend upon it. The evenings when Felicity was 'good' and did not intrude upon my time started to feel empty. We had the unwritten, unspoken agreement that we should continue to lead quite separate lives, but that, should we happen to coincide in the sitting room at about six thirty p.m., we would have a drink together before our separate suppers. In time, these separate suppers turned into joint suppers. I found myself deliberately hovering in the sitting room wanting her to return, eager for the glass of sherry, and the latest instalment of office gossip, while 'our' supper was cooking. By this stage, I was not quite sure who had taken over whom, or whether it was merely an arrangement which suited us both; perhaps it was a reversion to childhood, simply.

The rehearsals of Felicity's office day were among the features of the new dispensation which I valued most highly. Even more than when she had been a university teacher, Felicity now needed to talk about her colleagues. At the end of each working day, she had to relive it for at least a quarter of an hour before drifting into silence, or talk of something else. Sometimes, if the desire for work-talk was strong, or the details too esoteric for the layman's ear, she needed to share it with some colleague in the same department, and she would come home later than usual having been to a pub to discuss the minutiae of office politics with a colleague, usually with Rice Robey. At other times, my company would satisfy, particularly if she wished to speak of Rice Robey himself. These talks were the mental equivalent of stretching tired limbs in a hot bath after a strenuous walk; and because of them, I came to know, as well as I knew the Lampitts, or the Mulberrys, or the Fellows of Rawlinson, a whole new cast-list of the people who worked on Felicity's corridor, or those whom she encountered in the course of her work. She was in a department of the Ministry of Public Works which had charge of Ancient Monuments. Her work was purely administrative, and she never left the office, but there were colleagues, such as the much-quoted Rice Robey, who was occasionally in the office, and who spent much of his time 'in the field'. Rice Robey was not Felicity's superior – I never did quite work out the Civil Service hierarchy but I gathered that he worked several doors down from herself on the same corridor; he had charge of ancient sites in the southern region of England – stone circles, earthworks, Iron Age camps, White Horses, cairns, burial mounds, Romano-British floors. Sometimes, if no one else could be found to take them on, Rice Robey took an interest in later stuff, ruined castles and abbeys of Norman times, but his chief interest died out in the Dark Ages.

Rice Robey was by far the most colourful figure in Felicity's new box of puppets and I found him interesting from the first, not least because of Felicity's rapidly changing attitude towards him. So fast did the attitude change that I was slow in the early months to recognise that 'a really very tiresome man on the same corridor as myself', mentioned in her first week, was the same person to whom she contemptuously referred as the 'bull's-eyed poet' or that either of these individuals were to be associated with 'Mr Robey – he is a most fascinating conversationalist – he knows about everything – the Welsh Triads, theology, Egyptian hieroglyphics, William James's *Varieties of Religious Experience*'.

'That's everything?'

'Yes.'

She had laughed, a quite new laugh, liberated from the old despotism of fact which had enchained her academic existence.

'Whatever came of your theory that Mr Robey was a spy?'

'He certainly has the most extraordinary store of knowledge about people.'

She repeated the scandalous information which Rice Robey had told her about the newly elected Leader of the Labour Party.

'He should know. Mr Robey did work under the man during the last Labour Government.'

'You mean, Harold Wilson was Minister of Works, and Mr Robey happened to have a minor job in the ministry at the time. This made Mr Robey privy to the secrets of the minister's bedchamber?'

'I consider it rummer than this other business,' said Felicity, 'this stuff with the Cabinet minister.'

'If true, it would be *as* rum.' Now it was my turn to be pedantic. Since meeting Rice Robey, Felicity appeared to have an altogether looser attitude to language, and to truth. So much so, that it was difficult to build up a picture of the man which

539

hung together or 'made sense', in the way that one always wants a two-dimensional figure to make sense. When Felicity had first described Rice Robey to me as 'tiresome', she had not expanded, and I assumed that some minor verbal badinage had irritated her. As her picture of him grew rosier, she started to deny her early descriptions of the man if ever they were repeated back to her. Thus:

'How's the man with the squint?'

'What man with a squint?'

'You know, the poet. The man who's rewriting Dante's *Divine Comedy* on the back of memo-slips.'

'Rice Robey does not have a squint. But I do wish he did not always have a cigarette hanging from his lips when he pokes his head around my office door.'

When, a week or two later, I referred to his habit, which she had vividly described, of 'flicking ash all over the place', Felicity had crossly asked me what was wrong with 'having the odd cigarette' and reminded me that I myself smoked heavily.

A similar rewriting of recent office history took place with regard to Rice Robey and the women.

'He's auditioning us for the role of Beatrice in his *Divine Comedy*,' she had said, in the days when she could still describe him with detachment. 'I've no hope. He likes trecento maidens with long hair. Beattie – the girl I told you about in the typing pool – is the likeliest candidate at the moment.'

'You said she despised him; handed round the note he had written to her.'

'Only because she couldn't understand the quotation he had written on her blotter – she needed someone to translate it for her. *Incipit vita nuova.* How could he expect a girl like Beattie to understand such words? Perhaps he wants women to despise him. Some men need that. Anyway, he certainly likes hair. You know when we had a temporary typist with a high bun of hair on her head, he took her down to the basement of our building, supposedly to sort through some additional filing cabinets which we keep down there. Well, Brenda went down there quite by chance. . . .'

'Wait a minute. Brenda? She's the one two doors along from you. . . .'

'Yes. She's been transferred from Crown Buildings. Lives in Putney with a gym mistress, breeds cockers, it was her. She went down to the basement and found the two of them standing there. Rice Robey had a hairbrush in his hands, and the girl's bun of hair had been unwound. It was hanging loosely down her back. Brenda did not say anything.'

'Merely told you, and everyone else in the building.'

Since this incident had been related to me, I had more than once alluded to it. For some reasons, the image of the temporary secretarial assistant with her long hair falling about her shoulders haunted my imagination. I wondered why she had consented to play Rice Robey's probably harmless, if mildly unusual game. Felicity, it was clear, regretted having told me about it. The first time I mentioned it again, she dismissed my allusion with a crossness which reminded me of her mother. The next time I spoke about it, she more or less denied that the hairbrushing incident had taken place. She was in the middle of a fairly complicated narrative about some contretemps between the head of her department and the head of personnel. Not enough typists provided, something of the sort. I forget the details. I remember only that I made some facetious comment to the effect that I hoped any typists enlisted would have long tresses suitable for Rice Robey's requirements.

'I really don't know what you're talking about,' said Felicity.

'You know. Rice Robey in the basement with a hairbrush and the temporary secretary; Celia, you said she was called.'

'I don't remember a secretary called Celia. This sounds like one of Brenda's tall stories.'

'It was Brenda who discovered them together.'

'Brenda doesn't like Rice Robey. I don't remember the story. It sounds very unlikely to me.'

She fell to a meticulous analysis of a budget report and its ramifications. For most of our working lives, mind and emotions are caught up in details which, with the passage of the years, vanish totally from consciousness. I had taken to boring Felicity with analogous twingle-twangle in relation to my work for the BBC. I minded desperately, from week to week (not least because I was a freelance and my income depended on it) about the whim of the producer of 'The Mulberrys' and I was obsessed by the internal affairs of Bush House. It took Felicity no time at all after leaving Oxford to be neck deep in the trivia of office life at A1, as her branch of 'Accommodation and Buildings' was called in the Ministry of Works. Where the money was coming from for this or that project; the fate of particular papers, précis and memos; the abuse or exercise of power by those who pushed these documents from in-tray to out-tray: these things filled Felicity's mind, kept her awake at nights, throbbed through her waking thoughts as she caught her bus, or kept at bay those more disturbing thoughts of love and age and whither we were all hurtling as the weeks sped by. But they are gone now, these preoccupations, like the food we eat, and I find that I only recall those things which, at the time, seemed extraneous to work, supposedly unimportant matters of gossip such as who was in love with whom; and even those details became distorted and forgotten.

A myth to live by – that, Albion Pugh had suggested, was the one thing needful. An exercise such as the present narrative in which one selectively reclaims the past is such a piece of myth-making, no doubt, or a discovery of what myths I have been involuntarily weaving in my brain out of the day-to-day ordinariness of things. The lunch with Darnley had made me mildly drunk, but it had also awoken a disturbing chain of reflections. Memories of childhood, of the part played in life by the Lampitts, had all arisen, murky ghosts in the mind, drawing back further curtains of memory to reveal the north Norfolk coast, and my lost parents in the bright sunshine of 3 September 1939, a day which, for everyone who can remember it, however dimly, links the personal myth to the national. Albion Pugh was right. Everything since the war had broken up and old myths had not been replaced by anything with analogously cohesive power. And now the Cabinet minister was in disgrace and the bishop did not believe in Christ. Whether or not these two facts were, as Albion Pugh averred, mystically linked, they both threw into focus within my own head an atrophy which had overtaken me since my divorce. I had been living without love. What I had known with Anne had been for a short and delightful period something so real to me that I could no longer imagine consoling myself for its absence with casual affairs or the ersatz escapades apparently enjoyed by senior government ministers. With the sealing off of this area of experience, however, something within me had died and I had begun to fear that what I had lost was whatever gave one a motive for wanting to wake up in the mornings – the imaginative faculty or the capacity in any active role to love. I felt myself beginning to be doomed to be a spectator rather than a participant in life. That was why I derived such interest and satisfaction from Felicity's narratives of office politics and scandal. I could enjoy them at a voyeuristic distance with no danger of involvement. The very act of enjoyment filled me with the dread that I was turning into a figure like the Lady of Shalott who could not face life head on, but could only view it through her looking-glass. When she turned to look on Camelot, rather than its mirror image, she was cursed. Plato's figures in the cave, satisfying themselves with shadows cast by the fire and unaware of the existence, behind them, of the brightness of the sun, would have provided another image of my plight. And Albion Pugh's censure of the unimaginative bishop who could no longer believe in Christianity emphasised what was growing stronger in me with the years, a sadness at my own incurable agnosticism. As Uncle Roy's nephew, I had spent so many hours in church that I knew the Psalter and the Prayer Book and many passages from the Bible by heart. It did not worry me that I could not, in a conventional sense, believe: indeed, I did not see how an intelligent person could adhere to the orthodoxies. But it had begun to sadden me that I could put all this religious inheritance to no good or imaginative use. It lay around like lumber in my mind, but it did not quicken the heart. Stories from the Bible had inspired some of the noblest lives in history, some of the greatest music and paintings and architecture. As nothing else had done, it had provided a 'myth' for people to live by, and just as I regretted my present incapacity to love (or even to feel sexual desire), so I also regretted my unbelief, my failure to respond imaginatively to the Old Story. The great majority of Europeans for the last 1,900 years had lived with this story as a background to their lives and somehow made use of it. Imaginatively, I was cut off from them, and from it, unable to find the mental or emotional equipment with which to respond to it. I did not even share the vacuous bishop's worries about whether it was true. This, I think, was what Felicity had in mind when she spoke of a desire or need to go beyond common sense. At least she was now involved in the supposedly real world of work. Even this was denied me. I earned my living by pretending to be Jason Grainger, pretending to live in Barleybrook and purveying, each time the Mulberry theme music crackled through the loudspeakers into British homes, a fake England, disembodied and unreal.

543

With some such reflections adding melancholy to the late afternoon hangover, I fumbled for my door keys and entered my house. When I woke up in an armchair, having only slept for an hour or two, Felicity was entering our shared sitting room and putting down her briefcase on the upright chair beside the gas fire. I instantaneously wondered if she was about to launch into another Rice Robey saga, but in fact she was to do better than that. Her lips were pouting excitedly, moving noiselessly before she spoke in wheedling, uncharacteristically cooing tones.

'I hope you don't mind – I've brought Rice Robey home for a bit. Something' – her voice sank to a whisper – 'something has cropped up.'

'Use this room if you don't want to' – my mind flew instantly to hairbrushes – 'if you don't want to take him upstairs.'

'Could I . . .'

She hesitated. It was clear that she wanted me to leave the sitting room while she entertained her friend; on the other hand, she felt embarrassed to say that this was what she wanted.

'I've got to wash socks,' I said.

'Just say hallo to him anyway.'

'OK.'

I was not sure that I really wanted to meet the legendary Rice Robey of whom so many strong and conflicting reports had been delivered over the last year. He was a figure, evidently, whom Felicity could not get out of her mind, and nor could I. But was he not, from my point of view, better kept, like a character in 'The Mulberrys', unseen but vividly imagined? I had no choice in the matter, however, since Felicity was calling to him.

'Come in, do, and meet my cousin.'

A strong cockney voice in the hall said, 'Not if it necessitates the disturbance of the domestic tranquillities.'

The man who entered the room was the figure at Darnley's lunch table, the man called Albion Pugh.

'Mr Grainger,' he said, shaking my hand.

'Mr Pugh! What a coincidence!'

Felicity looked puzzled, and rather cross, as if we were excluding her from some private joke.

'A conjunction of personal destinies – it's not necessarily to be regarded as a matter of chance. ' As he spoke, he tossed his head backwards and his eyes became temporarily invisible as the lenses of his specs caught the reflection of the 100-watt bulb suspended from the middle of the ceiling.

Felicity, with a literalness which recalled her childhood self, explained to each of us that we were really named Julian Ramsay and Rice Robey.

'You two will want to discuss . . .' I hesitated, 'whatever it was you had to discuss.' I made to leave the room.

Rice Robey grinned.

'Connections, connections. What do you think of Lord Lampitt's chances of rising high in his party?'

'Negligible, surely? For a start, he's a peer.'

'He has the backing of the Marxians,' said Rice Robey. 'They are an important voice. If they dislike his title, they could find little in his private life which could bring down scandal on the party. Some day, someone is going to pin a great deal to the name of James Harold Wilson.'

'Really ?'

'Oh, yes.'

His face became cruel and slightly mad as he spoke of these political matters. He turned down the corners of his mouth and fumbled in his pocket for Fragrant Cloud. There is something particularly irritating about two friends, whom one had thought to belong to entirely different worlds, turning out to have topics in common which exclude oneself. I felt that Felicity was owed an explanation, if not an apology.

'Mr Robey met me at the *Spark* lunch,' I said. 'Vernon was there.'

'They are an interesting consanguinity, the Lampitts.'

'We've known some of them,' said Felicity. 'Someone called Sargent Lampitt is my godfather.'

'You never said' – Rice Robey's tone was sharp. 'The brother of James Petworth? Well, well!' His face broadened once more into a grin, and I supposed that he was going to repeat some Hunter-style scurrilous legend about Jimbo's private life. Felicity scowled and, standing beside the mantelpiece, moved from foot to foot.

'R.R.,' she said, 'Julian doesn't want to hear about our problem at the office.'

She normally had reasonable manners, but on this occasion she was desperate to have Rice Robey to herself, and there was a danger, if the Lampitt conversation continued, that I should hover about for the duration of his visit.

'You must forgive us, Mr Ramsay, if a little later we talk shop,' he said. 'A little trouble at the office.'

'Things are getting quite out of control,' she said wildly. Presumably she spoke of the behaviour of the head of department, but from her tone she could have been describing her own emotional condition.

'I knew Mr James Petworth Lampitt very well,' said Rice Robey.

He was, I should guess, a little more than fifty, which would mean that he was in his mid-thirties when Jimbo died. The belle-lettrist and biographer had occupied a flat in Hinde Street just off Manchester Square and had met his end falling from a fire escape just outside his kitchen door on the fourth floor. His young friend Raphael Hunter, subsequently the author of that indiscreet volume about him, had been in the flat at the time, but had been unable to prevent the old man cascading into the area. (It was said that he was found upside down in a dustbin by a policeman who was nearby at the time.) I remembered Hunter describing the incident (omitting the dustbin detail) when he came down to address the Lampitt Society when I was at school.

'In my youth I too wrote books,' said Rice Robey.

'I had no idea,' said Felicity.

'They're largely forgotten now.'

'Darnley is a great fan,' I said. 'So too is the professor who fell asleep at the lunch table.'

'Cormac? He wrote a very amusing article the other week about old Professor Wimbish.'

'Vernon mentioned it.'

'They are deadly enemies, of course, Cormac and Wimbish. There was said to have been more than academic rivalry.'

'Do you mean over a woman?'

'A neaniskos,' he said, without removing his cigarette from his lips. Smoke poured from his mouth and nostrils as he laughed. 'No, I am out of print, and out of mind. I could never write in that manner again.'

'Mr Robey wrote as Albion Pugh,' I said.

'*Memphian Mystery*!' exclaimed Felicity. 'I loved that book. Reading it was one of the great imaginative experiences of my adolescence. That scene between Pharaoh's daughter and Moses.'

She flushed with excitement.

'Incest is one method of not dissipating the sexual energy which unites the race of man to the cosmos,' he declaimed, 'and binds the humanities to the angelicals.'

'I was not talking about incest,' said Felicity. 'I was thinking of that discussion about the religious destiny of Moses, doomed to lead his people into the wilderness, but destined never himself to enter the Promised Land.'

'Because he was an Egyptian, not a Hebrew,' said Robey.

'It's a wonderful idea.'

'It's *true*!'

Felicity would never have allowed such an assertion of fancy in her early days as a philosopher. Now, evidently, the rules had changed. 'You see,' he continued, 'while I was writing those *fabulae*, I lived like young Samuel.'

'Consecrated to the Lord in the Temple at Shiloh?' she said hopefully.

'Samuel Johnson, not Samuel the prophet. The *fabulae* came to me in the evenings when I had finished teaching. It was not merely that I had time to write. My teaching did not consume me, as this job does, and we speak, of course, about the days before the commencement of the Great Attachment. All creation small "c" is part of the same process as Creation big "c" and the energies of Eros for the race of men are the channels through which creativity flows. When the distractions of Eros commence, the stream is diverted from Parnassus.'

I took him to mean that too much sex puts writers off their work.

'Surely if that were true,' I said, 'all true writers would be celibate which has not, historically, been the case.'

'It is probably truer than we know,' he said, 'but these mysteries are contained within the still heart of the Primum Mobile, and whether we make love or make art, we make ourselves not merely the partakers of that divine energy but also its rivals. Therefore a revenge is exacted. As we read in the Upanishads, there is Malice as well as Love in that still heart, though the malice was never shown in a more paradoxical chiaroscuro than on Golgotha hill.'

If Godfrey Tucker had been given the shivers by Rice Robey's comparatively mild talk at lunch, there is no knowing what he would have felt at these words. As I heard them, I had the sensation of cold slugs making their progress up my spine. If Felicity was seeking conversations in which it was possible to stray beyond the confines of common sense she had clearly found an ideal companion.

'James Petworth Lampitt was the vessel of grace for me,' Robey continued. 'Without Mr Lampitt . . . It was not just that he helped me to get my *fabulae* into print, found me my first job. . . . He was an enabler. He lent me books, gave me books. Books have been a sacred life-blood to me, Mr Ramsay. Mr Lampitt gave me a ticket to the London Library, no less. As far as I was concerned, it was a ticket to Paradise. You know how they tell you that if you wish to get on in the world you need an on-tray, you need to be introduced to all the right people? Well, Mr Lampitt introduced me to all the right people. He introduced me to Paracelsus and to John Milton and to the Pseudo-Dionysus and to Wilkie Collins. They were all there waiting to meet me on the shelves in St James's Square.'

It was almost independently of my Uncle Roy's Lampitt mania that I developed my own preoccupation with James Petworth Lampitt. At a certain point of my career at school, I had fallen under his spell as a stylist and had too often reread his mannered biographical studies of nineteenth-century life. Strangely enough there weren't, as I recall, many Jimbo stories in Uncle Roy's inexhaustible repertoire. Uncle Roy had the indiscriminate interest in the genus which marks the true collector. *N'importe quel Lampitt.* Stories of far-flung Lampitt cousins catching wrong trains or diseases or saying unremarkable things in shops and hotels ('Typical Lampitt saying, that,' he would murmur, satisfied, as he repeated their words) were just as fascinating to my uncle as those members of the Lampitt family who might by any dispassionate standards have been considered interesting. Jimbo was interesting to me not as a Lampitt, primarily, but as a writer. The fact that I had known his brother since childhood and later married his niece added to the interest, but it did not diminish his status in my eyes. As I changed my mind about 'style', so I changed my mind about Jimbo as a writer, but I could never entirely discard a feeling of gratitude to him, for the aesthetic pleasure which his writing had awoken in me, but more, because it was in reading his pages that I first consciously became aware of my own desire to be a writer, to encapsulate truth in words. The whirlygig of time brings in its revenges, and Jimbo, who had pinioned so many lives to his collecting case like the specimens of butterflies or moths, was destined himself to be the subject of a biography, that of Hunter, who never seemed even remotely appreciative of the distinctive features of Jimbo's prose and who regarded him merely as an appropriate coat-hanger from which to suspend social and literary history of a not unclodhopping kind. Most offensive to the family, as I have already mentioned, was Hunter's contention that Jimbo had been a rampantly promiscuous homosexual, at least in his youth. Where my new-found acquaintance Rice Robey fitted into all this, I was not sure, but his sudden appearances, twice in one day, and his three independent connections with Darnley, with Felicity and now with the Lampitts, gave plausibility to his theory of 'conjunction of personal destinies'.

In trying to convey the quality of Rice Robey's utterances, it is not enough to record his peculiar autodidactic idiolects, or his cockney accent. He had the power of drawing you in to his own peculiar imaginative world so that whether he was generalising about the supernatural or gossiping about the sex lives of politicians or giving the gist of an admired book, you had the same sense of being a child, led into a magic grotto by a grown-up whom the other grown-ups would not consider suitable company. Gooseflesh sometimes came and went as he spoke.

I now forget at what speed, and at what stages, I came to learn the outlines of Rice Robey's life, but I might as well set down a brief résumé here. His parents ran a small sweets and newspapers business in Gospel Oak. He was an only child of exceptional talents, but his education was interrupted by domestic tragedy, the death of his father when Rice Robey was twelve. The boy was compelled to leave school a year later, working as an office boy, first in a legal firm, and then at a publishers – James Petworth Lampitt's publishers. Duties included acting as a messenger to addresses in central London, and he came Lampitt's way when delivering parcels to the apartment which the writer occupied in Hinde Street. An invitation to tea turned into a conversation about literature. Jimbo lent Rice Robey a book – Jessie L. Weston's *From Ritual to Romance*. The next week, when he came to tea, the boy borrowed a volume of Fraser's

Golden Bough, and, another week, some Yeats. This was the period of Rice Robey's real education. Jimbo obviously liked the boy's company, and perhaps he was flattered that someone so young, and so different from himself, should wish to return, week after week, for tea and anchovy toast and literary talk. Self-taught, Rice Robey had an intellectual range which was idiosyncratic, but he was obviously clever. When he was about eighteen, and had known Jimbo for a number of years, the old man conceived a scheme for the furtherance of the boy's education. He was to be attached to a small private school on the borders of Metroland, somewhere near Chorleywood, an establishment with whose headmaster Jimbo was somehow acquainted. Rice Robey was given free board and lodging and a small allowance in exchange for teaching the younger boys. The headmaster for his part agreed to coach Rice Robey for the public examinations necessary to qualify for matriculation at the university. All this took place in the late 1920s and early 1930s. Jimbo's plans for his protégé, however, went badly askew. The headmaster of the school was an alcoholic and the academy was far from flourishing. When Rice Robey first went to work there, some thirty boys were in attendance, but after only a few years their number dwindled to twenty, fifteen . . . and the future of the school looked uncertain. Mention of Rice Robey's tuition for matric. was somehow forgotten, and as all the other teachers drifted away, the young man was left responsible for shoring up a collapsed system. Jimbo could, perhaps, have rescued him, or Rice Robey could simply have left, but this did not happen. Had he been serious about wanting to go to university, perhaps he would have left, but the circumstances were ideal for an aspirant writer.

It was at this period that he wrote his Albion Pugh novels. (Pugh was the maiden name of his mother, and a Blakean preoccupation must have made him choose Albion as a first name for his pseudonym.) The four novels so admired by a tiny coterie were all composed very rapidly when he was in his early twenties, and still nominally looking after the school. By now the headmaster was himself graduating from three-quarters of a bottle to two bottles of Scotch per day, and there were almost no pupils. Rice Robey had time, and stationery, to indulge his imaginative bent.

It was the period when he first read Malory's *Morte d'Arthur*.

Since he saw everything in analogical terms, he was easily able to envisage the collapse of the tenth-rate little school through the lens of high Arthurian fantasy; the departure of (doubtless ill-qualified) colleagues seemed like the dismantlement of Camelot when the friendship of the knights was broken partly because of the unattainable lure of a religious vision, the quest for the Sangreal, partly because of the adultery of Queen Guinevere and Arthur's most trusted knight, Sir Lancelot. From what he subsequently told me – the crack-brained idea that the exercise of the sexual faculty somehow or another diminishes the creative urge – I would guess that Rice Robey did not actually become Mrs Paxton's lover until he had finished *Towered Camelot*, though some of the steamier passages in that might suggest, to a relentlessly biographical critic of the Albion Pugh *oeuvre*, the direction in which his heart was leading him. An affair of some sort began with the headmaster's wife. I don't think anyone ever satisfactorily explained to me all the details of the final débâcle, but the upshot of it was that Rice Robey and Mrs Paxton eloped, leaving the school and the husband to sink into alcoholic collapse. We are speaking of a time close to the outbreak of the Second World War. Rice Robey was in his late twenties, Mrs Paxton getting on for twice this age. Her 'little bit of money' soon evaporated. They lived in hired lodgings, sometimes unable to afford more than one shared room. He tried to make a living as a writer, but the prose no longer flowed, and he was too eccentric a stylist to make much of a living from hack work. (A short spell of reviewing for the *New Statesman* – he covered crime writing – came to an end because he was unable to perform the task which the literary editor set him, that is, to give short notices of the latest detective stories; he was unable to write about anything without his metaphysical preoccupations rising to the surface, just as he was incapable of using 'ordinary' language – Bishops became 'episkopoi', young men, 'neaniskoi'; Marxists, 'Marxians'; families, 'consanguinities'; and so on. Once removed from the squalid little school – 'the Dotheboys of the suburbs', he had once described it to me – he could not get on with work. A projected novel about Druids never progressed beyond the stage of notes. He had the curious habit, which I had never come across before in a prose writer, of doing the first draft of everything he composed, including the published thrillers, in verse. The habit of doodling poetry continued, and he was still at work on an English version of his English *Commedia* (in execrable *terza rima*) when I first met him.

Money came his way from this source and that. Jimbo helped him on an irregular basis. Some of his cheques, as I learnt from Cecily Lampitt, were very generous. I myself disbelieve the suggestion (Darnley had heard it too and repeated it to me long after my first meeting with the man) that Rice Robey was formally employed in Military Intelligence. True, that branch of government service has employed some strange types in its time, but how would they have enlisted Rice Robey? How would he have come their way? I think he probably was in touch with those who did work for Intelligence. He had an astonishingly large acquaintanceship, and would seem to have known a little bit about everyone – politicians, churchmen, lawyers, senior civil servants and journalists. How this came about, that an unemployed young schoolmaster should have built up such a store of information, I shall never guess; but perhaps Rice Robey was merely an extreme example of the commonplace fact that one thing leads to another, and if you are prepared to follow up connections, to remember names, to work at gossip with the appropriate reference books and newspapers in your hand, it does not take long to build up a mental filing cabinet chock-a-block with damaging dossiers. It could well be the case that his friendship with Jimbo was the start of all this. The Lampitts may not be as important in the scheme of things as Uncle Roy supposed, but they are a large family with cousins and friends in the worlds of politics, business, universities and in what might once have been termed 'society'. Anyone wishing to build up a thoroughgoing knowledge of English life could do worse than to start with the cultivation of a Lampitt. Rice Robey was also a man who liked bars. He was not alcoholic, but he could hold a certain amount of liquor and was known to enjoy visits to pubs on his way home to Mrs Paxton. At the beginning of the Blitz, he and Mrs Paxton moved in with his mother, in the borderlands between Kentish Town and Gospel Oak. I do not know whether Mrs Robey and Mrs Paxton enjoyed one another's society, but Rice Robey's mother died some time during the war. His poor eyesight disqualified him for military service. He entered the Civil Service at the executive level, and was attached to an area of no immediate interest to his friends in MI5 – the Ministry of Works. It was a propitious moment to be starting a career as a civil servant. There were few rivals in the office of his own age or sex and his wide range of knowledge about ancient or prehistoric sites was soon recognised. Before long, he had been promoted and transferred to a job which carried the status and salary of the 'officer' class of civil servant, the so-called Administrative grade.

Since boyhood, all spare time had been spent exploring London on foot, and any available holidays had been devoted to walking or cycling in the British Isles. He had an encyclopaedic knowledge of the very sites which it was his task in the Ministry of Works to conserve. There was no henge, barrow, stone circle, or earthworks in the south of England about which he could not display knowledge (and, it is perhaps needless to add, cranky theories).

In peacetime, his job would doubtless have been given to someone with better paper qualifications, such as a degree in archaeology or medieval architecture. Needs must, however, and he was soon exercising a considerable responsibility for those sites which were under his control. After the war, the new government reorganised the Civil Service and greatly increased its numbers. Rice Robey felt himself diminished in importance. If there was truth in half Felicity's stories about him in her early months as his colleague, it was possible to see that he was not everyone's idea of the perfect civil servant. There was the gossip, and the compulsive trouble-making, perhaps exacerbated by the drying-up of his pen. He needed to weave romances, and when it was no longer possible to do so in print, the compulsion to do so in life became unstoppable. He came to believe, after one markedly unsuccessful year when he came up for his Board, failed to get promotion for which he had applied and found himself being 'shoved sideways' in some departmental reorganisation, into a job with less status or influence than he had been doing before, that 'they' were out to get him; that he was passed over for promotion not because of professional incompetence but because he 'knew too much', most notably about the Minister of Works in Attlee's administration, James Harold Wilson, the future leader of the Labour Party and three times Prime Minister. Others felt that Rice Robey ditched his chances by gross inefficiency at all matters of office administration, failure to do necessary paperwork, while among academics and archaeologists he was not taken seriously because of his unashamed willingness to link all the ancient sites with their supposed legendary or mythical background. There was also the talk of Robey and the women, and his eccentric, romantic ways of passing time with female colleagues.

Now he stood before me, this legend, and Felicity was conspicuously anxious to have him to herself. An expression of true anguish passed over her features when he looked at his watch and said that he should have been home half an hour earlier.

'The Great Attachment?' asked Felicity impishly.

'Masters' commands come with a power resistless,' he quoted, with a malicious grin.

There was scarcely going to be time to discuss whatever 'important' piece of business they had used as a pretext for this extension of their day together.

'I must leave you to it,' I said, 'but how fascinating – isn't it, Felicity? – that Mr Robey knew Jimbo Lampitt. We must talk of this some other time.'

I put down my sherry glass and overacted the part of a man bustling about his business, anxious to get on with chores.

'I not only knew him,' said Rice Robey. 'I also know something about him which I think escaped the speculum of the authorities, unless they chose to ignore it, unless there were a conspiracy of the magistrature.'

'You're not talking about that filth of Raphael Hunter's?' asked Felicity. 'Sargie and all the Lampitts are agreed that Hunter's book is a pack of lies.'

'Ah!' said Rice Robey. 'Raphael Hunter, a name which could not for long remain unmentioned in this connection.'

Felicity looked decidedly uncomfortable. It was inconceivable to me that she had ever spoken to Rice Robey of her own miserable time with Raphael Hunter; nevertheless, I believed it was possible that Rice Robey knew about it.

'I wasn't referring to Raphael Hunter's book, as a matter of fact,' he said. 'I was referring to Mr Lampitt's death, and the manner of his dying.'

'He fell to his death from the top of a fire escape,' I said.

In the brief silence which followed I thought of Jimbo, whom I had never seen; I thought of dead legs in tweed trousers sticking out of a dustbin.

'So we have been informed,' said Rice Robey.

'By Hunter. Who witnessed, or almost witnessed, the accident.'

'Ah, yes. Mr Hunter.'

Rice Robey's manner, smile, general demeanour, had already begun to give me the shivers, as they had done to Godfrey Tucker at lunch. I was now turning to such gooseflesh that it would not have surprised me to know that my hair was actually standing on end. He was a master of the pause. We waited breathlessly for him to spell out what he meant.

'One thing about Mr Lampitt is certain. He was not a self-slayer. Another certain thing in my mind' – again, a melodramatic pause – 'is that in recording a verdict of accidental death, the coroner was stretching the meaning of the word "accidental". I often stood at the top of that fire escape outside Mr Lampitt's kitchen door. He liked to stand there because on a summer evening, he could see the sunset behind the Wallace Collection, a view redolent for him of Italy and old Roman days. He was the lover, Mr Lampitt – but you know this . . .'

What morsel was to follow this appetising pause?

'. . . of the *Italianate*.'

Perhaps pruriently, I found this revelation a little tame.

'There are no accidents in my creed, Mr Ramsay; certainly, there are no accidental deaths.'

'But, let's get this clear,' I said, ' and then I really will leave you in peace with Felicity. Are you just saying that Mr Lampitt's death was in some way foreordained, fated?'

He turned to Felicity with a smile.

'I like your cousin's use of the word "just",' he observed. 'If the concept of Fate is a useful one, then the hour of our death is fore-resolved. But that is not all that I am saying. Outside the kitchen door at the top of the fire escape there are some railings. They came up to Mr Lampitt's chest, effectually. He was, I am sure you know, a small man. Now, the coroner said nothing about Mr Lampitt falling down the fire-escape stairs. He did not fall down the stairs. He fell over the railing which he would have considerable difficulty in climbing. If Despair had possessed his *anima* he would not have chosen to end his life in that way; not while he was in the middle of entertaining a neaniskos. He was the soul of courtesy.'

'You can't be saying that he was pushed? You're suggesting that Mr Lampitt was murdered?'

Rice Robey, however, would say no more at this meeting. His marbly eyes became mysteriously dead, almost invisible behind the thick lenses and he smiled his inscrutable smile.

Two

Lunch at the Rectory was over, and we were almost ready to depart for Mallington, Darnley and I. Throughout the meal, Uncle Roy had beamed at us with loving indulgence, as if, after the lamentable false start of my divorce from Anne, I was at last on the point of doing something sensible, that is, hobnobbing with Lampitts, extending and deepening my Lampitt acquaintance, brushing up on my Lampitt lore. Anecdotes and sayings of the great family had poured from his lips throughout the meal. The others round the table were Felicity, Aunt Deirdre and Granny.

Darnley did not go in for politeness. If someone bored him, he made no pretence to be interested in what they were saying. At the first possible pause in the Lampitt narratives he turned to my grandmother on his right and spoke to her, not uncondescendingly, but almost desperately, suggesting that any subject was better than my uncle's favourite topic of conversation.

'So Mary said – that's Sargie's second cousin – brilliant woman – "*Oui, mon capitaine*" – you do know French, don't you?'

'Enough to understand that,' said Darnley. Hoping we had reached the end of this particular story, he added, 'Is that it?'

'I've heard this one so often before,' said my grandmother without opening her eyes.

' "*Oui, mon capitaine, mais ça, c'est tout à fait une jolie bouilloire*". . . .'

He blushed, shook with the hilarity of it. Would he manage to finish his sentence before Aunt Deirdre snapped out the punchline for him?

'*Bouilloire de poissons*, we know,' she said.

While my uncle, convulsed, dabbed his lips with a napkin and murmured, 'Typical Lampitt story, that,' Darnley plunged in.

'Whatever happened to your nice friend who drove us about

in a Riley? Do you remember, Mrs Ramsay? We all went out to lunch together in Worcester.'

'Oh, Miles, that was ages ago, and you were a little lad,' said Granny. 'I'm afraid poor Mrs Webb has been gone a long time now.'

'Mrs Webb, that was it. Charming person. Laughed at all my jokes.'

'Mrs Webb and I always said as how Miles should go on the stage,' said Granny, making Uncle Roy wince at the phrase 'as how'.

Because it was Granny who said this, Aunt Deirdre reacted as if the remark had been mildly insulting.

'Different people want to do different things,' she said.

'Did I say otherwise?' asked Granny. 'I haven't seen this magazine of yours, Miles. Julian was telling me about it. Would it be this new satire?'

'Partly, some of it's serious.'

'I stayed up watching, you know, on the television.'

She laughed, just at the memory of it.

'It's far too late and it's absolute rubbish,' put in Aunt Deirdre.

'That was a Week, that was,' said Granny, at last able to remember the programme.

'*The* week, *the* week,' said Felicity. ' "That was the Week that was".'

'Very rude about the Prime Minister,' said Granny with a chuckle, 'and the other Harold. Both the Harolds.'

As she spoke, the very word *Harold* seemed richly comic. Granny had not opened her eyes for some minutes, and even now, as she indicated the need for cigarettes, she merely made her bodily gestures, from side to side, rather than opening her eyes to look for the packet of Craven A. '*Very* funny imitations,' she said, 'though I didn't like it when they made a joke about the Queen.'

'Honestly!' exclaimed Aunt Deirdre, 'I think that the standard of the wireless is vulgar enough, but the things they show on the television, not that I watch it. . . .'

'It was different in Lord Reith's time,' said Uncle Roy.

'They hardly had television in Lord Reith's time,' said Darnley, failing to see the importance of the BBC in the scheme of things – not that it was a great broadcasting corporation, in which many interesting people had worked, but that it had once figured in a Lampitt anecdote.

'Do you remember when they enlisted Jimbo Lampitt on to a committee advising the BBC on how to pronounce words? There was George Bernard Shaw, who was a bit of a chum of Vernon's papa, by the way – people sometimes make the mistake of thinking he only knew Angelica – and who else was there? Rose Macaulay, and dear old Jimbo.'

'We know,' snapped Aunt Deirdre, '*sausage* pronounced *sors-ij*.'

It was a little unkind of her to cut this particular story so relentlessly short, render it indeed into telegraphese. I began to think of reducing the other famous stories to palatable mouthfuls of less than ten words. 'Bobby Lampitt. Waiter. Duckling young duck not old horse.' Or, 'Tony – should have said you meant by *aeroplane*' or 'Sargie – poop-poop – car tyres – brilliant mind'.

'I heard a strange thing the other week about Jimbo's death,' I said.

'Do you need to worry about clothes, old thing?' my aunt asked. 'For Mallington, I mean? I dare say Roy's old dinner jacket's still wearable, if you need it for tonight.'

My aunt was manifestly unable to endure another Lampitt story, even if it were a murder story. Perhaps it was tactless of me to have embarked on the story of Jimbo's death. It could only upset Uncle Roy to think of a Lampitt being murdered, and I did not wish to revive the distressing memories of Raphael Hunter's book, nor of Uncle Roy's painful estrangement from Sargie. Probably, the idea that Jimbo had not met an accidental death was one of Rice Robey's fantasies.

'You won't need a dinner jacket at Mallington, of course,' said Uncle Roy, quietly amused at this little mistake of his wife's. '*Old* Lord Lampitt dressed for dinner, and of course down here at the Place, old Mrs Lampitt always liked men to put on a black tie. Sargie, bless him, always . . .'

'Penguin outfits,' said my aunt quickly.

'Yes, he always called them penguin outfits. But the Honourable Vernon – which is how I shall always think of him – is almost self-consciously informal.'

'It's all so put *on*, this Ernie nonsense,' said my aunt. 'I can't bear it on the wireless when they refer to him as Ernie Lampitt.'

'His father had that side to his nature,' said Uncle Roy. 'I'm sorry to say that Old Lord Lampitt was just a *tiny* little bit of a humbug.'

Felicity had resolved to stay with her parents, while Darnley and I went over to Mallington for the night. I did not blame Felicity for wriggling out of the engagement. I did not much want to go myself, as the time for departure approached, though I liked the idea of a jaunt with Darnley. I knew that I would be interested to see the house again, though, and a small part of myself was excited by the knowledge that Vernon was now a man of potential influence in the Labour Party. Mallington was known to be a place where senior trade unionists and members of the Shadow Cabinet sometimes congregated. I led such a very sheltered life that I was able to be snobbishly attracted to the notion of proximity to famous people, famous moreover in fields which were different from my own. Darnley, I think, was similarly fascinated by those who wished to exercise political power. He spoke a bit about this when, an hour after lunch, he was leaning forward in the passenger seat of his red Morris Minor, an ancient car which I liked to drive when I had the chance.

'I wonder who Ernie's got lined up for us,' said Darnley. 'Hope there aren't any other hacks. I could do with a rest from hacksville.'

'Really? You never seem to tire of it.'

'I shouldn't mind if Harold were there.'

'Harold Wilson? Is that likely?'

'Ernie was one of the people chiefly instrumental in getting Harold the leadership. Harold was the left's candidate, but the left knew they couldn't have a *real* lefty like Footy. They needed a man who would look after their interests and con the general public into voting for them.'

'What about Vernon? Is he a real lefty, as you call it?'

'Och, he's practically a communist.'

This last sentence of Darnley's was, for some reason, delivered in the voice of the Binker, our hateful old headmaster at Seaforth Grange. Darnley broke into different voices quite arbitrarily, and there seldom seemed much connection between the voice and the content – he could be Humphrey Bogart while talking about the Archbishop of Canterbury, Vernon Lampitt while telling me about his sister's latest (and unsuitable) bloke, which he did, as the car left Timplingham behind us, roared through the beech avenue beyond the church, passed the new bungalows and the petrol station until it found blank, mildly undulating country. The matter of Elizabeth's man disposed of, we fell to other areas of gossip, snatches of memory of Seaforth Grange and the army, and then – Rice Robey.

'Pughie's done a brilliant collection of diary snippets for *The Spark*,' said Darnley. 'Brilliant. It's miraculous how he gets hold of half his information.'

'Perhaps he makes it up.'

'Oh, no,' said Darnley airily. 'Pughie'd never do a thing like that. Besides' – he sniffed loud and long as if trying to inhale snuff through pints of mucus – 'all these little stories of his have the ring of truth. He's also given me some bits and pieces of this book he's writing about Jesus. I'll give them to you to read if I may. See what you think.'

'What sort of gossip has he fed you?'

'Well, there's some pretty good dirt on poor old Harold.'

'Which Harold?'

'Harold the younger. Pughie did work under the man when he was at the Ministry of Works. I must remember to ask Ernie about that – He and Harold were both in Attlee's Cabinet together, you know. He'd know the gossip. Then, on a completely different subject, Pughie's got a bee in his bonnet about Aldingbury Ring, this stone circle near Windsor which Pughie thinks they are going to demolish or plough up to build a road. He's trying to have it stopped.'

'He was in such a flat spin about it all,' I said, 'that he actually came round to my house, supposedly to discuss it with Felicity. You realise they work in the same office, she and Pugh?'

'Yes.' Darnley showed no interest in this at all. I was not actually sure that he did realise that Felicity and 'Pughie' were colleagues.

'From what Felicity said,' I continued, 'I thought they were both getting things out of proportion. They seemed to believe that people were out to get Robey, that they would somehow use this stone circle as a means to engineer his downfall.'

'I should think plenty of people would love to see Pughie sacked,' said Darnley. 'He's a dangerous man, he knows too much; and you see, you can't say that Pughie is motivated by malice.'

'Why not?'

'Pughie has nothing to gain by spreading these stories about.'

It was possibly true that Robey had nothing to gain in material terms by scandalmongering, but if this activity provided him with its own distasteful form of satisfaction, then this surely was malice? Did not malice provide its own satisfactions?

Darnley, it disturbed me to believe, did not quite understand what malice was, or did not choose to recognise it in his own nature. Yet, trying to be fair to Robey, I was conscious that my own reaction to him was instinctual rather than rational. He sent shivers up and down my spine, but this was not a reason for supposing he was a liar. The reason that I did not like him probably had to do with the fact that Darnley and Felicity did so. I was jealous of the man.

'Felicity is exactly of your opinion,' I said. 'She thinks they are doing their utmost at work to get rid of him. She wishes he did not make trouble, and she has tried to dissuade him from writing stuff for *The Spark*. '

I did not have enough imagination to suppose that Darnley might feel extremely jealous of Felicity for whatever degree of intimacy she had achieved with Rice Robey. One of Rice Robey's emotional talents was the ability to make his devotees compete with one another. They all wanted to show that they knew him better than the others – hence, presumably, their willingness to believe the worst about the Great Attachment, the woman with whom he shared his domestic life and who, presumably, in fact knew him best.

'Apparently,' I continued tactlessly, 'he has threatened to make a real stink in the office if they go ahead with plans to demolish this little henge. Rice Robey and Felicity and several others in their department have been sending in reports recommending that the Minister be informed, and that, if necessary, there should be a showdown with the Ministry of Transport. Oh, they've been going on about it for weeks. Fliss'll speak of little else.'

'It's not very interesting,' said Darnley. 'But the stuff about Harold *is*. '

It was odd that Rice Robey now dominated so many of my waking thoughts. Before Felicity changed her job, I had not even known that he existed. Then, in that mysterious way that

sometimes happens, his name cropped up in several miscellaneous and hitherto unconnected areas, rather as circuses, before
their arrival in a provincial town, advertise themselves by
posters stuck arbitrarily on trees and fences where you might
least expect them. I can remember my excitement as a child
when the beech avenue going into Timplingham suddenly
sprouted a crop of these brightly coloured posters. A clown
smiled out – over his head was the name of the circus, and in the
background, the hastily daubed rendition of the big top, a
ringmaster, performing beasts, awoke in me a longing to attend
the performance. Felicity (I could easily have killed her for this)
announced that circuses were boring and, worse, demeaning to
animals. Uncle Roy had kept repeating that, had old Mrs
Lampitt been alive, there would have been a rumpus about the
circus sticking posters to the beautiful beeches in the avenue. He
had also made some dismissive and contemptuous remark
about circuses in general, and I could see that by his standards
they were bound to be dull since, as far as history can shed light
on the matter, no Lampitt is known to have passed their life
balancing from a high wire on a monocycle, or jumping through
a hoop of fire, or coaxing elephants to stand one-legged on tubs.
Only Aunt Deirdre saw how much I wanted to attend the circus,
and she took me. The act which thrilled me the most was when a
firmly built young woman, her body taut inside a glittering
silver lamé bathing dress, spun round and round from the
summit of the Big Top, suspended only by her teeth. Afterwards,
Aunt Deirdre had said that Uncle Roy had spoilt the suspense by
talking; the sight of the girl spinning there had awakened, by an
inevitable train of association, the latest quarrel which Sargie
had contrived with his dentist.

Anyhow, if the analogy holds, the circus posters had by now
been going up for some time inside my head. A new show was
coming to town. Its name was Albion Pugh or Rice Robey. As a
grotesque, Rice Robey made me laugh, and I still could not quite
believe that Darnley meant it when he insisted that 'Pughie's a
great man'. Nevertheless, in that annoyingly proprietorial spirit
with which we regard our blood relatives, I was worried by the
growing attachment between Rice Robey and Felicity. Disregarding the fact that she was a grown-up person who was
allowed to make whatever mess she chose of life, I was anxious
that she would get hurt, as she had done during her fling with

Raphael Hunter. There was something decidedly odd about Rice Robey, sexually odd, I felt. Felicity spoke of the relationship in terms of Robey's need of her. He needed her as an ally, as an office friend, as a confidante. I was less sure than she was about all this, and not in the least sure that he had told her, or anyone else, the truth about 'the Great Attachment'.

There seemed such an absence of good taste, putting it at its mildest, in sharing his domestic secrets so openly with the world. I was astonished that Felicity felt sorry for Robey being 'shackled' to Mrs Paxton. Though specific instances of his antics were no longer referred to (we heard nothing now of hair-brushes nor of stenographers) there was a general, sniggering acceptance on Felicity's side that a man in Rice Robey's position deserved the occasional indulgence, added to the conceited (and I thought manifestly untrue) implication that, now that he had Felicity as a friend, he would be unlikely to look elsewhere. Felicity never spelt any of these things out; they were what I read from her manner, all of which suggested that he had found everything he needed in her company: intelligence and understanding hitherto lacking in colleagues; sympathy long absent from his relationship with Mrs Paxton. . . . God knows what fantasies she allowed herself on the erotic plane.

'Rice Robey – is he quite . . . ?' I had begun the question but I did not know how to put it into words without sounding priggish or snobbish. My ex-mother-in-law Sibs would have been anxious to know if Rice Robey was 'quite the thing', and this was the question which I actually wanted answered. How could it be translated into inoffensive terms?

'Pughie has a completely original vision,' said Darnley, 'a poet's vision.'

'What of?' I asked, realising as I asked the question that I am almost devoid, in this sense, of 'poetry'.

'You could call it a vision of England, but that would make it sound patriotic and boring; if you called it a vision of Jesus Christ, you would sound conventionally pious – and I'm never actually sure what Pughie *does* in that department.'

'You mean, whether or where he goes to church?'

Another big sniff answered this. Then Darnley continued, 'The thing about Pughie is that he makes categories redundant. He's *sui generis*. I used to think he was a bit bogus.'

'What made you change your mind?'

'The fact that he is so obviously genuine, the real thing.'

'The real what, though?'

When describing the foibles or weaknesses of those whom he liked, Darnley had a peculiar way of laughing. It involved shaking his head from side to side and slightly closing his eyes, as though any explanation for his laughter would have been impossible to put into words.

'This Jesus book' – more laughter – 'it will never get published.'

'He's published books before.'

'Ages ago. And they are thrillers, really. I forget if you ever read one.'

'No.'

'Well, the Pugh ideas are all buried in quite good yarns. Whereas this new thing he's writing . . .'

'It's fiction?'

'He's inclined to get a bit poetic, Pughie, if you don't watch him. And to have an idea which you can't tell – it might be batty, it might be rather brilliant. This new one's got two such ideas. The first is, that Jesus came to England.'

'That's hardly new. *And did those feet in ancient time?*'

'Well, old Pughie has Jesus going to Stonehenge, seeing the Druids, popping up to London, all that sort of thing.'

'What's he up to?'

'Jesus or Pugh?'

'The former.'

'Some kind of travelling salesman, or at any rate his uncle is, Joseph of Arimathea. I see signs that Pugh wants to extend the story into a vast epic history, so you will get the old legend of Sir Lancelot being a cousin in the ninth degree of Jesus, and the symbolic links continuing into modern times. I'm not sure that William Blake isn't scheduled to put in an appearance if the book ever gets finished.'

'You said the book has two ideas. What's the other, apart from the Holy Lamb of God on England's pleasant pasture?'

'It's about St Paul. Pughie thinks St Paul was one of the original scribes or Pharisees who followed Jesus about and agitated for his death. Batty idea in some ways.'

'Why?'

Darnley just laughed and did not say.

'Pughie's a mixture of things,' he remarked at length, 'an old-fashioned mystic, a newfangled psychological man. I'm not so sure about the newfangled bits. He sort of hints that St Paul was queer, almost in love with Jesus, couldn't get him out of his head. After the Crucifixion, Paul developed a bee in his bonnet about the Cross, couldn't shake off his guilt feelings. Then he has his moment on the Damascus Road – "I am Jesus whom Thou persecutest" and the whole thing gets turned round for Paul. Sublimated. The Cross which has been the greatest shame, becomes a thing of Glory. He feels it's all right after all. The wickedest thing he'd ever done, killing Jesus, has actually been a means of salvation, for him, and for the world.'

'Sounds terrible.'

Darnley sniffed.

We drove on for about five minutes without speaking. We passed a ruined windmill, beyond which stretched miles of flat fields.

'He's on to something, though,' said Darnley. 'You see, this bishop . . .'

'The one who doesn't believe in God?'

'It's hopeless, really, that. What old Pughie is so good at is seeing that if this thing is true, then it's true, and there's no getting round the fact that the material world just isn't what half the clever people say it is. There's *more*.'

'Of course there's more. But you surely don't believe all *that* rubbish do you?'

I blurted out these words too fast. It was obvious, from what Darnley had just said, that he was, in some sense, a believer. He must have known that by 'all that rubbish' I meant the whole Christian way of viewing the world, but he tactfully chose to assume that I referred merely to Rice Robey's particular idea about St Paul.

'Dunno. Pugh has a sort of intuition, you know. On the other hand, I don't believe everything he says or writes. This queer thing that St Paul is supposed to have about . . .' He ended his reflection with laughter.

'Is Rice Robey really queer underneath it all?'

This might have explained much, the early devotion to Jimbo, the need for a mother-figure in Mrs Paxton.

'Lord, no. Dirty old man with the girls, or so they always say.'

I was aware, as on other occasions, of Darnley's contrasting scale of values. He was loud in his condemnation of public figures who stepped aside from the strictest codes of chastity. The matter of the Cabinet minister, who had by now retreated in disgrace, with positively Dostoyevskian resolves to purge his guilt among the poor, had largely been dropped by the newspapers, but *The Spark* continued to mention it in every issue. Darnley must have half believed, as Rice Robey had been suggesting at that lunch in the Black Bottle, that such scandal spelt the end of something in Old England. In relation to his own personal heroes, however, Darnley took an entirely different line. Rice Robey could be described with a loving smile as 'a dirty old man'. Behaviour or proclivities which would have been abominated in Darnley's enemies here became rather endearing qualities which if anything enhanced our affection for the 'great man'.

'His home life is said to be absolutely wretched, so I suppose that's partly why he chases the girls,' said Darnley.

'I don't know why philandering should be regarded as a symptom of domestic unhappiness. It must often be the opposite. Having enjoyed something is a greater incentive for wanting more of it than not having enjoyed it. . . .'

'That's all too clever for me,' said Darnley. 'I've never met the Great Attachment.'

'Felicity talks about the Great Attachment. Does this mean that Rice Robey's married?'

I knew a bit about Mrs Paxton from Felicity's accounts, but I wanted to hear Darnley's version of events, and to see whether Rice Robey span the same story to all his friends, or whether he varied it.

'Pughie lives with this woman, they're not married. He met her when he was a schoolmaster, I believe. . . .'

He gave me an account of Rice Robey's early life which corresponded to what I already knew, or to what I have already set down in this narrative.

'So she ran away from her husband because of Rice Robey?' I asked.

'I forget all the details. He's very attractive to women. I don't know if you've seen enough of him to notice.'

'I have. Felicity, you know . . .'

'Anyhow, Pugh and the Great Attachment have been shacked up together for years, in Kentish Town or somewhere. He works

567

in some government department – he's a civil servant now. Pathetic, really.'

'He works with Felicity.'

'So you were saying. Good old Pughie.'

He smiled, as if the mere contemplation of Rice Robey's character brought peace and benediction. A similar expression would take hold of Uncle Roy's eyes and mouth when speaking of the Lampitts.

'I am actually very worried about Felicity and Rice Robey,' I said. 'She is obviously becoming very fond of him, and he doesn't strike me as the sort of person it is quite safe to love.'

This silenced Darnley. He was incapable of discussing the emotional life. When my marriage was tottering to an end, I had tried several times to treat Darnley as a confidant, and been greeted only by silence. I do not think it was failure of sympathy so much as a lack of rhetoric. All topics of conversation need a set of conventions to carry them along. An inability to handle these conventions leads either to brilliant originality of talk, or to no talk at all. Darnley simply did not know how to begin conversations about matters of the heart. It made me wish, sometimes, that he would 'grow up', and with a colossal failure of sympathy on my own part, I wished he would enter into my worries about Felicity and Rice Robey. It did not quite dawn on me that his own perspective on the matter was so different from my own that he could not have been sympathetic, even had he been able to speak of it. I was tacitly taking it for granted that Rice Robey was a grotesque joke, a figure whom it would be potentially calamitous to take seriously; and this fact seemed to me so fixed, so obvious, that I blinded myself, even then, to the extent to which Darnley did take him seriously.

After a longish silence, Darnley said, ' ⌐ugh's given me some truly extraordinary titbits for the "Diary". Can't decide whether to use them.'

'What sort of thing?'

'Well, do you remember that shit Raphael Hunter?'

I could hardly fail to remember Hunter, even if he had not been, at that date, a figure who was constantly on television and radio, as well as writing regularly for the Sunday newspapers. After all, he had dogged my steps ever since my boyhood, seducing the art mistress with whom I was so much in love at Seaforth Grange, ruining Felicity's life, destroying, by the rows set in motion after his life of Jimbo, the friendship between Sargie Lampitt and my Uncle Roy, alienating the affections of my wife. . . . Yes, I remembered Hunter.

'He wrote that big biog which so annoyed your family.'

'Not my family, my wife's family.'

'The one about the old homo.'

'James Petworth Lampitt. He claimed to be an intimate friend of Lampitt's, but it would seem that in fact he hardly knew the man.'

'Well, guess what Pughie thinks.'

'He told me himself. Unfortunately, Felicity was so anxious to have a tête-à-tête with Rice Robey that I could not get him to expand, but he thinks Jimbo Lampitt was murdered.'

'Who's Jimbo?'

'It's what they called Petworth Lampitt in the family.'

'So Jimbo was the old shirt-lifter.'

Darnley laughed again, a snigger turning into a continuous burst of laughter.

'The homosexuality was only alleged,' I said.

For some reason, this produced near hysterics in Darnley. At one point I thought he was going to put his head through the windscreen, he was laughing so much.

'It's only a hunch of Rice Robey's,' I said. 'He could have committed suicide; he could have died by accident, whatever Rice Robey says. I'd take anything he said with a pinch of salt.'

'I'd trust old Pughie's hunches,' said Darnley lovingly, still chuckling a little.

'Evidently, you would.'

'It has a kind of plausibility, don't you think?'

It would have seemed churlish to point out to Darnley that he did not know anything about Jimbo, nor about Hunter, so that the criteria by which he judged the plausibility of any information concerning them must be completely valueless. Without having any of Felicity's academic interests or ratiocinative skills, I was beginning to notice how few people in my acquaintance ever employed rational processes of thought to arrive at conclusions. Darnley was not unique in this regard; in fact, I do not remember meeting a journalist who was capable of 'thinking', in Felicity's sense, that is, of sifting evidence, or of seeing that one thing either does or does not necessarily follow from another.

'It all has the ring of truth to me,' said Darnley. 'I'll probably run the story.'

'What – say Hunter murdered Jimbo Lampitt?'

'I don't see why not.'

'Won't you be sued for libel?'

It was like asking someone at a firework party on November the fifth whether there might not be a danger, should lighted tapers be put to the fuses, of catherine wheels revolving, or Roman candles shooting their brilliant fountains of sparklight into the dark sky, or of rockets making their satisfyingly noisy ascent beyond the treetops. Darnley's laugh reminded me of school. Teasing people, 'rotting them up' had been the phrase then, was fun, but it was not enough to give him his real kicks. For pure satisfaction to result, he needed to go too far, to make the other person, master or prefect, lose control, lash out with (in those days) lines, runs, or the cane, or (nowadays) writs. There had already been several threatened libel cases in *The Spark*'s short history, a sure sign to Darnley that he was holding the strings and making the grown-ups dance to his tune.

'In a way, it is stronger stuff than his Harold Wilson stories. I mean, the Wilson stuff is all predictable, though I'm not sure I quite believe Pughie's suspicions about Harold's contacts behind the Iron Curtain. The smutty stuff has the ring of truth, though. Perhaps it will all come out, and Harold will resign. Then we might have Ernie as the next Prime Minister.'

'I wouldn't mind a chimpanzee as Prime Minister so long as he wasn't Conservative.'

'Ernie's a bit like Pugh in this way. He's got a vision of England. His whole political philosophy is really summed up in that Chesterton poem. You know the thing.'

' "The Donkey"?'

'No – "We are the people of England, and we haven't spoken yet".'

'He sees a sort of invisible thread connecting Magna Carta, the Peasants' Revolt, oh, all the predictable things, leading up to Tom Paine and all those enthusiasts for the French Revolution, of whom his ancestor, Jo Lampitt, was one.'

Darnley said, 'I don't know much about Ernie's family,' and I said, 'I don't know much about anything else,' realising with a thud that these words, intended as a joke, were probably true.

'Well, Jo Lampitt – Radical Jo – was really the founding father of the dynasty,' I said. 'Rolling in money from his successful brewery, and wildly revolutionary in politics.'

'Sounds much like Ernie himself.'

'He was one of the first provincial brewers to open alehouses in London, and he made a fortune out of property. He bought a lot of burnt-out houses at the time of the Gordon riots and refurbished them as inns. At the same time, he was a genuine radical, an intellectual. He was friends with men like Benjamin Franklin, Josiah Wedgwood, Joseph Priestley, Godwin. It was he and his Quaker wife Naomi who bought Mallington. The house was the ancestral home of the Isleworths. Funnily enough, Radical Jo's son Joseph, Jo the Second as Uncle Roy calls him, married an Isleworth heiress, Selina. They were already advancing themselves in the world, the Lampitts, and when Selina Isleworth's Uncle George sat up all night in Brooks's playing whist with Charles James Fox, he was said to have lost £40,000 in a single session – though the session lasted through two nights and a day, as Isleworth tried to win back his fortune, only losing more and more heavily. Mallington had to be sold, and the Lampitts had the money to buy it.'

'So all that passed into the hands of the lefties,' said Darnley waving at the view which suddenly came before us, as we turned the corner of the coast road and found ourselves at the south gates of the park. A long drive stretched before us, and beyond the clumps of ilex were pines, and beyond the pines the light of the sea. But in the distance was the house. Twisted brick Jacobean chimneys rose from the gabled roof. The stucco had been allowed to crumble, revealing here brick, here flint, the whole a pleasing variety of gentle colours surrounding the high oriel windows. Emblazoned at the top of the bays was the stone legend in simple capitals, the heraldic motto of the Isleworths: HONOR INSULAE AMOR PATRIAE. The house nestled in the trees which, to the east, crept up to the stable wings and garden rooms. The west front was in complete contrast to the remainder of the building, a stately wing added in the mid-eighteenth century, of pale pink brick symmetrically spaced with tall, well-proportioned windows. Further west still, beyond the smooth velvety lawns, stood the orangery, now housing a riot of azaleas.

I stopped the car.

'Yes,' said Darnley. 'Let's enjoy the view and prepare ourselves inwardly for a dose of old Ern.'

He chuckled, but I had not stopped in order to savour an aesthetic moment, irresistible and strong as that was, seeing Mallington in the haze of a warm summer afternoon. I had been jolted back with unexpected violence to the day the war broke out, a quarter of a century earlier, and reminded with horrifying clarity of the happiness of my early childhood. I had known, with my mind, that those days were happy, but it felt at that moment in the car as if I was remembering it all for the first time. I remembered with an intense vividness, the cottage a mile or two away which my parents had rented that summer. The holiday had never been so clear in my mind as it was then, sitting with Darnley. It had been summoned up for me more luminously than if a film of it had been made at the time and was now being replayed to me for the first time. I remembered quite uninteresting facts like the texture of the wooden draining board beside the sink, and the sliminess of the soap suds which had splashed there from the washing-up bowl. I was too small to see the draining board, I could just reach it and touch the edge, this mixture of rough, slightly splintery wood and soapy slime. And I remembered Mummy saying, 'Don't get a splinter, darling,' and reaching down – all this had been forgotten until this second – and moving my hands, and kissing them, and then stooping down to kiss me. I remembered the exact texture of her lips and cheeks and arms as she embraced me then, and the smell of her was brought cruelly back, a wonderful smell in which the sweetness of soap was mingled with a very faint suggestion of sweat. Even as I sat there, I could feel my nose pressing into the softness of my mother's bosom. This particular snapshot of memory, overpoweringly strong and beautiful, retreated before recollections which were perhaps not memories in the same sense of the word. I think they were part memories and part recollections of things I had been saying to myself about my childhood ever since. I remembered Daddy laughing at the idea that Uncle Roy aspired to know people such as the Lampitts. Now, what separated me from my parents was not the trivial barrier of class but the unbridgeable gulf of time. God had pulled the plug out and my parents were gone. They had been dead for more than twenty years and yet I was not sure as I sat beside Darnley in the Morris whether I had ever come to terms with their deaths, still less accepted them. With unquenchable longing, I still wanted them, and only them. I think that ever since they died, I had been waiting for the moment when this alarming state of things would be undone; surely, my subsconscious hoped, they would come back, and life could resume its 'normal' course, when Mummy and Daddy and I lived together in harmony, with only the occasional interruption from the likes of Granny, Mrs Webb, or Uncle Roy. Until Mummy comes back, I had felt throughout life, I am just marking time. There seemed no need to pursue a 'proper career' with a university degree or a professional training, no need either to put my emotional or personal life on a more grown-up footing. Why did I put up with the unsatisfactory arrangement of sharing a small rented house with a cousin I only half liked? Was it not because at the back of my mind there was this crazy idea that one day things would right themselves, return to normal, and until that day, there was no need to make an effort, no need to get life right? I sat there at the wheel of the car looking over the thick grasses and cow parsley and buttercups which occupied the foreground of the view and knowing with chilling clarity and certainty that there would be no getting back to normal, no reunion, no healing of old wounds, no sham wiping away of tears from every eye. All that was an illusion. I wanted Mummy then with a desire which was so strong that I felt myself shaking, heaving with grief. If Darnley noticed, he would have been deeply embarrassed.

I started the engine of the car. Darnley, once more, was speculating about the composition of the house party.

'Ernie and Pat are pretty thick with the Foots. I shouldn't be surprised to see Dick Crossman.'

These were not names which were above every name; they were no Lampitts; but I had heard them in childhood on the lips of Sargie and Uncle Roy. The Labour Party had a shadowy preexistence until the moment (after his quarrel with Lloyd George) that Lord Lampitt (humbug and father of Vernon) had decided to join it. Thereafter, the Labour movement becomes a subject of interest to the historian, it becomes real, and the names of its luminaries, in so far as they were known and loved by the humbug and the Honourable Vernon, came to be learnt as part of the Lampitt catechism. Thus, from early years, I could lisp the names of Nye, and Ellen Wilkinson, and Stafford Cripps. They did not figure largely in any great, central stories, but flitted in and out of the narrative rather like the lesser-known angels in Milton, attendant upon the great characters upon whom our fullest attention was fixed. Clem Attlee, for example, was not an important figure in himself; it did not matter in the least that he was the Prime Minister. The important thing, from the Timplingham perspective, was that the Honourable Vernon was a member of his Cabinet.

In those days, Vernon had not been very far to the left of the party, though he had shown early signs of subsequent developments by resigning, with the others, over the issue of National Health charges. ('They say it cost him the Chancellorship – a great misfortune because the Honourable Vernon, as you may know, is a brilliant economist' – Uncle Roy.)

Now that the party was poised to resume power, after more than a dozen years of Conservative governments, it was a very different thing from the Labour Party of Clem Attlee. Nevertheless, Vernon had somehow overcome the disadvantages of his upbringing and won the favour of the left wing. The surprising thing about this when I came to analyse it, had nothing to do with class. The title could be dismissed as his 'dad's little bit o' nonsense'. There was no reason, once prejudice had been discarded, why the more revolutionary wing of the party should not have been happy to welcome as their champion a man who was extremely rich and sat in the House of Lords. What was surprising about their enthusiasm for Vernon was the lack of Marxist, doctrinaire bite in any of his reported speeches, published articles, or, in my experience, private utterance.

He stood for an old-fashioned, sentimental radicalism – the abolition of the monarchy, the House of Lords, the honours system. These were things which, as far as I could see, could be removed from the scene without changing the fabric of English society in the slightest degree. There was nothing in Vernon's programme of reforms, set of private fantasies, call them what you will, which even remotely resembled Stalinism, Trotskyism, or Leninism – still less a fashionable new variety of the creed now gaining popularity, Maoism. The newspapers, however, had chosen to depict Vernon as a communist. He was always adorned with hammers and sickles in the cartoons, and the role of 'mad red' was evidently one which he was happy enough to act out if interviewers or reporters came his way.

Now, after its spell of political impotence, the left was in a position where it could once more exercise power in Britain.

Having seemed electorally immovable for years, the Conservatives had become unstuck. Economic and political reasons for this were advanced by the pundits, but perhaps it was just as plausible to believe that portents had appeared in the sky, and that the Harlot and the Episkopos were ushering in a new era, uncertain in its creeds, morals or social order.

The Morris made its slow way down the rutty drive towards the house. I was recovering from my sad reverie, but was not sufficiently concentrating on the driving, and was taken completely by surprise when a large black limousine swooped towards us at great speed in the opposite direction. For a second, a head-on collision seemed an inevitability, but lucky instinct made me swerve, and we juddered to a halt on the grass beside the drive, and the engine stalled.

'Bloody fool! Driving at us as if they wanted to kill us!'

'You saw who it was,' Darnley asked, 'in the back of the car?'

'No.'

He adopted the voice of the pompous High Court judge.

'The Leader of Her Majesty's Opposition.'

'That's no excuse for driving like a maniac.'

'He wasn't driving.'

I tried to be as blasé as Darnley seemed, and assented to the derogatory remarks which he was offering about our leader. I did not hold his views or career in any particular veneration; but I did revere the fact that he was powerful and famous, and the thought that we had nearly been involved in a motor accident with him produced an excitement which dispelled all my previous anger and fear, an excitement which was absolutely snobbish, based purely on a sense of proximity to the mighty in their seats.

The tall woman in slacks, waiting by the front door as the Morris scrunched to a halt in the gravel was Vernon's wife Pat, whom I had only met a couple of times before. The trousers were made of green artificial fibre and she had on a pink blouse. She was substantially built with rather mottled brown skin and thick silver hair.

'We nearly didn't make it here alive,' said Darnley. 'Your Leader almost collided with us in the drive.'

She shook us both warmly by the hand. My childhood catechism had told me that Pat Lampitt (née Dawnay) had been in the Wrens during the war. At seven years old, I could have told you, 'If Pat hadn't been a woman, she'd be fighting this war as an admiral.' Not Uncle Roy's own words, of course, but a 'famous' quip of old Mr Michael Lampitt, bless him.

Pat spoke with rather a surprising voice, in its way as idiosyncratic as Vernon's. It was fundamentally posh, but it had a nasal, cockneyfied twang to it, and one wondered whether she had always spoken in that way or whether she had adopted the vowels in early adulthood. Her voice could have been based on the Edwardian cockney known to have been spoken in some aristocratic families in her parents' time, but it is conceivable that she had decided that this highly eccentric way of speaking the English language would put Vernon's proletarian supporters and constituents at their ease.

'Let's go round the back way' (pronounced *why*), 'and then we can have a nice cupper in the kitchen.'

She led us through the conservatory at the side of the house and into a stone-flagged corridor littered with decades' attrition of junk. The bells on the walls, each with a coil of metal attached to them and, beneath, the name of a room, were rusty and cobwebby, eloquently indicative of the present generation of Lampitts' unwillingness to summon, or employ, servants. The shabby gloss paint, peeling from the walls, was a reminder of Mallington's incarnation as a field hospital during the war. Old prams, one of Edwardian vintage, groaned under the weight not of baby clothes but of political leaflets and pamphlets. The urgency of the headlines and the excitement of the exclamation marks on these documents were mocked by the yellowing and curling of the paper on which these messages, once so arresting, now so obsolete, were printed. In one ancient pram which might well have conveyed Vernon for walks, pushed by his nurse, there was a pile of papers headed, in scarlet capitals, A LIST OF TORY MISDEEDS. I paused to read them. They included the usual Conservative faults and flaws, but they concluded PRIVATEERING FROM THE SOUTH AFRICAN WAR. The advice VOTE LAMPITT FOR A FAIRER WORLD had been addressed not to our generation, but to the electorate of 1906 – one of the last elections he fought, before purchasing his barony from Lloyd George. Political bumf from Vernon's career outnumbered his father's relics. There must have been a thousand copies each of his pamphlets STOP THIS SUEZ MADNESS!, THE TRUTH ABOUT HANGING and HAVE YOU REALLY HAD IT SO GOOD?, an essay composed in 1960 but which,

on brief perusal, seemed almost identical in its general thrust to
A LIST OF TORY MISDEEDS of the 1906 era. There were also many
posters lying around, begging us to VOTE LAMPITT.

'Do you know Harold?' Pat asked. 'He likes journalists. He
mixes with them all the time; image-building, I call it.'

'I've met him a couple of times,' said Darnley.

This was news to me.

'He brought that secretary woman with him.' Pat sighed. She
heaved a huge black steaming kettle from the range and made
tea. As she did so she pulled a 'funny face' as though it was
perhaps wiser to say nothing of the secretary. It was almost the
expression of a woman who thought her kitchen was 'bugged'
and that anything she said might one day be taken down and
used in evidence.

'We last met when you were married to Anne,' she said with a
violent change of theme. 'And that was quite a little time ago
now.'

She was a Joe Blunt, Pat. I felt reassured that we did not have
to tiptoe round the subject of my divorce or feel that it was
unmentionable.

'It was at Sibs's house, right?' (*roit*).

'Wasn't it when Jimbo's papers were being sold to that
American?'

'That's right. There was a great family pow-wow' (*piaow-
wiaow*). 'We thought we'd all been so clever taking the papers
out of the hands of that man who wrote the book. In fact, he was
ahead of us in the game. He had the Americans eating out of his
hands, long before we came on the scene. We were conned!'

This series of events, which Pat was describing fairly accurately, had made most of the Lampitts extremely angry at the
time. Now, it made her roar with laughter.

'Like ginger biscuits?' she resumed abruptly. 'I made 'em
moiself.'

Momentarily, we were schoolboys being given a treat by
matron.

'Still, he's a right little bastard, our Mr Hinter.'

She saw the puzzlement on my face. Was 'Hinter' her funny
way of pronouncing, or had she forgotten Hunter's actual
name? I felt very stupid when she had to explain.

' 'Cause he hints! You're thick. Hints about Jimbo being a
pansy; never says so much, but hints. Mr Hinter.'

Now we had got the general idea, it seemed unnecessary to spell it out so repetitively.

'And did you see the paperback of *Prince Albert*, Jimbo's book?'

'No.'

'Didn't you? I'll show it to you.'

She went over to the dresser where she fumbled for a spectacle case amid electricity bills, seed packets, cookery books. On the shelves of the dresser stood ranks of Staffordshire figures, an enthusiasm of the late Humbug's. They were mainly political characters of the last century: Gladstone, Disraeli, Peel, Parnell, the Prince Consort, Bradlaugh (a great hero of the Lampitts) and Palmerston all stared down in their unreal garishness of whites, blues, oranges and reds. Other characters from the radical past – Wat Tyler and Milton caught the eye – were joined by a few religious figures. Wesley held up a glossy black sleeve from his pottery pulpit. Ridley and Latimer were eternally confined to streaks of red and orange earthenware flame. Some of these figurines recalled the subjects of Jimbo's popular biographies, most noticeably that of the Prince Consort. Others, if Jimbo's own biographer could be believed, had actually crossed the penman's path in his boyhood. The austere little statue of Cardinal Manning, the glaze faded from its biretta and its emaciated features, stared across Pat's kitchen icily unaware of the scabrous suggestions made in Hunter's book about that tea party, some time in the 1880s, when the prince of the church supposedly took the infant James Petworth Lampitt on the knees of his watered-silk cassock.

Hunter's life of Jimbo seemed to have ground to a halt after Volume I. Other things had happened in my life and I had not given any thought to it all until Rice Robey had revived my interest in the matter.

'Here we are,' said Pat, who had donned some surprising American-looking spectacles of butterfly design and retrieved the paperback of *Prince Albert* from the pile of rubbish on the dresser. She was reading from the blurb on the back of the book.

'Listen to this. "The engagingly written introduction is by Raphael Hunter, Lampitt's biographer, and for many years his close friend and private secretary." Well, that's a whopper. Jimbo had no need of a secretary. He always had Cecily.'

'Do you mean Sargie's wife?'

Sometimes one makes a remark to another person which reveals that one knows nothing, absolutely nothing, about the matter under discussion. Such blunders elicit looks which are akin to pity. As such an expression passed over Pat's face, I remembered, from my Lampitt catechism, that Cecily and Jimbo had been 'as thick as thieves'. But, Jimbo's relationship with Cecily, still less my ignorance of it, were not what Pat wished us to consider.

'You know,' she said, 'there is no one close to Jimbo' – she listed some members of the family and one or two writers – 'who ever met Mr Hinter until Jimbo died. Elizabeth Cameron said, I remember, when these books started to come out, "Pat, who *is* Hunter, we never heard Jimbo mention him?" That's the truth. Isn't it the *limit?* Sibs has written to the publishers to complain.'

We drank our tea and ate our biscuits.

'Was the Leader staying with you?' Darnley, perhaps understandably, was more interested in the recent departure of a man who, in a matter of months, was bound to become the next Prime Minister, than in the length or extent of Hunter's acquaintanceship with one of Vernon's cousins.

'Harold? Just came to lunch. Now, I haven't told you who *is* staying,' said Pat.

Even as she spoke, I could hear two familiar voices in the stone-flagged corridor outside the kitchen door.

'I said to the man, "Syringe the bloody things again. They're my ears. I'm paying." '

'Payin'? Shame on yer, Sargie, fer not usin' the Health Service.'

'Anyway, bang goes another bloody doctor. Had to sack him. I'm not deaf. Just needed my bloody ears syringing. I couldn't get another doctor that night. Though I rang three, it was past midnight by the time the other bugger was finished. . . . '

Sargie's narrative continued as he entered the room. Whether he was deaf was in the nature of an academic question since in my recollection of him, going back to my early childhood, he had never been interested in anything that anyone beside himself was saying. He was always affectionate towards me, however, and when he saw me in the kitchen, he abandoned his ear saga and exclaimed, 'Julie, my dear!' with apparent pleasure.

I introduced Darnley and while Vernon pumped my hand and

said how glad he was we could spare the time to come to this 'dirty great place – absurd intit?', Sargie said, 'So you edit *The Spark.*'

Darnley grinned. It wasn't often he met a reader of his paper.

'Bloody amusing cartoon in the last issue. The one about old Harold Mac's water-works.'

'That was several issues ago.'

There was a paradox about Darnley's journalistic efforts to be outrageous. He truly wanted to be offensive, indeed considered it almost a duty to make those in authority squeal; but he also coveted praise and Sargie's expressed enjoyment of *The Spark*, whether or not genuine, caused a sheepish grin of uncomplicated pride to appear on Darnley's face.

'Wouldn't have laughed some years ago when I was having wee-wee trouble myself. I asked my bloody doctor then, "Why do we *need* a prostate gland?" He couldn't answer. Have you noticed how many doctors are stupid? I mean, really stupid, much stupider than average? Anyway, I couldn't help chuckling over your thing about Harold Mac. But how did you know about it? That little titbit of yours appeared about a fortnight before Harold actually went into hospital, and no one knew – except his friends.'

'A bloke told me. Friend of Julian's.'

Darnley smiled at me and it was somehow immediately apparent that he spoke of 'Pughie'. I could not begin to guess then, nor can I now, how Rice Robey was *au fait*, before the great majority of the British people, with the Prime Minister's urinary difficulties.

'The Tories will have to have a new leader, Mac's on the way out,' Sargie decreed. 'Who'll put up the best fight against our Harold? Rab's the man they oughta have. Vebba clebba febba, Rab. But my guess is that they will choose Quintin – bloody fools that they are.'

Darnley laughed. I laughed. We all laughed.

'You could be right there, Sargie,' said Vernon, applying his light to his pipe and speaking jerkily between puffs. 'It'll be hard for Quintin ter lead iz party frum the Lords but it could be done, it could be done.'

The slightly insane gleam as he said this made me aware that Vernon would not be averse, if the chance came his way, to exercising power without abandoning his peerage.

'Verra much betwin a-selves,' added Vernon, 'Harold was here ter-day. Jus' came ter this terribly informal lunch, but it was nice uv 'im to come.'

'He's a devious bugger,' said Sargie. 'You always wonder what he's up to. He's not really left-wing, not *innocently* left-wing, like you, Vernon.'

'Oh, I think yer wrong, there, Sargie. I'm sure Harold's got a real socialist commitment. We wouldn't 'uv backed 'im if 'e hadn't. No. We're going to see real economic planning for the first time since 'fifty-one. We're going ter see an extension uv the nationalised industries, a total reform uv the educational system. My old school will go!'

'Julie's old school,' said Sargie.

'So it is.' Vernon could not possibly have remembered where I had been to school but he nodded as if this were the best-known fact in the world.

My school had been chosen for its Lampitt connections. Old Mr Lampitt, who married a sister of Archbishop Benson's, had been headmaster there during the last century; James Petworth Lampitt himself was one of the school's more illustrious literary sons.

'I'd be happy to see it nationalised,' I said.

'We'll see the House of Lords go,' said Vernon, '– in the very first session I shouldn't wonder. We'll see the American air-bases wound up, we'll see the banks nationalised, and the money put where it belongs.'

'Down the drain,' said Sargie, and laughed. 'You were right to back Harold, my dear, but don't get carried away. He only hinted about that Cabinet post anyway. You thought he was promising you something, but I listened to his words very carefully.'

'Sargie, we did agree not to talk about that,' said Vernon. 'For Harold's sake. It really was confidential.'

'Have some tea and stop talking about boring politics,' said Pat.

As he sat down at the kitchen table, the cigarette-holder clenched between his yellowing dentures, I noticed for the first time that Sargie was carrying my novel. It was the only book I had ever published and by now, five or six years on, I was so heartily ashamed of it that I was almost literally unable to bear the sight of it. I wondered what conceivable reason there could be for Sargie to carry it in his hand. He was no devotee of contemporary literature and, with the visitation of each bad bout of depression over the years, the habit of reading had slowly left him. If the Leader of the Labour Party could have been described as devious, it was an art in which he could have taken lessons from Sargent Lampitt who was the most successfully manipulative person I had ever known.

'Our house revolves around Sargie's moods,' my aunt once crossly and accurately averred; and certainly, during the days of their friendship, Sargie was able to command in my Uncle Roy the most unwavering and spaniel-like devotion. If high spirits seized Sargie and he felt like a few days in London, accompanied by a friend, then Uncle Roy would go with him, at a moment's notice, cancelling church services and leaving his own household to manage without him. Similarly, when Sargie was in the thrall of one of his very terrible black moods, wanting only to sit in Timplingham Place and watch the rain trickle down the window-panes, Uncle Roy would be there, to sit in silence with his friend, sometimes, when the gloom was at its worst, holding Sargie's hand. Whether as chauffeur, dinner companion, reader aloud, chess partner, or in other dogsbody roles, my uncle never failed Sargie. Now that they had quarrelled and neither met nor spoke, there was a great emptiness in Uncle Roy's life. He jabbered more obsessively than ever about the Lampitts, but was this a substitute for Sargie's daily, hourly companionship? Sargie must have missed my uncle, too, though he would have been too arrogantly proud to admit it. He found a succession of Roy-substitutes. My ex – Anne – had for a time run errands for him; for all I knew, she still did so. Any paid employee, whether medical or domestic, was lucky to last six months before some impossible quarrel necessitated an end to their association with Sargie, who was never happy with helpers or servants; slaves and serfs were what his nature craved.

He looked at me though his horn-rimmed spectacles and exhaled cigarette smoke through both nostrils over the well-trimmed moustaches. My eyes fell to the dust-wrapper of the book and passed up to his again. We eyed one another like two strange cats unable to decide whether the other wanted to rub noses or scratch eyes. I braved it out and said nothing about the book. It was too soon after my arrival at Mallington to be drawn into one of Sargie's plots. I was already experiencing the sinking sensation which had visited me more than once before in life, of having believed myself to be moving into uncharted territory only to find that I was still in the same, circumscribed world of childhood.

'Yer've told 'em we've got the kids comin'?' asked Vernon, gesturing towards Darnley and me with his pipe. 'Jus' the girls. Yer've not met me lads have yer?'

'Christopher I've met once or twice at Rupert Starling's,' I said. 'William was in America at that period.'

This parrot-knowledge of the names, doings and whereabouts of the Lampitts flew out of my lips easily. Sargie smiled. Vernon showed no surprise that I should remember, some five years after, his younger son's period in Massachusetts, the exact course he was pursuing at the MIT.

'No, Bill's in advertisin' now,' said Vernon. For a good socialist like Vernon to have spawned a boy who wanted to go into advertising seemed a bit sad. Hearing the information on his lips was like hearing a director of the Bank of England inform his company that a child of his loins was a dab hand at forging banknotes, or a Moderator of the Methodist Church confess to his brethren that a daughter of his had a prominent position in the chorus line of the Folies Bergères. I have noticed, however, that parents who are ashamed of their children's activities often speak about them with an added heartiness, and this was what Vernon did now.

'And then there's Tommy Wimbish upstairs. Have you met Professor Wimbish?'

'No, but I like his books.'

'Verra disciplined man, Wimbish. He's writing the history uv the party. He's done one volume. Not everyone was kind about it.'

Cormac, the portly young academic I had met at *The Spark*, was one of those who had been less than generous.

'You had to laugh at the review of Wimbish's book by young Cormac,' said Sargie.

'No yer didn't. It was malicious.'

'That's why you had to laugh at it. They're too similar, Cormac and Wimbish. That's why they hate each other. They are both good historians, they both became professors young, and wrote their books, but that wasn't enough for them. They wanted to make a splash. Always a mistake for academics to want that. So, Cormac hasn't written a word about the Crusades since he got his chair; he's written pop biographies of Nazis and articles for the Beaverbrook press.'

'Cormac's revoltingly right-wing,' said Vernon. 'Wimbish is loyal to 'is working-class roots.'

'In his fashion, doubtless. But there again, they are similar. They're both clever grammar-school boys. It just happens that Cormac is so-called right-wing and Wimbish is so-called left-wing. I more and more think it doesn't matter *what* opinions people have. Both Cormac and Wimbish just use their opinions as instruments of self-publicity.'

Not knowing either of the professors, I could not contribute to this discussion. I had not read Professor Cormac's books. Wimbish's briskly written popular histories of the Tudor Age had entertained me, though. The history of the Labour Party, in which he was now engaged, was evidently a work which would bring him less cash or kudos, and he was loyally pressing on with his task, in spite of the vilification of his colleagues.

'There's masses uv stuff me Dad left behind. Wimbish could tell the whole story from Dad's diaries alone,' said Vernon.

'If he wanted to get the story wrong,' said Sargie.

'He writes three thousand words every day,' said Vernon admiringly. 'Rain or shine. So 'e wuz tellin' Harold.'

'It's not often you see Harold stumped for words,' said Sargie, 'but since Wimbish wouldn't stop talking about himself, our dear leader hardly had time to spell out his policies or offer Vernon the job, or whatever it was he had come for. We had to hear all about Wimbish's low social origins, Wimbish's brilliant mind that rescued him from the gutter, Wimbish's original historical research. And you'd think Wimbish had invented the bloody Labour Party from the way he talks about this book he's writing.'

'Anyway,' said Pat. 'That's who we've got for you, Julian. Not exactly a glittering house party, I'm afraid.'

She stood behind the seated figure of Vernon and ran an affectionate hand through his hair as she spoke.

'The girls are coming by train,' she continued. 'If you were feeling like an angel, Julian, you'd drive over to Lynn and meet them at the station. Such a bore since they Beechinged all the railway lines in these parts. Some of the trains always stopped at Mallington Halt in the past, and if they didn't, you could always get out at Burnham, Wells, Walsingham.'

'All the LMS trains, of which me dad was a director.'

'And my brother Martin was LNER,' said Sargie wistfully. 'They were rivals in trade. We had decent railways in this country until this Great Movement of Ours nationalised the bloody things.'

'Closin' the branch lines had nothing ter do with nationalisation. If I'd a' bin Minister of Transport, I'd 've kept 'em open.'

I thought of this claim as I waited on King's Lynn station for the arrival of the Lampitt girls. It was strange to think that there were some people in the world sufficiently interested, or adult, to make decisions about our system of transport. I had never conceived, for a single instant, of being involved with the practical running of affairs. Felicity, with her files and in-trays, was now involved with such matters in a minor way. Her obsessive conversations with Rice Robey, animated as they were with an emotional interest which extended far beyond the prosaic sphere of civil service departments, were nevertheless concerned with such practical matters as whether the Ministry of Transport should be allowed to build roads through ancient archaeological sites.

I was glad of the chance to be alone. I had left Mallington with some eagerness. Darnley sank into a chair with *The Fifth Form at St Dominic's*. Sargie, still clutching *The Vicar's Nephew*, with no comment made upon it, had 'things to do' in his room, a compulsion which grew more conspicuous as the minutes in the kitchen had ticked past and Pat had poured him nothing stronger than tea. Vernon had gone to confer with Professor Wimbish, who had not yet descended from the library. Pat, who had beguilingly hinted at the existence of another member of the party by hoping that Gussy was all right on her own (who was she?) sliced peppers and counted plates in preparation for supper.

The drive along the coast road through Wells and Brancaster and Sandringham had brought many jumbled thoughts of past and present into my mind. I thought of Uncle Roy and Sargie driving me to London on the day of Jimbo's funeral and putting me on the train to Malvern, where I had been at school with Darnley. I thought of the moment, later that summer term, when I first glimpsed Raphael Hunter through a window in the school, embracing the art mistress with whom I was in love. The Lampitts' continued concern with Hunter's book and Jimbo's reputation came as something of a surprise. I did not know what to make of it. I was not having consecutive thoughts. Impressions, like a cascade of unsorted snapshots, filled the consciousness. I thought of Rice Robey and his youthful connection with Jimbo. All these images, apparently disparate, seemed linked by a golden string. It was ages since I had set eyes on Hunter's book *Petworth Lampitt: the Hidden Years, 1881–1910*, but the whole strangely connected matter did not seem to go away. The string of incidents which had begun on the day of Jimbo's funeral, begun, that is to say, in my own imagination and consciousness, had become one of those focuses provided by life as a way of observing the truth itself. Was it, simply, possible to be objectively truthful about the past? Hunter had based his book, or so he claimed, on Jimbo's diaries which no one but himself (and, fleetingly, Felicity) had ever seen. The family disputed the interpretation he had placed on these documents, now lodged in the Everett Foundation in New York. The Lampitts even went so far as to suppose that Hunter, for his own impenetrable motives, had fabricated the evidence. Certainly, the issue was complicated by the feelings we all had about Hunter himself. Were he, however, a purely blameless and scrupulous recorder, his selection and arrangement of evidence from Jimbo's diaries would still have been an interpretative act. Wishing to tell an objective story about another human life was perhaps an illusory desire. As I stood on King's Lynn station, mulling these ideas over, I think I began to have the glimmering of a wish which would one day turn into the present narrative. The half-thought, the almost-perception, was that all truth comes to us filtered through a mythological process. Was this what Rice Robey meant by saying that we could not live without myths? Wisdom would come, if it ever came, when we ceased to worry about the truthfulness or authenticity of the mythological instrument, language, memory, by which we discerned or shaped experience. It would be a mistake to try to make the focus of the image too sharp, for the most truthful impression of life's experience would have to convey its ambiguities, its smudginess, its half-enlightenments. Myths themselves help us use the inchoate collection of impressions we receive because they lack such fogginess, but even myths, or the best ones, are riven with ambiguities, we can take them both ways. The myths concerning Christ, for example, are riddled with contradictions

586

which give them a troublingly realistic quality of chiaroscuro, a quality garishly lacking (as it seemed to me when I read it) in Rice Robey's reworkings of the story.

And now I stood on the station platform, my mind full of confused remembrance, and tingling with the excitement, however slight, which must always come before meeting strangers of the opposite sex for the first time. I remembered that Kirsty was an undergraduate at Cambridge. Jo, her elder sister, was by all accounts save those of Uncle Roy a bit thick. I was to await them at the ticket barrier carrying a piece of card which had started life as a stiffener for one of Vernon's new shirts. On the back of it, Pat had written in bold characters the single word LAMPITT.

Like so much which had happened to me lately, this seemed portentous, emblematic. Was this a little image of what my life had been, and was to be, standing at a barrier where others came and went, with the legend LAMPITT on my cardboard shield? As I stood there, I tried to remember the various Homeric formulae or heroic kennings by which Uncle Roy labelled these two girls. He could scarcely have met them very often if at all; this would not have prevented him from thinking about them so long as Lampitt blood flowed in their veins. One of the more formidable female members of the family, perhaps Sibs, or possibly Ida (daughter of Bobby of duckling-in-Brighton fame) had pronounced Kirsty to be a 'handful' when a child. Jo's teeth, protuberant when she was twelve, had been put in a brace by an expensive dentist, said by Sargie to be 'an absolute something something' – Uncle Roy's way of conveying his friend's strong habits of speech. My wife Anne, several years older than these cousins of hers, used to speak of Jo as if she were mentally retarded, and it was true that there had been difficulty 'getting her settled' after she failed her resits at the secretarial college. It was then that Uncle Roy had pulled strings with someone he knew in the diocesan offices in Ely. The job entailed 'light office duties'. The world of archdeacons and minor canons' wives was not thought to be one where Jo would fit in cheerfully, but it was considered safer than letting her loose on London; Cambridge and Kirsty were near in one direction, Mallington and the parents in another. These were hazy snatches of Lampitt lore on which to construct any premonitory impressions; but there was not long to wait before coming face to face with the sisters themselves. Passengers were coming off the Cambridge train with that variety of unguarded facial expressions so often on display at points of arrival and departure. Some peered about, expecting a friend or relative to greet them, their anxiety melting suddenly into relief and glee and love at the sight of another human being standing there; it prompted the thought of how strangely arbitrary human affection is. Why should they be so delighted to see this person rather than that? Why did they gaze so fervently through the crowds of individuals, all similarly composed, all (or most) with their full complement of faces, arms, legs, desperate for the sight of one face, the clasp of one pair of arms? And I thought, too, of how vulnerable this made them, this rushing forward to be met, and how easily such expressions of happiness could be shattered, for example by the announcement over the loudhailer that some named individual was not waiting at the station, but lying unconscious in the intensive care unit of the local hospital.

Two girls came up to me. Both had short, blonded hair and duffel bags suspended from a shoulder; both had mouths wide with anarchic toothy grins, and both had an arm round Rice Robey. The trio were so intertwined as they approached, that they could almost have been some mannerist sculpture brought to life. At first glance, it was hard to see whose limb was whose, or where greasy navy blue sleeve ended and fluffy black jumper began.

'Fab!' said Jo as soon as she had made out the word on my piece of cardboard. 'I was expecting Mum. Nice to have a bloke. You're not married or anything, or queer?'

'Your mother's cooking supper. She asked if I'd drive over and fetch you.'

Rudimentary introductions began.

'Mr Robey's been giving this really brilliant talk at Cambridge to the archaeological society,' said Kirsty. 'Sorry – what's your name?'

'Mr Grainger and I are already acquainted,' said Rice Robey. 'This is indeed a propitious conjunction of the consanguinities.'

'He's nice, isn't he?' Jo asked me, with a sideways jerk of her head towards Rice Robey and a slightly crazy squint.

'It was all about stone circles, and ley-lines and temples and Druids,' said Kirsty, 'and it was quite simply the most brilliant talk I ever heard in my life. It beats all the lectures I ever heard in Cambridge.'

'Far too flattering a testimonial.'

'No, it was, it was.'

All these remarks passed as we walked to the Morris in the station car park. There was no need for Jo to spell out a reason for their bubbling merriment.

'G. and t. on the train!'

'I told Mr Robey that he must come home for the night and nobble Papa, and whoever else is staying. There's bound to be some Labour Party high-ups hanging around the place. . . .'

'I think not,' I warned her. 'It seems to be more of a domestic occasion.'

Rice Robey was basking in the glow of the two girls' affection. To be squeezed by two nymphs who took seriously his view of legendary Britain must have come close to his personal definition of Paradise, the equivalent of *foie gras* to the sound of trumpets. Kirsty never confided in me what her thoughts had been, but Jo, who was not noticeably reticent, announced when the effect of the gin-and-tonic had worn off that she was glad to get home.

'He's *sinister*! His fingers went too far in the back of the car.'

'How far's that?'

'That's a real wanker's question.'

We were standing about waiting for dinner by the time Jo and I had exchanged these words. Pat Lampitt was evidently so accustomed to unannounced arrivals that she completely accepted Rice Robey's eruption on to that scene. The only surprising thing, I found, was its unsurprisingness. One now expected him to turn up everywhere until what he called 'the symphony of destinies' had played its final chord, or at least reached the end of a movement. I knew, Felicity had so often reiterated it, that Rice Robey was much in demand as a freelance lecturer, and as a guide around the ancient sites of Britain. Given the fact that he managed to fit this in on top of a busy schedule of journalistic malice and office chores, it was perhaps not so very surprising that he had come Kirsty Lampitt's way. As soon as one began thinking of it as a coincidence, one began to remember that in his peculiar vision of things, such concepts as chance, coincidence and luck were to be discarded.

'Your friend – what's he called?' Jo persisted. She had sobered up a bit and become prosaically anxious to get things straight, sort out identities.

'Miles Darnley.'

'Miles, right. Why does he call you Percy Grainger?'

'Because . . . difficult to explain, really.' Difficult, that is, to someone who seemed virtually incapable of thought. I felt coy to admit that I was 'Jason Grainger' on 'The Mulberrys'; it would be too embarrassing if she never listened to the programme, and worse if she did. Darnley's tortuous need to relabel the human race with nicknames of his own devising was too wearisome to disentangle, particularly since the general family consensus that Jo was 'thick as a plank' seemed at that moment far more plausible than something Uncle Roy claimed to have heard from the Diocesan Secretary in Ely – 'that Lampitt girl's a live wire'. Darnley's doodling sort of brain had not been content to leave me as Jason Grainger. He had had to change it to Percy Grainger, a musical composer of whom Jo had almost certainly never heard. It was too boring to unravel nonsense of this kind.

'Anyway, he seems to be getting on well with Kirsty,' said Jo. 'Kirsty's just bust up with her boyfriend. It's really, really sad, I think.'

Kirsty, who certainly seemed to have hit it off well with Darnley, was unmistakably Jo's sister: they had the same sort of hair, straight and thick, which they had deliberately made more alike by cutting and dyeing it identically; both had the same rather beaky noses sticking out of fleshy faces; both had blue eyes. Both faces, however, were completely different; where Kirsty's was animated, Jo's was not. Jo stared uncomprehendingly, her eyes seemed half dead and the way in which she jutted out her lower lip somehow recalled the more truculent inhabitants of the ape house at London Zoo. Kirsty's face, by contrast, was lit up with intelligence; it seemed brightly and comprehendingly amused by the world it confronted.

'Bitch,' said Jo. 'She's always bagging blokes I fancy.'

'If you want to pitch in and break it all up,' I said, 'don't feel you have to waste time talking to me.'

'Oh, what's the use?'

She crossly exhaled a noseful of Number Six.

We were standing in the Cabinet, an octagonal room, whose high walls were hung with faded torn crimson damask. Ormolu candle-brackets and mirror-frames sprouted from the wall above the chaste white chimneypiece. Most of the furniture was gilt except for two or three large Boule *bureaux plats* which echoed the crimson of the wall hangings and added to the claustrophobic and vaguely infernal feeling of the place.

'Red curtains always make me think of *naughty* Lord Byron, you know,' Professor Wimbish's excited contralto rang out over the company. It was more like song than speech, the singing of some conceited bird or the uncontrolled warblings of some crazed old dowager. His pencil-thin wife, said to be rather grand, stood by, twitching her little lips with disapproval as he trilled out – 'You see! Byron woke up in the middle of the night and saw the red curtains hanging round the bed. He said he thought he was already in hell!'

Pat politely rocked with laughter.

'Horrible man, Lord Byron,' said Lady Augusta Wimbish. She looked so very old, and so wirily indestructible, that it was on the verge of credible that she spoke from actual memory of the poet.

'But, I say!' exclaimed Wimbish, ignoring his wife completely. 'What a mind Harold has!'

'He's brilliant,' Vernon agreed.

'You know, I've been thinking,' said Wimbish, 'all afternoon while I worked in your beautiful library, Harold is really the same as Henry VIII.'

Professor Wimbish was a small man, several inches shorter than his wife, with thick crinkly dark hair and nut-brown eyes which smiled madly behind specs. Joe and I had run out of things to say to one another, so we gathered round Wimbish in a circle while he expounded his theory of likeness between the Leader of the Labour Party and the sixteenth-century despot.

'Henry, you see! He was master of setting one faction against another. On the one hand you have your Boleyns, who might correspond, let us say, to some section of the party. Let's say the TGWU. Or Northumberland and the Fabian Society that Sargie's so fond of. Michael Foot and the Abbot of Glastonbury, you see!'

The comparisons were rather detailed and since the personalities of Henry VIII's courtiers and subjects were as real to the professor as the personalities of the modern Labour Party, it was difficult at times to follow his drift. Vernon protested at the likening of his new hero to the man who had put down the Pilgrimage of Grace which, in his view had been primarily an uprising of the people rather than a specifically religious movement. It was all rather lost on me, and probably on Jo, and it was something of a relief when Rice Robey turned towards our group and intervened.

'You speak of Henry VIII. What do you know, Professor, of Herne the Hunter?' he asked.

Wimbish cast a look of utter disdain in Rice Robey's direction, perhaps amazed that anyone with such proletarian diction should dare to open his lips at all.

'And what do *you* know about anything?' He wiggled his finger as he indulged in this ludicrous parody of point-scoring.

'I merely wondered, Professor Wimbish, whether you had come across references to Herne the Hunter in your extensive researches into the history of the Great Despoiler.'

'The Despoiler of *what*, pray?'

'Oh, come *on*.' Vernon leapt to Rice Robey's defence. 'Henry VIII was the Despoiler uv the Monasteries. Yer can't deny Henry did that, and brought into bein', at one stroke, the privileged classes. Gave the lands and the houses ter the people who could pay – all good Tory stuff. What uv we here – Fountains Abbey? Who's the highest bidder? Goin', goin', gone!'

'Well, Herne, you see, might well have existed,' said Wimbish. 'You probably remember that he is mentioned, in Shakespeare. Mistress Page, in *The Merry Wives of Windsor* says:

There is an old tale goes that Herne the Hunter
Sometime a keeper here in Windsor Forest,
Doth all the winter-time at still midnight,
Walk round about an oak, with great ragg'd horns,
And there he blasts the tree and takes the cattle,
And makes milch-kine yield blood, and shakes a chain
In a most hideous and dreadful manner.'

'The legend is that he was a keeper, either of Henry VIII's time or earlier,' said Rice Robey. 'He was a follower of the Old Faith, one of the *wicca*. He hanged himself, or so it is said.'

'All that is pure conjecture,' said Wimbish. 'There is not one shred of historical evidence for it. Why *do* second- or third-rate individuals insist on leaping to conclusions for themselves rather than coming to those of us who *know*, the professional historians? Here are you. I don't know who you are, but you are offering us opinions about a legendary character from Tudor times, without having consulted the most authoritative and important book ever written about the court of Henry VIII.'

'I have read your books, Wimbish, with great admiration,' said Rice Robey firmly.

At this confession, Wimbish became quite kittenish. His sternness melted into a coquettish smirk. He patted Rice Robey's wrist and said, 'Well in that case, dear, you're forgiven.'

'You ask all the old, empirical English questions,' said Rice Robey. 'It is your job to do so, or so you may consider it; but this is not the way that the collective unconscious operates.'

'What I think you are saying,' said Wimbish, 'is that people in the main are too bloody stupid to know the difference between truth and falsehood, which is why there will always be political oppression in the world. Tyrants like Hitler and Lenin knew this – they saw that people were far too stupid to see through their lies.'

'Lenin wasn't the same as Hitler,' said Vernon. 'Lenin was a good man, Hitler was a bad man – there's no gainsaying that.'

This assertion, which sounded uncomfortably like something out of Orwell's *Animal Farm*, was interrupted by Rice Robey.

'It isn't a matter of stupidity, Wimbish, it's a matter of the *way* we perceive truth.'

'Those of us with minds perceive truth by thinking. Those who can't bloody think – which means the majority of the human race – should just shut up, and leave the thinking to those of us who can.'

'We don't know our parents by thinking, we don't know ourselves by thinking, not by the narrowly empirical processes which you would call thought,' said Rice Robey. 'We recover the past by mythologising it, by forming connections which have no empirical reality but which possess what I call the verities of correspondence.'

'That's just waffle-talk,' said Wimbish.

'There's no such thing as "what actually happened",' said Rice Robey. 'It is a fantasy of the Age of Voltaire. Until that point, the race of man lived by myth and inference, not by what could be proved by the narrow rules of Leibniz or Hume.'

'No such thing as "what actually happened"? Are you trying to tell a professional historian, the foremost historian of the Tudor Age, that the Field of the Cloth of Gold did not happen, or the Dissolution of the Monasteries, or the execution of Thomas

More, or the Defeat of the Spanish Armada? And are you saying that we cannot distinguish between these events, which *did* take place, and those which did not – fairy tales about Herne the Hunter, for instance? Because, if you are saying that, then you can't bloody *think*! It is as simple as that.'

'I can think, but I can also breathe and feel. Those events which you describe were mythologies before they were even recorded in history. Their significance is not that they happened, but what they became in the collective mind. And this, incidentally, is why the current vogue for small-scale and local history is so dubious. In 1588, Jess Bundle of this parish shifted a bale of corn in Lammas-tide and, come Michaelmas, died of an ague. That may be true, but it isn't history, not in the sense the Armada is history. That was a mythology in the collective mind long ere your Froudes wrote about it in their books. Herne, likewise: just a man, perhaps, "sometime a keeper here in Windsor Forest". But in death he was translated, his verity corresponded to the deeper verities, to the memories in the collective mind which have their own necessity, or they would not be there. Perhaps, in life, he was no more than one Richard Horne, arraigned for poaching in the royal forests. In death – who knows how or why – he became identified with the great Antlered Huntsman whom we meet in the old Northern and Celtic mythologies. Cerunnos, the Antlered God and lord of the animals, brought fecundity. The Germanic tradition of the wild hunt saw the Antlered One as a sky-god, leading his pack of lost souls across the heavens. Garanhir, as the Stalker or Hunter is known in the English tongue, leading the Herlathing, the *Einheriar* as it is called in Norse. Herne the Hunter is a greater figure to me than Jess Bundle, and you have said nothing, O Empirical Dryasdust, nothing about him whatsoever, if you merely say that he does not exist; for to say that he does not exist is to say that human consciousness, human imagination itself does not exist! He appears, Herne, at times of national emergency. Herne flew in Windsor sky at the time of the Abdication crisis in 1936, and again at the commencement of the Germanic hostilities, and again when sixth Monarch George perished in 1952. Now, at the time of the Harlot and the Episkopos, might he not fly again?'

'These old folktales are interesting to an historian, of course they are.' Wimbish was visibly taken aback by this exhibition of knowledge and opinion, expressed by someone other than himself. 'But, to say that there is no empirical reality, or no distinction to be made between myths and pure historical fact, is just silly.'

'It depends what you call fact,' said Rice Robey.

'Fact is what happened, fiction is what didn't happen. I shouldn't have supposed *that* was difficult to grasp!'

'The piperade will be turning into rubber if we don't eat it soon,' said Pat, coming back into the room. 'Do we go in to dinner without Sargie, or will you go and rouse him, darling?'

Although she addressed Vernon, I heard myself interrupting with the suggestion that I should go in search of Sargie, and that they should start the meal without me.

Knowing Sargie of old, it was no surprise that he was unable to put in an appearance on time for dinner. Not least, he would have hated the notion of competing with Wimbish, Rice Robey, or Vernon to be the centre of attention. Pat the Wren officer gave such clear directions that I had no difficulty in finding Sargie's room, while the others trooped into the dining room.

Upstairs, the house continued, just, to contain its chaos. As in the kitchen corridors, so on the landings, heaps of paper littered the furniture. A bicycle – what was it doing upstairs? – was propped against turn-of-eighteenth-century Chinese wallpaper. A bust by Westmacott of old George Isleworth was adorned with a dusty opera hat. At the feet of the plinth on which it stood, piles of the *New Statesman*. Stuffed into the corner of the sub-Claude Lorraine harbour scene was a Vicky caricature of Vernon dressed as a matador, baiting a Tory bull – Selwyn Lloyd, I think. Some carved tables by James Whittle were scarcely visible beneath the mountains of newspapers.

Sargie was in a large, rather cold room at the front of the house, a room dominated by a huge four-poster bed festooned with shreds of moth-eaten green curtain. He sat on a little nursing chair as close as possible to the gas fire, staring at his trouserless legs and stockinged feet.

'Began to get dressed and couldn't finish,' he said, when he was aware of another presence in the room. He was still clutching my novel, *The Vicar's Nephew*.

'Bloody good book, this.'

'It's not really, Sargie.'

'Gets old Roy to the life.'

I pompously wanted to say that this wasn't the purpose of fiction, to caricature real people. (Now, I'm not so sure.) It was perhaps the first time Sargie had spoken to me about my uncle since their estrangement. Here would have been a chance to make a grand, intrusive, potentially embarrassing speech to Sargie; to say that I knew my uncle had missed him every day of the seven years or so which had elapsed since their quarrel, and that it would take nothing to effect a reconciliation, nothing at all. Roy hated scenes, and he would have picked up with Sargie as if nothing had happened, basking in his company, delighting in all his most infuriating characteristics, running his errands, listening to his talk.

There was a very long silence in which I could not speak, could not find the right words, felt sure that Sargie wanted me to speak about himself and Uncle Roy and for that reason felt unable to say anything.

At length, I said, 'I think Pat's starting dinner.'

'Don't give you much to drink, these people. Sittee down, Julie dear, have a little snifter with your Uncle Sargie.'

By the side of the nursing chair, on the floor, there was a bottle of gin and a tooth mug.

'Is there another glass?' I enquired.

He waved his cigarette-holder in the direction of the washstand. I found a chipped cut-glass tumbler there and wiped off the traces of denture-fixative with a grubby face-towel. I found that the faintly minty taste was not disagreeable when doused with two inches of gin.

'You should write another book.'

'I think about it a lot. Easier said than done.'

'Doesn't have to be a novel.'

The gas fire hissed. The chance to urge him to patch up the quarrel with Uncle Roy had floated away like a wisp of cigarette smoke.

'Know what I think?'

'Hardly ever.'

'I think you should beat Lover Boy at his own game, and write about old Jimbo.'

'Lover Boy' was Sargie's sobriquet for Raphael Hunter. Not realising that this was a considered suggestion – indeed the whole reason, I now believe, for my having been invited to stay at Mallington for the weekend – I responded at once with a little laugh.

'Don't know enough, Sargie.'

'Nonsense. You know all about my family. Roy's told you so much over the years. Sibs says you know more about the Lampitts than we do ourselves. You'd write a magnificent book about Jimbo. You could make it into a bit of family history, too. It needn't be just about him. You could even start the story with Old Jo and this place, if you liked. Radical Jo.'

Since Sargie's proposal was completely unexpected, I had no language to reply. I assumed that what he was saying belonged wholly to the realm of fantasy. Even supposing that I wished to write the book, and could rediscover within myself the energy to start writing once more, who would want to publish it? Certainly not Madge Cruden, who had published Hunter's first volume and anxiously awaited the arrival of the second.

'Think it over,' said Sargie. 'We'll have lunch one day, eh? Clabbages? Vebby clebber febbers, Clabbages.'

I drained my gin and rose to my feet.

'Well, Sargie, I think I had better go downstairs.'

'What's going on?'

'Dinner.'

'I know, but what are they talking about? Harold, I suppose. He's a bit of a shit, Harold. Between you and me and the bedpost, I think he'll keep Vernon out of the Cabinet when the time comes.'

'I thought he'd come over to lunch to suggest the opposite.'

'To suggest, yes; not to promise. Vernon's really the last of the radicals. Our comrades on the left like him because he is always prepared to argue their case, but by modern political standards, he is a dodo. The IP don't want to hear about the Chartists. They want tellies, fitted carpets, nursery schools and polytechnics for the nippers. Harold'll dish it all out to them and persuade Conference that this is socialism, even if it ruins the exchequer, which it will. He's just the same as Harold Mac, only he wears a Gannex raincoat instead of a norfolk jacket. They've both got the same cynical ideas. There won't be any social revolution of the kind which Vernon and the Comrades want. Our Harold's conning them, just as old Harold conned *his* party into thinking that Disraeli's One-Nation Toryism meant unlimited public spending, roaring inflation and indoor toilets for the masses.'

597

'In short, "Not Amurath an Amurath succeeds,
        But Harold Harold".'

'Worse luck, my dear. So we'll have to wait a few years before Vernon is able to Build Jerusalem.'

We sang the last few lines of the poem in slightly tuneless unison.

In England's green and pleasant land!

'Better go downstairs, anyway,' I said.

'Wimbish is a bore. Thinks he's the only living historian who knows anything.'

'He was just saying something to that effect.'

'Hope someone will shut him up. Your friend Darnley could pull the rug quite effectively. Come on, now, just a drop more.'

He leaned forward with the bottle and replenished my tumbler.

'Darnley's too smitten with Kirsty to be taking any notice of Wimbish,' I said. 'They've left Wimbish to the mercy of this man Kirsty brought from Cambridge, Rice Robey who writes under the name of Albion Pugh. Now, the strange thing is, Sargie, this man used to know your brother Jimbo.'

'Plenty of people did.'

'I know, but he evidently knew Jimbo quite well. Jimbo was kind to him.'

'He *was* kind. One of the reasons I want you to write the book.'

'He thinks Hunter is a liar and worse than a liar.'

I was almost drunk enough to blurt out to Sargie the theory that his brother had been murdered; but I held back and spared him the shock. Sargie had no reason, as I had, to be interested in Rice Robey.

'Shall I say that you aren't up to supper? Someone could probably bring something up for you on a tray?'

'I say, Julie, this place is bloody uncomfortable. Let's do a flit, eh? Drive back to town. Only take us three hours at this time of night. You've got a car.'

Had I been my Uncle Roy, I should probably have been immediately obedient to Sargie's whim, set off for London at once, and good-naturedly turned the car round, somewhere near Fakenham, when he changed his mind, decided that Mallington was a 'dear old place' and that he could not face the solitude of his flat in Kensington.

'I'm leaving in the morning, Sargie, not now.'

'Please, Julian. I can't stand this place. I *know* Cecily is always coming here and it makes me sick. She tries to poison their minds against me. Pat doesn't need much persuading, you know.'

'I'm sure it's not true, Sargie.'

'Cecily still hates me, Julian, after all these years.'

Knowing nothing of the case, I could not comment. Sargie's wife had disappeared long before Uncle Roy, let alone I, had appeared on the scene, though she still kept in touch with the Lampitts, and Uncle Roy had, I know, met her on a number of occasions.

'Well, I must go now, Sargie.'

'Come back when you've had some grub, Julie, please. Don't leave me here all alone.'

The company downstairs was not the most alluring I had ever encountered.

'All right, Sargie.'

It was with a slight feeling of dread that I descended the stairs. I had not yielded completely to his caprice, but I had allowed him much more than I intended, to exercise his will over me, and I knew from experience how all-consuming and absolute that will was. I was wondering, by the time I joined the others, what I let myself in for. Going upstairs to tell Sargie that dinner was ready had seemed such a slight act when I had undertaken it. Already I started to sense that the conversation which had just taken place between me and the old man could change my life.

The others had finished their first course by the time I entered the dining room. Lady Augusta Wimbish alone was still eating what might have been her second, or even her third, helping. Mounds of piperade, sauté potatoes and green cabbage were rapidly diminishing beneath the jabbing assaults of her fork. I noticed that for the remainder of the meal, she made no efforts whatsoever to converse; her one, apparently desperate, concern was to fill her emaciated body with food. She ate as if she had been deprived of nourishment for weeks. While Kirsty – 'Poor you!' – lifted the lids of serving dishes in the hope of finding something for me to eat and Pat shouted about the possibility of running up an omelette, and I said I was perfectly happy to eat cheese and fruit, Lady Augusta shot me frightened, jealous glances, a starving squirrel anxiously guarding its pile of beechnuts against a predator.

The long oval dining table stood in the centre of a magnificent panelled room whose ceiling was encrusted with decaying rococo plasterwork. The centrepiece, from which depended a vast dusty chandelier, was carved with spears, drums and hunting horns, wreathed in foliage, grey with neglect. Most of the portraits on the walls, blackened with old varnish, were of Isleworths, but on either side of the chimneypiece hung pictures by an artist called, I think, Jackson, of Radical Jo Lampitt and his Quaker wife Naomi. How often Uncle Roy had spoken to me of these unremarkable productions, in terms which would not have been too effusive had he been describing the most sublime canvases of Titian or Tintoretto. For him, they were icons, these depictions of the ancestors of those generations of Lampitts whom he so dearly cherished, even down to Kirsty and Jo, now placed on opposite sides of the table and beneath the gaze of their forebears.

Kirsty, still wearing her denims, was seated between Darnley and the place which had been set for me. Opposite her, Jo sat between Professor Wimbish and Sargie's empty chair. Jo stared impassively and glumly at her sister conversing with Darnley while Wimbish exclaimed about the magnificence of the library in which he had been working all day. Jo looked bored stiff by his praise of the copy of *Vitruvius Britannicus* to be found on the library shelves.

'Naughty me, you *see*! I should have been reading your grandpapa's political papers, but I just couldn't resist some of your folios, dear, and your positively delicious incunabula. But what a state they are in. . . .'

On her right, Jo had equally little luck with Rice Robey who was well into his stride doing what he had come to Mallington in order to do, buttonholing Vernon about this threatened henge. Vernon was nodding sagely and punctuating Rice Robey's impassionate talk with such phrases as 'We must see what we can do' and 'We're going ter stop all this wreckage of the countryside by the capitalists, you'll see'.

And Rice Robey was saying things like, 'But you don't understand! If you think it's just a question of keeping the countryside pretty and nice . . . it's not an aesthetic conundrum, it is one of the threatened sanctities, outraged divinities.

No good will come of it if you disturb the ancient scenes of sacrifice.'

Arriving at the meal late and finding nothing much to eat when I got there, only increased my sense of alienation from the company.

'As soon as Augusta's finished we can . . . ' Pat was unashamedly impatient. Impervious to niceties, she piled plates (something which poor Uncle Roy had taught me never was done) of good Coalport much mended with rivets. She clattered them as if they were cheap crocks in the NAAFI. I sat awkwardly and nervously between Pat and Kirsty.

Some apples, oatcakes and an excellent cheddar were produced from a sideboard when Lady Augusta had wiped her plate clean with bread and made her only comment of the meal.

'Scrambled egg, isn't it?'

Pat offered me some rather sweet cider of which she, her daughters and Rice Robey appeared to be partaking in modest doses.

'Sargie's got drink up in his room, I suppose?' she fired at me.

'I've often seen him like this. A cloud suddenly descends. He can't face society.'

'Sitting on your own getting squiffy is no cure for the blues.'

I thought that, with polishing, this could be the first line of a song, but there was no one round the table with whom I could share my thought.

'I'll take him some coffee later, if I may,' I said.

'Of course his mum spoilt him something rotten, that's the root of the trouble,' said Pat.

I had very often heard this explanation for the defects in Sargie's social behaviour, but I did not feel in a mood for a conversation about him. When Wimbish, who was an almost fanatical teetotaller, caught wind of our talk, it was certainly time to change the subject.

'I can speak my mind freely to you, dear,' he said, touching Pat's wrist. 'Sargent is just a bloody fool, swigging all that al-co-hol. He was my tutor, you know, at Oxford. I'd seen enough of oafish, drunken behaviour before I ever came up. Men staggering out of pubs! A miner's son, an illiterate Welsh miner, swigging *his* stupid alcohol, you *see*! But even then, when I was eighteen years of age, I can remember Sargent Lampitt was a byword for *it*.'

Turning to Jo and prodding her with his finger, he smiled the smile of a pantomime dame momentarily employed as the madam in a brothel.

'You think I mean "it", you naughty girl, I don't think Sargent ever took much interest in "it", certainly not in me! But in stupid al-co-hol, yes. And I haven't touched a drop of it in my life. Do you see the very simple difference? I am the foremost historian of the Tudor Age, who has written over thirty-five books. What's *he* done, bloody fool, except write one book about the House of Lords, telling them to abolish themselves?'

As it happened, I felt a greater empathy with Sargie than with anyone else present; I regretted leaving him, and I wondered what I was doing there. The fact that, in its way, it was a convivial occasion, made me feel even more distant from it all. Darnley's various imitations – at that moment he was amusing the daughters of the house with a shameless parody of Vernon himself – had everyone at his end of the table in a roar.

Over coffee, when we had all arisen and wandered into the drawing room, Augusta Wimbish buttonholed me and said, 'I really prefer plain English food. There were things in that scrambled egg.'

'I think intentionally.'

'Gussy,' said Darnley, kissing her. 'Do you know Jason Grainger? From "The Mulberrys"?'

'What is "The Mulberrys"?'

We tried to explain.

'No, well, you see, I should love to have things like a wireless set, but Tommy simply *won't*.'

At this, she fell silent again, drew in her lips and looked furtively about the room, eyeing it possibly for some more food or perhaps just for other devices or diversions enjoyed by others but denied to her by the professor. I was surprised by Darnley kissing her, and turning out to be a relation.

Wimbish himself approached, with Vernon and Rice Robey.

'So!' he said to me. 'You are to be Mr Hunter's rival!'

I'd been that often enough; or, rather, Hunter had been mine. The observation made me start.

'So Sargie's spoken to yer,' said Vernon. 'Good, good. And yer like the idea? Excellent.'

I hummed and hawed. The idea that I should write a book about Jimbo, possibly a history of the Lampitt family, was evidently one which had been discussed before my arrival at Mallington, but it was still new to me, and I had not decided what I thought about it.

'It's quite an undertaking,' said Wimbish, 'but you must get me to help you. I had quite a lot to do with old Jimbo one way or another in the days when I was starting out in the literary world.'

'It's all very speculative, isn't it?' I said. 'Sargie has only just asked me. I'm not sure whether I even want . . .'

'Splendid,' said Vernon, 'terrific.'

'I saw there was no point at all in my wasting all my talents on the academic fifth-raters,' said Wimbish. 'I shall read you the appropriate passages of my diaries. The struggle I had, you wouldn't believe it, coming from a filthy working-class home. Now, Jimbo saw my qualities at once. None of the academic fifth-rater about him. He was a very good *popular* historian, though it is a pity he wrote some of his books before I was born. Otherwise, I could have saved him from making some really silly howlers. That last book about him, though, rather missed the point, with all its *naughtiness*.'

He smiled archly and poked me with a long index finger. Kirsty came up breathlessly and said, 'There's going to be a full moon. We're going down to the beach. Come on, do.'

She tugged at my elbow excitedly.

'Oh come *on*.'

Darnley and she were so merry that I assumed that they were the only two going to the beach. I felt *de trop* and said that I had promised to look in again on Sargie.

'I'll say good night, then,' said Darnley. 'We might not meet before the morning.'

'OK.'

'I left that stuff in your room – the stuff I was telling you about in the car.'

'Which stuff?'

With comic movements of the head in the direction of Rice Robey, Darnley said no more. Rice Robey himself was excited by a not altogether affectionate rebuke from Pat.

'Here you, keep your hands to yourself and leave my daughter alone.'

He was stroking Jo's denim bottom as he waxed lyrical about

603

the moon. He ignored Pat's suggestion that he was behaving improperly and she did not repeat herself.

'Come, Lady Lampitt, come with us to see the moon,' he said. 'The chaste huntress of the sky.'

I had not realised that there was to be a party accompanying Kirsty and Darnley to the beach but I was too proud to ask if I could after all join it. The elder Lampitts and the Wimbishes were (rather to my surprise) devotees of contract bridge. They were rejoicing, as such enthusiasts do, when a 'four' materialises. It was time for me to slink away.

I wanted to go straight back to Sargie and say that it was quite out of the question, my writing this Jimbo book. When I went to his room, however, I found him snoring sonorously on the bed, and any further discussion of the idea would have to wait. It was not long after nine when I turned into my bedroom and found a brown paper envelope on my bedside table – the 'stuff', which I had supposedly discussed with Darnley in the car. I could not remember having discussed any stuff, and assumed that it was something to do with *The Spark*. I opened the envelope and found a bundle of extremely thin quarto pages closely typed on both sides. And I began to read.

> Wild man, goat-man, scrawny fist uplifted,
> Thin arm projecting from a shaggy sleeve.
> He stood and ranted by the waterside.
> 'Be changed, O very surface of the earth!
> Level each valley, low each hill and mount!
> Before the great and terrible day shall come,
> Before He comes, He mightier than I.'
>
> He stood on level stones which jutted out
> Into the Jordan water – desert man,
> A coney among rocks and barren land.
> His bearded face was gaunt and torn with grief,
> Though scarcely thirty years, he was careworn.
> Chronos had graven torture on his cheek,
> All-Father, Zeus the Maker chose this out,
> This locust-fed Joanes, desert man,
> And scratched on him prefigurings of death,
> A foredoomed martyr's death at Herod's hand.
> Wild place for wild man, desert place apart.

Yet near the waterside the ground was green,
And here and there a tree put out its leaves.
And hither thronged the hearers to his rant –
Some merely curious about a spectacle,
Some openly derisive, others swayed
Desirous of a cleansing from their sin,
Healing in Jordan water at his hands.
'The leprous Syrian, Naaman, in his pride
Scorned to be washed and healed in Jordan's flood.
"Are not the Syrian waters, Abana,
And Pharpar greater than this trivial stream?
May not my rivers wash me, make me clean?"
So Naaman scorned Jordan – so scorn ye!
But not until his heart was humbled low,
And not until he washed in Jordan's stream
Could Naaman be rid of leper's sores!
And not until you all repent of sin,
Receiving metanoia's baptism,
Can you wash out the leprosy of soul!
Turn! Change yourselves! For one is coming soon –
Mightier, oh mightier than I! Turn! Turn!
And he will thresh his wheat and purge his floor
And gather good corn into garners – but
The chaff will burn in an unquenching fire!'

Swarming, hysterical crowd converge on bank,
To be baptised of Joanes in Jordan.

Aloof from mob, the learned stand apart,
The learned men of Zion watch with scorn.
One of them, Tentmaking Saulos, deeply read
In sacred Scripture and the Torah's Book,
Gazed with peculiar intentness now.

Seeing this group of scribes, the goat-man shrieked,
'Vipers! A brood of vipers! Who warned you,
To flee the certain wrath which is to come?'
'I have kept to the Torah since my youth,'
Saulos said quietly to a Pharisee.
'How dare he now instruct law-perfect me,
Me to repent and turn? I have rejoiced

In the way of Thy testimonies,
As in all manner of riches. . . .
So shall I keep thy testimonies, even for ever and ever.
Such as I need no repentance.'
Saulos's companion turned and quietly said,
'I fear this man, because he stirs the mob.'
'And yet,' said Saulos, 'should the words be true,
And should Messias step among us now,
Desire of all the nations, should he come,
And should the end of all days be at hand,
The day foretold in prophecies of old,
And should the number of the Lord's elect,
Be shortly now accomplished, should the Christ . . .'

'Come, Saulos, come!' smiled his urbane companion.
'Your head is turned by ranting such as this?
Look at the creatures splashing there below.
Dogs chasing birds have more solemnity.
Is this the following of holy law?
Is this religion – splashing in the sun?
They should not look to this unlettered loon.
We are the true interpreters of Law;
We studied Torah-books both day and night. . . .'
And still they watched the Baptist with disdain.
'What is he saying now?' Saulos enquired.
'The ranter is gone silent, muttering.'
'To such a one as he,' said Saulos's friend,
A haughty Pharisee in costly robe,
'See how he mutters to the ragamuffin,
Some fool who heeds his tricks of rhetoric.'

Saulos walked down towards the water's edge,
Leaving his wise companions in their place.
He wanted to be witness to this scene.
Thigh-deep in water the Baptiser stood;
His raucous voice was for the moment still;
No more cries of 'Repent!' and for the while,
No more immersions in the Jordan stream.
Joanes stood quite still. His hands, like claws,
Clutched at a neaniskos's collar-bone,
Angelic young one, angel in his flesh,

Fleshly in his concealed divinity.
The crowds encircled the mysterious pair,
Poised, as it seemed, for passionate embrace.
A love-moment in which two human souls
Are lifted from their self-containing lives
Into new unity at Love's decree,
Enveloped in the unselfing of the Divine Eros.
Saulos approached and felt this emanation,
This soul-entwining of Joanes and the Stranger,
Felt the rays emanate of the spiritual warmth and the love-
    god heaving his heart of love!
Was Saulos then in the spirit of evil, and was this
    Beelzebub?
Was there one here whom water could not wash?
Was there a sin here which could not be baptised?
'No!' said the Baptist to the Stranger's face.
He held his shoulders, and he shuddered, 'No!'
Saulos was close, could see the Baptist's eyes
Focused upon the naked stranger there.
Neaniskos in the water standing before the wild man,
Speaking in words too low to be audible.
Saulos could see the Stranger from behind.
He saw thick hair fall on to pale shoulder blades
He saw the line of the vertebrae come down the thin back
    towards white buttocks,
He saw the buttocks touching the water's surface.

Baptiser Goat-man made his stern reply
To the inaudible mutter of the Stranger.
'I must be washed by you, not you by me!
I must decrease, dear man, you must increase.'

But still the Stranger mumbled in reply,
And must at length have won the Baptist round.
Joanes threw his head back, rolled his eyes,
And passed into a frenzied state of trance.
He forced the Stranger's shoulders under water.
With violent pressing held the young man down,
As if to drown him, not baptise a penitent.
Beneath the bony hands the Stranger crumpled.
He seemed all weakness as he fainted down,

607

And those who watched let out a gentle moan,
As if indeed the young man had been drowned,
Or dragged beneath the waters by wild demons
Called up by shaggy Joanes in his frenzy
Of love-imprecation and harsh benediction.
Joanes opened wide his terrible eyes.
They rolled ecstatically, and from his mouth
There came loud shrieks of some unheard-of tongue.
He shook like an exorciser who wrestled with Power
As he held beneath the water the head of his catechumen.
Then he removed his hands, and up he sprang,
The Stranger leapt, not like a drowning man,
But like a giant spreading wide his arms,
Hands up, up, towards the sun in a mime of purest joy!
The immersion and its consequence became a dance
Communicating an erotic gladness which was bigger than
    Eros.
The naked man looked innocently at the sky,
And Saulos, rapt, stood by and looked at him.
Something about these happy outstretched arms,
The tautened thighs, the dancing of his legs,
Made Saulos see that all men, not just this,
All, had within them a divinity.
He felt he was not watching one young man,
Exuberant and dancing in the river;
Rather, it seemed as if the human race
Had made itself anew.
Out of the shallow waters, Adam leapt,
New Adam, newly dancing for a new dawn.
And as in Adam sinners all had died,
So in this dance should all be made anew,
And out of death would come a newer life.
He shuddered, Saulos, for what fiend of hell
Could have whispered such blasphemous nonsense in his
    ears?
And now with eyes aloft, the Baptist yelled,
'I see the Heavens opened and the Dove,
The Holy Wind of God descending here,
Proclaiming our Messias and our Prince!'
Saulos could see no dove and heard no wind.

608

He saw a young man, eternally youthful and eternally
    naked
Lifting strong arms towards the stronger sun.
The Stranger turned and waded to the bank.
He dried himself a little with his mantle,
Then slipped it simply over his wet hair.
Saulos watched the dressing of this mysterious being,
Who brought no scrip, no purse, no staff,
Simply a chasuble through which his head,
Fresh-washed with Jordan-baptism jutted with joy.
And Saulos watched the face as it emerged.
Long, bony, thin, akin to the Baptist's face,
It was quite different.
Saulos discovered himself applying to this face
A host of contradictory epithets.
Terrible, strong, but it was vulnerable,
And it was wise, yet simple as a child.
It stared as madmen stare, but it was sane.
It had no conventional beauty,
But its beauty haunted Saulos, it was an unforgettable
    beauty
And it had haunted him before, as the beauty of a woman
    haunts a man.
And as he watched the Stranger throw back his mane of
    hair,
His thick, lustrous black hair over the shoulders of his robe,
Saulos assured himself that he was not in love,
He fought back the presence of Eros, but shook to know
The presence of some other, greater God.
Joanes had returned to his task of baptising in Jordan-
    water,
And the air was loud with his voice, and the shrieks of his
    idiot-followers,
And the Stranger was silent, aloof from this religious
    scene.
And Saulos followed the Stranger with his eyes,
As he walked through the crowds, and turned from the
    Jerusalem road,
Taking his feet over stony ground and wilderness,
Towards the brow of the deserted hills.

*

Twenty years earlier, and in another world.
The scene: Albion, new-Roman-named Britannium!
'Tarry,' the man said, 'tarry with the ass,
While I go yonder with the weary lad.'
The bearers drew the ponies to a halt
At the base of the primrose-covered hill,
The round, green, buxom, undulating breast of a hill.
The ponies were squat and shaggy.
Like the ponies, the Celtic bearers too were dark and squat,
Speaking to these foreigners in a strange sing-song patois,
But speaking to themselves in a lilting native music,
Which sang with sea-echoes and danced like the move-
    ment of the sea in caves.
'Wait here we shall then,' said one of these men.
Another, who had led the boy on his pony,
Lifted the child down on to the brilliant green of the turf,
And as he did so spoke an endearment,
'Here, get down, my little Lamb.
There is a long journey home awaiting us,'
Said Yusif, the tall foreigner to the Little Lamb.
'Let us walk on this hill to refresh ourselves.'
Much-travelled Yusif, merchant in many lands,
Brought with him his cousin's lad, not long past his Bar-
    Mitzphah.
They had been many months among the heathen, buying
    and selling.
Bales of stuff, carpets and spices,
They had brought with them on the outward voyage
To western lands. And they had travelled far,
Far to the west, to Lyonesse itself,
And seen the tin-mines and the mines of Gold,
Where Celts had delved like dwarves Gehenna-bound
With picks and barrows, dug for yellow ore!
Half a century ago, Great Kaiser Julius,
Had brought to the unformed poem of Albion's sons and
    daughters
The order and magisterium of law,
And placed beside the tufty mound of intuition,
The rod of military strength.
And the corridors of Hades threw up their all-corrupting
    ore,

Which Imperial majesty and military avarice required.
'We give to Kaiser only what is Kaiser's,'
One of the toothless Celts of Lyonesse,
Had laughingly told Yusif and the lad.
And he had implied that there was some mystery which
they retained,
Which Kaiser's legions could not buy or sell,
Something contained in songs they sang the Boy,
And tales they told of bird-gods, water-goddesses,
Of souls that slept in tombs a thousand years,
And then awoke to vitalise the world.
They sang, too, songs of sacrifice and death,
And told about the Coming of a King.
Returning from the west, and quite by chance,
Yusif and his companion had beheld,
Just such a heathen rite, horrid in blood.
As evening fell, they still were on the road,
And lighted on a certain place to sleep.
Waking before the dawn, they found themselves
Just on the edge of a great stone circle,
They heard within the enclosure of the high pillars,
Within the consecrated circle, petric and phallic,
The hierophantic wailing of the priests,
Hymning their Lord and Light before the Dawn.
And Yusif watched his boy-companion's face,
While these sounds, pregnant with the violence of mys-
tery,
And the yearning of natural man for the religion of
sacrifice,
And the hunger of the uninitiated soul for the satisfaction
of a cult,
Broke the grey, misty silence of a British spring,
The darkness and dampness of the half-hour before dawn.
Yusif could see the boy's face taut with fear,
And staring too with fascinated awe.
They crawled with stealth up to the outer edge,
Where the turf sloped outside the inner circle of the henge.
From here, they could be unseen witnesses,
To what would happen when the sun was up.
They saw the figures standing in the henge.
A priest in long white robes, stood with an upraised knife.

611

Before him, was a naked boy-child, younger than Yusif's
  strange companion!
And the child was pinioned like a wild beast to a stake.
And other white-robed figures sung a dirge,
Until their Lord and Light the Sun came up.
And when the first rays of the rising Sun,
Caught on the shining blade, the knife came down.
He did not even scream, the little lad.
A whimper, a weak whimper, he gave out, before the
  blood flowed.
Far, far away at home, both Jews had seen,
The sacrifices in the Temple at Jerusalem,
Lambs, Kids and Doves, they took each year
To fall beneath the sacrificial knife.
But in this foreign morning, this cold dawn,
They saw a different blood-pouring,
The slaying of a different Lamb.
And the priestly murderers ran with their cups to catch the
  child's precious blood.

Yeshua, the lad, had turned away,
And retched and vomited on the grass.
Quick as they could, they'd woken up the guides,
And hastened on their pony-slow journey back, back to
  Londinium.

This brutally religious scene of blood,
Silenced the boy through all the journey back.
Each night, he anxiously implored Yusif,
That they should reach an inn and not sleep out.
Each night, he begged Yusif to sleep with him,
And through the hours of darkness the cousins clung.
Yeshua hardly spoke, but one black night,
Silently weeping, he said to his cousin,
'Yusif, that boy they killed could have been *me*!'
He said no more, but wept and wept and wept,
While his elder cousin held his quivering shoulders in his
  arms.

And then to Londinium they returned
And at their inn they met the tentmaker,

The first Jew they had met in Londinium,
A travelling merchant like themselves.
A tiny creature, not five feet in height,
Sure in his views and hasty in his speech.
Yeshua spoke to him, tried to make friends.
Saulos was young – perhaps five years older than Yeshua.
And he was a Turkish Jew, of Tarsus born,
But more a Pharisee than those at home.
And Yeshua spoke to him of heathen men, and heathen
    prayer.
There was a Temple not far from the inn –
The Temple of Mithras over the Hill of Lud.
There was the cup of sacrifice upraised,
The chalice of blood worshipped by the Roman soldiery.

    NB. Some apostrophe cd be introduced here. The modern
        city. Lud's Hill. The Temple of the tentmaker on Ludgate
        Hill?

Yusif heard with surprise that Yeshua
Had visited this Temple for himself.
So that was where he was in early hours,
When he had so mysteriously 'disappeared'.
Yeshua was 'famous' in the family for this,
Teased by his brothers and sisters for his disappearing
    tricks.
Miriam, their mother, Yusif's cousin,
Became wild with rage when Yeshua disappeared.
She was not consoled when one of the brothers said,
'Mother, don't fear, your boy will be returned,
He'll come back in three days, you mark my words.'
This was allusion to that passover,
When Yeshua had lost himself in the Jerusalem crowds,
Thousands of people, swarming on pilgrimage to the
    Temple,
And the little boy lost!
They found him after three days, sitting in the Temple.
Baiting the clergy by asking them difficult questions,
Interrogation was his only mode.
He showed no interest in answers, only in questions.

When the answers were given, the boy's face seemed abstracted,

Almost idiotic, as if the words of human discourse and the rationality of John Locke

Made no *impresa* on this, the first *tabula-rasa* mind since Adam.

Yusif thought of this incident now, far away in the inn in Londinium.

For Saulos the tentmaker was enraged, and Yeshua had on his face that idiot abstraction.

'You went to the Temple of Mithras!' thundered Saulos.

'Temple! No temple, that!

There only is one lawful sacrifice.

There only is one temple in the world.

Salvation cometh to the Jews alone.'

Yeshua sat and stared into his drink,

He held his goblet firmly in his palms,

And looked down into it, seeing his face reflected in the blood-red wine.

'The nostrils of the Almighty will not sniff

The meat that's roast for idols by these scum!'

Saulos explained the Torah to the child,

Reminded him of how *Leviticus*

Decrees that meats be cut and stewed and burnt

For the savouring nostrils of the all-devouring Jew-divinity,

Universal in power but worshipped alone through the formulas of his chosen priests and people.

And then the silence of Yeshua was broken.

He drained his cup and said, 'The time is coming,

No, the time is come, when neither in Mount Sion,

Nor in these temples of the Roman gods,

Will sacrifice be asked, nor blood outpoured.'

Saulos, astonished, asked the little boy,

'Do you deny the Covenant of God?'

'I do deny no covenants, but covenants

Are not fulfilled as partners would expect.

Our Father loves all men, He called the Temple

Built by King Solomon my ancestor,

A house of prayer for all men on this earth.'

'But only for the children of the promise.'

614

'And did your earthly father make such laws?
Did he distinguish one child from another?
If one child spoke to him and did not use
Precisely the same form of words as you,
Would then your father say he could not *hear*
The voice uplifted by his own dear child?
Surely Our Father hears the voice of prayer?
Whoever speaks, wherever it is raised?
For unto him shall *all* flesh rise and come:
Whether from the Mount Sion in Jerusalem,
Or from the Mount Lud in Londinium.
For if men lift up their voices to the throne of grace from
    Londinium,
Then is Britain Mount Sion and the Heavenly Jerusalem is
    found here!'
Tentmaker's fury: 'This is blasphemous!'
Innkeeper comes to ask for no more noise.
' 'Ere, talking loud in all that foreign jabber!
Keep it quiet, will you, or I'll throw you out.'
And at a nearby table was a drunkard,
Who leaned towards them, and brought the flow of talk to
    an end.
Yeshua seemed to like this red-faced man.
He laughed at his jokes, and evidently enjoyed
His talk more than the earnest tentmaker's.
Saulos, indignant, rose and left the room.
They were not destined yet to meet until
Sixteen years later by the Jordan's bank,
When the eyes of Saulos the Pharisee met those of the
    anointed Messias.

Yusif disliked them both, the bigot Saulos,
And now this red-faced belcher with his jokes.
So, he proposed the ride, a few hours' air
Before the Tamesis tide allowed their ship
To sail for Gaul and turn their footsteps home.

From Hill of Lud, their guides led them north-west
Beyond the wattled walls and muddy streets
Outside the city wall, they rode through fields,
And from thick woods, finches and thrushes flew

Singing their bright songs in the grey cloudy air.
They passed through lush fields where the grass was thick,
Where green of bush and foliage was so bright
The colours shocked the eye. Much oak grew here.
May burst from bushes in abundant clouds.
Wild privet hedges burst with cow parsley.
High to the ponies' waists grew buttercups.
The boy's bare legs were brushed with wild barley-
    whiskers,
As they rode, rode, rode to the foot of a hill,
This round feminine hill, this breast on Londinium's edge,
Where they dismounted, and left their guides with the
    ponies,
And walking through the thicket, climbed the hill.
Beneath their feet the turf was soft and bright.
'This greenness soothes my heart,' said Yeshua,
'I still weep inwardly for that young boy,
Slain by the priests; now, I feel buffeted
By all the verbal onslaughts of that bore,
That bigot Saulos speaking of the Law.'
'There was no need,' said Yusif, 'for dispute.
Look at these flowers, this grass, these birds, this hill.
They do not argue, buffet, fight like men.'
Yeshua took in his hand the hand of Yusif of Arimathea,
And the two cousins who loved one another walked to the
    top of the hill.
The rain fell gently as they turned and looked,
Down on the city which they'd left behind.
The silver Tamesis wove like a snake
And slunk through fields and villas, camps and huts.
They saw the forts, the wooden palisades,
Built by the Romans at the water's edge.
They saw the temples, and the Roman walls.
Yeshua said, 'I love this little place!
It has no buildings worthy of the name,
No Temple like our own, Saulos is right!
The air's subdued, the light is dull and grey,
The population all seem mildly drunk.
But I don't want to leave . . . don't want to leave.'
Yusif replied in murmurs, 'Let my hand
Forget its cunning if I should forget

You, O Jerusalem, my mother, my city, my goal!'

The two stood silent on the fat green hill.
They watched a ray of sunlight penetrate
The lead-grey cloud and point into the Thames.
Over their heads from west to east there stretched
A rainbow, perfect arch formed in the sky.
Yusif felt bathed, suffused and washed
By this blest light and by these coloured rays.
He knew how heathen men could bow their knee
To worship the Magnificence of Light.
But as he stood in silence by the boy
He felt the light came not so much from the sky
As from this child himself. Yusif knew well
That he was standing on a little hill
On a grey day in a boring province of the Empire,
With a child born to his cousin Miriam,
Surrounded by bleating sheep and lambs.
But his heart told him that he had come to the mountain of
    the Presence!
The light which he saw was no ordinary light, but the
    shining of the Unutterable!
And this was the *shekinah* of the all-mighty, the glory of the
    Lord,
And he felt that he was come unto Mount Sion, and unto
    the City of the Living God,
And to an innumerable company of angels.
And then a silence followed, unmeasured by time.
A silence of a most refreshing kind,
Leaving the person washed and the mind renewed.
They did not speak again, the man and boy,
Until they'd walked down the hill and stopped halfway,
Amid the shaggy ewes and bleating lambs.
Yeshua stopped and broke the silence then.
'Yusif,' he said, 'tell no one what you saw.'

> *Notes:* All history is the reinterpretation of images. Memory
> the mother of the Muses. This supremely true in the
> true Mythos of the Anointed. Narrative to convey the
> actual numinous quality of Yeshua himself and the

Mythos of Sacrifice and Atonement in the mind of Saulos. The Mythos takes over Yeshua, he is obliged to enact it, like a man upon whom a spell has been cast. This obligation comes from the human yearning for a religion, a cleansing, an atonement.

The Crucifixion itself a sadistic love-moment for Saulos. Its repetition at the stoning of the Protomartyr Stephanos enough to precipitate the crisis known to Christendom as the Conversion of St Paul.

The Mediterranean world adopted Paulism, the religion of the Atoning Death, the Resurgent Body from the Tomb. Yusif of Arimathea travels northwards to the grey half-lights of Ambiguous Albion. The thorn crown hidden in Glastonbury and blossoming.

The whole cycle to include all histories and mythologies. Odin on the Tree Yggdrasil offers himself to himself. Herne the Hunter hangs himself on a tree. Messias Yeshua's kinsmen, the Knights of the Round Table, Lancelot and Galahad, imprisoned in the eternal gulf dividing desire and achievement, moral aspiration and human appetite. The failure of the cousin of Christ by ninth degree, Lancelot, to see the Sangreal: indicative of an eternal conflict between flesh and spirit, love and betrayal. The Holy House of Nazareth built in the Vale of Stiffkey, Walsingham England's Nazareth. The religion of Paul brought to mammon-glutted industrial Albion by itinerant Wesley. Contrast the true Jesus of the Everlasting Gospel who found his resurrection in the prophecies and engravings of William Blake. Revolutions. The necessary overthrow of images. Voltaire himself an unheeding witness to the light.

Rector of Stiffkey and the harlots; his death in the lion's den. The Abdication of Edward VIII; the casting down of the magisterium of Caesar before the throne of the Divine Eros. Herne the Hunter is seen in the sky in Windsor Great Park.

'Was Jesus chaste?' (Blake)

The sex-impulse and the fire of divine love. The blessing of the harlot by Christ the beginning of a great process, unfinished when Lancelot lost his vision of the Sangreal, but achievable through the sublimation of Eros by the Embracing of the Divine correspondences. *She wiped his feet with her hair.* The eternal libido throbs through the heart of the creation, and is the creation. The Cross for Paul the contradiction of this principle, the demolition of the phallus; the Resurrection of Man in Eternal Day a liberation of all sexual impulse through the means of the new *agape*. Paul fears his own nature; he projects it into the cosmos, peopled by demons, homo-erotic orgies (see *Romans* i) a sinful race eternally punished by a vengeful All-Father who hates mankind. Jesus hates mankind. He loves the All-Father and melts the hard principle of *nomos* with the liberation of *agape*. *He is at the centre of the most highly charged scene in all literature, when the harlot wipes his feet with her hair.*

Our Father. God in creation is big with desire and makes love to our mother the earth. Men and women are at one with this creative spirit only when they have discarded the fear of Paul and Augustine and moved with the Sun and other stars. It is sex which makes them anew in God's image and likeness.

And from Galilee, riots, and tumults of the people, and
    mob-hysteria,
Such as possesses a tribe or *res publica* at certain seasons,
A huge uplifting of the collective soul, a great longing such
    as makes bloody revolutions, and brings down kings.

Marginal note: Lenin came to power when the Russian Church had developed its holiest tradition of startsi, or enlightened ones. Cromwell ushered in an era of the saints, ushered it in with blood.

And they, the Galileans, would make Yeshua their King!

Galilee not really converted to Judaism until two or three generations before Christ. Galileans are not Jews, slaves of the law, but natural man in his instinctive quest for the divinities.

He fed his folk with fish and bloated them with bread,
Five thousand at a sitting, as he preached to them the
    coming of the new Kingdom.

Saulos is far from the Kingdom, far in Jerusalem.
Punctilious civil servant in the palace of the High Priest,
Favourite protégé of the rabbis and the professors,
The rising Promise of the Vatican secretariat.

What could they do, these men of greyness, these fillers of
    filing cabinets,
With the knowledge that a new King had come into their
    midst?
What if he seized, this Yeshua, his crown by force? for, he
    was of the blood royal and beloved of the people.
Saulos was in love with the face of Yeshua Bar Yusif whom
    they called Messias!
Yeshua's words and face made Saulos desperately afraid!
Ever since their first meeting, in Yeshua's boyhood,
Fatal encounter in the tavern in Londinium,
Saulos had been haunted by this elusive divinity,
And since the descent of the dove by Jordan water,
Shouted of by the shaman Baptiser, but unseen to Saulos,
He had followed the Son of Man, noted His preachings and
    felt the power of his proclaimed freedoms!
Yeshua made crowds laugh with his satires against the
    Pharisees.
He mocked the solemn faces of Saulos and his Sanhedrin
    friends,
And imitated the way that they prayed at street corners,
And ridiculed their devotion to the Holy Torah of the
    Almighty.
The sabbath was made for man, and not man for the sabbath,
Thus he overthrew the divinely given concept of Law, and
    made men into gods!
For the Law was not made for men, to suit their pleasure,
Nor to provide them with some arbitrary sense of how to
    order their lives.
The Law was the revelation of the mind of God; it was an
    absolute and given thing,
Law symbolised and enshrined in *shabat,* in keeping of
    diet, in recitation of set prayers.
The Jews were made and chosen by God to follow this
    Law.
Man was made for the *shabat,* not the *shabat* for man.
But Yeshua had set this at naught, and wanted to throw
    over religion itself.
Saulos thrilled to contemplate the liberty of the sons of
    God,

But he hated this feeling of excitement, and fought against
   it.
It was so much easier, so much safer, to believe that man
   was made for the *shabat*,
Than to think the *shabat* was made for man.
It was easier to believe that all our moral and spiritual
   obligations
Can be fulfilled by following a religious set of rules,
Rather than leaping out to the great anarchic liberty which
   is the birthright of the sons of God!

Today, Saulos had returned to the Jordan-bank, to the
   haunts of the old Baptiser,
Joanes the ranter, whose head had been cut off by Herod,
To hear Yeshua preach to the crowds who came down
   from Jerusalem.
And with Saulos were some of his friends the Pharisees,
Hoping to heckle the heretic, and to catch him with subtle
   questions.
To none of his Pharisee friends had Saulos confided
His strong feelings of attraction and revulsion,
And now they stood, Saulos and Shimon and Mordecai,
   and other scribes and Pharisees,
Listening once more to that maddening, beguiling voice,
With its succinct phrases, its humour, its innocence,
Speaking to the rabble, and making them laugh, with his
   absurd jokes and stories.
He told of a Jewish woman who had lost one small coin,
And searched her house through with serious diligence,
Turning over rugs and bedding, peering beneath cooking
   pots,
Until in her relentlessly serious quest, the coin was
   discovered,
On the muddy kitchen floor beside the sack of barley-
   meal,
And in the triumph of her finding, she summoned the
   neighbours,
To rejoice with her in triumph at this trivial finding!
Thus the Divine Love in pursuit of our little man-soul
Is reduced to a matter of laughter by profane analogy!
Shuddering at the blasphemy, Shimon by Saulos's side,

Catches the preacher off guard by changing his subject,
And calls out a question of Yeshua about marriage and
   divorce.
'Is it lawful for a man to divorce his wife? Tell us!'
And Yeshua turns the question back – 'My friend, you are
   young!
To ask such a question implies impatience! Live a while
   longer and she will get used to you!'
Shimon scowls with fury as the crowd yelp with laughter.
'Answer me the question,' he repeats hotly, 'is divorce
   lawful?'
'What? A Pharisee who does not remember the Torah?
   What did Moses command you?'
'Moses allowed that a man should put away his wife,'
   responded Shimon.
'Then for hardness of heart did Moses command you.
What God joins together can never be sundered.'
But this wasn't an answer, this was merely scoring a point!
For Moses merely decreed the Law of God, and did Yeshua
   set the Law at naught?
But in the heart of Saulos there stirred a deep yearning
For the law that was written in hearts and not graven in
   stone,
And he could not believe that Shimon had said anything
   serious,
Anything which described the human condition, or
   charted the mysterious prompting of God's voice in the
   heart of Man,
And when the meeting broke up, Saulos was still rapt in a
   daydream of thought,
And he allowed his friends to return to Jerusalem, leaving
   him standing,
Alone and aloof, watching the figure of Yeshua, who sat by
   the river.
Women approached him with children, and asked for his
   blessing.
And Yeshua picked up the infants and held them aloft,
And made each one laugh with a kiss or a grotesque
   grimace, or by tickling its ribs,
Each unwashed urchin-brat, he blessed them and held
   them.

And Saulos, who hated children, watched dismayed,
Jealous of the easiness with which Yeshua loved them,
And jealous of the children who received his love.
And then Yeshua arose, and set out with his followers,
Walking in a crowd down the dusty road to town.
Saulos was led by an impulse which he could not control
To run after the teacher, to run and to follow,
To push past the crowds until he was close to the Master,
And to throw himself, breathless, at Yeshua's feet.
'My good sir,' he uttered, 'my good . . .' His voice faltered.
And 'Good?' answered Yeshua, 'why call me good? Only
    One is good, our Father in heaven.'
'Tell me,' said Saulos, 'what must I do to inherit
The eternal life of the Kingdom of which you speak in your
    teachings?'
'Why, follow the Torah,' said Yeshua, smiling. And Saulos
    felt mocked.
For dozens of times, he had made this reiteration.
And this seemed like a *shabat*-school answer in a syna-
    gogue.
Why did this smiling man treat him like a little child?
'Do not commit adultery, do not bear false witness,
Honour your father and mother – you must know the
    Law?'
'I do,' said Saulos, woundedly. He had hoped for an
    answer,
Glowing with subtlety, suffused with the love of God.
'I have kept all the law from my youth,' said the Pharisee
    Saulos.
Then Yeshua looked at him lovingly. Saulos felt then
All the love of the universe penetrate him through those
    dark, smiling eyes.
'You lack only one thing,' said Yeshua. 'Though you speak
With the tongues of men and of angels, you lack the divine
    love,
And you are imprisoned in possessions, and do not know
    the freedom of dispossession.
So, friend, go and sell your possessions and give to the
    poor,
And you will have treasure in heaven, and come – follow
    me!'

And Saulos looked down at his chest, and his clean, well-
made tunic,

And thought of his house in the city, with its airy, spacious
rooms,

And the money his father had made in the family tent-
enterprise.

He knew that the words of the preacher were true, but
they stung with their truth.

He had wanted to be confronted with a theological
argument,

And he had been met instead by an all-embracing life-
demand!

And he stood, and felt foolish to have come so close to
Yeshua,

And foolish to have hoped that this man would take him
seriously,

And homesick for his own kind, and his small collegium of
confrères.

And he turned from the crowd and left Yeshua behind
him, saying,

'You see how the rich cannot easily enter the Kingdom of
God!

In this world, the bigwigs have lordship, but not in that
kingdom,

And anyone wishing to enter the kingdom as a lord, must
bow low as a servant,

The rich must be poor, and the great must be small, and the
last must be first.'

These words Saulos heard as he hastened away, and his
walk turned to running.

A mile down the road, he encountered a caravan of camel
drivers walking,

Who gave, for a fee, a rest to his limbs, and allowed him to
ride to the city.

And as they ascended the hill to the city, he saw his young
Pharisee friends,

And they too had camels, and rode them right up to the
walls,

But had to dismount as they came to the foot-entrance,

Built in Jerusalem's wall, the small gate, and known as the
Eye of the Needle.

Waking at one a.m., I found the leaves of Rice Robey's strange effusion spread out confusedly across my chest, sheaves of almost transparent paper, smudged with carbon. I put them into a pile on the bedside table, lit a cigarette, switched off the lamp, and walked to the window. My bedroom was in the eighteenth-century wing of the house, overlooking the orangery.

A full moon lit the scene with eerie brightness. The branches of the cedars cast long black shadows on the smooth silver lawn. There were two figures discernible there, and in that strange light, they were possessed of a non-human quality. It might have been almost credible if they had turned out to be elves or fauns, or angels, they seemed so colourless and silvery as they walked beneath the sky. It was Kirsty and Rice Robey. He stood with both his arms above his head, and I could hear that he was speaking, without being able to make out what he said. He appeared to be looking up towards the moon, and perhaps it was to the moon, rather than to Kirsty, that he spoke. Then, in a moment of unforgettable intimacy, Kirsty, who had been standing some yards apart from this hierophantic figure with his outstretched arms, paced towards him, stroked his shoulder, and buried her face in his collar. His arms came down and enfolded her. I hastily withdrew from the window.

Earlier in the evening, Darnley and she appeared to be getting along together so well. I felt sad on his behalf. Involuntarily, I remembered the look of sadness on Darnley's face when I married Anne for whom (I suspect, but will never know for certain) he had nursed a soft spot. His extreme emotional diffidence did not seem to grow less with the years. I hoped that Kirsty had not been cruel, on the beach, when, presumably, she had shaken loose of him in order to walk alone with Rice Robey.

Breakfast was a help-yourself affair in the kitchen. Jo was frying eggs and bacon when I came down at about half-past nine. The older members of the party had all made a start on the day. Wimbish, who had no sabbatarian principles and to whom one day was exactly like another, was already at work on the Lampitt papers in the library. Lady Augusta had, I gathered, been to the early service in the parish church and returned, ravenous for the fry-up which she and Pat had consumed at about nine. Sargie had been taken a pot of coffee and some dry toast in bed. Kirsty and Rice Robey were not yet down. Only Jo and Darnley were in the kitchen when I entered it. Since I had not really eaten dinner, I ravenously accepted Jo's offer to cook me a plateful. I looked at Darnley pityingly. How bitter for him that, rather than sit with the clever, attractive sister, he should have been stuck there with Jo.

'I read that stuff,' I said to him.

'Great man, Pughie.'

I was not sure that this was true, still less sure that there was any evidence for such a belief in those crumpled quarto pages; but it wrung my heart to see that Darnley would be loyal to Rice Robey even though he had lost 'his' girl to him.

In the area of other people's emotional lives, one can leap to conclusions on no basis. Darnley had in fact given no indication that he was in love with Kirsty, or even that he found her sexually attractive. The fact that he had made her laugh at dinner did not mean anything. He was making Jo laugh now, and actually seemed in very good spirits, not in the least requiring my pity or sympathy.

Darnley was reading aloud from the Sunday newspapers in a different range of funny voices. It made Jo laugh so much that she broke my fried egg as she slithered it on to a slice of buttered toast. Absolutely anything Darnley said was capable of inducing in her new hysterics.

'Ah!' he said, in a simpering, Third Programme voice with a slight lisp on the 'r's. 'A new novel by Deborah Arnott . . . sensitive . . . the eternal triangle reworked in the setting of a Hampstead kitchen . . . a *tour de force*.'

Jo, who had almost certainly never heard of Deborah Arnott, found this so funny that she spewed out her coffee like a porpoise, a stream of brown liquid all over her jumper.

'Look . . .' she spluttered, 'I've spat all over my . . .' She could hardly utter the word 'tits', so funny she found everything.

When two people are in the grip of truly uncontrollable laughter about matters not in themselves remotely funny, there is something embarrassing about it, you feel like an intruder.

'I thought I'd go about eleven, if that suits you,' I said to Darnley. 'Give us time to reach Timplingham before lunch, and pick up Felicity as agreed.'

The arrangement had been perfectly clear, spoken about more than once on the previous day.

'You go,' said Darnley quietly and – for once – in his own voice. 'I'm going to stay on here for a bit.'

'But how will you get back to London?' I clumsily pursued.

'There are trains. I'll see, I'm staying a bit longer, that's all. You take the car – no difficulty about that.'

This was not meant as a joke, but it still made Jo guffaw.

When I had finished my breakfast, there seemed no point in hanging around. Vernon was having an interminable conversation with someone called Dick. I heard him saying, 'Yer should oppose it on the National Executive. . . . Granted, Dick, granted, but yer should oppose it now, or we'll have to carry it into the Election and it'll be a millstone round our necks. . . .' Pat had settled down in the morning room with Lady Augusta, who was reading a newspaper and silently munching her way through a plateful of custard creams, washed down by coffee. Kirsty had not yet come down; nor Rice Robey, nor Sargie. I was anxious to be on the road before Sargie surfaced, with more plots and schemes for a proposed biography of Jimbo.

'I think you should do it,' said Felicity, when we drove back to London together that afternoon. 'If Sargie helps out financially, that is. It might be absorbing and – perhaps it *ought* to be done. Perhaps you alone can set the record straight.'

'I hardly conceive it as a duty.'

'Telling the truth is always a duty. That sometimes takes the form of needing to contradict lies.'

Neither of us wished to discuss Raphael Hunter, so five or ten minutes of silence elapsed.

'Wasn't it a coincidence – Rice Robey turning up at Mallington?' Had she known that Rice Robey was to be of the party, Felicity would no doubt have felt differently about coming along with Darnley and myself. I did not know how she would have responded to Rice Robey's evident *tendresse* for Kirsty Lampitt.

'He's so anxious to save Aldingbury Ring from this new road development. He's exploring absolutely every avenue – even Vernon! I don't know what influence Vernon has, or will have, when there's a new government.'

'That seemed to be the excuse for Mr Robey coming to Mallington.'

'Dear R.R.,' she said quietly. 'I do worry about him.'

'He seemed perfectly cheerful yesterday evening.'

'Well, you don't know him as well as I do.'

I freely admitted that this was so, omitting to mention that I was happy to leave it that way.

'I think Darnley may be a bit in love,' I said. 'I'm sure he's only staying on at Mallington because he's smitten with Kirsty.'

I don't know what, exactly speaking, 'happened' at Mallington that weekend. I do not know now whether Darnley ever felt remotely in love with Kirsty, or whether it was always Jo that he loved. Because I had it in my head that he loved Kirsty, I disregarded all the evidence, of Jo and Darnley laughing together and hitting it off so well.

'Are his feelings for Kirsty reciprocated?'

'Not exactly.'

Not wishing to hurt Felicity's feelings, I had given a heavily edited version of events, and made no mention of Kirsty's moonlit walk on the lawn with Rice Robey.

Felicity stared out of the car window with infinite sadness. Then she spoke with a false, brittle brightness.

'No doubt I shall hear Rice Robey's stories about the weekend when I get to the office tomorrow morning.'

Three

Of my two small broadcasting jobs, I much preferred the work
for the World Service of the BBC. There was something different
to do each week for the literary programme on which I was
engaged as a reader. Sometimes I would be asked to read a
poem, or an extract from a recently published novel before the
book in question was discussed by a critic. Sometimes, Freddie
Vance, who produced the programme, got me to read a passage
from some well-established author, or from a book which he
considered ready for revival. One week I might therefore be
reading a few paragraphs from the latest Deborah Arnott novel;
the next, an ode by Keats or a passage from Sir Thomas Browne.
It was in the best sense of the word a bookish programme,
designed for those who enjoy reading, rather than for those who
merely wished to keep up with the latest publications. Freddie
was rather a charming man – a clergyman's son. He was about
ten years older than myself and his parsonage-upbringing was
more rarefied than my own, his father having become a
Catholic. We sometimes had a drink or a meal together after the
recording. We were not intimates, and we did not discuss our
personal lives. I think he was married to a schoolmistress in
Amersham. I once knew, but have now forgotten, whether or
not he had himself once been a teacher. If so, he would not have
been a teacher like my own old English master, Treadmill, with
a gift for projecting his personality, but instead, the quiet,
colourless sort of schoolmaster of whom, having left school, one
retains no memory at all. He wore tweed jackets, corduroy
trousers and was half bald. His talk was punctuated with archaic,
sub-Wodehousian locutions. He tended to call me a dear fellow.
One could imagine him refereeing games of rugby between
teams made up of the less able players.

One day, when we were in the canteen of Bush House
discussing the contents of future programmes, he put a couple of

old green and white Penguins beside his plate of baked beans on toast and tapped them with stubby fingers.

'I'm wondering whether to do five minutes on this writer,' he said. 'There used to be a bit of a cult of his novels during the war – you're too young to remember that, my dear fellow. Oh, damn.'

A baked bean had fallen from his fork on to the back of *Memphian Mystery*. He retrieved the bean with his fingertips, ate it, and then, with a paper napkin, he rubbed at the small stain left by the tomato sauce just to the left of the photograph of the author on the back of the book.

'These are the author's own copies,' he said.

'Albion Pugh's?'

'Yes. I don't normally let my arm be twisted by authors – got to be tough with these blokes, my dear fellow, don't you know, but my missus has rather a thing about these particular books. Tickled pink when she heard I'd met Albion Pugh.'

'Where was this?'

'He didn't want to meet at our regular, and he wouldn't come and meet me here. Said it wasn't quite safe for him to be seen on Corporation premises. Said he needed to meet on neutral territory. All very hush hush. So we had gin at a strange old tavern behind Charing Cross station. Dripping old place, practically had stalactites coming down from the ceiling, or is it the stalagmites which come down?'

'Stalactites come down,' I said, remembering a useless piece of information which Lollipop Lew, a master at my prep school, had once taught us – 'Little mites grow upwards.'

'Eh? Oh, mites! Rather good. I'll remember that. Albion Pugh told me this bar where he took me had been there ever since the reign of Charles II. I think it was actually below the river. He said that the Popish Plot had been hatched there.'

'I thought the Popish Plot never happened – wasn't that the whole point of it – Titus Oates made it up?'

'Strange bird, Mr Pugh.'

'Really?'

'He was very keen that we should read his stuff on the programme; he brought along these two, and said I was to guard them with my life.'

'Oddly enough, I read *Memphian Mystery* for the first time not long ago. It's a favourite book of a cousin of mine.'

'What did you think of it?'

'A very gripping story, almost unbelievably badly written; so badly written, you could not imagine that it was not done deliberately, for some bizarre reason.'

'I told him my missus dotes on his books. He told me *his* missus loves "Bookrest". She particularly liked the one we did a few weeks ago about Pepys. By the way, Pepys used to go to this bar Mr Pugh took me to. I never knew he was a Rosicrucian, did you?'

'Albion Pugh or Samuel Pepys?'

'Pepys. Apparently, that cipher the diary is written in has all the hallmarks of a secret cabalistic cult or something. He had a whole theory about it.'

'Really?'

This was all too predictable. I was much more interested in the woman referred to by Freddie as Mr Pugh's 'missus', that is, 'the Great Attachment'.

'So he told you he was married?' The crude approach seemed easiest with Freddie.

'Had some name for her – what is it now? The Great something. Obviously very attached to her, as all right-thinking blokes are to their missuses.'

This was so much at variance from my own way of viewing human relations, this assumption that it was a matter of virtue, rather than of luck, whether one happened to enjoy the company of a domestic partner, that I said nothing.

'Full of weird talk, though.'

'About this woman?'

'Funnily enough' – Freddie's voice sank to a whisper – 'it was about the dear old Beeb. First there was some stuff about our esteemed DG. Albion Pugh had some very wild things to say about him. You would think the DG was a communist agent to hear Mr Pugh talking. I shut him up pretty quickly, of course. We don't want that sort of talk. Oh, he's not really called Pugh, by the way.'

Freddie was one of those innocents who clearly did not enjoy, as, say, Darnley did, wild speculation about his fellow mortals, nor a suggestion that all is not as it seems in the various organisations and establishments (the Civil Service, the BBC) by which society is run. I took it that there was some moral virtue in Freddie's distaste, without being able to see what it was. In spite of finding Rice Robey a strange bird, Freddie decided, in the event, to do a short feature on the Albion Pugh novels in a few weeks' time. There was to be a reading by myself and then a brief analysis of the books by a critic.

Much of the material for these programmes was recorded but Freddie liked, if possible, to assemble the separate items of his 'magazine' during the space of one afternoon; so, I quite often bumped into my fellow contributors. I was scheduled to read out the prepared passage – it was the moment in *Memphian Mystery* when the professor opens the mummy and finds the ark of bulrushes in which the infant Moses floated on the Nile – after the critic had recorded his say. I reached the studio and sat in the outer room with Freddie and the production team until it was my turn to sit in the sound-proofed glazed box with a microphone. The figure at present occupying this position, slouched at the round, baize-covered table and rustling his script nervously, was my old schoolmaster Treadmill, who quite frequently gave broadcast talks.

'If we can just have one more sentence for level, Val,' said Freddie.

Treadmill made the weary sound which one of my school contemporaries once described as an old sheep having an orgasm, a sort of 'yeair' sound, but muted, mumbled.

'I've already given you one sentence,' he said.

'Just a small technical difficulty. We weren't receiving you very clearly. Is that all right now, Jake?'

Whatever Jake, the sound recordist, had to say was drowned by a deafeningly piercing high-pitched squeak. There was then a silence. Through the glass which divided us from the studio I could see Treadmill talking but no sound communicated itself to the equipment on our side of the glass. Freddie good-humouredly made semaphore-like gestures with his script, and then spoke again.

'Bear with us, Val. Small technical fault.'

Treadmill was ageing. His moustaches were whiter, his skin sallower. His clothes, a capacious suit of stuff not unlike sacking, hung yet more loosely from his thin shoulders. He was by now glaring at Freddie. In a school setting, his cold rages, whether real or simulated, had a power to wither the most boisterous of childish high spirits. Nobody had ever been known to misbehave in Treadmill's classes. In this context, confronted by another grown-up supposedly in charge, Treadmill's display of

632

wrath seemed merely petulant. When the sound mechanism was made to function properly, he read his well-turned four minutes of reflection upon the novels of Albion Pugh. The point he made about them was that they were a wartime phenomenon. At that date, the conflicts in which Europe was engulfed appeared to call for metaphysical answers. Fighting against Hitler, the Allies had felt themselves to be wrestling with principalities and powers of darkness. In such a world, a writer with a blatantly supernatural viewpoint made an immediate appeal. His stories all had the qualities of a good yarn, as if Rider Haggard or Conan Doyle had chosen to highlight the implicit moralism of their stories by the introduction of quasi-magical themes. He rounded off his four minutes with one of his favourite old chestnuts, Samuel Johnson's 'Nothing odd will do long – *Tristram Shandy* did not last.' Some oddities did, like Sterne's great novel, last, Treadmill stated, but it was too early to say whether the novels of Albion Pugh would sink without trace or be remembered, as he would think they deserved to be remembered, as one of the most distinctive contributions to English fiction during the Second World War.

It did not take long, when my turn came to sit in front of the microphone, to read the required passage. When recording 'The Mulberrys' in Birmingham, I never, strange to say, had much sense of the devoted audience who day by day lapped up the doings of the inhabitants of Barleybrook. With the broadcasts from Bush House, it was all different. There, the magic of radio often gripped me, the fact that sound waves could transcend time zones, land and sea and be picked up by transmitters all over the world. I sat in a studio in the Aldwych reading a book. Later that night, insomniacs like the Great Attachment could lie in bed at two a.m. and listen to my voice in Kentish Town or Cumberland. At the same time, with clocks set to different hours and with the sun in a different position in the sky, the voice would, or could, be heard in Malaya, Africa, the United States. Far-flung Lampitt cousins could hear it in Mombasa or Johannesburg. In the suburbs of Los Angeles it could be picked up in broad limousines gliding along the freeway. In some downtown bar in Rio de Janeiro the same voice, at the same moment, could be crackling out Albion Pugh's words, while simultaneously they could be heard in some mission hut in Borneo or a sheep station in New Zealand. It made me think of the evening hymn,

As o'er each continent and island
The dawn leads on another day,
The voice of prayer is never silent,
Nor dies the strain of praise away.

The voice of the BBC was similarly unstoppable, a disagreeable fact if considered in the wrong mood but by another token strangely consoling, bringing the sense that since the advent of this incomprehensible invention the inhabitants of our planet will never quite know solitude in the sense that their ancestors knew it. I did not delude myself into believing that everyone in the world tuned in to 'Bookrest'. Of course, hardly anyone knew of its existence. It was not the numbers of those listening which moved me, it was the possibility of their doing so and their infinite distance from my own circumstances.

I handed back *Memphian Mystery* to Freddie who said, 'Now I've got to toil up to the blighter's house. He insisted on having the books delivered back to him by hand.'

'Where does he live?'

'Gospel Oak, roughly. Miles out of my way.'

'I could take them.'

'I say, my dear fellow, could you really?'

'If you could give me the address. It doesn't sound as if it is too far from where I live myself.'

A curiosity to see Rice Robey's ménage, more than any charitable impulse to spare Freddie trouble, explained my offer. It was soon arranged that I should deliver the books at 77 Twisden Road, NW5 on my way home.

'We had Albion Pugh down to speak to the Lampitt Club,' said Treadmill afterwards. We had woven a path through swing doors and subterraneous, ill-lit corridors to the canteen for a cup of tea.

'No one would say that his novels were – yeair – well *made*, but as Louis MacNeice, surprisingly an enthusiast, said in a pub not two miles from where we sit – as it happens, the Black Bottle which you know well; Joyce Cary was there, I remember, and Julian Maclaren Ross – "Pugh can hear the music of the spheres".'

'He can certainly hear something inaudible to the rest of us.'

'When I asked him to address the Lampitt, I had absolutely no idea – how could I? – that he had actually *known* . . .'

'James Petworth Lampitt himself; he was something of a mentor.'

'Did he come to address the Lampitt, then, in your time in the school?'

'No. I happen to have met him since.'

Treadmill did not look particularly pleased by this claim.

'I wonder, though, if you were in the school when a very much *less* interesting writer, Raphael Hunter, came to give a talk on Lampitt himself?'

'That was when I first met Hunter.'

It was tactless to have intruded the word 'first' into that sentence.

Treadmill really preferred to be the one with literary acquaintances. For a second or two his face assumed the indignant expression it had worn if a boy had the temerity to be late handing in prep, or displayed some other failure to play life's game by Treadmill's rules.

'Don't overstretch yourself, Julian. I mean, *socially*. Was it Evelyn Waugh who said that only bores know everyone? The remark was not made to me by Waugh in person but quoted to me, when he came to address the Lampitt Club, by an old chum of mine and his, incidentally, called Henry Yorke.'

Treadmill seemed the natural person with whom to discuss my professional dilemma. As briefly as possible I explained that, a couple of months before, Sargie had asked me to write the 'official' life of his brother.

'I could give you a certain amount of help over Lampitt's schooldays,' said Treadmill. 'I investigated the matter in some detail. It's not all – yeair – as you would quite imagine. My only fear about a *book* on Lampitt is that he is not perhaps sufficiently a heavyweight. You perhaps remember the disobliging phrase used by D. H. Lawrence in one of his letters about J.P.L.'

'I don't remember, but I can guess the kind of thing.'

'I see the justice of the gadfly comparison, though the part of the sentence about excrement . . .'

Treadmill laughed into his tea.

I continued to explain myself. It was not that I was burning with an immediate desire to write the life of Jimbo Lampitt. Sargie and Vernon between them, however, had made me a kind offer which was highly alluring. They would pay me a small retainer in exchange for being Sargie's assistant and secretary for two or three days each week. During those weeks when Sargie could find nothing for me to do, Vernon would enlist my help in making his own notes and papers into an orderly archive. In the meantime, they were scouting around the London publishers for someone who would take on, either a one-volume life of Jimbo or – an idea which Vernon slightly preferred – a general history of the Lampitt family, from Radical Jo to the present day.

The objections to this scheme were obvious. I did not wish to be Sargie's creature and slave as, for years, my Uncle Roy had been. Nor, if I wrote the book, did I want the Lampitts looking over my shoulder and determining what I said. If, upon investigation, it turned out that Hunter's 'hints' were accurate, for example, and if Jimbo had indeed led a very irregular sexual life, then I wanted to be at liberty to say so, regardless of the feelings of Pat, Sibs, Sargie, Vernon, Ursula and the rest of them.

On the other hand, if I wrote the book, it would provide me with the excuse to escape Jason Grainger. Treadmill was the man who had got me this role, being himself an occasional scriptwriter for 'The Mulberrys'. I knew that he would be able to offer sensible advice.

' "The Mulberrys" provide you with very regular work,' he said.

'But is it work I can continue for ever?'

'Your slightly bizarre friend Kempe has settled down very happily as Stan Mulberry, though in my consideration . . .'

I always forgot how seriously Treadmill took this drama series. He brought as much critical weight to his analysis of Stan Mulberry's nature as to the many old essay themes, so endlessly rehearsed in his classroom, of character and motive in Shakespeare.

We wandered out together towards the Aldwych.

'And there's always the simple consideration, as Wystan, of all people, sensibly once said to me – *Never turn down easy money.*'

'I don't intend to.'

'Good. You never knew Aaron Samuelson at school, did you? He's a year or two older than you.'

'It's not a name that's familiar.'

'My God, what an able boy *he* was! Abler, if I may say so, than you were yourself. He was no mean poet as a boy, and then surprised us all by getting a job in the Bank.'

'Mr Eliot would have understood.'

'Indeed. Samuelson and his charming wife are – yeair – putting me up tonight. There'll be several old pupils coming to dinner. Do you remember Garforth-Thoms?'

'Yes. What's he up to?'

'A parliamentary career in prospect, though not, I regret to say, as a member of the party which I, and I suspect you, would support. Had I known I was going to bump into you, I should have suggested to Samuelson that you came along.'

'No, really.'

A reunion of old schoolfellows was not my idea of a congenial evening.

'I'm beginning to scent victory in the air. They'll have to have an election soon, and I think the Tories will lose. The tactlessness of appointing a fourteenth earl as our Prime Minister, the undemocratic way in which it was done, these things will have their just reward. . . .'

'I wish I found the Labour leadership more attractive.'

'One step forward, two steps back. I believe that was how Lenin defined socialism. I never knew Lenin, of course, but Beatrice Webb, who knew him well . . .'

'This is my bus.'

It was rude of me to break him off in mid-sentence, but in those days Number 27s were a rarity. The appearance of one at the bus stop as we spoke was not an opportunity to be passed over lightly. I was particularly anxious to call on the Great Attachment.

I had not set eyes on Rice Robey in the months which had intervened since I stayed at Mallington. This by no means meant that he had been absent from my thoughts; in fact, he had been almost more vividly present to me through the conversations of other people than if I had been meeting him on a regular basis myself.

Human beings, particularly those of a vaguely mysterious character, exist for us less in their own impenetrable essence than in the mind of others. In the case of Rice Robey, my own inability to decide what he was really like was increased by the extraordinary vividness with which others, notably Darnley and Felicity, had imagined him, so that in hearing their projections of his character, I was confronted by a far more assimilable figure than the man whom I had so fleetingly met. That is to say, they had a coherent picture of the man, whereas I, if I had to rely on my own impressions alone, could not put together the disparate signals which I felt myself to be receiving in his presence.

Jo Lampitt, who had thrown up her job in Ely and was now working in Darnley's office in some supposedly secretarial capacity, had a different vision again. When I met her and Darnley one evening in a pub, she spoke with a lack of subtlety which enabled me, at any rate, to adjust the figure of Rice Robey into some kind of focus.

'Kirsty's *really*, really' (she pronounced the word *rarely*) 'got the hots for him. You'd have thought he'd have done it with her by now, but poor little Kirsty! She thinks, now, he never will! He's the opposite of a cock tease.'

'You don't mean the opposite,' said Darnley, 'you mean the male equivalent.'

'Shut up, you.' She biffed him good-humouredly with an elbow.

'Cunt tease, I suppose it would be. I think Kirsty's nuts, but that's not surprising after the things they've been taking together.'

'What sort of things?'

'I wouldn't touch his concoctions, but Kirsty does, she's crazy! She offered him a joint, right, and he smoked it with her. But then he took her for this really, really creepy late-night walk in Cambridge and they found these mushrooms he made her eat. They're really, really mind-blowing, apparently, and I think it's really, really frightening.'

It was a number of years before I heard of anyone else exploiting the hallucinogenic properties of mushrooms. Rice Robey did not regard it as a fad of the age. He thought it was a secret which had been transmitted, not through fashionable representatives of the 'drug culture' but through the same hidden oral traditions which handed down cures and spells, guarded the secret whereabouts of ley-lines and magic circles, or preserved the old tales of King Arthur, or of Herne the Hunter.

'They don't do anything, though!'

'Isn't this true of most people who make friends?'

'Of course it is,' said Darnley.

'Shut up, I tell you!' She was fiercer with Darnley now, and evidently felt that she should do all the talking. She certainly did not want to be contradicted. I do not know why it should have been so sinister that Rice Robey had not actually made love to Kirsty, but somehow this was what one did begin to sense, even before Jo's next revelation.

'You see, they have been to bed – he insisted. But nothing happened.'

'That was bad luck,' I said.

'It wasn't bad luck, dumbo!' I thought 'dumbo' was ripe, coming from her. At this point Darnley interrupted her narrative with a shorter version of his own.

'Rice Robey missed his train back to London from Cambridge and got Kirsty to put him up. It would seem that there was only one bed, which they shared, but with no intention on his side that they might have any leg-over.'

'Doesn't it give you the creeps, Mr Grainger?' Jo asked me, wide-eyed. 'Think of it, all night long, lying there. Kirsty really, really having the hots.'

'We've got the general idea,' said Darnley.

Jo put her tongue out at him and said, 'What's the matter, aren't I allowed to talk, or something?'

'I always knew that Pughie was a bit of a dirty old man,' said Darnley. 'But it's all slightly different with him.'

'You could say it was different! I wouldn't want to go to bed with a dirty old wanker if he didn't want to do it. Different! Kinky, more like.'

I saw what Darnley was trying to say, though I was not really convinced by his words. What was striking was that Jo so obviously missed the point. She genuinely supposed that 'different' was being used by Darnley to convey a bizarre erotic preference.

'Kirsty was practically starkers, and there he lay with his clothes on – that's different, if you like.'

I wondered how long I myself would survive with a girlfriend who did not quite understand anything which was said to her. Darnley appeared to be very happy. Her abrasiveness with him, and her willingness to speak so openly of matters which in grown-up life he had always seemed too embarrassed to discuss, seemed very congenial to him. He held her hand and smiled. I had never seen him hold anyone's hand before, or display any physical signs of affection for another human being.

'I've told Miles he shouldn't print this wanker Pugh's stories in *The Spark*,' said Jo. 'That one about the old poof being murdered – my cousin – there wasn't a shred of – Mama said he wasn't a poof anyway – always having it away with Sargie's wife.'

'I don't think that's quite true,' I said, with the condescending certainty of someone who regarded himself as an expert in the subject.

'We'll have to see about printing Pughie's stuff about Hunter,' said Darnley.

'Well, I say you're not to put it in.'

Three months earlier, if a typist in Darnley's office had offered her opinions on the verisimilitude of Rice Robey's stories, he would have laughed her aside. It was now obvious that he would take some notice of Jo's desires and opinions in the matter.

To Jo's disconcerting evidence about Rice Robey, I had to add the daily chronicles fed to me by Felicity. Jo Lampitt was too stupid to make things up. I was sure that there was something between Kirsty and Rice Robey. I was also prepared to believe that he was a person of intuitive power, an accomplished gossip and perhaps, in spite of Jo's malice about him, something of a sage. The fragmentary leaves of his religious epic, or however you chose to categorise it, were not in the least to my taste, but in their crude way they drew attention to a fundamental truth about the way we view the world, a truth which Rice Robey himself exemplified in his effects on those around him. That is, that it matters far more how a person is perceived than what they are actually like. However one viewed his theory that St Paul had a hand in the Crucifixion itself, it was incontestable that Christianity had begun, as far as the literary records shed light on the question, not with documentary or eyewitness memories of Christ, nor with any biographical details concerning his appearance, habits, marital status. Nor had this religion begun with Christ's reported sayings. As it first arrived in the Mediterranean ports of Asia Minor – Corinth, Ephesus, Thessaloniki – Christianity was something buzzing about in the mind of St Paul. It was Paul's perception of Jesus as a mythological being of cosmic importance which converted the members of the early church. They could not read the Gospels, which did not exist, and probably did not know stories of the goodness or wisdom of the actual historical personage who walked the roads of Galilee, teaching and healing. To the Thessalonians, Christ was a figure imminently expected to appear on the clouds to gather them up into the sky before they had known bodily death; to the Corinthians, he was the New Adam, the man who undid the death of the Old Adam by dying on a Forbidden Tree. It was Paul's capacity not merely to mythologise, but to communicate his vision, which transformed the world and brought Christendom to birth, with all its arcane theological preoccupations, its acrimonious councils about the exact nature of the person of Christ, its savagely cruel defences of intellectually untenable propositions, its persecution of heresies, its formulation of creeds, its wars of ideas, its sects, its factions. 'Albion Pugh', by contrast with the unbelieving bishops of the Anglican Church, could see that the craziness of St Paul did not, when recognised, diminish the Christian religion so much as place it within a comprehensible range of human experience. It was precisely because St Paul did not produce 'facts' which were capable of empirical discussion in the prosaic world of 'Either/ or' that he was able to revolutionise the world.

The journey to Rice Robey's house was rather more of a trek than I had foreseen. Between Tufnell Park and Gospel Oak, there is an infinite sea of dull Edwardian houses. Twisden Road was no nicer, if anything rather nastier, than the other streets in the vicinity; Number 77 (was the mystic number of importance to its occupants?) was much like all the other houses in the road. Darkness was closing in by the time I approached the front door, but by the garish street-lamp, I could make out the diminutive front garden, the peeling paintwork on the front door (colour indiscernible in that light which made of everything a fluorescent orange) and window-boxes sprouting dried-out sprigs of plants which had long ago died of cold or thirst; the remains of Michaelmas daisies, swamped, like the good seed in the Bible, by weeds. Across the windows themselves were drawn greyish, yellowing Nottingham lace curtains, beyond which a chilly electric bulb was visible, shining unshaded.

My offer to return the two paperbacks to their author began to seem rash. Curiosity had prompted me to it, but now my intrusion on that scene filled me with foreboding. Rice Robey had never been quite a serious character to me. My failure to get him into any sort of focus, or to understand him, sprang largely from this fact; the knowledge that Darnley and Felicity took him on the whole completely seriously only increased my own inability to do so. Now, however, before his own front door, the joke wore thin, and evaporated altogether. Domestic unhappiness, the source of so many good jokes when viewed from the blessed distance where mothers-in-law, errant wives or husbands and sexual incompatibility are all matters for ribald laughter, cannot be enjoyed close up. Already, in my various discussions about Rice Robey I had found myself censoring details and not passing on to one party what I had learned from another; and this was because I could not mistake his power of making other people, especially Felicity, unhappy. I had told her nothing, for example, of Rice Robey's behaviour at Mallington except to report that he had badgered Vernon for promises that the Labour Government, when it came, would protect his beloved stone circle, and all other sacred and magical places of old Britain. Felicity therefore knew nothing of his midnight walk with Kirsty, of the girl pawing his arm and looking at him with such adoration, nor of his subsequent visits to Cambridge. My desire to protect Felicity had made me similarly diffident when talking to Darnley, the more so since Jo now seemed privy to all his thoughts, and I certainly did not want her crude misrepresentations of Felicity's devotion to Rice Robey to be circulated for the entertainment of Jo's friends. It was obvious that Felicity was suffering acutely. The office dramas which she recited to me nowadays had a much reduced cast-list. All the figures in it, from the head of department down to the office boys and, when she dared to mention them, the temporary typists were now brought in to her evening narratives not as characters in their own right but as extras in the grand Rice Robey play.

Darnley's hero-worship of 'Pughie' enabled him in effect to turn a blind eye to Rice Robey's foibles. Felicity's devotion to the man took the more dangerous form of believing that she saw his faults, but that she, and she alone, could cure them. His mischief-making in the office, his sense that the hierarchy of the Civil Service were out to 'get' him, his wandering hands whenever a pretty girl popped up from the typing pool, his stream of little letters, notes, quotations jotted on cards and memo-slips, to a wide variety of female acquaintance – were all signals to Felicity of his need to be loved. It was a need which she felt manifestly ready to supply. Abject love, when viewed from the outside, has something pitiable in it, even when it is reciprocated. It looks like a sort of lunacy. The cliché of popular phraseology seemed entirely apt to describe Felicity's position. She was 'mad about' Rice Robey, crazy on him. When I first became aware that her interest in him was out of control, I assumed that there was a level of artifice, even of playful deception, in her idea that Rice Robey and she positively *needed* to meet for snatched, semi-secret, sandwich lunches or drinks after work, in order to discuss office politics, or his famous 'ideas', or his state of mind. After a while, it seemed so obvious to me that they were just meeting for fun, because they found it emotionally compulsive and not because of the threatened henge nor because Rice Robey's battle with the head of department could conceivably have been advanced towards its conclusion by yet another three-quarters of an hour with Felicity.

'He *needs* to talk, he needs *me*,' she said.

I soon came to see that she believed this, and that she had come to see herself as his saviour, above all as his consolation for what Darnley called 'the wretched situation' at home.

'I think if we knew everything R.R. has to put up with from that woman, we should realise that he was a saint,' Felicity once remarked with quiet intensity.

Another time, she said, 'He stays with her out of pure goodness. Anyone else would have had her put away years ago. The strain of living with mental unbalance, paranoia on that scale, is bound to exact its toll. I'm just thankful that I've come into R.R.'s life at this juncture. I know it sounds conceited, but I honestly think he might have collapsed if it had not been for me.'

This sentence, not really characteristic of my cousin – one could not imagine her boasting about how good she was with her parents, for example – made me recognise how deep Felicity had plunged.

Now that I stood before the Great Attachment's front door, I felt every possible misgiving.

'She hates him to have friends,' Felicity had told me once of

Mrs Paxton. 'If she hears he has been seeing a friend she really makes him suffer for it afterwards; even a male friend. Mentioning his friendship with me just wouldn't be *worth* all the tears, and shouting and explanations. That's why we meet in secret now.'

The bell which I tried at Number 77 did not appear to work, so I lifted the doorknocker, a cast-iron dolphin solid with paint, and gave three raps on the door.

A rasping voice, with the faintest tinge of the Edinburgh accent, said, 'I heard the bell. There was no need to knock as well.'

I looked about for the source of this apparently disembodied sound. It would have been fitting for Rice Robey to share his life with a spirit, a banshee, a poltergeist. An upstairs window was thrown open and the filthy lace curtain flapped in the damp evening wind. The voice came from behind this veil, and when I had taken a few steps backward and looked up, I could make out, behind the lace, the silhouette of a woman's head and shoulders.

'Is this where Mr Robey lives?'

'We don't belong to any Christmas Club. We don't fill in the football pools.'

'If this is the wrong address . . .'

'You're not a Jehovah's Witness, are you?'

'No.'

'They *do* want shooting.'

Her tone implied that we had already been conversing for some time, that I had been consigning whole categories of comparatively innocent people to the firing squad, but that she had at last found some worthier candidates for this particular form of punishment.

'No, no. I've brought Mr Robey some books.'

'So you *are* a Jehovah's Witness. That was how you got in the last time.'

'His own books. This is Mr Robey's house? Mr Rice Robey? He lent them to the BBC. I've brought them back.'

'You see, this is such a very awkward time.'

'I'm sorry.'

'I don't know, really. You see . . . Look, I'll come down.'

The window slammed. After two or three minutes, there was a sound from the other side of the door of bolts being drawn back, chains unhitched, the full paraphernalia of the suburban portcullis raised.

'Only,' she said as she opened the door, by way of explanation for the elaborate barricades, 'you get some funny people down this road.'

She herself was living proof of the statement.

Her shortish hair was iron-grey. A completely colourless face was brightened by a splash of scarlet applied to thin lips, lipstick which both in shade and texture might have been left over from the war. It was slightly smeared.

'Only,' she repeated (it seemed her sole conjunction), 'I have to listen in just now, if you will forgive me.'

It was years since I had heard anyone speak of 'listening in', the phrase my parents always used when preparing themselves for a session with the wireless.

Steel-rimmed spectacles gave her an intellectual appearance belied by her general manner and her talk. At first glance, she might have been some lesbian science professor, possibly German. She wore a severe navy blue suit on the breast of which had fallen a certain amount of cigarette ash. Ancient peep-toe shoes revealed the red-painted toe-nails, themselves ancient. I had not reckoned on her being so very old. We moved through the shadows of the hallway and into the back parlour at a tortuous pace, the Great Attachment with one mottled hand pressing the wainscoting for support as she went along; the other hand held the ignited cigarette.

'Silly, really,' she said, 'but I'm afraid I shall have to ask you to . . .'

As we reached the back parlour she scanned the ludicrous Tudorbethan long-case clock of 1910 vintage and murmured, 'We're all right.'

She conveyed the sense that if we had not arrived in the room on time, it would have been a disaster.

'Could you? Thanks!'

The gnarled claws which clutched the cigarette gestured frantically towards a wooden wireless set which made my Aunt Deirdre's obsolete Bakelite affair seem *à la mode*. The train of association was not inapposite; I realised a split second before turning on, and hearing the familiar Mulberry music, the reason for the Great Attachment's anxiety. Like Aunt Deirdre, and a million other people in the British Isles, she clearly found

645

intolerable the possibility of an evening passing without tuning in to the fictitious world of Barleybrook. She gestured me towards a chair, herself collapsing into a bulbous chintz armchair by the gas fire, stabbing her cigarette in the already brimming ashtray at her elbow and lighting another immediately as her face became abstracted, lost in Mulberrydom.

Jason Grainger was being a particular shit at that juncture of village history. I had been getting on badly with the ever-volatile producer, and it was touch and go whether, before I had decided myself to bow out of the series, Rodney would not have had one of his 'little words' with the scriptwriter, ensuring that Jason had an extended holiday or, if I was really out of favour, some nasty accident. The way Jason drove that E-type, it was always on the cards that he would crash it into the back of a horse-box or a tractor. It was one of the more curious features of the BBC stinginess that none of the actors on 'The Mulberrys' had any guarantee of tenure, nor even of regular work. This was as true of the national institutions, such as Stan Mulberry or Harold Grainger, as it was for the more peripheral characters in the drama such as Jason. If Rodney were feeling miffed, or if the scriptwriter just felt unable to write a particular character into the story-line for a few weeks, then the actor concerned went unpaid. The more colourless characters such as the vicar or the doctor sometimes had no work for months. I at least could not complain of Jason leading a dull life. Having tried to seduce Stan's daughter in a hayloft – she had run away screaming – Jason had consoled himself by smoking a cigarette and throwing the lighted butt into a bale. Thanks to the foresight of Stan's teenage boy Trevor, the extent of the fire damage was contained (what a crush Rodney had at that time on Johnny Bateman, who played Trevor), but there was talk of prosecuting Jason for arson; the further hint that Jason dealt in stolen property provided Rodney with another excuse, should he need one, to give me my marching orders.

That evening's episode found Miss Carpenter, the district nurse, local mercury and purveyor of gossip, with a gaggle of her fellow church-fowl cleaning the church in readiness for the Advent carols. A fairly boring antiquarian element had been introduced (the chief scriptwriter liked that sort of thing) but even this harmless tedium had been shaped, on Rodney's instructions, to point the accusing finger at Jason.

'They do say that old chalice the vicar discovered is medieval,' said Miss Carpenter. 'I say, Dol, you've left some polish on the eagle's beak.'

'Soon have that clean, Miss Carpenter.'

[Exaggerated huffs and puffs. The amount of energy the women were exerting in burnishing the brass eagle-lectern sounded as if it would have been sufficient to project the bird on to the church roof.]

'Much too valuable to be left lying for long in the vestry cupboard, the vicar says. That flimsy padlock on the cupboard door wouldn't deter a really hardened thief.'

'Oh, but Miss Carpenter. You don't get that nasty type of behaviour in Barleybrook.'

This was in general true. Barleybrook was an Elysian England almost untainted by the inheritance of original sin. True, the Swills ran a pretty filthy farm and had been known to water the milk. Reg, the landlord of the King's Head, drank too much and got on badly with his wife. The general impression conveyed by the programme, though, was of a bucolic paradise which would have been much to Shakespeare's taste when in Forest of Arden vein. There was no attempt to convey either the stultifying dullness of life in the real English countryside, nor the boot-faced oikishness of its actual inhabitants. Barleybrook had none of the smouldering feuds which I knew divided the farming people of Timplingham. No one in Barleybrook sodomised their sisters or their rams. Sheep could safely graze there. It is true that the villagers drove cars and tractors, and the women had perms, but nothing fundamental appeared to have changed in the rural paradise of old England since Justice Shallow sat in his orchard or Rosalind gambolled with Orlando in the woods. No one emphasised 'The Mulberrys'' place in the old pastoral traditions more exaggeratedly than the village blacksmith, Jason's Dad, Harold Grainger, whose memories of the place in the old days when swains sang folksongs and used hand ploughs owed more to the scriptwriter's weakness for minor Thomas Hardy novels than to any observed feature of behaviour among contemporary agricultural communities.

'Pointa scrumpy, ole dear,' Harold Grainger was saying to the barman at the King's Head, 'oh, 'ow oi loiks moy scrumpy.'

'There yar, then, 'Arold. 'Ear about this valuable goblet what the parson discovered?'

I mulled over this exchange as we sat, the Great Attachment and I, listening to her wireless, and I tried to imagine myself, during my own career as a barman saying it; tried to think of any bar in the kingdom where such a sentence could plausibly have been uttered.

'Oh, ar, the goblet. Moy Jason, 'eem a bin talking to paarson about it. Noice ter see the boy with a bit of an interest. Go all the way to Selchester 'e done to borra a book from the libree, primeval treasure or summat.'

'Medieval the vicar says it was.'

'Ar. Medi-um-eval, ole dear.'

We listened in reverent silence. Unlike Aunt Deirdre, the Great Attachment did not answer back to the Mulberry characters. No words escaped her lips. She sat rapt, until the last scene, which switched back to the church vestry where (a little predictably) Miss Carpenter found the padlock wrenched from the cupboard door, the ancient chalice stolen and a packet of flashy cigarettes of the brand smoked by Jason and no one else in Barleybrook, lying on the floor.

The Great Attachment sighed and smiled impishly.

'Hope he gets away with it – just between ourselves,' she said. 'It's only an old goblet, after all.'

'I'm sorry to have called at such an inconvenient moment.'

'I can't help having a very soft spot for Jason Grainger,' she said. 'Are you a regular listener?'

'Not really.'

'It was always the way when we ran our school that it was the naughty boys that you found yourself getting a soft spot for – the ones who really wanted putting across your knee and spanking.'

I found it difficult to reply to this.

'And I know someone else who'll get his botty spanked if he doesn't come home soon,' she added.

I assumed this was said in a spirit of pleasantry.

'So,' she continued, 'you've brought some books back for my boy.'

'For Mr Robey, yes.'

'And where are you from again?'

I gave a brief explanation of how I happened to have the books in my hand.

'Well, my boy's a dark horse! He never said anything about

being on the wireless! And I like listening to the . . . you know . . . the one after the Home Service finishes.'

'The World Service.'

'Because it goes on during the night.'

'Yes.'

'Well, he *is* being a time. He works hard.' She smiled the same indulgent smile she had done for Jason Grainger. 'And then there are all the young ladies! They keep him busy.'

She seemed entirely untroubled by the idea. So much for Felicity's understanding that the Great Attachment was thrown into hysterical fits of grief by the mention of Rice Robey's female acquaintances. The Great Attachment was smiling at me innocently, or perhaps not so innocently. Darnley had been told by Rice Robey that his home life was 'wretched'. Felicity had been told that so much as to allude to his trysts with her 'would not be worth all the tears and shouting'. It was not for me to decide how unhappy Rice Robey might have been, but it became immediately obvious that he had, to put it mildly, adapted or edited the truth, and in a manner which was in its way more disturbingly disloyal to the Great Attachment than any physical betrayal.

'There are two main ones at the moment he likes to talk about,' she continued merrily. She lit another cigarette. 'But I must see to the toad-in-the-hole; he'll be home in a moment and wanting his tea. There's little Kirsty he likes to go to visit in Cambridge. She's rather posh. He's *shy* about her, bless him. I think he thinks I . . .'

What Rice Robey thought Mrs Paxton thought was either censored or forgotten, and she reverted to the urgent question of the evening meal.

'Only I've got to open a tin of peas. I don't suppose *you* are any good at tins?'

'Depends on the tin-opener. I could try.'

'Could you? There's a step-ladder in the cupboard under the stairs.'

'Will I need it?'

'Fetch it, will you.'

She spoke quite authoritatively and for some reason there seemed no option but to obey. Amid a clatter of buckets, mops, cardboard boxes containing pieces of wire and old tins, I found a very paint-stained old step-ladder whose divided legs were held together by frayed pieces of rope.

'Only the light bulb's gone in the downstairs toilet, and it needs changing. If his nibs had been back, I'd have got him to do it.'

I changed the light bulb – it involved returning to the cupboard under the stairs to scrummage in one of the cardboard boxes for a 40-watt, and – 'while I was about it' – moved some surprisingly heavy flower pots from a high shelf in the lavatory wall. She wanted them for planting Christmas hyacinths. Then I came back to the kitchen to address myself to the tin-opener. 'Only, he gives these talks, you know. Would it be ley-lines? And there are standing . . . They're very interesting, and he *so* often comes back from having given a talk and says he's met another little friend!'

'Lucky for him.'

She snorted with amusement.

The kitchen was steamy with the vapour of overboiled potatoes. With the cigarette between her lips, she drained off the potato-water into a pyrex jug with a Bisto paste lurking evilly at its bottom.

'That's the gravy made.'

This was very much Aunt Deirdre's approach to cooking.

'The tin-opener's there. Thanks. You can't stop those men – unless they're like my husband used to be, they're romantic. You are, I shouldn't wonder. So at the moment, it's little Kirsty. Oh, dear, and next month it will be little someone else. And then there's this woman at the office.'

'Oh, yes?'

'Well, she's more of a friend. She sounds a nice sort, and clever. Oh, *clever*! But a bit too intense, my boy says – wanting a bit too much, you know. I dare say she's been holding him up again tonight. She makes little excuses to see him about things, says it's all frightfully important business, only she really just wants to be with him. Only, it's *understandable*!'

It was disloyal of me to allow her to tell me so much. I felt the sinking feeling of having been betrayed. It was also a feeling of embarrassment on Felicity's behalf. She had spoken so clearly to me about these trysts with Rice Robey. The version he gave to the Great Attachment was clearly very different. Where the truth lay, who could guess?

'But I'm thrilled,' said Mrs Paxton, 'about the wireless. He'll have been keeping that for me as a nice surprise. He used to be quite a well-known author – before the war, and a bit during. He was really ever so young when he first came to . . .'

'To your school?'

'That's right. He came and helped my husband run the school; before it was all wound up.'

'Was it a Mr Lampitt who recommended him to you?'

'James Petworth Lampitt.' She said the words without looking at me, with one hand on her waist and the other taking the cigarette from her lips.

'Yes.'

'Now, he was an author, and he happened to know my husband. How odd that you should mention that.'

'I simply wondered if Mr Lampitt recommended Mr Robey for the job at your school.'

She either missed the point of this question or she did not think it was worth answering.

'He was always writing, you know. All those stories were written while he was working for us at the school. My husband ran this school.'

'Yes.'

'It was quite a *distinguished* school. Now, how are you getting on with that tin of peas? Don't cut your thumb.'

'Nearly there.'

'Oh, *good*. He still writes now, of course. Bits of poetry. And there's some great long thing he's planning. He won't tell me a *thing* about it. "Another mystery?" I'll ask him. "You could say so," he says. "Does it have a murder?" I'll ask, and he'll say, "You could say it has *the* Murder." Only, you see, the trouble is, he doesn't have the time for books now that he has all these other things. But it's nice to think – did you say, would it be, the producer, is that what you are?'

'No, I just help.'

'Oh, only I'd like him to make a name again for himself. And the money would be nice.'

The kitchen doorway was at that moment filled with Rice Robey. Presumably, he had come through the front door in the usual way, but I had not heard him do so and it seemed equally probable that he had simply materialised; or even that he had not materialised, that this was a spiritual emanation of his

651

personality making its apparition while his body bilocated in another place.

'I'd nearly given you up,' said Mrs Paxton. 'Only it's Thursday.'

He bowed down to kiss her white cheek and I noticed how tenderly and lovingly he did so.

'Then it's toad-in-the-hole,' he said.

'This is Mr . . . He's brought you your books. He says you are going to be on the wireless, boy, isn't that good?'

'Mr Grainger and I are acquainted,' he said.

'Grainger! I wonder if you're related to our friend Jason,' she said waggishly.

'I was going to tell you about the wireless programme, Audrey, only I didn't want to say anything until it was definite. You'd only have been disappointed. The Corporation of British Broadcasting can be very unreliable.'

'Perhaps your books will become real sellers! It would be nice to have the money. Have you ever read one, Mr Grainger?'

'I read *Memphian Mystery* not long ago. I was much impressed.'

This did not seem the moment to reveal that I had also read some fragments of his strange religious poem.

'Well,' said Rice Robey, 'it was very kind of you to bring the books, but we generally have our tea about now.'

Mrs Paxton moved over to him as he said these words, visibly delighted that he had shown the strength of character to bring my visit to an end. She stood very close to him. Her grey hair and ancient white cheeks reached his dandruffy shoulder. He spontaneously put an arm round her and squeezed her. It was not done for effect. The gesture could not have been made by a man who hated or feared his companion. I noticed too, that in her company, his voice was different. There was a cockney twang to it all the same, but it was not such a marked accent as it had been at Mallington Hall or the lunch in the Black Bottle. In the company of his admirers, I do not think he would have let fall a simple sentence about the hour when he preferred to eat. There would have been some Pugh-like phrase for it, and toad-in-the-hole itself would have become pregnant with mystic meaning. He appeared to be at ease with the Great Attachment in a way that I had never witnessed before during my other encounters with the man. It was also obvious that he could not wait for me to leave the house. My intrusion there had blown his cover, the secret of his domestic harmony, its ordinariness.

Since that moment of leaving Number 77 Twisden Road, and walking back through the dingy street, I have formed various theories to explain his shocking compulsion to tell other people that his home life was unhappy. One explanation was that they were fundamentally miserable together, that I simply happened to catch them on a good day when hostilities had momentarily ceased. Another possibility was that he chose to dramatise those periods of discontent which descend upon almost any pair of human beings living together; that, by making a story out of these bad patches, and depicting the Great Attachment as the cross he had to bear, he had mysteriously made life more bearable. The immediate explanation which came to me, however, as I made my tortuous way on foot and by bus to Camden Town, was that Rice Robey was simply a liar. He liked the company of young women; he was emotionally, if not physically, promiscuous, and he had discovered that the women themselves found it easier to square it with their consciences if he pretended that he needed their company since all was not well at home. Had they believed that he was perfectly happy with Mrs Paxton, then the more scrupulous of the adorers, Felicity above all, would surely have been inclined to keep their distance. I felt fury with him on this account. She would never have intruded upon him, and made herself so unhappy, had she known the truth. He seemed to be causing emotional havoc in Felicity's heart wholly arbitrarily. What was he gaining from their association if, as he told Mrs Paxton, it was not something he needed or wanted for himself? Was it simply the unclean pleasure to be derived by the exercise of power over another human being?

As a man who exercised a spell (perhaps in a literal sense) over a wide range of women, Rice Robey naturally invited comparison with Raphael Hunter. In both cases, I found it completely mysterious why otherwise intelligent women queued up to be treated so badly. The difference between the two men would seem to have lain in the area of emotional self-control. Hunter was a purely manipulative person. I do not believe that he was ever remotely in love with any of the women whose hearts he so easily broke. They happened, at whatever juncture they crossed his path, to serve some purpose. With Rice

Robey, things were different, I am sure. He obviously had nothing to gain from displaying a passion for temporary typists. He must have been, for short spells at least, rapturously unable to stop himself doodling poetry on the blotter in his office and dreaming wild dreams about the latest girl.

At this period in my life I was in the strange position of having forgotten what love was like. I *had* been in love, or I supposed that I had been – with Miss Beach, with Barbara (a little), with Anne (besottedly). I did not wish to deny this, but I was unable to summon back any of the sensations which might have enabled me to empathise with the emotional predicaments of my friends. Why, for example, should a man with Darnley's intelligence, humour and melancholy good looks have 'chosen' a girl with Jo's apparent limitations? The question, which nagged me, was absurd. It implied that love was a matter of the will. The shock I so unreasonably felt was comparable to the first visit to the house or rooms of some new friend, whose good taste had somehow been taken for granted, and finding there shop furnishings and uncongenial pictures. Viewing the effects of love from the outside, it just seemed like a form of capricious silliness. Now, if Darnley had fallen in love with Kirsty . . . Yes, of course. In the case of Felicity's attachment to Rice Robey, I felt not merely aesthetic disapproval, but also an appalled pity. I ached with pity, but at the same time I made the mistake (as with Darnley and Jo) of wondering why – why had she *chosen* Rice Robey? Why not choose some handsome, intelligent, presentable young man? Why fall in love with a scruffy, myopic man in his fifties who had an ugly voice, and a lot of bloody silly ideas?

Even to ask the question was a corrective to rationalism. *Incipit vita nuova* were words which Rice Robey had once written on a memo-slip and placed on the typewriter of a young stenographer to whom he owed a brief devotion. It had happened early enough in her acquaintanceship with the man to make Felicity laugh, and it was she who told me about it. Since the girl had been called Beattie, the highly charged Dantean reference had been apposite, though not one which the recipient of the note had understood. She had asked one person, and then another. Finally, she had asked Felicity, who obliged her by translating the three words. As it happened, that morning, Beattie's boyfriend, a car salesman in Cricklewood, had been offered promotion by his firm on condition that he moved to St Albans. He had been sufficiently confident in his increased prosperity to be able to catch Beattie before she left for work and propose marriage, an offer which she had accepted. Her new life had indeed begun, and she had disappointed Rice Robey by the insensitive assumption that he knew all these things; she had taken the words to be an elaborate expression of pleasure at her good news. Rice Robey had felt crushed, so much so that Felicity had bought him a drink at lunchtime by way of consolation. Perhaps her own New Life had begun on that day also, the establishment of herself as Rice Robey's confidante, and the incipient dawn of her own devotion to the man. In a way with which I had not yet come to terms, it was the beginning of a new life for me also. I found myself thinking about it all as I alighted from the bus in Kentish Town.

Drizzle fell through the darkness, lit up in mysterious shafts of sparkling light by the headlamps of cars. Light shone, too, from dusty shopfronts above which jutted the jerry-built houses of blackened brick. Here and there were signs of change. The first Chinese restaurant in that part of London, and a Laundromat. These were harbingers of some new creation, but already, after less than two years in the place, they wore the tired, dank aspect of the surrounding shops, the baker's, which still, after it had closed, left the less edible of its wares on display in the window, sticky buns erupting with currants which looked more like bread spattered with soot; or the barber's shop whose sun-faded Brylcreem advertisement grinned out to passers-by like a ghost, growing paler each hour it had been exposed to the light of day; or the pawnbroker's, stuffed with the merchandise whose value could not be redeemed in the betting shop next door. This was Kentish Town which William Blake (and perhaps Rice Robey) saw as a place where the pillars of an imaginative Jerusalem had been set up, ground trodden by the feet of the Lamb of God.

> Pancras and Kentish Town repose
> Among her golden pillars high
> Among her golden arches which
> Shine upon the starry sky.

Here, the imported labour force of the nineteenth century had crammed their sickly and ever-expanding families into mean terraced houses; here, ten-year-old factory hands had swarmed in tenement buildings. Sometimes, the sheer indignity of the life of the poor, even when viewed from a perspective in time or place where it might be imagined that life has improved, has a power to oppress and torture the soul. Lloyd George and Vernon's dad, and later Clem Attlee and Stafford Cripps and Vernon himself, had done their best to make existence more endurable for subsequent generations. That could not alter the fates of those who had lived and died like slaves in this place, their stomachs pinched with hunger, their lungs clogged with soot, their brains wandering through God knows what corridors of despair which only alcohol could numb.

Kentish Town deepened into brick-blackened Camden. On my left was the tube station, infested, as always, with human wreckage, blue-nosed contemplatives clutching ragged blankets to their shoulders and wodges of newspaper to their knees; shiny-faced inebriates, eyes swollen and cut, murmuring snatches of old songs; a woman who might once have been a flower-seller, a black straw hat rammed jauntily over scrubs of unwashed hair, sprawled in a pool of unidentifiable liquid, her neck and shoulders pressed against a newspaper-placard reading CLOSING PRICES, her bulbous legs spreadeagled on the chilling paving-stones and coming to a halt in a pair of dusty brown shoes from which the soles were yearning to part company. Could they, these people, remember who they were, or once had been? Was there any link between the bodies slumped there and the undeveloped limbs of their childhood, when their lives had been all in the future, rather than a fuddled nightmare past? I turned into Parkway, where more such figures lingered in doorways. The pavements were also full of sober men and women, all on the move. Thin-faced crones in headscarves, lighted cigarettes at ninety degrees to their sharp noses, paced homewards to evenings of solitude.

The comparative architectural elegance of Arlington Road, as I turned into it for the last few yards of my walk home, did little to console. Sadness in that sort of mood seems the only truth. To be conscious is to be sad, and anything else seems like an illusion. Approaching my own front door, I was visited by self-disgust. I had gone to Twisden Road as a voyeur, I had intended it as a guerrilla raid in some emotional war that I was fighting against Rice Robey inside my own head. Now, I felt merely that I had intruded on his privacy. Having met Mrs Paxton, it was no longer quite possible to regard her as no more than a joke – 'the Great Attachment'; nor would I ever be able vicariously to enjoy accounts of her rages against Rice Robey, accounts which I would now believe to be lies.

Entering our common drawing room, I found Felicity sitting by the gas fire. A thick pile of foolscap typed pages was balanced on her knee.

'I'm just trying to work out next year's Budget Bids,' she said by way of greeting. She had not looked up from a page which had the word VIREMENT typed in capitals at the top of it. I resolved to say nothing to her about Rice Robey. Very likely, she would soon disappear into her own room or, as she quite often did, go out for the evening with a friend. If she *were* to discuss office politics, I hoped that it would be possible to vary our theme, and speak of other colleagues. I longed to hear more about Brenda and her friend Henri, and their dog-breeding life in Putney; or about Brenda's war with the surly Dr Jack, who countermanded her orders and proposals and made dark hints that paperwork had a way simply of disappearing when passed through her in-tray. Dr Jack was not saying in so many words that Brenda was throwing paper away, rather than filing it; this, after all, would have been in a civil servant the ultimate professional dereliction, the equivalent of a doctor disregarding the Hippocratic oath, or a Catholic priest celebrating a Black Mass.

These harmless matters were not, however, uppermost in Felicity's mind. She put down her work and sipped at a glass of pale sherry.

'I'm afraid that R.R. is in trouble up to his neck,' she said quietly. 'Our head of department . . . oh, Julian, it just makes me so *angry*. Rice Robey is worth ten of them. He is a person of such talents.'

'Being the discreetly anonymous civil servant isn't one of those talents.'

'He isn't a civil servant. He is an inspector of Ancient Monuments with an unrivalled range of knowledge. He really does not *need* to waste his time in administration. It is all so footling. You know, quite apart from his work for the ministry, he is in constant demand as a lecturer; he gives guided tours, he . . .'

'I heard of him going to Cambridge not long ago to give a talk: I think it was about ley-lines. Kirsty Lampitt was certainly much impressed.'

'He's respected. And yet these stupid people . . . Since he isn't a grey man in a grey suit, why should he behave as if he were one ?'

'He is technically a civil servant.'

'True, he entered the Civil Service at the lowest level of the Executive Grade with no qualifications. It was towards the end of the war and they were glad of anyone they could get. But, he very quickly became involved in the practical supervision of these old sites. He never was a paper-pusher. He loves his work. And in this particular case, he is right to make a stink. The Ministry of Works holds these places in trust and what they are proposing is that Aldingbury Ring should simply be wiped off the face of the earth.'

'This is the cut-price Stonehenge which you have mentioned before?'

'He calls it his sacred grove,' she said lovingly. 'It's in Berkshire. R.R. thinks that it is an ancient sacrificial site. There is very little to *see*, it has never been dug. There is a strange slab of stone at one end of a grove of trees, and a little way away, there are the remains of a small stone circle. R.R. thinks that if it *were* dug, there is no knowing what might be found – swords, helmets, rings, human remains . . .'

'If it has never been dug, how can he be so sure?'

'He works by instinct, but his instincts are often right.'

This was very like his approach to journalism, gossip, perhaps to religion. Like Darnley, Felicity seemed to place absolute trust in Rice Robey's hunches.

'Has he ever taken you to see it?' I asked.

She very slightly flinched. Doubtless she would have loved a day out with Rice Robey; in admitting that she had not so much as set eyes on the Sacred Grove, she was also having to admit that her association with Rice Robey was not as intimate as she would have liked. She did not answer my question. Rootling about in her capacious black bag she produced a cardboard folder, opened it, and took out a drawing of Aldingbury Ring.

'He gave me this,' she said.

Rice Robey was no draughtsman, but there was something undeniably distinctive about the thick black pencil-work with which he depicted this strange place. The trees were after

Palmer. In the sky above the grove, he had drawn an antlered figure hurtling across the clouds, accompanied by four-footed creatures, perhaps meant to be hounds but bearing more resemblance to goats.

'There's Herne,' I said, 'sometime a keeper here in Windsor Forest.'

'Aldingbury Ring is very near Windsor. That's the trouble. It's bang in the line of the new fast road they're planning to build between London and Bristol. That's the MOT's problem, though, not ours. It's the MOW's job to preserve ancient sites, not to allow them to be overrun by lorries and tarmac.'

'Can't the road be resited, so that it curves round the Sacred Grove?'

'It would wreck it if it did. R.R. takes it really seriously, Julian. He says that the Gods will exact their revenge.'

'That's certainly their usual way of behaving.'

'He thinks that the head of our department positively wants to destroy Aldingbury Ring, just out of spite against him. He has been out to get R.R. for years. Do you know, he had the cheek to ask R.R. to step into his office the other day and warn him that his Staff Report for the last six months was very unfavourable. ' To speak the final two words of the sentence, Felicity adopted a mock-pompous tone reminiscent of her mother's 'joke' voice. 'The head of department is about ten years younger than R.R. I know that isn't the point; but it was a threat. They are afraid of him rocking the boat. They somehow know about his friendship with your Mr Darnley and they don't like it. Civil servants are terrified of journalists. They think R.R. will feed Mr Darnley with scurrilous gossip.'

'They would be right to think that.'

'It is almost a resigning matter. They want R.R.'s head on a charger; they won't be satisfied until they have destroyed him.'

We stared at the gas fire. It seemed so clear to me that, if I were in charge of a civil service department, I should find Rice Robey an uncongenial colleague; it was no surprise that they wanted to get rid of him, if indeed they did, and this was not merely a piece of persecution mania of Robey's own imagining. What was so eerie was to hear Felicity's account, and realise that she saw things so totally from Rice Robey's point of view. She was not even attempting to be rational or dispassionate.

'I believe civil servants are always made edgy by political

change, and it does now look as if the Tories haven't got a hope of winning the next election.'

'I wouldn't be so sure. Think what snobs the English are. The clever journalists mock Douglas-Home, but I suspect he's really quite popular.'

'Rice Robey thinks Labour will win,' she said. She did not need to say that this was what she thought too.

She stretched and closed her eyes momentarily as she spoke. When she lifted her arms, the jacket of her navy blue costume fell open and I could make out the shape of her breasts beneath the sleeveless, schooly jumper which she had knitted for herself some months before.

I wanted to change the subject, but I also wanted to have the last word. I think that was why I made the next few tactless remarks.

'If they boot out Rice Robey, he'll get by perfectly well as a lecturer. You have said yourself that he is much in demand. Possibly, he'll do more writing. You shouldn't worry about him so much.'

Felicity had been looking at the floor. She lifted her oval, fleshy face towards mine and I could see that her eyes were full of distress.

'Get by? Get *by*?'

I saw that I had completely failed to come to grips with the reason for her sadness. The supposed persecution of Rice Robey was bad enough, but what truly distressed her was the prospect of losing him, the chance that he might no longer be a presence in the same corridor as her own, a head stuck round the door at periodic intervals during the day. It would spell the end of their secret little lunches and their drinks after work. Rice Robey would move on, and, of course, Felicity was realistic enough to realise that once she was removed from his immediate sphere of work, he would be unlikely to keep their friendship in good repair. He would find other women, other causes, other ruins and earthworks in which to be immersed, other audiences for his fantastical ideas; and she would be left alone. How bitterly this would pain her, was now written on her quivering strangely pale lips, on her harrowed brow, and in her tearful eyes.

'I've become very fond of him,' she said.

'Yes.'

'You probably can't see why. You probably think I'm just an

hysterical middle-aged woman, past her best, fantasising about a much older man.'

'I don't think anything.'

'You suppose it's like women who fall in love with vicars. Do you remember Miss Dare?'

She sniffed, and we both laughed at this shared childhood memory, a phase of two or three years when a spinster, living in a village quite some way away from Timplingham, formed an attachment to Uncle Roy. Miss Dare had come to Norfolk from London, where she had attended St Mary's Primrose Hill, and someone had recommended Timplingham Church as an appropriate rural substitute. Here was the same loving reconstruction of an English ritual based on the Sarum Missal, with vestments modelled not on modern Roman Catholic rubbish but on illuminated books of hours from the fifteenth century. Miss Dare's addiction to apparelled albs, full, Gothic conical chasubles and the profound *inclinatio* (in preference to genuflection) had strayed into a devotion to the person of my uncle, who liked to talk of these rarefied ecclesiological matters in those very fleeting intervals of waking life when he was not talking about the Lampitts. Even here, Miss Dare had followed the form very closely and could claim to have taught in a school with a lady who had known Miss Bean, the very close friend of the unfortunate Angelica Lampitt.

'No, you're not like Miss Dare.'

'Oh, Julian.'

And she began to weep, copiously and silently, only occasionally letting out moans of grief. When she did so, I wanted to comfort her. She was sitting in the armchair where she had been working; it was not an object of furniture on which two people could sit and hold one another. Our embrace was clumsy. Perched sideways on the arm of her chair, I could neither kiss her, nor even quite fit my arm around her shoulder, nor could our faces meet without her jutting her chin almost vertically in the air. So we clutched one another awkwardly, lost for words as she moaned. I no longer thought especially of Rice Robey, still less held him responsible for the unhappiness of my cousin. Love had done this, not Rice Robey. Holding her as best I could, and putting my head on the top of her head, I realised that I was not doing this merely to comfort her. Something was awakening within me which had been dead for well over a year.

'Come on,' I said, 'I'll take you out for some dinner.'

'Couldn't. Couldn't face it.'

'It'll take us out of ourselves.'

'I don't want to be out of myself. I am more unhappy than I have ever been in my life, but I want to be hurting and bleeding with the pain of it. I don't want to be taken out of this state.'

I stroked her head. It was a signal for a change of posture. She stood to light up a cigarette from the matchbox on the mantelpiece and I remained sitting on the arm of the chair. For the first time in conscious memory, I found my cousin's calves in their thick tan stockings beneath the navy blue skirt hugely alluring.

'I've quite often been fond of men,' she said. 'You and I have never shared confidences, except once, when it was unavoidable' – she meant the affair with Hunter – 'but there have been others.'

'I guessed there might have been.'

One of my worst habits is stating, out of shyness, the precise opposite of what I think.

'But nothing like this,' she said.

'Is it worse because . . .' – I toyed with various delicate ways of asking her whether it was all made worse by the absence of sexual expression on both sides, the heightening of emotions which soared uncontrollably inside her head; or was it worse because he regarded her as no more than a friend, but had come to depend on her for friendship, so that she could not declare her love without destroying the friendship? Or was it something different, which made it worse?

'He set something free in my mind. When I gave up Oxford and went to the Ministry of Works I was determined to have a rest from thought. There seemed nowhere further to go, and yet my mind was still working away, hammering at a wall which contained no secret door, but which I had to get through. All the methods of penetrating this wall were either ineffectual or intellectually inadmissible. There was a very, very serious danger of my going mad, since the ratiocinative process continued in my head even when I was asleep. Nothing would stop it, not even work. It rampaged in my head like toothache. At first, I regarded Rice Robey as an entertainment, a sideshow to distract me from this fruitless intellectual churning. It was when I discovered that he was, in some sense, my saviour, that I knew I was lost. No, no. Don't worry. I'm not soft in the head. I mean, quite literally, that Rice Robey offered me salvation.'

'Would this have to do with his thinking Either/or the two falsest words in the English language?'

'Yes.'

She lit another cigarette from the glowing butt of the first. 'I thought – this has all been done before, it's back to Bergson, it is really a retreat from thought, the struggle between the idealists and the realists was a true one and we must resolve it, either by an honest silence or an out-and-out empiricism; but the latter became as impossible as the former.'

'I don't really follow.'

'It doesn't matter. It does. It matters more than anything, actually, but it doesn't matter that you, individually, at this moment don't follow what I'm saying. I'm expressing myself badly. Rice Robey offered me a way of viewing things, of chucking ideas about at a simple level, which was liberating because it was totally unlike the way I'd been trained to think. I also began to see that in many, many areas he was right. So, all our early talk was about this philosophical stuff.'

'I see. Not office politics at all?'

'Well, yes, we talked about that; but the burning, essential thing we both needed to discuss each day was thought, ideas.'

Her hand was sweaty and she let me hold it in the way that people do hold hands, kiss, cuddle one another when sex is far from their mind.

'Then, quite simply, I became involved in his story.'

'There was a change,' I said. 'When you first met him, you found him tiresome.'

'I still do,' she said indulgently. 'It wasn't just pity for him. You know, he lives with this monster of a woman. He has not said so, but reading between the lines I can tell that she is actually mad. She would be locked up in a padded cell if Rice Robey weren't such a good Christian. She rails at him all the time. He has to do all the cooking – he has told me that much – but he never complains, not so much as a murmur. She has absolutely no interest in his work. There's no wonder he stopped publishing; she took no interest in his books, never read them.'

'You derive all this from reading between the lines?'

'He lets things fall sometimes.'

'I see.'

'You probably think that love has made me silly, but if you really knew Rice Robey, Julian, you would realise that he was practically a saint. Mrs Paxton is the cross he has to bear. She is the real torment of his life. The rest – the campaign against him at work, the destruction of Aldingbury Ring – that, I suspect causes less pain than the hell that woman has made for him.'

I urged her once more to come to the trattoria in Parkway and this time, somewhat surprisingly, she accepted the idea. (Felicity hated restaurants.)

As she was putting on her coat, she said, 'You must read something R.R. has written and tell me what you think of it.'

'Is it about Christ, because . . .'

'I'll show it to you.'

The trattoria was five minutes' walk from the house, and we were soon established in the corner sipping a rather acidic Valpolicella and leaning backwards to allow a waiter to grind too much pepper into our minestrone from a huge phallic mill. We settled; we made no strenuous efforts to be cheerful; we reposed, conversationally, on the unplumbable store of Timplingham memories, which no one but ourselves could share. Neither of us could remember what happened to Miss Dare, but the mention of her name inevitably led us to talk of Felicity's parents, and to speculate how long Uncle Roy would stay in his parish before retiring.

'I don't think Ma's ever enjoyed being a vicar's wife; she'd had enough of being a vicar's daughter.'

We left on one side the more general question of whether Aunt Deirdre had enjoyed any aspects of married life, or how far this was effected by her husband's choice of profession.

'She'd miss the garden if they retired,' I said.

'I say,' Felicity burst out impatiently, 'they're being noisy.'

A very pretty, animated woman, of about my age, was shrieking with laughter in the opposite corner of the restaurant. She was sitting facing us, and opposite a heavily built man with thick blond hair; she had heavily mascara'd eyes, and very full red lips, parted in her laughter to reveal magnificent even white teeth.

When her companion turned his head, I recognised him.

I said, 'That's Blowforth-Bums, and he is meant to be having dinner with Treadmill.'

I explained that I had met Treadmill, and heard how much he was looking forward to a dinner with old pupils, Garforth-Thoms among them.

Like his friend, Garforth-Thoms was laughing fit to burst.

One felt excluded by the joke, whatever it was.

The waiters in the restaurant were being tolerant of their high spirits, but hovering, their smiles a little fixed, to make sure that things did not get out of hand.

Felicity said, 'I'm not up to joining them, Julian, I hope they don't notice you.'

'We can just wave at them as we leave. They won't want to join us.'

At that moment, a voice at our table said, 'Look at Hedda! My dear, I always told you my family were mad.'

William Bloom stood there.

I had never seen him on a regular basis since army days, when he had managed to make even the dreariest of occupations such as square-bashing, spud-bashing, or cleaning equipment an occasion for high camp humour; very welcome it was, in those days. Inevitably, there had been some calming down since his return to civvie street and the passage of something like a decade. He had made such a success as the employee of a well-established London publisher that he had decided to set up on his own, in partnership with an Irishman called Byrne. 'Bloom and Byrne' had already made quite a solid reputation, and Bloom had been astute enough not to restrict himself to the 'literary' end of the market. It was said that they made most of their money from books about cooking and gardening.

'Hedda's meant to be giving a dinner party for her husband,' said William. 'I forget if you've ever met.'

'She's your sister?'

'She rang me at the offfice and asked me to buy her dinner. I said I couldn't – I've been entertaining an American author all afternoon – but she insisted. I see she's not been entirely without companionship in my absence. I wonder who that piece of beefcake is. Darling, where does she *find* them?'

'He's called Garforth-Thoms. He wants to stand for parliament.'

'You know everyone, darling, don't you?'

'I was at school with Patrick Garforth-Thoms.'

'Look at the way those lips of hers pout.'

I would have said that if this sentence had been spoken to Felicity in most circumstances, she would have frowned and been embarrassed. Two minutes earlier, she had been writhing with distaste at the behaviour of Bloom's sister, and preparing for a retreat from the restaurant had there been the slightest question of our joining the rowdies. Perhaps because she had so lately been weeping, and her emotions were wound up to an uncharacteristic pitch, she found Bloom's remark very funny.

'You haven't met my cousin Felicity?' I said.

'This is perfect. I've been *pining* for a philosopher all week.'

Bloom has a very good memory, which is one of the most necessary components of social charm. It is hard to warm to anyone, met three or four times, who has difficulty remembering the circumstances of one's life. By contrast, the man who after a couple of meetings, has an instant recall of where you went to school, the number and extent of your family, makes an instant appeal. Bloom had often talked to me about my family, and I must have mentioned Felicity to him dozens of times. On the other hand he had hundreds of acquaintances, and I thought it was impressive that he had retained so much information about her.

'There are plenty of philosophers about.'

'Listen, my dear, you can tell me, does anyone nowadays read G. E. Moore?'

'Fewer than read Agatha Christie or Deborah Arnott,' said Felicity.

'No, but be serious, my dear. ' He explained that someone had asked him to publish a book about Moore and his Cambridge circle and he was uncertain until he had spoken about it to a professional philosopher. This was, as it happened, very much up Felicity's street – I rather think her PhD thesis had touched on Moore – and she spoke about the subject animatedly for about five minutes. Then Bloom asked her about various friends he knew in Oxford.

'How's Geoffrey Cormac?' he asked.

'Is he a rather cherubic-looking drunk in a leather jacket?' I asked. 'A strong Ulster accent?'

'He can be a bit tiresome,' said Felicity. 'He hasn't altogether mastered the difference between argument and fisticuffs.'

'Isn't he a great enemy of Professor Wimbish?'

'Tommy!' Bloom rolled his eyes. 'Isn't he divine! I want him to write a book for us when he's finished this boring history of the Labour Party. A nice sort of sex romp through the court of Henry VIII.'

'Hasn't he written quite a lot of those already?' asked Felicity.

Bloom bent double with mirth at this question, shot out his tongue, rolled his eyes.

I was clumsy enough not to sense that there had been an immediate rapport between Bloom and Felicity, and I ploddingly continued to 'keep the conversation going' by spelling out the fact that I had met Professor Cormac and Professor Wimbish for the first time that year. I mentioned that Cormac had come my way at one of Darnley's lunches in the Black Bottle.

'Oh, that squalid little rag *The Spark*. I get more spark out of wanking. But I mean, darlings, it won't do, will it – not quite?'

'I think it's pretty feeble,' said Felicity. 'Then you find, just occasionally, that there are some things in it which make you laugh.'

'Wish I'd found them. I suppose that pathetic 'Diary' thing at the front is penned by our little friend Miss Malice herself?'

'Darnley?'

I could not help remembering the time when Bloom was so passionately in love with Darnley. 'The real thing,' he had said. 'Shakespeare's *Sonnets*, *Tristan und Isolde*, *La Prisonnière*, the whole horror story.' Now he spoke of Darnley as little more than an irritant, and I realised that in time Felicity herself would be delivered from the torments of loving Rice Robey, that this inexplicable pain which love brings does not last, any more than love itself lasts.

'Did you see their feeble thing last week about little Hedda?'

'About your sister?'

Bloom's sister had now spotted him and was waving, calling out, beckoning him to join them. Garforth-Thoms, at about the same moment, had noticed me and was looking, I thought, a bit sheepish.

'They made her out to be a sort of nymphomaniac. Her husband wanted to sue. Luckily, I managed to persuade him not to. As for Miss Malice.'

'Darnley?'

'You've heard the latest, I suppose?'

'What?'

'She's getting married. She may kid herself, but she doesn't kid Mother.'

'He's marrying the daughter of Vernon Lampitt.'

It took very little to persuade Felicity to cross the restaurant and continue our meal in the company of Bloom, his sister and Garforth-Thoms.

'Can you imagine anything more boring?' asked Bloom's sister. 'My husband Aaron had organised a dinner party consisting entirely of old school chums. No girls, just a lot of boring men.'

'Darling, I thought you were like me, I thought you never found men boring.'

'He didn't *want* me there,' said Hedda. 'It was perfectly obvious I was doing him a good turn, getting out of the house.'

'It was a dinner for Treadmill,' said Garforth-Thoms. 'You remember Treadmill?'

Having been accused of knowing everyone, I was almost non-committal in my reply, and certainly did not wish to advertise the fact that Treadmill had himself expressed the hope, that very afternoon, that he would be dining with Garforth-Thoms.

'He used to teach English in our school,' said Garforth-Thoms, ostensibly to Felicity, but partly, one felt, to me, in case I had forgotten. 'I should have gone to the dinner myself, but Hedda was bored and wanted . . .'

It did not seem entirely polite to dwell on what Hedda, at any stage of the evening, had wanted.

'I think we'll find the pundits have got it all wrong,' he said confidently. 'Journalists get bored, they like a change, that's why they keep saying that Labour will win the election. If you look at the actual situation in the country, if you talk to people in the constituencies, as I have, you realise that there is a tremendous groundswell of support for the Conservative Party.'

'Yawn, yawn,' said Hedda, 'let's all go to a night club.'

This suggestion was repeated at various junctures until Felicity said she was tired and wanted to go home to bed. Hedda and Garforth-Thoms appeared quite happy to be left on their own. She was running through the possibilities, and had finally selected Ronnie Scott's as their next port of call. When we had parted from them, Bloom, Felicity and I walked slowly down the street together.

'I saw Sargie Lampitt last week,' Bloom said, 'so I'm glad I bumped into you. Isn't it a good idea, Felicity?'

'For Julian to write this book about Jimbo?'

'I want it to be a book about the whole tribe. It'll be *far* more interesting than Hunter's crap. The Lampitts are one of those great Victorian dynasties.'

'Radical Jo was dead fifty years before Queen Victoria,' I said.

'No, but by the time they were *established* – they'd married everyone, read everything. They're just a vanished phenomenon, families like that – the Bensons, the Sidgwicks, the Wedgwoods. They're not really aristocrats, they're the intellectual aristocracy of England. They're actually one of the best things this country has ever produced, those large educated, enlightened families, and I think you'd do it *frightfully* well.'

I had no such certainty, and it came as a surprise to realise that the idea for the book had advanced so rapidly in the minds of others. Bloom, who had shown no desire at all to publish my novel, would have been prepared, I felt, to sign me up on the street corner to write about the Lampitts. It did not occur to me to wonder whether money had passed hands during the conversations he had been having with Sargie.

'Sargie himself always meant to write the book,' said Felicity. 'It could be very good indeed.'

We lingered. The moment we parted from Bloom, both Felicity and I might return, not merely to our house, but to the painful preoccupation which had so wracked her with tears and grief before dinner. The meal had been an unreal respite, an interlude, the sort of holiday, which even in the most terrible emotional circumstances, the heart allows itself.

'I have to start early in the moming,' said Felicity, 'but I'm so glad we met.'

'Maybe,' said Bloom, 'you would let me buy you lunch, so that I can quiz you further about Moore?'

'That would be very nice,' she said.

When we had returned home, we made no more explicit allusion to Rice Robey; only, just before she went to bed, Felicity fished in her briefcase for a brown envelope and said, with a sad smile, 'You could read this if you liked.'

669

(*Second draft*)

On the beautifully unformed juvenility of the face of Stephanos could be read the terror of a cornered animal. His large dark eyes could not avoid glancing first this way, then that, as he looked at his tormentors, wondering who should cast the first stone. He had not been stripped quite naked. They had permitted him a loincloth before leading him down into the rocky hollow which dipped from the quarry on the edge of the Field of Blood.

The trial had been absolutely legal, inescapably conclusive. Stephanos was a blasphemer and the Law demanded the death, by this means, of those who took the Name of the Lord in vain. Stephanos, a young Hellenised Jew, was the most eloquent of the little gaggle of heretics who preached the error nicknamed the Way. He had made fervent speeches, attracting considerable crowds, in which he argued with great erudition that Yeshua had been the fulfilment of all the ancient prophecies, the promised Messias of Israel, the dear Desire of all the Nations, Yeshua who had been crucified. Cursed is he who hangs upon a tree. No clearer manifestation could have been vouchsafed to Israel that Yeshua had been a pernicious corrupter of the Jewish faith than in the manner of his death. Would the Lord the Unutterable have allowed his anointed to perish on a tree? Why, even to admit the thought was to suggest that the Holy Torah could be disregarded; and this was to say the impossible, it would be to say that the Law of Moses was not the Law of God. Stephanos had maintained that the divinely ordered priestly hierarchy of Jerusalem had always persecuted the mouthpieces of the Most Holy, and that they had not heeded the prophets, and that it was no surprise that they had failed to recognise the divinely chosen Christ. He had even said that they had called down God's curse on their heads by murdering the Holy One of God. Such wild words called for blood-letting, not merely as a punishment to the blasphemer but as a Manifestation that the Holy Torah could not lightly be traduced. The trial, therefore, had been hastened to its conclusion and now the neaniskos, with wrists bound, was led outside the city as an example to the many. He had been pinioned to a stake on the edge of the hollow, and his accusers stood around him in a semicircle. Behind the judges and the guard, massed the crowds who saw here no more than a ghoulish spectacle such as might be provided by any criminal execution, for example the crucifixions which were carried out every week on the common criminals on Golgotha hill by the imperial military.

Saulos had in his hand a rough boulder and for a moment the high solemnity of the occasion was lost for him by the self-regarding fear that he was going to miss his target and make himself look ridiculous. As a boy, with hoops and quoits, he had been clumsy and the other children had not wanted him as their companion. He had never been practised at such games as delighted the Hellenes. He had never in his life thrown a javelin or a discus. His delight, rather, had been in the Law of the Lord, which he had made his study both day and night. He could not waste time developing the muscles on his dwarf-like body, when he had more important things to think about, more demanding faculties to develop, such as his knowledge of the Torah, his capacity to understand its intricacies and to master the commentaries of the rabbis. Now, as he stood with a stone in his hand, he was conscious of the crowd at his back. They would jeer, as at the pagan games, if he threw and missed; thus the dignity of the Sanhedrin would be tarnished, and the high religious significance of the scene would be lost; for this was no secular punishment; it almost had the nature of a sacrifice, since this death, the atoning for a blasphemy, was an offering to the Unnameable and Holy One himself.

Then Stephanos ceased to glance this way and that, like a frightened animal. He looked up at the sky. Saulos saw the muscles of the youth's chin, throat and chest tauten as he stared upwards and intoned, 'I see the Heavens open and Yeshua at the right hand of God.'

With automatic horror, Saulos hurled his stone. It was as though he had been visited with strength not his own. The stone hurtled through the air and caught Stephanos on the temple, stunning him instantly. After this first stone had been projected, the others followed and before long, the animate beauty of the neaniskos had been reduced to a bloody heap of

671

butcher's meat, a bruised bleeding *thing*, lying in its own blood like the carcases of the sacrificial lambs in the Temple.

Blasphemy called forth the necessity of blood-letting; it could only be appeased by the execution of the evil-speaker. Only the atonement of blood could pay for it. In all the weeks since the stoning of Stephanos, this thought had never left the fevered brain of Saulos. Inevitably, the young man's death recalled that other death, of Yeshua himself, some years previously, in which Saulos, still then a very junior member of Sanhedrin and secretary to the High Priest, had played a minor role. Yeshua had blasphemed. True, it had been necessary to bribe false witnesses to say so, but that was only because at the time of the trial, the Galilean had been so abominably silent. He who had disturbed the whole fabric of religion and society by his words during the previous three years would then say nothing to his accusers. The stream of jokes, stories and paradoxes with which his public speeches and his tavern-talk were larded had dried up. So, Annas had arranged for the usual false witnesses to come forward and claim that Yeshua had put himself on a level with the Almighty, or even claimed to be the Almighty. Saulos could have saved Yeshua. He knew that this, most precisely, was what Yeshua had never claimed.

'Why call me good?' he had asked in that maddeningly quibbling, seemingly frivolous tone. 'No one is good but God.'

That made it quite clear that Yeshua did not think he was God; but when the false witnesses said otherwise, he would say nothing to contradict them; nothing to gainsay the preposterous claim that he had made himself the King of the Jews.

When they brought Yeshua back from the torturers, that was the last time that Saulos had seen the man at close quarters: the thorn crown rammed on to his bleeding brow, the robe of purple around his naked, bruised body. The rest – when they compelled Yeshua to drag his cross through the streets of Jerusalem out to the Place of the Skull – Saulos had been unable to watch. It was the just penalty of the law, of Roman *lex*, for by making himself a king, Yeshua had defied the authority of Imperial Kaiser. From a window in the High Priest's house, Saulos could look out of the city towards the hillside where the crucifixions took place. There were always crosses erected there, holding up their victims like bloody scarecrows until sundown. He had not needed to watch. He knew that somewhere among the forest of crosses, the divine Jester of Nazareth was receiving his reward. It had been the ending, as Saulos believed, the purging of a lifelong obsession. Until Yeshua was dead, the faith of Saulos would never be safe. It had become as bald a choice as that. The love-hate which he felt for Yeshua would not rest. The humour of the Carpenter was one of the things which most disturbed Saulos. Someone would ask Yeshua to explain the love of God. Yeshua would describe his mother fussing because she had lost a coin she put down on the kitchen table for the shopping, and how no one in the household was allowed to rest until she had found it. And then when she found it all her agitation turned to joy and the neighbours would be asked to celebrate as though the discovery of one lost coin were worth a festival of rejoicing. And Saulos could see that the story, as told, was funny; not because he himself laughed, not because he had himself ever found anything funny in his entire life, but because it made the crowds laugh. And their laughter, and his inability to laugh, made Saulos pine to be a part of the accepting and good-humoured moral world which Yeshua inhabited, even though with another part of himself it made Saulos shudder, to hear Yeshua speak so familiarly of God. The Galilean had taught illiterates, buffoons who could not possibly understand all the implications of the Torah, to believe that they could approach the unapproachable majesty of the Almighty Mystery, and call It 'Our Dad'.

Saulos had wanted Yeshua dead, and when there seemed a danger that Yeshua's followers would revive his heresies and group themselves together in a new movement called the Way, he had been uncontrollably anxious that they should be eliminated. Gamaliel, his old teacher from university days, had been puzzled by his fury. Was it not better, and kinder, to let the Way die its own death, in the manner of all previous such enthusiasms? There had been so many other prophets, particularly from Galilee, troubling the tranquil surface of life for a while, attracting followers by their supposed miracles, and then passing into the obscurity of the grave. Their credulous disciples claimed for them miraculous powers, the

673

capacity to heal lepers, or to give sight to the blind. Who could know the truth of such things? The air was full of demons, spirits and powers, which could be harnessed for the good or evil of mankind, and wizards and shamans had always been able to harness them, just as in times past, the Witch of Endor had brought back King Saul from the dead. Safe, cynical, religious old Gamaliel had been in favour of allowing the Way to go its way. To persecute would merely make its adherents into martyrs.

Gamaliel had put his scrawny old arm round the small simian shoulders of Saulos.

'Let it be, let it go,' he had counselled. 'You have this man of Galilee in your mind, and he is swelling out of all proportion. Perhaps, my dear, you feel guilty about your part in his trial. It was a shabby business, if the truth is told.'

Saulos had stiffened.

'There was nothing shabby about it and I feel no guilt. The Torah had to be defended against blasphemy.'

What business of Gamaliel's was it, how Saulos *felt?* Part of Saulos had wanted to disclose his heart to his wise old tutor. In his awkwardness and uncontrollable anger, he envied the old man's urbanity.

'Yeshua was a very good man,' said Gamaliel. These words were a bitter gall to the young fanatic who wanted to block his ears as the old man continued. 'I am thankful that in the end it was the Romans who executed him and that he was not given the Jewish condemnation of stoning. We should all have known that that was wrong. Even Caiaphas was saying to me the other day that the thing should never have come to trial. Maybe it never would have done so, my dear, if you had not made friends with Judas Iscariot, and started that rumour that Yeshua was in league with the zealots and planning an uprising against the Romans. It was that which tipped the balance against Yeshua in the mind of Pontius Pilate. I am sure of that. You, though, became too involved emotionally.'

'It was simply a matter of law, of principle,' said Saulos stiffly.

Gamaliel smiled at him kindly.

'You know, Saulos, I think you envied Yeshua.'

'Why do you say that?'

'Because Yeshua was one of that rare class of being, a man

674

who was at one with himself and at one with God. He had somehow learnt the secret of how to live, how to be simple. That was what made him invulnerable, even when he had been beaten by the soldiers and dragged out to die on Skull Hill he was still in his own mysterious fashion strong, because he had never been, as most men are, at war with himself. He had always been the same person. I've known the family for years. He is a cousin of Yusif of Arimathea, you know, that charming man in the treasury who arranged his funeral.'

'I know.'

'Oh, I can remember Yeshua coming to argue with us when he was just a little lad, preparing for his Bar-Mitzphah. He *was* a clever little thing. He knew the Scriptures as well as the wisest doctors of the Law, and yet he had an almost idiot simplicity. Miriam, his poor distracted mother – you know it is always said she has blue blood in her veins – a direct descendant of King David.'

'I've heard that.'

'I remember her, anyway, saying to me, Yeshua says that we should live like the birds. "What, I say to him, do we do for money, answer me that?" "God feeds and clothes the birds," said Yeshua, "why should he not feed you, Mother?" Yes, Yeshua was at one with himself and at one with God. Most of us are at war with ourselves. We want to be chaste, but we find it hard; we want to live simply, but we crave riches. When we meet a figure like Yeshua in whom these conflicts do not seem to exist, we find it disturbing. That happened to you, didn't it, my dear? And so you wanted to kill him; you wanted to kill his freedom, his ability to live without conventions, his natural goodness. If all men were like Yeshua, there would be no need for laws, or the Law.'

'He mixed with harlots,' said Saulos, 'drunkards, quisling collaborators with the Roman authorities, as well as with the zealots whom you mentioned, hothead terrorists who are willing to put innocent civilian lives at risk for the sake of their political ideas. Yeshua had no morality at all.'

'No,' agreed Gamaliel. 'None at all. That is what I have been saying. Morality is only for sinners. Do you remember how he broke up the rabble when they were going to stone that adulteress?'

'Typical interference in the due processes of the law.'

'And he said, "Let the man who has no sin cast the first stone".'

'The casuistry is typical of the man,' said Saulos. 'That is the sort of thing he was always saying. But it is all perfectly clear. The Law prescribes, in cases of flagrant adultery . . .'

'Yes, yes, the Law prescribes. But I wonder if you would have thrown a stone at that woman after Yeshua had said those words.'

'Certainly I should.'

'Saulos – my dear – what is the Torah?'

'That is a schoolroom question. The Torah is the mind and will of the Almighty, graven on Sinai stone by His own right hand, the gift of the all-Holy to his chosen people, written in our hearts and inscribed in the holy scrolls of our scriptures. He has spoken to our race, alone and select throughout the entire world. While the rest of humankind sank into moral chaos and depravity, the Jews have kept alight the sacred knowledge of how mankind should live.'

'True, the Jews are the conscience of the human race. But even the sacred Torah itself is no more than a shadow, an echo of God's mind in man's mind. It was drawn up because men and women are sinful. But if there were another way, if there came among us a man who was so in tune with the mind of God and so at one with God, that he felt no instinct to murder, to steal, to commit adultery, what then? Would he not be entitled to show no interest in what you and I call morality?'

'There is no such man and never was,' said Saulos, but the words scalded him as he spoke them.

'I think we might have wanted to kill such a man if he had been born of our race,' said Gamaliel. 'That is why I ask you, "What is the Torah?" There are the laws of the schoolmasters and the armies and the judiciaries. Those who break them are punished and, in time, those who exercise authority come to believe in law for its own sake. They fall in love with punishment itself, they enjoy condemnation, they forget that Our Father in Heaven is a loving God who forgives our sins and cleanses us from all unrighteousness. There are other sorts of law, however, and those are what we call the laws of nature. Fire burns, so it is not wise to put your hands in the flame. Weights fall to the ground, so it is not safe to step off a cliff top. What if the laws of morality were really laws of this order, part of His loving care, mere warnings to us that we shall suffer in our inward selves if we seek only to live for ourselves, if we nurse anger or pursue greed and lust? Then, could we not feel that these laws, implanted in the hearts of all, and not just in the hearts of Jews, were not the end of life, but merely the beginning of wisdom, and that those who transgressed these laws were not to be punished but to be pitied, as we might pity the folly and carelessness of a child who had thrust his hand into the fire? You remember what they reported Yeshua as saying when he was lifted up on to the cross?'

'Yes.'

'They are not easy words to forget, are they, my son?'

'No.'

' "Father, forgive them – they know not what they do." '

Gamaliel was right. The words could not be forgotten. They were intolerable. Saulos did not want such forgiveness. He did not want the liberty of living as Yeshua had taught us to live. If there was need for forgiveness then this was only another way of saying that there was a cause for condemnation. If those who condemned Yeshua to die on the cross needed to be forgiven, then they were guilty of a terrible crime, at best the killing of an innocent man, at worst, something much graver and more mysterious. Stephanos in his homiletic martyrion had declared the crucifying of Yeshua to be the killing of the Holy One of God, the slaying of the Christ. Among those who followed the Way there was even talk of Yeshua himself being the promised Messias. The wilder among them even claimed that they had been granted visions of Yeshua after he had died, but since a large proportion of these were women there was no need to take them particularly seriously.

So, Saulos had led the persecution of Stephanos and yes, yes! Saulos had cast the first stone. Saulos had torn with a boulder at that smooth skin and cracked the beautiful temple of the young man. And he would go on killing followers of the Way until he had stamped them out and rid the world of their immoral poison.

'Father, forgive them – they know not what they do.'

677

Yeshua had been speaking, presumably, only of his perse-
cutors as they nailed him to the Cross at Passover time. Saulos
had subsequently come to believe that the utterance was of a
far broader consequentiality. If the race of mankind knew not
what it did, if they were in fact a race of moral idiots, ethical
imbeciles, then forgiveness or contempt were the only
possible reactions they deserved. But, if that were the case,
what was the position of the Jews, who were very far from
being moral idiots? For they *did* know what they were doing –
they had the Torah! Was their self-discipline, honesty,
sobriety to count for nothing in the eyes of the Almighty?
And if virtue counted for nothing, what *could* win God's
favour and love? Yeshua in his stories and apothegms spoke
as if we could not, did not need to, bargain with God. His love
was poured out for us without our asking for it, like the love
of that father in the story of the prodigal son. The boy did not
have to earn his father's favour when, having wasted all his
substance, he turned for home. The father was waiting for
him at the gate, ready to kill the fatted calf and put the best
robe on his lost child, now found again. Saulos had so easily
identified with the elder brother in that story who sulked and
refused to come to share in the festivities of the fatted calf.
The father seemed to want to place the two brothers on the
same moral level. The love of the father was not won or
earned by all the loyalty and hard work of the good elder
brother. Did this mean that the sin of mankind was not going
to be *paid for*? Surely, Saulos believed, there must be
punishment for wrongdoing? The patterns of natural justice
demanded it. And if the words of Yeshua had been true it was
hard to see how moral imperatives had any seriousness, how,
indeed, they remained imperatives at all. If the reward is
fatted calf, whether you work hard or waste your substance,
what is the point of working hard?

Such questions throbbed through the mind of Saulos in
subsequent weeks, as he continued to persecute the followers
of the Way. He found it extremely easy work to persuade
most of the fools, when they were arrested, to recant the
error of their ways. He began to notice within himself the
capacity to persuade people. The more simple-minded ones,
in particular, were putty in his fingers. It interested him,
moreover, that none of these enthusiastic followers of

Yeshua and his Way even began to see his religious significance or importance. Of course, this was chiefly because they
were too stupid, but even the intelligent ones like Yeshua's
cousin Yusif of Arimathea seemed woefully unable to concentrate on the central, pivotal thing. Yusif believed that
Yeshua offered a new Way of living, but this was little more
than an extension of the baptism of Joanes the Baptiser. Turn
again! Change! Find newness of life in the knowledge that
God is Abba, Father.

Did they not see the paradox in Yeshua's vision of the
universe and of the human race, that such a turning was
impossible? Oh, men could turn, but they could not change
what they were inside. Saulos remembered the scorching
love in Yeshua's eyes when he said, 'You lack one thing – go
and sell all and give to the poor.' Always, in Yeshua's vision of
mankind, it would lack one thing.

Chastity, as defined by any sane or legal definition must
mean an abstention from lustful behaviour. 'But I say to you,'
Yeshua had proclaimed, 'that anyone who looks at another to
lust after her, has already committed adultery in his heart.' It
was not enough to abstain from violence. Yeshua searched
out even the involuntary anger of the human heart. 'Be ye
therefore perfect, even as your Father in Heaven is perfect. . . .' 'Why call me good? No one is good, only God. . . .'

Precisely by his goodness, and by his searching reappraisal
of the very nature of ethics, Yeshua had revealed the great
ache in the universe, the gulf between our good desires and
the divine perfection. He had placed the virtuous Pharisee
and the sinful publican on the same level before God, because
both fall short of the divine perfection. His shortlived
popularity with the mob could partly be explained by his
humorousness, his attractiveness, his apparent easiness.
'Learn from me – my yoke is easy and my burden light.' And
they had been drawn to that, the fools, and not realised that
this was itself a condemnation of the human race, a nullifying
of all the ethical codes and moral systems which good men
had been painstakingly devising since the dawn of consciousness.

Yeshua's religion derived from the Psalter and explored
with relentless and unsparing extremism the implications of
those haunting songs. The relationship between God and the

Psalmist was that of a tempestuous love affair, a catalogue of reconciliations, estrangements, battles, tenderness, desolation. Yeshua's last words on the Cross were reported to have been a quotation from the Psalms – 'My God, my God, why hast thou forsaken me?' In those words, Saulos now began to see, Yeshua had spoken not only for himself in his loneliness, he had spoken for the entire human race. Why were the race of men God-forsaken? Had the Psalmist not also written that God was a loving father who forgave men their sins? As far as the east is from the west, so far hath he set our sins from us? But how, how, was this forgiveness to be achieved? 'Thou desirest not sacrifice, else had I given it thee. . . . The sacrifice of God is a troubled spirit, a broken and contrite heart, O God, thou wilt not despise . . .' Yet the voice of the Almighty in the face of sin must always be the same: 'Forty years long was I grieved with this generation and said: it is a people who have erred in their hearts and who have not known my ways, unto whom I swear in my wrath, that they should not enter into my rest.'

This was the rub. Even God could not undo sin. Merely to say that God *forgave* would be to destroy all moral imperatives in the world, for if God merely forgave and overlooked all wrongdoing, why should we esteem virtue more than vice? Why not steal?

'Why call me good? Only God is good!'

'Thou desirest not sacrifice, else . . .'

God did desire sacrifice. Of this, Saulos became increasingly convinced. He felt that he, and he alone, could see clearly what Yeshua had been saying, and, more than saying, what Yeshua had been doing. During those final ignominious days of Yeshua's life, Saulos and the others had collected the witnesses against him, had him arrested, beaten, tortured, killed. . . . Ever since, Saulos had lived with the guilty knowledge that he had condemned an innocent man. But there was something further, a feeling of disjointedness about the whole experience, and he now began to ask himself whether Yeshua had not in some mysterious fashion been in control, whether he had not wanted this death, whether this death of a pure, innocent victim, this offering of a perfected humanity, was not the arcane healing for which the universe yearned and travailed. No one is good but God. We can only call God Abba if we are reconciled to him through the death of Yeshua. . . .

Saulos felt the attractiveness of these new and wholly strange ideas as others might be drawn to the sensualities of Eros or to the lure of narcotics. He knew them to be a terribly, explosively dangerous set of assumptions. He felt that he himself, and all his religion, and the very Temple itself at Jerusalem with all its hierarchies, laws, rubrics and formularies, its priests and levites, its screaming goats and birds spattering their blood in the area of sacrifice, its money-changers and treasurers, would be overthrown if Yeshua had been right. By Yeshua, Saulos meant his vision of Yeshua. This was what made it so imperative to destroy the religion of Yeshua, the followers of the Way. Yeshua was not merely an itinerant exorcist, who told people funny stories in order to inspire them to become better Jews. If Saulos was right . . . If Saulos was right, Yeshua was not merely claiming to be the Anointed Messias of God, but in his deliberate act of self-sacrifice on the Cross . . . Such thoughts stopped being thoughts and became wild visions in which Yeshua had a superhuman status, in which his death had undone the profound ache in nature's heart and reconciled the erring hearts of men to the fountain of goodness. And this was to make him into a being of divine power. Saulos thought of that long, strange face which he had first seen as a little child in Britain so many years since, and then of Yeshua the man, the disturbing combination of absolute love and absolute knowingness in those dark, humorous eyes. Even to have the thoughts which were now possessing Saulos was an act of blasphemy. The thoughts held out to him the supreme temptation. His guilty part in the Crucifixion would become, not the worst thing he had ever done in his life, but the best. The murder of the innocent of Golgotha became a triumph of God's purposes. He could positively glory in the Cross!

No, no, no! He must suppress these thoughts, and he must suppress the followers of the Way before they realised its significance. The heart of the Way for these simpletons consisted in brotherly love, holding things in common, being diligent in their Temple-observance, and generous in alms. They still spoke of the death of Yeshua as a disgrace to those Jewish authorities who had not recognised him for the great prophet he was. These fools thought that Yeshua had been teaching them a simple ethical system, and they were trying to put it into practice. They did not see ... Pray God, they would never see ... It was Saulos's own secret, the knowledge of what Yeshua had been doing, alone in the darkling desolation of Golgotha. It was the ultimate witchcraft, the deepest magic, the strangest and most terrible, and most wonderful idea, one which would transform the world even as it was trying to transform Saulos. But he would not let it, he would not.

The Way was even attracting adherents in the Diaspora. Saulos heard a rumour that it was infecting the synagogue at Damascus. Gamaliel and the older members of the Sanhedrin had laughed when Saulos had announced this. So, a few Jews in Syria were being kind to the poor, and living in a commune where they shared all their few possessions! Was that a reason for becoming so angry? What authority did the High Priest in Jerusalem have over Damascus? Saulos spoke as if it was the end of the world. Yes, he had retorted, furiously, to Gamaliel. 'It *is* the end of the world!'

'Oh, let him go,' said Gamaliel. 'There is a good Jew there called Ananias. He'll explain what they are doing.'

Saulos had insisted on getting letters from the High Priest to the leaders of the synagogue in Damascus, telling any followers of 'the Way' that they must return at once to Jerusalem and justify themselves in Sanhedrin.

It was an excessively hot day, one in which the sun dazzled, the dust choked and merely to be out of doors was a species of torture. Saulos felt heady in such weather, though frightened that he would be revisited by the mild epileptic convulsions with which demons had tormented him since childhood. If it had been possible to stop thinking, if only it had been possible to stop thinking for five minutes about Yeshua, and the Way, and the Cross .. ! What peace would follow. But his brain raced and churned with it. Sometimes, within the space of a minute, Saulos had experienced violently contradictory emotions: sentimental pity for kind, humorous Yeshua being killed on a cross; gnawing guilt for his own part in that death; certainty that it was all for the good, the more so if it were a death of necromantic power in which Yeshua was himself summoning up great strengths and powers by his sacrifice.

And all the time, throbbing through his whole being, Saulos had the appalled and grief-stricken knowledge that he loved Yeshua, he loved that man as he had never loved anyone before and now he was separated from the possibility of that love for ever . . . Jangling of bridles, flash of sunlight on the horse-furniture of the servants who accompanied Saulos on his journey, high sun and further along the road, a figure . . . A beggar – the roads were dotted with them, always. A leper? Saulos blinked and the man was no longer there. He blinked again and his eyes were dazzled by the sun. There *was* a figure, standing now directly in his horse's track. The beast reared. Saulos gazed towards the sun and saw the face of Yeshua Messias.

'Saulos, Saulos, why are you persecuting me?'

'You? Who are you?'

'Yeshua Bar-Yusif, whom you are still persecuting. But it is hard for you to go on fighting . . .'

Saulos had fallen from his horse. He lay on the road with his eyes closed, but he could still see that beautiful face and it no longer caused him any torment. It was looking at him with absolute love.

Four

A year passed, possibly a little longer. I had not got very far with
my book on the Lampitt family, but I now made a weekly visit to
Sargie notionally to 'help with his letters'. His correspondence
was in fact negligible, and on most weeks, my secretarial duties
did not extend beyond a walk to the local off-licence where I was
expected to procure half a dozen bottles of 'what killed Auntie'.
Of course, no reference was implied, by Sargie's rather hackneyed kenning, to either of his actual aunts, Gloria Boyd-Fleet,
his mother's sister, nor to old Michael Lampitt's sister Lavinia. [I
remember her architectural watercolours hanging on the
Rectory walls. 'Well in the Shotter Boys league' was Uncle Roy's
verdict on these accomplishments. Critical rigour was never
brought into play when surveying the achievements of Sargie's
family. Uncle Roy, for example, was the only person whom I
ever heard to praise the Symphonic Poems of Campbell Dilkes,
Lavinia's husband, a minor musician, a friend of Elgar's, and a
collector, with Vaughan Williams and Cecil Sharp, of English
folksongs. (Strangely enough, Campbell Dilkes achieved
immortality through one air, though few who listen to it know
the name of the composer: the melody from his 'Surrey
Rhapsody' is used as the theme tune for the Mulberrys.)]

   After a session with Sargie the essential difficulty of the man
would sometimes overwhelm me. His whims and violent mood-
swings would have repelled any but one like myself who had
known him a long time and fallen into the habit of making
repeated allowances. On that particular afternoon, when my
narrative resumes, Sargie had been shedding gin tears on my
arrival (supposed fear that I had forgotten the appointment,
certainty that no one really liked him, fury with Vernon for
having Cecily to stay at Mallington the previous week) to a quite
different mood. Within half an hour of the deep, self-pitying
melancholy which greeted my arrival, he had been cackling

with ruthless glee at the latest edition of *The Spark*. He flung it across the room for me to read.

'Second para, my dear, on the gossip page, the "Diary" thing. What's Lover Boy going to make of that, do you suppose?'

The paragraph read as follows:

To the House of Lords to lunch with my old friend Lord ('Ernie') Lampitt to commiserate with him for not being chosen as a member of the new government. Harold, it would seem, had more or less promised him a Cabinet post, but a certain lady who has the Prime Minister's ear was said to be opposed to the appointment.

Ernie can perhaps turn his attention to family matters. Jason Grainger of 'The Mulberrys' (otherwise known as Julian Ramsay) is to undertake the history of the Lampitts, and looks likely to drag many skeletons out of the family cupboards.

We have not been able to gauge the reaction to Mr Grainger's work by that other Lampitt biographer – televisionary and man-about-literary-London Raphael Hunter. No doubt Mr Grainger will be able to shed light on the mysterious death, seventeen years ago, of James Petworth Lampitt, the bachelor man of letters, who fell to his death from a fire escape into the area beneath his flat in Manchester Square. Did Lampitt fall, or was he pushed? Since only his biographer, Mr Hunter, was present on this occasion, he is perhaps in a position to supply this vital information. We wonder how many cases there are in which a biographer has been the agent of his subject's demise?

I was astonished that Darnley had chosen to print all this stuff. My first reaction was one of selfish annoyance that he had somehow involved *me* in the story. I was in no better position than anyone else to know how Jimbo died, and by suggesting that I would tell the story, *The Spark* managed to implicate me in their scarcely covert assertion that Hunter had murdered the old man. Since it was over a year since Robey had begun to voice this thought, it seemed extraordinary that Darnley should have chosen now, of all times, to print the story.

When I had absorbed the surprisingness of the story being

printed, I was able to feel further surprise at Sargie's reaction. Probably there is no appropriate reaction to the discovery, or suggestion, long after a brother's death, that he had in fact met a violent end. I was shocked, none the less, by the absence of sadness in Sargie as he crowed over the story. He appeared to view the whole matter as a weapon against Hunter, detestation of whom grew with the passage of time.

'So – Lover Boy's got his come-uppance at last!'

'I don't quite see that, Sargie.'

'He's only been exposed as a murderer!'

'Accused, not exposed. He's bound to sue the paper for libel, and I should think he'll make a lot of money out of it.'

'Wouldn't dare, my dear. Your friend Darnley's got him on toast. If he comes to court, Darnley will produce evidence. Vebba clebba febba, Darnley. I'm only sorry they've abolished the rope. Perhaps Harold will bring it back; he seems so bloody keen on giving the IP what they want, and apart from an indoor *topos*, it's the one thing most English people most ardently desire, the restoration of the gallows.'

'Darnley hasn't enough evidence to hang his hat on, let alone hang Hunter.'

'You'll see, my dear. Lover Boy won't sue, too much of a coward, and that'll be an admission of guilt. You'll see – he's guilty as hell.'

These were the words which were still repeating themselves inside my head as, one evening, I stewed in the Miller Street baths. For some time, I had been a devotee of Turkish baths. To be lightly poached in the steam rooms, to be so intensely hot and moist that all physical strains and all thoughts were purged by the mere concentration of breathing in that atmosphere, produced sensations of well-being which were incomparable. I would always emerge from the baths with my worries in better perspective and the general melancholy of life momentarily assuaged. I had tried several Turkish baths, but the Miller Street ones were my favourite, not least because they were only a very short walk from my home. That proud old Victorian building off Camden High Street was pulled down long ago. It constituted a weird place of architectural eclecticism. Outside, its plain brick façade and pillared portico suggested the Queen Anne revival of the 1890s. Inside, you passed through a sitting-out room lined with cubicles and divans whose décor blended music-hall and pub in its riot of Edwardian baroque, its gilded electroliers and lamp brackets, its green flock fleur-de-lis wallpaper. Changed, wrapped round with towels, one descended the gradual stairs to an area of cold pools, a poor man's version of the Arab hall at Leighton House, where a fountain splashed against sub-de Morgan turquoise tiles. Beyond the cold baths, the showers, and beyond them, the steam rooms, Vales of Lethe where libel, *The Spark*, the emotional lives of friends, the problems of what to do with one's life, all slowly sweated themselves into nothingness and evaporated in the steam. The atmosphere was as thick as one of the old pea-soup fogs evoked in the Sherlock Holmes stories, or as the profoundest sea-mist in a late canvas by Turner. One was aware that there were electric lights shining some-where, giving a yet more ethereal quality to the thick vapours, now purest white, now evanescent silver, through which the eye was aware of other human figures, but so dimly aware that it would not be quite true to say that one *saw* them. Only thick smudges of grey appeared to the sight, sometimes assuming form, sometimes fading to whiteness again, as, in the first shock of extreme heat, I breathed through my mouth and peered about to find my way to the edge of the room and the benches which lined the wall.

The room, for all I knew, could have contained two or twenty people. It was impossible to gauge. Only when my nose was almost touching the wall tiles could I discern a patch of empty bench and deposit myself upon it, waiting for the next faint evaporation of the steam to see whether I could stretch myself out without kicking another man in the face.

One's eyes accustom themselves gradually to such an atmos-phere. It grew more possible to sense, at least, if not to see the presence of others. Then the steam lessened for a while to the point where the grey smudges took human shape and colour and one saw here a scarlet pot-belly, there a hairy shoulder blade. There is a passage in the Bible which Uncle Roy enjoyed declaiming where the prophet Isaiah had a vision in the Temple: the Holy of Holies is filled with smoke, and through the fumes and the rays of light he makes out the presence of six-winged angels. Miller Street baths conjured up visual experiences comparably remote from everyday. I knew that there was a figure quite near me, and when the mist cleared and I could make out its shape, younger than the last pot-bellies glimpsed but not unflabby in its soft sloping shoulders and rather full breasts, making me have a moment of wondering whether I had accidentally strayed into the baths during a women's session, and whether the hirsute limbs half glimpsed earlier had been figures of my imagination. The figure who had arrested my attention was, I decided, just too close to me on the bench for it to be easy to stretch out my legs, so I swivelled myself once more into a sitting posture and buried my face in a towel for a further five or ten minutes of pure thoughtless sensation. (Keats, in the mood which made him exclaim, 'O for a life of sensations, rather than of thoughts!' would have been happy in the Miller Street baths.)

When I removed the towel from my face, it seemed as if the soft, womanish body on my left had edged nearer. Certainly now, there would have been no question of stretching out horizontally on the bench, as I had originally considered. He was so close that he was visible all the time, even at the thickest swirling of the steam, close enough for me to be able to see him, and to be aware, though I could not make out his face, that he was peering intently in my direction. Moreover, his hands clutched the edge of the bench, and one of them, his right hand, was now within inches of my thigh.

I was not so naïf as to suppose that everyone attended Turkish baths purely for the enjoyment of steam and heat. The proximity of scantily clad sweating male bodies never happened to be a temptation to myself, but – *chacun à son goût*. I had never seen any man at the Miller Street baths behaving in a remotely suggestive manner, but for some reason on this occasion, the hand of my near neighbour, even though it was not yet touching me, made me think that I was unquestionably in the presence of a man on the prowl for a sexual partner. It seemed the moment to cross one's legs and fold one's arms. The only irritation it caused me was that it forced me to think, or to have semi-coherent thoughts, until the remedy occurred. I could stand up and find a space on the bench on the other side of the room. I did so, wandering somewhat more cautiously now through the Dantean fogs and half-embodied shapes on the mosaic floor. It was only when I crossed the room and found a completely empty bench, where I could stretch out with ease, that I realised that I had been followed. The womanish form was there at my side. In quite insistent, nasal tones, it spoke.

'Shall we sit down together?'

'I don't think so,' I said.

As I replied, the steam cleared momentarily to reveal our faces to one another and I found myself looking into the eyes of Raphael Hunter.

The embarrassment of the situation was potentially enormous, not least because I had an irrational fear that he might think I had been pursuing *him*. As a young man, I worried very much about how other people would assess my own sexual proclivities; it is one of the blessings of age that one ceases to mind about these things.

My ex-mother-in-law, Sibs Starling, used to assert that 'there was a pansy on the top of every omnibus', an article of faith not often substantiated, I should guess, from a personal experience. She considered herself rather an expert at nosing 'them' out, and often hinted that she thought Hunter was 'one of them'. When her daughter Anne formed her disastrous infatuation for Hunter, about a year after I married her, I had given little credence to Sibs's suggestion that Hunter was ambivalent in preference. Bloom had once told me that Hunter was homosexual, but Bloom believed that this was true of most men, even though some, for their own baffling reasons, chose to conceal this taste by the casting up of contrary smokescreens. The fact that a man like Hunter had a string of female conquests behind him (I myself knew, from first-hand observation, of Miss Beach, Vanessa Faraday, Felicity, Isabella Marno the actress, and my wife Anne) was all the more reason, in Bloom's eyes, for guessing that Hunter's interests really lay elsewhere.

'It stands out a mile, darling.'

'What does?'

This, on my part, entirely unintentional *double entendre* provoked one of Bloom's explosions of abandoned mirth, tongue out, eyes rolling, a laugh which seemed to bear relation to narcotic or religious ecstasy.

'Well, perhaps not a mile. Not on that young lady. O, darling, you'll kill Mother if you make too many cock jokes.' He dabbed the corner of tearful eyes with a red and white spotted handkerchief. 'But those women in Miss Hunter's life – little lesbian affairs for her – they don't fool Mother. They never last, you see. A whole string of women, all for show like a little string of pearls on her little twinset. It's the way queens behave. We

689

can never be happy with a good thing when we see it. Straight men give up the chase eventually.'

'Not always. What about Casanova?'

Another pause for manic eldritch laughter.

'By this view, any deviation from pure, heterosexual, lifelong monogamy would really be a sign of . . .'

'Don't be shy, darling, you can tell Mother.'

Bloom patted my hand.

'Mind you,' he added, 'I think that's true. Faggots flit from flower to flower, busy little bees that they are, cruising down the river, popping in and out of the cottages.' His eyes rolled at this strange pair of expressions, more redolent of *Wind in the Willows* than the actual range of activities denoted. 'You know, I think the straightest guy I've ever known is you, Rikko.'

He stroked the shoulder of Rikko Kempe's windjammer. Everyone else with us at the pub that evening had laughed. Rikko patted a violently blonded perm with his carefully manicured hand, pursed glossed lips and fluttered mascara'd eyes crossly.

'This is a very boring subject,' he said in his gravelliest, most manly, Stan Mulberryish tones.

Fenella, his wife, never quick on the uptake even when sober, had stirred herself on her bar-stool and grinned winsomely at Bloom as if imploring him to hold the lid on this Pandora's box and keep his reflections to himself. She began an anecdote about Lord Kitchener.

'Shut up, Fenella, you did not know him,' said Rikko petulantly.

'My father and he were best friends. They knew everything about one another.'

'Lord Kitchener liked buggering women, we know,' said Bloom. 'That's not what we're talking about.'

'Oh,' said Fenella.

She grinned yet more fixedly, hoping that no one would ask her at that vodka-soaked stage of evening, to make any comment to demonstrate that she had been following the previous line of argument.

That conversation with Bloom, and the judgements of Sybil, probably came to mind after my Miller Street encounter with Hunter, but the essence of their theme, and the whole question of the ambiguity of human emotions, and the fallibility of judgements based on appearances, did sweep into my mind there and then.

Hunter, however, was nothing if not brazen in his approach to social difficulties. How else could he have smiled in the faces of so many men whom he had cuckolded, or heartbreakingly contrived to offer friendship, the very last thing they at that stage wanted, to women whom he had discarded as sexual partners? So now, semi-naked in the steam, and very nearly unmasked as the sort of faintly pathetic individual who might risk arrest and imprisonment for making a nuisance of himself in a public place, Hunter stepped back from the moment and resumed control. It had, after all, only been a split second during which his guard had dropped and, if his next sentence were true, then his first – 'Shall we sit down together?' – was stripped of any suggestive purport.

'I was fairly sure it was you, Julian. Well met.'

This was a matter of opinion. I considered walking away from him into the steam. Certainly an encounter with Hunter was calculated within seconds to undo the therapeutic effect of the steam room and to bring to mind not merely the women he had made unhappy, but also, all those Hunterish questions about life itself, the extent to which one was a success or a failure, the degree to which one had got on.

'We could go and sit in the hot rooms where there is no steam.'

He spoke quietly. We could, I thought, do as he suggested. Alternatively, he could stick his head in the toilet and pull the chain on it.

Strangely enough, though, it was impossible, in Hunter's presence, to allow the slightest unpleasantness to show through. His own smiling gentleness of manner neutered all situations, making them pappy as his prose, pasty as his skin. I found myself obediently following him into the hot rooms.

He held the door open for me as he said, 'You will have guessed that there are a couple of things I wanted to talk about.'

His words and manner put the embarrassing moment of a few seconds earlier firmly out of mind, implying almost that I had come to Miller Street baths specifically for the purpose of talking literary 'shop' with Hunter, even, perhaps, that this was something we did together quite regularly.

'First let me say, I'm thrilled, truly, about the idea of your Lampitts book,' he said.

'Who told you I was writing it?' I asked, hoping very much that he had not read about it in *The Spark*.

'Madge' (his publisher) 'keeps her ear to the ground. Now, some people have already spoken as if you've been setting yourself up as my rival. They'll say anything to create mischief. I've already made it clear that I regard you as a friend and the book you are writing will complement my more *literary* biography of Petworth.'

To whom had these assurances been made? For a few more sentences, he prosed on about his own difficulties in getting started with Volume II, his readiness to help me in any way he could, for example with introductions to Virgil D. Everett, the American collector in whose archive the papers and literary remains of Jimbo were, thanks largely to Hunter's machinations, deposited.

'The Everett Foundation have already said that I can see the Lampitts Papers,' I said. 'Sargie has squared it with them.'

'Oh, he *has*?' That weasely look came into Hunter's face. 'Good, good. I'm not saying this *will* happen, but just in case Sargent has unintentionally queered your pitch . . .'

'How could he have done that?'

'He may think he has arranged everything with the Everett Foundation, but in fact, by the terms of the purchase, I have the ultimate say-so about who is permitted to consult the Lampitt Archive.' He paused for a while so that I could gasp at the production of this trump card. 'No one can lay a finger on the Lampitt Papers without consulting me, and in this case' – Hunter's voice always became more nasal when emphasising a point – 'no one has in fact consulted me.'

'I thought Virgil D. Everett might have some say in the matter,' I said shortly. 'After all, he owns the Lampitt Papers.'

'I'm sure there'll be no diffficulty,' said Hunter. 'It's just a good example, that's all, of how one's got to be – shall we say' – he smiled that indulgent, amused smile of his, creasing and half closing his eyes with mock, or perhaps actual, affection – 'a *little* cautious with some of Sargent's wilder utterances.'

It was hardly a wild utterance of Sargie to say that he had written to the American who had bought his brother's literary remains. I had typed the letter myself and we had received a reply, which I now only understood for the first time, stating that Sargie's request (permission for me to visit New York and read through the manuscripts in the Everett Collection) would almost certainly cause 'no problems' and that the letter had been passed on to the Custodian of the Lampitt Papers to whom all future correspondence should be addressed. Until this encounter in the Miller Street baths, I had forgotten that the Custodian of the Papers was Hunter himself. It was, on the face of it, unlikely that anyone had ever asked before to consult the Lampitt Papers. This was another thing which only began to occur to me then. I had breezily assumed that people were coming into American libraries all the time, leafing through documents for their own obscure purposes, perhaps for no purpose at all other than to pass the time. I had therefore assumed that 'the Custodian' was a busy person, dealing with such requests as my own on a regular basis. But who, now one came to think of it, would wish to consult the Lampitt Papers? The Everett Foundation was in any case a private collection, not a public library or an academic institution. Virgil Everett bought literary manuscripts in the way that other men bought blue chips, as an investment. Hunter had persuaded Everett to make him the 'Custodian' of this particular archive solely to safeguard his own position as Jimbo's biographer. Since my own enterprise could be regarded in some sense as a threat to Hunter, I was not optimistic about my chances of his allowing me to see the papers. I had that feeling which had visited me before in his presence, if not quite of being in his power, at least in a position where he could make a fool of me.

'I've been absurdly busy as usual,' he said, appearing to answer the question I had not asked; more, seeming to indulge me with titbits of information for which I was open-mouthed, ravenous. 'The London Library Committee takes up a lot of time, and I've been co-opted on to the Leverhulme thing, and I'm judging no less than six prizes this winter. Then the Government – this is rather between ourselves – wants to set up a committee to advise the new Arts Minister.'

'I think poor Vernon Lampitt was rather hoping for that appointment,' I said.

'Is this another of Sargent's ideas?' He smiled good-humouredly, making me feel that I had made a rather feeble joke which he was trying to find amusing, for politeness's sake. 'Thank goodness, anyway, that we have an Arts Minister at last. I've been pressing to have one for years. Jennie is somewhat at sea, which is why I – she – thinks that such a committee would be no bad idea. I've talked to Charles Snow a certain amount about it, and we've been throwing some very interesting ideas about.'

He shrugged and smiled. Where there were twenty blotters around a table, with Minutes and Apologies for Absence and Any Other Business, there would be Hunter in the midst.

'It leaves little time for writing,' he added. For a moment, as if consulting an order paper he looked down at his navel. 'The other thing which I wanted to pick your brains about is rather more delicate.'

For a moment, I expected an embarrassing confession, a description of the compulsion which led him to follow naked men about steam rooms.

'I know that you are a friend of Miles Darnley,' he said. 'The last time I was in Malvern, Robbie Larmer told me that you and Miles were at Seaforth Grange together.'

Hunter was at least ten years my senior, so we had not overlapped as pupils at Seaforth Grange. He had evidently been one of the Headmaster's favourites. In common with most people who attended this hellish establishment, I regarded Mr Larmer as an almost criminal monster, and I could not imagine wishing to remain on terms with him in grown-up life.

'Margot's very much crippled with arthritis. ' He sighed to contemplate the sorrows of the Headmaster's wife, a figure if anything more insufferably cruel than the Binker himself.

'They are thinking of moving into a bungalow down on Barnard's Green. Robbie's as alert as ever, still manages the *Telegraph* crossword each morning.'

'Surely not a very difficult accomplishment?' This observation of mine sounded harsh, ill-mannered.

'Naturally,' Hunter said, 'I talked over with Robbie what to do about Miles.'

Hunter was leaning forward now, pressing his palms together.

'I've nothing against Miles personally. Nothing. Robbie's view is that I must sue, however, in order to establish the truth. It's a very serious charge, Julian.'

The idea that libel trials clear the air, or establish the truth, is not one borne out by a study of legal history. I did not then know enough to be able to say so to Hunter. I was chiefly arrested by the thought that he still regarded the Binker as a friend and confidant. The Binker had made life insufferable for generations of boys at Seaforth Grange. He was a pervert and a sadist, a criminal whose activities should by rights have been brought to the attention of the police, not a wise old Nestor to whom one would naturally turn in grown-up life for advice about how to conduct one's affairs.

'I suppose Miles wrote the piece himself,' said Hunter. No aggression was visible in his features. He wore the same impassive smile, and spoke in the same toneless voice which would have been adopted had he been presenting the cheque at a poetry prize-giving or making a speech at the AGM of the Royal Society of Literature or the PEN Club. 'I simply have no idea how he could have got hold of such a story: that I, who did so much for Petworth, and so much for his reputation after he had died, that I could have . . .' Words failed him. 'We've got nearly all his stuff into paperback now, many of them with introductions by myself.'

His tone implied that not marble nor the gilded monuments of princes could be a more enviable memorial for a deceased writer.

'I think they felt . . .'

'They?'

I was completely convinced, by the testimony of all the Lampitts who had spoken to me about it, that Hunter's claims to have been very close to Jimbo were fraudulent. This was not to say that he was a murderer. I did not know what to think about it all.

Years had passed since I had trusted Hunter, or taken him at his word, but it was perhaps not until this meeting in the Miller Street baths, talking of James Petworth Lampitt, that I reached the view that Hunter was through and through a creature of artifice, a person whose true identity, if it existed at all, had never been displayed and whose projected self, offered to the world as a substitute for actual encounter with a real man, had as little substance as vapour. So forcibly did this image present itself to me that I would hardly have been surprised, now that we were in the dry room where the air was clear and the outlines of benches, chairs, lockers and other bathers were sharp, had Hunter's form evaporated from my sight as it had done in the Stygian fogs of the steam room. The absolute non-existence of the self he had been presenting through the years, and the capacity for inflicting suffering which his fraudulence had explored, had a curiously weakening effect on me. For years, I had supposed that I hated Raphael Hunter, because women I had loved had loved him so distractedly, because his presence in my life had created so much suffering; but I did not really hate him. I realised that for all those years I had been peering into an abyss, confronting an emptiness. My 'jealousy' of Hunter, for example, my obsessive certainty that he had had an affair with my wife, had been hatred of a phantom. I felt, sitting with him, tricked and puzzled. I also felt the extraordinary contrast between Hunter and Rice Robey, the new bane of my life. Both men, certainly, were capable of an impressive series of emotional conquests, but Hunter's success in this area was explained (I now felt) by what he wasn't, not by what he was.

Some great paintings convey their effect by leaving everything out; much oriental art depends on such a principle. This was Hunter. Rice Robey, by contrast, was like some full-square grotesque primitive painting, perhaps one of those curious Ethiopian renderings of Coptic saints or biblical characters, strong in outline and colour. There was nothing subtle about Rice Robey. Perhaps the confrontation between the two men was an archetypical clash of opposites, just such a conjunction of thesis and antithesis as Rice Robey liked to describe and expound. Undoubtedly – as I will now admit to myself, though I would not admit it at the time – I wanted a confrontation. I had come quite bitterly to resent Rice Robey's power over Felicity. I was jealous of it, though this was something which I did not fully appreciate. Instead, I told myself that I found it *boring* that she spoke of him all the time, tedious that she was deeper in with him as month succeeded month, and that he was not worthy of her. In fact, I was simply jealous of his hold over her, and over Darnley. It was only during that conversation with Hunter in the Turkish baths that I realised that my feelings about Rice Robey were not in control. I was ready, if necessary, to destroy him. Hunter was fishing for information about the authorship of the libel in *The Spark*. My motives from now onwards became base; I cannot defend myself, but any reader may be puzzled by my behaviour unless recognising that I did not understand the law of libel. I thought – it was probably a measure of my obsession with Rice Robey – that in a case such as this, the litigant would select the author of the offending sentences. It did not quite occur to me that several parties might be sued for the same offence – that Darnley could be sued for publishing the article, the printers for printing it, the news-agents for distributing and selling it. I thought that if responsibility and blame could be shifted to one man – the actual author of the story – Darnley and *The Spark* would escape Hunter's lawyer.

'When you knew Lampitt,' I began. I was never able to indulge in the absurdity of referring to Jimbo as 'Petworth'.

'Yes,' came Hunter's suspicious, nasal reply.

'How much part did a novelist called Albion Pugh play in his life?'

Hunter's smile momentarily vanished; then he laughed nervously.

'Oh, dear,' he said. 'I might have known that *he* was behind all this. You think it is likely he wrote the piece?'

'Certain.'

An expression passed over Hunter's face which made it clear that he had received the information he wanted. It was not an expression of triumph, so much as of finality. The chairman, having seen that there was no more to be discussed under the heading AOB was about to bring the meeting to a conclusion. We parted very shortly afterwards, I to the showers, he for another session in the steam.

I spent that evening dining at a cheap Greek restaurant with a girl. Our affair was not going well, and would soon come to an end. Since my moment of awakening with Felicity – when I held her and tried to comfort her some twelve months earlier, and she admitted to being in love with Rice Robey – girls had come back into my life. There was nothing worth writing down here. It is simply worth noting that life was once again punctuated by affairs. Evenings now were likely to include the cheapest restaurant supper I could find, or a visit to the cinema. I was back into the routine of looking for the perfect mate, an everlasting quest. In my case, ordinary standards disappear when I am engaged in the pursuit: that is, in seeking or finding friends, I have been guided by fondness, liking, or shared interest. Many of the girls I saw during that year were, by contrast, not necessarily people I would otherwise have liked. I do not think any of them fell in love with me; they certainly failed to engage my imagination.

Falling in love is the greatest imaginative experience of which most human beings are capable. What happened between myself and my Greek restaurant companion possessed as much imaginative significance as an encounter between two cats on a dustbin lid, possibly less. It was not to be compared with the Wagnerian opera which must have played inside Felicity's head whenever she thought of Rice Robey, a figure with whom she had indulged in no physical intimacy.

I envied Rice Robey's capacity to mythologise existence, to draw out of it shapes, stories, significance. I envied him his charm and his whatever it was he had instead of genius. I was also, as I have indicated, simply jealous of the devotion he excited in Felicity. Since the conversation in which she wept and we had hugged one another, everything had changed between Felicity and me. I saw no signs that she was aware of this. She still came and went. We still ate an evening meal together if no alternative materialised, but continued to have an independent social life. She had quite a number of friends, and I am sure that I was not the only ear into which she eagerly poured her stories of office gossip and the latest utterances or adventures of her sage. But life in Arlington Road was utterly different for me. What had been a companionable, cosily domestic arrangement, had turned into a torment. Visits to the bathroom, for example, were now charged with potential shocks. The size of her large wet footprints on the bath mat caused me paroxysms of frustration, and I more than once caught myself out in strange fetishistic and secret gestures, such as removing my own shoes and socks so as to place my own bare feet in her damp footprints, or taking one of her stockings from the towel rail where it hung to dry and pressing it to my lips.

Felicity, since confiding in me the state of her heart, had settled down. I was her Dutch uncle, and she still spoke obsessively about Rice Robey, but I think she had begun to be able to accept that their relationship would never go further than it had done already. What I had not fully absorbed, since I am not a philosopher, was Rice Robey's importance to her as a man of ideas. He had, though, effected in her an intellectual transition which was as extreme as could have been. My puzzlement, my inability to take in what was happening, could not be blamed on any reluctance of Felicity's to talk about it. Some days, she talked about it for hours at a time. Put simply (which she always refused to do) Rice Robey had converted her to a belief in God. As far as I am aware, this is a belief which has never left her and since religious conversions, in my circle of acquaintance, are rare, I wish I could provide a more coherent account of it.

The subject is one which interests me extremely, not least because I fail to understand it. I suppose that Felicity must be one of the most intelligent people I ever knew, perhaps the most intelligent. It is a pity she was so unwilling to put her ideas in a form which would have been intelligible to the layman. To my untrained eye, it seemed as though what happened was like this. When she withdrew from her job at Rawlinson and entered the Civil Service, she seemed to have reached the limits of her own rigidly empirical view of the universe. Rice Robey's idiosyncratic world-view had an effect on her which I felt to be highly comparable with the effect which reading William Blake had had on me several years before. Felicity denied the points of comparison, insisted that I did not begin to understand the religious viewpoint and further insisted, truthfully and not meaning to be unkind, that my use of language was too imprecise for it to be worth discussing the matter. Blake had changed and enriched my way of viewing life. I supposed that his conflict with eighteenth-century rationalism was comparable with the movements of Felicity's mind as she thrashed around the problems of logical positivism. Blake's importance for me was to make me see that the world of phenomena and of other people is not a fixed set of *things*, to be described or investigated in only one particular manner, but rather, a story which we tell to ourselves, a set of impressions capable of an infinitude of explanations or non-explanations, but which can only be intelligently perceived through the exercise of the imagination. Thus, for each of Sir Isaac Newton's scientific explanations of how the world appears to us, Blake provides an irrational but imaginatively satisfying alternative.

> The atoms of Democritus
> And Newton's particles of light
> Are sands upon the Red Sea Shore
> Where Israel's tents do shine so bright.

I took it that Rice Robey's unfinished scraps of verse and prose about St Paul were exploring similar territory. The significance of St Paul was not that he knew more about Christ than Caiaphas or Pontius Pilate had done. His importance, rather, was imaginative. Questions of theology were not empirical ones. I thought I now saw the point of Rice Robey's distrust of those two words Either/or. *Was Christ Divine?* was a question which deceived us because it appeared to be grammatically comparable with sentences such as *Was Napoleon a Corsican?*, an enquiry which could be settled one way or another by empirical analysis. Had the question of Christ's divinity been like this, his advent into the world could not conceivably have haunted the imagination of mankind for two thousand years. I could not admire the style of Rice Robey's new book, but I was excited by what seemed to be the central idea, an idea which had application far beyond St Paul: *Each of us comes to fullness of life only when we have learnt how to mythologise it.* My own experience had been shaped by the intricately extensive Lampitt drama being played out inside Uncle Roy's head, a vision wholly at variance with Hunter's plodding account of the same events and people. The Lampitts themselves hated Hunter's book because of its inaccuracies, or what they would see as downright lies. This was certainly one way of viewing Hunter's claim to have been Jimbo's secretary and years-long companion.

I believed Rice Robey's doctrine that we need stories by which to live. Each life needs, and probably creates, a mythology. For me, this makes sufficient sense of the religious question to enable me to leave it alone. For years, I was puzzled by the fact that religious opinions for which there was no shred of evidence or justification were those to which people clung most tenaciously, being prepared to die, or kill, for them. How could this be? In a suffering universe, why had religious people chosen to add to the suffering by resorting to physical violence, torture, wars and murders over such questions as whether the Holy Ghost proceeded from the Father alone or from the Father and the Son; or whether certain legends about the prophet Mahomet were true; or whether men and women were predestined or elected to divine grace? These were things in which it was not, strictly speaking, possible to believe; not in the sure and certain way we can believe in observable phenomena. Then I read in a book that 'religion is what we do with our madness', and I began to understand. The activities of the uncontrolled and unexplored self create religious belief, and it is in this unexplored area that we are most vulnerable. We protect the cloud-capp'd towers and gorgeous palaces of that insubstantial pageant more fervently than we would protect the quantum theory or Newton's Law of Thermodynamics because that is where we have learnt to come to terms with life's pain and muddle, if we have come to terms, which perhaps we never shall and perhaps we should not hope to do. That was what I had come to feel, anyhow, reading Blake, and recognising within myself all kinds of religious impulses which I knew could never honestly be translated into belief.

But Felicity had been rather quiet when I tried to put this point of view to her. This was partly a polite quietness since she evidently did not want to show up the inadequacy of my language, my looseness of expression; but there was more to it than this, for after a while she had quietly said that we evidently had rather different views of the religious question.

It was on some other occasion that she told me why. Apparently 'my' idea that the world is really something which we make up inside our own heads had been in circulation for centuries, certainly since Samuel Johnson refuted the ideas of Bishop Berkeley by kicking a stone. *I refute him thus*. The point, Felicity laboured it, was that there really was a stone, it really existed. I have never said that the stone did not exist, of course, but Felicity said that the logical corollary of my position was that truth did not matter, that we could, if we chose, decide that the stone kicked by Dr Johnson was a phantom, or a spoonful of mashed potato, and once you had gone down that path, Fliss said, of truth not mattering, there was no point in having any discussions or views about anything. And then we had a brief moment of agreeing that probably 'views' weren't very interesting, certainly less interesting than gossip; and we talked of the novels we liked reading, and remarked on the fact that in English, 'gossip' or interest in human character had called forth all the best writing; that even writers who could easily have devoted their writing lives to the cerebral exploration of ideas, like George Eliot, were at their most riveting when discussing and describing human character, and though 'ideas' might come into their books, they would not spoil the narrative flow by long disquisitions on metaphysical subjects. And at the mention of metaphysics, Fliss returned to the fray and said that I entirely misunderstood Rice Robey, probably misunderstood William Blake too, and that I had certainly misunderstood the nature of the things I was discussing. The fact that these things were so intensely difficult to grasp with imperfect linguistic tools did not diminish the supreme importance of trying to do so, which was what philosophers ever since Pythagoras and Plato had been trying to do. And this was one of the reasons that philosophy was so supremely important. The mystery was, that we do not, in fact, make up the world out of our heads. We receive it. We find ourselves in a universe where stones are not mashed potatoes, and there is an all-but-universal consensus of agreement about which is which. Much more intensely important and mysterious, we find ourselves in a universe where there is a similar consensus about the difference between good and bad. We cannot claim that this is just something happening inside our own heads. From the beginning of time, no one has been able to invert moral value. Different societies and religions might differ over inessentials such as the legality of eating pork or sleeping with a sibling, but the universality of moral values was far more striking than the minor points of difference. Here was something which was outside ourselves. It required our patient homage and intelligent attention. Perhaps too it required our silence, and our contemplation. And another thing, she had then surprisingly interjected, I had been quite wrong to think that Rice Robey suggested, in his writings, that Christianity was no more than some crazed fantasy buzzing about in the mind of St Paul, utterly wrong. The reverse was the case. All that Rice Robey was exploring in his book was the manner in which the imagination of St Paul worked on certain facts, certain given and authentic data. (I did not agree with her then, and I don't agree with her now about this matter, but this was how she argued.) She said that when Paul spoke of Christ as the Eikon of the Living God, he was presenting the authentic and revealed doctrine of the Incarnation – what Rice Robey called the God-enfleshment. You could not escape this, any more than you could escape the challenge to the imagination which it presented. Rice Robey believed, Felicity said, with Coleridge, that the primary imagination was the repetition in the finite mind of the eternal act of creation in the infinite I AM. I take it, this really means that the pictures drawn in our minds,

702

the stories we tell ourselves, are not, as I would contend, internalisations; they are actual invasions of the consciousness from outside. If I say that St Paul *imagined* his theology, I mean that he created myths about Christ which were a response to his own profoundest psychological needs (Rice Robey's speculation that it began with a guilt complex about the Crucifixion would make some kind of sense to me) and to which, for various reasons, many, many human beings have responded at the same deep level ever since. The myth that Jesus would come on the clouds to take the living and the dead to live with him in the sky was the first central story of Paul's message to the world and it set the tone for all the rest. Biggest and strangest myth was the idea that the Cross of Jesus itself had been able to remove the sin and guilt of the human race, or the guilt of those people who turned towards the Cross in faith. For me, the meaning of this idea will always be elusive, but I see that it can only be explored on an imaginative level. Clearly, when I thought of all the millions of human beings for whom the Cross has been the symbol and focus of salvation, I did not dismiss lightly what St Paul had set in hand. I did not think, and never have thought (since the coming to an end of my early adolescent quarrels with Uncle Roy about religion) that Christianity was a mere sham, or lie. I considered it a profoundly important thing, but something which existed on the level of the inner being, so that its truth could not be regarded as universal, it was not a commanding, undeniable truth before which everyone must bow, like the truth of mathematics. If an imaginative life has been focused on the Cross, then to kiss a crucifix or to sing 'When I Survey' might touch the deepest part of a person's soul, and be the most important thing in their lives. But for someone whose imagination had been shaped in a different way there was no obligation to believe in the Cross, or, indeed, in any of St Paul's other myths. It was not a truth which compelled.

This was not, however, how Felicity viewed the matter. She said that there were not various sorts of truth; it made no sense to talk of imaginative truth, or of things being true for one person, but not for another. In the case of Christianity, it ultimately came down to something unknowable, that is, whether God himself had actually been enfleshed, and entered history, and been born of Mary. This could never be investigated as an historical phenomenon, but in Felicity's mind it related to her increasing sense that truth is not something inside ourselves which we are fashioning out of our own psychological experiences as much as something utterly external to ourselves and which, in the case of great truth, religious truth, for example, or ethical or aesthetic truth, can only be perceived by the exercise of virtues, such as patience and humility. So, slowly and inexorably, she moved towards the acceptance of Belief – though it was some years before she joined the Society of Friends. I remained, and remain, on the borders, revering Felicity's mind as much as I revere her heart, but wondering, always, how truly intelligent and grown-up people could believe in stories of Jesus ascending into the clouds, or walking about on water, or rising from the dead – and if they did not believe these things, why did they call themselves Christians? It is rather an Anglican question, and no one quite seems able to give the answer, since Christ and Christianity continue to exercise such a benevolent and powerful hold on the human heart that some men and women will never leave go of Jesus even if they did cease to believe in miracles, or angels or perhaps even in God.

I do not mean to disparage Felicity's religious journey when I say that it had largely to do with Rice Robey. Her obsession with the man made it quite natural that she should follow his intellectual interests; to some degree it was inevitable that she should have come to think his thoughts, just as it sometimes happens when a person falls in love that, all unconsciously, they come to imitate the mannerisms, locutions, even on occasion, the handwriting of the adored one.

From Jo Lampitt, either direct, when I met her in pubs with Darnley, or through the indirect intermediary of Darnley himself, I gathered that Rice Robey's association with Kirsty had fizzled out. The last time he had tried to visit her in Cambridge she had pleaded a prior engagement, or pressure of work.

'She should have told him to piss off,' Jo opined, 'from the very beginning.'

'But presumably she found him charming.'

'He's a prize wanker.'

There seemed no point in rehearsing with Jo, whose approach to human psychology Darnley at least found reassuringly unsubtle, the possibility that charmless behaviour had never yet been an obstacle to strong attraction growing up between the sexes. I wondered slightly about Jo's reliability as a witness. She varied her accounts of what Rice Robey did or did not do with Kirsty. It may be said at this distance of time that it did not really matter, but I am one of those who is never reluctant to know these details about my fellow mortals, provided the information is authentic.

Felicity had for some time known of Rice Robey's visits to Cambridge, and she had duly absolved him. He had expounded to her the view which is mentioned in more than one of the Albion Pugh novels, of Sexless Eros, a doctrine which I think he invented, but which he claimed to derive in slightly wobbly descent from the writings of Plato, St Paul and Dânte. According to this view, when two people fall in love, or grow fond of one another, they immediately involve themselves in the chemistry of mutual attraction which was called in Pugh language 'the Mutualities of Unselfing'. Part of the boy flies off to join the soul of the girl and vice versa in a process he called 'the Coition of the Psyches'. So lofty a view did he take of these fleeting moments – indeed, for him, they held the seeds of the secret of the universe – that he enunciated the view that all those who had been involved in such feelings were held together in a perpetual spiritual link, of sexless Eros.

Why sexless? He pointed out that Plato's Symposium recommends passing on from adoration of a boy's beauty to the contemplation of spiritual love. 'At no point,' Rice Robey would insist with eyes ablaze behind his thick lenses, 'does Plato recommend a free-for-all of the homosexualists.' St Paul urged virginity on his followers. Dante had not bestowed so much as a kiss on the face of his beloved Beatrice. Of course, Rice Robey had not invented the idea of chastity as an important adjunct to spiritual advancement but he added refinements of his own to the traditional notions. Sexual energy in his view was a divine fire which could be harboured. As the professor states in *Memphian Mystery*, 'Man and woman, when seized by the divine fire of mutually experienced carnal attraction, may choose to dissipate and waste it by unchastity, but if they choose to cherish the fire in the crucible of chastity they will become as gods, empowered to see mysteries, to exercise psychic control, to call down angelicals to the terrestrial plane and to raise up their confused consciousness to high knowledge.'

Poetry, the intellectual achievements of philosophers and

scientists, the insights of mystics, all sprang from the human ability to link up with the Divine Energy, and this ability was intensified, he believed, by the Mutualities of Unselfing. Assuming that he practised what he preached, it did not suggest that Felicity, the Great Attachment, or any of his other female admirers could look forward to a very vigorous sex life. Perhaps this was part of his charm.

For Felicity, a large part of the attraction appeared to be the belief that she was rescuing a fallen archangel, so that the most glaring contradictions in his character and the most off-putting faults positively increased his attractiveness to her. She even seemed to relish the fact that he was, by any ordinary criteria, a quite stunningly bad writer, and to blame this fact on Mrs Paxton.

'The early books are half formed; they are brilliant but they do not add up. He should still be capable of writing a book which brings together his great spiritual and intellectual powers, his imaginative powers. That woman just fails to stimulate or expand his imagination. Do you know what he had to do all last week?'

'I can guess from your tone that it was something tedious.'

'Go round the shops and buy her a washboard.'

Felicity's laugh at this point was both girlish and conspiratorial: it could have been a confidence shared after lights out in the dorm or the Girl Guides' camp. 'Of course he could not find one, they went out with the Ark. People have washing machines now.'

'We don't.'

'We don't have a washboard either. He had to go to umpteen hardware shops in Kentish Town and Holloway.'

'Skiffle groups had them. They must still be around somewhere.'

'Julian, that isn't the point. What is a man of R.R.''s distinction *doing* in a hardware shop searching for washboards?'

'Presumably, Mrs Paxton felt that she needed one.'

I had not met the Great Attachment since my visit to Twisden Road of a year before. I wondered if Rice Robey had ever mentioned to Felicity my visit to his house. I had said nothing about it, and continued to allow her to repeat her stories of 'R.R.''s domestic hardships without overtly suggesting that the man told lies about them. Felicity herself found all domestic chores tedious. I had once suggested to her that many people positively enjoy shopping, cooking and indulging in humdrum household chores. I enjoy it myself, and thought it possible that Robey did too.

'He's trying to read his way through the *Enneads* of Plotinus but he can't concentrate because she insists on having the wireless on all the time, and she makes him sit and listen to it with her. If his attention wanders for an instant, she flies into a rage. If he goes out for half an hour to take a turn in the open air, she suspects him of having an affair with another woman. No wonder there's so much unresolved anger in R.R. I told him the other day that he should pipe down about Jimbo Lampitt, and all that business.'

I somehow guessed that Rice Robey knew nothing of Felicity's former attachment to Raphael Hunter and that she did not intend to confess it to him. There was no reason why she should have done, but it is always a little surprising to think, when two people develop deep emotional bonds, how little each knows of the other, compared with old friends and family. That Hunter had 'jilted' Felicity was one of the great unmentionables in our family. It lay behind all our thoughts about James Petworth Lampitt. Since it was in the past, and since it was unmentionable, Rice Robey knew nothing of it. He had his own personal memories of Jimbo and it made sense to suppose that he disliked Hunter for reasons of his own which had nothing to do with Felicity.

I made some remarks to the priggish effect that if Rice Robey was so anxious to pursue his study of Plotinus, he should have not wasted so much time on gossip. And I developed the theme by suggesting that two aspects of his nature sat oddly beside one another: his mystical and religious interests in private and the unbridled malice of his journalistic pen.

'R.R. is never malicious,' she said. 'I never knew a less malicious man; but he is angry, which is different, and sometimes the anger is misdirected. If he expressed to that woman Mrs Paxton the anger which he actually felt – why, he'd kill her!'

'So, he libels Hunter because he doesn't want a row with Mrs Paxton?'

'He has rows with Mrs Paxton whether he wants them or not, poor lamb.' She did not develop or take up my question. She had once told me that she hated Hunter, and at the time of the abortion this was probably true. The quality of hatred which we nurse for those who have caused us pain in love is unlike any other form of hostility: it is in fact just a continuation of love itself, nothing less, and I wondered whether some of the old flame for Hunter did not continue to burn in Felicity's heart and make sad clashes with her new fondness for R.R.

'I wish he hadn't written that thing about Raphael,' she said quietly.

'Do you think it's untrue?'

'No *good* will come of writing like that.'

That was as much as we said about the matter before Darnley's wedding party, a function to which both Felicity and I were invited. The union which (to my mind, so unaccountably) he had finally decided to make official, between himself and Jo Lampitt, had been solemnised at a register office earlier in the day, and friends and relations were bidden to celebrate the occasion at a party in the Savile Club, beginning at, roughly speaking, the cocktail hour, and continuing through dinner. Darnley was my oldest friend, and I wished him well; there would have been no question of my staying away from such a gathering, even though I knew in advance that it would be one of those parties where as much energy would be devoted to the avoidance of those whom one did not want to see as to devising themes of conversation with those whom one liked. Such forebodings were well judged. Within seconds of stepping into the room I found myself standing next to my ex-wife.

After we ceased to 'get on', Anne had more capacity for communicating anger than any other human being I have ever known. Encountering her, I at once felt waves of it, and remembered the disastrous evening, the beginning of the end really, when we had gone backstage after a particularly good production of *Uncle Vanya* and discovered Raphael Hunter in the arms of the actress Isabella Marno, a conjunction which had plunged Anne into a moody rage from which she could not escape. There was no guessing what had set her off this time. Perhaps she by now made a habit of fuming disgruntlement. The most obvious explanation, namely that my own appearance on the scene embarrassed and irritated her, or at the least awoke painful memories, oddly enough did not occur to me.

708

'I can't think why Vernon and Pat have asked all these people,' she said by way of greeting.

'To swell the throng? Because Jo and Miles wanted them?'

Anne's taste for the company of the human race, never marked, was fast evaporating into non-existence. The thought that people might choose, actually choose, to see one another in great numbers, was puzzling to her. She knew about families: *they* saw one another, naturally, and one saw a very few old friends, in her case, her poisonous friend Lesley, a fellow student at the Courtauld, or the slightly less poisonous Elizabeth, with whom Anne had been at school, and who was Darnley's sister. She was worlds away, Anne, from my feeling that the circle of acquaintanceship was infinitely extensible, that it was always interesting to meet new people and that, as far as something like the present party was concerned, the more the merrier. She stared bleakly at the people who milled about on the upper floor of the club. It was a place where I had more than once seen Sargie become drunk. It was in fact, though I did not witness this, the place where Sargie and Uncle Roy ate lunch on the day of Jimbo's funeral.

'It's an entirely unsuitable place for a party,' said Anne.

There was space, elegance, beauty. Waiters were moving gracefully among the guests distributing glasses of wine or fruit juice. A female trio, bespectacled, crop-haired, all girls with pale, intensely serious faces (they looked like girls who might have got on well with Simone Weil) played a jaunty selection of tunes, ranging from near-contemporaneous favourites like 'Fings Ain't What They Used to Be' to revivals such as 'Pasadena'.

One of the girls, fascinatingly plain and serious-looking, occasionally abandoned her mouth-organ or clarinet (she played both) so as to croon into the microphone in an icily academic, tuneless whisper.

I was unable to see what made this an unsuitable place for a party.

'How are you, Anne, anyway?'

Her silent shrug told me that the banality of the question did not even compel good manners on her behalf, still less a reply. She walked away from me without a word. I wondered, since she seemed so determined not to enjoy herself, why she had troubled to attend the party. Possibly Sibs, her mother, had put out what she would have termed a three-line whip and insisted that all her family should be there, lest Darnley's friends and relations be seen to swamp the Lampitt contingent.

When I approached Darnley himself he was standing with Jo and a soignée blonde whom I took to be aged about forty.

'Mr Grainger!' he said. 'Excellent! Mummy, you remember Julian Ramsay.'

'It is funny that we have never met before,' said Darnley's mother, whose name at that point was, I think, Mrs Fitzgerald.

'We saw you!' Jo interrupted.

'When?'

'Just now, trying to chat up that dark-haired piece.'

Darnley's grin became a little fixed and he shook his head to indicate that she was being tactless and should shut up. Either she did not read these signals, or she chose not to do so.

'You didn't have much luck, did you, Mr Grainger?'

'I'm sorry?'

'Chatting up that bird. Nice tits, boring dress, though, you're better off without her. . . .'

I could avoid the embarrassment of telling Jo her mistake since she continued to prattle without a pause.

'. . . Frances has asked me to call her Frances, haven't you Frances – Miles already calls Dad Ernie, some call him Ernie, some call him Vernon. Bit of a pose, calling himself . . . But what do you think of Frances, Mr Grainger, eh? Nice mother-in-law for me? Do you think?'

The directness of the interrogation made any response impossible, anyway in Mrs Fitzgerald's hearing. There could be no doubt that Darnley's mother was beautiful. Whether she would be a 'nice' mother-in-law, not the easiest of roles in which to exercise pleasantness, remained to be seen.

'I think we met a number of times actually, when I was at Seaforth Grange. You kindly bought me lunch at the Foley Arms.'

She seemed ageless. Her cool smile implied that if the rest of the human race knew her secret formula (frequent divorce? vitamin pills?) they too could defy the ravages of time. When she had entertained me as a schoolboy twenty years earlier, her head had appeared to be encased in a helmet of mouse-coloured perm. Now her hair was drawn gently back from her forehead in loose swathes of platinum blonde. The suggestion that she had once bought me lunch did not disconcert her. Certainly she saw no need for the elaborate apologies which most English people, quite insincerely, would have introduced into the conversation at this point.

'Miles said you were married to a Lampitt once.'

'To Anne Starling, standing over there.'

'Would you recommend it?'

'Say you do, Mr Grainger,' said Jo eagerly. For the first time in my life I felt tenderly towards her. Mrs Fitzgerald had turned the tables on Jo's tactless prattle (whether she herself would make a nice mother-in-law) and was showing her mettle in retaliation, by holding up for assessment the Lampitts and all their tribe. Were the Lampitts marriageable? Perhaps this was an example of the empiricist fallacy and the falsehood of the words Either/ or.

'They vary,' I said.

'You can give it a go, darling, anyway,' said Mrs Fitzgerald, stroking Darnley's cheek.

'Oh, do shut up, Mummy.'

'Come on, Julian,' said Mrs Fitzgerald, lightly taking my arm. 'You'll know far more people here than I do. Show me round.'

There was no evidence in her gait or speech to make me suspect inebriation; in fact, I am sure she was not drunk, but she seemed, in her poised, quiet way, to be in an anarchic frame of mind which most of us are only able to achieve with alcohol. The suggestion that I would know more people than she did was a ludicrous one, and her request for me to show her round had the sort of condescension which one would display to a child. Perhaps she really did remember our lunches together on exeat from Seaforth Grange and still, subconsciously thought of me as a little boy. I record these feelings as I believe I had them at the time. It was years before I heard the strange stories about her very distinctive predilections, and the impressively varied catalogue of men who had submitted themselves to her charm.

'He can be so prickly, can't he, Miles?' she said as we left her son alone with his bride. 'You've known him for ever, I know. Do you think he's doing the right thing?'

'He and Jo seem very fond of one another.'

This was no answer, but she must have been pleased that I did not reply in the negative. As it happened, I thought that anyone who wanted to marry Jo Lampitt was raving mad, but one could hardly say this on their wedding day to the bridegroom's mother.

'You see,' she said, 'you *do* know everybody.'

As we walked through the room, I had nodded here and there to the arbitrary miscellany of people there assembled. Presumably, Mrs Fitzgerald herself had been consulted about the guest list, or perhaps Vernon had approached Darnley himself. One saw some strange conjunctions. Peter Cornforth, his existence only semi-imaginable outside the Black Bottle, was resting his full weight on his metal foot and holding an ignited Park Drive rather threateningly close to the nose of Dame Ursula Lampitt, who giggled appreciatively at what he had to say. They both waved to us as we glided past. The best parties provide the chance for such surprising confluences. Was Pete treating Ursula to one of his usual foul-mouthed diatribes against her sex – is that why she was laughing? Or was she telling him about the latest fruits of her research into Anglo-Norman literature? Or were they both revelling in the chance to talk to someone of a kind they would never normally meet, and had they found some common ground which the rest of us could not guess at? We did not stay to discover.

After the celibate years, in which sexual feeling had been all but quiescent, I was easily over-excited by discovering that I was attracted to someone else. It tended to make me behave in a way that Aunt Deirdre, perhaps others, would have categorised as 'silly'. Mrs Fitzgerald certainly made me want to be very silly indeed. The last girlfriend whom I had entertained at cinemas and Greek restaurants had lasted about a fortnight. I was feeling, on that evening, game for anything. Between Mrs Fitzgerald and myself, there was, undoubtedly, what Sibs would have called (and oh dear, there *was* Sibs at the top of the stairs talking to the Home Secretary) chemistry. Mrs Fitzgerald's light touch on my arm seemed charged with significance and when I reached up to strengthen my hold on her elbow and lightly to squeeze her fingers, she made no resistance.

'That's Lady Augusta Wimbish,' I explained. 'She is married to an historian.'

'She's my aunt,' said Mrs Fitzgerald. 'It would be a cruelty to disturb her while she's at the trough.'

Not much in the way of a buffet had been provided, since there was a dinner afterwards for twenty or thirty of the guests.

Lady Augusta had none the less managed to arm herself with a side-plate and heap it with some salted nuts, about eight olives and some sausage rolls. She was the only person in the room who was eating. Perhaps she had brought the sausage rolls with her in her pretty silver-mail reticule which was suspended from one tiny, bony wrist. Upon the comestibles assembled on her plate her entire attention was fixed. Thin, tall and pale, she stood firmly in the middle of the floor eating with nervous speed and occasional glances to left and right. It would certainly have been an unkindness to approach lest she mistook a harmless social advance as a covert attempt on her salted peanuts. Her husband, the professor, was not far away, and I saw that he was accompanied by William Bloom.

'Are these two men screwing?' she asked me quietly, as they approached.

'I've no reason to suppose they have even met before this evening.'

'That's not a reason for not doing it.' Her fingers squeezed mine in return.

'George is just making a fool of himself,' said Wimbish, loudly. The only reason that he addressed us was that we happened to be there. The remark would have been made had Wimbish been standing on his own. He made no distinction between conversation and monologue, dialogue and soliloquy.

'Just look at the bloody fool! Thank goodness our party for once in its life saw some sense and voted Harold into the leadership. Can you imagine if that buffoon over there were now our Prime Minister?' He pursed his lips in mock-dowager distaste. 'Very Prime Ministerly behaviour, that!'

It was a surprising sight, certainly to me, but then, in spite of the impression I hoped I was making on Mrs Fitzgerald, I was unused to the ways of the world. George Brown, the Deputy Prime Minister, and at that stage in charge of the newly formed Ministry for Economic Affairs, was attempting a dance. He was generously undiscriminating about his choice of partner. When a waiter had shaken free of him he had seized a potted bay tree near the piano, and after a few steps he had swayed into the arms of my old landlady, Fenella Kempe. Rikko, standing by, was pinching his forehead. I don't suppose that he minded anyone being drunk. He was doubtless dreading the incident being exaggerated in the telling by Fenella when she described it to their friends and lodgers.

'It's a bit early in the evening for all that,' I said.

'I wonder,' said Mrs Fitzgerald, 'where Vernon and Pat found that extraordinary band. I know quite a lot of good musicians. They should have asked me.'

Wimbish's smile was unamiable, even threatening. It suggested that, just this once, he would brook interruption, but in future would we jolly well shut up and listen to him.

'I believed they're friends of Kirsty's,' said Bloom. It was clear that he knew Mrs Fitzgerald quite well. Did she know that, in army days, Bloom had been so much in love with Darnley?

'I love the fact that they don't smile,' he said.

The palest and most humourless of the girls, the one who sometimes played the mouth-organ, was whispering,

My love for you
Makes everything hazy
Clouding the skies
From view--oo-hoo.

'And Hugh, you see, bloody fool, was the same, always swigging from the bloody bottle.' Wimbish was allowing himself to become quite worked up. 'Thank goodness we've got Harold, who in my view is one of the most distinguished leaders this country has ever had since the Tudor Age. I don't know if it had ever occurred to you, but Harold Wilson is just a *tiny* little like Henry VIII . . .'

'My dear!' said Bloom, 'does this mean that poor Mary is going to have her head chopped off on Tower Green?'

He made some other remarks which made it clear that Mrs Wilson was something of a friend of his.

'Who writes that thing in *Private Eye*?' asked Mrs Fitzgerald. 'It's meant to be Mary Wilson's diary. It's screamingly funny.'

'. . . a man, you see, of brilliant intellectual accomplishments. He knew French, Latin, Italian. He could compose music and songs . . .'

'It's funnier than Miles's paper really, *Private Eye*, wouldn't you say?'

'And yet with this vein of tremendous ruthlessness. Really,

714

Machiavelli might have been thinking of him when he wrote . . .'

'They're called the Newnham Norns,' said Bloom. 'Aren't they heaven? I must apologise, my dear, for the other evening.'

'What on earth for?'

'Now, you see, no one would have been able to predict that he would dissolve the monasteries. What? Catholic Henry? Author of a book on the Seven Sacraments . . .?'

'My sister and I spoiled an evening for Julian and Felicity some months ago,' Bloom explained.

'Who's Felicity?' and 'You did not spoil it at all,' said Mrs Fitzgerald and I in unison.

'My sister's married to the most extraordinarily boring man called Aaron Samuelson,' said Bloom. 'At the moment she seems to have lost her head to an old schoolfriend of Julian's called Patrick Garforth-Thoms.'

The evening in the restaurant, which I had already begun to forget, had ossified in Bloom's mind into an anecdote. He changed a lot of details, but his description of Garforth-Thoms's raucous behaviour was quite funny. Aeons later, someone told me that Mrs Fitzgerald herself nursed a *tendresse* for Garforth-Thoms, even that he had at one stage been one of 'her boys'. This discovery made sense, as nothing did at the time, of the momentary spasm of distaste which disturbed the haughty passivity of her face. At the time, I barely noticed it and certainly failed to interpret her reaction, a good example of the fact that we frequently fail to catch the meaning of events until years after they have happened, and also of the fact that our interpretation of the past depends on more than mere powers of recall.

'Come on,' said Mrs Fitzgerald. 'Let's go and talk to Mia Eggscliffe.'

She began to walk away before Bloom had finished speaking, which provoked him to an exaggerated shrug, hunched shoulders, pouting lower lip, palms upturned, for five seconds the parody of a stage Frenchman.

'Funnily enough,' I said to Mrs Fitzgerald, 'Miles and I were at school with Garforth-Thoms.'

'Mia!' exclaimed Mrs Fitzgerald, 'how wonderful to see a sympathetic face amid all these *strangers.*'

As we drew level to the celebrated Mrs Eggscliffe (as Bloom

used to say, 'one of the last great hostesses, present company excepted', a phrase he managed to make even cheaper than it looks by emphasising the second syllable of the word *hostess*) a cruel alchemy took place in my perception of Mrs Fitzgerald. In the twinkling of an eye, I realised that these two women were roughly of the same generation, if not of an age. Mrs Eggscliffe's bouffed-out dyed black hair encased a thin face fast turning to scrawn, though gallantly disguised by well-applied make-up. Already, however, she seemed poised to enter that penultimate phase of human decrepitude when a face has become prune-like, a phase which in women can last as long as twenty years. As soon as Mrs Fitzgerald approached Mrs Eggscliffe, her own face appeared to age, like the countenance of 'She' in Rider Haggard's story when the spell of her agelessness is broken. The platinum streaks in Mrs Fitzgerald's blonde hair now seemed like wisps of grey and the blue-grey eyes were visibly edged with crows' feet which I had not noticed before. With the complete heartlessness of youth, I released the pressure of her fingers in mine. The strange ten minutes or so in which I had found Darnley's mother the most beguiling being in the universe had passed.

If I knew how you did it to me

sang the Newnham Norn,

I would do it to you.

'I've asked a waiter to take George in hand,' said Mrs Eggscliffe, speaking of the Minister for Economic Affairs whose light fantastic with the bay tree had been resumed. 'It was Vernon's responsibility, I suppose, but I took it upon myself.'

She was manifestly incapable of behaving in any social setting other than as a hostess, giving orders to waiters and gazing about the room to make sure that the 'right' people were talking to one another. Seeing a roomful of people, instinct made her speak as if we had all been summoned at her command. This fact was emphasised by the roll-call which was now fired at myself and Mrs Fitzgerald. Since I never moved in the world, I had no idea who the people were that she was talking about. It was a rapid rehearsal of names, not unlike the roll-call at school with which

716

each day began and ended, almost like the low-toned announcement of the dentist to his assistant as he makes a rapid survey of one's mouth and declares, for the record, which teeth are missing, or which require attention since the patient's last session in the chair. In this litany Mrs Fitzgerald was cast in the role of acolyte or assistant, giving me no more than a minimum response before the rapid interrogation continued.

'Is Frank here?'

'Over there.'

'He's so dotty. With Elizabeth?'

'In every sense.'

'Where's Isaiah?'

'Couldn't get.'

'Naughty. Now, Dick I've seen, but . . .'

'Oh, he's somewhere.'

'I suppose the PM . . .'

She smiled with triumphant malice.

'My dear.'

Mrs Fitzgerald whispered something to Mrs Eggscliffe, who responded by talking down the back of her hand, which she held up to her lips. This gesture evidently announced that her words were supposed to be 'classified information'. They weren't exactly whispered, but they looked as if they were being spoken from behind an arras in some Renaissance tragedy.

The two women were discussing Vernon's political disappointment. Since his failure to be chosen as a member of the Cabinet, there was bad blood between the Prime Minister and the Lampitts; Harold Wilson's failure to choose the second Baron Lampitt as a minister, however lowly, was now being reinterpreted as a danger signal to the left. Not to have chosen Ernie, the people's man, marked down the Prime Minister as at best a fair-weather socialist.

I was naïve enough, since they were discussing the matter, to suppose that this was of interest to Mrs Eggscliffe and Mrs Fitzgerald. I assumed, since Mrs Eggscliffe was evidently on such easy terms with so many senior members of the new government, that she was herself a committed Labour supporter. I did not realise that she had just as many friends, probably more, in the Conservative Party, and that her *salons* (it almost seems appropriate to use such an obsolete term), though frequently places where politics were discussed, were far from being easy to classify in political terms. She chiefly loved the pursuit of success, the worship of chic and the exercise of power. Hence her preparedness to be married to rich men who bored her (two of them had been newspaper proprietors) but who provided her with the means to exercise her curious range of influence.

It was something of a concession that Mrs Eggscliffe had accepted the invitation to these nuptials. Several years afterwards, Darnley used, laughingly, to relate that she had 'had her eye on him for one of the Rothschild girls'; since the surname was pronounced in this phrase in the continental manner, he assumed that the girl in question belonged to a French branch of that illustrious dynasty. Mrs Eggscliffe was related by blood neither to the Darnleys nor to the Rothschilds. This did not prevent her from believing that the marriages of members of these families somehow fell under her responsibility. The Rothschilds and the Darnleys both belonged to the elect, as far as Mrs Eggscliffe was concerned, a category which it would be difficult enough to define. Being rich, or famous, or aristocratic, or all three, were by no means qualities which Mrs Eggscliffe undervalued, but you might possess all three and still be regarded by her as 'a bore'. Others, such as the columnist Godfrey Tucker, hardly conspicuous for any obvious style or breeding, was one of the men on whom Mrs Eggscliffe most doted, insisting, in those phases of life when she was married to Fleet Street magnates, that Tucker's columns of opinionated reflections be given pride of place in whatever newspaper the husband of the day happened to own.

The Elect were present at the wedding party but by Mrs Eggscliffe's mysterious but also, one suspected, rather rigid standards, their number had been almost irredeemably diluted or coarsened by the admission into the assembly of riff-raff such as myself. I slightly hated Mrs Fitzgerald for introducing me as 'a madly famous radio actor' before mentioning my name. Mrs Eggscliffe's 'Oh?' made it excruciatingly clear that my name meant nothing to her, a fact which is hardly surprising when it is remembered that 'The Mulberrys' so invariably clashes with the cocktail hour.

'Sargie here?' she continued.

'No,' said Mrs Fitzgerald, 'but one would not expect him to turn out.'

'He comes to my parties,' said Mrs Eggscliffe. No one had in fact tried to excuse Sargie's absence, for example by the suggestion that he feared crowds or was of a generally unsociable disposition, but she spoke as if wholly inadequate excuses had been offered to her. 'I got him round the night we really badgered Harold to give Dora a peerage. My dear, is that Violet Bonham-Carter?'

'Talking to the clergyman?'

'Canon Collins – he's an ass, but a bit of a charmer. I wonder who that handsome man is with them, the one with the sort of metal frame on his foot; looks frightfully uncomfortable. I wonder who chose this *ghastly* music! No, you're right, my dear, Sargie would never come to a clan gathering like this. Too many skeletons rattling in cupboards.'

'Sargie said to me this morning that he never attends weddings,' I volunteered. 'He finds them too depressing, can always see what is going to go wrong for the bridal pair. . . .'

Mrs Eggscliffe stared at me as if she wished that I would simply go away, possibly as if my claim to know Sargie was spurious.

'I haven't seen Cecily for ages,' said Mrs Fitzgerald. She had lit a cigarette, and her words seemed to be borne on the two perfectly straight diagonals of nicotine smoke which issued from her nostrils.

'I met *the* most extraordinary man just now,' said Mrs Eggscliffe, 'but he was really very charming. I asked him to one of my parties at once, he's coming next Tuesday. He was dressed in a sort of demob suit, my dear, you never saw anything like it, and he was telling one of the Know-Dutton twins, Jilly, the pretty one, the one I call Tinkerbell, how they practised human sacrifice in the ancient pyramids of Mexico.'

'Poor Jilly.'

'Lapping it up.' Mrs Eggscliffe let out a short barking laugh, a strangely countrified noise, the sort of sound you might have expected from a distinguished MFH if you had told him that you had moral objections to field sports. Young girls, her tone suggested, jolly well should learn about human sacrifice, if necessary, perhaps, even offer themselves up as candidates if the occasion, or Mrs Eggscliffe's social arrangements, demanded such a thing.

'What was so interesting about this scruffy man, my dear, was that he knew all about . . .'

Once more, Mrs Eggscliffe lifted the back of her hand to her

719

mouth and spoke down her flattened knuckles like Midas whispering secrets to the earth. Whatever it was that Rice Robey had said, it made Mrs Fitzgerald roll her eyes and gasp with astonishment.

'No!' she said.

I now felt like an eavesdropper.

'He's great friends with Miles,' said Mrs Fitzgerald.

'And he's a poet isn't he?' said Mrs Eggscliffe. 'I must get hold of some of his stuff before Tuesday. I'll ring up Heywood Hill in the morning, and they can send the books round.'

'He writes under the name of Albion Pugh,' I said. 'Even though his name is Rice Robey.'

Grateful for this information, Mrs Eggscliffe said, 'I must remember that. Albion Pugh. I think people talked about his novels during the war.'

'That's what everyone seems to say.' Her facial expression made it possible for me to imagine that I had said something to offend Mrs Eggscliffe. First I had claimed acquaintance with Sargie, she seemed to think, and now I knew about Albion Pugh. Enough was enough. I did not particularly wish to attend one of her famous parties, but I could not help wondering what it was about Rice Robey which had made her so instantly desirous of his company. I had been standing beside her for ten minutes, and I knew that she was never going to suggest that I dropped in to see her.

'I wonder how he could have *known*,' said Mrs Fitzgerald.

'You won't say anything?' said Mrs Eggscliffe.

'Of course not.'

Darnley had been afraid, and said so several times before his wedding, that Pat and his mother between them would manage to fill the party with 'awful people', by which, roughly, he meant relations, and those individuals whom Mrs Eggscliffe would have regarded as most acceptable. It was to offer some kind of antidote to 'awfulness', thus defined, that he had scoured the hedgerows and ditches for such a wide variety of unfashionable characters, many of whom could have been no more than casual acquaintances of his or Jo's: hacks, barflies and oddballs. Fenella Kempe was there, for example. I saw her shouting something in the ear of Godfrey Tucker and went over to join them; as I did so, I heard Mrs Fitzgerald repeating to Mrs Eggscliffe that I was a schoolfriend of Miles.

Fenella was boasting about Rikko's national fame as the son and heir to Dick Mulberry.

'It's absolute rubbish,' said Godfrey Tucker in his voice which recalled sackfuls of gravel being emptied into trucks. 'It's completely beyond my comprehension why anyone should be fascinated by such a concentration of pure gibberish.'

After five years of acting in 'The Mulberrys', this had become more or less my own view of the series, so I waved aside the heavy-handed apology with which he concluded his diatribe when Fenella reminded him that I was the man who played Jason Grainger.

'I'd better watch what I say,' he reflected.

'So you'd better,' said Rikko hotly. He had come up to join us and looked extremely displeased by Tucker's opinions.

'Who are you?' asked Tucker incredulously. For the previous sentence or two, Rikko had been standing by Fenella's side, one hand on a hip and the other holding a wineglass at shoulder level. He resembled some slightly overweight Renaissance sculpture of Bacchus. When Fenella explained that Rikko was her husband, Godfrey Tucker spluttered with astonishment.

'Then what did you let me go on for, you stupid woman?' he grumbled. Probably, like most successfully opinionated journalists, Godfrey Tucker did not entertain any sincerely held views at all. The regular production of strongly worded observations on the world was his means of livelihood and had become habitual to him. He could not help doing it. If the views expressed provoked a response, he had done his job, whether the response was one of outrage or of rapturous agreement. He deftly demonstrated this facility by sketching out aloud an absolutely opposite viewpoint from his earlier assessment of the series.

'If it gives a lot of people completely harmless pleasure,' he began.

'Which it does,' said Rikko.

'You could almost say that it was the closest thing we have in our culture to the Pastoral. *Some Versions of the Pastoral*, now who wrote that?'

This question, being put to Fenella, produced in her a frightful fit of coughing until the moment passed in which she might be expected to answer it.

'Within a certain conventional framework, it works

721

extremely well,' said Tucker. 'And don't let's forget, the real tests of a thing like that are, Has it lasted? Do people still want to go on listening? To which we must answer a triumphant Yes!'

Though pretty bored with my role as Jason Grainger, I was at that stage in a state of suspense, not having been 'used' for some weeks. Rodney, our producer, had no qualms about leaving a story-line in the air. This had happened the previous year with the Mystery of the Stolen Chalice. It looked as though Jason had been responsible, but no one pinned it on him. The latest thrilling possibility was that he might become a reformed character and attend a horticultural college with a view to becoming a landscape gardener. Listeners agog to discover whether he would pursue this harmless avocation were now to be left uninformed for some weeks, perhaps for ever. Interest had switched to an outbreak of fowl-pest at Daisy Farm, the chance that little Ginger – Reg's daughter – would be bought a pony for her tenth birthday, and a bumper dairy yield at the Swills' farm, leading to a repetition of the perennial suspicion that they watered the milk.

'I was talking quite seriously to Rodney the other day,' said Rikko. 'He really shouldn't do this to well-established members of the cast.'

'Kind of you,' I said. 'As a matter of fact, I don't really know how much longer I shall be going on with it all anyway.'

The time would have been, in his early days as Stan Mulberry, when Rikko would have seen some of the absurdities of the series, though he was always impressed by its power to attract a large and faithful audience. His touches of merry cynicism had, however, vanished with the years, together with any discernible ambition to pursue a career as a serious actor.

'What on earth do you mean?' he asked. 'You are surely not contemplating leaving "The Mulberrys"?'

I mumbled something about the Lampitt book taking up a lot of time, and how my conscience was pricked by my failure so far to settle down to any research into the matter. Meanwhile, Sargie expected me to call once a week, and I was still doing my book programme for the World Service.

'But none of these compares with being . . . a national institution,' he said earnestly.

Rikko was no less effeminate in manner than when I had first known him, but over the years there had been a perceptible transformation. He no longer said 'your'. There was a touch, in the way he pronounced the word, of Vernon's mock-earthy 'yer'.

'It would be madness to give up yer part in the series now.'

Stan Mulberry was quietly taking him over. Perhaps in some moods, he thought he was Stan Mulberry. Fenella and he even spoke of giving up the house in South Kensington where I had lived as a lodger and taking a cottage in Worcestershire, to be within easy distance of Birmingham and the recording studios. Stan Mulberry was not simply a voice speaking into a microphone. He had begun to do such things as open village fêtes, and to reply to fan-mail in his own name.

'I'm not sure that I want to be in "The Mulberrys" for ever,' I said.

Rikko believed himself to have been instrumental in having secured me the role of Jason Grainger in the first place. I now felt him bridling, and I had not quite realised how he had come to take his own part in 'The Mulberrys' with complete seriousness. It was like the moment, after an uncongenial year working at Tempest and Holmes, the shirt factory, when I had tactlessly told Mr Pilbright that I wanted something more interesting out of life. Pilbright had worked for the firm for the greater part of forty years. To admit that I did not take 'The Mulberrys' seriously was to suggest that I did not take Rikko seriously. It was understandable that he pursed his lips. I could tell that he was on the point of saying, in one of his habitual phrases, that some people did not know what was good for them. By rational standards, the various other activities in my life were not so serious or exalted as to justify the sense of superiority to Rikko which had so embarrassingly been allowed to show.

'What an unusual band,' I said.

'She can't sing,' said Rikko peevishly. 'I can't think why they've hired her.'

'Isn't the point that she's not even trying to sing?'

The vocalist now looked really cross, far crosser than Rikko. Barely bothering to project her voice into the microphone, which she was almost kissing, she whispered,

> I don't stay out late,
> Nowhere to go,

723

I'm home about eight,
Just me and my radio.

She injected into these words a desolated sense of the tedious manner of life which they depicted.

'Good heavens,' I said, 'I've just seen my Uncle Roy.'

'Then you'd better go and talk to him,' snapped Rikko, and he turned aside to tell Fenella that if they did not go soon, the Afghans would have shat all over their drawing-room carpet. I heard him saying, 'I sometimes think you simply don't care about my Persian rugs.'

Since schooldays, when Uncle Roy sometimes helped me to change trains from Liverpool Street to Paddington or, later, Euston, I had hardly ever seen him in London. I thought of him primarily as the *genius loci* of Timplingham and his appearance at a gathering such as this was almost like an apparition of the dead.

He looked, however, far from moribund. His cheeks were as pink and his smile as fixed as I had ever known them. He was almost the only person present, apart from the waiters, and the Secretary of State for Defence (just leaving) who wore evening dress, so that he cut a conspicuous figure in the throng as he leaned slightly forward, cocking an alert ear to the neat little woman with whom he was conversing. She had a short bob of white hair, rather mischievous eyes and a sharply intelligent face which could have been peering at you out of a burrow or a sandy hole. To say that she was rodent-like would mislead if it suggested anything unpleasing in her appearance. It was simply that she seemed like one of the smaller mammals, though not necessarily one which you would want to keep as a pet. Her clothes, her neat paisley blouse and her rather long black skirt had a faintly incongruous air, somehow recalling the world of Beatrix Potter, where hedgehogs, rabbits, rats and mice disport themselves in human garb.

'I don't *think*,' said Uncle Roy laboriously, 'that you've met . . .' He looked at me and paused. I wondered if, in the excitement of being surrounded by so many Lampitts, he had in fact forgotten my name. 'Er, my nephew, er Julian.'

'No, but you're the one who's going to write the book,' she said with almost exaggerated directness. 'Is it the family as a whole or is it mainly about Jimbo?'

I half guessed at once who she was, but no explanation or

724

introduction were offered. I suppose that Uncle Roy thought that all members of the Lampitt family were as instantly recognisable as film stars or royalty and did not need the superfluity of an introduction.

'It's really . . .'

I hesitated. She was not asking out of politeness – there was far too much eagerness in her tone for that – and I did not want to commit myself too far before knowing why she was so interested.

'I so hope, that's all, that you won't be too much in Sargie's pocket,' she said. 'It was entirely because of him that we had that *frightful* book about Jimbo, *wicked* book, scandalous book.'

She spoke very emphatically, gabbling the words which were not important, but stabbing the air with a finger when she wanted to underline part of a sentence which demanded close attention. Her vowels were strangely coy. For all its vehemence it was a cooing voice; the sort of voice some people might have thought appropriate for reading aloud to children.

'Dear Sargie!' said Uncle Roy, who had now been excluded from Sargent Lampitt's company for years. 'He *can* be maddening!' I could see that he would be unable to resist telling the very old chestnut about his drive to Cromer, and Sargie's belief that the tyres of the car were first too hard, then too soft, all the way to the coast.

Our companion's method of listening to Uncle Roy's anecdote differed from, say, Aunt Deirdre's, who was anxious to cut these stories as short as possible, or from those others who listened, either in amusement or lost in their own thoughts, until the narrative was done. This lady had no sense of anecdote, no idea that this particularly deadly conversational mode requires nothing except an audience on the part of the speaker. She would not play the game. She punctuated Uncle Roy's story with repeated interruptions. For example, when our heroes had reached the garage in Fakenham, and Sargie had leaned over my uncle to sound the horn in the middle of the steering wheel – thus throwing the garage man into a fury – she did not laugh. Instead, she said, 'That's one of the things I find so *hard* to *understand* about Sargie, that he has always been so rude. Do *you* understand it?'

Uncle Roy, I could see, found these interruptions trying. By the time he had reached his punchline, the discomfort of

Sargie's bedroom and his insistence that Roy change places with him, the lady had made so many interjections that her identity was plain to me. She was Cecily, Sargie's long-estranged wife.

'Typical! It was the Hotel de Paris, I expect, overlooking the pier. ' (She pronounced the word pee-er.)

'I think it was. Yes.'

Since no one else laughed, Uncle Roy did so. This particular narrative was one of his favourites. During my childhood, I heard it on average every ten days.

'He liked going to Cromer with *me,*' said Cecily. 'Once upon a time. You see, the *trouble* with Sargie, and Jimbo used to be driven *mad* with *rage* about this, was that he was always spoilt. That was why I couldn't live with him. No one *could.*'

She glowed at this confession.

'Extraordinarily difficult,' Uncle Roy agreed, only he said it as though being difficult was the most charming quality in the world, the one thing we should all look for in a friend or life's companion.

'You should have been *firmer,*' she said. 'Firmer with Sargie. I should have done. We *all* should. And now, you too, Julian. You must be firm with Sargie. Oh, Julian,' she suddenly changed gear, 'I've just had the most *extraordinary* thought. Over there with Vernon. The man with the crumpled dark blue suit . . .'

'His name is Rice Robey,' I said.

The effect on Cecily was electrifying. She brought a mottled hand to her quavery lips and her dark eyes shone.

'Oh, but he is so *old,*' she moaned. 'It couldn't be *our* Rice Robey, could it? Mine and Jimbo's? Our little urchin boy?'

I remember now Sargie's repeated assertion that Cecily and Jimbo had been thick as thieves, and his paranoid claim that they plotted against him. My uncle had barely known Jimbo, nor Cecily, and so it was hardly surprising that he had never come across Rice Robey in his juvenile incarnation; but when I explained that he wrote under the name of Albion Pugh, my uncle's interest quickened.

'The very best is about Herne the Hunter,' said Uncle Roy. 'It is a most remarkable book. That opening chapter of a gamekeeper thinking he has surprised some poachers in the wood at night, the sudden rustling of branches above his head and then his sighting of this terrifying antlered creature, silhouetted in the sky against the pale moon . . .'

'I've not read that one.'

'We've got them at home. We all read them during the war, though,' he smiled, 'they weren't really your aunt's cup.'

'I would imagine not.'

Cecily was almost dancing with excitement to have discovered that Rice Robey was at the party.

'We must go and look for him, Roy, we *must*, oh this is *too* extraordinary, it's years, *years* . . . Jimbo was heartbroken . . . We just felt, you know, that we had lost him. We found him this little job at a prep school, oh, out in the sticks.'

'Was it in Chorleywood?'

'It might have been. It seemed perfect, for him. He wrote his books, which of course Jimbo got published for him. Oh, I remember the Egyptian one, and his coming to us for the books, you know, that he had to read and saying, "Oh, Mr Lampitt, my hieroglyphs are rusty, they need burnishing!" Wasn't it wonderful? And then he just got swallowed up, he just vanished from our lives. There was no explanation, but this *ghastly* woman took him over *completely*. He came to Jimbo's funeral, of course, but I was too distressed to talk to anyone that day. . . . Oh, where *is* he?'

In the minute or two that it took Cecily to utter these words, I realised how very little I knew about Jimbo Lampitt. I had read all his published works, and some of his books, such as the biography of Prince Albert, I had known so well that I knew paragraphs of it by heart. Of his life, I knew little. Hunter's published account of Jimbo's early years, discounted by the family as inaccurate, largely failed to bring him to life, since, in spite of the reputation which it created for Hunter – a fearless exposé, etc., etc. – it is in point of fact a very wooden, inanimate sort of book. For the rest, I knew only a few snatches of information about Jimbo. I knew that he spoke with a high squeaky voice, that he had an old-womanish manner (about which Harold Nicolson made that famously barbed comment) and I knew that he had a fondness for Italy. The personality who survived in his books was powerful enough, but it was chiefly a style, a voice, a way of describing the world and people which had bowled me over when I first read Jimbo's books. Yet, I had no sense of what it would have been like actually to spend a week in Jimbo's company. I realised for the first time, what must always have been known in the family but never openly discussed, that Cecily must have been very close to Jimbo, perhaps in love with him. The idea that any woman (apart from the 'extraordinarily nice' old Mrs Lampitt of Timplingham – 'what a woman') had ever been involved with this famous bachelor man of letters had never once crossed my mind. All the testimonies I had heard had suggested to me an emotional history in which women played no conspicuous part; and this was true even before Hunter's book came out, with its hints at emotional conquests, on Jimbo's part, as varied and surprising as Cardinal Manning, Lloyd George and Lawrence of Arabia. It now occurred to me that the Lampitts had always cast a certain veil over the story of Jimbo's life, which was not really to be explained by the rumours of his homosexuality. Now I came to consider the matter, it struck me as odd that they were so united in the certainty that Hunter's allegations were untrue. It was not as if they regarded homosexuality as an entirely unmentionable subject in the family. One thought of Angelica and Miss Bean; or Frankie, the one who was so keen on the Boys' Brigade, and had to leave the country for a while before settling in, I think, Eastbourne. Would they have all been so sure about Jimbo, if they had not possessed evidence that Jimbo's emotions were in fact engaged in some other area? That evidence, I now realised, stood before me. Cecily's association with Jimbo was no secret, but, as so often in families, its nature was unexplored. Some time later, the whole story was told me, partly by Cecily, and partly by Pat Lampitt, of Cecily falling in love with Jimbo not long after she married Sargie, of Sargie's desolation, and the beginning of his worst period of depression and alcoholism, of Jimbo's devoted attachment to Cecily which did not, in either of their minds, rule out the possibility of emotional attachments being formed for members of his own sex (though they seem always to have been emotional rather than physical attachments) and of the curious ménage which they retained, never quite living together, never quite apart, for at least a quarter of a century.

Before we found Rice Robey at the party, Cecily let fall another piece of information which strengthened my strange feeling of life possessing a shape which I had only begun to understand or interpret.

'You must remember, Roy,' she said, 'when you were looking about for a school for this one.'

She tapped my arm.

It was the first I heard that the Lampitts had played a part in the choice of my prep school, though I knew that my public school had been chosen because of its Lampitt associations.

'What did Albion Pugh have to do with it?' Uncle Roy asked. 'I rather forget now how Seaforth Grange was chosen. . . .'

Uncle Roy was unable to refer directly to his dead brother, my father.

'Your brother wanted advice about a school for Julian,' said Cecily, 'and you asked Sargie and Sargie asked Jimbo, and Jimbo suggested sending the little boy – that's you, Julian – to this place in North London where Rice Robey was teaching.'

It was a strange thought that, had this plan been put into operation, I might have been taught by Rice Robey, and that those hierophantic cockneyfied utterances might have become part of the inner world of childhood memory and imagination, never lost in after years, like the sayings and mannerisms of Treadmill. What Cecily continued to say, however, was even stranger.

'Your wife – where is she, by the way?'

'Deirdre?'

'That is your wife's name?'

'Oh, she's not one for parties.'

I wondered whether Aunt Deirdre had excluded herself from the evening or whether Uncle Roy had simply chosen to come on his own. It is perfectly true that my aunt would have hated it all.

'*Deirdre* said you *couldn't* send the boy to school in London, with the *Blitz* going on, and most of the boys were being *evacuated* anyway, or transferred to that woman's brother's school. It was in the West Country, wasn't it?'

'Malvern,' I said. 'Seaforth Grange.' A name of dread to me still. I shudder slightly even to write the words on the page. 'But are you saying that Mrs Paxton's brother . . .'

'Mrs Paxton, that was her name – she took Rice Robey over *completely.* '

'She was my old headmaster's sister?'

'I think that was right.'

There was no time to develop this now, nor to make sure whether it was true, which it was. It merely accentuated my sense of destiny having fewer cards in the pack than I had supposed, and of life having a shape which is hidden from us except in strange moments of illumination such as this, which we label coincidence.

'There's Rice Robey – there!' I said.

He was standing in a group which contained Vernon, Darnley, Jo and Felicity, who kissed her father and introduced him to her beloved.

Rice Robey looked hard at Uncle Roy.

'Felicity's sire!'

He was rather red in the face as he said this, and sweat had formed globules on his Shakespearean brow which were running down his temples.

'You can always tell, with a woman,' he added, 'when the blood of the sacerdos runs in her veins.'

This was mere Robey talk for saying that Fliss was a vicar's daughter. I did not know whether my uncle was more disconcerted by the words themselves or by the accent in which they were delivered, having striven so successfully to banish from his diction all trace of the London vowels which still lingered in the voice of his mother, and which my father had had.

'Good ter see you, Roy, good ter see yer,' said Vernon, pumping my uncle's hand. 'Fliss said yer were here.'

My uncle fell at once to Lampitt talk with Vernon, leaving me to take Cecily by the elbow – she seemed in that moment very small – and introduce her to Rice Robey. When he recognised her, he folded her in his arms and clutched her for a full minute of silence.

'It's an *age*,' she said.

'I wanted to write to you, Mrs Lampitt.'

'Lost your pen?' she asked sharply.

'I mean, lately,' he said.

'I suppose you mean, about *The Spark*.' She turned to Darnley, whom she evidently knew a little, and said, 'Did you write it?'

Darnley smiled in a non-committal way. So much had passed through my mind since meeting Cecily that I had not yet allowed myself to speculate about her likely reactions to the allegations in *The Spark*. The idea that someone we love has been murdered, could not, one supposed, have failed to be upsetting. Sargie, however, had been so oddly elated by the suggestion that his brother had been pushed off the fire escape that I no longer knew how anyone would react to the story of Jimbo's death.

'No one could have written that paragraph unless they *knew* something, you see. Oh, it's so *long* ago, so *long*, but darling Jimbo . . . I could say so much about it all, if I wanted. I wouldn't *speak* to that man who wrote the book, I wouldn't *see* him. He's insufferable, with all his claims to have known Jimbo so well. I saw Jimbo every day of his life, every single day in those last years, and I should think he met Mr Hunter at most six times. He was an . . .' she dithered for a suffficiently devastating word, 'an upstart! I know it sounds awful to say that, but that's what he *is*. But the idea that he had *killed* Jimbo . . . And in cold print . . . Rice Robey, it wasn't you wrote the article, was it? Or who told Mr Darnley the story?'

'I'm sure it's true,' said Darnley before Rice Robey had the chance to reply. 'It has the ring of truth about it.'

'After all these *years*, to have it raked up again. I'd always supposed that it was the most terrible *accident*. *No one* knew Jimbo better than I did, and I'm quite sure he would never have . . .' The word suicide would not quite come. 'He just wasn't the type. He loved life! But, oh! If the dead could only rest in peace!'

The air of theatricality in Cecily – Sargie had sometimes made disobliging comments about it – was never more marked than when replaying her memories of Jimbo. Conversation in the little group had rather stopped. We all looked and listened, except for Vernon, who was talking to Felicity about the virtues of a planned economy.

As Cecily was speaking, a young man came to join our group, evidently unknown to the company, a pale young man with a lot of spots on his forehead and a strangely elderly manner of dress – a dark suit and a watch chain. He moved awkwardly from one foot to the other. Sometimes a smile played across his weasely face and sometimes he held his mouth open as if, should anyone care to listen, he was about to speak.

'Oh but I miss him, I miss him,' Cecily was saying.

And Vernon was rubbing pipe dottle on his fingertips and saying, 'Ur aim shud be to take all manufacturing industry into public ownership within the first three years. There's no good in beatin' about the bush.'

'I think this young man . . .' said Felicity.

She did not develop what she thought about the stranger.

Vernon slapped the youth on the shoulder.

'Good ter see yer, good ter see yer. Friend of Miles? Where's yer drink? There's lemonade if, like me, yer a teetotaller.'

'I haven't come for a drink, ' said the young man, now gulping with embarrassment.

'And look, um forgettin' me manners. Um Ernie Lampitt – Roy Ramsay, Julian Ramsay . . .' He began a round of tedious introductions. 'Miles Darnley, yer know.'

'My name is Tongue,' said the young man, blushing at the admission. 'I represent the firm of Widdell and Blair.'

Jo Lampitt, silenced for the previous few minutes by her inability to say anything sufficiently fatuous about either the planned economy or her great-uncle's demise, squealed with merriment at the mention of the word Widdell.

'I see in you,' said Rice Robey to Mr Tongue, 'the neaniskos of Gethsemane, the unknown young man who appeared at the arrest of Christ and who fled naked when the guards seized his outer clothes.'

Mr Tongue blinked like a cornered rabbit at this assertion which might well, in the circumstances, have been the prelude to debagging him and sending him out naked into the night with no clothes.

'Mr Rice Robey?' he tentatively enquired.

'Yes.'

Without another word, Mr Tongue reached into his pocket for a folded paper and placed it into Rice Robey's hand.

'Mr Miles Darnley?' enquired Mr Tongue again.

'This is like Christmas,' said Jo. 'Little cards and prezzies for everyone.'

'Who are you?' asked Felicity fiercely. 'Are you from a lawyer?'

Mr Tongue placed into Darnley's hand a document identical to the one which he had given to Rice Robey. Darnley smiled, but I felt it was a stung sort of smile, and I remembered Rice Robey's very odd assertion, made to me long before, that Darnley had in him something of John the Baptist, a prophet doomed to martyrdom. By the time we had all absorbed the fact that these pieces of folded cream paper, sealed with scarlet wax, were writs for libel, Mr Tongue (in this respect, at least, like the biblical young man who so interested Rice Robey, though fully clothed) had vanished through the throng.

Because of the creakingly slow processes of the law, it was at least eight months before Rice Robey's case came to court. At Darnley's wedding I had assumed, knowing nothing of such matters, that the police might arrive at any moment and prevent the newly-weds from departing for their honeymoon. In fact, for a long time nothing much seemed to happen. I was not, of course, privy to the long exchange of solicitors' letters between the various parties concerned. I felt intensely embarrassed by my own part in the affair, and, in the way that the marriage of one's friends can make them into strangers, Darnley did not bother to keep in touch with me. My life was taken up with other things – with 'The Mulberrys', with Sargie, with unattainable girls.

The first I knew of what had happened in the case was on a blustery evening the following April. I had returned from Birmingham (a recording session of 'The Mulberrys' during which Jason had started an improbable flirtation with the Barleybrook village schoolmistress) and found Rice Robey sitting with Felicity in the downstairs sitting room of the house in Arlington Road. When I entered the room, they were sitting next to one another on the sofa, and she sprang up with such nervousness that I wondered if I had surprised them in an embrace.

'Julian! I wasn't expecting you so soon.'

'The intrusion is my own,' said Rice Robey.

'Sit down, R.R.,' said Felicity sharply.

'If you'd rather I went out again,' I said, awkwardly, not knowing how I should finish the sentence. I saw no reason why I should be driven from my own home by Rice Robey and Felicity having yet another of their little trysts.

'We'd better tell him,' said Felicity.

For a second of horror, I guessed that she was going to announce her intention of marrying Rice Robey.

'Mr Darnley has settled,' he said, instantaneously putting my mind at rest.

'Settled the case with Hunter? Oh, but that's marvellous news.'

'How can you say that?' asked Felicity reproachfully. 'You see where that places R.R.?'

'I don't see anything.'

As far as the intricacies of law were concerned, I was an

innocent. They patiently explained to me that Hunter had issued three writs. He intended to sue Darnley and Rice Robey as individuals, and also the small limited company that owned *The Spark*, which consisted of Darnley and a couple of 'backers'. Darnley's family lawyer had eventually put pressure on him to settle the case with Hunter out of court. It was not, apparently, something to which Darnley agreed very readily, but when he had realised the extent of the likely damages and legal costs, there was really no alternative. His mother and the family lawyer did not wish Darnley's assets (which I was somehow not surprised to learn were considerable) to be poured into Hunter's bank account in a limitless flow. They had agreed to pay Hunter £10,000 and to close down the paper – which could not by any standards hope to sustain a loss of this magnitude. (At that date £10,000 could buy you a substantial house in the middle of London.)

These were big stakes. As I heard the story, I felt crushed by self-hatred; by the knowledge that my indiscreet words to Hunter in the Turkish baths had helped to bring about the downfall of my friend and the closure of *The Spark*.

Since the whole painful business began, Rice Robey had refused to employ his own legal adviser. Any letters which had been written to him by Hunter's solicitor had been answered by himself – no doubt in his own distinctive manner. When, however, Darnley's solicitor reached a settlement with Hunter, they approached Rice Robey and asked him to come in on the deal. Darnley had generously offered to pay all Rice Robey's costs; and I have no doubt that he would also have paid any out-of-court settlement in lieu of damages on Robey's behalf out of his own pocket however much this was frowned upon by the guardians of the Darnley family money.

This development was not to be. Robey had spent about three hours with Darnley's solicitor. It had been pointed out to him that he had only two alternatives. He could issue a full retraction of the libel, and come in under the umbrella of their collective settlement with Hunter, or he could be left on his own. Since his legal liability was inextricably linked with that of Darnley and *The Spark*, Darnley's lawyers were skilfully anxious to distance themselves from the risk which Rice Robey now constituted. In spite of Darnley's protests, they warned Rice Robey that if he did not accept the settlement, he would be on his own. The prosecution could sub-poena Darnley as a witness *against* Rice Robey, by making it clear that he had published the accusation in good faith, and that the libel, the suggestion that Hunter was a murderer, was a lie originating solely with Rice Robey. Hunter was evidently in no mood for clemency. He would sue Rice Robey for all he was worth, perhaps more. Robey and the Great Attachment faced total financial ruin, and Robey could very well face a prison sentence.

This was the sobering news which Rice Robey had come to my house to relate to Felicity.

Now that Darnley was out of the running, it was more than ever clear to me that I was directly responsible for the case having been brought. If it had not been for the fact that, in his guileless letters to Hunter's solicitors, Robey had already admitted to the authorship of the articles, I might have myself been summoned as a prosecution witness.

'So, what are you going to do?' I asked.

'*Magna est veritas*', Robey intoned, '*et praevalebit.*' The shock of the whole experience had made him momentarily forget his own language, and it seemed that he was only capable of speaking in Latin – pronounced, as always, in his highly idiosyncratic tone. When I asked – 'Apart from anything else, how will you pay for your trial?', he merely smiled and said: '*Deus providebit . . .*' Even I knew how that quotation ended – God would provide a victim for the slaughter – whatever deities of wrath had been unleashed by the libel, they would exact their revenge.

The trial, when it happened, was conducted in a small room in the Courts of Justice in the Strand. Cinema-going had led me to believe that trials – however few the participants – happened in vast theatrical settings – a crowded public gallery, rows of bewigged clerks and counsel, a judge on his bench set apart like Zeus in a Greek drama. In reality, the whole place had an almost embarrassingly intimate air. There was very little space for spectators, and these benches were filled to capacity, partly by journalists, partly by myself, Darnley, Cecily – who put in faithful and regular apearances on each of the three days of the trial – and Felicity. The jury were squashed into benches on the other side of the court.

The judge was a man called Mr Justice Howell, a small-lipped, scarlet-cheeked Welshman whose face suggested that he might

735

at any moment become uncontrollably angry. His appearance on the Bench, for which we all respectfully stood to attention, did not bode well for Rice Robey's chances. Hunter sat behind his own counsel, a clever barrister called Oliver Leslie. He did not, as Rice Robey did, look around the courtroom or attempt to catch anyone's eye. He sat pale, and impassive, as the proceedings got under way.

There was a great deal of palaver before the trial proper began.

The judge greeted the prosecution counsel with effusive good manners which were immediately switched off when he came to address the defendant.

'I employ no counsel, my lord,' Rice Robey said. 'Partly because it is beyond my means to do so, partly because the Truth needs no . . .'

'Please do not try to explain yourself to me, Mr Robey,' said the judge.

'I thought that this was the function of the present assembly, my lord – that I should explain myself to you.'

This sally of Robey's made the judge's already scarlet face deepen to the colour of purplish bricks.

'Since you clearly have no idea of what constitutes the law, Mr Robey, I should leave it to me to decide what the function of this assembly might be,' he snapped.

'As your lordship pleases. Except to say this.'

'What is it now, Mr Robey?'

'We were not forbidden to judge one another because it is improper – merely because it is impossible.'

'Forbidden? Forbidden? What on earth are you trying to say, man? Who has forbidden me to judge you?'

'Another judge, my lord,' said Robey with his mysterious, and on this occasion infuriating smile. 'Another Judge.'

'I should be interested to know his name,' snapped Howell. 'Whoever he is, he has no function in this court. I am trying this case. I apologise to you, Mr Leslie' – once again, he switched on an ingratiating smile – 'for the amount of your valuable time which we are wasting.'

'I'm sure it is valuable time, my lord, for which my client will not be paying,' said Oliver Leslie smoothly.

'I'm sure,' added the judge, thus making it abundantly clear, before a single word of the trial had begun, how he intended that it should be concluded. Since Rice Robey was no lawyer, he did not pick the judge up on this, and so the farce began without further interruption.

Oliver Leslie QC arose, and began to explain to the jury the nature of the libel. He told them that Raphael Hunter was well known to them, a proposition with which I am not sure that they agreed. He told them that they had all seen Raphael Hunter on television, and admired his 'many contributions to the arts'. (It made it sound as though he was recommending Hunter for a knighthood in the New Year's Honours rather than defending his good name in court.) Some of them would read Hunter's column in a Sunday newspaper. Others would have read his biography of James Petworth Lampitt.

'It could be said,' pontificated Oliver Leslie, 'that Lampitt was a distinctly minor writer, who owes his survival very largely to my client. When he died, I should say that very few people read the works of James Petworth Lampitt. Very few indeed. His was a vanished reputation, if, indeed, ladies and gentlemen of the jury, it was a reputation at all. He was, I gather, a lonely man. He was what you could call the literary world's equivalent of a has-been – if I may use so vulgar a phrase. And this was the man, ladies and gentlemen, whom my client, out of the goodness of his heart, befriended, the man whose loneliness he . . .' Oliver Leslie paused. It was by no means clear what Hunter had done to the supposed loneliness and neglect of Jimbo.

'After he died,' continued the QC, leaving the loneliness and neglect somewhat in the air, 'Mr Hunter, my client, worked tirelessly for the restitution of his work. It is entirely thanks to him that some of that work is now available in paperback. It is thanks to him that the name James Petworth Lampitt is known. And it is known, very largely, I should submit, because of Mr Hunter's magisterial biography of the man – a man whom he knew, and whom he respected, and to whose friendship and conversation, he owed much.

'Ladies and gentlemen, this is a libel trial, and not a murder trial. There is absolutely no question that James Petworth Lampitt died an accidental death, on that April day in 1947. You will hear from my client, when he takes the stand, how that death occurred. A coroner returned a verdict of accidental death on the man, and accidental death it unquestionably was. If – and of course, the very possibility is unthinkable – if anyone had suspected otherwise, there would have been every possible opportunity for them to state their suspicions to the police at the proper time, and in the proper manner. Of course, no such suspicions existed. It was only after sixteen years had passed – sixteen years, ladies and gentlemen of the jury – that the defendant chose to perpetrate this foul and damaging libel on my client, the very direct suggestion that he had been responsible for the death of the man whom he so much revered and to whom, as I have already stated, he owed so much.'

Mr Oliver Leslie QC proceeded to acquaint the jury with *The Spark* – which he described as 'a vulgar news-sheet of which they had probably not heard'. He told them that it was now defunct but that it developed a reputation for printing scurrilous verbal attacks, often upon persons unable or unwilling to defend themselves. He described the magazine as 'malicious with the malice of the school playground – and we all know how cruel that can be'.

It was, he stated, an open secret that Rice Robey was the author of many of these items which appeared in the anonymous 'Diary' item at the front of the magazine, and that he had enjoyed extraordinary good luck in not being prosecuted for some of the libellous things he had printed about other well-loved and much-respected figures in the public eye.

Rice Robey smiled through all this. He did not rise to his feet, or object that he was being tried for a libel upon Raphael Hunter, rather than upon these putative and unnamed public figures. He did not even protest as Oliver Leslie began his description of himself.

'Mr Robey, it would be true to say, ladies and gentlemen of the jury, is a bitter man. He is a failure. You will learn how he wished to pursue a career of learning and literature, but that poverty and various character defects made this impossible. He was in early days a protégé of the late Mr Lampitt's and he would dearly have loved to enjoy the same position in Mr Lampitt's affections that was occupied by Mr Hunter. He was, in short, envious of Mr Hunter, eaten up by envy and malice for sixteen years, and probably for longer. He had known when he published his libel in *The Spark* that it was the most dastardly libel, and he had still persuaded the editor, much against his better judgement, to print it. He had done so for reasons of envy and pique and malice, knowing them to be foul lies. There is no worse libel than to accuse another man of having killed one of his best friends. This is a very simple case, ladies and gentlemen; an extremely simple case. I have absolutely no doubt how it will be concluded.'

I gather that it was not Oliver Leslie at his best, but the judge seemed to like it. He beamed solicitously at the barrister as he sat down, and then said, with ill-concealed distaste, 'Mr Robey, you may make some statement for the defence if you wish before the case proceeds.'

Oliver Leslie had been a little verbose, but his manner had been reasonable, his tones quiet. His eyes had moved from his papers to the jury, and back; he spoke as a reasonable man speaking to other reasonable beings. It was obvious from the moment that Rice Robey rose to his feet that this was not to be his technique.

Thrusting his head right back so that he looked at the ceiling, and raising both arms in the air, he called out, 'What is truth?'

Such a long silence ensued, that one wondered if this was to be his defence. Then he turned, not to the judge or jury, but to Hunter himself, who refused to meet his gaze, but sheepishly examined his finger-nails as the Robey harangue unrolled.

'It is a good question at a trial, and you will recall at which trial the question was first posited, by the representative of the *saeculum*, by the *magisterium* of Empire, what is truth? And he managed – I speak of Pilate – to find no answer in his process, and so through the handwashing ritual he demonstrates the impotence of the empirical lie, and the illegality of the Roman *lex*, and the worse emptiness of the Torah, written in scrolls and not on hearts. . . .'

'Mr Robey,' said the judge, 'this is nothing to do with the case.'

'Ah! We shall remember that, your honour, and so will the jury when they come to their verdict: that the question *What is truth?* has nothing to do with the case.'

'Mr Robey, you are here to defend yourself against a very specific and I might add a very serious charge. I really must insist that you restrict your remarks to what is relevant to the charge against you, and not treat us to this – *generalised* tirade.'

'My lord Caiaphas, my lord Pilate, I stand rebuked,' said Rice Robey.

'I am sure that the jury agree with me that it is extremely

improper, not to say blasphemous, to introduce all these other considerations into the case,' said the judge testily.

'*I'm sure this Jesus will not do – Either for Englishman or Jew,*' agreed Rice Robey. 'Very well, I shall present my defence in terms which even a judge might find comprehensible. I feel no malice towards friend Hunter – merely a confidence that he shed innocent blood. I knew Mr Lampitt – Mr James Petworth Lampitt – for many years. Witnesses will be called who knew him for much longer.'

There was a rumble of excitement in the courtroom at this news. We had all assumed that there would be some witnesses for the prosecution, but (in so far as Felicity would let me be privy to details of Rice Robey's plans for his own defence) I had not heard that there would be any defence witnesses.

'James Petworth was no self-slayer. He was possessed with no suicidal *daimon*. He was not – though you could consider this, O Pilate, to be an irrelevant detail – he was not the watery figure whom we meet in the pages of Mr Hunter's compilation, published some winters since. He was, for one thing, not homo-erotic.'

'Mr Robey, I have warned you,' said the judge.

'But have you warned *him*, O Pilate?' and Robey pointed a long and hieratic finger at Hunter. 'Have you warned him of the consequences of shedding innocent blood? No! For the judgement is not yours or mine to give. All we are here to do is to arrive at the truth; and we shall! We shall!'

The sing-song manner of Robey's delivery – and the volume (he spoke, for that little room, far too loud) did not seem to have made a very favourable impression on the jury. They looked distinctly as if they were in the presence of someone embarrassing and distasteful, and there was laughter among them – the embarrassed laughter of relief when the comparatively 'normal' judge spoke and the trial went on.

It was during that first day that Hunter took the witness box. Whereas Robey was wild and mad-seeming, Hunter, particularly when cross-examined by his own counsel, was quiet, and his smile suggested that he was being extraordinarily good-humoured about a matter in which other men, less reasonable or kind, would have been violently aggrieved.

Mr Oliver Leslie QC did not have many questions to ask of Hunter. He took him through the article in *The Spark*.

'Mr Hunter, it will distress you if I repeat that sentence once more, that foul libel, but I feel that I must do so. Here it is: "We wonder how many cases there are in which a biographer has been the agent of his subject's demise." Those are the words. Do you believe that these words can be interpreted in any way other than to make it seem that you murdered James Petworth Lampitt?'

'No, sir,' said Hunter. 'I do not.'

'And, in order to save Mr Robey the trouble of asking you the question, let me, Mr Hunter, ask you the question myself: did you, sir, murder James Petworth Lampitt?'

'No, sir, I did not.'

Quiet, hushed, reasonable. It was an odd occasion for one of Hunter's smiles, but he did smile at the jury, with an almost flirtatiously nervous curl of the lips.

'No, sir,' Rice Robey repeated, as he rose to cross-examine Hunter, 'you did not. And that is your reply.'

'Mr Hunter's reply was perfectly audible, Mr Robey,' interrupted the judge, 'without your repeating it. I must also remind you that you must address the bench with an appropriate deference or I shall punish you for contempt of court.'

'A not inapposite description of my feelings, m'lord,' said Robey, which caused laughter in the public benches.

'Now, Mr Hunter, may I ask you some questions?'

'Mr Robey, ' said the judge, 'we know that you have stood up to ask Mr Hunter some questions. That is all we wish you to do. Kindly hurry up about it.'

'Do you believe in God?'

'Mr Robey, really!' exclaimed the judge.

'I think I am entitled to the question, my lord.'

'I consider it improper,' said the judge.

'Perhaps I may ask some other questions of you, Mr Hunter,' continued Rice Robey, who was fishing in his pocket and produced from the inside of a dirty cheque-book some yellow newspaper cuttings. 'Did you, in a review in the *Sunday Times* last summer, review a book about the modernist movement in poetry?'

'Yes,' said Hunter. 'I did.'

'Did you write these words: "I" – referring to yourself, Mr Hunter – "must be one of the many who found 'The Four

Quartets' an inspirational work while being unable to share T. S. Eliot's religious beliefs"?'

'Yes,' said Hunter. 'I wrote those words.'

'Did you, in a review in the same newspaper of a biography of D. H. Lawrence dated some months earlier, state that "few intelligent people nowadays accept the old religious orthodoxies"?'

'Yes,' said Hunter, 'I wrote that.'

'And would you consider that you are among the few or among the many?'

'Mr Robey,' said the judge hotly, 'I must warn you that I see no relevance in this line of questioning.'

'My lord, Mr Hunter has made it very clear in his journalism that he is not a religious believer. He makes it clear, I should say, by every uninspirational sentence that he pens. . . .'

'I should remind you, Mr Robey, that this is not a symposium on the merits of Mr Hunter's prose style.'

No one except the judge laughed at this pleasantry.

'Mr Hunter began his evidence, my lord, with an oath. He swore by Almighty God that the evidence he would give would be the truth, the whole truth . . .'

'We all heard Mr Hunter take the oath, Mr Robey.'

'I think, my lord, that the ladies and gentlemen of the jury might be illuminated to discover that the man who swore by Almighty God does not believe that Almighty God exists.'

The judge turned to the jury.

'You may disregard all those questions,' he said hotly. 'Now, Mr Robey, will you kindly get to the point?'

'I cannot get to the point, my lord, if you and I do not agree as to what the point is,' said Robey. 'I began by asking – What is truth? I was told that it was of no interest in an English court of law, and that will be an interesting lesson to have learnt, if nothing else is to emerge from these proceedings. I then began by asking if Mr Hunter's oath was to be understood to have the slightest meaning. You directed the jury to disregard my question. Now we know where we are. We are in a room where it is not considered important whether there is such a thing as truth, or whether we live in a godless universe. And in this place, this infernal place I should say, we are required – by what means I do not know – to establish truth by some means which will be beyond me.'

'If it is beyond you to establish the truth, Mr Robey, you had better shut up and sit down,' said the judge.

'Not yet, my lord. I have some more questions for Mr Hunter.'

Hunter smiled patiently. I noticed, as on the first occasion that I met him, and he was describing the death of James Petworth Lampitt to a small literary society at my boarding school, that he pressed his hands very firmly down on the surface in front of him, in this case, the wooden railing at the front of the witness box.

'Once again, I ask you – were you alone with Mr Lampitt when he died?'

'I was not with him. I was in the sitting room of his flat. He had gone into the kitchen. He liked to stand on the fire escape just outside his kitchen and look at the sky. I heard a crash – a cry – and I ran out to the kitchen to see what had happened. He was not there. I looked over the balustrade at the top of the fire escape and saw that he had fallen into the area below.'

'And nobody else was there?'

'No.'

'How high is the railing outside his kitchen?'

'My lord, this incident happened seventeen years ago,' said Hunter. 'I seem to remember that it was about waist-high, but I could not be certain.'

'How tall are you, Mr Hunter?'

'Five foot ten inches.'

'And how tall was James Petworth Lampitt?'

'I do not know.'

'You wrote a very long book about him, but you do not know his height. You knew him well, but you do not know his height. You were, according to a recent paperback of his life of the Prince Consort, his close friend and private secretary, but you did not know his height.'

'I meant that I do not remember his exact height.'

'Quite so, Mr Hunter,' said the judge sympathetically. 'There is really no need to submit to this hectoring from the defendant.'

'He was five foot five inches in height,' said Rice Robey. 'Would you agree that he could not have fallen over the railing? He could have climbed it – a very unlikely eventuality – or he could have been helped over it. Would you agree?'

'There is no need to answer that question,' said the judge. 'It was an impertinence even to have suggested it.'

'Thank you, my lord,' said Rice Robey. 'And it is an impertinence to suggest that a man fell over a railing which he would in point of fact have had the greatest difficulty in climbing. I have no further questions of this witness.'

It was on the following day of the trial that Robey made his most dramatic coup.

'My lord, I call Mrs Sargent Lampitt.'

In the witness box, Cecily looked smaller than she was. More than on previous occasions when I had looked at her, I was put in mind of the dressed animals in Beatrix Potter's illustrations. Her pretty rodent-like eyes darted sharply about the court, and then fixed themselves accusingly on Raphael Hunter.

Cecily did not take the oath. She made a declaration that she would tell the truth, but that she would not invoke the deity in whom she did not believe.

'Your name is Cecily Horatia Lampitt.'

'It is.'

'And you are married to the brother of the late James Petworth Lampitt.'

'I was. I am.'

The judge leaned forward and peered at Cecily contemptuously.

'Well, are you or aren't you married to him?' he asked.

'In law, I am still married to Sargent Lampitt.'

'Speak up!' snapped the judge.

'I said in law, my lord, I am still married to Mr Lampitt. We have not lived together for many years.'

'Why waste words?' asked the judge. 'How else can you be married to someone except in law?'

This rebuke excited Cecily's indignation. Her lips pursed, and then she said vehemently, 'There is no need to be so *rude*! Just because you are a judge . . .'

'I must remind you, madam, that if you do not restrict yourself to answering the questions, you could be in very serious trouble.'

Rice Robey smiled and stared at the ceiling as he said, 'Mrs Lampitt, you knew your brother-in-law very well, and for a long time.'

'Yes,' said Cecily.

'When were you married?'

'In 1917.'

'And James Petworth died in 1947.'

'Yes.'

'So you knew one another for at least thirty years.'

'Most of us can count,' said the judge.

'Did you read the biography of James Petworth Lampitt by the plaintiff Mr Hunter?'

'I did.'

'Did you consider that it provided an accurate account of the man?'

'No, I did not. I considered it a mean book, a cruel book, a foolish book. It was not the man I knew so well. It wasn't him at all. It was full of innuendo. No one in the family liked it. None of us recognised James Petworth Lampitt in Mr Hunter's book. No, we did not.'

'In particular, you were displeased that Mr Hunter made James Petworth Lampitt out to be of homo-erotic proclivities; is that not the case?'

'I have said, there are many innuendoes in the book which I disliked.'

'And that was one of them.'

'Yes.'

'And you considered that this was untrue – that James Petworth did not indulge in the vices of Alcibiades and Alexander the Great?'

'If you mean did he make love to boys, then I would say very decidedly not.'

'And you knew him very well – you knew him well enough to feel confident about this?'

'I do feel confident. Mr Hunter told lies. He pretends that he knew James Petworth Lampitt really well and this wasn't true, it wasn't *true*. I used to visit Mr Lampitt many times, oh, often each week. And yes, in the last few months of his life, I heard him mention Mr Hunter. I forget where they had met: at some literary party, I believe. They certainly did not know each other well. Mr Hunter used to come to tea with Mr Lampitt sometimes, that was all. He came to tea on the day that Mr Lampitt died.'

'And you were due to call on Mr Lampitt later that afternoon, were you not?'

'Yes, yes I was.'

'Can you tell us what happened that afternoon?'

'I arrived at Jimbo's flat – at Mr Lampitt's flat, as I often did, and let myself in, I had my own key, and I was astonished.'

'By what?'

'I was astonished to find that Mr Hunter was sitting in the flat on his own. He had been going through Jimbo's desk.'

'How do you know?'

'Jimbo was a very neat man. He never left papers or notebooks lying about, he never left drawers open. But when I came into the room, his bureau was open, and there were papers spread out all over the desk. Mr Hunter had obviously been going through his things – going through Jimbo's things, Mr Hunter. He was, he was.'

'What did you say or do?'

'I challenged him. I said – "Where is Mr Lampitt? You aren't supposed to be here on your own" (hee-er). 'He said that Jimbo was dead, that he had fallen from the balcony at the back of the flat, and that he was very glad that I had come. He said he had wanted to tell me in person.'

'Did you believe him?'

'No, I did not. Why should he wish to tell me anything? He was surprised by my coming into the room, startled – he looked fishy, guilty, up to no good. He was not shocked by Jimbo's death, not at all. But he was shocked by my appearing. He was trying to rifle through Jimbo's desk, and he was trying to cover his own tracks.'

'Can you guess what he was searching for in James Petworth Lampitt's bureau?'

'No.' She paused. 'I have often wondered.'

For me, who had so often thought about the day on which James Petworth Lampitt died, all this had an extraordinary interest. Since Cecily was not really on terms with Sargie, it was not surprising that her presence in the flat, so soon after Jimbo's death, had never been mentioned by Uncle Roy.

As Mr Oliver Leslie QC was soon to demonstrate, Cecily had not provided any new evidence of a kind that would, as the phrase goes, 'stand up in a court of law'. She had not proved that Hunter had murdered Jimbo. But in an imaginative sense, as far as I was concerned, she had changed the whole of that day for me. I now saw it, and all the actors involved, and to some extent everything which had happened thereafter, in a different light.

It was the little details which changed things – the fact that she had her own key, for example; and her vivid word-picture of Hunter, startled like a guilty thing surprised as he sat at Jimbo's bureau. And it was all so long ago, and yet it all had such power, still, to change us.

Mr Oliver Leslie QC was not kind in his cross-examination of Cecily. I do not know whether the judge knew what was coming, but he leaned forward as soon as the prosecuting counsel was on his feet, and a malign smile lit up Howell's mean little features.

'Mrs Lampitt, your brother-in-law was a bachelor, was he not?'

'Yes.'

'He had many friends in the literary world, I believe.'

'Yes, he did.'

'Stretching back over a number of years?'

'Well, yes.'

Mr Oliver Leslie QC picked up a fat paperback edition of Raphael Hunter's biography.

'For instance, I believe he knew slightly Henry James.'

'Yes, he did.'

'And Hugh Walpole?'

'Yes, Jimbo knew Hugh Walpole.'

'Is it true that he also knew Baron Corvo?'

'I can't remember. I did not know all of Jimbo's friends.'

'Ah. That is very interesting. You were close to Mr Lampitt, but you did not – er, know *all* his friends.'

'I don't see what's wrong with that!' Again, Cecily was losing her temper, and she turned to the jury for support. By now, it was clear in what direction Mr Oliver Leslie QC was leading his inquiry, and Cecily was presumably angry that she had allowed herself to be led into a trap so easily.

'We are told in Mr Hunter's book that, as a young man, James Petworth Lampitt even went to Paris in order to meet Oscar Wilde. That was an event which took place, would you not say?'

'Yes. He described it to me.'

'Mr Lampitt told you he had met Oscar Wilde?'

'Oh, really, what's all this got to do with it?'

'I'd like to ask you a few more questions, Mrs Lampitt. Do you remember that James Petworth Lampitt wrote a short introduction to the sonnets of Michelangelo?'

'Yes, I do. It's a very fine piece of work.'

'And do you remember that in that introduction he described the love of Michelangelo for his own sex as "an ennobling thing, this love which Shakespeare celebrated in his Sonnets, and Plato in his Symposium, a love, perchance, which can never be found between a man and a woman". Do you remember that sentence, Mrs Lampitt?'

'The substance of it, yes.'

'And do you remember the sentence which appears in a later paragraph – "It is not merely in the pages of the sacred texts that we find love 'passing the love of women' ". A reference of course to the love in the Bible between David and Jonathan.'

'I am perfectly well aware of the Bible story,' snapped Cecily.

'Do those sentences please you, Mrs Lampitt?'

'I think they are very interesting,' she said.

'And you think they are true?'

'I beg your pardon?'

'Do you think it is true that for certain men, there is a love which is "passing the love of women"?'

'You have just told us that there is. In the Bible.' She smirked, as if she had scored a point, and not realising that he was about to pounce on his prey.

'Were you in love with your brother-in-law, Mrs Lampitt?'

A pained silence fell on the courtroom. Rice Robey jumped to his feet.

'My lord! This is not relevant to the case. My witness is being subjected . . .'

'It is of great relevance to the case, Mr Robey, to know in what direction witnesses are biased,' said the judge with a satanic gleam in his face. 'Please answer the question, Mrs Lampitt. We are all agog for the answer.'

'Why should I answer such a question, in such a place?' Cecily asked furiously.

'Because I have said that you must,' said the judge sharply. 'Were you in love with James Petworth Lampitt or weren't you?'

Another aching silence. Then, Cecily's voice, very quiet, and serious and low.

'Yes. Yes, Jimbo and I loved one another.'

'That is not what I asked you, Mrs Lampitt,' said Oliver Leslie.

'I put it to you that you were in love with James Petworth Lampitt, but that your affections were not returned.'

'That's not true!'

'I put it to you that you knew James Petworth Lampitt was homosexual by inclination, and that you had a jealous hatred for the young men to whom he formed attachments. I put it to you that you suspected him of loving my client Mr Hunter, albeit in a platonic sense. I put it to you that you were jealous of Mr Hunter and that you are still jealous of him, and that in all your remarks about him you are motivated by sexual jealousy. I put it to you that you are a bitter woman whose judgement is clouded by years of nursing a foolish and hopeless passion for a man who had no interest in you whatsoever.'

'No, no, no . . .'

But Oliver Leslie had sat down. He had no further questions.

The summing-up occurred on the following day. As Oliver Leslie had said in his opening speech, it was a very simple case. Rice Robey had accused Hunter of murder. The coroner's verdict on James Petworth Lampitt's death had been produced, and they had even managed to find the doctor who had performed the autopsy in 1947. No evidence had been produced that Jimbo's death had been other than accidental. Therefore, Rice Robey was guilty of libel. In his own summing-up, he was crushed. He still looked aloft, and he still waved his hands in hieratic gestures, but he knew that he had no case.

'Ladies and gentlemen of the jury, I began by asking you Pilate's question – "What is truth?" And like jesting Pilate, our learned judge would not stay for an answer. You have heard the testimony of Mrs Lampitt which Mr Leslie has attempted to twist and distort. She knew James Petworth Lampitt; and I knew him too. We knew he was not a suicide. We knew that he had not died by natural means. There was only one who could have hastened his end, and that one is Mr Oliver Leslie's client, the plaintiff in the case today.'

The jury were out for about twenty minutes. They found him guilty, and Rice Robey was ordered to pay £1,000 damages, and almost as much again in costs.

It was from Felicity, in the subsequent days, that I heard the last details of these costs. I had gone away again to Birmingham, and did not follow the final stages of the drama. Darnley's offer to pay Rice Robey's costs had been refused. Nobly, but surely

749

foolishly, Rice Robey had said that he had got himself, and Darnley, into the case and he would pay his own way out of it.

'Julian – it was so wicked: when one thinks of that rich judge, and that rich barrister, being prepared to reduce R.R. to ruin. He would barely have got £2,000 for that house in Twisden Road.'

'So, what happened?'

'I went through a terrible twenty-four hours of believing that R.R. wanted to go to prison, wanted to become a martyr for the cause of truth. Oh, Julian, he is a noble man.'

'What saved him? – or should I say – who saved him? Felicity – you didn't . . .'

'I offered, of course. I haven't quite got that money, but I have about £1,000. Of course I've made it available to R.R. from the beginning of all this.'

I did not know this fact and it made me furious; but I kept my counsel.

'So, who bailed him out?'

'Guess.'

'I can't.'

'The Great Attachment.'

'I thought that she was as poor as he was.'

'They are both desperately poor – particularly now that he has lost his job.'

'It's not certain that he's lost his job, is it?'

'They'll get him out,' she said with great sadness. 'He was so unpopular with those *fools* in the Ministry that they can easily get rid of him now. It is really because he was going to stop them building a road through Aldingbury Ring. But now that this case has come to light they can dress it up as a disciplinary offence. They can say that he was leaking secret, civil service information and writing in *The Spark* about things he could only have known from classified documents.'

'True?'

'It's so unfair.'

'But, how did the Great Attachment come to have two thousand quid?'

'Julian, it is such a strange story. They had a couple of really hideous paintings by this man that you used to work with in the shirt factory.'

'Not Mr Pilbright?'

'Yes. The one who's just been "discovered" after a lifetime of

obscurity. One of them in particular – R.R. calls it the Woolworth Magdalene – is said to be a really "important" Pilbright.
Mrs Paxton sold it a couple of months ago. Apparently it will pay
for the damages and the costs and leave a little over for' – she
smiled wanly – 'a washing machine.'

Five

William Bloom's large flat overlooks the Westminster School playing fields in Vincent Square. In idle moments, of which, for both of us, there are nowadays so many, he can gaze down on the boys at play, occasionally even lifting field glasses from his desk to survey, in summer, some particularly decorative figure in white flannels at silly mid off, or, in winter, the more tempestuous beauties of a Rugby scrum.

A quarter of a century had passed since Rice Robey's trial for libel. I was lunching with Bloom that day I saw the 'Mr Pilbright At Home' exhibition at the Tate, and we fell to talking, inevitably, about our lives, the forty or so years we had known one another, the singular threads of cognition and coincidence which had run through experience like Blake's Golden String.

'Extraordinary to think of all those years that Mr Pilbright worked at the shirt factory,' I said, 'and the total obscurity of his life when Daddy worked with him, then me . . . '

'You'd still be working in a shirt factory today, my dear, if I hadn't talked you into lodging with Rikko and Fenella, and set you on the move, so to say.'

This was true. As we spoke, sipping coffee (how abstemious we have both become – no smoking, and barely any desire for alcohol) I thought of all the parallels between Mr Pilbright and Rice Robey. Not only were they both men with an idiosyncratic religious vision, translated without apparent awkwardness into their chosen medium; they also both achieved their effects of imaginative projection entirely uncowed by the way in which 'the world' expected them to earn a living. Rice Robey's career in the Ministry of Works is now remembered as little as Pilbright's forty years in Accounts at Tempest and Holmes. What remained was their imaginative achievement, Pilbright's hundreds of canvases, Robey's Albion Pugh novels, which still have their admirers, not to mention the charismatic effect which Rice

Robey was to make as a minor cult figure in the late 1960s – something which lies outside the scope of the present volume.

Speaking of Robey, Bloom said, 'All that mingling of sex and religion – my God, he had it *made*!'

He threw back his snowy head and his wrinkled old face (the same age as mine – it is incredible!) creased into its familiar manic laughter.

'The chicks couldn't have enough of it!' he guffawed. 'His great secret was never for one instant doubting his own fantasy life. A very rare quality, that. Most of us lack faith in ourselves and call that process of disillusionment growing up. Not Robey-baby. Nor old Pill-prick. I haven't seen this latest exhibition, but I remember the important one at the Hayward Gallery which they put on after Raphael Hunter did that big interview with Pilbright on telly.'

While Bloom talked, I looked about his flat and tried to fashion into words what it was about these figures which had become significant for me with the passage of the years. My eyes fell on the comfort of Bloom's huge room, its wall lined with books, and the impressive Matthew Smith nudes, the gleaming, slightly too new leather sofas and armchairs, the huge round table where we sat alone, the two of us, looking out over the treetops and the boys in the distance playing hockey. The point at which I identified with Pilbright and Rice Robey was precisely in this area of the disparity between their imaginative and their workaday lives. Bloom was probably right to say that they had never grown up, never doubted their fantasies, always lived, as William Blake had done, within the self-confidently discovered borders of their own imagination, and refused to accept any secondhand vision of the world doled out to them by others.

My imaginative history lacked such cohesion. Mine had been a story of many visions and revisions, a chronicle of doubting everything, especially myself. Yet, when it occurred to me that my life was defined in anyone's eyes by the way in which I earned a living, I experienced the same sense of shock which could have been felt if Pilbright's life-story were told with no reference to the paintings, only to Tempest and Holmes, or if someone were to write the story of Rice Robey, schoolmaster and civil servant, without ever mentioning the Albion Pugh novels, the cult following, the pursuits in mind and on foot of legendary Britain.

Bloom had asked me to write a short book about my thirty-five year career as Jason Grainger. 'The Mulberrys' are as popular as ever, and Jason, as I need hardly remind regular listeners to the programme, is barely the same man as his youthful self. Successive scriptwriters have been sentimentalising his role to the point where all that remains from the bad old days is the occasional expression of verbal cynicism, which does not really conceal a heart as nauseatingly warm and loving as that of his sainted father, old Harold. Since the Mulberrys are so popular, and Jason Grainger is one of the longest-surviving members of the cast, it was not surprising that some publisher should see a saleable book in the subject.

William Bloom's idea was that I should actually write the book in the persona of Jason, describing his early adolescent quarrels with dear old Harold Grainger, his sorties into criminality, the unscrupulous affair with the lady of the manor turning into a love match, his mysterious absence from the village (during that period when I really believed that I had shaken free of him and might pursue my own career – he was meant to have gone to Canada, but Bloom wondered whether he might not have had a spell in prison for the sort of sexual aberration which is now regarded so much more sympathetically than then) right down to the present when, after Lady Tredegar's demise, Jason found himself the heir to Barleybrook Manor which he promptly converted into a 'country-house hotel' with himself as the increasingly oleaginous proprietor.

Bloom's money tempted me, but I could not write the book. After several false starts, I realised why. I wanted, before I died, to explore another story. It was not an urge to pure autobiography.

> I will give you the end of a golden string,
> Only wind it into a ball:
> It will lead you in at heaven's gate
> Built in Jerusalem's wall.

All lives are intertwinings of such golden strings. Mine, thanks to Uncle Roy and the way I was brought up, had been peculiarly connected with a family which was not my own – the Lampitts – and in particular to Sargie's brother Jimbo. James Petworth Lampitt had been the first writer to fill me with the desire to be a writer myself. Reading his work had produced in me an epiphany to which I had never lived up, a vocation to which I had been unfaithful. I had allowed life to float by, never disciplining myself, as Professor Wimbish was said to do, to 3,000 words a day, rain or shine. Had I pursued a 'literary' career, I suppose I should have been able to improve on my first disastrous autobiographical novel and to produce books which might have been in the same fashionable league as, say, Deborah Arnott's books, reasonably well-turned stories of domestic life in contemporary Britain. Looking back, I realise that it was not what I wanted to do, and that James Petworth Lampitt had haunted me all my life, not simply because of his writings, but because of the Pandora's box opened up by contemplating his death. I find myself increasingly interested in the past, in the way that the past, just as much as the evanescent present, is always on the move, always changing, only percept-ible by imaginative means. Blake distrusted representational art. 'I question not my corporal or vegetative eye any more than I would question a window concerning a sight. I look thro' it and not with it.' This vital perception illuminates everything for me, though it illuminates in the manner of a child's kaleidoscope, shaking all the constituent ingredients into shapes which will never stand still. The Petworth Lampitt created by Hunter in his fat tome was said by one reviewer to have 'a full-square reality', comparable with the subjects of other great biographies, Froude's *Carlyle* or Sartre's *Flaubert*. This illusion of reality, just like the realism of Sir Joshua Reynolds so much abhorred by Blake, was achieved by Hunter's invariable ability to look with a window, not thro' it. In this connection, it makes almost no odds that most of the 'facts' in his biography are untrue, any more than it would matter to subsequent generations who had not known the original sitters, whether the canvases of Reynolds were true likenesses. Jimbo Lampitt, then, began to acquire a significance for me which Rice Robey, using the term in his own distinctive way, would have described as mythological. Jimbo's reality was beyond question. I knew two of his siblings well, and I came to know Cecily, who had loved him for more than a quarter of a century. In time, I would visit the United States and open those notorious boxes, labelled THE LAMPITT PAPERS, and discover what they revealed. The whole experience of reflecting upon Jimbo, and by extension upon my own experience of the

Lampitt family, not to say upon my own life, has caused me to make endless readjustments of vision, with which I can only come to terms by writing them down. This act is itself an act of 'mythology', a fixing of things which are fluid, a series of still photographs of moving objects. Felicity, when I have discussed it with her, reverts to her merciless belief that there is no point in writing about such subjects unless one can, in her terms, *think*. My own ratiocinative defects, and my consciousness of them, have deterred me again and again from the task. In other moods, however, I have believed that it is precisely because I cannot approach the matter as a philosopher that I am qualified for the task. Very few human beings can think, and perhaps those rare ones who can, like Felicity, necessary as they are as puncturers of nonsense, will never be able to understand, as intuitive artists can do, the way that reality presents itself to the human imagination. What nagged me about Jimbo, and the Lampitts, and my own past, turned out, the more I considered them, to be perennial questions with which Rice Robey, and other Christians before him, had been wrestling for two thousand years. We inhabit a world of facts, a world where things either are, or are not, the case, where events did or did not happen; but facts and events actually possess no significance until they have been lit up by imagination. Truth-telling is impossible unless we see thro' and not with the eye. And yet I could not entirely sympathise with Rice Robey's dismissal of 'the empirical fallacy'. There are facts. There is Either/or.

Death, my own approaching and certain death, sharpens all this. My days are empty enough now, but I am haunted and terrified by the greater emptiness which stretches ahead, when my sentient being has ceased to exist and there is nothing. Memory floods back. I am one of those who 'lives in the past', and whole phases of existence come alive while I go about humdrum domestic chores or lie awake at night, phases which I had imagined were lost and forgotten. My early childhood in London, life in the Rectory at Timplingham, the awakening of love, the dawning of my obsession with the story of Jimbo Lampitt, all these swirl into the brain, sometimes welcome visitants, as often not. Each time they do so now, I am stung by the knowledge that all these experiences are lost and irrevocably past. I know that the return of these memories does not mean that they can truly, still less permanently, be recalled.

They are not for me intimations of immortality; nor are they hints that, after my bodily death, all such consciousness, refined and purified, will remain with me for eternity. (This, presumably, or something like it, is what religious people believe when they speak of the survival of consciousness or of the soul.) I feel reasonably certain that there is nothing to look forward to but total blank. At the end of the day, before the mind drifts off into the oblivion of dreamless sleep, half-dreams come, and the preoccupations of the previous twelve hours flit in and out of the mind, sometimes assuming playful shapes and muddling themselves into fantasies. The mind thus automatically stretches its limbs before the dark unconscious. In the same way, before the endless sleep of death, whole tracts of experience resolve themselves into stories in the mind. The cards are being reshuffled before they are put back in the box. I cling to them. I do not want them to go.

During childhood, I would become hysterical at the prospect of returning to boarding school. My grief was not wholly rational. 'You'll be all right once you are back at the school,' my exasperated aunt would say briskly to me as I sobbed and moaned and struggled. This had a broad truth. I did not cry because Seaforth Grange was horrible, though it was. (In many respects, the company of Darnley and my other friends there was more congenial than that of my uncle, aunt and cousin at the Rectory.) It was the separation itself which terrified me. Awaiting death is much worse than the 'back to school' feeling. What is there to dread if there is no future consciousness? Such common sense should console more deeply than the belief, at an earlier stage, that I should be all right when I got back to school. But I am not ruled by common sense; and it is precisely the nothingness, the non-being, the absence of thought, memory, or desire, which fills me with terror. In this state of mind, it no longer matters whether I have had a happy life or whether there is not much of it which I should prefer to forget. In such a mood I cling to memory as to the only thing, in my remaining years, which can ward off the emptiness of eternal death, and I cling to it with a horrified desperation, unable to tolerate the knowledge that it will go. In reality, the years have passed, the time is gone, and writing about it all will not bring experience back.

The last time I saw Mummy was on the railway platform at Paddington station before I went back to school. She thought it would upset me less if she left me there before the train pulled out, but I implored her to stay, which she did – quarter of an hour's anticlimax in which we had nothing to say to one another, nothing to do but cry, until the carriage juddered into motion and I pulled away, separated from her for ever. My present existence, the writing of these pages, has something of the same pointlessness, I know. Soon the guard will wave his flag and the train will pull out, and what will have been the use of clinging to these memories until the last moment? No use, but compulsion, a necessity like love. So long as I write, my aloneness, and my sense of the future abandonment of consciousness itself, are held in check; but, together with the self-indulgence of the exercise, I feel a duty to tell it all as honestly and truly as I can. These compulsions inspired my first volume of childhood reminiscence which Bloom had just read and which we had met that day to discuss.

Throughout our meal, we had tiptoed around the subject, swapping memories and gossip as we ate an excellent goulash and looked out at the bleak magnificence of the wet afternoon sky.

'Well, my dear, it's not what we had in mind,' he was eventually brave enough to say. 'I'd thought you were writing a book about "The Mulberrys".'

I think the phrase 'Christmas market' came into the next part of the sentence, reinforced by the earnest hope that I wasn't planning, in my old age, to turn into 'Miss Proust'. This transposition of the sexes, which used to be a regular feature of Bloom's conversational style, had now largely been abandoned, and 'Miss Proust' was a deliberate allusion to the old days, a plea based on old friendship that I was not going to land him in grave financial difficulties.

'I mean,' he said, 'it's just going to be this one volume?'

He eyed me suspiciously.

'I thought, as many volumes as it would take.'

Bloom sipped his coffee and stared out of the window.

'You'll get piles if you lie in bed all day long – scribble, scribble, scribble!'

Bloom's wife (a perhaps surprising addition to his ménage, but they seemed very happy together in a slightly quarrelsome way) entered the room to help herself to coffee and to join in the laughter.

'I read your book,' she said shyly. 'Hope you don't mind. I've told William he ought to be bold and publish it – even if,' she added with dispiriting realism, 'not all that many people will want to buy it. Who wants to hear about the fucking Mulberrys?'

She squeezed her husband's ear before going back to her desktop printer in another part of the flat.

One of the reasons they got on well together was that Alice seemed totally unabashed by the flare-ups of anger which so often occur when two strong characters are sharing one another's lives.

'Only about two million people, who listen to the fucking programme every fucking day!' Bloom yelled at the door which Alice had just shut.

She opened it again. She is about thirty years younger than Bloom, tall, pretty, fine-boned.

'Why publish crap?' she asked hotly. 'Isn't there enough crap in the world?'

Her high-pitched New York voice rose to a squeal at the end of the question.

When she had slammed the door again, and begun to tap and whirr with her computer in a distant room, Bloom grinned. In that over-emphatic way he has of speaking, he slapped the forefingers of one hand into the palm of another in time to his words, as he enunciated, 'Because crap, as she calls it, is what people want to read. Look, Julian. Here you are. My dear, a national institution.'

'Hardly.'

'You'd make so much more money if you'd do a nice little Jason Grainger book.'

The glacial silence after this felt like eternity.

'Are you saying that you don't want to . . .' I could not quite bring myself to suggest that he did not want to publish my book, lest this make it easier for him to slither off the hook.

'The *fleuve* novels have to be *bloody* lucky to make publishing sense.' He prodded his hand once again. It was a gesture more suitable for soap-box oratory than for private discussion. 'You pick up Volume Five or Volume Seven and ask yourself, "Who the fucking hell *are* all these people?" It's like arriving at a dinner party a couple of hours late and not being introduced to the other guests and spending the whole evening picking up the fag-end of their conversations.'

'I first got addicted to Proust by dipping into the middle. It didn't matter that I had not been introduced to Mlle de Vinteuil or Saint-Loup. . . . One picked it up after a page or two.'

'Authors expect readers to make such *efforts* these days.'

'You mean, actually *read* their books?'

'It's years since William read a book,' said Alice, re-entering in search of cigarettes.

'Oh, rubbish, Alice, you know that's rubbish,' he added crossly, 'Over *there*! They're on the arm of that chair. And stop interrupting us. This is important. Julian is on the verge of conning me into losing money so that he can lie in bed scribbling about the old days.'

'Thanks. ' She retrieved her Marlboro Lights. 'I read aloud to William in bed. Beatrix Potter. I'm quite sure, they're the only books he reads now.'

'They're *heaven*,' he purred. The eyelashes of his old face were still abundant and boyish. Unlike the rest of his features, they had not altered, and they provided one of those little shocks which I frequently have when looking in a glass, bafflement that one should have come to inhabit this prune-faced old carcase while still remaining in many observable areas the same person who once had smooth cheeks, some white teeth, ungnarled knuckles, cornless toes and the same vulnerable emotions.

I probably have Alice Bloom to thank for the fact that her husband accepted my book. As I had already written the second novel in the sequence, it would have been disconcerting if he had turned down Volume I. From this point of view, the problem was how to make each separate division of the *fleuve* into a plausible unit which could be sold on its own.

'Each book must be able to be read in its own *right*,' he has kept saying defensively, since he started to publish the story.

For me, the problems have been more technical; wondering how much to leave out, which scenes to place in which order, how much to reveal without burdening the reader.

There could have been much to say to Bloom that afternoon about the architectonics of the projected work, had I thought that he would be remotely interested. I might have wanted to explain that he was wrong to think of 'Miss Proust' as the only possible structural model. His own preferred Beatrix Potter could be another, a writer who, like Balzac, wrote a series of separate chronicles in which we might meet as major protagonists figures who in previous volumes of *La Comédie* had only walk-on parts. Within the over-all structure of my Lampitt obsession and my desire to snatch some parts of my own experience back from the consuming entrails of oblivion, I intended, should fancy take me, to turn aside and to relate stories which were extraneous to what might be regarded as the main story. A church-crawling analogy occurred. The visitor to a large church which had been a long time a-building, might never take in the whole edifice at once, but on one visit might find a single place in which to beguile half an hour, now the Lady Chapel, now the choir. On one visit, he will want to sit at the back and gaze at the light pouring from the east window and take in the edifice as a whole. On another visit, it will be the detail for which he searches; turning up a misericord in order to concentrate on one carved scene from medieval life, a housewife at her distaff, a monkey-faced demon tormenting a lecherous friar, a drunkard downing his knobbly, black carved pot. Then, looking up from these tiny intricacies, the eye might take in the structure, and in some transept arch see how each piece of carved stone or wood formed part of the whole. In any human life viewed from a long perspective there may be found these linking points, analogous to roof-bosses or the meeting points of the arches, where different parts of the building are held together, and where, in medieval times, the craftsman might have chosen to place some grinning face or winged angel.

A case in point would be the Great Attachment. I have not written much about her in the previous pages, and indeed I hardly knew her, but in some ways she is as interesting to me as Rice Robey himself. As first depicted to me, in Felicity's accounts and Darnley's, Audrey Paxton had been no more than a grotesque gargoyle in the edifice, a monster of domestic horror who kept Rice Robey in her trivial thrall, forcing him to perform menial tasks when his mind might have been given to supposedly more important concerns. I had accepted that Rice Robey was completely miserable with her, and that this in some way excused or explained his wide circle of female acquaintanceship beyond the confines of Twisden Road. When I actually visited their house, and saw them together, and discovered that other women were not unmentionable in her presence, I had felt a considerable shock. It made me believe that Rice Robey was purely a bogus figure, stringing all the other women along. Then I came to realise that human relationships are never simple and that his projected descriptions of Mrs Paxton as a tyrant whom he hated probably would not have been necessary to invent unless they corresponded at least some of the time to a felt reality. Probably, he did hate her, as well as love her. With part of himself, he must have resented the limitations on his freedom which followed their elopement from the school. Cecily's vision of things, that Mrs Paxton had wilfully cut off Rice Robey from his friends, broken his association with Jimbo, deprived him of all imaginative and intellectual stimulus, and prevented him from developing as a writer might have been true, but whether he considered this a price worth paying for the emotional fulfilment which she, and perhaps no other woman, provided, we shall never know.

Cecily had astonished me, at Darnley's wedding party, by revealing that Mrs Paxton was the sister of the Binker, my old headmaster at Seaforth Grange. In itself, there should have been nothing so surprising about this. What more probable than that her husband and her brother should both have pursued the same unpleasant Dotheboys line of business? When Cecily told me this, however, it was one of those moments when the eye strayed from mere detail, the grotesque gargoyle or carved misericord, and took in the structure of the whole edifice. My vicarious interest in Rice Robey's ménage had already changed by the time that I realised that Felicity was in love with the man. It was a shock to discover that this bogus gargoyle, who had so beguiled my friend Darnley and my cousin, who had appeared arbitrarily and suddenly on the scene like a comet flying across the night sky, was not, in fact, a man who had arrived in the drama from nowhere. He had been part of that interconnected pattern of personal destinies which were one of the given truths of his own metaphysic.

'Branches and shoots of the *arbor cognitionis*!' he had intoned one night in the Spread Eagle, when Felicity had persuaded me to meet him there for a pint. 'Each of us has a tree of cognition, which we could sketch and trace; no uninteresting exercise for a winter night – how meeting X led us to know Y and love Z and change our views about ABC. In most lives, the relation of the branches to the parent stem is uncomplex. Your life, I suspect,

Mr Ramsay, has a number of interstices which are somewhat further from the central trunk.'

'I'm always amazed,' said Felicity, 'by Julian's capacity to remember trivia about the people he meets.'

Rice Robey had launched into a far from trivial disquisition on the transmigration of souls.

The fact that Rice Robey was a branch off the tree who connected my Lampitt life with Seaforth Grange was odd enough in itself, but I had been even more surprised to discover that Mrs Paxton was the owner of two or three important Pilbrights.

I have already said enough about Pilbright to convey how astonishing it was when he burst upon the world as a stupendously successful painter. I had known him, as my father had done before me, as an infinitely tedious office companion, to whom I would have attributed no powers of imagination, let alone artistry. For forty years or more his painting life and his copious work were unknown to the world. The secret was contained in his dingy house in Balham, where he worked during the evenings and at weekends. Then, just as he was retiring from Tempest and Holmes, he was 'discovered'. Raphael Hunter made him the subject of one of his 'Perspectives' programmes on television, and there followed that huge exhibition at the newly opened Hayward Gallery.

That day I lunched with Bloom and discussed my literary future, the day I had just been to see 'Mr Pilbright At Home' in the Tate, it was inevitable that I should recall this earlier and showier affair.

Merely to get there, to reach the newly built gallery itself, was an experience which jolted eye, mind, heart, into a recognition that a great change had occurred in England, and perhaps in oneself. Vernon was not in the Cabinet, and the Socialist Government had disappointed those of us who voted for it by being scarcely distinguishable, in most of its attitudes and policies, from the previous administration. This did not matter. The changes which were coming upon us all did not need to be authorised by government. The excitement of walking to the South Bank to see that exhibition was intense. The boldness and apparent anarchy of the vast expanses of concrete offer numberless visual delights, an effect partly achieved by the varieties of level on which the even grey lines of rough-hewn planes are arranged. The particular walkway which I crossed was from Waterloo station. Behind me was an old railway bridge, where commuter trains still rattled in and out of the terminus. The blackened London brick of the railway bridge, the train, even the faces of the travellers, seemed, in scale, to be like a child's toy. Old London, old England, old Life were swept behind us; we were all soaring to something newer, freer and infinitely more exciting. Gulls circled above my head, letting out their poignant seaside sounds, and the sun shone brightly. Now and then, the clean sweep of concrete, which from some aspects appeared to stretch for numberless yards, gave place to a little gap through which was momentarily visible a Canaletto scene – the Thames as blue and clear as in some idealised canvas, and, beyond, the dome of St Paul's. To one's left, there was a different vista, of buses and cars passing at eye level, and for this reason seeming, as the trains did, like toys. The world itself seemed like a plaything.

> Then felt I like some watcher of the skies
> When a new planet swims into his ken:

but the new planet was earth, and life was now possessed with a thousand exciting possibilities, not so much of action as of sensibility.

That the new gallery should, within months of its opening, be housing a large exhibition of P. J. Pilbright, was symptomatic of this change which had come upon myself as well as upon the world. Hitherto in my mind, Pilbright had been the embodiment of everything that was inimical to imaginative release. He was a man who stood for plodding work, slavery to routine, unbounded domestic dullness. Of no one I had ever met did I feel more confident that he was a slave to dullness, a man without a soul. The fact that he had pursued a secret artistic life for the previous forty years, covering canvas after canvas with his strangely self-assertive projections, was cause for reassessment not merely of Pilbright, but of the world itself. At first seeing, probably because I was simply jealous of the talents displayed on wall after bare concrete wall of the new gallery, I could not throw off my dislike of Pilbright the man. I did not like the pictures, even though I could see that such huge set-pieces as *Matthew Forsakes the Inland Revenue to Follow Christ* had an undeniable originality. In the many interviews which he gave about his work, Pilbright fought shy of defining his own religious position, and I suppose that it is possible that he did not really have one, the paintings being their own statement, and not requiring a theological justification. Seeing them at that particular juncture of life was to be reminded of the powerful hold which the Christian story exercised on my friends, notably on Felicity. Pilbright did not paint exclusively religious scenes but when he did so, it was to represent Christ as a contemporary figure, the events in the New Testament occurring in the setting of London and its suburbs. (Critics at the time of the exhibition at the Hayward Gallery made much of *The Marriage Feast at Canonbury* in which the Virgin Mother, far from demurely wishing that the other guests be given more wine, is herself a chaotic, plump cockney girl, not unbrassy, with one hand reproachfully holding out an empty glass towards her son, and with the other clutching a cigarette. The empty glass might once have contained white wine or champagne, but from her general appearance – there were affinities with the fat women in Donald McGill cartoons and postcards – I would guess that hers was a port and lemon.)

Not all Pilbright's representations of the human form were so earth-bound. I was haunted at once by the so-called Woolworth Magdalene whom he painted more often than any other female form. It is hardly original of me to say so. She became the favourite of everyone who saw the exhibition. Sometimes the pictures have no obvious biblical link and appear to be simple portraits of the girl, sitting on a chintz sofa with her scarlet-varnished toes tucked under her buttocks, or standing beside some municipal flower bed admiring the zinnias. She is also to be seen as the girl in a hat in that picture so strangely full of movement, about which the critics differed. Some wanted to call it merely *Girl Running for a Bus*. Others accepted the judgement by the author of the exhibition catalogue that the bundle under her arms was not laundry but a baby, and that this was the picture referred to by Mr Pilbright in a notebook as *The Flight into Egham*.

Her most celebrated appearance at a bus stop, of course, is as *The Angel of the Resurrection Informing the Balham Bus Queue, 'He is not Here, He is Risen!'* Her short dark hair and gamine features might almost make the spectator believe that the angel was an androgynous creation of Mr Pilbright's fantasy, or perhaps, even, a boy. Turning to the justly famous Woolworth Magdalene, however, you see this figure (same face, larger breasts) as unmistakably feminine. In her role as the penitent, she is kneeling on a pub floor at an angle of three-quarters to Christ. Her eyelids are beguilingly cast down in an expression of self-reproach. Are the eyes shut, or does she gaze, as we do, on that half-buttoned blouse, and the perfect moulding of her young breasts? Everyone when looking at the picture (now part of the permanent collection at the Tate) always notices the torn big toe of the fishnet stocking, the scarlet toe-nails jutting through, the peep-toe stiletto cast aside as she bathes with tears the socks and sandals of her Redeemer who looks as though he might have been a schoolmaster, possibly with a fondness for the Aldermaston March where Vernon made so many friends, demonstrating against the existence of nuclear weapons.

Since first seeing the picture, I have often wondered about its significance and formed my own ideas about the biographical sources for its inspiration. As with so many other depictions in art of Mary Magdalene, one wonders quite how penitent she feels, and whether, in the light of the liberal absolution she receives from her Master, it would in any case be appropriate to feel abject misery. My own feeling is that the title of the picture is only half serious. (That's another matter which divides the Pilbright critics, the extent to which he expects us to take the religious content of the work seriously or whether, as some believe, the pictures do not betray a perkily irreverent not to say blasphemous point of view.) She is sorry, the Woolworth Magdalene, but she is also resolute, sad more than penitent and more than a little angry. Are we quite sure that the young man in the picture is in fact meant to be Christ? Might she not be more of a Guinevere than a Magdalene or (the reader will have guessed my reason for asking the question) a wife or a mistress, sorry that she now has some other attachment, but taking leave of the figure at the pub table? Take a closer look, if you will, at that pub table. Critics have neglected it. Only one figure is sitting there – the bearded man. The other characters in the bar are all holding their drinks. In front of him on the table, however, we see a barely sipped half and several glasses which have obviously contained 'shorts', probably whisky.

['Medieval man,' said Abbot Denys to the ex-garage

mechanic, *castrato* novice in *Glastonbury Tor* by Albion Pugh, 'made the drunkenness of Noah a type of Christ's Passion and since then, we have been blind to the complementary verity, that Christ's drunkenness is a redeeming answer to the lonely passion of Noah. The Celestial All-Father poured out his promise of benediction in the bow of rain and the rainbow of his wrath. But the Divine Humanity came to birth in a tavern and he was condemned in life as a wine bibber and a drunkard since the innocence of the inebriate abandonment releases the glad heart of redeemed humanity and numbs the mind which poses those questions which would rend in twain the Temple veil. For only one could challenge the All-Father for the broken promise of the rainbow, the promise to withhold pain from the sons of men on earth. Only one could turn water to wine, and wine to his own blood, a chalice which he wished could pass from him, but which he raised in the noonday on a lonely hill as a salutation to suffering mortality and a reproach to the indifference of the Father who forsook him at the last. The sun of nature turned the grape to wine, and the indifference of Zeus turned the wine to vinegar on the lips of the Crucified' etc., etc.]

Supposing, in other words, that the Woolworth Magdalene is in the presence not of Christ, but of the very man she has wronged? Or, by total contrast, could she be kneeling at the feet of a serious young man whom she is about to seduce?

The reader will have seen the way in which my mind is moving; though, when I say 'mind' I mean that curious and intuitive part of consciousness which prepares the ratiocinative faculty for the absorption and comprehension of surprising pieces of information. Before reason could possibly deduce the facts from a given set of information, instinct has helped us to knowledge. On a trivial level, it is manifested in the phenomenon of discovering the answer to crosswords momentarily before understanding the clue. In this case, the clue was, I suppose, the scarlet nails poking through the Woolworth Magdalene's torn fishnet stockings. I did not 'place' the scarlet nails, nor realise that I had seen them in the gnarled and ancient flesh some twelve months before.

'Hallo. It's Mr Grainger, isn't it?'

I swung round on hearing this voice, deeper and throatier than when heard in the domestic context, because for an instant, I believed it to be that of the Binker, my old headmaster at Seaforth Grange. It was a misapprehension which called up a succession of painful reactions; for a split second, I was at school once again, locked in the never-forgotten fear of the Great Dictator, before I recognised his sister, the Great Attachment. And then I looked at the feet, which were enclosed in soft suede bootees trimmed with lambskin at the ankle. When I had last seen those feet, the scarlet toe-nails had been visible.

'Mrs Paxton.'

She smiled conspiratorially.

'You're too modest. That day you came round. You should have said. You know, when you came round with his book.'

'I felt a bit shy.'

'And to think we sat and listened to "The Mulberrys" together. I was so *cross* with him when he told me – not for weeks afterwards, mind. I said to him, "Why didn't you *tell* me that was Jason Grainger. You know I've got a soft spot for Jason." '

Rice Robey had already left the Civil Service. Felicity and he now saw one another less often, but, in view of my obvious feelings about the man, she did not always tell me when they had their little trysts and lunches. I half wanted to know very much, and half did not want to know at all. He had managed to get a number of engagements as a lecturer and guide to the sites of legendary Britain. There was some travel agent who employed him, I believe, to inform or entertain American visitors, and I was told that he was not above placing advertisements in the newspapers, proposing walks, for interested clients, around Blake's London. I had not been on one of these walks myself. Apparently, he had been known to attract as many as a dozen followers. The advertisement requested that any interested party should convene at the West Door of Westminster Abbey at eleven o'clock on Saturday mornings. There, apparently, he would show them the Gothic tombs of the old church where the young Blake had studied when an engraver's apprentice. A bus ride would take them to Soho and if there were few enough, they would repair to the Black Bottle in Poland Street. Darnley had come across him one morning, annoying Cyril's regulars by declaiming the Songs of Innocence to a bemused gaggle of Blake enthusiasts. Then, if time and weather allowed, he would take his followers north of Regent's Park to stand on Primrose Hill and look down on London.

One of these days, I half intended to join this walk of Rice

Robey's myself. Thinking about it at the Pilbright retrospective, I could see the many points of comparison between the painter's view of London and Rice Robey's own. Mrs Paxton, however, was obviously under the impression that I shared her purely commercial view of Pilbright's pictures.

'Wasn't it a stroke of luck! To think of those pictures hanging in my bedroom since – oh! before the war. The funny thing is, I never particularly liked it. 1934. No, 3.'

Her little shoulders hunched. Her teeth were very brown when she grinned.

'It was Mr Pilbright himself who approached us,' she said. 'He thinks it is his best painting. Well, you know the rest.'

In my foolish way, I grinned, shy to admit that I knew nothing at all.

'It was the Tate Gallery who wanted to buy it,' she said.

For a few moments of silence we stared at the canvas together. I was still slow to realise that she was the Magdalene in the foreground. Grey, and small, and wizened, she no longer bore any resemblance to this sulkily voluptuous woman, kneeling on the pub floor. Even if she had been instantly recognisable, it was not possible to deduce how she and Pilbright had met. It was later that I heard about it all from Rice Robey himself. She and Pilbright had not met very often; most of Pilbright's pictures of her, and there were dozens, had been done from memory, becoming increasingly stylised over the years, icons more than portraits.

'It was my husband, you know, who *knew* Mr Pilbright – not . . .'

'I thought perhaps that Mr Robey and Mr Pilbright . . .'

What did I think?

'His nibs? Oh, no. Only, my husband was always very particular about his shirts. He always bought them at a particular shop, usually patronised by the legal profession, in High Holborn. He liked black and white striped shirts, and a clean collar every day. Now, one day' – her voice, like that of her brother, entirely lacked euphony, and I could imagine the shirt anecdote lasting for ever. She did spin it out much longer than necessary – her husband's penchant for a particular type of stiff round collar which had become obsolete before 1939, the retailer's inability to procure the desired item, Mr Paxton's decision to write to the factory – Tempest and Holmes. She did

769

not explain, and I now kick myself for not asking, how Mr Paxton and Mr Pilbright became friends, or what it was about Paxton which enabled Pilbright to reveal his secret: that he was not simply the man in the Accounts department at Tempest and Holmes, but also a painter. As she told the story, I was distracted by the curious thought that all this was going on when my father was still alive and working with Mr Pilbright. Perhaps it was Daddy himself who opened Mr Paxton's first letter about the collar, and took it over to Mr Pilbright's high clerk's desk. The upshot of Mrs Paxton's tale was that Pilbright was able to get hold of some of the preferred collars out of 'stock'.

'There were dozens of them, dozens. Only, my husband had a bit of a thing about shirts, you know. I took some for his nibs to wear after we, you know . . . Well, he's still *wearing* some of them. And that's what? Thirty years?'

I would give anything now to have the much more interesting part of the story filled in: that is, how Pilbright met Mrs Paxton, and persuaded her to sit for him. I do not think she was being secretive. She probably assumed that I knew it already. Rice Robey said that he thought the Paxtons had occasionally asked Mr Pilbright to Sunday lunch in Chorleywood during the school holidays. Presumably, while Mr Paxton quietly drank himself under the table, Mr Pilbright produced a sketchbook and began to immortalise the female form who plays so important and repetitive a role in his work.

When I told Bloom that I wanted to bring some mention of Mrs Paxton into the present story, he said, 'There must have been *something* about this woman, and you haven't said what it is! She inspired these two crazy geniuses, Pilbright and Pugh. . . .'

'Half geniuses.'

'She inspired them. Pilbright made her the Angel of the Resurrection – what *was* it about her?'

I agreed that there must have been 'something' about Mrs Paxton, and I freely admitted that Bloom was right. I had not captured the 'something' because I had insufficient faith, or vision, to see what it was. Presumably, sex played some part in her power over Pilbright's imagination, but having said that, one has not said much. Pilbright must have seen hundreds of young women in the course of his life, on his bus journeys between Balham and the works. Many of the girls at Tempest and Holmes were probably prettier and cleverer than Mrs Paxton; none of them had been transformed into the Woolworth Magdalene.

The modernist outlines of the Hayward Gallery provided an incongruous enough setting for Pilbright's pictures. Mrs Paxton seemed even more out of place there than her images on canvas. I found, having fallen in with her, that I was stuck with her; and perhaps in an infinitesimal degree I recognised how she had managed to keep Rice Robey in thrall for thirty years. After five or ten more minutes looking at the pictures, she was announcing that she was ready to go, and making it clear that I was responsible for seeing her safely on her way.

'You don't have to see me all the way back to Twisden Road,' she said, with the air of someone who was offering a tremendous concession. Since I had met her in the gallery purely by chance, it had not crossed my mind that I had any responsibility to convey her several miles across London. I had, after all, only met her once before. As soon as that sentence had been uttered, however, I felt mildly guilty and bowed to her superior willpower. It felt as if the very least I could do was to walk her to the train.

'I had a job finding this place,' she said. 'Only, it's a long walk for someone my age.'

By now we were hobbling along the concrete walkway in the direction of Waterloo. I was carrying her bag, which she had chosen to weigh down with some potatoes and a change of shoes, and a large frayed umbrella.

'I tried to put it up, there was a nasty shower earlier, only the wind nearly blew me away.'

I wanted to ask her why it had been necessary to bring a bag of potatoes to the picture gallery, but instead, I tottered obediently at two miles per hour and allowed her to hold my arm.

'You must remind me to get toilet paper,' she said, 'only we're running out.'

Why was this obligation thrust upon me? In a cowardly way, I murmured an assurance that I would, at some later stage, remind her of the necessity.

'Only, I really wanted to take our electric kettle to be looked at on the way home, only I couldn't carry that *and* the potatoes. I suppose you wouldn't come back and fetch it?'

'The thing is, I've promised to be somewhere else.' The lie

flew out desperately, and I felt an absolute brute for suggesting unwillingness to become her slave.

'Some of the girls gave it to, you know, his nibs when he . . .'

'Left?'

'No, no. It's up there, Waterloo. To the right.'

We veered slowly over a footbridge.

'I mean, when he left the Civil Service?'

'I said it wouldn't work.' She did that laugh which I remembered from my first meeting; perhaps it was what she did when Rice Robey's female acquaintances were under discussion: a sucking-in of spit and air through brown teeth. Her lips curled into an impish grin.

'I'm much happier using, you know, our big old . . .'

'Your old kettle is working, then?'

Having established this fact, there seemed no urgency about the electric kettle which she had already admitted to not liking.

'Only, we'll have to get it mended. No use having it if it doesn't . . . And in the early morning, it saves a thermos. Bother!'

'Are you all right, Mrs Paxton?'

She had stood quite still and her face had become concentrated with anxiety.

'Knew there was something else. Hot water-bottles! You see, it's just as well I bumped into you!'

The previous night, Rice Robey had screwed the top too tightly on to her hot water-bottle. He was not expected back until late that evening, and it was essential that she had a fresh hot water-bottle for her afternoon rest. It was an inevitability that I offered to traipse all the way back to Twisden Road.

'Only, now he's a free . . . free agent, you might say, he is busier than ever. He's taken the bus to Glastonbury today to show . . . And they were anxious, you know, to see . . .'

I have no idea what he was up to in Glastonbury, nor who 'they' were. Evidently, being sued by Raphael Hunter and being made to give up his job had not after all done much damage to Rice Robey's career.

Ever since I had heard that Mrs Paxton had sold a Pilbright to the Tate, I had ceased to regard her, or Rice Robey, as figures of pathos. And anyway, had she known it, financial considerations were not to bother her much longer. That journey to see the portraits of herself in the Hayward Gallery must have been one of her last major expeditions.

It was not simply infirmity, however, or old age, which allowed Mrs Paxton to dominate the rest of my day. She was a time-waster of a stupendous calibre. Effortless expertise is always recognisable: the difference between a good average cook, who has plodded along with the help of cookery books, and the magician like Thérèse before whom soufflés obediently rose, fowls grew golden and pastry delicate, soft. Compare the heavy thump of a child practising its scales and the rippling diapason as another set of fingers runs over the same ivories five minutes later. All of us have made bids for sympathy or have wanted at some stage to enlist another person to help us mend a fuse, wash up our dirty dishes, take a cat to be wormed or injected, or to unscrew a too tightly done-up hot water-bottle. Few of us have had the cheek to ask even our nearest and dearest to perform such menial tasks on our behalf. With the abolition of the servant class, everyone does these things for themselves. Not so, Mrs Paxton, the *maestra* in this department of life, who effortlessly established a situation in which I should have felt churlish to refuse any of these chores. By the time I had taken the kettle to the electrician (an awkward journey by bus and not made easier by the presence of Mrs Paxton's cat Smudge, mewing at the prospect of the vet) most of the day had gone by. Her secret, I suppose, was that it never crossed her mind that I should refuse. When it was allied to sexual attractiveness, as in earlier years with Rice Robey, it must have been a powerful combination. Ever since Darnley had begun to speak to me of 'Pughie' and Felicity's Rice Robey obsession began, I had been told that his domestic life was hell; and yet this had not been the impression I received when I saw them together. The mystery had remained in my mind, why had he *chosen* to be her domestic slave ? A few hours with Mrs Paxton made me see that choice did not really come into the matter.

When I returned to Twisden Road with Smudge, Mrs Paxton insisted in reimbursing me for my troubles and a tediously exact calculation was made – nine and six for the veterinary fee, eightpence bus fare each way, one and three for a magazine called *Woman's World*, which she had requested me to purchase at a newsagent en route. Needless to say, she did not have the exact money in her purse and she would not hear of merely giving me a pound note and owing me the rest. I was sent out on another expedition to the newsagent for change, and while I was there, I was commissioned to buy some sweets. Having destroyed the better part of my day, Mrs Paxton glowed with satisfaction, smiled with the look of an artist who had achieved particularly satisfying results. While I ran my errands, she had been recumbent with a hot water-bottle. On my return from the newsagent with the Chewies and the change, she was in the process of making tea, and we were soon settled in the back parlour with cups, milk, cigarettes and some rather stale buns.

'Kind of you to make the tea, only my wrist . . . that big steam kettle is so heavy. That's why I wanted the electric . . .'

'The man said it would be ready in ten days.'

She grinned at me through fumes of Fragrant Cloud. She smoked desperately, hurriedly. There was so much that I should have liked to discuss with her: her importance in the life of Mr Pilbright, her life with Rice Robey. . . . And there was her brother to talk about, too, the criminally sadistic Headmaster of my old school, Seaforth Grange.

'You know the man who sued Mr Robey,' I said.

'Would he have been a Mr Herne?'

'Mr Hunter.'

'His nibs has just a slight bee in his bonnet.'

'About Raphael Hunter? He wouldn't be the first.'

'Well, as you know, he came to us on the recommendation of Mr Lampitt, you know, when we ran . . .'

'You mean Rice Robey came to you: when you ran your school.'

'Graham knew Mr Lampitt, of course, that was how it happened.'

'Graham was your husband?'

'Mr Paxton to you,' she said sharply. 'I don't like this Christian names thing, do you?'

I was not suggesting for an instant that, had Mr Paxton been alive, I should have aspired to be on Christian name terms with the man. I had merely been establishing his identity. An awkward little silence followed. She had lost the thread of whatever it was she had been about to say.

'His nibs has had . . . since our little bit of money with the, you know, with the . . .'

'With the money from Mr Pilbright's pictures?'

774

'He didn't want a whole book, but he's had a poem published. I shouldn't think he'd mind if you took one. There they are on the table.'

A pile of about fifty pamphlets stood on the table, bound in stout purplish card. I accepted Mrs Paxton's gift as a reward for my day's labours. I was not to receive any more confidences. Seeing me to the front door, she said, 'Only Graham always thought that Mr Lampitt was just a bit *too* fond of his nibs. . . .'

They were the last words which I heard her utter.

On the bus which took me southwards to Camden Town, I opened the purple pamphlet, which had been rather handsomely printed and which was entitled *A Return to Glastonbury*.

Yusif began to hear the silence now,
The silence of Yeshua, the silence Yeshua enjoined.
'Tell no man.' 'Say nothing.' How often had such words
Parted from Yeshua's lips after moments of strangeness,
When the corner of the created curtain had been lifted up,
And the brightness beyond had been revealed!
In the days of his flesh, the friends of Yeshua,
Yusif among them, had tried to explain the silences.
'He is modest,' Yusif had said, 'it is part of his modesty.'
But since the dark day of Golgotha and the in-tomb-
    laying,
Yusif had pondered the nature of Yeshua,
The boy he had loved since childhood, the man whom he
    buried in tomb;
And 'modesty' was not a quality Yeshua had, nor diffi-
    dence either.
He had loved verbal quips, and the engagement of debate.
He was not short of words when the Pharisees were
    present.
Only in moments of secret glory with those whom he
    loved
Did he say, 'Silence! Tell no man. Say nothing.'
For some new believers who never knew Yeshua, silence
    meant 'mystery'.
They believed that Yeshua Christos had made a cabal.
'Tell no one' meant 'Keep the cabalistic lore
From those outside our secret confraternity.'
Just such cabals had now been started up

By little Saulos whom the church named Paul.
Yusif had journeyed round the Great Sea's coast,
Before in Spain he reached his greater ship
And sailed back to Britannium in rain.
He had seen Mediterranean synagogues,
And heard in gentile towns the word as preached
By Paulos of the mysteries of Christ.
In some such towns, new 'synagogues' arose,
And followers of Yeshua's simple way
Were dubbed the Men of Christos, 'Christians'.
Corinth had been the very worst of all.
The drunken love feast there had taken place
In some rich merchant's house. He'd never heard
Of Yeshua's injunction to sell all, and give to the poor.
The 'gathering together' in this house
Disgusted Yusif with its vinous din.
The merchant lolled in the triclinium,
Surrounded by inebriated friends.
And there a Greek – Apollos was his name –
Held up a cup of wine, and said it was
The Fruit of Gnosis – 'Who would drink thereof
Would know the secret given to the world
By Yeshua the secret-bearing, messenger of God.'
Part mystic orgy, part erotic feast, the dining room.
Outside, the fountains gurgled in the Atrium.
Throats gurgled too, when incomprehensible slaves
Shouted out incomprehensible sounds, gibbered with
    tongues.
Another slave vomited on to the mosaic floor.
A wild-eyed youth explained it to Yusif.
'He drink the blood of Yeshua, but he no good.
He drink unworthy like Lord Paulos say.
He cursed. He have bad spirits, so he spew.'
Another figure (female) stood and wailed.
A mirthless glossolalia made her laugh.
Yusif had left the merchant's house displeased.
How well he saw why some of his fellow-Jews
Wanted to silence Paulos and his mysteries, Paulos and the
    Secret Chalice.
At Thessalonika, he landed next.
Much smaller there, the little Paulist band.

Fifteen or twenty followers of 'the Way'.
They welcomed Yusif to an evening meeting.
He did not tell them he had known 'the Lord',
Known him in his enfleshment, shared indeed
Kinship with Miriam the Mother of the Christ!
The Thessalonians had made of Yeshua
A demi-god who rode upon the clouds.
Soon, soon, he would come, on his chariot in the sky!
Soon, he would come and gather them up to meet him!
And then, beloved Yeshua would call
The dead in Christ to meet him in the clouds,
And then the end would come – destruction fierce
Of world, and all the race of human kind.
No need to ask who first had brought this word
To Thessalonika – 'Lord Paulos said.'
Paulos had told them all they had to know.
They knew no saying of Lord Yeshua's lips,
None of his parables or witty tales,
None of his moral paradoxes, none of his high comic jokes,
Only the manner of his dying they knew,
And the fact that he would return on the clouds,
And save their souls from certain death and hell, so Paulos
    said.
Paulos had not been there for several years.
He was, men said, en route to mighty Rome,
Led as a prisoner for his lord the Christ.
In Sicily, when Yusif landed there,
He met some women who had heard the word,
Imbibed from Paulos the great Mythos which would
    transform Europe
More than the journey of Aeneas to the Latium shore.
The universe was doomed, the women said.
The God who made it cursed it in his wrath!
Only the blood of Yeshua could avail
To quench the anger of Jehovah's heart.
Their certainty wrung anger from Yusif.
He spoke! 'Yeshua was my friend –
He loved the Psalms of praise, the songs of love,
God was a father, loving to us all!
Forgiveness was the message that he preached!
He has not dealt with us after our sins!'

There was a story Yeshua had told,
Yusif repeated it in Sicily.
A father waiting by a garden gate,
Yearning with love for his rebellious child,
Kissing the boy on his crestfallen return,
Kissing his neck, killing the fatted calf.
There was no need for sacrifice for sin.
'Thou desirest not sacrifice, else had I given it thee.'
The women of Sicily heard the tale impassively.
Paulos had said, Paulos had said . . .
Their God and His was not a loving Father,
But a monster of Cosmic wrath and malice,
Placing the universe under his inescapable curse!
The blood atoned, the mystic blood of Christ –
Else were the universe consigned to hell.
So Paulos said, and Paulos they believed.
Yusif had said no more. 'Say nothing to any man.'
'Tell no one.' 'Hearing they do not hear.
And seeing with eyes, they do not understand.'
He thought of Yeshua the little child,
Disputing with the doctors of the Law,
Wrangling with the hard men, the men who lived by rule,
He remembered the raised voices in the Nazareth home,
He remembered the overturning of the money-changer's
    tables.
These outbursts of noise and rage had all occurred
When Yeshua spoke to the hard men of malice who
    worshipped the Cosmic Sadist.
And by contrast, Yusif remembered Galilee.
Those hours of silence in the flower-strewn hills,
The silence of the blue sky, and the lake.
And nothing had been gained by the words, for men and
    women would not hear them,
And everything had been contained in the silence,
And the 'Consider the lilies of the field'.
There was no need to fashion into words
What need not be said and what could not be articulated.
Miriam the Harlot had run from the garden terrified.
The tomb in which Yusif laid the body of his friend
Was empty on the first day of the week.
Its emptiness was what was frightening.

Before long, the stories had begun,
For it was easier to fashion into stories
Something which could never be understood.
Yusif had heard the tales of resurrection.
The followers of the Way had pitied him
Because he had not seen the risen Lord.
Yusif preferred the silence of unknowing, and the mystery
    of emptiness
And the non-knowing to the knowing, and the not-seeing
    to the seeing.
And now, in Mediterranean ports and small towns of Italy
    or Asia Minor,
Those who had never known Yeshua heard the words of
    Paulos and Apollos,
And sang to a mystic Christ, a demi-god.
Yusif did not suppose that it would last,
This cult of Paulos. Even now, the dwarf
Buzzing with tales of a redeeming god,
Who sacrificed himself on Calvary's hill
And poured his blood out for the sins of men,
Would be confined in Rome, out of harm's way.
Mercantile interest gave the first excuse
For Yusif to return to British soil.
But memory took him, too. He would go back
To those grey, misty, ambiguous lands where he had
    travelled
With Yeshua the boy,
Back to the land before it all began,
Where he had made his promise not to tell
The unutterable mystery which shone forth
From the height of Jerusalem's mount on Primrose Hill.
Back to the Western Lands he'd travel too,
Die there, perhaps, and bury with himself,
The object which he carried in his bag.
For twenty years, he'd kept it,
He could not throw away something so hauntingly sad,
A symbol of all that was most pointlessly cruel,
Of all that was base in human nature, he could not destroy
    it.
For Yeshua had worn it at the last,
Worn it as if it was a triumphal crown.

Yusif could not forget the darkest hour.
He lived with it for every day he breathed.
Nothing could be more abject, pitiful
Than that pale body, bloody, thin and bruised,
Which Yusif and the women had wrapped round
With winding sheets and laid within the tomb.
This was the reward given by men to one
Who saw what could not be uttered and refused at the last
    to utter it,
Who preached only by riddle and story the divinity of man,
Who saw the human face divine in children and lepers,
Who loved the drunkards and harlots because they did not
    believe that goodness consisted in the following of
    ethical codes,
Who challenged the malice of the All-Father with a grand
    gesture of impenitent defeat!
And from the body, from the battered head,
Yusif had taken it, the cruel thing,
And now would bury it in Glastonbury.
Blackened and dry it was, the crown of thorn
Which thugs long dead had forced with brutal hands
On to the temples of the Son of Man.

I did not read more that day. I put the poem in my mackintosh pocket when I got off the bus, and did not discover it again for several weeks.

Not long afterwards, Mrs Paxton died of some pulmonary conditions. They took her to the Royal Free Hospital in the end, the place where my old friend Day Muckley had died. Rice Robey was in the north of England at the time, conducting a coach party of Americans to the Roman wall, and probably giving them an oration laced with his thoughts about the Celtic divinities, about Mithras God of the Morning, and about the arrival of Cuthbert and the other Christian missionaries in Northumberland. No doubt, in some sense, his audience would get their money's worth. I forget if it was this particular American party, or another, who had been spotted by Darnley in Trafalgar Square during the London leg of their tour. One of the party, a septuagenarian curly-haired woman clad in tennis skirt and shoes, was attempting to record the Speaker's reflections in note form, perhaps for personal perusal during the winter months in Ohio, perhaps for regurgitation to some group of interested coevals on her return home. She was looking up at Nelson's Column.

'So, let me get this right. It's a phallic symbol, it's a ship's mast with an eyeless boy at the top of it? Eyeless? Have I got this right? And . . .'

'In the death of the great, there is a perfect marriage between the heroism of sacrifice and the sacrifice of the hero,' Rice Robey had replied. 'I mean sacrifice in its pure, ritual and arcane . . .'

'*Ark*-ine. What's ark-ine?' another member of the party had enquired.

The old lady in tennis shoes had relentlessly returned to her spiral-bound pad. 'And a totem-pole? Right? It's a totem-pole?'

This was one of the many snapshots which Darnley preserved of 'old Pughie' and which he would produce for the entertainment of anyone in the pub who was interested. I imagine that Rice Robey was almost perpetually engaged in such conversations, baffling most of those whom he met but exciting a gratifyingly intense appreciation from the Faithful Few.

Felicity certainly belonged to this latter category however fiercely she would defend her own independence.

'Rice Robey has brilliance, but he has not actually got this matter right,' she had said to me about some esoteric metaphysical concern. What was memorable about her saying it was the brave expression on her face. She obviously thought that it was daring, almost outrageous of her, to disagree with the Master. There can have been few *cleverer* Robey-maidens – 'daughters of Albion' as Darnley had dubbed them – than Felicity, and the book on which she now laboured was perhaps the highest compliment that anyone ever paid him.

Felicity was to rewrite the book many times, and I found the work, when it was eventually published under some academic imprint, totally impenetrable. It had chapters about Frege, Heidegger and Wittgenstein. The second half of the book was devoted to Felicity's own thoughts or notions about the Metaphysical Question. It was couched in terms which the ordinary intelligent layman could not possibly have understood. In some circles, however, it was regarded as a philosophical breakthrough, rescuing the subject from the arid borderlines in which, in England, it sometimes too readily rejoiced. Evidently, to judge from things people in the academic world have occasionally said to me over the years, the book was 'difficult' even for professional philosophers to grasp. I believe that there is even some dispute about whether the book was the ultimate refutation of Theism or an extremely subtle justification for it. I assume, the latter – but perhaps there is more mystery than my mind can grasp in the hours of silence which Felicity, nun-like, has spent in her attendance at meetings of the Society of Friends.

The book's dedication – 'To R.R.' – also tells its own tale. Until she had met the 'really rather awful man' on her corridor at the ministry, Felicity had been interested in very different philosophical concerns. I do not know whether he took this fact as a compliment or whether he was so consumed with egotism that he assumed that any woman would wish to conform her way of thinking to his own.

Jo, who improved on closer acquaintance and whose marriage to Darnley seemed very happy at that date, used to complain that a faraway look still came into Kirsty's eyes whenever she received one of Rice Robey's strange postcards or letters, even though a considerable time had elapsed since their brief period of intimacy. I began to think that Kirsty was entirely typical of the 'daughters of Albion', and that there might well be dozens of such women, dotted about the country though mainly in London, whom he had loved intensely for about a fortnight, and who still gazed dewy-eyed at the coconut matting if the postman delivered on to it one of Robey's communications in his large babyish handwriting.

In the bosoms of all these Daughters of Albion, there must have been a certain relief, if not actual hope, when the demise of Mrs Paxton became known. It had not been my intention to attend the obsequies of the Woolworth Magdalene. I had only met her twice in my life, and it seemed intrusive to go to her funeral. During the singing of the hymn, I asked myself why I was there. Was it really, as Felicity had said, that we owed Rice Robey our support and comradeship at this time of trial? Or was it somehow the egoism of the Great Attachment herself which drew me there? I am sure that she would have been delighted to know how extremely inconvenient it had been to rearrange life in order to be present at her funeral. It meant cancelling a visit to Sargie – with all the emotional upheaval which that provoked –

782

and missing a rehearsal in Birmingham for 'The Mulberrys'. (Tight lips from Rodney.)

Felicity had wanted to be at the crematorium, however, and I had accompanied her, not sure whether I did so to lend her support or to keep a jealous eye on her. We had been lovers ever since the night of Darnley's wedding, and the affair had now entered the phase of wondering whether it was what either of us actually wanted, or whether we had been duped by physical attraction into a state of things unconducive to personal happiness.

One of the least pleasing aspects of this, on the whole, rather happy period, had been her continued obsession with Rice Robey. It baffled me completely. Felicity and I did not pretend that we were, exactly speaking, in love with one another. But it had been a surprise to find, after we had been lovers for a few weeks, that her pillow-talk consisted almost entirely of the saying and doings of 'R.R.'. Because of his famous devotion to the Sexless Eros, I was apparently supposed to find acceptable her continued devotion to him. The fact that she had no chance of going to bed with him made it wholly acceptable for her to continue regular trysts with the man when he was available for them, to exchange long letters with him when he was not, and to discuss his genius and character with me for hours, when I should rather have whispered sweet nothings or read a book.

I had assumed, and certainly hoped, that when they ceased to be colleagues, Felicity and Rice Robey would see less of one another. I thought the preoccupation would somehow simmer down to more manageable, less boring proportions. At the time of Mrs Paxton's funeral, there was no sign of this happening. During the hymn – 'Lord Dismiss Us' – my lips were sealed. I thought of the conversation which Felicity and I had had the previous evening.

'This of course has solved nothing.'

Felicity's words had implied that we had a shared problem to which all manner of solutions had been sought, the present activity, that second over, being one of them. I had not been aware that we were seeking to solve anything, but her stiff shoulders and her serious eyes looking up at the ceiling told me that all was not well.

'Not that it isn't very nice,' she had said.

'Good.'

783

'I could make us both a pot of tea.'

'That would be nice too.'

She had turned once more to hold me in her arms. When I kissed her naked shoulder, she murmured, 'Earl Grey, or Indian?' And when she had returned with a tray, and a pot of Indian, she had said, 'If he wants to be alone with me after the funeral tomorrow, you won't mind, will you?'

'He?'

She ignored my absurd implication that she might be discussing anyone other than her hero.

'He might prefer to be alone with me, that's all,' she had said.

'You do what you like.'

Beside me in the chapel of the crematorium, I could hear Felicity's tuneless voice singing

> Pardon all, their faults confessing,
> Time that's lost may all retrieve . . .

a school hymn perhaps appropriate in Mrs Paxton's case. We had sung it at Seaforth Grange on that speech-day when Darnley used my five pounds – a present from Sargie – to order a ton of manure to be delivered outside the marquee during the Binker's sermon.

Felicity was not the only Daughter of Albion to imagine that Rice Robey would want a shoulder to cry on after the service. Considering the fact that Mrs Paxton was a virtual recluse, seldom leaving 77, Twisden Road in latter years except to remonstrate with the newsagent for failing to deliver the *Daily Mail*, I could not believe that many of those present at her funeral had been closely attached to her. The chapel, though, was quite full. We had arrived late and found places at the back. We watched the proceedings over twenty or thirty heads, most of them female. Beyond the hats and scarves and perms, I could make out the back of Rice Robey's Blakean crown. He stood entirely alone in the front pew on the right. On the other side of the chapel, another group of mourners were huddled, but I could not see them very clearly from where I stood.

The parson who conducted the service was a fat, bespectacled figure with a red face and sleeked, possibly brilliantined, hair framing a podgy brow. The lubricious self-importance of his tone was not unfamiliar, but I could not place him until the end of the service when he began to read some prayers.

The congregation was kneeling. At that stage of my life, I had not abandoned the adolescent feeling that unbelievers such as myself should not compromise, when attending church services, by bowing head or knee. I was prepared to take my shoes off in a mosque, but I would not kneel in church. Sitting upright, I was therefore able to get a better view of the assembly.

'Shall we pray for Audrey's family . . . and in particular, at this time, our thoughts go out to Robbie . . .', there was a significant pause, '. . . and Margot.'

Not being a praying man, I have never seen the point of these meaningful pauses during extempore prayers. They somehow imply that the Godhead is rather slow on the uptake, and needs a moment – as I did not – to recall who Robbie and Margot were. There they were, in the front row, the Binker and his horrible wife. The parson, I instantaneously realised, had been the head boy of Seaforth Grange in my time, a bloke called Timpson.

Someone (Bloom?) once told me that clergymen who find employment in crematoria have usually been withdrawn from regular parochial life to avoid scandal. During the unctuous prayer for my old headmaster, I allowed myself to speculate about the nature of Timpson's indiscretions. To have landed up, at a comparatively early age, as a functionary in this dismal suburban furnace, the offence must have been glaring. If Darnley had been there, perhaps one would have found this thought funny; as it was, the picture of Timpson indulging in any erotic activity was unpleasing. Public lavatories? Choir-boys?

In fact, of course, Timpson did not work at the crematorium. He had come along at the Binker's request to take the funeral. When he had finished begging the Almighty to soothe the supposedly grieving hearts of the Binker and Mrs Binker, Timpson pressed a button, and we waited for the coffin to disappear through the hole in the wall which, now I come to think of it, resembled the food hatch in the dining room at Seaforth Grange. I remembered reaching through that hatch for a dish of vegetables (we all took turns to wait at the table), and Mrs Binker, who happened to be standing there with a ladle, arbitrarily rapping my knuckles and drawing blood.

The button which Timpson had pressed produced a recorded

rendering of 'Sheep May Safely Graze', but the coffin refused to budge. I was delighted to see Timpson's face become cross and flustered in a manner which recalled his losing his temper with Darnley and myself aged twelve.

'There appears to be some fault,' he said. One of the undertaker's men came forward to the little desk where Timpson stood and indicated the button to push.

'I've already done that,' said Timpson hotly. 'It simply makes the music play.'

'It looks as though . . . ' said the undertaker's man awkwardly.

He retreated to the back of the chapel while we waited for something to happen. Then he came back up the aisle with a workman in overalls, who disappeared into the pale oak pulpit or lectern where Timpson waited.

Timpson, I thought rather foolishly, had opened his floppily bound leather Bible, and was reading a passage at random from one of St Paul's epistles. It was an apostolic utterance which I thought showed particular confusion of mind, but it was hard to concentrate on it very carefully, since everyone was by now desperate to see whether the coffin would finally shift, or whether Mrs Paxton's mortal remains would be stuck in the chapel for ever.

While Timpson read aloud, one couldn't help hearing the man in overalls, who had been tinkering with a screwdriver, observe, 'It looks to me like a faulty connection.'

Probably only a few minutes passed in which Timpson continued, with smarmy false emphasis, to harangue us with suggestions about how to behave at a dinner table in the event of being offered meat which had previously been sacrificed to idols.

Then, in his front pew, the Binker stood up.

'There appears to have been,' he said, and then he cleared his throat. 'If Timpson would kindly turn down the music – thank you, Timpson. There appears to have been a mechanical difficulty. I think it might be a more fitting conclusion to the ceremony if we were simply to leave our places now and . . . '

And, what? We all wanted to know what was going to happen to the coffin.

The Binker did not look in the least grief-stricken; he looked pleased, if anything, to be given the chance to address us. It was school all over again. One half expected him to tell us to leave the chapel in twos, and that anyone seen talking would have to come to his study afterwards for a thrashing.

It was presumably because Mrs Paxton had not been married to Rice Robey that her family had taken charge of the funeral arrangements, a fact which would have accounted for their extreme dreariness. We shuffled out with a sense of profound anticlimax. Even as we did so, two more workmen in overalls and the undertaker's men were advancing on the coffin. It seemed appropriate that Mrs Paxton was causing maximum trouble to the last.

Outside, in the arcade, the congregation stood about in awkward little groups. Some members of the party leaned over the pathetically few wreaths and bunches of flowers which had been sent to attend Mrs Paxton's last journey to the flames. Natural curiosity made me lean forward to read the labels attached to these tributes, and my eye fell on words and handwriting which were immediately familiar.

With deepest sympathy and all good wishes from P. J. Pilbright.

These words were identical to those with which Pilbright had concluded his letter of condolence to Granny when my parents had been killed during the war. Similar formulas adorned the Christmas cards which he still regularly sent to her. One might have supposed that something more heartfelt would have been appropriate for a painter's leavetaking from one of his greatest sources of inspiration, but it would not have been in Pilbright's nature to stray outside the borders of convention.

'Oh good,' he said, 'mine arrived! You never know with florists.'

And there he was, looking as he had always looked when we worked together in Accounts at Tempest and Holmes: white hair *en brosse*, steel-rimmed spectacles, a very good colour in his unlined face. Retirement and fame were evidently congenial.

'I saw Mrs Paxton not long ago,' I said to him, 'at your exhibition.'

'Oh, yes?'

He looked a little quizzical, but from an emotional point of view quite unmoved. There was nothing in his face to suggest that I was talking of a huge exhibition which had whisked him from total obscurity to prodigious celebrity, nor that I was discussing a person who had been of immense importance in his imaginative life.

'She was always a very good friend, Mrs Paxton was to me,' he said. 'And, of course, Mr Paxton. Mr Paxton was also very kind.'

Once this fact had been established, there seemed no more to say. This was certainly not the moment to talk about the Woolworth Magdalene. I was not even completely sure that Mr Pilbright knew who I was. I asked him if he knew Kirsty Lampitt, who was also leaning over to look at the floral tributes.

'No,' he said crossly, 'no, I can't say I do.'

'Hallo, Julian.'

'Hallo.'

'I thought I'd come,' she said quietly. She looked as if she might have been crying. The resemblance between her and Jo was certainly very striking. I had now spent a lot of time in Jo's company, and almost none in Kirsty's, so it was hard to remind myself that they were in fact different people.

'That was P. J. Pilbright,' I said, adding slowly, as if to a dim-wit, 'he is a painter.'

'Wasn't the exhibition extraordinary,' said Kirsty. 'Did you read the catalogue? He'd been working in total obscurity for years, until he was discovered by Raphael Hunter. The man Mama and Papa blow so hot and cold about.'

'I know.'

'Good news about Jo-Jo, isn't it?'

'What news is that?'

'Hadn't you heard – she's having a baby.'

'That's marvellous.'

Kirsty did not want to be wasting time talking to me. Her eyes were darting around nervously in search of Rice Robey. The Binker and Mrs Binker were now emerging from the chapel, treading short, slow steps and looking about them timorously. Raphael Hunter held the Binker's arm. To Kirsty, and to anyone else who did not know them, they probably looked like a couple of harmless old people being helped along by a middle-aged man. For me, there was something about the defiant way in which the Binker looked about him which recalled the behaviour of impenitent war-criminals seen on those newsreels of the Nuremberg trials.

'I think I can say, a very beautiful ceremony,' said the Binker.

'It was lovely,' said Hunter. 'Just as Audrey would have wished.'

'A pity about the mechanical failure,' said the Binker, sounding more than usually Scotch.

'Can't stand gloomy funerals,' barked Margot Larmer with some savagery.

'Just mind that step, Margot, dear,' said Hunter, carefully guiding Mrs Binker every inch of the way.

The Binker turned aside to thank Timpson for the manner in which he had conducted the service.

'I can always rely on my boys,' he said.

'Very good to see you,' said Timpson to me, pumping my hand and staring into my face without a glimmer of recognition.

I could not tell whether the Binker recognised me. I thought on balance that it was unlikely. Hunter, who clutched his elbow, certainly did know who I was; since, until a few moments before, I had been accompanied by Felicity, it was not surprising that he decided to cut me. Soon, he, the Binker, Mrs Binker and Timpson were piling into the back of a hired limousine. The funeral party was beginning to disperse.

'Phew,' I heard one of the undertaker's men say to another as they re-emerged from the chapel. 'Never had to do that before – shove 'em through *by hand*.'

Kirsty and Felicity had both made a bee-line for Rice Robey, who was bending over to kiss a woman in a headscarf. As I approached, he was saying to her, '. . . just such an immortality as Plato envisaged, a striving for the union of the Psyche with the eternal Agathon, the melting away of *sarx* to be reborn in *gnosis*.'

Not being a Greek scholar, and never being quite used to Rice Robey's strange vowels, I thought he was telling this lady that divine wisdom came after the dissolution of *socks*.

'Remember, dear man,' she said, 'any time! You have my number.'

They were all queuing up to say the same – Kirsty aged twenty-two, Felicity at forty-odd, this older woman, who was perhaps sixty.

'Mr Grainger – Felicity – it was kind of you to come.'

'I couldn't have stayed away,' said Felicity.

Even as she said this, and Kirsty made some almost identical remark, I was saying to Rice Robey that I had seen Mrs Paxton at the Pilbright exhibition. I was going to remark on Pilbright's presence at the funeral. (Where was he? Presumably, he had walked briskly to the nearest bus stop or to Golders Green station.)

We had seldom slept together, Felicity and I. After an hour or two in bed, I would get up and return to my own room. Sometimes, in the mornings, we would greet one another as lovers, and hold one another tightly in our pyjamas and dressing gowns. Sometimes, more often, we would be overcome by shyness, by wondering, quite, whether the previous evening had actually happened.

I felt paralysed, humiliated, by her continuing need to be a Daughter of Albion. She had no treachery in her nature; and we were both perfectly well disposed towards one another; but I knew, as she stood there beside Rice Robey, that our lovemaking of seven hours before meant absolutely nothing to her.

She did not need to say anything. Without speech, she could convey to me an overpowering desire that I should be gone. She wanted to be alone with Rice Robey. In spite of the others who hovered with similar attentions, I could see that Felicity rated her own chances high, of being able to take him home in a taxi, and spend an evening cooking for him and listening to his talk.

I began to wish that I had teamed up with Mr Pilbright and gone home with him on the bus. It would have been interesting to renew our old acquaintanceship.

'You'll be wanting to take a taxi,' I said to Felicity. 'I'll go. Kirsty, if you're not . . . '

'I'm fine,' said Kirsty, who also waited by Rice Robey's side with a hopeful expression on her face.

I half thought of walking home across the Heath.

Rice Robey was seriously discomposed. He looked more than usually peculiar, since the blue pinstripe had been discarded for a suit of deepest black fustian, the property, I suspect, of the late Mr Paxton, to judge from how very short the trousers seemed on Rice Robey's legs and how bulkily the coat sat upon his shoulders. His cheeks were wet with tears, and he was shaking.

'You look tired, R.R.,' said Felicity. There was something bossy and school-matronly in her tone, something falsely no-nonsense, a manner which she was adopting, partly to put him at ease, but chiefly, I felt, to differentiate herself from the more gushing or quasi-mystical of the Daughters. Some of these looked like very strange creatures indeed. I thought that the one with a woolly hat and spectacles wore such an idiot smile that she could only have been released for the afternoon from some institution. Another figure, with iron-grey shoulder-length hair, had, one assumed, arrived at the funeral by broomstick. Neighbours in Twisden Road? Members of his lecture audiences?

It was humiliating enough to know that Felicity yearned for Rice Robey's company rather than my own; but I also felt humiliated on her behalf, to see her competing with this gaggle of slightly strange individuals: secretaries from the Ministry of Works? Deaconesses? What about the heavily moustached young woman with red hair and a shopping bag from Harrods? And what did *that* contain? Rat's bane? A pot of basil? Or some sacred relics?

'I think I should perhaps be going,' I said. 'Mr Robey, I'm . . . '

The conventional words of condolence seemed more than usually pointless on this occasion.

'We shall meet again,' said Robey. 'You were very kind to Audrey.' It looked as if he might be going to weep again. Perhaps to guard against such an eventuality, he changed the subject, and his face assumed some of that malicious glee which Darnley always found so infectious.

'You saw our friend – with Audrey's brother? Mr Hunter! Sometime a keeper here in Windsor Forest!'

'Hunter was at Mr Larmer's school,' I said. 'I was there myself, though at a later date than him.'

'Those people did nothing for Audrey.' He fumbled in his pocket as he spoke and produced a packet of cigarettes. When he had got one alight, he spoke with it still between his lips. 'Through all her years of unhappiness with her husband, through all her years of poverty, they did nothing.'

'Come on, Rice, you need a drink.'

This sentence was uttered by the young woman who now came to join us, and who was waving her car keys temptingly in the air. I had not seen her at the funeral, but she had presumably been there. Her dark hair was shorter than when last seen, as the lead vocalist singing at Darnley's wedding. She wore jeans and a black T-shirt.

'R.R., you're very welcome to come back to my house,' said

Felicity, shameless now, flushed with disappointment. 'We could share a taxi, or we . . .'

'Miss Nolan has a conveyance,' he said quietly. He had perhaps hoped to shake off the Daughters of Albion and leave as a mystery his manner of getting away.

Miss Nolan obviously did not wish to waste any further time on conversation. She looked as pale and plain and cross and mysterious as she had done that evening when she had sung. Her spoken tones were no less educated, but, without a microphone, almost inaudible. In fact, as a passing aeroplane flew overhead, it was impossible to hear what she said, though her lips were visibly moving.

Rice Robey could hear her and was apparently turning down, on our behalf, an invitation from Miss Nolan to drive us back to Camden.

'It's hardly out of our way,' whispered the Newnham Norn.

'Felicity and Mr Grainger will have their own arrangements,' said Rice Robey firmly. 'And, anyway, we shall meet again soon.'

'Oh, R.R. !' With a sudden gush of affection, Felicity placed her hands on Robey's shirtfront and buried a kiss on his neck. Miss Nolan watched with the impassive distance of a dog-owner waiting for its charge to empty its bowels before resuming a walk.

'Ready?' she said to Rice Robey when Felicity had blushingly stood back from the kiss.

'I'm ready,' said Rice Robey.

We stood, Felicity and I, both for differing reasons vaguely shocked, and watched him climb into the front seat of a van adorned with the legend PSYCHEDELIC LIGHTS. It was a primrose yellow van, and the letters, of varying shapes, colours and scripts, danced unevenly over its side. Rice Robey did not acknowledge us as he sped past, in the passenger seat, though Miss Nolan gave a little wave, not entirely unable to banish a smile of triumph, as she turned her van left, out of the crematorium gates, and into the afternoon traffic of Golders Green.

No logic could explain this, but as I watched Rice Robey and the Newnham Norn lurch away in the van, I knew that Felicity and I had ceased to be lovers. From the beginning, it had been a somewhat questionable development. We still loved one another, and would always continue to do so, but this particular period of life, during which – not all that often – we had wandered into one another's bedrooms, had now come to a close, like a phase of childhood. We never discussed the matter, never alluded to it in any way, but the night before Mrs Paxton's funeral was the last which we spent in the same bed.

Watching the Newnham Norn's departure, I felt a great surge of jealousy, and once again asked myself, as I had often done in the preceding weeks, whether I had gone to bed with Felicity simply in order to compete, emotionally, with Rice Robey. Certainly, there was satisfaction to be gained from the knowledge that whatever power he exerted over Felicity, here was one Daughter of Albion who had come, albeit physically, albeit for a brief half-hour or so, beneath my imaginative thrall; yet, even here I could not be consoled, for who could guess what had passed through Felicity's mind as we made love?

'What a rude girl,' she said.

'A woman of few words, certainly.'

'I *hate* unnecessary rudeness.'

'I vary. Most unfairly, I know, I rather like rudeness in girls; some latent masochism, I suppose.'

'She's just a *silly* person,' said Felicity vehemently. 'All the same, it is a pity to see . . .'

She did not finish the sentence. Was it a pity to see Rice Robey, as usual, making a bit of a fool of himself over a girl? Me, slightly, ditto? (Already, in my fantasy life, I was concocting plans to pursue the Newnham Norn.) Pity that Mrs Paxton was dead, and that we never appreciated in her what it was that had inspired Pilbright's artistic vision? Pity that Felicity was in love with Rice Robey, and was doomed to be one of the Daughters of Albion for the rest of her life, her heart – however much she told herself that she had 'got over' the experience of Robey – always missing a beat when she heard his name or saw one of his books? Pity to see that people age, but they do not grow up? Or that England ages, and is being, has been, destroyed? Pity to see the world, turning on its sad old axis, learning no lessons, solving no problems, and increasing, with each of its revolutions, the sum of human misery? I do not know how Felicity's sentence would have ended. Some time, not long after that, she returned to Oxford: not on a permanent basis, but for a space of several weeks, in order to get started on her great philosophical treatise.

I missed her. Before her arrival in Arlington Road, I had luxuriated in my solitude. Now it hung upon me like a burden. I wandered the streets in the evenings, rather than to endure the oppressions of my own society in my own room. I became, then, one of the night people, the men and women who for some reason or another are out when the rest of the world is indoors. Some of them are insomniacs searching for late-night cigarette vendors. Some are dog-owners with an obvious need to pause at lampposts and street corners. Some, however vaguely, are searching out some sexual encounter, and some are strayed revellers, too drunk to know where they are or why they are there. I felt a kinship with all the night wanderers whom I passed, even those whom I suspected of being violent psychopaths, prowling in search of victims to cosh or knife. Sometimes, sexual feeling would be so heightened by the night, and the gloom, and the fear, that one could imagine oneself inside the skin of a rapist, whose needs were momentarily so intense that the humanity and fear of their prey become entirely forgotten in the overwhelming need to assuage lust. Sometimes, these lusts could, on my night prowls, be satisfied, usually for an exchange of cash, and I would return home, hoping that sleep would bury the experience, blot it out, make it as if it had never been. Then dawn would come, and remind me. During my nocturnal walks, my mind would normally become so confused that its movement could not be dignified with the name of thought. Impressions, sometimes of the day just past, sometimes of my life, would jumble together, and mingle with the immediate sensations of the night. On other such walks, however, particularly if I had reached just the wrong stage of drunkenness and begun to sober up, I would be confronted by a vision of life's emptiness, of the terrible pointlessness of my own way of life. This made returning home even harder, and when the cruelty of the perception was sufficiently strong, I would pace and pace until dawn, sometimes finding that I had walked for miles, across the entire expanse of London. On one night, having set out from Camden Town, I found myself breakfasting at a workmen's café in Wimbledon.

Self-estimation, my good humour in general, were low at this point, so low that I did not voluntarily seek out those friends and

794

haunts which would restore to me my sense of common belonging to a world of good humour and sense, a world of day, not night. A telephone call out of the blue from Darnley restored these things instantaneously.

He said, 'I've tried you several times. You always seem to be out.'

'I've been busy.'

'You wouldn't like a drive in the country tomorrow, would you?'

'Love one. Where to?'

'Jo and I think we've found a house.'

'That's good news.'

'We thought we'd drive out and have a final look round before making up our minds. Before that, I thought of having a squint at Aldingbury Ring.'

'The threatened henge?'

I heard Darnley laughing down the line.

'A friend of mine went there the other day. . . . ' He paused for more laughter. 'They found this party of Americans gazing up into the trees. Pughie said there'd been a sighting of Herne the Hunter there during the previous week. They were all looking to see if they could see him. . . . ' Darnley switched to his 'Pughie voice', which had become eerily accurate. 'The Hunter appears in the skies at times of spiritual undoing and rebirth. . . . ' Darnley added in his own voice, 'He also appears when you've had one too many drinks on a Friday night.'

The next morning, early, Darnley and Jo appeared at my front door. Jo, heavily pregnant, seemed to fill the Morris, and it was with some difficulty that I clambered on to the back seat. As we drove out of London westwards, she prattled excitedly about the new house.

'There are two spare bedrooms, Mr Grainger – aren't there, darling – '

Darnley assented with a nod of his head.

'One for junior' – she touched her belly – 'but one for our friends, so you must come and see us often if we buy it. And there's a garden – huge garden – and it's near Henley – and you see, there's an old garage which I think we can convert and make into a sort of study, lair thing, for Miles. It'll be perfect.'

'We shall see,' said Darnley.

He was glowing with happiness, and for a period, as the car

bowled along, and they talked intimately among themselves in the way that married couples do, I felt wholly excluded by it, more of a pariah than I did on my night prowls. I knew that they were doing what the human race naturally wants to do – settling down, buying a house, starting a family, declaring their belief in the future. Something within me held back from wishing to join in, and I felt it to be my loss not theirs.

'Darling, you put the rubbish out before we left?'

'Yes, yes.'

'And you moved those chops from the meat safe to the fridge?'

'Yes, yes.'

'Thank you, darling.' She leaned over and kissed his cheek.

'We'll drive through Windsor,' said Darnley, 'and then out by the road which is going to go smack through Aldingbury Ring – if they get away with it. Pughie was organising some sort of protest. He was telling me about it last time we met. Real Gandhi stuff – lying down in front of the bulldozers if necessary.'

'He would enjoy that.'

'Darling,' said Jo, 'tell Mr Grainger what Pughie said that time we bought him lunch in the Café Royal.' And she burst out laughing.

'Julian knows that story,' said Darnley.

'Darling – what was the word he said – the word Pughie used for rent-boys?'

'It wasn't quite rent-boys. It's any young man, really – *neaniskos* – it's a Greek word. It's even used for angels in the Gospels.'

'Anyway, Mr Grainger . . . '

Jo relentlessly pursued this little piece of narrative – it was not strictly speaking a story – about Rice Robey's behaviour at the lunch table in the Café Royal, and his speculation that Oscar Wilde might have sat just at such a table with a neaniskos. He himself had been an angel there in younger days, dining and lunching with Jimbo, who went on patronising the Café Royal long after it had ceased to be fashionable among literary or theatrical celebrities.

'Oi think the roast fowl with bread sauce,' she spluttered, in a very inaccurate imitation of Rice Robey ordering from the menu. Darnley was visibly delighted by her chatter, certainly did not manifest any of the irritation or embarrassment which would have come over me if I had elected to share my life with Jo.

'I think if we drive up this little road here, we come to Aldingbury Ring from behind,' said Darnley.

There was no sign of the earthworks until we were nearly upon it. Darnley parked the car in a lay-by of a narrow road, and it was only when we had climbed a stile into a field, that we could see, on the brow of the gentle hill, surrounded by trees, a row of mounds.

'The Ministry of Transport say that they aren't burial mounds.' Darnley sniffed hard and long. 'Old Pughie says that if they dig 'em up, they'll find a dragon's hoard or something!'

'Just before he was sacked – I remember Felicity telling me – he went to his head of department and asked him if he had ever read *Beowulf*. The head of department asked him if he had read such and such draft memo or report which referred the whole matter to such and such committee.'

Darnley laughed.

'Typical Pughie, that. Still' – sniff – 'I shouldn't be in the least surprised if that hill was not stuffed with Iron Age treasure.'

'Anyway,' said Jo reasonably, 'it's a shame to build a road there.'

None of us at the time could have guessed how prescient Rice Robey had been about this ring. The Ministry of Works and the Department of Transport had both insisted that it was not an 'important' site, and that the extension of a motorway to ease London's traffic problems was of far greater importance than some low-lying grassy mounds which might simply, in their view, be the remains of a badly ploughed field.

'No good can come from raping the earth,' said Darnley in his Pughie voice. 'From disembowelling the earth, and disturbing the dragon's gold. They should read *Beowulf*' (pronounced *By-a-wolf*).

Now, as we know, there is a whole room in the British Museum containing artifacts bulldozed up at the time of the destruction of Aldingbury Ring: well over thirty complete swords and daggers, and the fragments of dozens more; an eighth-century BC bronze helmet – the oldest military headgear to be found in Britain; bracelets, pins, brooches, rings, harness fittings, were, if we had only known it, but a few inches beneath

797

our feet as Darnley, Jo and I paced the turfy slopes. Archaeologists seemed, after twenty or more years of research, to accept Rice Robey's hunch that Aldingbury Ring was a sacrificial site. Perhaps the most haunting and painful 'exhibit' in the Aldingbury Room in the British Museum is the tiny skeleton, thought to be that of a child, with a fractured skull, preserved by chance in what had been a peat bog, long since hardened.

I can certainly testify that Aldingbury Ring possessed an 'atmosphere'. As we climbed the gentle slope towards the copse, Darnley, Jo and I became silent. It was a palpable silence, as if some unseen presences commanded it: the sort of silence which comes upon all but the most insensitive visitors to a great cathedral. Behind us, fields stretched through Windsor Forest towards Eton, and in the mist we could make out the outlines of the College chapel, and on the further hill, the turrets of the Castle. Nearer, there was a nondescript row of houses; a gas works, where large iron frames encased the huge grey cylinders and stood out against the pale misty sky like the buttresses of a Gothic church. On our other side, there was an illusion of open country, and a bluish smudge of forest, whence, presumably, the antlered figure of Herne could be seen flapping his bat-like wings by night and driving his hounds of destruction across the sky. Hedges gave way to open land. The Thames snaked into invisibility, streaked with silver from the sun which now began in arbitrary shafts to penetrate the clouds. The sun was invisible, but the sky was filling with light. We had reached the first of the stone circles. By the standards of Stonehenge or Avebury, it was small. Some of the stones were little more than boulders. Others, vaguely phallic in shape, poked up from the tufts of grass some four feet in height. One of them, from an angle at which I first glimpsed it, suggested a gaunt face with high cheekbones.

'They can't be going to destroy *this*!' I exclaimed.

'Shh.'

It was Darnley who hushed me. I thought at first that he was objecting to my speaking because it was no place for idle chat. Certainly, the atmosphere was potent, the ancient presences induced a gooseflesh. But Darnley wanted us to be quiet so that we could catch the mysterious noise which came to us on the cold air.

'Listen!'

A thin, high-pitched voice, euphonious but not especially

tuneful could be heard. It would have been credible at that point if one had been told that it was the song of the elves, disembodied or invisible to mortal sight.

When we left the small henge behind us, and tramped through the copse at the brow of the little hill, the song grew more audible, and one saw that, just beyond the trees, the ground sloped with some abruptness towards the west. Just out of sight, but somewhere down that slope, someone was singing.

Following a small mud track through the bracken, we came upon the source of the song. It was a mysterious incantation, and I guessed that the words might have been Welsh.

Two figures were sitting on the grass at the mouth of a minuscule tent. One of them, the one who sang, wore a tweed cloth cap, a blue jersey and trousers, and seemed to be a young boy. The other was much older – a balding mage-like man who sat hunched in meditation against the boy's knees. The pair were immediately suggestive of figures from old stories: Merlin and the boy Arthur, or the prophet Samuel with David the young shepherd-king. The misapprehension was dispelled in an instant when I recognised Rice Robey and Miss Nolan.

When he stood up, Rice Robey showed absolutely no surprise at our presence. Indeed, his opening sentence implied that Aldingbury Ring was his own personal domain, to which he was welcoming guests.

'I knew that I could rely upon you to appear,' he said. 'It is at such time that the loyal *animae* conjoin. We came last night.'

Miss Nolan scowled silently. She looked thoroughly displeased to have been interrupted.

'It is any day now,' said Rice Robey. 'They think to take us by surprise, which is why Persephone and I have encamped. Lord Lampitt has said that he will join us, and Kirsty is hoping to come; I had not thought it right to enlist her sister in view of her condition.'

'Enlist them for what, Pughie, old boy?'

I was glad that Darnley asked this blunt question, since I was beginning to wonder myself why Rice Robey should be so pleased and unsurprised to see us.

'The engines of destruction and rape are poised – just down the road. You probably passed them as you came.'

'No,' said Darnley, 'we drove by the back way.'

'Darling, we can't stay here all day and wait for the bulldozers,' said Jo. 'We promised Mr Fanshawe – he's the house agent – that we'd get to the house by half-past ten.'

'But Mr Grainger will stay and support us?' asked Robey.

It soon became clear that Rice Robey had organised a 'demonstration' against the proposed road development, and was planning to camp in the line of the road until the Ministry of Transport changed their plans or until the police came to carry him away. I cannot now remember exactly how it came about, but within minutes – as it now seems to my memory – Darnley and Jo had driven off to keep their appointment with the house agent, and I was left sitting on the hillside with Rice Robey and the Newnham Norn. This seemed to please her even less than if we had made up a party of five. She said nothing at all, even when Robey praised her singing, and explained to me that it was an old Irish song, something to do with the Daughters of Cohoolin. Miss Nolan did, however, consent to boil up some cocoa for me on their spirit-stove. When she handed me my mug of steaming chocolate, our knuckles touched. She wore black woollen mittens and the fingers which obtruded from them were small and cold and white. Her round petulant face must have been as cold; her little snub nose was quite pink. She refused to meet my gaze during this transaction, and this somehow heightened for me her attractiveness.

In the course of the morning, a group of about thirty people assembled there on the hillside. Some of them seemed like professional vagabonds, weighed down by haversacks, pots, pans, tents. Others, like Vernon Lampitt, obviously had no intention of sleeping there and had come dressed as for a vigorous hike. The dignity of Vernon's appearance was some-what diminished by his wearing a bright red woollen hat, not unlike a tea-cosy, with a pom-pom on top. He did not remove it as he explained to a group of the protesters why he was there.

'I'm not against progress, I'm not against roads, but I am against *people* not being consulted. I'm against the present government. I'm ashamed of it, ter tell yer the truth. Like a lotta me comrades, I'd thought it'd be a socialist government. . . .'

'. . . a place of sacrifice,' Robey was saying to another gaggle of young people. It occurred to me that these older men, who believed themselves to be engaged in discourse, were in truth little more than sideshows, engaged in entertaining the demon-strators until the more exciting action began. That such action was about to start could not be doubted. In the course of the morning, we heard that the bulldozers, only a few hundred yards away from us, had begun to gouge out the earth, and at about midday, a police van appeared containing ten or fifteen uniformed officers.

'It is my intimation – something stronger than what the world would call a hunch – that here was a place of sacrifice. Indeed, I have even written about it as a place where Yeshua Himself witnessed the slaying of a child in a sacrifice of the old dispensation.'

'It's an interestin' theory,' said Vernon, 'but yuv got ter admit that the issue which confronts us ter-day is one of accountability. Government accountability.'

One of the policemen was advancing towards the huddle of protesters, of whom I now realised myself to be one.

'Now, we're not tryin' ter stop yer doin' yer duty,' said Vernon to the policeman.

I wonder what it was about Rice Robey. Although Vernon was trying to make it clear by this intervention that he regarded himself as the senior person present, the officer took no notice of him at all. Uncle Roy would no doubt have considered this extremely surprising. The policeman spoke to Rice Robey.

'Are you the leader of this lot?'

'Not the leader, though it is my idea that we should convene here.'

'Now we don't want any fuss,' said the policeman, 'but in half an hour, the bulldozers are coming through this site and they are going to continue with building this motorway. As I say, we don't want any fuss. You are obstructing, and if you don't move quietly, we'll have you for obstruction.'

'I'm pleased to be obstructing,' said Rice Robey, 'because I can tell you what it is that I and my friends here are obstructing. We are obstructing the obliteration of the sacred past.'

'That may be your opinion, sir. In our book, you are obstructing what might turn into a public highway.'

'Every valley shall be exalted,' said Rice Robey, 'in this Satanic New Jerusalem, which you are allowing to be built. But no new Jerusalem can be built without stretching forth with faltering hand to touch the old Jerusalem.'

'I must warn you, sir, just as politely as I can, that if you aren't out of here in half an hour we'll put you under arrest.'

Vernon began talking about Magna Carta and the rights of an Englishman, but Rice Robey was still intoning, 'The past is what helps us to define ourselves, to define the present, which is why it has to be continually rewritten, revisioned, retold. For you, my friend, this is just a piece of rough ground, with a few stones and a few trees, and doubtless, when its rough places have been made smooth, a few old swords and shards and helmets. I do not doubt that it is a place of what some might denominate a site of archaeological interest. But that is not why we are here. We are here because it enshrines our true past – the past which your empiricist academicians would define as fantasy, but which we know to be . . .'

His voice was drowned by the noise of the vans and lorries and bulldozers which relentlessly, though slowly, were churning and trundling in our direction.

We had been given our instructions by Robey, and some instinct in all of us recognised him as a figure of authority. We closed ranks and sat down: a crowd of about forty by then. The bulldozers came closer and closer, but still we sat down. Then two large white police vans, with sirens screeching, came bumping over the field, and at that point, in a vigorous, rollicking loud voice, Robey began to sing. Like Uncle Roy on the Day that God pulled the plug out, he had found that William Blake's words matched the hour. The first few lines he sang as a solo –

> And was the Holy Lamb of God
> On England's pleasant pastures seen . . . ?

but by the time he had reached the end of the first verse, we had all joined in, and our voices made the sort of raucous but moving noise that I associate with chapel at school, when as boys we roared out hymns during the morning service. A disproportionate number of policemen had been assigned to the task of bundling us into the vans. One officer took my feet, and the other was holding me under the armpits as I continued to sing

> I will not cease from mental fight . . .

Vernon was being carried into another van, and he too sang –

Nor shall my sword sleep in my hand . . .

Inside the van, as it rolled away, we were squashed quite tightly together. Most of them were a hippyish rent-a-crowd whom I don't believe I have ever met since: but good fortune had allowed me to be dumped by the policeman next to Miss Nolan. Her thighs and legs squashed beguilingly against my own. In the van, we sang 'Jerusalem' again. This time, because her delicately formed, boy-like lips were so close to my ear, I could hear her tuneless, breathy voice chant –

Bring me my arrows of desire . . .

I knew in that way one sometimes does that we were destined for further intimacies.

A.N. WILSON

Hearing Voices

THE FOURTH NOVEL IN THE LAMPITT PAPERS SERIES

In 1968, Virgil Everett Jnr, an extremely wealthy and influential businessman, falls to his death in New York in mysterious circumstances. Lawyer, political activist and collector, Everett's business interests are so diverse that the motive for murder seems undetectable. His ownership of the Lampitt Papers seems an unlikely starting point.

Over thirty years later, the actor Julian Ramsay, Lampitt's rival biographer, finds himself in New York with his 'one-man show' on Lampitt's life. It is here that Julian experiences an epiphanic insight into that part of his life which up until now he has been unable to address. It is a fascinating journey back to the late 1960s at a time of ground-breaking scientific research and intense theological debate; a journey that may ultimately reveal the true content of the Lampitt Papers.

DEBORAH MOGGACH

Changing Babies

Changing Babies will delight both die-hard fans of Deborah Moggach's books and those readers new to her charm and wit.

In it she writes of a woman who thinks she has found the perfect man until he becomes too mysterious for words; of a rock star writing his memoirs who can't remember a thing; of harassed teenagers and harangued fathers; of opera lovers, Belgian lovers, young lovers and romance on the Costa del Sol courtesy of Sunspan Holidays.

Here are fifteen brilliant stories – all sharp, funny and painfully accurate.

Praise for Deborah Moggach's previous books:

'Intelligent, persuasive, sensuous, perceptive . . . what an achievement'
Fay Weldon

'Extraordinarily skilful'
Anita Brookner

'Warm, tolerant shrewd and exuberant'
Sunday Times

'Just delicious'
New Woman

LEE LANGLEY

Persistent Rumours

A childhood mystery has haunted James Oakley all his life: the disappearance and unexplained death of his mother far away in India. Years later, in an attempt to unlock the past, he returns with his unhappy wife Daisy to the islands where he was born; a place of treacherous seas and hurricanes, which conceals an appalling secret.

'The closest thing to a faultless novel that I have read for years'
Daily Mail

'. . . beautifully written . . . Langley has a very definite and original voice of her own, with the power to portray a real sense of deeper truths about humanity within the context of a gripping and moving story'
Sunday Times

'. . . skilful and poignant . . . Langley writes with passion, verve and rare tenderness'
Literary Review

'Flawless, lyrical writing and vivid evocation of place make this a hauntingly beautiful novel'
Sunday Telegraph

PAUL SCOTT

The Jewel in the Crown

India: 1942. When fifty-seven-year-old Miss Crane is found sitting on a dusty roadside holding the hand of a dead Indian, the troubles in Mayapore are only just beginning.

As the uprisings escalate, the brutal rape of Daphne Manners, a young English girl, in the Bibighar Gardens, is savagely re-enacted in the defilement of India by the British – the racism, violence and hatred launched upon the head of Hari Kumar, Daphne's young Indian lover, symptomatic of the terrible rift in Anglo-Indian relations. A rift which eventually prises India – the jewel in the Imperial Crown – from its setting.

'A major work, a glittering combination of brilliant craftsmanship, psychological perception and objective reporting . . . Rarely have the sounds and smells and total atmosphere been so evocatively suggested'
New York Times

'One of the most important landmarks of post-war fiction . . . a mighty literary experience'
The Times

A Selected List of Fiction Available from Mandarin

While every effort is made to keep prices low, it is sometimes necessary to increase prices at short notice. Mandarin Paperbacks reserves the right to show new retail prices on covers which may differ from those previously advertised in the text or elsewhere.

The prices shown below were correct at the time of going to press.

All these books are available at your bookshop or newsagent, or can be ordered direct from the address below. Just tick the titles you want and fill in the form below.

Cash Sales Department, PO Box 5, Rushden, Northants NN10 6YX.
Fax: 01933 414047 : Phone: 01933 414000.

Please send cheque, payable to 'Reed Book Services Ltd.', or postal order for purchase price quoted and allow the following for postage and packing:

£1.00 for the first book, 50p for the second; **FREE POSTAGE AND PACKING FOR THREE BOOKS OR MORE PER ORDER.**

NAME (Block letters) ....

ADDRESS ....

....

☐ I enclose my remittance for ....

☐ I wish to pay by Access/Visa Card Number

Expiry Date

Signature ....

Please quote our reference: MAND